The
CALLING
DREAM

The
CALLING
DREAM

Karlyle Tomms

Fresh Ink Group

Guntersville

The Calling Dream

Copyright © 2022
by Karlyle Tomms
All rights reserved

Fresh Ink Group
An Imprint of:
The Fresh Ink Group, LLC
1021 Blount Avenue, #931
Guntersville, AL 35976
Email: info@FreshInkGroup.com
FreshInkGroup.com

Edition 2.0   2022

Book design by Amit Dey / FIG
Cover art by Anik / FIG
Cover by Stephen Geez / FIG
Associate publisher Lauren A. Smith / FIG

Cataloging-in-Publication Recommendations:

FIC042120 FICTION / Christian / Romance / Suspense
FIC074000 FICTION / Southern
FIC043000 FICTION / Coming of Age

Library of Congress Control Number: 2021913596

ISBN-13: 978-1-947893-79-5 Papercover
ISBN-13: 978-1-947893-80-1 Hardcover
ISBN-13: 978-1-947893-81-8 Ebooks

"I can say without hesitation that it is a good story and well-written. The characters, the dialogue, etc. ring true and clear, and portray the flavor of life and the people who live in the back country in Arkansas vividly. Well done. Karlyle Tomms has a wonderful gift of expression, and the reading is easy."

—Su Sherry, author of *My Three Girls*

DEDICATION

This story is dedicated to my roots, to the Ozark Hills of Arkansas, which bore me and molded me. This is dedicated to the resilient people of the Ozarks, who dug their livelihood out of the rocky soil and forged a resilience, and dedication to survival that is unmatched in many places of the world. This book is dedicated to those who overcome abuse, prejudice, and mistreatment, and it is dedicated to God, to faith, and to those who truly come to understand that love is the bottom line, for this is a book about love.

TABLE OF CONTENTS

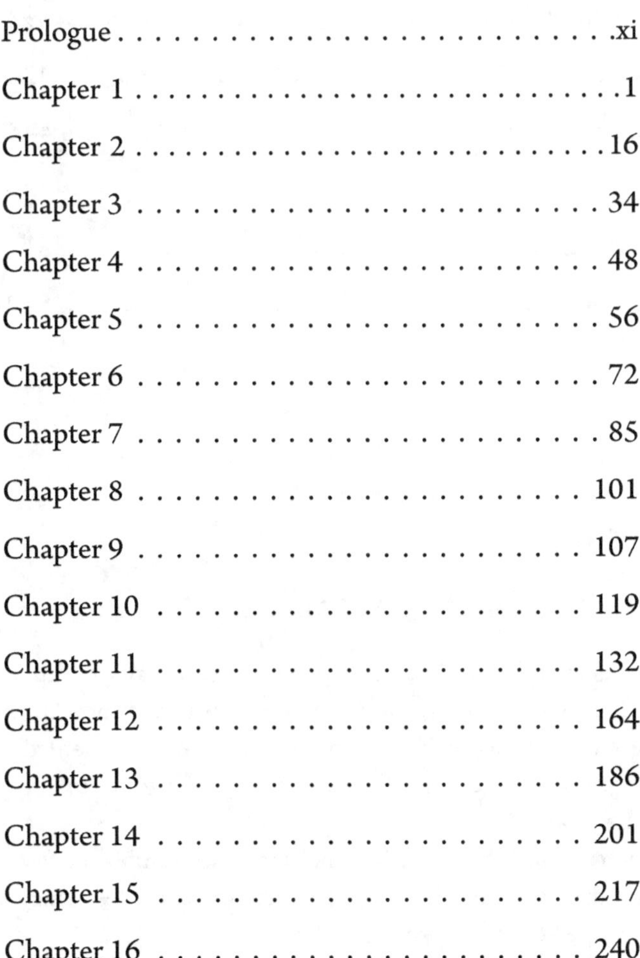

DISCLAIMER:

There are words and phrases in this book, which by today's standards, would be considered offensive. However, the terminology was common during the time frame of the story. These words and phrases are not intended to be offensive toward any persons or social group, but are intended to accurately portray the language of the time.

All characters in this book are fictional and any resemblance to any person or persons, other than the author, is purely coincidental as these characters are not drawn from any person known to the author.

PROLOGUE

There are wars we fight within ourselves. We all do. The wars take different forms and vary with intensity and lethality, but we all fight them. Sometimes there are little skirmishes over whether we should have a piece of cheesecake or remain committed to our goal to lose weight.

Sometimes the wars become chronic, dangerous internal battles fought over the course of a lifetime. The casualties may be our sense of self-worth, our feelings of dignity, and sometimes even the loss of our own physical freedom when those wars spill over into legally forbidden behavior. The casualties might be the loss of relationships when our battle invades the lives of others and they decide they can no longer tolerate being around someone in such constant turmoil. Most of the time the wars are about behavior based on our judgment of what we or others should or should not be doing. Often the wars are about an internal judgment as we pretend to think and feel one way while we hide the unspoken.

There are some people in the world who are quite adept at reading the truth on a man's face. Even if micro expressions or the dart of eyes do not give away true feelings, the one being read may remain paranoid that others see into the forbidden secret he carries. When, on rare occasion, someone does spot it, paranoia can grow until the subject becomes even more determined to hide what he considers to be his dirty little secret. There are secrets inside us all, some things we will never tell a soul for as long as we live, and some we share only with very trusted few. We all fear it—the judgment of others, the constant dread that someone will condemn us for who we are, how we behave, or what we think. Those who judge may become so attached to their beliefs that they not only hold themselves to their standard of judgment but demand that others must conform to it as well. Sometimes the standards demanded of others are not applied to oneself. The torment of judgment toward self or others can become a maddening fire that consumes the soul to the point of utter destruction. The fires of hell for a tormented soul are not so much an inferno of eternity but the burning anguish of conflict between belief and truth. If there is one who has never begged in anguish, "How can I be saved?" that is the only one who cannot be saved. For all have sinned and have fallen short of the glory of God.

CHAPTER 1

I discovered I was called to preach the day I woke up with a hard-on and the smell of fried chicken in my nostrils. I must have been about ten years old back in 1945.

I lay down on the back porch for a nap after church on a summer Sunday afternoon, and I had the strangest dream. I was standing there by the pond in the barn lot of our family farm over in north Arkansas. There were no cows around, and it was like the barn wasn't there anymore, but I knew it was. The pond water shimmered silver like a pool of mercury. All around the pond stood tiny little Roman soldiers, each one about a foot high. Their breast plate armor was notched with scroll-like designs, and each one had a metal spear and a shield. When I approached the pond, they all stamped one foot and stood at full attention with their spears pointing up to the sky and their shields pulled round in a defensive position.

I knelt down by the water's edge and reached two fingers into the water. The water shimmered on my fingers as I brought them to my lips. When I touched the water to my lips, the pond began to stir. Then the waters parted from side to side like Moses had parted the Red Sea. When the water parted, up from below came the most beautiful woman I had ever seen. Her dress was white and thin, like gauze, like pure white window sheers. As she walked toward me, the fabric flowed back as if it was blown in a soft breeze. I saw the full outline of her body, taut breasts, and perfect womanly hips beneath her thin waist. Her hair was red like fire embers, and it flowed back off her shoulders in the breeze. She came walking straight up to me out of the parted waters. She was tall like a grown woman, and her lips were red like communion wine. Then she leaned over, cupped gentle hands on both sides of my face, and kissed me. I felt her soft lips gently touching mine. Then her tongue went into my mouth, and I woke up, startled.

I found myself lying on our back porch cot. The overhang shaded me from the hot summer sun that gleamed a golden soft shimmer across the grass in our backyard. I realized that my little soldier—that's what Momma always told us to call our penis when we were little—was standing at full attention. It was pressing toward the front of my britches like it was trying to get out. It pushed firm and hard against the contour beside my zipper, but the fabric held it captive. Then I smelled fried chicken and I realized Momma must have a meal about ready to serve.

I got up and went in the back door leading to the kitchen. There was Momma turning crispy chicken in the cast iron frying pan, and it was sizzling hot, browning up. I walked up to Momma and said, "Momma, I just had a strange dream."

"Ronnie, go wash up for dinner," she said in a hurry. Now let me explain something here. Hill folks in those days had no word for lunch. You didn't have breakfast, lunch, and dinner; you had breakfast, dinner, and supper. So Momma was fixing the midday meal right after church that morning.

"But, Momma," I said, "I had this dream where I was down at the pond, but it was filled with water that looked like liquid silver, and all around the pond was these little Roman soldiers about a foot high, and they was all standing at attention. Then the waters parted, like Moses parting the sea, and this beautiful woman came up out of the waters, and she walked straight over to me and kissed me right on the mouth. What do you think that means?"

Momma looked at me sternly while she was forking chicken from the frying pan to a bowl.

"What do you think it means, Momma?" I asked again.

"I think it means you were called to preach," she said as she wiped hands on her apron then carried the bowl of chicken to the table. "Now go wash up. Find Teddy and Hannah. Get them to wash up too, and go call your daddy for dinner. He's out in the garden."

Now, our house was on a farm near Ravenden, Arkansas. That's where the Ozark Mountains begin to melt into the Mississippi delta. It ain't exactly flat, but it ain't exactly hill country either. The house wasn't much. There were four rooms inside a square. There was a living room and a kitchen on opposite corners with a doorway between them slightly overlapping in the middle. The kitchen was rudimentary at best, and Momma cooked on a woodburning stove that made the kitchen awful hot in the summertime. Nonetheless, our table was in the kitchen, and that's where we ate our meals whether it was hot or not.

On the other corners were two bedrooms. One corner was Momma and Daddy's bedroom with a door off the living room. My older brother, Teddy, and I slept in the other corner bedroom back on the north side of the house, and it also had a door off the living room, but the kitchen door was right next to our door. Teddy and I shared a bed, and Hannah, my baby sister, had a little cot on the opposite side of Momma and Daddy's room. Hand-cut cedar posts held the porch roofs up. There was a porch in the front and one in the back. The back porch was on the north side, and it was also shaded, so good for summer naps.

I went straight out the back door again and saw Daddy off in the distance past the yard fence. He was working a hoe in our garden, cutting weeds back from the vegetables. "DAADDDDYYYY!" I shouted. "Dinner's ready."

"Go round the side of the house and get your brother and sister!" he shouted back. "I'll be right there."

When I went around the house, Teddy was leaned up against the northeast side reading a book. Hannah was three years old then. She was lying there on the grass with her homemade doll, fast asleep. Teddy looked up at me and asked, "Dinner ready?"

"Yeah," I said as I walked over and started picking Hannah up off the ground. "Come on, sissy. It's time to eat."

She moaned a little bit and sat up with her rag doll. I picked her up and carried her on my hip. Then we all went around the house to get washed up. Normally, Daddy would've had me and Teddy working with him in the garden, but he gave us a break on Sunday.

My daddy was a preacher at a little country church, and you would think he would not be doing work on the Lord's Day, but he said it wasn't a sin for him to work the garden on Sunday because he had such a good time doing it. He said it was fun and relaxation for him instead of work, but it sure felt like work to me and Teddy.

On the porch, next to the kitchen was what they used to call a dry sink. We moved it inside in the wintertime. We didn't have running water, so everything had to be pulled up with a zinc bucket from a rock-lined well. The well had a wood brace over the top and a pulley for lowering the bucket into the water with a rope. A couple of buckets sat on the dry sink next to an enameled wash pan. One of the buckets had a dipper in it so we could get ourselves a drink of water, and the other was for washing. Teddy took the wash bucket and poured a little bit into the wash pan, and then we all took turns picking up the bar of homemade lye soap and swishing it around on our hands in the pan of water. Sissy couldn't reach the pan, so I took a washcloth and got some soapy water to wash her hands.

Inside, Momma had the kitchen table set for dinner. The big bowl of fried chicken was in the middle, and there was a mashed potato salad that Momma had made before church that morning and kept in the icebox till dinner. We didn't have electricity in those days, so Daddy had to buy block ice in town and put it in our icebox to keep food cold. The ice would last the whole week in the wintertime, but it didn't last but a couple of days over the summer. Momma had sliced salted tomatoes from the garden, and she made a wilted salad from lettuce, green onions, and hot bacon drippings. She baked some cornbread while she was frying the chicken, but most of it she had put together before we went to church that morning. She warmed over a pot of pinto beans she had made earlier in the week. The more they were reheated, the better they got. It was a downright feast.

We all sat down quietly at the table and waited for Daddy to get washed up and come in. We weren't allowed to talk till after Daddy said prayer. Before we sat down, Momma had us hold our hands palms up then flip to the back so she could see that we washed up before we ate. If she wasn't satisfied, it was right back to the dry sink and only come back when they were clean.

After a while, Daddy came in and sat at the head of the table. Momma always sat on the opposite end, and we kids sat between. Daddy reached out his hands to each side, and we all held hands around the table. Hannah sat on a wood box in a chair next to Momma so Momma could help feed her. Everybody held hands on either side except for Hannah. She couldn't reach Daddy's other hand, so she just held Momma's hand. After all hands were clasped, Daddy looked around the table and bowed his head. That was our cue to do the same. With my head down, I watched the flower patterns in that china plate and wondered what I was going to fill it with, then Daddy started to pray.

"Dear Lord, we thank Thee for the bounty that is before us this day and for this food that will nourish our bodies. Dear Lord, we thank Thee for bringing Teddy some wisdom so that he knows when he ought to behave. We thank Thee, Lord, for little Ronnie and for how he always tries to be good help. Lord, we thank Thee for little Hannah and for bringing her sweet countenance into our family, and yes, Lord, I thank Thee for Marylee, for her faithfulness and for being a hardworking, good wife. Lord, we thank Thee for the health and well-being of this family and for the blessings we are about to receive. In Jesus's name, amen."

Now, after prayer, everybody sat quietly, and nobody said a word till Daddy acknowledged us. He would start with a fork to the chicken bowl, serving the oldest child first. That would be Teddy. He was thirteen years old when I was ten. "Teddy," he would say, "what kind of meat would suit your liking today?"

Teddy always asked for the same thing. He picked up his plate and held it out toward the chicken bowl. "I believe I would like thigh and leg please, Daddy."

Then Daddy forked out a thigh and leg for Teddy and asked me what I wanted. I always wanted the breast meat and sometimes the gizzard, but a gizzard by itself wasn't quite enough. If Daddy felt like I had been good, he would go ahead and put the gizzard on my plate too. After he served me and Teddy, then Momma served Hannah. After that, Momma and Daddy served themselves. Then, we started passing the bowls around the table. By the time it was all done, we each had a heaping plate full of good food.

Momma's fried chicken would make you want to sing praises to the Lord. It was so good you had to fight the urge to moan when you tasted it. The skin was always crispy and brown, fried up in some lard, and she somehow got even the breast meat to stay moist on the inside. I took a big bite of chicken and chewed it well before I swallowed. I had to get a bite of that before I did anything else. Then I said, "Daddy, Momma says I was called to preach!"

Daddy held his chicken in both hands in front of his face and looked at me with a kind of smirking grin on his face. "Oh, she did?" he mumbled while chewing chicken and looking over at Momma.

Daddy was kind of a handsome man, kind of. He was bald, but he had blue eyes and dimples on his cheeks that made his smile look twice as wide. He was a tall man and thin. Everybody always said I looked like my daddy in the face, but I never got that tall or went bald like him. Whatever clothes Daddy wore looked kind of like they flowed around him instead of clinging to him, and thick chest hair always curled above the top button of his shirt. He had big hands, and the veins on the back of his hands made them look manly and strong. This time of the year, the sun had darkened them so much you could barely see those veins, but in wintertime, when his skin lightened a bit, the veins looked like road maps across his hands. He was such a strong, fine-looking man, you would have thought he would have been called to war, but Momma said he didn't go because he had rheumatic fever when he was little. I guess that must have done something to him to keep him from fighting, along with the fact that he was already older with a family when World War II started, and he was too young to fight in World War I.

"Yeah," I said. "I had this really weird dream when I was off taking a nap, and Momma said it means I was called to preach."

He glanced over at Momma again. She sat quietly chewing, not looking up much from her plate except to make sure Hannah was getting properly fed without too much mess. She gave him a shy glance, and he turned his attention back to me.

"Did you dream about angels coming down and telling you to speak the Word of the Lord?" he asked.

"Well, not exactly, Daddy," I replied. "I dreamed I was down at the pond in the barn lot, and the water was all silver like, and there were little Roman soldiers standing around the pond. When I came to the pond, they all stood at attention and pointed their spears to the sky. Then I touched the water to my lips, and it parted like the Red Sea, and up out of the parted waters came this beautiful redheaded woman wearing white flowing robes. She had bright-red lips, and she came up out of the pond and came over to me and put her hands on my cheeks and kissed me right on the lips. Then I woke up."

Daddy looked at me stern and scornful for a second like I had just done something terrible to him. Then he glanced around the room like he was checking to see if anybody saw his reaction.

"That sounds to me more like the dream of a sinner than a man called to preach," Daddy said. "Cavorting with some red-lipped Jezebel that rose up out of the pond don't exactly sound to me like a dream that a man of God would have. That sounds to me like you were giving in to lascivious temptation."

Teddy was snickering by this time, and I was mad that he made fun of me. He was sitting right next to me, so I slapped him on the leg and said, "Shut up, Teddy!"

Daddy immediately reached over and smacked me flat handed and hard on the back of my head. "You stop that nonsense and behave yourself at the table!" he said firmly.

"But, Daddy, Momma says the dream means I was called to preach," I pleaded, "and Teddy was laughing at me."

"Was not," Teddy defended.

"That'll be enough of that!" Daddy snapped. "I don't care what your Momma says. That's a sinner's dream! You dreamed about fornicating with a strange woman, and your momma thinks that means you were called to preach?" He looked up at Momma with an angry stare. She didn't say anything but just kind of looked down at the table. The truth is she was disciplined by him just like we kids were. Daddy kept staring at her. Then in a moment she said, "I'm sorry. I really didn't hear the boy. I was busy and just wanted to rush him on out of my way."

"Well, you gotta be careful what kinds of things you say to a child," Daddy scolded. "An impressionable child gets the wrong idea about things like that. If anything, he should have been scolded for having smut like that in his mind."

"But, Daddy," I started imploring.

"Shut up, boy!" he snapped before I could finish my sentence. "Eat your dinner!"

We didn't say much for the rest of that meal. Even Teddy kept his mouth shut. We all knew better than to push when Daddy was in a bad mood.

After dinner we rested a little bit for the remainder of the afternoon and then had to do evening chores before supper. That meant that the cows had to be gathered into the barn for milking, the hogs had to be slopped, the chickens fed, and eggs gathered. Our chickens were free range, but it was easy to feed them in the coup to lure them in for the night. We locked them in the coup at nighttime to protect them, but varmints still got to them pretty often. Now and then, Daddy would get hold of a wood shipping crate that we would fill with straw and place in a corner of the coup in hopes the chickens would take to nesting in it. Sometimes they would still nest out in the weeds, and some old hen would come marching up one day with a passel of fluffy yellow chicks trotting around her.

I didn't say another word about my dream through supper or Bible study at church in the early evening, and that night after we went to bed, we heard Daddy chewing Momma out for saying "frivolous things" to children. I felt sorry for Momma because she got scolded and punished just like one of the kids. I wanted to go in there and tell him it wasn't her fault, but I knew better. Besides, I would have had to crawl over Teddy to get out of the bed, which was shoved up into a corner by a window. He would have just pushed me back and told me to go to sleep. Sometimes I couldn't tell if Teddy was protecting me from Daddy or helping him out. After a while the yelling stopped, but I didn't fall asleep right away. I just lay there on my back, staring into the darkness and thinking, *What if Momma was right? What if my dream means I was called to preach?*

Before Daddy came to get us up for chores the next morning, I had another dream. I was back down in the barn lot. The pond was still shimmering with silver water, and the little Roman soldiers stood at attention all around it, but this time I heard wailing and crying off to the side. I turned around, and there was Jesus nailed to the side of the barn with arms outstretched like he was nailed to a cross instead of the old gray barnwood. He hung on the side of the barn just above the opening to the corn bin. He had thorns all around his head, and they were poking into his forehead, so little streams of blood ran down his face. He had big iron nails through his wrists and hands. He had big nails through his knees and his feet, so they were bleeding too. Streams of dripping blood ran down the side of the barn onto the ground. There on the ground before him was the red-headed woman who had come up from the pond in my other dream. She was kneeling down and crying in great horrible sobs. Her pure white dress was stained with his blood. She looked up at Jesus and said, *"My Lord! My Lord! Why have you forsaken me?"* Then Jesus looked down at her and said, *"Wait, wait patiently, for the time will come when all will be revealed."* After he said that, he looked over and saw me standing there looking up at him, and he shouted in this voice that echoed all over the whole farm, *"YOU ARE MY WORD!"* The next thing I knew, Daddy was shaking me awake, shaking Teddy, and telling us to get up.

Summer wasn't much fun for us. There was always a lot of work for us to do on the farm, and Daddy always got us up just before the rooster crowed. By the time he woke us though, Momma already had pork chops, eggs, biscuits, and gravy ready on the table. The smell of breakfast and fresh coffee filled the house so sweetly you could almost float into the kitchen on the aroma.

Since it was summer, there was no school to attend, and Daddy would have us out on the farm working all day. We would be fixing fence, cutting firewood for winter, or something similar to that. There barely ever was a day Daddy didn't have us working. All year round we worked. As soon as we came home from school, we had chores to do. Through the colder months, Teddy and I attended school together in a little one-room schoolhouse that was about a two-mile walk from our farm, and all year-round we worked.

After we washed for breakfast, we came in and sat down at our places at the table. Daddy said prayer, as he did before every meal, and then he began to pass the biscuits around. I waited for him to say something to me because I wanted to tell him about the other dream, but he didn't speak to me. I knew I would only get smacked if I spoke first, so I didn't say anything. He never asked me if I wanted a pork chop—nothing. He just passed the bowls around and motioned for us to take what we wanted. Momma didn't say anything either. I guess she didn't want to upset Daddy after he got mad the day before.

After we finished eating, Teddy and I just sat there looking at empty plates not saying a word. Finally, Daddy said, "After you feed the stock, you boys go get the mule hooked up to the plow. I think we need to be prepping the south side of the truck patch for some winter crops today."

We didn't say anything but "Okay." Then we got up and headed for the barn. We didn't feed hay this time of year, but we would put some grain mix out for the milk cows to get them into the barn for milking. I would be doing that while Teddy mixed some table scraps with wheat shorts to slop the hogs. Catching the mule was sometimes a problem because he always seemed to know when we were thinking about hooking him to the plow, and he didn't like to work. I don't know how he knew, but he always knew. It was like he could read minds or something. Any other time when we weren't thinking about putting him to the plow, any one of us could walk right up and pet him, but he always knew the difference. I always held off on the mule's feed till last, trying not to give him any ideas, and I waited long enough for Teddy to get the hogs slopped so he could come help me.

I would lead the mule into the corral with a feed bucket. Teddy would try to get the gate closed behind him before the mule figured out what was going on and took a run for it. As likely as not, we would end up having to get Daddy to help us because the mule would push through the gate and run off. Then we would both be in trouble, and Daddy would be telling us that we were stupid, and we couldn't do anything right.

On that day, we lucked out though. We got the mule locked in the corral all right and got him fed, but when we started trying to hitch him up, he started slinging his head and kicking. Then, we ended up chasing him all over the corral. It took Daddy coming over to get him settled down. Teddy and I were chasing the mule around, yelling at him to stop, when we heard Daddy from behind. "Yelling at him ain't gonna get him to take that harness!" he shouted.

We turned to see him come strolling up from the gate. I wished Daddy would think that yelling at us wasn't going to help. He didn't yell at the livestock, but he seemed to think yelling at us would do the trick. Apparently, it did, because I always did what Daddy said. Teddy misbehaved some, especially as he got older, but I always did what Daddy said. Daddy helped us get the mule into a chute, and then we got him cinched up and led him to the plow. After all the excitement was over and we were getting ready to go to the truck patch, I finally got my courage up to talk to Daddy.

"Daddy," I said hesitantly. "Can I tell you about another dream I had, a different dream?"

"What is all this interest in dreams you suddenly have?" he questioned as he stared like he was angry at me, between glances up to the mule reins.

"Well, don't the Bible say there were interpreters of dreams?" I went on. "I was thinking maybe my dreams had to have some meaning."

Teddy led the mule out in front of us and occupied himself with pulling the seed heads off stalks of grass that came within reach of his opposite hand. He pretended not to hear.

"Well, those were prophets, some, and priests of Pharaoh that interpreted dreams," Daddy said. "I don't know nothing about interpreting dreams, but I do know the kind of dreams a man of God should not be having."

"Well, this dream is a little different. Can I tell you and maybe you might get some idea?" I questioned. "People are always wanting to tell their dreams. There has to be a reason why people want to tell their dreams."

"All right then," he reluctantly agreed. "Tell me your other dream."
"Well, Daddy," I began nervously. "It was back down in the barn lot again. Those little Roman soldiers were still standing around the pond, and the pond still glimmered silver, but I looked up, and there was Jesus being crucified on the side of our barn. It was awful. He had nails in his hands and feet, and he was nailed up to the side of the barn with old rusty nails, and blood was running down the side of the barn. That redheaded woman from the first dream was at his feet, and she was crying. She said, *'My Lord, My Lord. Why have you forsaken me?'* Jesus told her to be patient, then he looked up and saw me standing there watching. When he saw me, he shouted in this loud voice that echoed across the whole farm. He looked at me straight and said in a big echoing voice, *'You are my word!'* Then I woke up."

Daddy said nothing. He just kept walking. I waited patiently for him to say something but he never did. Finally, I said, "Daddy? Are you thinking about it? What do you think it means?"
He said, "I think it means you better quit snacking before bedtime."
Teddy snickered.
I shouted, "Shut up, Teddy!"
To this, Daddy popped me on the back of my head and said, "You boys behave and get on down the path."
I knew enough not to say anything else. I could read Daddy's moods as easy as the Sunday paper, and I knew when it was best to just shut up and drop things. We got the south side of the truck patch plowed by noon and then went back to the house for a bit of dinner while the old mule stood under a shade tree.

That afternoon we took the disk to it to break up the clods, and Daddy had us out there sowing turnips and other things that would come into make in early October. Food was what the farm was about. We were always working on how to feed ourselves. That might be milking the cows or cutting a crop of hay to feed the cows over winter. It might be growing vegetables for Momma to can for the winter or selling some animal or crop so we could buy other things we needed. The farm was always turning over and over, bringing a living up out of the soil. We didn't think much about "consider the lilies of the field" because we were too busy plowing them up to plant something else in their place.

Supper time came with a little fried meat, potatoes, and some leftover beans, and cornbread. After supper Daddy sat down in a corner of the living room under a couple of kerosene lanterns to read the Bible and prepare his sermon for the next Sunday. I had watched him do this my whole life, but I began to see it with a new fascination after I thought I had been called to preach. He would scribble little notes onto pieces of paper and tuck them in various spots of the Bible as bookmarks. Sometimes he would go to the indexes and scan for the verses that supported something he wanted to talk about. Then he would flip over to those verses and read them, sometimes aloud, sometimes not. Other times, he would sit staring at his reflection in the dark glass of the window by his chair and tap his pencil on the back of the Good Book.

That evening, when he got to one of those stopping places where he was staring at his reflection and tapping his pencil, I asked him, "Daddy, can I ask you something?" He half startled when I broke the silence. He turned to me with a foreboding look. "What?" he said irritably, "No more of that crazy stuff about your dreams!"

"No, Daddy," I said shyly.

"What?" He continued to sound irritated, and I hesitated.

After a hesitant pause, I asked, "How do you do it? How do you know what you are going to preach about and then pull it all together into a sermon?"

He sighed deeply. "Sometimes, it just comes to me, and it all falls together like God meant it to be that way. Sometimes, I see something that is going on in the congregation or hear about something that somebody has done wrong, and I know I need to preach about it. Sometimes, it just don't seem to come at all, and I struggle all week thinking about what I'm going to preach on Sunday morning. Other times, I just rewrap an old sermon with new ribbon and present it in a different package."

"Will you teach me?" I pleaded. "Will you teach me how to write a good sermon?"

The Bible had sat open on his lap. He placed his pencil in the fold of the book, closed it, and then set it on the table beside his chair. "I think it's time you kids were in bed," he said firmly.

Momma had already put Sissy to sleep in her little cot an hour or two back. She sat on a chair, opposite Daddy, working on mending one of Teddy's shirts. Teddy sat on the floor by Momma fiddling with a pocketknife and a stick of hickory. He was whittling the shavings into an empty dish pan so he wouldn't make a mess. We didn't have a sofa or a radio in those days or electric light. Daddy had refused the first time the county came through offering to hook us up to electric. He said it cost too much money. I thought Daddy was kind of stingy, but I didn't know what it was like for him to survive the Great Depression. Momma set Teddy's shirt down into her lap and said, "You boys go get ready for bed."

Teddy and I both got up and went out to the dry sink to wash up a bit. We brought one wet wash rag back to wash the dirt off our feet before we got between the sheets. We stripped down to our underwear in our room, and then I got in bed first. I sat half in and half out till I could wash the bottom of my feet with the old wash rag. Then I snuggled up next to the wall, and it was Teddy's turn.

The room wasn't big enough for the bed to sit out from the wall, and we had no solid doors in the house except for those leading from the front and back to the outside. Momma had hung homemade curtains on nails over the doorways to the bedrooms so we might be lying there in bed, and they might think we were asleep, but we could hear everything that went on in the house.

After we were in bed for a while, I overheard Momma say Daddy's name. "Paul," she said, "don't you think you could at least humor Ronnie a little bit? The boy has a good heart, and he's just curious."

"The boy is too young to preach," Daddy retorted.

"Well, I know he is," Momma replied gently, "but at least he wants to be like his daddy, and it's better he learns it from you, don't you think?"

"If he is genuine about it and this ain't some passing whim, he has got plenty of time to learn when he gets a little older," Daddy commanded.

Momma didn't say anything else, but I drifted off to sleep comforted that Daddy was going to teach me how to write and preach a sermon when I got older. He didn't rule it out or say "No way." He said I had plenty of time to learn when I got older.

I didn't recall a dream that night or for several nights to come. Life went on the way it was supposed to, I guess, and I waited for another dream, or for Daddy to tell me it was time for me to start learning how to preach. In the meantime, he was too busy teaching me how to be a farmer, and that wasn't an easy thing to do in the 1940s. You earned your muscle from the back side of a plow, and you burned every calorie you ate. You begged the sun for mercy in the summertime, and the snow and ice for mercy in the winter. If you were good at it, you would eat well. If you weren't good at it, or if nature was unforgiving that year, you relied on your neighbors to get you through. It was a hard life the way I grew up, but it was the only life I knew, so maybe it didn't seem so hard at the time. I learned the value of hard work and the value of good friends and neighbors. I learned that the seed doesn't come up overnight, and the plant does not bear fruit for months to come. I learned, if nothing else, to be patient.

CHAPTER 2

As I grew older, my little soldier stood at attention more and more, or maybe I just noticed it more. Along about the time I was turning twelve years old, there was a different feeling down there, like some kind of itch or urging that wouldn't go away. It was like my little soldier was just begging to be touched and petted kind of the way a dog likes to be petted. Now, at first, I was a little hesitant because we had basically been taught that the only time you were supposed to touch it was to wash it or to hold it while you pee, but it seemed like I couldn't keep my hands off it, and I knew that Teddy had been touching his for quite a while. Maybe he thought I was asleep, or I didn't know what he was doing, but I knew he was touching his little soldier too.

One night after we got in bed, about thirty minutes after the light went out, I felt the covers move. I would probably have just passed it off as nothing and would have gone back to sleep except that the covers kept moving and moving. He was lifting them up and setting them back down quickly over and over. He had been doing that for a couple of years almost every night, but that night I was moved to a curiosity that I didn't have before I started wanting to touch my own little soldier. Finally, I asked, "Teddy, what in tarnation are you doing?"

"Nothing!" he exclaimed in a whisper. "Go back to sleep!" I tried to go back to sleep. I really did, but it was hard to sleep in a bed with someone squirming even if it is just a tiny little bit.

Finally, I reached over to his elbow in the dark and ran my hand quick down to his hand, and there it was. His little soldier was out of his underwear, standing at full attention. It was hard, and his hand was on it. He immediately threw my hand back and exclaimed in whisper shout, "Don't ever do that again!"

"Well, what are you doing?" I whispered.

"Nothing," he muttered. "Go back to sleep."

"Well, I might have an easier time sleeping," I told him, "if the covers wasn't moving back and forth all the time."

"Fine!" he quietly blurted kind of angry. Then he rolled over on his side away from me.

"Teddy, why are you mad at me?" I queried.

"I'm not mad. Go to sleep."

It was less than a year or so later that I began to figure out what Teddy was doing. My own little soldier kept calling me and calling me till I practically couldn't keep my hands off it.

One night I was playing with my little soldier when Teddy suddenly rose up in bed, propped his head on one hand, leaned on his elbow, and whispered. "Why, Ronnie, what in tarnation are you doing?"

My eyes popped open, and I saw him propped up there staring at me with the moonlight shining gray on his face through the window.

"Nothing!" I exclaimed and quickly pulled my hands away from my little soldier. My heart was pounding like I had just been caught robbing a bank.

Teddy snickered, rolled over on his other side, and said, "Kind of fun, ain't it?"

"What?" I said, pretending I didn't know what he was talking about.

"It's okay," he said. "I won't tell."

Those were comforting words, but I still wasn't sure. On one hand, it was comforting to have permission to do what I needed to do. On the other hand, I felt like I was doing something terribly wrong. Still, my little soldier was urging me like it was hungry or something, like it needed to be fed with touches.

Teddy stayed on his side with his back to me, I guess to give me some privacy. Finally, I moved my hand back to my little soldier and began to play with it. It always stood at full attention when I played with it. Sometimes it felt like it was never going to relax. I played with it for a while, and then I said in my mind, *Go to sleep.* This was a command more for my little soldier than for me because I knew that I wasn't going to be doing much sleeping as long as it was standing up and demanding attention.

Nothing changed. My little soldier kept standing at an upright angle and refused to lay down. I took my hands away from it and said again in my mind, *I said go to sleep!* Nothing, it just kept standing at attention, aching to be touched. *At ease, little soldier!* I commanded in my mind, but it just kept standing up, pushing against my underwear. Every time it pumped, the rub against my underwear sent surges of urgency through me. Either it had to be appeased, or it had to be squelched.

A little bit upset with it, I reached down, pulled my underwear back, and slapped it against my belly. Gritting my teeth in a low but audible whisper, I said, "Go…to…sleep!" It just popped right back up, so I slapped it down again and again. I was slapping it against my belly so much it must have sounded like a broken fan belt flapping on a wheel—*flap, flap, flap, flap, flap.* Teddy didn't turn over. He didn't move. I was scared with all the commotion that Teddy might turn back over and tell me to stop it, but then I heard him snoring. I had no idea how he could sleep through that, but he seemed to be asleep.

Suddenly I felt the strangest feeling like something was pulling all the way up into my insides. I felt like every muscle in my body tightened up then released in spasms as this warm, wet stuff came out of my little soldier, pulsing all over my belly. It took everything I had to keep from groaning like I was in pain. I reached over with my other hand and felt that stuff on my belly. In the dark I couldn't see, so the first thought I had was, *Oh Lord! I'm bleeding! I have slapped my little soldier so much he is bleeding!* The fear rose up in me. I didn't know what to do. There were after-pulses, as though my little soldier was still trying to stand up, but it couldn't. Gradually, it began to deflate like a balloon slowly losing air.

Oh Lord, what am I going to do? I questioned myself. I could maybe have told Teddy, but I didn't want to wake him or bother him in the middle of the night when he was sleeping. So I carefully crawled over the foot of the bed and sneaked into the kitchen. Then I felt around carefully, trying to be quiet, till I found one of Momma's kitchen matches. I struck the match and held it down near my little soldier. The light was dim, but I couldn't see anything that looked like blood. The match burned down to my fingers and burned me. I shook it out, biting my lips so I wouldn't say "Ouch!" and stuck my fingers in my mouth. Then I thought I needed more light, so I eased over in the darkness and used a match to light a candle from the kitchen table and held it close to my belly. I didn't want any light to wake Momma and Daddy, but I had to take the risk. I had to see what was wrong with my little soldier. I don't know what I would have told them if they had gotten up to find me standing in the kitchen with my underwear down to my knees and a candle over my privates. Thankfully, they didn't get up.

By this time, my little soldier was completely limp, just hanging there. My belly was still wet, and try as I might, squint as I could, I could not see blood. What I saw was a semiclear liquid all around my navel with a tinge of white to it. Then I thought, *Oh, dear Jesus. I have an infection. That's why my little soldier was all swollen. I must have made it pop like a boil when I was slapping it around.* My mind could not wrap around why the feeling was so strange and pleasurable, not really like pain, and it never occurred to me that I didn't feel the least bit sick.

I had no idea what to do. I didn't really want to talk about it at all. It was too embarrassing, but I knew I had to tell somebody. Finally, I pulled up my underwear, pressed the cloth into the liquid so it would absorb some of it, blew out the candle, and went back to our bedroom. I could hear Teddy snoring a bit when I got there, so I knew he was still asleep. I carefully crawled over the foot of the bed and didn't get under the covers because it was a warm night anyway. I didn't sleep much. I just lay there on my back, wondering if this was a symptom of some terrible disease and if I was going to die a horrible death.

The next day, Daddy got us up as usual before the crack of dawn. The sun was just a tan light on the horizon still trying to wake itself up. Momma already had breakfast ready. I got up and put on my pants, noticing that overnight, my underwear had stuck to my belly where the white stuff had been. I turned to the wall and kind of pulled the cloth away from my belly where it was stuck almost like glue. It was uncomfortable pulling my underwear off my belly, and there was this kind of musty smell coming up from down there. *It must be the smell of death,* I thought to myself. *I have a terrible disease, and I am going to die. My little soldier is probably going to rot off, and then it will rot the rest of my body, and I am going to die!* I kept the anxiety to myself and finished dressing.

After breakfast, Teddy and I went to the barn with Daddy to do morning chores. This included feeding the cows that had come to the barn for milking. Once they got used to being fed and milked, they just kind of always showed up on time. You didn't have to go herd them in from the field much anymore. Teddy and I each milked into zinc buckets, while Daddy made sure there was feed in the bins or went out to select the next cow for milking. We got more milk than the family could use, so Daddy took the excess and poured it into milk cans that had been cleaned with bleach water. We usually filled up one or two ten-gallon cans of milk each morning. A little later in the morning, after milking, the milk truck would come by our house and load up our milk to take over to the dairy in Pocahontas. We always had plenty of milk, and Daddy got a check once a month from the dairy. It varied depending on how much milk we had sent in that month. We also got a discount on cheese if we went to the dairy store.

Ravenden was about twenty miles from Pocahontas, so we didn't get over there much before we finally got a car. Even though cars had been around for a long time, out in the Arkansas woods, a good many people still only had a horse and wagon all the way up into the 1950s.

After milking, we packed up to go to the cotton fields. Daddy raised a little cotton, and after it was picked, we would load it onto wagons and take it over to the cotton mill in Pocahontas. At that time of year, the cotton had to be hoed. Teddy, Daddy, and I would do most of it, cutting out the weeds from around the cotton plants with a garden hoe. Momma did a little bit of it, but she also had to pay attention to Hannah, who was old enough to be in the fields with us but still too young to be left on her own. Momma would give her a short-handled hoe and was trying to teach her how to push and pull the weeds from around the cotton, but most of the time, she sent her to a part of the patch where she could be watched but also do the least amount of damage.

All morning long, my mind was nagging me about my little soldier and the terrible disease I must have. I hadn't noticed any pain or anything. In fact, my little soldier had even stood up a couple of times since then like it wanted to be touched again, but I couldn't keep my mind off the fact that a terrible ooze came out of my body and that it must be a sign I was awful sick.

We worked all morning, and you would think that would keep my mind off things, but it didn't. Every time I cut a weed from between two stalks of cotton or happened to accidentally cut down a cotton stalk, I thought about how maybe my little soldier might have to be cut off to stop the infection and keep me from dying. The thought horrified me, but I had to consider what could happen.

I saw Teddy coming down the opposite direction from me on the next row over, and when he got up even with me, I went "Psssst! Teddy!" in kind of a loud whisper.

"What do you want, knucklehead!" he said out loud, never looking up from his hoe.

"Shhhhh!" I said. "I don't want Momma and Daddy to hear."

"What?" he exclaimed.

"Not too loud!" I pleaded in a whisper.

"What?" he finally whispered back.

"When we break for dinner, I need to talk to you really bad. Can we go off and sit somewhere separate?"

"Whaaaaaat?" he implored.

"I got a problem," I explained. "I need to talk to you, something I need to talk about really bad."

"Okay, fine," he replied. Then he kept on chopping the weeds in his row.

When noontime came, we all retreated to a shade to get a bite to eat. Momma had put a gallon-sized Mason jar of tea down in the creek so the water flowing over it would keep it kind of cool. She had wrapped a farmer's lunch in a table cloth, and when time came, she untied the table cloth and spread it along the ground under the thick canopy of a big oak tree. There were biscuit sandwiches with ham that were left over from breakfast. She had made some fried apple pies and some batter fried potato wedges. It was food you could pick up with your fingers and that saved having to carry forks and knives over to the field. We each had tin cups for cold, sweet tea.

There wasn't much we could do about hand washing. Momma brought a rag up from the creek that she had wet in the cool water, and we all kind of wiped our hands on it. However, when you work the fields, you get used to a little grime in your food. Some folks said it made the grub taste even better. I grabbed a sandwich, some fries, and a fried pie and made a pocket for them by pulling up my shirt tail. Then I said, "Teddy, the shade up on that knoll there looks like it might be a bit cooler than down here."

"Huh?" he said, having initially forgotten what I had asked. Then he went, "Oh, yeah—it does look pretty cool up there. Just let me get a handful of taters and I'll come up there with you."

When we got up to the knoll, Teddy spread his handkerchief out on the ground to put his food on it, and I just let my shirttail down so mine was in my lap. We had to be careful about setting our cups on the grass because it wasn't a very level surface, and the cup could tip over. Neither one of us wanted to waste a drop of Momma's sweet tea.

"Now what is so all-fired important for you to talk about?" Teddy asked. "And why have you been moping around all morning?"

I looked down at my apple pie and fingered around the edge of the toasty brown crust. "Teddy," I said at last, "I think I am really bad sick. I think I might have some terrible, awful disease like cancer and I might even die. I'm scared how I am gonna tell Momma and Daddy."

He looked at me and grinned as though he had just seen a circus freak. "Ronnie, what in the world would make you think that?"

"Well," I began hesitantly, "last night, I was playing with my little soldier. You know, like you said, it's all right, but I still don't think it's right. So I was trying to stop touching it, but my little soldier just kept standing up and pushing. No matter what I did, it kept wanting my attention, and I needed to go to sleep. So I slapped it and told it to go to sleep."

Teddy snickered.

"Well, it wouldn't lay down," I continued, "so I slapped it again and again, trying to get it to lay down, and then suddenly this warm mush came gushing out of it. I thought it was blood and I had maybe hurt myself slapping it, but when I got up and checked by a candle in the kitchen, it was kind of white and watery looking. It must be some discharge of sickness. I know I have to have some terrible disease."

Teddy got the freakiest look on his face. He stared at me for a second with his eyes popping wide. He had a huge grin came on his face, and then he couldn't contain himself any longer. He burst out laughing like I had just told the funniest joke he had ever heard. I was horrified. There I sat thinking that I was dying, and he was laughing like it didn't even matter.

"I can't believe you would laugh at me like that!" I exclaimed. I got up, forgetting that I had dinner in my lap. My food went rolling off into the grass. I marched off in the opposite direction, crying as I went. I was mad, scared, and hurt.

"Wait! Wait! Ronnie, come back," Teddy said pleadingly as he came after me. He might have been half genuine with concern, but more likely was afraid that Daddy would get onto him for picking on me. About twenty feet away, he caught me by my elbow and spun me around toward him. "Ronnie, you are not dying," he said, still wanting to snicker.

"How do you know?" I exclaimed.

"Because I know what happened to you," he affirmed. "Come on, let's go sit back down and I'll tell you what is going on."

I reluctantly went back to our spot with him. Teddy picked up my biscuit and pie off the grass and handed it to me. "Here, you better eat," he said. "Daddy ain't gonna let us sit out here much longer." I took the food, brushed grass and twigs off it, and took a hesitant bite.

"What happened to you last night is called cumming," he said. "Men and older boys do it all the time. It means you are becoming a man. If it hadn't happened to you from slapping your little soldier, it would have happened pretty soon in a dream or something. It happens to me every time I play with my little soldier. It's supposed to happen."

"How come something like that is supposed to happen?" I inquired.

"Cause it's where babies come from," he said, glancing back toward Momma and Daddy.

"You mean I'm gonna have a baby?" I exclaimed once again, half-horrified.

He laughed again. "Boy, you do have a lot to learn. No, goofball! You have been on this farm all your life. You know where baby animals come from—out of their mommas, same as we came out of our momma. That stuff on your belly last night is called jizz, cum. Some people call it semen. It is what makes a baby if it gets inside a girl. You know we breed cattle and hogs. They have it too. If it don't get inside a girl, it don't do nothing, and even if it gets inside a girl, she has to be at the right time of her period for it to make a baby, even then."

"What's a period?" I pondered.

"It is like when the cow comes in heat and the bull breeds her. If the cow ain't in heat, then she don't get bred, but even if she did, she couldn't make a baby then."

"You mean people go in heat and breed like cattle?" I questioned, my sense of wonder mixed with disgust.

"Yep," he replied. "It's how you, me, and sissy got here."

"Oh, Lord of mercy," I said, looking away from him.

"It's okay," he continued. "Almost all adults do it. Haven't you ever heard the bed squeaking from the front of the house in the middle of the night before? Hasn't that ever woke you up?"

"Yeah," I replied, not looking back at him, "but I just thought it must be the wind blowing the screen door or something."

"Nope," he went on. "That was most likely Momma and Daddy breeding."

"Don't you talk like that!" I exclaimed as I turned directly toward him with sudden anger. "They don't do that!" Suddenly, I had this image in my mind of Daddy mounting Momma like a bull in the field.

"Yes, they do," he said. "If they didn't do it, we wouldn't be here. Just like if the bull didn't breed the heifers, we wouldn't have any baby calves to take to the sale barn. It's nature, Ronnie. It's normal, and so is slapping your little soldier around. It's just something boys do till they get married."

"You mean that's okay?" I questioned.

"Yeah. I said it was, didn't I? Just don't let Momma or Daddy ever catch you, especially Daddy." Teddy looked back over toward Daddy and Momma and then back to me. "Daddy would give you some line from the Bible like, 'It is better for your seed to be buried in the belly of a whore than spilled needlessly on the ground.' Then he is likely to swat your bottom."

"Well, if Daddy would spank me for it, then how can it be okay?" I questioned.

"'Cause I said it is," he replied. "Daddy gets all high and mighty with that preaching stuff and wants to tell everybody how to live, but truth is, he ain't so perfect himself. There are things he does that ain't right."

Teddy never did get along too well with Daddy. There were plenty of times he defied Daddy's authority and plenty of times he got his butt beat for it. Part of me wanted to believe Teddy that it was okay to play with my little soldier, but part of me was half scared I would be doing something terribly wrong. Yet as much as we spatted, I was close to Teddy, and I looked up to him.

"Boys," we heard Daddy call from off down at the edge of the cotton field, "time to get back to work."

Teddy and I scrambled to our feet and walked fast toward the cotton field because we didn't want Daddy upset with us for lollygagging. I shoved the rest of the fried pie in my mouth as we went.

After that, I had mixed feelings. On one hand, my little soldier seemed to demand more and more attention all the time, but after I heard what Teddy said about Daddy not approving of it, then every time I did it, I felt awful guilty about it.

Teddy, if he noticed, never gave attention to it, and once in a while I would wake to catch him rubbing around on his little soldier as well. We didn't talk about it much after that. It was just an understanding we had between brothers that we would be touching ourselves, and we wouldn't tell nobody. I learned to just keep rubbing my jizz stuff into my belly when

I was done, and then it would all kind of disappear into the skin like lotion. I battled with myself over touching my little soldier all through fall and winter and prayed that Daddy would never catch me. It was like I couldn't stop, like my little soldier made demands on me, extracted payment. My body and my needs could not be denied. I had no idea at that young age that it would become the biggest battle of my life. My talk with Teddy helped some by letting me know it was natural, but it didn't help in the way of my guilt, and I felt like I needed to talk to someone else for that.

My Grandma Miller lived just over the hill from our house. She was my grandmother on Momma's side, and she lived just across the back side of our farm. Grandpa Miller, they say, died in World War I after he volunteered to go. Momma was just a toddler when he was killed, and she was the only child he had. Grandma Miller never married again and raised Momma all by herself—well, except for a little help from my great-grandparents, I guess. She said Sam Miller was the only man she loved and the only man she would ever love, so she never allowed another man to court her.

She probably seemed a lot older to me than she really was when I was a kid, but country women spend a lot of time out in the sun working the fields just like their menfolk. That can make a body look older than someone who has never had that lifetime of exposure to the elements. Even though she might only have been just past middle-age, she still needed a little help. Daddy, Teddy, and I cut and hauled wood for her so she could build a fire and stay warm in the winter. Daddy would plow her garden in the spring, but she pretty much did all the rest by herself.

She had a tiny cabin down at the bottom of the hill on a flat space. There was a porch straight across the front, and she loved to sit out there in her rocking chair on warm days. There was a stone well just off to the side of the porch, and through spring and summer, mint grew around the stones. If she made you a glass of tea, she would pinch a bit of a mint leaf into it for flavor. She kept the tea in a half-gallon mason jar. Then she tied a rope under the lid and lowered it into the well to keep it cool during the summer. Cool well-water running over the jar in the bottom of the well cooled the tea just right.

I always loved to go visit Grandma Miller because I knew she could soothe a broken heart or a worried spirit like no one else in the world, and there were a lot of times I made that trek across the hill to talk to her, sometimes even when I didn't ask Daddy for permission. There must have been a reason Momma had so much love in her, 'cause she got it straight from her own Momma.

Daddy said I could go visit Grandma Miller after supper one night in late April and said it was okay if I spent the night as long as I got back the next day in time for chores. It was a Friday night, so there was no school the next day.

It wasn't a long trek over there and took me a half an hour on foot. When I got there right about six o'clock, Grandma Miller was sitting out on the porch in her homemade hickory rocking chair. It had been one of those days with a temperature in the upper seventies, warm for spring, and Grandma was resting on that porch enjoying the evening breeze when I came walking up.

"Well, mercy me," she exclaimed, "looks like my handsome grandson has come to see me."

I walked right up onto the porch and gave her a hug while she still sat there in her rocking chair. "Hi, Grandma," I said as I felt her warm cheek next to mine and her hands softly patting me on the back. She wasn't all that old really, maybe along about sixty at the time, but when you are fourteen years old, someone that age can seem ancient.

Grandma always kept her hair pulled back in a rolled bun on the back of her head, and sometimes she would stick a couple of knitting needles in it to hold the bun in place. You had to be careful when you hugged her lest you put an eye out on one of those needles, but she usually had them point side down.

"So what brings you to these parts?" she said, like I had come from some far-off land.

"Oh, I just thought I would come spend a little time with my granny," I said as I plopped down on the porch floor with my back against a post and one leg dangling off the side just above Granny's flower beds.

"Have you eaten?" she asked.

Of course, she asked. Country women would feed you like nobody else.

"Yes, ma'am, course I have."

"But you ain't had none of my pie though, have you?"

My grin was a dead giveaway. It didn't make any difference what kind of pie it was or whether I had already had pie at home. Granny made the best in the county, and she knew I would be wanting a piece.

"I'll just cut you a little slice," she said as she got up from the rocking chair.

"What kind you got, Grandma?" I asked, watching her pull open the screen door and go inside.

"I think you like cherry, don't you?" she shouted back from inside the house. "I opened a jar of cherries yesterday that I canned last summer, and it turned out a real good pie."

"Yes, ma'am!" I shouted after her. "You know I like me some cherry pie."

The next thing I knew she came back through the screen door with a big piece of pie on a saucer with a fork. She handed it down to me, and I wasted no time digging out that first bite.

"How have you been, Grandma?" I questioned as I chewed my pie.

"Been okay," she replied. "Kind of nice to see some good weather, but it won't be nice to see the ticks a crawling."

Grandma had guineas and chickens wandering free range around her yard, and they did a pretty good job of eating up the ticks, but nobody got through an Arkansas summer without tick bites.

"Yeah, I know," I said. "I hate them ticks and chiggers, but it ain't much fun scrunching your butt up next to a wood stove trying to keep warm in the wintertime either."

"How have you been?" Grandma asked with a sly look.

She knew I came to see her when I had something troubling me. "Oh, I don't know," I said. "I guess I have been doing okay."

I could not figure out how I was going to discuss feeling guilty about touching my little soldier.

I set my pie plate to one side, having already wolfed down my treat. Finally, I asked, "Grandma, how do you know when something is wrong?"

"Hmmmmm," she pondered. "I guess it's wrong if the Good Book says it's wrong." She kind of moaned as she sat forward in her chair, leaning toward me. "But then I guess the basic definition of the word wrong is something that hurts somebody."

"So if it don't hurt nobody, but the Good Book says that it's wrong, then it's still wrong?" I questioned.

I looked out across her yard where a yellow cat was napping under a tree.

"What does your daddy say about it?" she asked.

I had not dared to discuss touching my little soldier with Daddy.

I could only imagine that his response would not be good. "Well…I…I haven't really asked Daddy that question yet," I replied. "He don't seem to be much open to talking about things with me. Most of the time it feels like he just wants me to stay out of his way."

"Your daddy can be a stubborn man," she said as she gazed off in the same direction that I was looking. She must have been wise enough to know what kind of things I might be struggling with just coming into puberty.

"You know," Grandma said, leaning back into her rocker and clicking it back and forth over the cedar boards of her porch, "when boys and girls get to be about twelve to fourteen years old, something starts happening to them. They start to have changes in their bodies and start feeling things they never felt before. You been having anything like that happening to you?"

I nervously nodded my affirmation, but I couldn't bring myself to look at her.

"Hmmmmmmm," she pondered as she kept rocking. "You know there are some things that a person might do all to themselves in private that they wouldn't do around somebody else, and there are certain needs that the body has that have to be taken care of, like when you need to go to the toilet. You would do that in private. People don't talk about going to the toilet. There might be other things that need to be done in private. It is just important that you only take care of that which is absolutely necessary, and you don't let yourself start thinking things that might get you in trouble or might hurt somebody."

My Grandma Miller was definitely a very wise woman. She had essentially answered the question that I wanted to ask without my even having to ask it. Feeling a little resolved, I changed the subject. "Grandma, I know God wants me to preach. I know He does, but Daddy won't hear of it. He won't even show me what he does to get ready for a sermon."

"You still think those dreams mean that you are called to give the gospel?" she asked.

"Yes, ma'am," I said. "I keep having them, and it seems like Jesus and the redheaded lady are in every one of them."

"Well, what would you preach about if you could give Sunday service?" she asked.

I didn't have to ponder. I had already thought about it. Daddy never had taught me about how he planned his sermons and since the dreams told me that I am Jesus's Word, I figured I would let him do the talking. I leaned forward, picked up a twig that had blown up on the porch. I began swirling it around on the porch floor like I was drawing something.

"Well, Grandma," I said as I watched the stick going around, "I assumed I would just let Jesus do the talking. I would just get up there, give Him my voice, and let Him say whatever He wants to say. I mean, in the dream He said, 'You are my Word,' so that ought to mean He is going to speak through me."

"Hmmm…well," she said as she leaned back and began thinking. "I guess that might work. You got any idea what Jesus wants you to say?"

I sat there silent. Truth was, I had no idea.

After watching me sit there in confusion for a while, she said, "Most of the preachers I have ever known have *not* just gotten up there and let

Jesus talk. Now it ain't that Jesus maybe didn't take what they started and then speak through them, but most of them had some idea what they were going to talk about before they ever got up there. Seems like they spot something going on in the world that is wrong, and they look up what the Bible has to say about it, then they preach on that. Maybe they find some Bible story or a parable or some passage in the Bible, and they start looking up other places in the Bible where that same topic is addressed, and they preach on that, but they have got some idea where they want to go before they head there."

I had gone back to stirring the invisible pot with my stick. I didn't look up. Finally, I said, "Grandma, what is fornication?"

"Why are you asking about that?" she questioned.

"Well, the Bible says that fornication is a sin, and daddy said my first dream about the red-headed woman was a dream of fornication, but I don't really have no idea what it is."

"You thinking about preaching on that?" she queried.

"I don't know. I might preach on it if I knew what it was."

She smiled and leaned back in her chair again. "Seems like there is a lot you still have to learn about that Bible and things you need to understand before you start preaching."

"Daddy won't teach me nothing!" I snipped. "He just keeps saying I'll learn when I'm old enough."

"Well, there are a lot of ways of learning about the Bible," she said, "and it ain't all found in the Bible. You ever thought about looking that word up in the dictionary just like you would if you found a word in a schoolbook that you didn't understand?"

"No, ma'am," I said.

"Well, maybe you might want to think about doing that."

She got up and went back into the house. In a moment, she came back with a dictionary. She handed the book to me and said, "See what you find." I looked up the word, and it said, "Consensual sexual intercourse between two people who are not married." I really didn't know much more than before.

"Grandma, I really don't know what that means either—*consensual*."

"Well, then you may have more words to look up," she said. Then she asked, "What has your daddy taught you about things like fornication?"

Because I had a little bit of an idea what it meant, I began to breathe heavy, and I began to tear up a little. "Not much of nothing I guess, just that it's bad."

"Well, truth be told," she continued, "I think your daddy needs to be the one who is teaching you about things like that, not your old granny. Now you can go on and keep looking up words in the dictionary or you can ask your daddy what he thinks you ought to know about at this point in your maturity, or you can let it go and maybe assume if there are things in the Bible you don't yet understand, you are not ready yet and certainly not ready to be preaching about it."

I set the dictionary down on the porch floor. It was getting late in the day, and the sun had already hidden below the horizon, leaving the pale gray mist of dusk. It was getting too dark to read anything without a lantern anyway. "I guess maybe I'll wait and see," I said.

"Your time will come, sweetheart," Granny said as she got up and walked over to me. She reached out her hand for me to give her the book. I handed the dictionary to her.

"Come on," she said. "Gonna be bedtime soon." I followed Grandma into her house.

Everybody on the farm went to bed early in those days. Before there was electric, there wasn't much use in staying up past dark anyway. You could read by an old oil lantern, but it wasn't easy to do. After we got electric at our house, Daddy got a radio so we could listen to music and shows, but Grandma Miller still didn't have electric. At her house, when the sun went down, so did you.

Grandma lit a lantern and led me to the bed that had been Momma's bed when she was growing up. She turned back the covers and said, "Sleep tight." Then she kissed me on the forehead. She left the room and closed the door. The bedrooms in Grandma's house had doors instead of curtains.

I think Grandpa Miller had installed those when he built the house before he went to war. I guess Daddy just didn't think doors were necessary.

After Granny left, I stripped down and got in bed. It was kind of nice to sleep in a bed that I didn't have to share with Teddy. For a while, I just lay back staring at the darkness thinking about what I was going to preach for my first sermon. Then I fell asleep before I even knew what happened.

CHAPTER 3

A family that came to our church had a beautiful daughter named Lynetta. She was the oldest of three girls in the Jacobs family, and she was about a year older than I was. She stood maybe two inches taller. She had wavy light-brown hair and the prettiest dark- brown eyes you ever did see. You don't see girls with dimples very often, especially in the chin, but she had a little dimple right at the bottom of her chin. Somehow that dimple seemed to make her even prettier. Her lips were full and soft, like two little pink pillows resting one on the other.

Lynetta's momma and daddy, Martin and Edith, had become friends with my momma and daddy. They lived about ten miles away over at Imboden. Still they came to our church on Sunday even though there were lots of churches closer to their home. I think Mr. Jacobs got upset about something with the church he was attending and went shopping around for another church to attend. He said when he first heard my daddy preach that he knew he was a man of the Gospel, so he decided to start bringing his family over to our church. That was fine by me because every Sunday I got to look at Lynetta.

When I was younger, I realized she was pretty, but I didn't really start to understand just how pretty she was till my little soldier started contributing to my opinion. By the time I was fourteen years old, it seemed like I couldn't keep my eyes off her. Now and then she would catch me looking, giving me this pretty little smile that said "I caught ya!" and I would look away embarrassed.

For a couple of years, once or twice a month, the Jacobs family would come to our house and have Sunday dinner with us after church. Sister Jacobs would get in the kitchen with Momma and help with the dinner fixings, and usually she brought something to contribute to dinner, most times a cake or pie, but they owned a grocery store at Imboden, so sometimes we got treats we wouldn't normally get, like soda pop or potato chips.

In the colder months after dinner, Daddy and Mr. Jacobs would sit in the living room discussing farming, the Bible, politics, and such, while us kids would, most of the time, be on the floor of our bedroom playing Chinese checkers or dominoes. In the summertime, Daddy and Mr. Jacobs sat on the front porch after dinner, and we kids would run around the farm, finding things to do and play. Hannah stayed behind to play in the yard with the two younger Jacobs girls, Ruth and Kathryn. Teddy, Lynetta, and I would play hide-and-seek or fantasy games down in the barn lot.

One June Sunday when I was almost fifteen, Teddy had gone after church to spend the day with one of his friends and then meet up with us again at Bible study that Sunday evening. That left just me and Lynetta to play hide-and-seek after dinner, and it is a whole different game with just two people.

I buried my eyes in the crook of my elbow and leaned up against the big oak tree that stood to the east side of our barn. Lynetta said I had to count to a hundred and give her plenty of time to find a good hiding place. When I finished and turned around, I didn't have a single clue where she might have gone. I checked behind bushes and behind the pond bank. I looked in the cow stalls inside the barn. I was about to give up when I heard an almost whispered voice from the hayloft say, "You're not a very good seeker."

"Shucks, Lynetta," I said as I stuck my head inside the hayloft. "Where are you?"

I heard a giggle over to the left of the hayloft and went over in that direction. I might have stepped on her if she had not been fairly high up in the hay pile. She had covered herself completely over in loose hay. I was turning this way and that when she shouted "Boo!" then reached out and grabbed my leg.

"Aggghhhhhhhh!" I turned, and there she lay laughing like she was about to shake apart.

"You're not a very good seeker, Ronnie." She laughed.

"Well, you sure are a good hider," I admitted. I knelt down beside her on my knees in the hay. "Ain't that scratchy on you?"

"Maybe a little." She grinned. "But it was worth it."

She started pulling stray bits of straw off her dress and out of her hair. I just knelt there watching her when she asked, "Well, aren't you gonna help me? I can't get it all."

I reached over and pulled some straw off her shoulder and then pulled some out of her hair. One piece was a little stuck, so I needed both hands to pull the strands of hair apart from the straw and finally get it out of her hair. I had never been that close to any girl before, and without even thinking, the next thing I knew my little soldier was standing at full attention. I was embarrassed that she might see it so I said, "Here, let me see what you got on your back." I ducked around behind her and began pulling straw off the back of her dress.

"You're not hiding anything from me, Ronnie," she said. "I know boys get hard, and I know why."

"I'm sorry, Lynetta," I said. "I don't know what you are talking about."

"Yes, you do." She giggled. "I saw you. I know you have a hard-on."

"I'm sorry. I didn't mean to," my embarrassed voice replied. "It's kind of like it has a mind of its own. Sometimes it just does that for no apparent reason."

"Oh, there's a reason," she said.

She turned around toward me and looked me square in the eyes. "Ronnie, have you ever thought about what it would feel like to be inside a girl?"

My breath half went out of me. I know my face must have turned the color of a tomato because I felt it flush hot. "I, ah…ah…ah…I don't know what to say."

She just kept looking at me with those brown eyes, scanning my face, smiling. It seemed like she had looked at me forever when she said, "Would you like to know what it feels like to have it inside of me?"

"Oh heck, Lynetta, I haven't even kissed a girl before." I felt myself trembling, heard my voice quivering.

She grinned, eyes gleaming like a couple of twinkling stars on a cool summer night. "Well, here is your chance," she said.

My face went flush again. I knew exactly what she meant because, by that time, Teddy had fully educated me about sex. I felt my heart pounding like it was going to leap from my chest. Part of me wanted to jump up and run out of that barn as hard and fast as I could run, but my little soldier was pushing hard against my pants, telling me that it wanted something else entirely.

Lynetta took my hand and moved it to her breast. I felt weak and vulnerable, like there was nothing I could do to stop it even if I had wanted to, and I didn't want to. I knew Daddy wouldn't approve, and I knew the Bible said it was wrong, but I just couldn't seem to help myself. My knees were trembling.

"Do you want to learn how to kiss?" she said softly.

"I…ah…ah…ah…"

"Here, follow my lead," she said as she reached her hands out and placed them on either side of my face. She pulled me slowly and gently toward her and touched her lips to mine. Then she moved her lips gently over and around my lips. I opened my mouth, and her lips moved with mine. Her tongue moved in to touch the tip of my tongue. I felt like every cell of my body was charged with electricity. Slapping my little soldier sure felt good, but it had never felt anywhere close to this. I put my hand behind her neck and leaned into her, wanting her lips on mine, devouring her softness and her sensuality. Suddenly, I wanted to touch every inch of her. I wanted to feel her skin against mine. I wanted to melt into her like candle wax flowing over onto a tablecloth.

"Slow down," she softly commanded as she began to unbutton my shirt, "and not quite so hard. Be gentle."

Her hands went across my chest where my chest hair was just beginning to grow. Then she moved her hands around to my back. Everywhere she touched felt like ecstasy. Never, ever in my life had I felt anything like it. I knew in that moment if there was a drug that could make me feel that way, I would take it every day, all the time, constantly, if I could.

We slowly and carefully undressed each other, and when at last I slipped my little soldier inside her, I felt the exhilaration immediately building toward crescendo.

"Now just move," she said softly. "Just remember to pull out before you let go. I probably won't get pregnant because I'm not on my period, but just to be on the safe side, pull out. Promise?"

"Uh-huh," I said with stilted breath, and I began to push.

"Promise?" she questioned.

"Uh-huh."

It didn't take much. I had only rocked back and forth a few times when I felt myself shiver all over. I didn't want to stop. I wanted to stay right there inside her and let it go. Suddenly I realized I had promised. A feeling of emergency ran through me. I needed to keep that promise, but I knew that if I didn't pull back in a split second, it was going to be too late. Pulling out was the hardest thing I had ever had to do at that point in my life. I quickly pushed myself off, rolled over on my back, and my little soldier exploded like fireworks on the Fourth of July. Guttural moans, animal noises, came out of my mouth as I convulsed and grabbed fists of hay. Lynetta cupped her hand over my mouth to stifle the sounds but that could barely contain the noise much less the seizures that pulsed through my body, especially when she reached down and began to gently stroke my little soldier as I released. When it finally subsided and I began to catch my breath, Lynetta giggled.

"Did you enjoy that?"

"Jeepers! I exclaimed. "What was that?"

"You came, silly," she said. "Haven't you ever cum before?"

"Well, yeah," I said and motioned my hand weakly up and down toward my little soldier, "but only by myself and never anything like that!"

"It's different when you are with a girl than when you are by yourself," she said.

"I'll say!" I exclaimed.

After that, I couldn't get enough of Lynetta. I found myself peeking at her in church more and more and feeling more and more guilty about it because I knew I was there to be worshiping the Lord, not to be looking at girls. By that time, I had learned what fornication and consensual meant, and I knew what we were doing was against the Word of the Lord, but it was like I had been administered some kind of drug that made my will to resist completely futile.

Lynetta began encouraging her parents to come to our house on Sunday after church. Her daddy invited us to come to their house for Sunday dinner, and even though it was a long way off, there were a couple of times that we went. We rode over there with them in their car, and then they brought us back because we didn't have a car at that time. Lynetta's family had a nice house. It was an old farmhouse, but her daddy kept it pretty much updated and in good repair. They had running water in the house even though it was basically an outdoor pump over a sink. Still, they didn't have to go hauling water from the well like we did. Their house was a two-story white house with a long wide porch all the way across the front. I guess her daddy could afford a good house as he owned a grocery store at Imboden that got good business from the surrounding area. Their house was located on the north edge of town just off Highway 62. They didn't have a big farm like Daddy, but they had several acres and kept livestock for meat. About a mile from their house, there was a great big pond with a high bank that sloped way down into a clump of trees, and when the weather was warm enough, we would go out there on Sunday afternoon to make love, any chance we could. By that time, I was barely past sixteen, and Teddy was nineteen, so he wasn't around much.

Lynetta and I had been spending time together for almost a year. The folks knew we were sweet on each other, but there were just things that boys and girls were not allowed to do, and when you got to that age, the adults kept a close eye on you.

Lynetta and I would say we were going to walk over into town to window shop, but we would sneak around behind the house, through the fence, and over behind that pond bank. Lynetta hid a blanket up inside in a hollow tree so it wouldn't get wet, and we would take it out to lay over the ground when we were making love. I got better at it as time went on. Lynetta taught me things so it didn't end as quickly as it did that first time, and I learned how to bring her to orgasm too.

It was a lot more difficult to get away when the Jacobs's came over to our house. There were no stores nearby so we could have an excuse to take a walk downtown. Sometimes, we would say we were going to walk over to the church house a, couple of miles away, and then sneak off into the woods. When Teddy or Hannah were there, we couldn't take a chance of going to the barn for fear of getting caught, and often the menfolk would walk down around the barn to look at cattle or pastures.

One autumn day when it was getting a little bit cool, we made a fatal mistake. There had come a cool rain the day before, and it had just stopped raining that morning. Although there were bits of clearing, the skies were still filled with dark gray clouds. So not only was the temperature dropping down into the upper forties, but the leaves were wet, and the roads a bit muddy.

"I don't guess we are going to be able to do anything this week," I told her, "except maybe stand a little off the road out of sight and kiss."

She put her arms around me and pulled herself close. "The church is warm," she said. "There is still a fire going in the wood stove from services this morning."

"Oh goodness no, Lynetta!" I said in shock. "We can't do that. Not only are we more likely to get caught, but it's the Lord's house. We would be defiling the house of the Lord."

"I figure the Lord is everywhere," she said. "So if making love is defiling the Lord's house, then we have been defiling it everywhere we have been. Besides, nobody is going to be coming back over to the church till Bible study this evening."

"I feel awful about it, Lynetta."

I took a deep breath and looked away into the woods. A little stream of water trickled over some rocks in the ditch beside the road. "I hate when I sin," I said. "Every time we do this, we are breaking the Commandments. I love it when we are together, but then I feel horribly guilty."

"Maybe," she said, "but I don't really understand why God would give people such intense urges and then demand that we ignore them. It seems kind of cruel to me, like giving a baby some candy and then telling him he can't eat it, letting him have one little piece, and then slapping his hand if he reaches for more."

"We are allowed the candy," I said looking back at her. "It just has to be within the sanctity of marriage. The baby doesn't get candy all the time, but just as a special treat. The parent decides when the baby can have it. God decided we get our candy within marriage."

"See, I don't even understand that," she said. "It's not like we are hurting anyone. I could understand something being a sin if it hurt someone, but we are not hurting anybody, and why are only married people given the privilege of making love?"

"It's about family," I told her, "having a unit of support that allows us to grow up in safety. Women who have babies all by themselves without the support of a family don't fare very well."

"So we have to be careful about not having a baby," she argued. "As long as you don't cum inside me, we'll be fine." She reached down and cupped her hands over my butt, then leaned back, and looked at me straight with those enticing brown eyes. She smiled a broad, beautiful, alluring smile and kissed me. My little soldier was already standing up, eager and urging toward her. Every time we even kissed, there was a battle that I fought inside me, a battle between everything I was taught that is right and proper and the longing of my little soldier. My little soldier always won. I had long battled with myself even touching my little soldier at night. I tried to tell it no, and I would go for days resisting the urge, but the longer I waited, the more intensely it begged to be touched. In the end, it always won.

"We don't have to do anything," she said, touching one soft palm against my cheek. "We can just sit on the pew and talk, be together where it is warm."

"I guess," I said with a nervous smile, gritting my teeth and regretting what a terrible sin it would be if we did anything sexual in the church. I took her hand and turned toward the church, which was only about a hundred yards away. When we rounded the curve, there it sat on the edge of the dirt road, a little gray clapboard building with a tiny makeshift steeple that could not have been more than eight or ten feet high above the front crest of the roof. Through the week, it had doubled as a one-room schoolhouse where Teddy, Hannah, and I had all attended. However, when school consolidation laws had passed a few years back, the bus came to take us to Oak Ridge school after that. It didn't really affect Teddy. He was nineteen and talking about joining the Army. So it was just me and Hannah still going to school. Even at just sixteen years old, that old building held lots of memories for me.

We walked up the front steps of the building and through the door that was never kept locked. By the time we arrived, I reckoned it to be about 3:00 p.m. We had plenty of time to at least sit and visit before Bible study would convene at about 5:30 p.m.

The school desks that once sat in lines from wall to wall were traded out for pews on Sunday and had all been taken away by that time. In some respects, the church looked bare to me. I had stopped pestering Daddy to let me preach, and in fact, my religious dreams had all but gone away. After I met Lynetta, preaching didn't seem so urgent to me anymore.

The church was warm but somewhat dark with the residual rain clouds still lying gloomy over the autumn sky. A bit of gray light filtered through the clear window panes that lined the walls on either side. The church was simple. Wood pews sat atop wood floors, and a wood podium sat on a platform in the front that was elevated about a foot above the rest of the floor. A chalkboard crossed the wall behind the podium, and Daddy sometimes used this to write out Bible verses during his sermons or during Bible study so people could look them up. The walls were painted an eggshell color, and the window frames were varnished wood with a walnut stain.

I led Lynetta to the very front pew of the church because it was the only one that didn't face another pew in front of it. On the front pews, hymnbooks lay in the seat, each about three feet apart. All the other pews had slots on the back where hymnals could be placed. When we sat on the pew, I put my arms around Lynetta's shoulders and pulled her close to my side. "I have a lot of memories here," I said. "I attended school here from the first grade. I miss it now that we are going over to Oak Ridge."

"Your daddy ever come up here through the week?" she asked.

"He has a time or two," I responded. "More, since they don't have school here anymore. I think he finds it a quieter place to study for his sermon than home."

"You look like him," she said. "You are handsome like he is with dimpled cheeks, dark hair, and pale-blue eyes. Do you think you will go bald like your daddy?"

I turned and looked at her thinking the question to be odd. "I hope not," I said. "Why do you ask?"

"I'm just trying to imagine what you will look like in your forties," she responded. "If you stay as handsome as your daddy, I would not mind continuing to make love to you even as you get old."

I somewhat snickered. "What are you saying here," I asked, "that you still want to be with me when I'm forty, or that you have lustful eyes for my daddy?"

She giggled. "Maybe I'm saying both."

I thought Lynetta was a sweet girl. I very much enjoyed her company and I was exhilarated about making love to her, but I had never thought about the proposition of growing old together. The idea of marrying her and starting a family had not actually crossed my mind until that point. "Are you saying that you could see us making a family together?" I asked.

"Well, yeah," she replied. "Don't tell me you haven't thought about it too."

"Well, I—ah—I guess I was giving more thought to just being a teenager than making plans for the future."

She sat back and lay her arm across the back of the pew. "Didn't you tell me you thought you were called to preach like your daddy? Isn't that thinking about the future? Wouldn't that also involve family?"

"I don't even know about that anymore," I said. "I probably haven't thought about it in a year or more now. Whatever I do, I would kind of like to take my time and figure it out."

"You are saying you are not sure about me," she said.

"I'm saying I'm not sure about anything, Lynetta." I placed my hand beside her head and ran my fingers through her soft hair. "I know that I really like you, and I know that I am extremely attracted to you."

"But you don't know that you love me," she snapped and pulled away from me.

"I didn't say that," I said, leaning toward her to take her hand.

"That's just the point," she snapped with her smile becoming sadness. "You didn't say that. You didn't say that you love me."

"I do love you," I affirmed, "but for goodness' sakes I'm only sixteen."

"A lot of people are married and have babies by the time they are sixteen," she said. "I'm seventeen. I don't think that is too early to start thinking about a family."

"Okay," I said, giving in. "We will start thinking about a family, but for right now, only that, just thinking, not making a family, not looking so far down the road that we trip over what's before us today."

Her look turned to one of mischief, and she began to giggle. "You are so funny," she said, laughing. "Some girl is going to wrap you around her little finger so tight someday that you will never get loose."

"What?" I grimaced in confusion.

"I was just joking!" She laughed. "We like each other. We enjoy each other. That's enough for now." She grabbed me by the collar, pulled me over, and began kissing me. I felt her soft lips engulf mine, and our tongues met. She pulled back with those big brown eyes perusing my face and then kissed me again. Then she leaned into my ear and nibbled as she whispered, "Why would we want to give this up just yet for the drudgery of changing diapers?"

A mix of feelings ran through me. One of them was anger. One of them was lust. Truthfully, I did want a family someday, but I wasn't ready. She got me to admit that. I did want to enjoy the freedom that comes with no commitment, just sex, just fun. I loved being able to surrender to abandon with Lynetta.

My little soldier ached for release and pushed firm against the fabric of my khaki pants. I kissed her back, ran my hand over her breast, down her side, and up under her skirt. I ran my fingers around the edge of her panties to the band over her butt and began pulling them toward her knees. As I did this, she unbuttoned my shirt and started loosening my belt. I undid the buttons of her blouse, pulled one breast up out of her bra and began urgently rolling my mouth over her nipple.

"GREAT GOD IN HEAVEN!"

I heard a man's voice scream and realized immediately it was Daddy. I pulled quickly up from the pew to see Daddy and Mr. Jacobs standing at the door. Before I could even stand up, Daddy had crossed the room, pulled me up by the back of my shirt, and slugged his fist into my face. I fell backward to the floor with my lip cut and blood running into my mouth.

"SINNER!" he screamed as he picked me up from the floor and hit me again. "FORNICATOR! DEVIL'S SPAWN!"

His fist was drawn back to punch me again when Mr. Jacobs laid a hand softly on his shoulder and said, "Paul, stop. Please stop now."

Daddy turned around with the rage of Satan on his face and screamed, "HE HAS DESECRATED THE HOUSE OF THE LORD!"

"I know, Paul," Mr. Jacobs said softly, "but surely we can handle this calmly and quietly."

Daddy let go of me and pointed at Lynetta who was scooted back to the end of the pew terrified, nervously trying to button her blouse. "Well, he is not the only one!" Daddy snarled in a low growl. "Obviously, your daughter is a Jezebel and a whore!"

Anger crossed Mr. Jacobs's face, but he held himself. "Paul, I don't see how name-calling and accusing is going to help these children."

"Think not that I came to send peace on earth," Daddy snarled, quoting Matthew, "I came not to send peace, but a sword!"

"I understand that you are angry," Mr. Jacobs responded. "I am angry too, and I agree that they need to be punished, but I think we need to step back and collect ourselves a little bit."

"Who being past feeling have given themselves over unto lasciviousness, to work all uncleanness with greediness?" Daddy quoted again. "How dare you defend this atrocity?"

"Paul, please," Mr. Jacobs pleaded. "I am not defending the behavior, but they are just foolish kids. Doesn't the Bible also talk about forgiveness?"

"Take your harlot daughter and get out of my church!" Daddy commanded. "Get this whore out of my sight!"

"Paul, my daughter is not a whore." Mr. Jacobs tried again. "I will thank you not to call her that. Both your son and my daughter are just stupid kids doing stupid things."

"The Lord will not suffer the soul of the righteous to famish, but he casteth away the substance of the wicked!" Daddy quoted as he took a step toward Mr. Jacobs and put a finger in his face just two inches from his nose. "I SAID…GET YOUR WHORE OUT OF MY CHURCH!"

The look on Mr. Jacobs's face was one of sadness, anger, and despair. He was losing a friend, losing a church, perhaps losing a daughter. There was a moment when I thought he was going to hit Daddy. Instead he turned to Lynetta. "Gather yourself," he commanded firmly.

Frightened, Lynetta scrambled quickly to her feet. Mr. Jacobs walked over to her and first put one hand under her arm as though to guide her by the arm. Then he stopped, caught himself, and changed what his body was saying. He put his arm around her shoulder and said quietly, "Come on, child, let's go."

I watched them march quietly through the front door of the church, wondering what would ever become of Lynetta. Daddy stood silently and watched them as well.

Just as Mr. Jacobs exited the door, he looked briefly back over his shoulder and softly said, "Forgive them, Father, for they know not what they do."

Then, Daddy turned to me, said not a word, but punched me square in the face again. Then, he hit harder and knocked me back into the podium. My head hit the sharp corner, and I fell to the floor. He kicked me hard in the gut and hissed, "HELL IS CALLING FOR YOU, SINNER!"

Consciousness faded. I don't know what Daddy did after that. I passed out. Then I had a dream of the redheaded woman. She found me crying and naked in the corner of the corn bin in our barn. She came to me, gently lifted me up, and led me by the hand, still naked, down the road toward church. When we arrived at the church, she stood before the door and waved her hand in an arch across the doorway.

The church door opened, and a bright yellow light came forth shining on us. It was hot and bright like the sun, so I couldn't look at it. I squinted my eyes and turned toward the redheaded woman. When the light hit her face, she turned to me, and for a moment, her face looked like Lynetta. Then she cupped each hand beside my head, leaned over, and kissed me on the forehead. "Go and sin no more," she said sweetly. Then she stood back to look at me, and her face began to melt like candle wax.

I awoke when I felt a splash of cool water on my face. Then I painfully opened my eyes. Daddy was standing over me with a bucket of water and a rag. He set the bucket down on the floor and threw the wet rag into my face.

"Clean up the blood," he commanded. "You have about forty minutes before Bible study starts." He then turned and walked out the door, down the steps, and out of sight.

I got to my knees and washed my blood from the hardwood floor. Then I carried the bucket out, tossed the bloody water onto a nearby tree, and set it at the corner of the church building. I struggled painfully back up the steps to close the door of the church. Then I staggered home.

CHAPTER 4

Momma did not ask how or why I got black eyes and a busted lip. Maybe she didn't really want to know. Maybe she knew but was afraid to say anything. I had never seen Daddy beat her, but I did see him slap her once. She didn't question anything. She just held the cold compress to my head while tears trickled slowly down her face.

When Momma went back to the kitchen to put some fresh ice in the wash rag that she had been holding to my head, Teddy sat down at the foot of the bed and said, "I told you he was an asshole."

"He's not an asshole," I said. "I defiled the church. I deserved what I got."

"He's a hypocrite!" Teddy insisted. "He wants everybody to follow the rules he is not willing to follow. He thinks he has the right to tell the whole world how to live."

"He is called of God," I said painfully through my sore jaw. "It is his job to make sure people follow the Commandments."

"Bullshit!" Teddy defended. "It is not his job to act all high and mighty and pretend like he is hot shit 'cause he can quote the Bible."

"You don't understand," I said. "He's troubled by the sin in the world."

"He is troubled by the fact that he can't rule the whole world," Teddy said as he laid a comforting hand on my leg.

I said nothing.

After a while Teddy said, "I'm getting out of here."

"What do you mean you are getting out of here?" I questioned.

"I've talked to an Army recruiter over in Jonesboro. I'm joining up, going to fight in Korea or something. It's gotta beat dealing with the old man and his crap. Besides, if I don't join, they are likely to draft me anyway."

I lay there, silent for a while.

"I don't know what to say," I said, finally. "I knew you would be going sometime. I mean, you are nineteen, but I figured you would be getting married or getting a job or something.

Teddy smiled, and a little hiss came out of his nose as he looked at the floor.

"Just got to get out of here. There ain't nothin' around here. Try to scratch a living from the land all your life. Go over to Jonesboro or Blytheville and get a job in a factory? Ain't worth it."

"So when does this happen?" I queried.

"Be going to boot camp down in Louisiana in about two weeks," he smiled. "Fort Polk."

"Have you told Momma and Daddy?" I asked.

"Told Daddy," He quipped, looking off into the corner like he was going to see something there. "He don't give a shit. Haven't told Momma yet."

"She ain't gonna like it," I said.

"I know," he said quietly, "but life's gotta go on."

World War II had come and gone while Teddy and I were growing up. We knew little about it except for huddling by the radio listening to the evening news after Daddy finally signed up with the electric cooperative and that was after the war was already over. The Korean War was just as confusing to me. I really didn't even know what a Communist was or why they were such a threat to the world. I just knew that it seemed like there was never much of a time that America wasn't at war with somebody or that some terrible thing was happening somewhere around the globe. I knew I didn't want any part of it, but I had no idea how I was going to stay out of it, especially when they were drafting boys left and right for military service. It seemed like I had my hands full just dealing with life in Ravenden. If I was going to play my part in saving the world, it was not going to be by going to war, not if I could help it.

Teddy finally told Momma that night that he had signed up for the Army. She cried practically all night. I guess she was losing one boy to war and one to sin. It had to be a painful thing.

After that, the Jacobs never came back to our church, and I didn't hear from Lynetta again. I never found out what happened to her until way into my adult life, that she had married some boy from over at Hardy a couple of years later, that she had three kids by the time she was twenty- five, and that she was a divorced single mother before she was thirty.

I determined that I wasn't going to sin again. Every night I buried my face in the Bible. I read it from cover to cover and then read it again. I didn't touch my little soldier, and every time my loins ached, I fell to my knees and begged God to take the affliction of lust from me. Sooner or later I would give in and masturbate, or I would have a dream that released it. I dreamed about having sex with different women. I even dreamed about doing it with a fat old lady from church who had hairs growing out of her round chin. It didn't matter because each time, I woke up angry, angry with my mind, angry at the devil for putting things like that in my mind. I felt guilty every time. Each time, I determined to try even harder not to let it happen again. I had learned the full meaning of the word fornication, and I had learned how it could hurt someone. In church, I humbled myself and prayed. I held my hands to the heavens and spoke in tongues. I praised the Lord with every fiber of my being, and still the relentless urgings of sex would not turn loose of me.

Sunday after Sunday, time went by. Then when I was seventeen, a little bit after Easter, I woke from a dream in the middle of the night. I sat straight up in bed screaming, and my heart was pounding like it was going to pop right out of my chest. It might have scared Teddy, but he had gone away to the military, and in those days, I was sleeping alone. I had no more sat up in the bed screaming when I heard Daddy say, "You all right in there?" In a moment, Daddy shined a flashlight into my room. I felt like a panting dog and must have looked like a prisoner in an interrogation room under that light. Daddy reached up to the ceiling and twisted the light bulb into the socket.

After we finally got electricity, there were still no light switches on the wall and no plugs. You turned the light on by twisting the bulb till it connected, and anything that needed to be plugged in was on an adapter that screwed into the socket above the light bulb. You turned the light off by unscrewing the bulb a little.

When Daddy turned the light on, I startled, sucked air in like it was going to be my last breath, and lunged backward in the bed. "Mercy, son!" Daddy exclaimed. "What's the matter here?" By that time, Momma and Hannah were peering in at the door.

Finally, I caught myself so I could speak. "I had a dream, Daddy," I gasped. "I had another dream like I used to have. This one was real scary."

"Well, ain't nothing but a dream," Daddy said. "Go back to sleep."

"I don't know if I can sleep, Daddy," I pleaded. "What if it comes back on me? It was real bad."

"Most of the time nightmares won't repeat," Daddy said. "Now we all need to go back to bed."

I sucked tears back in my chest. "Daddy, I don't want to go back to that. Maybe I might just sit in the kitchen for a little while."

"Suit yourself," he said as he turned around and gave a hard look at Momma.

Momma said, "Maybe if I fix him some warm milk, it might soothe him to go back to sleep."

"All right then," Daddy commanded. "Go with your momma, but keep quiet. The rest of us are gonna go back to bed."

I followed Momma into the kitchen and sat at the table. Momma took some milk out of the icebox and poured it in a sauce pan. We still had the wood cook stove and still used block ice in an old icebox to keep the food cold, but after we got electric, Momma used a hot plate to supplement cooking when she didn't want to stir up a fire in the stove. Momma plugged in the hot plate and set it low to warm the milk, then she came over and sat across the corner of the kitchen table from me. I looked up at her, and she smiled. Momma had the warmest smile and the softest eyes. I always knew she loved me. She never had to say it. I could feel it run through me every time she looked at me.

"What you been dreaming this time?" she asked as she pulled her nightgown up around her neck because, even though it was spring near Easter, it was still a bit chilly at night.

"Same kind of stuff I dreamed before," I said, "except things are getting kind of riled up."

Momma reached over and patted my hand. "Tell me about it."

I was halfway scared to tell, like talking about it was going to bring it back on me. After a moment, I started to talk.

"Well, you know Jesus has been in most of these dreams since the second one, and the redheaded woman from the pond is in all of them. This one started with a hard rain falling, and Daddy came through the house shouting that a storm was coming and everybody needed to get to the cellar fast.

"Off in the west, I could see through the window there was a big black tornado coming this way, and we all went running for the back door, trying to get to the cellar. Everybody ran out of the house except I was behind everybody else, and I couldn't get out before the wind hit."

I could feel terror rising in me as I told the dream, and it seemed almost too frightening to repeat, but I went on.

"I saw through the kitchen window the tornado ripped the barn into little shreds of wood that went flying everywhere, slamming up against the house, and the roof began to peel back. The wind was blowing something awful. I was trying to get to the back door, but it flew off the hinges and went flying through the air. There was nobody left in the house but me, and I heard demon voices in the wind shouting my name and telling me that I was bound for hell. I looked out the back, and I saw Jesus nailed to a cross, but the cross was blowing in the tornado, and it went tumbling off into the woods with Jesus still nailed onto it. I heard my name called from behind me, so I turned around. There stood the redheaded woman, and she was right up in my face real close. She shouted, 'SINNER!'"

Momma said "Shhhh" and patted my hand to remind me that the rest of the family was trying to sleep. We both knew if Daddy said to keep quiet, that was exactly what he meant.

I dropped my voice to a whisper.

"Well, she yelled, '*Sinner!*' Then she grabbed my face and started kissing me. When she did, the windows blew out, and shards of glass flew across the kitchen, and demons flew all about the room, cackling and yelling, '*Sinner! Sinner! Sinner!*' I thought the whole house was gonna blow away with me in it. I heard something behind me from the other way, so I turned back around toward the back door. That whole end of the house was blown away, and Jesus came crawling up the back steps toward me. He had the crown of thorns around his head, and he was bloody and bruised with blood running down his face. He raised one hand up to me and he shouted, 'YOU HAVE BEEN TOLD!'"

I caught myself and lowered my voice back to a whisper. Then I continued.

"Anyway, He shouted, '*You have been told that you are My Word, but you have defied Me!*'

"Momma, the words were like a shock wave from a bomb, and when the wave hit me, it blew me back into the wall, and I woke up."

Momma took a deep breath. She got up to pour some warm milk in a cup. She unplugged the hot plate from the extension cord that ran to the light socket, brought the cup back to the table, and set it in front of me. "That sounds like a really powerful and scary dream," she said.

I took a sip of the milk and looked up at her. I started to take another sip but had to set the cup down as I broke down into deep sobs. "Momma, I'm so scared!" I pleaded.

"Honey, it's okay," she comforted. "It's just a scary dream."

I looked at her with begging eyes. I couldn't say it, but I was begging her to give me an answer, tell me what I should do. "I'm a sinner, Momma. I'm a sinner bound for hell 'cause I have defied my calling."

"Ronnie, you have not defied your calling," she said insistently.

Momma sat back in the chair and looked toward the night-blackened window. Then she looked back at me and sighed. "You remember when you told me your first dream?" she questioned.

I nodded.

"Well, I'm sorry, Ronnie."

She laid her hand on top of mine.

"I should never have told you that your dream meant that you were called to preach. I didn't mean it. I just wanted to tell you something to get you out of my way 'cause I was busy fixin' dinner. I never knew that it was going to torment you the way that it has."

"But, Momma," I debated, "what if it wasn't really you speaking? What if it was God speaking through you, letting me know that this is my calling? The dreams have come back. Since I was ten years old, they have repeated in one form or another, and now they have come back stronger than ever. It has got to mean something."

Momma knew that she could not convince me.

"I can't say that I ever knew of a time that God spoke through me," she said, "but I doubt that I could convince you that He didn't."

"How would we know for sure?" I debated. "Maybe sometimes God speaks through us, and we don't even know it."

Momma sat silent for a while. Then she said, "You know, Ronnie, when you have children, you are making a path for the future. When you have a baby, it is not just that God gives you someone to love like you could love no other, it's that you can see that baby, in your own mind, walking off into some distant world that you will never see yourself. You hope and pray that they will learn some bit of wisdom from you, that they will develop a good heart and a gentle spirit. Maybe you hope they might become successful or wealthy or something, but probably what you hope most is that they will simply find a way to be happy."

Momma saw that I had finished the cup of milk. She picked it up and took it back to the counter and dribbled a little water in it from the dipper so it would be easier to clean in the morning. Then she turned around and sat back down in front of me.

"Ronnie, I got no idea whether you have been called to preach, and it is not for me to say. I know that you are convinced that you have the calling, and maybe that's all that it takes. I do know that God's will *is* done, and if that is what you are meant to do, then somewhere, sometime, whether your daddy agrees to it or not, then that is what you will end up doing, but the time might not be now. So for now, trust your daddy that he knows his church, and he knows you. If he says it isn't time, it isn't time."

A sadness came over me, and my face fell. "Okay, Momma," I said.

There was nothing else for me to say. I thought to myself that there was no reason for God to choose a miserable sinner like me to preach His Word, especially after I had desecrated His temple.

"Are you ready to go back to bed now?" Momma asked, patting my hand.

I nodded and headed back to the bedroom. The light went out behind me, and I knew that Momma was making her way in the dark back to her bed.

When I got back to my room, I took careful fingers to unscrew the hot light bulb in the ceiling and felt my way back to the bed. I rolled over next to the wall where I always slept when Teddy was there and fumbled a little to get under the covers. I didn't sleep much, and I did a lot of thinking that night.

CHAPTER 5

Late in October of my seventeenth year, Daddy caught a terrible case of the flu. He was throwing up, had diarrhea, and could barely even keep water down. Momma kept making him drink some of her home-canned tomato juice mixed with a little cool water, or she would feed him her chicken and vegetable soup.

"I don't want that!" he snarled at her.

"I don't care if you don't want it, Paul, you need to drink it," she returned. One of the few times Momma ever stood up to him was when he was sick or when one of us was sick. At those times, Momma's word was law.

Daddy would drink it, throw it up, and exclaim, "I don't want no more! It will just make me puke."

Momma was relentless. "Paul, if we don't try to keep some fluids down you, then you are going to dehydrate, and then you will be really bad sick."

Along about midweek, Daddy started affirming, "I gotta get up and prepare my sermon for Sunday."

Momma said, "You will do no such thing. You are too sick even to get out of bed."

Come Friday, Daddy was still bad sick and still insisting that he had to get up to prepare his sermon. Momma was still arguing with him.

"Curse it, woman!" he exclaimed. "I have got to get something ready for Sunday."

"Well," she replied, "if you are well enough to preach Sunday, then you can either preach off the cuff, or you can reuse one of your old sermons, but I don't think you are going to be well enough to go anywhere Sunday."

Late Saturday evening, the argument went on, but Daddy was sicker than ever, mostly too weak to argue. "If I don't do something," he wheezed, "there is going to be no Sunday service."

"Well, you are not doing anything," she told him. "Either they can congregate Sunday and just have singing and Bible study, or Ronnie can preach. He's been wanting to preach anyway. Maybe this is his time."

"That boy is NEVER going to preach in my church!" Daddy hissed.

I heard bits and pieces of these conversations most of the week. When Daddy said that, I happened to be standing at the door because I had come to see if there was anything Momma needed. My heart dropped when I heard him say that. I knew after that incident with Lynetta, he was never going to respect me. Despite all my dreams and being convinced that I had the calling, I had the feeling that my sins had blocked the way, and God had decided that a miserable sinner like me had no place in the pulpit.

Momma saw me standing there, knowing that I overheard. She turned back to Daddy after looking up and giving me a forlorn look. "Paul, that is a terrible thing to say," she responded. "Why would you not want your son to preach when it is something he has been wanting to do since he was little?"

Daddy didn't care that I was standing there. He didn't care that I overheard.

"He doesn't deserve to be called a man of God," he wheezed through stifled breath.

A look of shock crossed Momma's face, and she shot a look quickly back to me. There were some things she would push him about and others she wouldn't. That was something she would not confront. Instead, she got up, came to the door, and pulled me into the other room.

"I don't know what in the world is the matter with your daddy," she whispered, "but there is no reason why you shouldn't take care of Sunday service. You know everything you need to do to conduct the normal service, and Ronnie, if you want to preach, now is your chance."

"Momma, I don't want to go against Daddy's wishes," I said, defending.

"His wishes and God's will are likely two entirely different things," she responded. "You got any idea about what you might preach on?"

"I guess, kind of," I said.

The truth is, I had been thinking about it ever since I had the talk with Grandma Miller. I had been studying my Bible, and I had been thinking about quite a few things.

"Then go put yourself a sermon together," she encouraged, "and don't worry about what your daddy thinks about it. He is so sick right now he is probably not even going to know it's Sunday."

All week long, I had been doing all the farm chores, work Daddy and I normally did together. After Teddy left, a lot more work fell on me. By that time, Hannah was ten years old. She helped with a few little things, like feeding the chickens and gathering eggs, and that was a lot easier since we finally got a hen house, but other than that, it was a lot of work, and I was really tired. I would rather have just gone to bed and forgotten about it all, maybe have used Daddy being sick as an excuse to not go to church on Sunday, but I had been waiting my whole life for an opportunity to preach. Trouble is, even though I had thought about what I might want to preach on, I had never really done anything to prepare a sermon. I had no notes, no Bible references, nothing. I went back to my room, twisted on the overhead light, and began flipping through my Bible. I was as nervous as a cat in a mouse trap factory. I found a few Bible verses, jotted down a couple of notes, and then felt stumped. It wasn't going to do me any good to stay up half the night preparing a sermon because I had no idea what to do with what I had. I only had an idea and a couple of verses. That's it.

Daddy slept more than he was awake, and I saw the light go out in Momma and Daddy's room early. I wasn't up much past that time, but I couldn't sleep. I just lay there staring at the ceiling, rehearsing in my head what I might say or how I might say it and praying that God would use my voice to speak His truth.

Dawn came early, and there was work to do on the farm on Sunday. When it came to farm work, Sunday was the same as any other day of the week. Before church, the pigs still had to be slopped, the cows milked, and hay put out for the calves that we would soon take to the sale barn.

Hannah got up and came to the barn with me. She helped me move the cows in for milking, when each had its turn. Momma stayed with Daddy. By Sunday morning, he was half delirious, and Momma was debating whether to send for the doctor.

After chores, I took my Bible and walked with Hannah to the church. Even though we had gotten a truck about the same time we got electric, Daddy didn't want me to drive it for fear I would damage it. The church wasn't that far anyway. When we got there, Hannah helped me bring in some wood and light a fire in the wood stove because it was a little chilly that morning. After the fire was going, I sat on the front pew opposite to the side where I had last been with Lynetta and prayed. I had not sat there since the last time I saw Lynetta. I didn't want to sit on that side of the church anymore. It seemed like I was still doing something wrong if I sat over there. I missed Lynetta, not just because we were having sex together but because we were friends, and I really liked her. Maybe I had even been in love with her. I thought about her as I prayed, and I asked God to bless her and her family and to bring her peace. Then I prayed for God to heal Daddy.

A little before ten o'clock in the morning, people started arriving for Bible study. At first, I heard a car pull up outside, and then the Jones family came in, Brother and Sister Jones and their three kids all under the age of six. Their baby was about two years old, and Sister Jones had her hands full just keeping him occupied every Sunday morning. There was nothing in the way of babysitting in a small country church like that. If a child started crying or acting up, one of the parents had to get up and take them outside so it wouldn't disturb the service too much. In just a few moments, others began to arrive, and people began to ask about Daddy.

"Oh, he won't be here today, Brother Parker," I said humbly. "He has been bad sick with the flu."

"Yeah, yeah," said Brother Parker, "bad strain been going around. Well, tell your daddy we are praying for him."

I looked up at the clock that hung on the back wall of the church, where Daddy could see it when he preached but nobody else could because they would all be facing the front of the church.

"Yes, sir, Brother Parker, I will," I said and realized that it was about time for Bible study to start.

We all called each other Brother and Sister because we were a church family, and it felt like family. We relied on each other, helped each other in times of crisis, grieved over one another's losses, and rejoiced with one another in times of celebration. There were hardly ever more than fifty people in that little church, and some Sundays, depending on the circumstances, quite a few less. On that Sunday, it was almost full. I think I would have felt a lot less nervous if it had been one of those Sundays when only about half the congregation showed, but I couldn't think of a single person who was missing that Sunday morning except for Daddy and Momma.

At ten o'clock, I got up in front of the church and announced, "In case any of you have not already heard, Daddy has been bad sick with the flu this week, and he is not able to attend Sunday service, so I will be conducting Bible study and the service. If you don't mind, let's bow our heads and say prayers for Daddy to be well and back to preaching soon."

The church then hummed with a rumble of different people saying different prayers for Daddy out loud and at various different levels of audibility. Some prayed in tongues. I prayed along with them. Then briefly, I said a bit louder than the others, "Thank you, Amen."

Everyone raised their heads and looked again to the front of the church.

"Well, Ronnie," spoke Brother Clark from off in the back, "are you gonna preach the sermon today?"

"Well, sir," I responded nervously, "I'm going to do the best I can with that."

"Praise be!" Brother Clark exclaimed. "I know you will do well."

I didn't dare thank Brother Clark for his praise because I figured to say thank you would be a show of arrogance like I knew somehow what I was doing or thought that I was better than others because of it. I simply said, "Shall we start the Bible study with a prayer? Brother Clark—Johnny— would you lead us in prayer?"

I remember Brother Clark saying, "Let's bow our heads" and "Heavenly Father," but I don't recall much of anything between that and the "Amen." We all had places marked in our Bibles from the study the week before, and so Bible study pretty much took care of itself. More than anything, it was taking turns reading passages and then discussing their meaning in context to our lives.

After Bible study, we had a short break, and then I prepared for the main service at eleven o'clock. I think if someone had said "Boo," I would have jumped completely out of my skin. I was about to deliver my first sermon feeling like an imposter, feeling vain and unworthy.

We had song leaders who got up to the front of the church to lead the singing, and I had led singing a time or two myself. Folks said I had a real nice voice, but it wasn't the singing I wanted to do. It wasn't the singing I felt called to do. We had a beat-up old piano angled back away from the corner to the far right of the podium, and Sister Matthews would bang out the rhythm behind the hymns, even though most of the time it was barely in tune. It didn't matter. We made a joyful noise unto the Lord. Sometimes people would shout "Hallelujah" or dance about during the hymns. Sometimes people would raise their hands and speak in tongues.

After a few hymns, I kind of danced my way to the podium and shouted, "PRAISE JESUS!" This was a sign that I was ready to speak. From the back, I heard a resonating, "Hallelujah!"

It felt so strange to be there, to be up in front of these people, most of whom were old enough to be my parents or grandparents, and the majority of the rest were old enough to have children of their own. Yet there I was, arrogant it might appear, but humbled in the presence of these fine and faith-loving people.

I had studied a little of what I might say that morning, but in truth, after the opening, I had no idea where I was to go from there. I truly believed, despite my sins with Lynetta, that I was called to speak His Word and to share the Gospel. A moment after the Hallelujah was spoken, I said, "My name is Ronald Dennison, and I am a sinner."

The words fell on a silent congregation. I don't know that they had ever heard such a thing proclaimed from a preacher before. I had certainly never heard Daddy admit to the congregation that he was a sinner, yet according to the Bible, we are all sinners.

"For all have sinned, and come short of the glory of God—Romans 3:23," I proclaimed and scanned the congregation with eyes needing to be affirmed of the truth I was preaching. A twinge of fear scratched at my heart as I wondered if any of them had found out about what I had done with Lynetta.

I felt nervous and unsure of myself. I didn't know what to do from there. I had assumed the Spirit would move me, but at that moment, I felt more moved to run out of the back of the church and never come back than to preach. My hands trembled as I held the Bible close to my chest. I said nothing for a moment, and then with a crackling voice, I turned to Sister Matthews and said, "Sister, I do believe I could feel more moved to speak if you might just play a gentle refrain on the piano, soft like, in the background."

Daddy had never made such a request. There was no music playing in the background when he preached. Sometimes, he would stand with both hands gripping the podium and shout the Word with the veins popping out on his neck. Sometimes he would prance back and forth across the front as he spoke.

Sister Matthews had sat down on the front pew and when I made this request, she seemed a bit taken aback, but she smiled and said, "Certainly, Brother Ronnie." Then she got up to the piano and began to play softly. That old out-of-tune piano never sounded as marvelous as it did to me on that day. It gave me motivation and momentum. After a few moments of listening to the music, I began to speak again.

"My name is Ronald Dennison, and I am a sinner, and oh, how I hate that I have sinned. How I hate, Brothers and Sisters, that I have fallen short of the glory of God. I hate that I have to battle the spirit of sin within me. I HATE that my Heavenly Father has been displeased with me. Because, Brothers and Sisters, there is nothing I want more than to please the Lord."

I held the Bible out away from my chest and waved it across between me and the congregation. "Do you hate that you have displeased the Lord, Brothers and Sisters? Say Amen if you want nothing more than our Heavenly Father to find you worthy in His sight."

A resonating "AMEN!" came back from the congregation, and I began to feel empowered. I began to feel energized, and I felt the spirit of the Lord move within me.

"We have all sinned!" I proclaimed. "We have all sinned, every one of us, going back to the dawn of time and the original sin. We have all sinned ever since the sin that caused Adam and Eve to be cast from the garden. We have all sinned and have fallen short of the GLORY of the Lord! We have all sinned and displeased our Father in Heaven. Yet a solution was given to us. We have a solution to our sin. Our Heavenly Father looked down on our wickedness! He looked down on our depravity! He looked down and saw how we suffered from our sins! He looked down and saw how we suffered from our separation!" I took the Bible up into the air above my head with one hand and then slapped it across the palm of my other hand as I shouted, "AND HE HAD… MERCY…ON US!"

Shouts of "Hallelujah!" "Praise Jesus!" came from the back of the church and resonated to my ears as though the words of God Himself cheered me on. Sister Matthews raised the volume and tone of the music to match the energy that became present, and I continued.

"HE HAD MERCY ON US! HE HAD MERCY ON THE SUFFERING THAT SIN HAD CAUSED HIS CHILDREN! OUR HEAVENLY FATHER LOOKED DOWN FROM THE HEAVENS AND HE PROCLAIMED 'I CANNOT LET THIS HAPPEN! I CANNOT LEAVE MY CHILDREN LOST WITHOUT A WAY TO COME HOME!' AND SO HE SENT HIS ONLY BEGOTTEN SON THAT WE MIGHT BE SAVED. JESUS DIED…THAT…WE…MIGHT…BE… SAVED! SHOUT HALLELUJAH, MY BROTHERS AND SISTERS IN CHRIST, IF THIS IS WHAT YOU BELIEVE!"

"HALLELUJAH!" came like a wave from the congregation sweeping over the church. It practically rattled the windows like thunder. More shouts resonated through the church. "PRAISE GOD! AMEN!"

There was an energy building, a praise, a fullness, and I felt it like hairs standing up on my arms in a heavy electrical storm. I shouted at times and almost whispered at times. All the while, Sister Matthews's piano music followed me like a minstrel of the Lord.

I don't remember everything I said on that day. I don't remember every quote from the Bible I used, but as the sermon was winding to a close, I heard myself say, "Jesus is my refuge! He said, 'Come unto Me and I will give you rest.' Jesus is my comforter! He has told me to lay my burdens down, to give it ALL to him. He has told me to give Him my sorrows and my concerns, my anguish, and my guilt. Jesus…is…my…REFUGE! He is the forgiveness of my sins, but in His forgiveness, there is a price to be paid. When Jesus saved the adulteress who was about to be stoned, and He said to her accusers, 'Let he among you who is without sin cast the first stone.' What did He say to her? Sure, He let her accusers know that they were sinners too, but what did He say to her? He said, 'Go and sin no more.' He did not say, 'Keep on doing what you have been doing that will be fine!'—No! No, my brothers and sisters! He said, 'Go…and sin…no more.' For if we are to be saved, we make a commitment! Our sins are forgiven, but we make a commitment, and IF our forgiveness is to stand, we must hold to that commitment that we will…GO…AND SIN…NO MORE!"

I looked quietly around the room, making eye contact with one person after another, after another. I stood there in silence quite a long time before I spoke again.

"He died for your sins, Brothers and Sisters. He died that you might have forgiveness of your sins and that you might have everlasting life. WHAT ARE YOU GOING TO DO FOR HIM? He does NOT require that you lay down your life as He did! He only requests one simple little thing. Go and sin no more. Now, I don't know about you, Brothers and Sisters, but I plan to dedicate my life to fulfilling that simple request. I plan to dedicate my life to keeping that commitment to my Lord and Savior Jesus Christ that I WILL GO AND SIN NO MORE!"

Again, I raised the Bible over my head and slapped it against my other palm as I shouted, "BECAUSE IF HE CAN LAY DOWN HIS LIFE FOR ME…SURELY…I CAN CHOOSE NOT TO SIN…FOR HIM!"

Again, I stood silent, looking out across the faces in this small group, and finally, I spoke again gently and softly, "Brothers and Sisters, do you have need of prayer today? Do you have need of anointing and the laying on of hands? Do you need to confess your sins to the Lord? Won't you come and let me pray with you? Won't you come forward now and bring your burdens that we may pray together for the forgiveness of our Lord?"

For a time, nothing happened, and for a brief second, I thought that I must not have preached a good sermon. Then Brother Wilson stood up. He was a man in his fifties who had farmed the Arkansas land since he was a child and the sweat of his brow watered his crops almost as much as the God-given rain. He was a man whom I knew to be of good character, a man who cared for his family and worked hard to supply them. His grown sons now shared his farm with him as he had shared it with his father before inheriting it. For all I had ever seen, he had been a gentle, loving, and honest man who had wonderful relationships not only with his family but with his community. He had taken care of his frail mother at home for many years after his father died, until she eventually passed as well. I could not have imagined how he might have sinned, but he stood and made his way, slowly, to the front. He knelt down in front of me and burst into tears. He said only, "Pray for me."

I knelt down before him, put my arm across his shoulder, and leaned my head up next to his. At first, he only sobbed in my arms, placed his arms around my back, and held me close the way no one ever had except maybe for Momma and Grandma. It felt strange, at first, to have a man hold me that way. It felt strange to be a seventeen-year-old boy comforting a man in his fifties, but I held him. Eventually, he began to whisper his sin into my ears. He told me something I never would have believed of him if I had not heard him say it himself, and I will not repeat it here. His grief over his wrong, and the sincerity of his heart, touched me. Instantly I forgave him. I felt no more judgment of him in that moment than I would have felt for a newborn infant. I forgave him completely for what he had done. In the years to come, I forgave many others before I could ever forgive myself.

When he had finished his story and had become silent, I said softly in his ear, "Your sins are forgiven, Brother Wilson." I leaned back away from him, stood up, and placed my hands on his head. Then I heard myself speaking in tongues, "Cala saga toolata! Chaga nata sola hala cala que hala coe usha saga la! IN THE NAME OF JESUS, I REBUKE THE SPIRIT OF SIN! I REBUKE YOU, SATAN!"

I barely nudged my hand toward his forehead, and he fell over onto the floor and began to shake like he was having a seizure. Animal sounds were coming out of his mouth, and for a moment I was scared. We had never done anything like this in our church before, and I wasn't sure what kind of reaction the congregation might have to it, but Brother Carter stood and shouted, "WE REBUKE YOU, SATAN!" Then others followed.

For a short time, Brother Wilson shook, and then he began to cough. He rolled over on his side and panted like he had run a marathon, and then he sat on the floor, looking around like he didn't know what had just happened to him. I walked over to him and reached out my hand to him. He reached out and took my hand. I said, "Get up, Brother Wilson. Your sins are forgiven." He stood. Then I pulled him to my side and put my arm around his shoulder. I said to the congregation, "Will you greet with me our brother in Christ after we say our prayer of closing. Please bow your heads as we pray."

I said a prayer of blessing for the Lord to watch over us all in the coming week and bless all our endeavors. Then everyone came to the front of the church. Brother and Sister Clark both came immediately to me, and Sister Clark reached out her hand to take mine. She cupped her rough farm wife hands around mine, smiled at me lovingly, and said, "Oh…oh…Brother Ronnie. The spirit of the Lord moved in this church today!"

As she was still holding my hand, Brother Clark slapped a huge muscular arm across my shoulder and said, "Son, you have the calling!" Others began to come up from the pews with exclamations of, "Oh, Brother Ronnie!" and "What a miracle we have witnessed here today!"

I was both elated and humbled. In all my life, I had never seen the congregation react to Daddy the way they reacted to me on that day. There was a part of me that wondered how Daddy was going to react to all this, and there was a part of me that was filled with such excitement that the dreams might have been true. Maybe they had been a true calling that I was meant to preach the Word of the Lord.

After church, Brother and Sister Clark gave Hannah and me a ride home. Hannah said hardly anything about the morning's events. When we got home, Brother and Sister Clark came in to see Momma and asked if there was anything they could do to help. Daddy was sleeping. Momma said his fever broke, and he had not been throwing up anymore. She figured, more than anything, he just needed to rest. Sister Clark scolded Momma for not sending one of the kids to let them know she needed help, and Momma insisted that she had it all under control. Sister Clark pronounced to her, "Well, this evening you are going to rest! Don't you dare even think about cooking supper! I will bring it, and Ed will come by after a while to help Ronnie with chores."

That afternoon Sister Clark came by with a basket full of supper for everyone. Brother Clark, as promised, stayed around and helped me with chores before going home to do his own.

The Clarks were an older couple, a little bit younger than Grandma, who lived down the lane a bit. Their names were Johnny and Rosalee, and their kids had grown up and moved off to raise families of their own. I heard their oldest son was studying over in Memphis to be a doctor. We didn't visit with them all that much, but they were always there to lend a helping hand if we needed it, and sometimes we helped them as well.

By the time Sister Clark brought supper, Daddy had woken up, and Momma, as well as Sister Clark, began insisting that he try to eat. Sister Clark had made a whole loaf of sour-dough bread, and she brought all kinds of things to go with it like slices of fried ham, some skillet-fried German- style potatoes, and home-canned green beans from her garden.

Daddy had not eaten solid food in about three days. Momma got him up to sit on the side of the bed and laid a tablecloth over his lap. She cut his ham up in bite-sized pieces and put a little bit of everything on the plate.

He first sank his fork into the potatoes, and when he put the bite in his mouth and began to chew, Sister Clark exclaimed, "Praise Jesus!"

Daddy looked at her a bit forlorn and a bit stern and choked out through a hoarse voice, "Thank you for the food, Sister Clark. You are a true blessing."

"Shush now," Momma chided. "You just eat now and save your voice." Then she turned to Sister Clark and said, "Sister Rosalee, we are, indeed, blessed to have you in our lives."

I stood at the door and watched all this.

Sister Clark replied, "Blessing! You want to know who is a blessing?" She turned a bit to point at me. "This young man is a blessing!"

Then she started saying things I really wished she had not said. "Brother Paul!" she went on. "Oh, my! You should have heard this boy preach the sermon in church this morning!"

Daddy shot me one of those looks where if eyes had been knives, I would have died a bloody death. I could see that he wanted to say something. I could see the displeasure on his face. Then he simply nodded to Sister Clark and picked up another bite of food.

"Brother Paul!" Sister Clark continued. "This boy has a true gift! I know that you preach a marvelous sermon! You do! But I haven't heard anybody preach like that since I went to this huge revival over at Memphis a couple of years ago."

Momma looked up at me and smiled then darted an embarrassed glance back at Daddy.

"Sister Clark," she said, "I am so pleased to know that Ronnie did well this morning, but perhaps we could talk about it sometime when Paul is feeling a little better and can join in on the conversation."

"Oh, I am so sorry, Brother Paul!" Sister Clark responded. "I didn't mean to go on at a time when you are too hoarse to enter in rejoicing."

I knew Daddy was not going to be rejoicing. I dreaded to face what he might have to say or do when he got well enough.

It was not long after that when Brother Clark and I headed for the barn to do chores. After helping me and Hannah with our chores, they drove home. While we were yet doing chores, I asked Brother Clark if he wouldn't mind conducting Bible study that evening. I didn't want to risk Daddy becoming even more upset with me, and I wasn't sure how it might turn out given the events of the morning. I told a little white lie when Brother Clark offered his enthusiasm that I would be conducting Bible study. I told him I wasn't feeling well, and perhaps, I might be coming down with the flu like Daddy. Brother Clark agreed to conduct Bible study. That evening, Daddy continued to sleep a lot. I spent a little time listening to the radio and a little time reading my Bible.

Then I went to bed fairly early and dreamed that I was making love to the redheaded woman while Jesus was laughing. The next morning when I woke from that dream, my guilt and my shame were palpable. The stain on my underwear was proof I had reached full climax while I dreamed of sex with the redheaded woman. The fact that I dreamed that Jesus was standing there laughing made me feel even more miserable. Why would I dream such a thing? I couldn't make heads or tails of what it could possibly mean for Jesus to watch and laugh as I sinned in front of Him. Specifically, I remember the redheaded woman's glossy red lips, kissing them, and smearing the lipstick across her face as I fornicated with her.

As soon as I dressed, I fell to my knees beside the bed and prayed. After all, I had promised from the pulpit the day before that I was going to commit my life to sin no more. Yet my mind had done things with my body that seemed to be out of my control. On my knees with my elbows on the bed and my hands clasped tightly together in front of my forehead, I prayed over and over, "Dear Lord, take this affliction from me! Dear Lord, take this affliction from me!" Tears rolled down my cheeks and dropped into little wet spots on the sheets. I felt completely ashamed and defiled. I pleaded with God to wipe away my desires that I might never sin against Him again. Momma must have heard me because she came to the door and lifted back the curtain.

"Ronnie, are you all right?" she questioned.

I looked up from my prayers and said, "Sure, Momma, I'm fine. I…uh…I just miss Teddy, and I am praying that God keeps him safe in the war."

Another lie, another sin. Even as I said it, I knew that I was sinning. I wiped the tears off my cheeks with the back of my hand and said, "It's about time for breakfast, ain't it?"

"Make your bed," Momma said, "then come on in the kitchen."

When I got to the kitchen table, Daddy was sitting there at the head of the table looking very pale, Momma was at the other end, and Hannah was sitting across on the other side from my chair. She was big enough now that her reach completed the circle. Daddy held out his hands on either side, a signal that we were to all take hold. I gripped Daddy's hand. As soon as Daddy saw that everyone was holding hands, he started to speak but couldn't get out even a word before he started coughing and turned his head to the side without letting go of our hands. When the coughing fit subsided and the evidence of grimacing pain from a severely sore throat finally left his face, he looked at me and whispered, "Please give prayer." I bowed my head humbly and gave prayer of thanksgiving that Daddy was getting well and that we were cared for in abundance.

After prayers and breakfast, cores were to be done. Momma made Daddy go back to bed. She sent Hannah on some feeding chores and came to the barn with me to help with the milking. She knew the chores as well or better than I did, and she didn't say much except for the conversation necessary to coordinate what we were doing. After the chores were finished, when we were walking back to the house, Momma said, "Ronnie, I am proud of you for yesterday. I wish I could have been there to hear you preach."

"Probably the only time I'll get to preach is when Daddy is sick," I said.

She stopped in her tracks and caught my sleeve. She looked at me a moment with those loving eyes and said, "Ronnie, I know what happened with Lynetta, and I know what your daddy did to you. Teddy told me what he did, but I think I knew, and I was too afraid to challenge your daddy about it."

I didn't say anything. I stood there before her, ashamed and loved at the same time, like I might have felt if I was facing the judgment of the Lord.

"Your daddy is wrong," she said after a silence. "I don't agree with how he is handling any of this, but the man is the head of the household, and a woman's place is to submit." She put a soft hand to my cheek and continued. "I know you cared about Lynetta, I know, but what you did with her was wrong. Part of youth is figuring out what is wrong and why. All kids make mistakes. The problem comes if you are still doing those things in later years when you should have learned better."

"I'm sorry, Momma," I said, almost quivering.

"Ronnie, you are going to preach," she said, stepping back and putting her hand under my arm to walk with me. "If the enthusiasm the Clarks showed yesterday after that service is any indication, your daddy is not going to be able to stop it. Besides, it don't matter whether your father endorses it or not. It only matters if God does."

"Sometimes I think I sin too much to preach the Gospel," I half mumbled under my voice.

Momma stopped walking again, reached out and grabbed my shoulder, and turned me toward her. "You ever notice in the Bible that some of the most beloved of God have committed great sins?"

I nodded my head.

"Don't you worry about it, my little boy," she continued as we turned to walk again. "Just follow your soul, and the Lord will lead you right."

When we got to the back door, Momma stopped one more time and said, "By the way, I miss Teddy too, and I pray every day that the Lord will keep him safe."

She patted me on the back and said, "Now go on in there and get ready for school. I'm going to the cellar to pick out some canned goods for supper."

CHAPTER 6

Daddy did not intend to let me preach again. People from church asked him about it, and he would make some excuse like he wanted me to have a better understanding of the Bible first, and he wanted more time to train me in the Word at home. Sometimes he would say that he wanted me to mature into my gift. I knew he thought I was not worthy of the pulpit because of what I did with Lynetta in church. The congregation, so far as I could tell, never knew about that, and I knew there was no way Daddy was ever going to tell about it. If anyone knew, it would have been from something Mr. Jacobs might have told someone.

If Daddy had had his way, I was never going to preach, but word spread about the boy preacher, and Daddy never quite recovered from that bout of the flu. He was sickly off and on for the rest of his life. So between days when Daddy was not physically able to go and days when people of the church would pry at him to let me preach, he finally started giving in. He never came to hear me preach, so he didn't know what I could do or what I couldn't do. He only let me preach on Sundays he didn't feel well, and he told me that I had better always have a sermon ready. People in the congregation began asking him to let them know when I was going to preach because they had friends they wanted to invite to hear me preach.

After a while, some folks began asking me to conduct a revival. I considered what all this might be doing to Daddy as he had been preaching at that church since before I was born. All those years it had been his church. He had been the shepherd of the flock. People came to him for weddings and funerals, for baptism, and to pray for the sick. There had been times in my childhood that someone came to get Daddy because of some illness of a church member or some family or friend of a church member, and Daddy would get up and go with them to their home just like a doctor making house calls. There were times that people had come to the house asking him to pray for them, and he always did. I knew that it had to feel like a betrayal to him that after all these years, people were asking more for his son than for him. I don't know that people even thought about that. Maybe folks thought that he should be proud of me and that he should want me to preach as much as they wanted me to.

Our little church began filling up. More and more people began to come to Sunday service, and I simply did what came to me when I was before the congregation—and all this happened before I turned eighteen years old.

One Sunday, just after I turned eighteen, when I called people to come forth for prayer at the end of the sermon, a woman came forth with a sick-looking little girl who appeared to be maybe ten or twelve years old. The woman was plain looking with her hair pulled behind her head into a bun. She was thin herself, but you could tell hard work in the sun had darkened her skin and had begun to make wrinkles across her face. She wore a simple tan-colored cotton dress and tie-up men's shoes with no socks or stockings. The girl she brought forth was wearing about the same except her dress was plaid and her shoes were black, Mary Jane style, and looked almost new. The child was pale and thin. Dark spots sank in her eyes, and she looked like she could barely walk. The woman brought her to the front with hands on her shoulders and presented her to me.

"Please, Pastor Dennison," the woman spoke. "My child is so sick. She has been sick all her life, and we can seldom afford a doctor. When we have had her to the doctor, most of them say they don't really know what's wrong. One of them said he thought it was something called Crohn's disease, but I don't really know what that is. Lots of times she can't keep much of nothing down, and when she does eat, it goes right through her, or she can't pass hardly at all. Sometimes, she bleeds, and you can see what she eats don't nourish her. Please, Pastor Dennison, pray for my child."

The girl barely looked at me. There was a sadness on her face wrought by a lifetime of seldom feeling well. It was obvious to me that she would have been a beautiful child, had it not been for the sickness. Her hazel-green eyes stood out like lighthouses from the sea even over those pale, gaunt cheeks. Her thin brown hair fell straight down the sides of her face and was dull like a pencil lead and almost the same color. She didn't smile, and I wondered if this was just another in a long line of desperate efforts her mother had made to save her. I wasn't sure what I was going to do in that moment, but in my mind, I quietly prayed for the guidance of the Lord. Then I reached out to her.

"Child, take my hands," I said.

She reluctantly reached out and let me take her two hands in each of my own.

"Look at me, please," I continued, and she looked up at me with a face so empty of joy that the void seemed to go directly to her soul. "What is your name, sweetheart?"

"Alissa," she replied, so softly that it was barely over a whisper. "Alissa, do you believe in Jesus?" I questioned.

She barely nodded, and I knew that she wasn't sure what she believed and that maybe she was just doing what she thought was expected of her.

"Well, Alissa," I said, "I very much believe in Jesus, and I believe here today that Jesus can heal you. I believe that His saving grace can wash over you and cleanse all the sickness out of your body and all the despair out of your soul. Will you let me pray for you today? Will you let me ask Jesus to help you?" Again, she barely nodded an affirmation.

I smiled at her, feeling a compassion and a love like I had never felt before. This was different from other times when I loudly praised the Lord and raised one hand to heaven while the other lay upon someone's head. This was different from when I shouted, "Praise Jesus, and I rebuke you, Satan." This was quiet and tender. This was a frightened child, and I heard my Lord and Savior speak in my mind that I should not frighten her any more than she already was. I knelt down before her on my knees and was just a little lower than she was as she was standing. I reached out my hand to her head, pulled her to my shoulder, and embraced her. As I held her to me, I said to the congregation, "Will you pray silently with me as I pray for this child?" Then I began quietly to pray, "Heavenly Father, giver of all life and all hope, we know that You have seen this child suffer at the hands of Satan. We know that You see her spirit being crushed by this terrible disease. We call upon You, Lord and Savior, to bless and heal this child. Bring the color back to her skin, the light back to her soul, love back to her heart, and let her play and rejoice as any child is made to do. Let her body be comforted, and let her laughter rise to the heavens in praise of Your name that she is well."

I said nothing more after that but simply held the child in an embrace for a while longer. I held her back from me and placed a gentle hand on her cheek. "Do you believe that you are healed, Alissa?"

A smile came to her face, and a tear drifted silently down her cheek. She raised both her hands straight up and shouted, "THANK YOU, JESUS!"

The congregation responded with shouts of "PRAISE THE LORD! THANK YOU, JESUS! HALLELUJAH AND AMEN!"

Alissa's mother stepped forward to me and took my hands. "Thank you!" she cried with tears streaming over her smile.

"Not I, but the Lord," I said. "Thank the Lord. Don't thank me. I am only a tool for His use."

After church that day, I saw Alissa playing with the other children in the yard as though there had never been anything wrong with her. The color seemed to have returned to her face, and she had as much joy as any other child.

Alissa and her mother, whom I learned was Susan, came to church a few more times, and then I didn't see them after that. I began to look forward to seeing them. I looked forward to seeing how Alissa continued to look healthier every week. On Sunday, I scanned the congregation looking for them, but one Sunday they didn't show up. After that, Sunday after Sunday, they failed to show, and at one point I accepted that I was probably never going to see them again.

Daddy almost stopped coming to church. He refused to come hear me preach, and he told people that his health just wouldn't allow him to sit that long in one place anymore. Still, he got out and worked the farm, even though it was obvious that he couldn't do what he once did. There were times that members of the congregation would come by to see him and ask him to come back to church.

One day, Sister Clark was over for a visit. She had asked Daddy to come back to church, and he gave her the same story, that his health just wasn't up to it, but he would be praying and praising the Lord at home. Sister Clark reached out a hand and placed it on Daddy's arm.

"Paul," she said, "You should let Ronnie pray for you. I've seen him many times heal the sick in Jesus's name. Surely he could do the same for you."

Daddy shot her a look as though Lucifer himself were baring down upon her. You could tell she felt it. She immediately pulled her hand away and nervously stammered, "Well…I…ah…well, Paul, think about it. Maybe you and Ronnie should pray together sometime." Sister Clark made an immediate excuse to leave and never asked any such thing of Daddy again.

Daddy's visits from Brother and Sister Clark became more and more rare, and eventually, they stopped coming to the house at all, unless they thought Momma needed help with something. After that, I was doing all the preaching. There were times that folks in the congregation would say they missed Daddy, but they didn't complain much.

In the summer of my eighteenth year, some of the folks in the church convinced me that we should have a tent revival to save souls and heal the sick. There was plenty of room in the churchyard to set up a tent that would easily hold two hundred people. Brother Clark and a few others said it would not only be good to save souls, but it should bring money into the church as well, and maybe we could use some of the funds to spruce up the building, maybe even build a real toilet instead of just having a couple of outhouses behind the building. I agreed to it, and Brother Clark put together a committee to get hold of a tent, print fliers and posters, and provide water and facilities during the revival.

It took a while to plan, and along about the middle of September that year, the tent went up with plans to hold a revival every night from Sunday to Sunday. We figured folks could park along the road and walk to the tent if necessary. We had no idea how many people would be attending, but the fillers and posters went out as far as Truman to the east and as far as Ash Flat to the west. Some folks even took fliers and posters up into Missouri. One of the new members of the congregation, Brother Jones, who had started coming from over near Walnut Ridge, had taken me to a photography studio and got my picture taken to go on the fliers. When the fliers were printed, he said he was sending some to family he had living in Memphis.

Come that first Sunday of the revival, I was as nervous as a cat. Momma had helped me pick out a couple of nice suits with two new dress shirts and ties, and the church paid for all of it. Collections had increased along with the size of the congregation since I had been preaching. So there was more money in the coffers. Momma never told Daddy that the church paid for the suits, and he never asked, even though we could barely afford much beyond subsistence from the farm. The church was giving me 50 percent of the collection on Sunday, and each week I brought it home and handed it all to Daddy. Each week he would look at it with a kind of a snarl, hand it to Momma, and say, "Do what you want with it." I assume he thought the suits must have been paid for out of that money. I didn't realize at the time that I was bringing home far more from the ministry than Daddy ever had.

Daddy would get out and work a little, but I had almost taken over all the work of the farm as well as the church. I tried to understand how Daddy might feel, and I tried to be sympathetic to it. I wanted nothing more than for Daddy to be pleased with me. I wanted nothing more than for him to tell me I had done a good job with anything. I never got that from him, so I accepted it from others.

On the Sunday the revival started, Momma, Hannah, and I got in the truck, and I drove us to church early so we could help with the setting up. The men of the church had been working on getting the tent and the chairs set up since the week before. Metal fold-up chairs had been rented, and by the time the tent was rented, a platform was built across the front, and the old piano tuned, there was precious little left in the funds of the church. If the revival brought in a lot of people, we would profit greatly, but if it didn't, we would be lucky to break even.

We had regular Sunday services in the church building the morning the revival started, and in the afternoon the revival committee set about getting the piano moved to the tent. The men had run an electric cable from the church building and had strung lights all around the inner rim of the tent. By the time we got there that afternoon about 5:00 p.m., there wasn't much left to be set up, but we were there early anyway. The revival was to start at 6:00 p.m., and even in September, there was plenty enough light left that we might not have to use the electric, but they turned the lights on anyway. We certainly would need the lights before each evening service ended.

Momma began helping some of the women of the church set up some water coolers and paper cups. Hannah went with Momma and hung around more than she helped. I went to Brother Clark and asked if there was anything I could do to help, but there was little else to do. So I sat on a fold-up chair that had been placed near the podium for me, held my Bible in my hands, and prayed.

I spent a good thirty minutes or more in prayer, and as I prayed, I could hear crisp in my ears the rumblings of activities around me, people's voices, some whispering in an attempt, I suppose, not to disturb my prayer. Then I heard the sound of cars pulling up and parking and the sound of car doors opening and closing. I looked up to see that what appeared to be an entire extended family not familiar to our church had parked their vehicles near the front of the tent, and they were walking up the middle aisle between the chairs. I stepped down from the platform and greeted them.

"Ah, you are Pastor Dennison, the boy preacher," the man, whom I assumed to be the elderly patron, said. Behind him were a couple of young men who were the younger spitting image of him as well as what I assumed were their brides and children. A very welldressed and permed elderly woman stood beside him in a floral dress with her gloved hand through the crook of his arm.

"Yes." I smiled as I shook his hand. "Welcome."

They all filed past me, smiling. The young men reached out to shake my hand as they passed. Each one was wearing a dark suit and smelled of cologne. Their wives were very modestly dressed young women whom I assumed were not much older than me.

There was still a part of me that felt like an imposter. There was a part of me that cringed at the sound of being called Pastor or Reverend. Even though this was something I had wanted since I was a very small boy, a part of me kept saying that I didn't deserve it. I excused myself and went into the church building for a little while. I prayed for God to guide my words, to make me worthy. In a few minutes, I was going to go do something I had never done before, something that both excited me and frightened me, something that Daddy had never done and probably would never have considered doing. I paced in the church, rehearsing passages in my mind, thinking how I would approach different topics. I had no idea how I was going to set about preaching a different sermon every night for a week, but I knew I was determined to do it.

About six o'clock, Brother Clark came and stuck his head inside the door of the church. "Brother Ronnie." He smiled. "It's time."

I immediately turned and followed him out of the church. As soon as my eyes fell on the tent, they fell in astonishment. It was full, and there were some people standing at the back because we had run out of chairs. Strange vehicles filled the grounds and lined the old dirt road back as far as I could see. My heart pounded, but I went, and I preached. I shouted and I praised. I quoted the Bible and admonished the forgiveness of sins.

Each night the tent filled up. There were not quite as many through the week as on that first Sunday, but every night it filled up. On the following Friday, the tent filled to overflowing again. This time there were almost as many people standing around the tent as were seated inside. I came early that Friday and walked about the grounds as I prayed. I thanked the Lord for blessing our little congregation for by Friday we had made almost 200 percent past our original investment, and the revival was still going. The following Saturday night would be the last night of the revival, and I was thankful for the opportunity to preach as well as the opportunity to bring financial blessings to our church.

On the next to the last night, about five thirty, the tent was full again, and I heard another car pull up onto the grounds. I turned to see a brand-new jet-black Cadillac pull up beside the road. When it parked, a single driver got out, who caused me to be taken aback in many ways. She was one of the most beautiful women I had ever seen, taller than most, with an hourglass figure sweetly outlined by a body-hugging knee-length pink summer dress. Her blond hair was styled like she stepped off the pages of a fashion magazine, and her face was painted the same. My eyes were immediately drawn to her full pillow-like lips, which were painted in a wine-colored lipstick. I guessed her age to be early thirties, and I almost gasped when I saw her. Her striking beauty tugged at my body, and I felt my groin tighten with delight at the sight of her, but my mind and my upbringing judged her. She looked more like she was going out on a fancy date than attending a church service, and never would a woman of our church, or any woman of our faith, I thought, ever go out in public painted up like Jezebel, much less go to church dressed that way. My little soldier said, "I want her!" and my soul cried, "Be careful!"

I was not about to tell her she couldn't attend our service for I would never tell anyone they could not come to the Lord, but I wondered in my mind if I might think about including something about the story of Jezebel in my sermon. Daddy told me, when I was a small boy, that Grandpa Dennison used to say that the first woman who ever painted her lips was eaten by dogs. It was a frightening thought to me at the time, and I was too young to realize that he was referring to the story of Jezebel. However, I knew my Bible well enough on that day to think that this could be a woman who was up to no good.

After getting out of her car, she came walking straight up to me even though I was standing alone a good fifty feet away from the tent. However, when she had pulled up, I had stopped and watched her as though I was seeing a movie unfold. She had a black belt around the waist of her pink dress and black accessories. When she walked across that uneven lawn toward me, she had such control over her black high heel shoes that she looked more like she was walking on a cloud than rough ground.

It occurred to me that perhaps she was lost and merely about to ask for directions rather than attend the service, but when she approached me, she reached out a perfect hand with red-painted manicured nails and said, "How do you do? My name is Wanda Moore. You must be the Reverend Dennison."

"Yes," I said, nervously, torn between my role as a pastor and the lust of my flesh.

"Reverend, I have heard a great deal about you over the past week, and I told myself that I simply must make the trip up from Memphis to hear you speak."

Her smile gleamed, and I fought the image of myself putting my hand to the back of her neck and kissing those delicious lips. "Well…uh…we have been quite blessed this week from the turnout and people coming from parts we never expected," I replied.

"I hope you don't mind if I take some notes during your service," she gleamed.

"No…ah…no, that would be quite acceptable," I half stuttered. "I very much encourage anyone in the study of the Word."

"Thank you," she said. "I hope to talk to you after the service." She then turned and walked toward the tent.

I stood there for a moment, watching those perfect heart-shaped hips sway in her pink dress as she glided across the lawn, thinking, *Lord have mercy!* not because I wanted God in that second to have mercy on me for what I was thinking, but because I couldn't believe that God could possibly make such physical perfection. I caught myself and turned away, held my Bible to my chest, and prayed, "Lord, remove these sinful thoughts from my mind and help me stay focused on what You have brought me here this night to do."

During my preaching, I tried as much as possible not to look at Wanda Moore, but I noticed that she had taken a small spiral notebook from her purse with a pen. From time to time she would jot things in it, but it did not appear that she was writing anything down after I had quoted the Bible as most folks would do. Her notes seemed random. After the service, there were many people who crowded around me, giving me praise, and I found myself repeating over and over, "Not I, but our Father in heaven."

Wanda waited until everyone else had cleared away and there was no one left except the folks on the church committee who were doing cleanup. Momma and Hannah busied themselves with the cleanup as well. Then when the last elderly woman shook my hand and ambled off down the aisle with her cane on one side and her husband on the other, Wanda walked up to me and held out that most beautiful and delicate, feminine hand again. "Reverend," she said, that was quite a performance."

I wasn't sure what to make of her wording, as though I had just completed a stage show, rather than preaching the Word. "Thank you, Mrs… Miss Moore?" I questioned as I released her hand from my grip.

"It is Miss, I suppose," she responded. "It used to be Mrs. Moore, but I am a widow.

"Oh, I am so sorry," I blabbed, half sorry for her loss and half not for the knowledge that she wasn't married. "You are so young to be a widow."

"It can happen to anyone," she replied. "My husband died in a car crash shortly after we were married."

"I am very sorry to hear that," I solaced. "I know that there are a great many widows of the world, especially with wars and other consequences of the modern age."

"Reverend," she said, changing the subject, "I know you must have thought that I was taking notes about the content of your sermon, but the truth is I was taking notes about you, and I have to say that I am quite impressed."

"Why would you be taking notes about me?" I asked.

"Well." She smiled. "I had a friend from Jonesboro who had been to your service early in the week call me the other day and say that he was quite impressed with you. I then called a friend of mine in Nashville who is putting together a Christian broadcast ministry, and he asked that I come to see you and give him some feedback."

"Oh?" I questioned, having the ambivalent assumption that this could be a longer-than-usual conversation. I pulled one of the folding chairs around and said, "Won't you have a seat?"

She sat and carefully positioned herself on the chair in a ladylike fashion. I pulled another chair around to face her and said, "I have heard some broadcasts of church services locally from time to time. I know that it is a way of sending the Word of God to a greater number of people."

"Yes," she continued, "however, the person I am representing is seeking to expand Christian teachings far beyond local broadcasts. You have heard of television, I assume."

"Yes, I have heard of it." I motioned with my hand as though TV was something way off into the distance. "But I don't think I know of anyone around here who has one. Most of us still rely on the radio for our connection with the outside world. It is fascinating that they could broadcast a picture across the air just like they can a voice, but truthfully, it hasn't been that long since radio started."

"Well, my friend, actually my employer, in Nashville, Jacob Clayburn, is convinced that television is the wave of the future and that it will allow us to reach far beyond what we might previously have expected." She leaned forward in her chair. "Would you like to be on television, Reverend Dennison?"

"And Jesus said, 'Greater things will you do.'" I smiled.

My mind wandered off into the possibilities. I recalled the dream of Jesus hanging from the side of our barn shouting, "You are My Word."

"Reverend, I would be happy to introduce you to Mr. Clayburn," she said, calling my mind back to the moment.

"I…ah…I don't know," I found myself saying as my mind raced to all kinds of possibilities, from becoming a nationally known minister of the Word to what Daddy, or Momma, would think, to how the members of my congregation might feel. "Would this mean moving to Nashville?" I questioned. "You know that I am only eighteen, right?"

"Right now, it wouldn't mean anything except meeting Mr. Clayburn." She reached a hand over and patted me on my knee. "I know you will need time to think about it." She reached into her purse, pulled out a business card, and handed it to me. "Call me when you have had some time to think about it. Talk to your family and your congregation about it. There is no hurry."

I looked down at the card which said, *Wanda Moore, Christian Broadcasting Consultant, Christ Beacon Broadcasting.* Her address and phone number were printed below the title. She then rose from her chair and reached out her hand to shake mine again, elbow straight, very business-like. I stood up and took her hand, not knowing what to say.

"It was very nice meeting you, Reverend, and very nice to be a part of your service. I will look forward to hearing from you."

She turned and strolled out the side opening of the tent toward her car. I did not hesitate that time to watch her heart-shaped bottom swaying all the way back to her car and was slightly startled to hear Hannah's voice behind me.

"What was that all about?"

I jumped around. "Oh, Hannah, don't come up behind somebody if they don't know you are there."

"Okay," Hannah responded. "What was that all about?"

I heard Miss Moore's car start as I spoke. "They want me to preach on radio and television," I said.

"Are you going to do it?" Hannah questioned with innocence.

"I don't know," I replied. Then, I turned to see Wanda Moore's black Cadillac pass perpendicular to the tent and head down the dirt road. A soft cloud of Arkansas clay dust floated up behind her tail lights as she drove away.

CHAPTER 7

In the night that I met Wanda Moore, I dreamed that I made love to her. I kissed those burgundy-red pillow-like lips, and my tongue played around with hers inside her mouth. There was never a thought during the dream that it was wrong or that I shouldn't be doing what I was doing. I just gleefully and passionately made love to her. The sensation of my body pulsing in climax woke me up. I rolled over onto my back, looked straight up at the ceiling, and cried, "God, no!" The guilt and shame of what I had done in my dream pressed my emotions like a huge stone. My body had betrayed me again. Ever since Daddy had caught me with Lynetta, I had tried hard to control myself. I viciously fought never to touch my little soldier, but even in my waking state, there were times when I couldn't stand the urge any longer and allowed myself to relieve it. Every time, I was overwhelmed with guilt. Every time, I felt as though I had betrayed the Lord and my calling. I didn't understand, but I became more and more determined to beat Satan in this quest for my body.

I reached down, pulled off my wet underwear, and threw them to the floor. I leaped out of bed and scrambled for another set of underwear. I quickly pulled on clean underwear and then my pants. I snatched my semen-stained underwear from the floor, wadded them into a fist, and raised them over my head so fast and hard that my knuckles popped against the low ceiling. "Why, Lord? Why?" I cried. Then I paced in a circle around that tiny bedroom, slapping myself hard over the shoulder with the dirty underwear, gritting through my teeth, and chanting, "The Lord is my

Shepherd. I shall not want! The Lord is my Shepherd. I shall not want! The Lord is my Shepherd. I shall not want! Let me have no desires, Lord! Take my desires. Let me desire only to serve you!"

Then I heard a tapping on the doorframe outside my bedroom, and I heard Momma's sweet voice saying, "Ronnie, are you okay?" I stopped dead still, tears streaming down my face.

"I…ah…I'm fine, Momma," I replied. "I'm just in fervent prayer."

"Breakfast will be ready soon," she said. "Get yourself ready."

"Okay, Momma," I said. Then I began scrambling around, looking for a shirt. My mind was reeling. What if this Moore woman was a temptress from Satan sent to lure me away from my calling to preach the Gospel? What if she was an emissary from Jesus sent to call me to a greater vocation? Was I supposed to just forget what happened? Was I supposed to call her back? I went to the dress shirt I had worn to service the night before and pulled her card from the pocket. There was an instant I wanted to tear it into little bitty shreds, but I didn't. I put it back into the shirt pocket, took a deep breath, and went to the kitchen to meet the family for breakfast. There in the kitchen sat Daddy at the head of the table. Momma and Hannah were already seated, and the table was filled with Momma's usual cooked bounty.

"I'm sorry," I said as I took my seat and reached out my hands for the prayer circle and began to give blessing. Daddy had long since stopped even giving blessing. He had stopped everything except some of the farm work. It was as though he felt like I had replaced him, and there was no longer a need for him in our lives or at church.

After the blessing, Hannah looked over at Daddy, and he nodded to her that it was okay to speak. "Ronnie is going to be on television," she said, and I gave her a stern look of displeasure.

Daddy gave a sarcastic, half laughing snort as he forked a piece of ham into his plate. "Is that so?" he said.

Momma looked over at Hannah and back at me. "Hannah told me that strange woman at the service last night, who stayed and talked to you, wants you to do something with this television thing."

"She just said she wants me to meet a man in Nashville, Tennessee, who has a Christian broadcasting ministry." I nervously reached for a biscuit. "She didn't say anything else, except to talk it over with my family and the church and give her a call with my decision."

"Gonna be famous like Amos and Andy," Daddy quipped with sarcasm.

"What do you think?" Momma asked, ignoring him.

"I don't know what to think," I replied. "I'm torn."

"You can always ask the Lord for a sign," she affirmed.

Daddy grunted and ladled gravy over his ham and eggs.

"I suppose I could," I pondered. "Will you all pray that the Lord sends me a sign what I should do?"

"I think you should do it!" Hannah spouted with excitement.

"Settle down, girl!" Daddy snarled quickly.

"Well, watch for a sign," Momma assured quietly. "I'm sure the Lord will guide you." Then she changed the subject. "I got a letter from Teddy yesterday all the way from Korea. I can read it to everyone after breakfast if you wish."

"No need to read it," Daddy quipped. "We can all read. What did he have to say?"

"Well, he said Korea is very cold, that he has seen a lot of strange and terrible things, and that he is going to be discharged and sent home in a few months. He is not choosing to re-enlist and is about to serve out his enlistment." Momma smiled. "It will be so good to see him home, safe and sound.

"I sure miss Teddy," I said.

Daddy said nothing but continued to eat his breakfast. It didn't occur to me at the time that Daddy might have slipped into a depression. He certainly was not the same, and I think he thought I had taken from him the one thing he had valued most in his life, and that was his church and his ability to preach. I didn't take it from him, though. I only wanted to share it with him for a while. Most everyone in the church at one point or another asked him to come back, told him they missed hearing him preach, but he refused.

After breakfast, I went on with chores and thought about some of the things I was going to say that night as it would be the final night of our revival. I also thought about Teddy and how wonderful it would be to have him home. I questioned how I would recognize a sign from God that I was either to call Miss Wanda Moore or continue what I was doing in my little community in Arkansas. I figured I could never have a chance with someone like her, but I had never met anyone since Lynetta who even interested me much, except for Miss Wanda Moore. It might not have been a very Christian thought. Thoughts run through your head when you are doing mundane things like farm chores, but I thought, *There are women you fuck and women you marry.* I had no sooner said it in my mind than another voice in my mind chastised me for even having entertained such a thought. Still, I wondered if Miss Moore was a woman you fucked or a woman you married.

There was always something to be done on the farm over and above morning and evening chores. After I had finished at the barn, and after Momma and I finished milking, the whole family went to the truck patch to dig up the last potatoes. Momma and I dug potatoes, while Hannah and Daddy came in behind the row, dusted the rest of the dirt off them, and put them in buckets to carry to the barn. Down at the barn, there was a bin just for the potatoes. We packed them with a little hay so they wouldn't freeze when it got really cold, and then we had potatoes lasting us most of the winter. I chatted with the family a little as we went about the chore, but I also continued to think all kinds of things, like what if I did go to Nashville and become a radio and television preacher? How was that going to change my life? I had been to Memphis a time or two, and I knew that Nashville was a big city too. I had no idea what it might be like to live in a big city. In those days, there were radio broadcasts that came out of Nashville of the Grand Ole Opry and country music stars like Hank Williams and Lester Flat and Earl Scruggs. All I had to go on was what I heard on the radio and my imagination. I thought about Teddy too, and how he had gone to war in Korea. He had enlisted, but I wondered about the draft. I had to register for the draft when I was eighteen, and if I got drafted, it could mean the end of being able to preach, maybe at least it might mean the end of it for a couple of years. My mind went all over the place. Sometimes, it went back to the dream I had of making love to Miss Moore. Then it would go to getting onto myself for bringing that dream up in my mind again. Still, it was darn near impossible to get the image of those beautiful lips and heart-shaped hips out of my mind. When she walked away, it looked just like someone had turned a pink heart upside down, and it pulsed with life on every step she took. When that image came back to my mind, I prayed, "Lord, take this affliction from me." The thought of her still returned.

I got through the day and went that evening to preach the last sermon of the tent revival. All through the service, I looked for Miss Moore, watched for that black Cadillac to pull up out front again, half expected, half wished that she would come swishing up the aisle wearing that pink dress, but she never arrived.

The next morning, we held services in the tent as there was not enough time to move everything out the night before. A gentle rain was falling, and it was a bit moist and cool, but no one complained. That afternoon amid light sprinkles, the men of the revival committee and I dismantled the tent and got everything ready to go back to the rental company over in Jonesboro. I was sad in a way that it was over and sad that Miss Moore had not come back for one more visit. Despite how I had perceived her, and where my fantasies had gone with her, I guessed that she really was all business. Besides, despite how she was dressed, and despite what my mind made of her, I had no way of knowing that she did not otherwise practice good Christian values.

The rest of that year I watched for a sign from God whether I should or should not call Miss Moore. I took her business card out of my shirt pocket and placed it in the upper left corner of my top dresser drawer. The passing of the year came, and if there had been any sign that I should call her, I must surely have missed it.

In April of the following year, I had turned nineteen, and Teddy came home. I took the truck over and met him at the bus station in Jonesboro. I asked at the window of the bus station about Teddy's bus, and when it was going to arrive, then I sat where I could see the bus when it pulled into the station. When Teddy got off that bus in his Army uniform with his bag, I thought I had never in my life seen anything more beautiful.

Lynetta and Miss Moore were going to have to take a back seat to my big brother coming home from the war. I went running up to him quick as I could, shouting, "Teddy!" I hugged him flat out around the neck before I even thought about how he had reacted. When he heard me shout and saw me run up, he first jumped back like he had seen a ghost, but by the time he jumped, I had my arms around his neck, slapping him on the back. He hesitated a moment and then began patting my back and gave me a big hug.

"It's good to see you, little brother!" he said smiling. "Let me get a good look at you." He then pushed me out a couple of feet away from him and said, "Hell, you ain't half as ugly as you used to be."

"Well, you are a darn sight better looking than you used to be," I said. "Come on, let's get your bags. I got the truck just over here."

"This is it," he said as he pointed to the stuffed canvas bag sitting on the ground beside him.

Other people had been getting off the bus all around us and were being greeted by family or friends. I had barely noticed that Teddy had backed up with his back flat against the bus, and his eyes were darting around like he was looking for someone else to show up.

"You expecting someone else?" I asked when I noticed him looking around so much.

"Nope, just looking," he said. "Come on, let's go."

He reached for his bag, but I grabbed it first. "I got it. You are probably tired from your trip."

We walked on over to the tuck, and I set his bag in the truck bed, then we got in for the forty-minute drive home.

"So tell me about Korea," I said as I began steering the truck away from the bus station.

"Ah…you don't want to know anything about that," he said.

"Yes, I do," I responded. "You have been off on the other side of the world to some exotic, far-off land. I want to hear about it."

A deep sigh came out of him. "Well," he said finally, "for one thing, it is so cold there in the winter that you can take a piss outside and it will freeze into little crystals before it hits the ground and send up a steam cloud. I don't half understand why my dick didn't freeze off."

"Goodness!" I exclaimed. "I don't think I ever want to be that cold."

"No, you don't want to ever be that cold," he said, gazing out the window. "Arkansas sure is pretty this time of year."

I said, "Yep, nice to see some flowers blooming."

"How's Momma?" he queried.

"Momma is doing fine, and you ain't half gonna recognize Hannah. She's growing so fast," I replied. "Daddy just don't seem right though. He's depressed or something. I preached my first sermon at the church last year when he was sick, and he ain't been right since."

"What do you mean he ain't been right since?" he questioned.

"It's a long story, Teddy," I said as I gripped both hands on the steering wheel. "See, he didn't want me to preach."

"I know that," he said. "Selfish old bastard don't want to share nothing. So what excuse did he use?"

I took a deep breath like I was about to confess my sins. "Well, he said I wasn't worthy to preach 'cause of that thing that happened with Lynetta. He said I am a sinner, and a sinner has no place in the pulpit."

"Oh, bullshit!" Teddy exclaimed. "He points that damn judgmental finger at practically everybody else and has the rest pointing back at him."

"Daddy tries to be a righteous man," I defended.

"No, he don't!" Teddy snarled. "He's a hypocrite. He tries to make everybody think he's a righteous man."

"I ain't ever seen him do anything except study the Good Book and try to go by the Word of the Lord," I defended again.

"Yeah, well maybe there are things that I know that you don't," he snapped.

"You and Daddy just ain't ever got along, have you?"

"No," he popped off. "And we ain't ever going to. First chance I get, I am gonna get the hell out of here, but it ain't gonna be in the damn military this time."

"Well, I can understand not wanting to go to war anymore," I said.

"No, you don't understand," he quickly retorted. "In the military, you got a whole fucking team of daddies telling you every fucking move you can make and every fucking move you can't, and every damn one of them is just as big a hypocrite as Daddy is, even if they ain't really Christian."

"Well, I'm sorry you didn't have a good experience with it," I said. "I hoped maybe, the war notwithstanding, that the military might be able to give you something to help you along in life."

"What it gave me was a lot of bad memories," he said sullenly as he gazed out the passenger window at the passing landscape.

"What about the GI Bill?" I questioned.

Air spewed out of his mouth almost like a cat hissing. "What about it?" he asked.

"Well, you could go to school or something."

"Yeah, and what the hell is that going to do for me?" he quipped.

"Maybe learn a trade, get a better life?" I pondered.

"My life probably ain't gonna get no better, Ronnie, no matter what I do."

"Teddy," I questioned with concern, "what happened to you?"

"I don't want to talk about it." He sighed. "You talk about it, it all comes back, and it will tear your heart out all over again. Best I just shove that off in the back of my mind somewhere and forget about it."

"War must be a really awful thing," I said.

"Yeah," he said sarcastically, "must be."

"So!" he proclaimed, changing the subject, "dating anybody?"

"No, don't seem like I have the time. What time I don't spend preparing sermons and preaching on Sunday is spent taking care of the farm 'cause there is a lot Daddy can't do anymore."

"What do you mean there's a lot Daddy can't do anymore?" he questioned.

"Well, he got really bad sick. Been getting worse. I guess almost two years ago now, and he ain't really recovered from it since," I explained.

"The first time I preached was 'cause he was really too sick to get out of bed and go, and Momma wouldn't have let him anyway."

"So how did the old man feel about you taking his pulpit?" he questioned.

"He wasn't very pleased about it," I said. "He could have gone back to preaching after that, and did for a little while, but folks kept asking him to let me preach again, and then he just stopped—stopped everything. He won't even go to church anymore."

"Yeah, his way or no way," Teddy snapped. "So you are doing everything, the farm, the church, everything?"

"Well, Momma and Hannah help with the milking and a lot of the chores," I responded. "Daddy helps a little bit, but he seems to tire out easy."

"Yeah, I bet he does," Teddy quipped again. "If he can't have his way, then he ain't doing nothing."

"He tries," I defended, yet again.

"You ever pay attention to how much you defend that asshole?" he questioned. "I have never been able to understand why you keep standing up for that old bastard when he ain't fit to wipe your shoes."

"Daddy is a good man," I replied calmly.

"Yeah, well, you just go right on believing that if you want to, little brother. It ain't the truth, but you believe whatever you want," Teddy said and changed the subject. "So how is this preaching thing going for you?"

"Well, last fall I did my first tent revival." I smiled, thinking back on the success of it.

"Tent revival?" he questioned, grinning. "Daddy would not have done that in a million years."

"It went pretty good!" I said excitedly. "We brought in a lot of money for the church, and that has really helped to get some things fixed up around there. We got regular bathrooms now with flushing toilets and everything! Of course, you still have to go out back to use one, but we dug a well, put in a septic tank, and replaced them little outhouses with a freestanding bathroom."

"Well, praise the Lord!" he said in his usual sarcastic manner. "What else?"

"Well," I went on, "there was this woman who came up from Memphis to hear me preach one night and said she represented a Christian broadcasting ministry out of Nashville. She left me her card and told me to call her, and I could meet this fellow in Nashville who owns the ministry, maybe preach on radio or television."

Teddy turned around in his seat facing toward me and sat up on one leg. "You're shitting me!" he exclaimed. "Well, did you call her?"

"No, I haven't yet," I admitted.

"What in the hell are you waiting for?" he asked.

"I'm not sure, Teddy," I replied. "I don't know if this is something that is right for me. I don't know if I want to move to a big city or do something like that. Maybe I am meant to be a country preacher just like Daddy. I don't know what I want to do, so I have been waiting for a sign from God to guide me what to do."

"Well, here is your fucking sign!" he shouted. Then he whipped off his hat and began slapping my shoulder with it for every time he spoke a word. "Get…your…fucking…ass…on…the…phone…to…that…woman!"

"Hey, hold on there!" I said laughing. "You are gonna make me wreck this truck."

"What the hell?" he questioned. "Somebody offers you an opportunity like that and you don't jump on it like a dog on fresh meat! What the hell is the matter with you?"

"Teddy, it ain't that easy," I replied. "I can't just pick up and move away from the only life and only family I have ever known."

"By God, I can," he snapped.

"Daddy and Momma need me now," I went on. "Daddy can't do what he once could, and Momma can't handle that farm by herself."

"And that is somehow your responsibility?" he asked. "If Daddy can't work the farm, sell the motherfucker! They can move into town or something."

"Well, how are they gonna live if they can't make a living from the farm?" I asked. "Teddy, it just ain't that easy."

"They ought to have enough money left over from the sale of that farm to live for a while," he responded. "Besides, did it ever occur to you that if you become some big famous preacher or something, you might have enough left over to support them?"

"It ain't about making money, Teddy, it's about serving the Lord."

"The hell it ain't!" he quipped. "Look what you just told me a few minutes ago. A woman representing a Christian broadcasting ministry came and left you her *BUSINESS CARD*. The purpose of a business is making money! I don't care if they call it a ministry. They can call it anything they want. It is still a business, or they wouldn't have business cards…and…did you ever consider that you could serve the Lord AND make money?"

"It is easier for a camel to go through the eye of a needle than for a rich man to get into heaven," I semi-quoted scripture.

"Well, seek the Kingdom first and ALL the rest will be added to you," he debated. "Prove me now, herewith, SAITH THE LORRRRRRD, if I will not open the windows of heaven and pour you out a blessing that there shall not be room enough to receive it!"

"Wow!" I said giggling. "You actually paid attention all those times Daddy forced us to sit down and study the Bible."

"Ronnie, who says you can't serve God and be rich too?" he asked.

"Lay not up treasures on earth," I replied.

"Doesn't it occur to you," he questioned, "that the verse you just quoted means don't be attached to all the stuff here? Don't it maybe mean that you can have all you want just as long as you don't make having it more important than God?"

I took a deep breath. "I suppose that would be one way of interpreting it," I said.

"Ronnie, if you want to preach, go preach. Take it wherever it goes." He turned back to face the front of the truck and waved his hand across in front of him. "Don't waste your life on this shit hole. There is nothing for you around here. If you ain't a rice farmer, then there damn sure ain't nothing for you, especially if all you got is a little scratch-a-living piece of shit land like Momma and Daddy. That ain't you, little brother. That just ain't you."

I didn't say much else. I looked over at him and nodded and then just kept driving toward home.

When I pulled the truck up in front of the house, Momma came running out of the house shouting, "Mercy! Mercy! Mercy!" Tears were streaming from her eyes as she went running up to Teddy to give him a big kiss on the cheek and a hug. She exclaimed, "My boy is home! Thank you, Jesus, my boy is home!" Hannah went running out after Momma and started hugging Teddy from the other side.

I left Momma and Teddy to talk while I carried his bag to our room. I wondered how the two of us were going to sleep in that bed. We weren't boys anymore, and the bed hadn't gotten any bigger. We were two grown men, and at least for a while, we were going to be sharing that same bed just like we did when we were little boys.

Daddy didn't even come out of the house to greet Teddy. He just sat there in his living room chair, thumbing through the Bible. When Teddy came in with Momma and Hannah, he looked over at Daddy and said, "Hello, Daddy."

Daddy didn't look up from the book. He simply turned the page and said, "Welcome home, son."

Everything went on as usual that evening except that Teddy went out to help me with the farm chores, while Momma stayed in the house and fixed him a special supper with big juicy cuts of rib eye steak, mashed potatoes, and a homemade orange cake for desert. Daddy came to the table for supper that evening and looked over everything on the table. All he said was, "Who's paying for this?"

"I am," I said quickly. Then Daddy just sat down and held his hands out for prayer.

Bedtime came not long after dinner. The bed we had slept in as boys didn't seem quite as big with two grown men in it, but we had slept together our whole life, and there was no expectation for anything to be different. We settled in, kind of butt to butt, and got comfortable. Not long after that,

I heard Teddy snoring and was soon asleep myself. Later that night, I was awakened by a kick to the back of my leg. Teddy was moaning and flailing, jerking here and there, and his arms were moving in the air above his head. "Teddy?" I questioned. "Teddy, are you all right?" He didn't say anything but kept flailing around. I began to get scared he was going to hit me. I figured out pretty quickly that he was still asleep, and I thought maybe I should wake him. I reached out to touch him on the arm, and when I did, he was all over me. He had me out of that bed in a choke hold on the floor before I half knew what was happening. I had a sharp pain in my ribs where he had punched me in the process of taking me to the floor, and then he was choking me and snarling through clenched teeth, "Fucking gook! Goddamn fucking gook!"

"Ted…eh…dy," I wheezed, barely able to breathe. "I can't br-br-eathe." He never for a second loosened his grip, and when I thought I was about to pass out, Daddy twisted on the overhead light above us.

"What's going on in here?" Daddy asked loudly.

As soon as the light came on, Teddy let go, and slid back on the floor, looking around, summing up the scene, which at that moment, suddenly seemed new to him. I fell back against the bed choking and reaching for my aching throat.

"Oh God." Teddy sighed. "I'm sorry. Oh God…Ronnie, are you all right?"

He came toward me with a concerned look on his face, and I reached up my hand to wave him back. I wasn't sure, in that moment, what had happened or what else he might do. I just knew I didn't want him too close to me right then. He knew he had done something. As soon as the light came on and he snapped out of it, he knew he had been choking me.

"I'm sorry. I'm so sorry, little brother," he moaned. "I don't know what happened. I don't know what happened."

You could see the anguish on his face, the remorse, and the tears welling up in his eyes, but no tear ever fell. He just kept repeating how sorry he was. Daddy just stood there.

"It's okay. It's okay, Teddy," I soothed, groaning through my own pain. "I will be all right. I'm fine."

The pain in my ribs told me I couldn't be sure I was fine, and as soon as I tried to get to my feet, it told me even more clearly. I grimaced and winced in pain as I tried to get up.

Daddy just stood there and said nothing, did nothing.

Teddy got to his feet and said, "Can I help you?" I nodded affirmation. Then Teddy came over and helped me to sit up on the bed. Momma and Hannah had come to the door by then. Momma winced when she saw me.

"What in the world is going on here?" she gasped.

"It's okay, Momma." I tried to calm her, barely able to speak. "Teddy just had a bad dream."

"But you're hurt," she pleaded. "Where are you hurting, son?" Momma came and sat on the bed beside me, wanting to comfort me, solace my pain like she used to do when I was a little boy. She could see a knot and a bruise starting to rise up on my rib cage under my left arm. She motioned to Hannah, "Sissy, go get some ice in a washcloth."

We had finally gotten a real refrigerator instead of the old icebox, but in those days, there was barely enough room in a refrigerator to freeze more than a couple of trays of ice, and that had not had time to fully freeze since the trays had been put in after supper. I heard the crack of the ice tray in the kitchen, and soon Hannah came back in and handed Momma a cold, wet washcloth. Momma touched it to my ribs, and I winced as much from the cold as from the pain.

"We probably ought to get you to see the doctor tomorrow," she said, trying to acclimate me to the cold cloth. Then she turned and looked at Daddy. "Paul, do we have any aspirin in the house?"

"How should I know what's in the house?" he snapped and walked out of the room. In just a minute, we heard the bed squeak from Momma and Daddy's room and realized he had just gone back to bed instead of looking for any aspirin.

"Sissy, go check the medicine box and see if we got any aspirin," Momma said.

Hannah dutifully left and came back shortly with an aspirin bottle and a glass of water. I took a couple of aspirin, and after we sat there for a while, Momma asked, "Pain any better?" I nodded a yes, but truthfully, I didn't feel much different. "You think you can sleep now?" she asked.

"I'll try," I said.

Teddy had gone back over and sat in the corner on the floor with his arms around his knees and his head folded over on his arms. He just sat there.

Momma said, "Teddy?"

Then he startled like he had just seen a ghost. He caught himself quickly and said, "What, Momma?"

"Are you okay, son?" she said softly.

"I'm fine, Momma. What?"

She stared at him for a moment with a worried look on her face and then said, "How about if I fix you a quilt pallet on the living room floor for you to sleep the rest of the night."

"Fine, Momma," he replied.

"You think that will be comfortable enough?" she continued.

"Momma, I've slept in a lot worse."

Momma got up to go fix the pallet, and Teddy got to his feet again.

When he stopped to look at me, I said, "I'm sorry."

Teddy sucked air through his teeth like he was choking back tears and gritted, "No, I'm sorry. You didn't do nothing."

He stood there for just a second longer and turned for the door. He reached up and twisted the bulb down to dark as he left.

I lay back on the bed and tried every position I could think of, but it didn't matter. No matter how I turned, it hurt, and turning itself, hurt more than anything, so I finally just lay there on my back, staring up at the ceiling with the little bit of moonlight that crept through the window. I drifted in and out of sleep I guess, but mostly, I just thought. Try as I might, I could not imagine what war must have done to my beloved brother.

The next day, Teddy drove me over to Jonesboro to see a doctor. I don't know how long we sat in the waiting room, but they didn't really have appointments in those days. Neither of us talked much. When I finally got to see the doctor, he told me there wasn't really anything he could do about a cracked rib. He gave me this wrap thing to go around my chest that made me feel like I could barely breathe. Then, he gave me a prescription for some kind of pain killer that made me loopier than a vulture circling a rotting rabbit. I took the first one right outside the pharmacy and don't half remember the ride home. However, I do remember asking Teddy, "What happened to you over there in Korea?"

All he said was, "I don't want to talk about it."

I remember saying, "But something happened to you over there. Something messed you up. You never used to have fits in your sleep before." He didn't say anything, and a long silence ensued. In time I pressed,

"Teddy?"

"SHUT THE FUCK UP!" he snarled, never wavering his gaze from the road directly ahead. "I don't want to talk about it!"

For the rest of the drive home, we sat in silence.

CHAPTER 8

In time my ribs healed, but Teddy never healed. I could tell his wounds weren't physical. They ran much deeper than that. I prayed for him, prayed for him a lot, but it didn't seem to do much good. I guess prayer really only works on another person if their faith matches the prayer you give.

Teddy didn't have much in the way of faith anymore. I never saw him pick up his Bible, and he got in more spats with Daddy than ever before. I figured Teddy might get his own place and move out, especially when he wasn't getting along with Daddy, but he didn't. He kept right on sleeping on that quilt pallet that Momma put down on the living room floor. Sometimes, I could hear him flailing around, talking in his sleep. Sometimes, he would scream out, and then it would be silent for a while before I heard him snore again.

Teddy got a job at a sawmill up near the Missouri line and bought a car. On a fairly regular basis, he crossed over the border into Missouri, where he could buy legal liquor, because liquor wasn't sold in northern Arkansas. There were times he came home so drunk he could barely stand up. Daddy would scream, "No son of mine is going to behave like a derelict in my house!"

Teddy's response was usually a loud, "Fuck you, old man!" Then, Momma would get between them. In time, Momma would have Teddy lie down on that quilt pallet, sitting beside him on the floor, stroking his hair and singing him to sleep like he was a little boy again. Nothing was ever going to be the same.

In early December, a state trooper came and knocked on our door very late on a Sunday night. Teddy had not come home the whole weekend. Momma had worried and paced the floor like a tin duck in a shooting arcade. Everybody was in bed sound asleep when the trooper knocked. Momma got up and went to the door. I heard the noise and got up myself. I walked out into the living room just as Daddy twisted on the overhead light, and Momma answered the door. There on the other side of the door in the darkness of the porch stood a handsome man in his state police uniform.

"Ma'am, is this the Dennison residence?" he asked when Momma pulled the door back to reveal him standing there.

"Yes," she said quietly, probably knowing, as we all did, that it ain't no good thing when the state police come to your door in the middle of the night.

"And you would be?" the trooper questioned.

"Marylee Dennison," Momma said. "And this is my husband, Paul." She motioned toward Daddy still standing beneath the overhead light.

"You are the parents and next of kin of Theodore Jonas Dennison?" the trooper asked.

"Yes, sir," Momma said with trembling voice, pulling her nightgown up around her throat against the cold winter air coming through the door.

"Ma'am…Sir." He nodded up at Daddy. "I am Officer Benton of the Arkansas State Police. I regret to inform you that your son Theodore Jonas Dennison was killed in a single-car fatality on Highway 67 this evening between Corning, Arkansas, and the Missouri border."

Terror crossed Momma's face, and a wail came out of her like an animal caught in a steel trap. She fell half to her knees on the floor, sobbing and grabbing at the air like her very soul was being torn out of her. I ran to her side, unable to hold back my own tears, and Hannah, also crying, came up behind her on the other side with a comforting hand to her back.

"Momma…Momma…Momma," I cried.

I knelt down beside her, clasped her hand in mine, and pulled her head to my shoulder. I cried, torn between comforting Momma and feeling my own grief that was tearing away at my heart. "Oh, Jesus, Lord Jesus, bring comfort," I heard myself pray as I held Momma's head to my shoulder. Momma shook and cried in my arms so much that it felt like she would never stop. I didn't know what to do at that moment. I didn't know how to give a mother's hope back when her firstborn child was yanked away from her like a feather in a storm. I just held her and waited for her to stop.

Daddy stood there silent. He said nothing until it seemed that Momma was beginning to soften in her grief. Daddy did not shed a tear, and as far as I could tell, had no feeling at all when, finally, he asked, "How did he die?"

Officer Benton, who had stood there and waited as well, said, "Sir, as I said, it was a single-car fatality. Mr. Dennison lost control of his vehicle and hit a large tree near the pavement. We are unsure why, except…"

"Except what?" Daddy queried.

"Except that we believe alcohol may have been a factor in the accident," Officer Benton replied.

"Wages of sin," Daddy snarled in a cold matter-of-fact tone.

I looked up from the floor where I had been holding Momma while she cried.

"What?" I asked, looking up at him in disbelief.

"You heard me!" Daddy snapped crisp like a breaking pencil. "Wages of sin is death! Teddy was a sinner, a drunkard."

I got to my feet and left Hannah to comfort Momma. "You have lost your firstborn child, your son, and that is all you can say?" I questioned. "'Wages of sin'? That's it?"

"It was Teddy's sin that killed him," Daddy replied.

"I cannot believe you!" I said as I crossed over to stand in front of him. "You have no love, no feeling, for the son you have lost?"

"The Bible is clear," he said. "The wages of sin is death."

I wanted to hit him. I held back the urge to punch him square in the face. I knew it would do no good. I stood there staring at him, boiling in anger and unable to express what I was feeling. My only brother, my teacher, and my guide was gone, and the man who bore him was able to write it off as if it had no more significance than pulling off a tick. I wanted to scream at him, curse him, degrade and belittle him. I wanted him to understand the suffering that I had seen in Teddy, but all he could see was the black and the white, the all or nothing. All he could see was that Teddy drank and, therefore, somehow deserved to die. He didn't even want to understand the suffering that drove Teddy to annihilate his emotions with alcohol.

"Your son has died!" I cried, finally. "I would think that there would be at least a morsel of remorse in your heart, but you didn't love him! You don't love me! You don't love anybody but your own miserable self!"

Daddy turned without saying a word, walked straight through the kitchen, out the back door, and into the darkness.

I turned back to Officer Benton, who stood patiently at the door while all the family dramatics unfolded. "Sir, what are we to do about claiming Teddy's body?" I asked.

"Contact the coroner's office in Piggott," he said. He reached into his pocket and handed me a piece of paper. "This is the corner's name and number. Give them a call in the morning."

I accepted the paper. The officer tipped the brim of his hat. He turned to leave but turned back at the edge of the porch and said quietly, "I'm so sorry for your loss."

"Thank you, Officer," I said and gently closed the door behind him.

Hannah helped Momma over to the sofa and sat beside her, holding her hand while she cried. I kept thinking, *Where is Daddy in all this? Shouldn't he be the one comforting Momma instead of a thirteen-year-old girl?*

I walked over, sat on the opposite side of Momma, and took her other hand. She looked up at me briefly and said, "Oh, Ronnie, my heart is shattered, shattered in a million pieces." Then she burst into tears again.

"I'm so sorry, Momma," I said, holding back my own grief and feeling like I had an anvil on my chest.

"Where's your daddy?" she asked.

"I don't know, Momma."

"Your daddy should be here. Why isn't he here?" She pulled her hand away from mine and pulled the corner of her nightgown up from her chest to wipe the tears off her face.

"I don't know, Momma."

"Ronnie," she said, picking up my hand again and looking at me square in the eyes. "I want you to preach the funeral."

The tears I had been holding back would not hold anymore. I still tried to stifle them, but they leaked out of my eyes. I looked at Momma, pleading unspoken words. *Please no. Please don't make me do this.* Finally, I quivered, "Momma…I don't think I can."

"It would mean so much to me. I know it would mean a lot to Teddy." Her entreating look tugged at my heart, and I felt torn between the guilt of disappointing my grieving mother and the treachery of my own grief.

"Momma," I begged, "I loved Teddy with all my heart and soul. My heart is breaking too, breaking so much that I don't think I could ever stand up and give that service without falling apart. It's not that I don't want to, I just don't think I would be able to."

"I'll preach the service," came Daddy's voice booming into the room. He had come back in unnoticed.

We all turned at once to see him standing there on the other side of the living room. None of us had any idea how long he might have been standing there, apparently long enough to hear the conversation.

"Daddy, do you think you can?" I questioned. "We can always get a guest minister to do the service." In that moment I had some concern about what he had said earlier, but I did not express it.

"I can and I will," he said firmly. "I got no problem with preaching my son's funeral. I want to preach my son's funeral.

Momma said, "Thank you, Paul. It will be good to see you preaching again."

With Momma's approval, I said no more.

"Best we all go to bed now," Daddy said. "Ronnie, you can take the truck and drive over to the Clarks' tomorrow and see if you can borrow their phone to make arrangements. I guess we can use Bates Funeral Home over in Imboden." Daddy said not another word. He just went into the bedroom and got back in bed.

I sat there staring toward the bedroom wondering how he could be so nonchalant about it, like Teddy was some stranger and his death meant no more than another soul passing. After what he said earlier, I worried about him preaching, but Momma had given him the go-ahead. I wasn't going to challenge her.

"I can't sleep," Momma said. "My mind is reeling like I am on some kind of mental merry-go-round. I keep seeing images of Teddy growing up. I keep flashing in my mind the first time I held him in my arms." The tears returned. "I can't…I can't…I-I…"

"It's okay, Momma," I comforted as I pulled her head to my shoulder. "As soon as we are conceived, we start to die. Ashes to ashes. Dust to dust." I looked over to see silent tears streaming down Hannah's face.

I darted my eyes toward the kitchen and said, "You know, Sissy, I think I would like to have a cup of hot chocolate. Don't that sound good to you?"

Hannah nodded, then went to the kitchen and began warming some milk for hot chocolate.

After a while, I nudged Momma and said, "Come on, let's go sit at the kitchen table. Sissy made some hot chocolate. Maybe that will help us relax enough to go back to sleep." I led Momma to the kitchen and sat her down in front of a steaming cup. Hannah sat over on the other side of the table with her own cup. Momma smiled.

"You kids are so sweet. I love you so much. I don't know if I can tell you enough how much I love you. I hope I told Teddy enough." She reached one thumb up to her cheek to wipe away a single tear. "I hope Teddy knew how much I loved him."

"Momma, we all knew," I insisted. "Teddy knew how much you loved him. He always did. None of us ever doubted that."

Then Momma began to talk. She told stories about Teddy when he was little. She told some stories we had heard before and some we never knew about. She began to weave us all together into those stories, and it seemed to comfort her. We did not sleep again that night. Whether Daddy slept, I don't know, but he did not stir till morning light.

CHAPTER 9

The next day we were all exhausted, but I did what I had to do. After chores, I drove over to the Clarks' to call the coroner. I knocked on the door about 8:00 a.m. because I knew it was not likely that anyone would be in the county office before that time. When I told Sister Clark, her eyes swelled with tears. She burst out crying, "Oh Lord, honey, I'm so sorry! Your poor Momma and Daddy must be devastated." Everybody in our church was like family. These folks had been almost like second parents to us, at least on Sunday. "Oh my," she said as she hugged me to her fat bosom. "Brother Ronnie, are you okay?"

"I will be okay," I affirmed. "I will be happy to pay you for the phone call as soon as the bill comes in."

"You will do no such thing!" Brother Clark exclaimed. "That little bit of nothing phone call is the least we can do."

The truth is there were no more than four or five people in a ten-mile radius who had a phone in those days, and those who did have a phone were on a party line sharing calls with their neighbors who might also have a phone. I was happy that no one else was on the line when I picked it up to make the call that morning. After I got off the line with the coroner, I called the funeral home. Momma let me know some of her wishes when we sat up talking the night before. I made arrangements for Teddy to be buried the following Thursday afternoon at 2:00 p.m., and I made arrangements to pay for it out of what I had been making for Sunday preaching. The funeral services would be held at the funeral home. Then the procession would take us to a little cemetery halfway between Imboden and Ravenden, where many of our family had been buried.

Brother and Sister Clark wasted no time in spreading word of the tragedy, and before that day was over, neighbors and church members were showing up at the house with food. The men of the community came by to help with farm chores so that neither Daddy nor I would have to work much for the next couple of days.

That afternoon, I walked over the hill to tell Grandma Miller and witnessed a reaction similar to what Momma had as she exclaimed in tearful wails, "Oh Lord Jesus! Oh Lord Jesus! Oh Lord Jesus!"

She sat, more like fell, backward onto the porch steps and grabbed the post like it was a dear loved one. She pushed her forehead against the post and sobbed. I sat down beside her and placed my hand between her shoulders. She turned to me, grabbed my other hand in both her hands, and squeezed it hard. She stared straight and hard into my eyes. "My baby! My baby! You be safe now!" she admonished. "Don't you let nothin' like this happen to you!"

"Yes, ma'am," I replied quietly. I didn't know anything else to say.

It seemed like it took so long for Thursday to come. Neighbors stopped by, and family came from other parts, although some family simply could not be contacted in time for the funeral. We could have written to Uncle Daniel and Aunt Stella down in Texarkana, but it wouldn't have done any good. By the time a letter got to them, there wouldn't be an opportunity to drive all the way from the southwest corner of Arkansas in time for the funeral, and they didn't have a phone. We wrote to them after the funeral to let them know. Aunt Wilma and Uncle Fred over in Newport and Uncle William and Aunt Janice down in West Memphis both had phones. Aunt Morene and Uncle Jake lived up at Poplar Bluff, Missouri. I was not sure if a letter might get to them in time, but I rushed a quick note off to them on Tuesday morning. These were Daddy's brothers and sisters. They were all older than Daddy, who was the baby of his family. Aunt Wilma and Uncle William were twins. Every one of Daddy's brothers and sisters had grown kids. Hannah was the youngest of the whole family.

Brother and Sister Clark were gracious enough to let me continue to use their phone to call family. Some family could make it, and some couldn't. To my surprise, Aunt Morene and Uncle Jake, along with their youngest boy, Mike, showed up on the day of the funeral. All the family that showed planned to drive back home after the funeral, but Brother and Sister Clark as well as others in the church offered their homes for guest room to all of Daddy's family.

On Thursday afternoon, a cold chill in the thirties filled the air, but the sun was shining, and the skies were a clear, cloudless blue. The limbs of the charcoal-colored trees drew lines across the blue sky, and here or there a residual brown leaf was left hanging. We all dressed in our finest and donned whatever coat we had to go over that. None of us drove to the funeral home. Aunt Wilma and Uncle Fred drove Daddy, Momma, and Grandma Miller over, while Hannah and I rode with the Clarks. There wasn't much to the funeral home, just a little squared-off brown brick building with a small chapel off to one side.

We were met by greeters, and everyone except Daddy was escorted to an area cordoned off at the front of the chapel just for family. At the front of the chapel was a copper-colored closed casket. Teddy had been practically unrecognizable after the wreck, identified mainly by his driver's license, which was in the wallet that was still in his hip pocket and the fact that he was driving the car he bought. We didn't want to see him like that and didn't want anybody else to see him like that. We simply solaced ourselves that he was lying inside that casket.

Momma fiddled with her handkerchief and squeezed it at times, like she was trying to get juice out of a lemon. Hannah and I sat silent. Grandma Miller sat on the other side of Momma and kept a comforting arm around her. Although tears were streaming down her face too, and she occasionally had to pull out her own hanky, Grandma Miller kept Momma pulled close.

The next thing we knew, Aunt Morene and Uncle Jake came walking up with Mike standing off to the side. Aunt Morene reached out her hand and took hold of Momma's hand, hanky and all. "Oh, Marylee," she cooed. "God bless you, sweetheart. I am so sorry you had to go through losing a child."

Momma looked up, nervous, eyes pleading like a wounded deer. She didn't say anything at first. Aunt Morene motioned for me to move over so she could sit down beside her. When I moved, she pulled Momma over to hug her and asked, "Is there anything I can do?"

Uncle Jake and Mike stood there like a couple of skinny scarecrows dressed in black suits. Uncle Jake was a very tall thin man with cheekbones that carved a sharp angle out on either side of his face, and Mike was pretty much a younger version of that. Aunt Morene, who looked a lot like Daddy, was wearing a black pillbox hat with a short black veil that crunched when she hugged Momma. I felt certain that had to hurt, but I said nothing. I just sat there watching everything unfold like I was watching some kind of dark movie.

Momma said, finally, "I'm so glad you could come, Morene. We weren't sure you would get the letter in time."

"Well, actually, the letter just arrived this morning," Aunt Morene responded. "We rushed around and got ready quick as we could, hoping we would get here on time. The good news about being dairy farmers is once morning chores are done, other things can be put off till evening, especially when you have something important to attend to."

"Well, I'm so glad you are here," Momma said.

"I am too," said Aunt Morene. Then she got up and motioned for me to scoot back over next to Momma. She motioned to Uncle Jake and Mike, who followed her like little ducks. Then, she came around to take a seat in the pew behind us.

The service started with some round, fat little woman with auburn hair taking a seat at a little electric organ over on the left side of the chapel. She started to play some mournful classical kind of music I had never heard before. Then Daddy came in and took a seat behind the podium. Brother Mills, who was a healthy young father of two small children and who had become the song leader of our church, followed in and sat in a chair next to Daddy.

At the appropriate time, Brother Mills got up with a song book and stood next to the podium. His blond hair glistened in some sunlight that was shining through a west window. He sang a song all by himself as the lady at the organ accompanied. The song was Momma's favorite hymn, "Nearer to Thee." Then he led the congregation in a couple of hymns that Hannah and I had each chosen. Hannah chose "Kneel at the Cross," and I chose "This Side of Heaven."

The service was much more subdued than our usual Sunday morning. It felt different and strange. I found myself wondering what Teddy was thinking about all this. When the song lyrics cascaded over my ears, "If we never meet again this side of heaven, I will meet you on that beautiful shore," I found myself wondering if I would ever see Teddy again. I found myself longing for him, hoping that one day I would meet him again on the other side, but doubt tugged at my heart that neither of us had lived right.

After the music, Daddy got up and walked up to the podium. His style of preaching at church had always been to pace back and forth in front of the congregation, so it felt a little strange to see him standing there at that podium with his Bible laying up in front of him. He seemed more like a judge in a courtroom than a preacher about to give a eulogy.

"Who was Teddy Dennison?" he started. "Teddy Dennison was my son. He was my oldest boy and the boy I placed most hope in. He was the boy I expected to take over my farm and continue in the footsteps I had made for him so that he wouldn't have to make his own."

"Who was Teddy Dennison? Teddy was a strong-willed boy, a boy with intentions of his own, a boy who didn't listen. Lord knows I tried to warn him of the ways of the world, of the pitfalls and temptations therein, but my son did not listen."

I felt my gut begin to tighten and my teeth clench. I could tell straight off where Daddy was headed, and I was furious. I found myself wishing I had told Momma I would preach. I found myself feeling an immense guilt. I glanced over at Momma to see a horrified look on her face, but there was really nothing we could do about what was happening.

Daddy continued. "In Romans 6:23 we read, 'For the wages of sin is death; but the gift of God is eternal life through Jesus Christ our Lord.'

My son rejected the gift of God. My son chose liquor and debauchery over eternal life, and here before you can be seen the result of that sin. This is not the coffin of an old man who lived a long and fruitful life for the Lord. This is the coffin of a young man who died a death so wretched that we dare not open it to look upon the carnage inside!"

My heart was pounding like the hooves of a running horse beating the dirt. I was livid that Daddy was not saying one good thing about Teddy, and I wanted to scream, "STOP IT!"

Momma burst into tears and I was torn between trying to comfort her and walking straight to the front of the chapel to pull Daddy off that pulpit and throttle him. I reached an arm around Momma to hug her, but I kept my face turned toward Daddy. He caught my eye and saw the look of disgust on my face. He paused for a moment and then went on.

"I would like to stand up here today and tell you that my son is going to heaven, but I can't. I can't do that because I know in my heart that his sins have taken him down. I know in my heart that he is hell bound, and the grief of this, my brothers and sisters, rips me asunder!"

Though Daddy reported grief, there was no look of anguish on his face. He was cold, cold like his heart had been frozen in a block of ice. When Aunt Morene saw Momma break down, she came around and got down on her knees in front of Momma. Grandma Miller had been trying to comfort Momma, but she just kept wailing, and I knew this was about more than losing a child; this was about having that child disgraced to the community by his own father.

I couldn't take it anymore, and when Aunt Morene came around, I saw an opportunity. I might not pull Daddy from the pulpit and beat him before that gathering of grievers, but I simply could not tolerate hearing one more word from him. I got up, shot him another dirty look, then turned and marched straight down the aisle and out of the building. I made no pretense to be anything other than angry. I couldn't believe what I was hearing, and I was not going to subject myself to any more of it.

To my surprise, others stood up and walked out as well. I saw people Teddy had gone to school with as I walked down that aisle. I saw the same disgusted look on their faces, and they got up behind me and followed me out. There were people who knew Teddy from church, including Brother and Sister Clark, who got up and walked out as well.

When I got outside, I walked over under a tree and began pacing. It hadn't even occurred to me that I left my coat back inside. Still, the cold air was not enough to cool me off. I stomped angrily over dead tan grass, first one direction, and then the other. Tears came running down my face, but I didn't know if they were tears of grief, tears of anger, or both. Brother Clark approached me, I suppose to offer some comfort, but I threw up my hand and gave a hard look to let him know *stay back*, and he retreated. I could hear people outside the chapel talking and caught a snippet here or there of "I couldn't believe that" or "Never in my life…" It didn't matter. I was lost in my own world, lost in my own anger. It was bad enough that we had lost Teddy and more than bad enough that he had suffered like he did when he came back from Korea, but for Daddy to say what he did at his own son's funeral was pulling at me like wild dogs ripping teeth into my soul.

After a while, the pallbearers brought the coffin out of the chapel and loaded it into the back of a black and chrome Cadillac hearse. I couldn't help but notice that it looked a lot like Miss Moore's car with exception of the covered back for carrying the dead. There was another black car, for transporting the family, parked just behind the hearse. I saw Momma, Daddy, Grandma Miller, and Hannah come out of the chapel. Then I saw Daddy motion to Hannah and point up at me. Hannah came walking over the grass carrying my coat. When she got to me, she held the coat out toward me and said, "Daddy says come on and get in the family car for the processional to the cemetery."

"I'm not going anywhere with him," I said firmly as I lifted my coat off her arm an put it on.

"What do you want me to tell him?" Hannah asked.

"I don't care what you tell him," I said. "It's not safe for me to be around him right now."

"What are you going to do?" she asked with a forlorn look across her face.

"I don't know," I replied.

I looked over to see Brother and Sister Clark who had stood nearby, waiting and watching. Brother Clark saw me staring at him and nodded a reassuring nod in my direction. I turned back to Hannah. "Tell him I'll ride with the Clarks."

Hannah didn't say anything but turned to walk back toward the family.

I walked over to Brother and Sister Clark. "Do you mind if I ride with you?" I asked.

Brother Clark smiled and put an arm around my shoulder. "Come on," he said. "Plenty of room."

Brother and Sister Clark didn't ask anything about what was going on with me or how I was feeling, and I was glad. I didn't want to talk. When we got to the grave site, I stood away from the rest. I could scarce believe how Momma, Hannah, or Grandma Miller managed to sit through the service or sit there before the casket, but they did. They endured it, sat through what I couldn't abide.

Daddy didn't stop. Despite my walking out and other people walking out of the service, which surely should have been a clear indication that he was doing wrong, he still continued.

"In Leviticus 20:9 we read, 'For everyone that curseth his father or his mother shall be surely put to death, he has cursed his father or his mother; his blood shall be upon him.' And in Genesis 3:19 we read, 'For dust thou art, and unto dust thou shalt return.' May God have mercy on your soul, my son." Daddy cast a handful of dirt onto the casket as it lowered into the ground, closed his Bible, and stood there in silence.

The few people who had come to the graveside service got up from folding chairs and walked away. Some stood over to the side and chatted briefly before leaving, but that was it. It was over, and Teddy was surely gone.

We caught rides home the same way we had gotten to the chapel. When we got there, Momma went to lie down in her room without even taking off her funeral dress. She would cry now and then, but mostly she just stared at the wall like she was looking off at some distant place, maybe trying to see

Teddy. Daddy sat down in his chair and thumbed through his Bible like it was a waiting room magazine. There were plenty of leftovers and lots of food that church people had brought to the house. Most of it didn't even need a warm-up. Years of Arkansas culture taught wives to make funeral food that was quick and easy and not something that required any effort, things like fried chicken that would keep a day or two. They knew the last thing a grieving mother would want to do is cook.

About suppertime, I went in to see Momma just lying there with that blank stare on her face. I sat on the edge of the bed and laid one hand over on her foot. "Momma…it's suppertime. Can I fix you a plate?" She didn't say a word but just kept staring at the wall. "Momma?"

"I'm not hungry," she said, finally.

"You need to eat, Momma."

Without wavering her stare, even for a moment, she said in a flat tone, "I'll eat tomorrow."

I went into the kitchen and picked up a couple of the dishes that had been emptied and began washing them in the sink. I tried to remember which family brought them so I could be sure they were properly returned. Daddy came in and picked up a piece of fried chicken out of a bowl on the table. "I thought it went well today," he said as he bit into the side of a chicken leg.

A shivering rage hit me, full force. I dropped the bowl I was cleaning into soapy water and whirled around to him. I pointed a trembling finger at his face and shouted, "HOW DARE YOU! HOW DARE YOU SAY THAT! HOW DARE YOU DENIGRATE YOUR OWN SON AND DESECRATE HIS MEMORY IN FRONT OF THE ENTIRE COMMUNITY!"

"You mean how dare I speak the truth?" he flashed back at me in a glib tone.

"WHAT TRUTH?" I screamed. "WHAT TRUTH DID YOU SPEAK? DID YOU SAY ANYTHING AT ALL ABOUT WHAT A GOOD-HEARTED, LOVING SON YOU HAD? DID YOU SAY ANYTHING ABOUT HIS SERVICE AND SACRIFICE TO HIS COUNTRY?

DID YOU SAY ONE THING GOOD ABOUT HIM…JUST ONE THING? NO! ALL YOU DID WAS DESECRATE THE MEMORY OF YOUR OWN SON!"

"Teddy was a sinner," he said calmly. "The Bible is clear."

"EVERYBODY IS A SINNER, DADDY! YOU'RE A SINNER! I'M A SINNER! EVERYBODY IS A SINNER! DID YOU STOP TO THINK THERE MIGHT HAVE BEEN A REASON FOR HIS BEHAVIOR OVER THE LAST FEW MONTHS, THAT MAYBE IT MIGHT HAVE SOMETHING TO DO WITH WHAT HAPPENED TO HIM IN COMBAT, THAT MAYBE IT MIGHT HAVE SOMETHIG TO DO WITH TRYING TO MAKE SENSE OF THE SENSELESS, AND MAYBE IT'S NOT JUST ABOUT SIN?"

I turned around and grabbed the counter with both hands, half afraid that I was going to hit him. I tried to calm down. All my life I had wanted nothing more than to please my daddy. All my life I had wanted to follow in his footsteps, but in that moment, on that day, all I could feel for him was disgust. I took a deep breath and let go of the counter. "I need to go to bed," I said as I turned and walked out of the kitchen.

When I got to my room, I fell to my knees in front of the bed and prayed for myself to let go of my anger, for Daddy to find some compassion in his heart, for Momma to find solace in her grief, for Hannah to find some way out of her confusion, but most of all, I prayed for Teddy, that our loving Savior would take his soul to heaven and abide with him until the time might come that I could see my brother again. I got ready for bed and lay there on my side, staring off into the darkness in the direction where Teddy would have, should have, been sleeping. Just like Momma, I lay there and stared. In time, I drifted to sleep.

The next thing I knew, someone was shaking my shoulder. "Ronnie," he whispered loud enough to get my attention but not so loud as to wake up the others. I opened my eyes, and there sat Teddy his eyes bright and gleaming like the time when he was happy, like the time before Korea.

"Teddy?" I said. "I thought you were dead."

"Come on," he said. "I got something to show you."

I sat up on the side of the bed, and Teddy took my hand to lead me like he did when I was a very little boy. He led me out of the bedroom, through the kitchen, and down to the barn lot. When we got there, the sun was shining overhead, there were flowers blooming, and the sky was filled with the most beautiful fluffy white clouds I had ever seen. The clouds really did have silver linings, and the light was glowing off the edge of them as though they had their own light within. Teddy led me to the pond, and it was silver like mercury. The little Roman soldiers were lying around the banks of the pond, eating bright-red grapes, and the redheaded woman sat beside the pond dipping her hands into the water and bringing it to her face, but when she brought the silver to her face, it became crystal clear water and poured over her face and her head like she was standing beneath a gentle waterfall. Lying on his back, across the top of the pond, I saw Jesus dressed in a pure white robe. His arms were outstretched, and He was looking up into the sky with a blissful look on His face.

"Watch this," Teddy said as he led me to the water's edge. He then reached his hand into the water and made a little ripple.

When the ripple reached Jesus, He stood up on the water's surface and reached out His hands to us. "You stay here," Teddy said.

He let go of my hand and walked across the water to Jesus. When he got there, Jesus enfolded him in a big hug. Then He held him back, turned him around, and baptized him into the silver water. When He lifted Teddy back up out of the water, he was no longer a grown man but a little infant wrapped in a white blanket. Jesus held baby Teddy up above His head. Then a light came down from the sky upon them. When the light came, Jesus let go of baby Teddy, and he floated up into the clouds.

"Teddy, don't leave me!" I cried out with tears rolling down my face. One moment I was looking up as Teddy floated off into the light and into the clouds, and the next moment Jesus was standing in front of me as though he had traveled the length of the pond in an instant. He took both my hands in His hands and gently said, "I have told you that you are My

Word." I looked at Him then looked up into the sky where Teddy was floating away.

"Teddy is in heaven," He said. "For on this day he shall be with Me in heaven. You have work to do and much to learn before you go. Teddy's time is over now."

Jesus then placed the palm of His hand against my forehead and swiped His hand down across my face. When He did, everything went totally dark, and there was nothing more that I could see.

I awoke to the sound of Momma's sweet voice coming from the kitchen. She was gently singing a hymn. "I surrender all, all to Thee, my blessed Savior. I surrender all." I knew, in that moment, what I had to do.

CHAPTER 10

It took me a few days to find Miss Moore's business card. For a while, I was afraid I might have accidentally thrown it away. I decided eventually to take everything out of every drawer and look through every box under the bed. Then I found it where I had previously overlooked it, in the back of my sock drawer.

Things had kind of gotten back to normal, I guess. Momma was doing her normal daily stuff except that now and then she would stop right in the middle of doing something, suck in a quick breath, fight back tears, and then move on with what she was doing. Most of the time, right after that, she would start singing, "I surrender all."

Daddy actually seemed to be coming out of his depression as though preaching Teddy's funeral had done something for him. I knew he was stuck in his way of thinking, and nothing I could ever do would bring him out of that. I had such mixed feelings about Daddy. There was a part of me that wanted to hate him for what he said about Teddy and for a lot of other things. However, I couldn't make myself do it. I had always looked up to him. I had always adored him and would have loved nothing better than for him to have said to me, just once, that I had done a good job or that he was proud of me. That day never came. Whenever my anger rose toward Daddy, I would just say to myself, "Seventy times seven. Jesus said forgive seventy times seven."

Hannah just stuck her nose in her schoolbooks every night. Christmas was coming, but we didn't pay it much attention. We never really celebrated it in our house anyway. Daddy always said nobody really knows when baby Jesus was born, and besides, he said what we call Christmas is just a pagan holiday that the Catholics adopted. Still, like as not, somebody would bring us a bag of nuts, oranges, or a coconut, the kind of things you just didn't find around Arkansas in those days, except on special occasions. Momma would make a few cakes out of the things we were brought, a coconut cake or an orange cake, so it was a kind of a celebration without really being a celebration. Despite what Daddy thought, I never could quite see anything wrong with picking the date to celebrate Jesus's birth, even if it had been a pagan holiday.

I didn't know how Momma was going to react to my calling Miss Moore. She had just lost one son, and I was afraid that going off to Nashville might make her feel like she was losing another one. I had already made up my mind that I was going to go. I felt like I had to go. The dream told me that much. I knew it was time for me to take some action. I just didn't know if I should wait a little while to let Momma get used to the idea first, or if I should just say it. I finally decided to talk to her.

It was actually on Christmas Day that I asked her to sit down. We would usually have a big meal on Christmas Day. Momma would do a big roast or something special like that, which she didn't do on any other day.

We didn't exchange gifts or decorate, but we would relax after Christmas dinner. Grandma Miller would either come over to our house for dinner, or we would all go over there. Often, we would sit around listening to holiday radio programming. I recalled days when Teddy and I would sit by the radio listening to Christmas Radio Hour on holiday afternoons. It was delightful to us, even if Daddy didn't really believe in Christmas, or if he said things like, "Now, there is not one thing that a Frosty Snow Man has to do with the birth of Jesus!"

"It's still a fun story, Daddy," Teddy would say.

"Well, I don't suppose there is any harm in it," Daddy would return, "but it don't have anything to do with baby Jesus."

After Christmas dinner that year, I went into the kitchen to help Momma and Hannah with the cleanup. We got most everything cleaned and put away. Then I asked Hannah if she would go into the other room so I could have a private talk with Momma. Good old obliging Hannah always did as she was asked.

"Momma," I said. "I think I would like to have an afternoon cup of coffee and maybe another piece of that coconut cake you made. Would you sit down and have a cup of coffee with me?"

"Are you making the coffee?" she asked.

"Yes, ma'am," I responded. Then I got up and began prepping the stovetop percolator for a little time on the hot plate. While that was heating up, I got out a couple of saucers and cut us both a hunk of cake. I set Momma's cake in front of her and sat down across the corner from her to take a bite of mine.

"We have had a lot of talks at this table over the years, haven't we, Momma?" I questioned as I chewed the sweet confection and watched for her reaction.

"Yes, we have." She smiled. "I was usually trying to comfort you in some little turmoil you were having."

"You've been my anchor, Momma," I affirmed. "I know that the winds of life would have blown me against the stones had it not been for you."

"What's bothering you this time, son?" she asked.

I glanced over to see that the coffee pot was beginning to perk. "I'm worried a little," I said as I got up to turn the coffee off. "Mostly about you."

"Worried about me?" she asked.

"Yes, ma'am," I said, pouring coffee into thick porcelain mugs that had been picked up at a cheap auction many years before.

She got a little nervous. "Ronnie, I think I'm handling things okay. I know I still get upset now and then, but it's not easy to outlive your child."

"Momma, that's not what I'm talking about." I smiled and set her cup of coffee beside the cake she hadn't yet touched. "I'm worried because I'm going to do something, and I'm afraid it will upset you, especially this close to Teddy's passing."

I heard the gasp she tried to stifle. Then she dug her fork into the cake for a bite and took a quick slurp of her coffee before she had finished chewing it. She didn't ask what I was going to do.

I sat back down and took a sip of my coffee, which I must admit was a little too hot just coming from the boiling pot.

"Momma, do you remember Miss Moore, that city woman who came up from Memphis for our revival meeting?"

"Of course I do," she responded. "I told you to look for a sign from God."

"Well, I think I have found one."

I took another bite of my cake and sat back in my chair. "Momma, Teddy came to me in a dream on the night of his funeral."

Her face filled with shock, and I could see little puddles of tears floating at the base of her eyes. I leaned forward and placed my hand over hers. "Momma, I know Teddy is in heaven. I *know* he is. It's okay." I proceeded to tell her about the dream and how Jesus lifted little baby Teddy up, and he ascended into heaven.

"You know," she said, upon hearing that part, "the Bible says, 'Lest ye become as little children, ye shall not enter into the Kingdom of Heaven.' Teddy became a little child again." She smiled and relaxed a little. I saw more peace in her at that moment than I had seen since before Teddy went off to war. Maybe that's not really what the Bible verse meant, but if it gave Momma some peace, that was more than all right by me.

I went on. "After Teddy ascended, Jesus was standing right there in front of me. He told me again that I am His Word, and He said that I have much to do and much to learn, and it is not my time yet." Another worry faded from Momma's face and then I said, "I think this is my sign, Momma. I think I need to call Miss Moore and go talk to these people in Nashville."

"I think you are right." she smiled. "Ronnie, there is no question that you have the calling. When you preach, you move people, and I have been a witness to your healing of the sick. If you can expand that and reach a broader following, who knows how many you could bring to the Lord."

"I worry about you and Daddy and Hannah," I said. "I worry that you might not be able to handle the farm without me."

"Ronnie, whether we can handle the farm or not is not a relevant concern," she argued. "If this is what you are meant to do, then you need to go and do it. You don't need to let concerns about this old farm or anything else hold you back. When the time comes that we can't take care of the farm, then we will think of something else. The Lord will provide."

I got to my feet, crossed over, and kissed her on the forehead and said, "I love you, Momma." Then I went back to my chair.

"I love you too, son." She smiled. "More than you can understand till you have children of your own."

I dug my fork in for another bite of cake. "You know, Momma, this is a very, very, fine cake. I think you missed your calling. Maybe you should be baking for some fancy restaurant in New York City."

"You know, if we get to where we can't handle the farm no more," Momma grinned wide. "I just might do that. I just might move up to New York City and start cooking for the Ritz." Then she giggled like a little girl and put two fingers over her lips. "Can you imagine?"

The next day I drove the truck over to Brother and Sister Clark's place. Then I drove right back home without stopping because I could see they still had company, and probably their kids and grandkids were home for Christmas. I waited another week, and then it snowed a couple of inches just after the New Year. The whole world seems to shut down when it snows in Arkansas. Nothing moves. Even the animals try to find shelter and stay still when the wet, cold white blankets the land like a suffocating glob. Arkansas snows are wet snows. It rarely gets cold enough for that powder snow they talk about in the magazines about ski resorts. The good news is it usually doesn't last for long. However, that snow didn't want to go away. It turned off bitter cold, and then it snowed again on top of the first one. This was after it had melted enough to make a glaze of ice over the crust of the first snow when it started to get cold again. We kept our wood stove burning full time, and it still got pretty chilly in the bedrooms overnight.

Finally, I just decided I would walk over to Brother and Sister Clark's since the truck was not safe to drive in that stuff.

I told Momma what I was going to do, and she made a bunch of cookies for me to take over. She boxed them up with a dish towel over them, and I headed off for the Clark place. Even with high boots, my feet got wet, so by the time I got there, my toes were aching and throbbing. The wind stung my cheeks like a swarm of wasps, and I know my face must have been the color of a Santa suit. When I knocked, Sister Clark came to the door, took a quick look at me, and said, "Lord have mercy, child. What are you doing out in this mess? Get in here!"

She tugged on my sleeve at the shoulder, and I entered the house to a wave of toasty warm air. They had a big, potbellied black stove in the middle of their living room hooked up to a brick flu on the east side of their house. Sister Clark kept a pan of water on top of the stove all the time to keep the wood heat from drying the air too much. Plus, it added a little humidity and warmed the air.

I handed her the box of cookies and said, "Momma made you some cookies—molasses, I think."

"I love molasses cookies." She beamed. "Look, Cecil, Brother Ronnie brought us some cookies."

Brother Clark had already gotten up from his chair and had come across the room to greet me. "It's good to see you, Brother Ronnie." He smiled as he reached out to shake my hand. "Take your coat off. Sit down, and stay a spell."

"Well, if you don't mind," I said, "I would like to do a little more than take my coat off. My socks got a little wet on the walk over here. Do you mind if I dry them out by the stove while I sit?"

"Oh, get out of those wet clothes," Sister Clark commanded. "I'll hang your coat up behind the stove to dry, and we can set your boots back there to dry as well."

I did as I was ordered, and Sister Clark, obviously prepared for similar situations, hung my socks with clothes pins on a wire that was strung between two nails behind the stove pipe. We all sat down around the stove after that. The bottom third of my jeans were also wet, but I just scooted up near the stove to give them a chance to dry a little. Sister Clark said, "It sure was nice of your momma to think of us during this storm and send you over here with some cookies."

"Well, truth be told, Sister Clark," I said, "I did have an ulterior motive for coming over. I was hoping you might allow me to use your phone again. I don't even know if you have gotten the bill yet for all the calls I made around the time of Teddy's funeral, but I want to pay you for every bit of it."

"Now, we are not going to worry about calls around a tragedy," Brother Clark spoke firmly. "Neighbors pitch in to help neighbors during times like that. If you have personal calls to make otherwise, when there ain't no emergency, we might let you pay for those."

"Well, I know it has got to turn into a hassle being one of the few people around who has a phone," I said. "I'm sure people around are pressing you all the time for the use of it when they don't take steps to get one of their own."

"Oh, it's not too bad," Brother Clark responded. "Most folks are pretty courteous about it and only ask to use it when there is an urgency. Only time it really bothers us is when people we don't even know have found out we have a telephone and come knocking on the door. I started telling those folks it's two dollars a call, so now they don't come around much no more." He chuckled and sat back in his chair. "I know that's a little high, but if they want to pay it, I get a little cash, and if they don't, then they can go on and find somebody else with a telephone."

"Well, sir," I began my plea, "I need to call all the way to Memphis, and I am more than willing to pay you two dollars."

"Memphis?" Sister Clark blurted. "Why would you want to call all the way to Memphis?" Then she caught herself. "Oh—oh, is this about that woman that came up for the revival and said she was with a broadcast ministry? Ronnie, word has gotten out all over about that."

"Yes, ma'am," I said shyly. "I have decided to go ahead and follow up on that."

"We knew you would come around, and there is absolutely no way we are gonna let you pay for that phone call. It is on us and happy to do it." Sister Clark beamed. "As much as we would miss you and hate to lose you, we have been praying for the Lord to lead you to greater things. I hate to say it, Ronnie, but God gave you a gift that your Daddy ain't ever gonna have. You have got a calling of the Lord, and you need to spread that as far and wide as you can."

"Ma'am, I don't know what to say," I responded. "Not I, but the Father through me. I'm gonna try to keep my ego out of it. I'm gonna try to keep myself humble."

"Oh, look at me!" she exclaimed as she got up and headed for the kitchen. "I'm not being much of a hostess. Would you like something to drink, Brother Ronnie, a glass of tea, cup of coffee? The kids even brought us some cola for Christmas if you would like to have one."

"No, ma'am," I said, resisting the urge to accept a cola since it was something I dearly loved and was a rare treat in those days. "That's your Christmas gift. You need to keep that and enjoy it yourself, but I would take a cup of coffee though, if you have some made."

"Come on with me," she said, "You can go ahead and call that lady over in Memphis."

Their phone was mounted on the kitchen wall by the table. I suppose that made it convenient to sit at the table and talk. I followed her into the kitchen.

"Go ahead and make your call, Brother Ronnie," she went on. "You can do that while I put the coffee on."

"No need to make a pot just for me," I said. "A glass of water would be fine."

"Nonsense," she scolded. "I might like to have a cup too, on a cold day like this."

"Cecil!" she called into the living room.

"Yes, my dear," he called back.

"Don't you think you would like to have a cup of coffee?" she half-shouted.

"That sounds wonderful," he called back. "It'll make them cookies taste even better."

"Go ahead and make your call, Brother Ronnie," she demanded, again motioning to the phone. Then she turned around and busied herself with making the coffee.

I pulled the card out of my pocket half trembling, part of me terrified for what I might be getting myself into, and part of me determined to do it. I first picked up the receiver to make sure no one was on the party line. Then I heard two women talking. I wasn't surprised, really. Calling up a friend on a snowy day was one way to pass the time, and everybody in those days had party lines with several people sharing the same main line. I simply hung the receiver gently back on the hook and decided to wait.

Sister Clark saw me hang up the phone. "Someone on the line?" she asked, and without giving me a chance to answer, she asked, "Who is it? Is that Sheila Johnson on there?"

"I don't know, Sister," I said.

Sister Clark already had the coffee on the stove to perk. She came across the room and picked up the receiver. "Hello? Hello? Who's on the line, please?"

I heard a tinny jabber softly coming from the receiver. Then Sister Clark said, "Well, Sheila, I hate to interrupt, but the Dennison boy walked all the way over here so he could use the phone. Would you mind postponing your call for a few minutes while he makes his call? I can call you back when he's done, if you like."

There was more jabber on the line, and then Sister Clark said, "Thank you both. You're sweeties. I'll be sure and give you a call back when he's done." She hung up the phone then turned to me and said, "Give it a second."

"I hate to interrupt," I said.

"Oh, that ain't nothing," Sister Clark replied. "Sheila and her friend Madge get on there and do little else but gossip. Ain't right by the Lord, but they do it. They tie that line up more than anybody else on the party, talking about who has done what. I know they listen sometimes too. See if they can get some snoop on something private so they can gossip about it. Most other folks on the party line have got to interrupt them if they want to get a call in anyway, and you can't receive a call as long as they are on the line neither. Some of us have talked about setting up a call schedule so we can get a little equal sharing of the line. Gonna have to get with everybody and talk about that sometime. In the meantime, go ahead and make your call now. I'll check the coffee."

I picked up the receiver again, and this time there was a dial tone. I nervously dialed the operator then gave her the number on the business card and waited. In those days you couldn't dial long distance direct. You had to wait for an operator to connect you. So long distance calls could be expensive. After the operator made the connection, I heard the phone ring several times and thought surely there would be no answer, when I heard the line click, and the voice said, "This is Wanda Moore. May I help you?"

"Ah…um…Miss Moore?" I found myself trembling. This was more frightening than I thought it was going to be. Suddenly, I found myself realizing that my whole way of life would change with this phone call. I would be giving up everything familiar to me, and no matter what I might have imagined, everything out there was unknown.

"Yes?"

"Ah…this is Ronnie…ah…this is Pastor Ronald Dennison." My hand was trembling. I sat down. "You came to hear me speak at our revival in Ravenden, Arkansas, last year."

"Yes! Yes, Pastor Dennison. How are you?"

"I'm fine," I replied into the line. Then I found myself saying, "Well, no, actually, I'm not fine. My brother died a few weeks ago, a little before Christmas."

Sister Clark set a cup of coffee on the table beside me. I reached over to take a quick sip and felt my lips burn in the process. "Aoum!" I exclaimed as I quickly set the cup back down.

"What was that?" Miss Moore asked.

"Ouch, that hurts," I blurted, not really as an answer to her question.

"I'm sorry, Pastor Dennison," Miss Moore said. "Are you okay?"

"I'm fine," I said. "I just burned my lips a little on a hot cup of coffee. I should have blown on it some, since it came right off the stove."

Sister Clark grimaced and whispered, "I'm sorry. You want me to get you some cool water?"

I shook my head and focused back on the telephone. "Ah…Miss Moore…the reason I called is to take you up on the offer of meeting the gentleman you told me about in Nashville. I'm sorry. I don't remember his name."

"Jacob Clayburn," she responded.

"Ah…is the offer still open?" I questioned with part of me hoping that it wouldn't be.

"Yes, yes, of course," she replied. "I will be happy to set an appointment for you. You can come to Nashville and meet him."

"Well, I don't know if it will be as easy as that," I explained. "My family has only one vehicle, and that is a truck most often used for farm work."

"Could you take a bus to Nashville?" she questioned.

"Yes, I suppose I could," I acknowledged. "I-I…ah…I just really don't know how to arrange all this. Actually, I have never been away from home before. I've never stayed in a hotel or taken a bus. I don't even know how to go about arranging for a hotel, and actually, right now, I'm at a neighbor's house borrowing their phone because we don't even have a phone of our own. I-I…think I'm going to need a little guidance."

"Hmmm," she pondered. "Where is the nearest hotel close to where you live?"

"That would probably be over at Pocahontas," I replied. "It is about twenty miles from our house, and it has a population of a couple of thousand, I think. I assume they must have a hotel there."

"Black River Motor Inn," Sister Clark blurted out, obviously listening in on the conversation.

I looked over to see her sitting on the other side of the table. I hadn't even noticed that she had sat down with her coffee or that Brother Clark had come in as well. Sister Clark had placed the cookies on a plate in the middle of the table, and they were both nibbling cookies with their coffee while listening to me talk. I was so engrossed that I hadn't realized any of that.

"My neighbor says it's the Black River Motor Inn," I told her.

"Hold on," Sister Clark directed. "I think I have a Pocahontas phone book. I'll be right back."

"Well," Miss Moore suggested, "if you can wait a couple of weeks to go to Nashville with me, I can come up to stay at the motel in Pocahontas and then pick you up the next morning to drive over to Nashville. Once there, you will be able to stay with Mr. Clayburn. You should expect to stay about a week."

Sister Clark came back into the room and placed a phone book on the table in front of me with her finger pointing to the number for the Black River Motor Inn.

"I have the number for the hotel here," I said. "When would we do this?"

"I can get the number from information," she replied. "Let me contact Mr. Clayburn to see when we might be able to arrange this. If you don't have any conflicts as to when you can come, then give me your mailing address, and I will write to you when I have the arrangements made."

"Ah…okay…my address is 169 Sassafras Trail, Ravenden, Arkansas."

"Tell her she can call here," Sister Clark interrupted. "Give her our number."

I looked up at Sister Clark. She wrote their number on a piece of paper and laid it in front of me.

"My neighbor says you can call them if you need to get hold of me," I said into the phone.

"Okay." Miss Moore questioned, "What is their number?"

I read the number from the paper, and Miss Moore said, "All right, Pastor Dennison. As soon as I have arrangements made, I will get back to you. Most likely I will simply send you a letter outlining the suggested dates and times. However, I will call your neighbor if I need to. In the meantime, please be patient as this could take a few weeks. Mr. Clayburn is going to want to make arrangements for you to speak to a congregation here, and he will want to do a screen test and some vocal tests. That could take some time to get arranged."

"Yes, ma'am. I understand," I said, but I didn't understand anything at all. I had no idea what a screen test or a vocal test was. The truth is I had no idea what I was getting myself into, but despite my trepidation, I had determined that I was going to do it.

"All right then," Miss Moore said, concluding the call. "Call me again if you need to, but otherwise, please wait a few weeks for me to get back to you."

"Well?" Sister Clark questioned eagerly.

"Well, they are going to take me to Nashville for some screen and vocal tests," I acknowledged.

"Praise be to the Lord!" she exclaimed, clasping both hands in the air before her. She had no more of a clue than I did what a screen test was, but she did know it could mean an expansion of my ministry, and the Clarks had supported me in my preaching more than anyone.

I was too much in shock to be excited. I sat there feeling stunned and humble. I reached for a cookie and dunked it into my now lukewarm coffee. As I was pulling it from the cup, the soaked half fell off and disappeared beneath the dark liquid. *Hmmm,* I thought, *I hope that is not an omen.*

CHAPTER 11

Weeks rolled past after I had my phone conversation with Miss Wanda Moore. It had been so long since our conversation that I wondered if she might have changed her mind or that maybe this Mr. Clayburn decided he didn't need some inexperienced upstart like me for his broadcasting ministry. I was trying to be patient and determined to have faith, yet the doubts etched into my mind. I thought about going over to the Clarks to call again, but I knew they wouldn't let me pay for it, and I didn't want to put them through that expense again.

On the fifteenth of February, I went out after dinner to see if the mail had arrived. I pulled the mail from our box and began flipping through the envelopes while I walked back to the house. The third envelope had a preprinted return address with the name Christ Beacon Broadcasting. My hand trembled, and my heart raced briefly as I pulled the letter from the stack. I paused for a moment then rushed quickly to the porch, where I sat on the front steps and opened the letter. A crisp winter breeze almost snatched it from my hands when I pulled it from the torn envelope. Miss Moore's business card was stapled on the upper right side.

February 10, 1954

Dear Pastor Dennison:

This is to inform you that I have made arrangements for you to meet Mr. Clayburn in Nashville on March, 22, 1954. I will come to

Pocahontas on the weekend prior, and stay at the Black River Motor Inn. If you need to call me there, I will be staying in Room 57. I have enclosed another copy of my business card and have written the number of the hotel on the back. Please make arrangements to meet me at the Motor Inn at precisely 8:00 a.m. on the morning of March 21, 1954, and be prepared to leave at that time. I realize this is Sunday and our travels will mean that you will have to miss church. I apologize for any imposition. However, we have a long drive to make.

Please pack enough belongings for up to a two-week stay. During the first week, Mr. Clayburn has several appointments scheduled for screen and vocal tests. On the following Sunday, arrangements have been made for you to be a guest minister at Evangelic Temple in Nashville. Mr. Clayburn wishes to observe how a larger congregation will respond to you. You may determine whatever topic you feel is appropriate for the theme of the service on that date. We will want to know the topic of your sermon at least by Monday, March 22, so this can be included with service bulletins.

If you do not have funds for a hotel, please do not concern yourself. Arrangements have been made for the two of us to have rooms at the new Vacation Inn hotel in Nashville on the evening of March 21. On the following morning, I will take you to meet Mr. Clayburn, and I believe he will plan to have you as a guest in his home for the remaining time.

I am sending this letter a little over a month ahead so that you will have plenty of time to prepare. Please either call me on my business line or write me to confirm whether these arrangements will be convenient for you.

I will be awaiting your reply.

Sincerely,
Wanda Moore,
Christian Broadcasting Consultant

I folded the letter and placed it back into the envelope. On one hand, I was excited and looking forward to an adventure like I had never previously experienced. On the other hand, I heard myself whisper, "Oh, Lord, what have I gotten myself into?" At that moment, a stronger and cooler gust of wind whisked across the front porch, created a vacuum, and popped the front door against the facing. The thumping sound of the door might have startled me if I had not heard it all my life. That same gust almost yanked the papers from my hand and put a bite to my face, so I thought it best I go inside. I never considered that also could have been an omen.

I walked through the living room where Daddy sat listening to the radio. I knew Momma was still cleaning the dinner dishes. When I entered the kitchen, she had finished all but wiping down the table and the countertops. She glanced over to see the papers in my hands and said, "Oh, we got quite a stack today."

I quietly pulled the letter from Miss Moore off the stack and handed it to her. She dropped her dish rag on the counter, took the letter, and examined the envelope. Then she opened it and read it while she leaned against the counter. When she finished the letter, she looked up at me and smiled a strange smile that let me know she was feeling the same kind of ambivalence I was. She pushed a breath out her nostrils so hard it could almost have been a hissing cat. "Well, you are off to see the world, my boy." She smiled.

"Momma, am I making a mistake by doing this?" I queried. "I just don't know. It seems so big and so far away, and I'm just a little country preacher who ain't even cut his milk teeth yet."

She sighed deeply and handed the letter back to me. "Ronnie, what I know is that God didn't give your life to me or to your daddy. God helped me and your daddy give life to you, but that life belongs to you and only to you. You get to do with that life whatever you want, even if it is to mess it up, and I don't think you are going to mess it up. The Lord may guide us, but He never forces us. The one true gift God gave, besides His love, is the gift of choice. What you do with that choice is up to you."

"I guess I'm scared, Momma," I said. Then I pulled out a chair at the table and sat down. Maybe this was my signal that I needed to have another one of our talks.

"Ain't everybody scared?" she asked, leaning back into the counter and folding her arms. "Every day of anybody's life there is something to fear."

"What if I mess up?" I questioned. "What if I get up in front of that big congregation in Nashville and make a total fool of myself. I don't even know how big that church is. For all I know, it could be a thousand people."

"Well, if you make a fool of yourself" she smiled "at least you will be a fool for the Lord."

"And then what?" I continued.

"And then you do anything you want to do," she replied. "Honey, you can always come home. Ravenden ain't going nowhere, but you have an opportunity that most people go their whole lives and never encounter. At least you need to find out if you are going to be a fool for the Lord. If you try and you fail, at least you will know that you tried. If you don't try, you have failed already."

"I'm scared like I have never been scared, a different kind of scared." I sighed. "I'm comfortable here. I know what to expect. I pretty much know that today is going to look a lot like yesterday, and tomorrow is going to look a lot like today. I feel safe here."

Momma walked over to the table, pulled out a chair, and sat down. Then, she leaned toward me and took my hand. "Two things," she said. "Two things I heard before; one of them is that a ship is safe in a harbor, but setting in a harbor is not what a ship is for. You got to set sail, son. You have got to float out into that great beyond and see what adventure the Lord has planned for you. The other thing is, somebody told me one time the statement *'fear not'* is found in the Bible 365 times. That's one for every day of the year. I don't know if that's true or not 'cause I never took the time to count, but I do know that the Lord don't want us to be afraid of anything. Faith is the opposite of fear. Faith is knowing that God is holding you in His loving arms no matter what happens. Faith is knowing that you and God can do together what you could never do alone."

A tear rolled down my cheek, and I thought of Teddy just then. "Momma, didn't Teddy have reason to be afraid? Isn't it likely that he experienced things in that war that tore him apart that overwhelmed him and gave him reason to be afraid?"

She looked at me, eyes gentle, but stern staring straight into mine, and a few tears rolled over her own cheek. "Maybe if Teddy had a little more faith, he would still be with us," she said. "I know he must have seen and experienced horrible things, and then he brought those things home with him. Maybe the problem is that Teddy didn't stop being afraid even when he was safe at home. He didn't stop being afraid when there was no reason to be afraid anymore." She sat back in her chair and pulled her apron up to wipe the wet from her face. "It seems to me," she went on, "that all of life is learning how to deal with fear. If we don't learn how to deal with it, then one way or another, it is going to tear us asunder."

I reached over and patted her knee. "I'm sorry, Momma. I guess by comparison to Teddy, I got nothing to be afraid of."

"Ronnie, I know you will do well," she said. "I know it, as sure as I am living, that you are going to be successful at the vocation you have been called to, and I'm going to love you as long as I live, no matter what you do. So you might as well go live your life the way you want, follow your heart, and follow your dreams."

I realized, in that moment, that as much as Daddy had expectations of me, Momma wanted me to be happy. She wasn't going to try to push me this way or that or try to tell me what I was supposed to do to be happy. She was going to let me discover that all on my own. It was my momma who taught me what love really is. She taught me all my life, but it was going to be a long time from that day before I would really understand.

The next day I dropped a letter in the mail to Miss Moore to let her know I would be ready to go on March 21 and that I was looking forward to meeting Mr. Clayburn. In the following weeks, I fought with myself about what I was going to preach at Evangelic Temple. I even took to just opening my Bible at random, and with eyes closed, I'd drop a finger on the page and read whatever was there in the hopes that I might begin to solidify an idea for a message. I lay in bed at night staring at the dark ceiling, imagining what it might be like to preach in a big church or to be on television. In those days, television was still pretty much a new medium. I had seen snippets of television shows on display model TVs at a store over in Jonesboro, but I had never actually watched a TV show from beginning to end. Just as telephones were scarce in north Arkansas in those days, so were televisions. For one thing, the closest TV stations were in Memphis and Little Rock, so if you didn't live in the city, there wasn't going to be much you could see anyway. Over the next five to ten years, things improved greatly. New TV stations opened; antennas got better and could pull from greater distances. After a while, TV started coming to rural communities, but at the time, I didn't really have a clue.

When March 21 finally rolled around, I had spent the Saturday before trying to think of anything that I might need in the following two weeks. I went to Jonesboro the week before and bought myself a set of luggage as well as some new clothes. I still got a little money for preaching, but it didn't go very far when it came to buying extras. Most of it went toward taking care of family. When I was gone, they wouldn't even have that. I worried about Momma and Daddy, but I took Momma at her word that I needed to move on, live my own life, and answer my calling.

On the morning of the twenty-first, Brother and Sister Clark drove me over to the Black River Motor Inn. Daddy said he couldn't because he was going to preach the service that Sunday. It seemed like, with me out of the picture, he felt more confident about going back to the pulpit. Most people forgave him for what he said at Teddy's funeral.

Brother and Sister Clark assured me that they could have me in Pocahontas in time to meet Miss Moore at 8:00 a.m. and still have plenty of time to get back for church. When we got there that morning, Miss Moore was waiting for us in the hotel lobby. I recognized her immediately when we walked in, such a stunning woman. Her physical beauty was almost overwhelming. She was wearing a yellow floral print dress that made her blond hair seem even more brilliant. She wore a white belt around her waist that pulled the dress in to accentuate her figure. In my mind, I wondered if she was what fashion models looked like in person. I had seen pictures in magazines, and she sure looked as good as, or better than, any of those women. As soon as she saw us, she got up from her seat and strolled across the small lobby to greet us.

"Pastor Dennison." She smiled, extending her hand as she approached. "So nice to see you again."

I reached out to give her a traditional business handshake although I only caught her fingers in my palm. "Very good to see you again, Miss Moore," I responded. Then I wondered if she had any idea how good it was to see her or that "good to see her" meant something bad in my mind. If I could, I would have sat there all day just looking at her. I stood there, dazed for a moment, fighting my sexual urges, when I realized I hadn't introduced the Clarks. I turned to Brother and Sister Clark, who were standing just to the side behind me. "Ah…this is Brother and Sister Clark," I stammered, "from our church."

"Very pleased to meet you," Miss Moore graciously smiled as she held her hand out to shake each of theirs in turn. I watched her smile and chastised myself for wanting to kiss those full, delicious lips tinted a deep red with lipstick. Her lipstick enticed me, called to me like a Siren song to a sailor's ears. It was not just that I rarely ever saw a woman around home wearing lipstick; it was more like an aphrodisiac. It made my libido surge just by watching those lips move when she spoke. I had a secret fascination for lipstick almost for as long as I could remember. When I was little, I thumbed through magazines staring at pictures of women in makeup, especially if they had on red lipstick. I had no idea why I had such a fascination, but I also had a sense of shame about it. I would sometimes lift magazines from waiting rooms and hide them in the barn so I could steal away to look at those pictures. I felt guilty, not only feeling like I had stolen the magazines, but also because there was something about looking at those pictures that felt like forbidden fruit. It was not like I was looking at pornography, but when I looked at those women wearing that red lipstick, it felt like I might as well have been looking at pornography. Now I was standing with a real woman with real red lipstick, and I fought the urge to let my eyes drink her like a warm glass of milk as she spoke to Brother and Sister Clark. Upon finishing her greeting with the Clarks, she turned immediately back to me and said, "Have you had breakfast?"

"Yes," I replied. "We do that pretty early in our household."

"Good," she said. "Then I assume you are ready to go."

"Yes, ma'am," I responded.

"Good, let's get your luggage loaded in my car, and we will be on our way." She marched promptly to the door. I closed my eyes for a moment because I no sooner watched her sway toward the door than the lust hit my groin like a wolf on prey. Then I opened my eyes and followed her. Brother and Sister Clark tagged along behind me.

When she got to the door, she asked, over her shoulder, "Where are you parked?"

I wondered if there would be any way I could run into her from behind and then pretend it was an accident, but I feared if I did, she would be too aware of my building erection. I fumbled to button my jacket to hide it. I should have known in those first few moments that I would be fighting with my libido all the way to Nashville. Miss Moore swung those hips gracefully to her car as though they were on some type of rhythmic timer designed to make each move back like a pendulum. She was parked just outside the door, but I hadn't even noticed as we entered. She leaned over to open the ample trunk of that big black 1953 Cadillac Eldorado, and I battled the desire to walk up to those hips and wrap my arms around her from behind.

Brother Clark blurted out, "I'll get your luggage, Brother Ronnie. Be right back."

His words shocked me from my daze, and I went trotting after him, "No, that's too much for you to carry by yourself," I called.

There were only two bags, and he could have gotten it on his own, but it was my luggage, and the Clarks had already done a great deal for me. We each took a bag, carried it over to the Eldorado, and placed it in the trunk. Miss Moore closed the trunk, and I turned to see Sister Clark grinning at me like I was the prize she just won at the county fair.

"Oh!" she exhaled. "You are going to do so well, Brother Ronnie. We are going to miss you around here." She reached out and hugged me into that huge bosom of hers. I felt like a little boy, and I knew there was a part of her that thought of me as a little boy, almost like one of her own. Brother Clark extended his hand to give me a firm and piston-like handshake and said, "I'm proud of you, Brother Ronnie."

"You both are acting like I'm already some big wig," I said. "This is just an audition. I may be home in two weeks with my tail between my legs."

"Oh, but the Lord knows better!" Sister Clark exclaimed joyfully. "The Lord does know better."

I tilted my head toward the pavement in humility. "Thank you for your confidence, Sister Clark," I said. "I will do my best to live up to it." Miss Moore walked around to the driver's side of her car and opened the door. I took this as my hint and said, "Goodbye now. Thank you for checking in on Momma and Daddy."

"Happy to," said Brother Clark. Then they turned back toward their truck.

I opened the passenger side door and sat down on the lush seats of the Eldorado. "Wow!" I heard myself exclaim as I ran my hand across the seat and over the dash. Miss Moore had just reached the key to the ignition when I said this.

"I love my car," she said as she turned the key. "It's very nice, isn't it?"

"Forgive me, Miss Moore," I said, somewhat embarrassed. "I have just never seen anything quite like this before."

"First of all," she announced firmly, before she began to back out of the parking space, "my name is Wanda, not Miss Moore, and you are welcome to call me Wanda. Second of all, it's just a car, and if you are half as successful as I think you are going to be, a car like this is just for starters."

I didn't know what to say. "I…ah…well, I'm very glad to be going to Nashville with you…Wanda," I said rather uncomfortably.

The next thing I knew we were on Highway 67 to Jonesboro, and it didn't take long for Wanda to say, "So tell me a little more about yourself, Pastor Dennison."

"I…I don't know what to tell you," I replied.

"Well, tell me about your life," she said as she drove.

I wasn't sure how much I wanted to tell her at that point. Finally, I decided I would just tell her about my childhood, growing up out in the butt crack of Arkansas on a farm, boring stuff, I thought. Still she seemed to be very interested. I told her about Grandma, Momma, Daddy, and Sissy. I told her about Teddy and how much I looked up to him. I struggled to hold back tears when I told her that he had died recently.

"Oh, I am so sorry," she comforted. "That must have been devastating for you. I remember you saying that during our phone call."

"What about your life?" I queried, hoping to get the attention off myself before tears came.

She took the bait and began to tell her own story. I found out that she had originally been from a small town in Kansas and that her husband, David Moore, died tragically in an auto accident. He had been a business partner with Mr. Clayburn in the Christian Broadcasting Ministry. He was a fair amount older than she was and, at the time of his death, was fifty-one, and she just was twenty-five. They had never had any children. At the time her husband died, as a widow of a business partner, she owned part of the ministry. Mr. Clayburn bought her out of her husband's part in the business then offered the option to work with him on further developing the ministry, and she took it.

I told her that Teddy had also died in a tragic accident. However, the conditions of her husband's accident had been quite different. He was on his way home from his office one day when a woman ran a red light and broadsided him on the driver's side of the car. A piece of the door frame broke off and impaled him through his abdomen. He was maintained in a hospital for about two days before he finally passed away, and this had been very heart breaking and difficult for Wanda because she had been deeply in love with him and expected to spend most of her life with him.

"I'm so sorry," I said, seeing emotion rise in her as she was telling the story. "I have no idea what that must be like. I loved my brother deeply, but it has got to be different when you lose the person you expect to spend your life with."

"You've never been in love?" she questioned.

"No, I guess I haven't," I said, somewhat embarrassed. "I've really only seen one girl, and my daddy put a stop to that. I liked her a lot, but I don't know that I was in love with her. I'm not sure I know what that kind of love feels like."

"Why did your dad stop you from seeing her?" she asked.

I hesitated in my embarrassment and most assuredly hesitated on just how much I was willing to tell her about what happened with Lynetta. At last I said, "We were doing something we shouldn't have been doing."

"Having sex?" she asked.

I felt my face flush with heat at her directness, and I know I must have turned beet red, but she thankfully had her eyes more on the road than on me. I wasn't sure how I should answer, or if I should just change the subject and avoid the question entirely. I mustered my courage. "Yes," I said, finally. "It was wrong. I knew it was a sin. I knew better."

"How old were you then?" she continued.

"Fourteen," I replied.

"Kids don't quite understand the complications of those things," she said in a matter-of-fact tone. "Still, what kid at that age doesn't have the urge to explore? The time in our lives when we are expected to save ourselves for marriage is the time when our hormones, urges, and curiosity are the most rampant. It is harder for teenagers to resist things like that than it is for adults, but we expect them to just be celibate."

I felt a strange mix of emotions. The lust I had for Wanda was mixed with my embarrassment at my confession and my guilt for having sex outside the sanctity of marriage, and I was shocked by the response I never would have expected from a Christian woman. I was wondering if I had said too much too soon when I realized we were passing through Jonesboro. I felt a little safer when Wanda didn't judge me, but still I wondered if I should have held back a little more from a person who was still very much a stranger.

Just by crossing over the Mississippi Bridge north of Blytheville, we could have gotten from Pocahontas to Nashville in about the same amount of time it takes to drive from Memphis to Nashville, but Wanda turned south toward Memphis. She apparently had the route planned to go through Memphis so she could stop by her office. At the time, I didn't know enough about the other side of Jonesboro to realize the difference. Between Jonesboro and Memphis, the conversations circled around the mundane musings of life in the 1950s, and the conversation lightened considerably. I thought about asking questions about Christian broadcasting, but I wasn't sure exactly what to ask or how to ask it. I assumed I would be shown everything I needed to know.

We pulled up to the sidewalk in front of Wanda's office at about 10:00 a.m., and it wasn't much, just a little one-room space she rented in a brick building on the northeast edge of town. I found myself walking into the office looking at religious pictures on the walls when she said, "I'm sorry to take you the long way around, but I'm going to be in Nashville with you all next week, and maybe the week after as well, so I have a few loose ends I need to get tied up before I'm out of the office for that long. I simply didn't get the chance to do much with it yesterday."

"It's okay," I said. "No problem." Truthfully, I had not known, until that moment, that we were taking the long way. It didn't matter to me anyway. While Wanda worked at her desk, I wandered about the room and stood for a while looking at the building across the street. Sunday traffic was scarce, yet still it was more common to see a car pass than it would have been at home. I would rather have sat and stared at her intriguing beauty, but I knew it would be unseemly and might cause her to feel uncomfortable. "If the broadcast ministry is in Nashville," I asked, "why do you have an office in Memphis, so far away?"

"My husband was from Memphis," she replied. "David's family is here, and though we were only married a few years, I still have a good relationship with his parents. He only had a sister. She contracted childhood leukemia and died when she was about fifteen, so at this point, they have no children. His father is disabled, and I just like to be nearby in case they need me. My own parents are younger and are doing quite well. Besides, my role in the ministry doesn't require me to be in Nashville. Most of the time I am researching new venues and ways that we might expand the ministry. I can be in telephone contact for most of that."

"Oh," I said, politely. "His parents are very blessed to have you, then."

"I'm blessed to have them," she replied. "They are wonderful people."

I wanted to ask about her husband and the fact that he must have married late or had been widowed or divorced to be so much older than she was, but I didn't want to pry. Instead I asked, "If you are going to be a while, do you mind if I take a walk around the area?"

"Certainly, go ahead," she replied. "The area is called Hollywood. You might find it interesting, and the Hollywood Café is just up the street here."

"Really?" I asked, "Like Hollywood, California?"

"Sort of." She smiled. "Just not quite as much glitz and glamor as one might expect from the stars."

"How long do I have?" I questioned.

"Give me about another hour, maybe," she replied. "I don't think anything will be open today, but you can window shop."

"Good, then I'll see you shortly," I said as I stepped outside the building. Since I couldn't comfortably sit and stare at Wanda Moore, I needed some distance to quiet my groin a bit.

As I walked, I noticed spring flowers blooming in flower cases along the street, and it was a particularly warm day for March. I perused up and down the street for quite a while, peeking in windows here and there, curiously noticing things that were different from home, even though it was less than a two-hour drive away from home. I found a little shop with Asian trinkets displayed in the window. There were curious little porcelain figurines of various sizes, and in the back, I could see what appeared to be embroidered tapestries. I was leaning in, holding both hands over the sides of my face to get a better look into the back of the store, when I was startled by a car horn. I jumped half out of my skin and turned to see Wanda sitting there in the Eldorado. She had pulled up to the curb behind me without my slightest notice. As soon as she saw me jump, Wanda burst out laughing. "I'm sorry." She giggled. "I didn't mean to frighten you."

"Oh, you are a vixen," I heard myself exclaim without even realizing what I was saying until it was out of my mouth. "You should be spanked."

"Come on. I'm done." She grinned. "Are you ready to get back on the road?"

In my wandering, I had lost track of the time, and the hour she allotted me had already passed. "Yes, ma'am," I smiled as I slid onto the leather seats of her car.

"Stop calling me ma'am," she chastised. "I may be a little older than you, but I'm not your school marm."

"Okay, I will work on that," I said as she pulled away from the curb.

"Are you ready for lunch?" she asked. "There is a truck stop up here on Highway 70, and we can have a bite there."

"A truck stop?" I asked, never having heard the term before.

Wanda smiled but was not critical of my ignorance. "It's a place where truck drivers, carrying freight across country, stop to have a meal or refuel. They have a café open there."

"Well, I definitely am ready for a bite to eat." I grinned.

"Good, then we will stop there," she exclaimed.

In very short order, we were pulling into a large parking lot with a big Standard Oil sign at the edge of the road. It was filled with big trucks, and there was a bank of gas pumps and a red neon sign over a building at the back of the lot that said, "Café." I had seen big trucks like that before but never really thought about the fact that they might be going all the way across country or that the truck drivers might need to stop and eat sometime.

Wanda pulled into a parking space in front of the café, and we went in. There were vertical chrome bars over glass double doors with red metal frames leading to the dining area. Directly across from the doors was a long counter with round stools. Several booths lined the edge of the room. Behind the bar there were a couple of male fry cooks working a griddle. Practically everything except the walls was red and chrome. One wall was painted with a mural of an old freight truck that must have been from the 1930s, and other places around the room had pictures of old trucks. The room was filled with men of various ages sitting on the stools or at the booths. When we walked in, I didn't notice a single other woman there besides Wanda, except for three waitresses who were all dressed in pale-blue cotton dresses with red aprons. It became quickly apparent that Wanda was a show these men had not planned on and one they greatly appreciated. One man whistled his appreciation as Wanda strolled over to a booth, but she acted like she hadn't even heard it.

"Will this be all right?" she asked, turning back to me when she reached the booth.

"Yes, this is fine," I said, sliding into the side opposite her as she sat down.

A chubby waitress, probably in her late forties, was quickly there with menus. She plopped them down between us and said, rather gruffly, "What'll ya have to drink?"

"I think cola for me," Wanda said as she looked across the table to let me know it was my turn.

"Things like that were kind of a luxury on the farm," I replied, "so I just avoided asking for it."

"Well, you are not on the farm anymore, Pastor Dennison," she scolded. "Don't worry about the tab. Mr. Clayburn is covering everything. If you want a cola, have a cola. Soon, you should be able to afford all the colas you want."

"Oh, okay then." I smiled. "I guess I'm going to have a cola too, then." The waitress didn't say another word. She simply stomped off in the direction of the bar as though she had to throw each foot out in front of her to keep from falling facedown in the floor.

"Mr. Clayburn sure must have plenty of money," I said. "I certainly am not used to such treatment."

"He does." She smiled. "And you need to get used to such treatment."

We began glancing through a very short menu, and I was struck quickly by the description of a plate lunch with meatloaf, mashed potatoes and gravy, with green peas, carrots, and a roll. I didn't need to look any further than that. I knew if the meal tasted half as good as it sounded in that description, it would be fine.

"I think I'll just have a burger," Wanda quipped as she sat her menu to the side.

About that time, the waitress was back with our drinks and was ready to take our orders. We told her what we wanted. She snatched the menus from our hands and stomped off again.

Wanda and I sat silent for a few moments, I suppose not really knowing where to go with a conversation at that point. I then asked, "So how long ago did your husband pass away?"

She glanced quickly at me with a hint of "Don't ask" in her eyes and then said, "It has been seven years."

"That's a long time," I said sympathetically. "At least it seems like a long time to me."

In my mind, I did the math, and figured she must be in her early thirties.

"Somehow," she said, stirring her cola with the straw, "it seems like just yesterday."

"I'm sorry that pain would still feel fresh to you," I said quietly, suddenly feeling as though I were intruding.

"It's hard to get past losing the love of your life," she said, still stirring her drink.

"Is that why you have not remarried?" I asked.

"I suppose," she said, looking up at me with a brief smile. "It just seems to be difficult to find another man who can measure up. I don't know that I'll ever want to remarry." She looked briefly out the window at the parking lot and beyond, then turned back to me with a nervous expression that I had not seen in her until that point.

"It sounds like you have tried," I commented, part of me hoping I might be the one who could measure up.

"Yes, a few times," she replied.

"Well, I pray that Jesus will guide you to another love of your life." I smiled nervously. "Someone who will love you as much and fulfill you as much as David did."

"That's sweet of you," she said quietly. Then she took a sip of her cola, holding the straw carefully between those lusciously painted lips so her lipstick would not be smeared.

I watched her intently for a second and then tore my eyes away. I seemed to always be torn between Jesus and my lust. No matter how hard I tried, the lust kept coming back to haunt me. I found myself wishing in the brief moment before I looked away that my little soldier had been that straw in her mouth. The waitress saved me from that struggle by plopping plates in front of us and announcing: "Meatloaf plate and a burger." I turned back around in time to see her slap silverware down on a paper napkin beside my plate.

"Thank you," I said, and she didn't even reply. She just turned and stomped away.

Wanda giggled. "She could use some table manners." Then she winked at me as she laid the top half of her burger bun to the side and began nibbling at the pickle, picking up each little slice between thumb and forefinger. It seemed strange to me, but I didn't question her approach. I stirred the gravy into my mashed potatoes and felt my little soldier pushing at the edge of my pants, thrusting against the fabric to express its intentions. I quickly unfolded the napkin and laid it across my lap, hoping no stranger's eyes had seen it throb. "So how does all this work?" I asked and then took my first bite.

"What are you asking, exactly?" she questioned back. "How this week is going to go, or how the whole broadcast ministry works?"

"I guess maybe a little of both," I pondered.

"Well," she began, "this week you will have several appointments during which you will be tested to see how you appear on camera and whether you can perform on film the way I saw you perform at the tent revival last year. You will have a couple of appointments for some vocal tests, and you will need to be preparing—if you haven't already—for your sermon at the Evangelic Temple service on Sunday. Depending on positive results of some of the screen and vocal tests, Mr. Clayburn may ask you to do a few other things."

"Perform?" I asked. "I'm not an actor or singer or something. It is not a performance. It is ministering."

"In a way, it is a performance," she replied. "If you don't hold the attention of a congregation, they won't hear what you have to say. You have to perform to keep their interest, or your teaching is lost. That's one of the reasons we were interested in you. You can hold peoples' attention."

"So how does the broadcast ministry work?" I asked.

"We are essentially like a church," she began. "The ministry has tax-exempt status just like churches do. However, in many respects, we are like a business. We have operating expenses, and we attempt to support ourselves and our employees as comfortably as we can while expanding the ministry to as many people as possible. Mr. Clayburn started the ministry several years ago through radio broadcasting. He engaged several ministers in the process. Some of them worked out pretty well, and some didn't. However, now he is recognizing that television is the coming thing, and it will be important to expand into television ministry as soon as possible. The problem is that, although a person might be excellent in a radio format, they may not do well in visual broadcast. There are a lot of factors to consider. You, Pastor Dennison, happened to show up at just the right time, and I think you have what it takes to handle the cameras. A little over a year ago, Mr. Clayburn charged me with the task of locating some possible candidates to serve in the television ministry. When I was informed about your revival, and it was so close to Memphis, I was delighted at the opportunity to come hear you speak. As I have told you, I was quite impressed."

"I don't know why people are impressed with me, really," I said, glancing away. At the time, I had mixed feelings about personal praise. My ego loved the attention, but I constantly told myself to be humble and that it was God doing the work through me. It wasn't me, but when Jesus had told me that I was His Word, I knew it meant I was to speak His Word, teach what He taught. Whether it meant staying home and preaching in little country churches or speaking on television and radio, part of me knew I had the calling.

"Well, you obviously have a gift for speaking, and for touching people's spirit," she countered. "What first got you interested in the ministry?"

"You know my daddy is a minister, and that gave me my first interest." I was feeling a little more comfortable with her by that time. So I went on to tell her more. "I began having dreams when I was about ten years old. Over the years they became more intense. In my second dream, I saw Jesus crucified on the side of our barn. There is a redheaded woman in all my dreams. In that dream, she was crying at the feet of Jesus, and blood was running down the side of the barn. Then Jesus shouted to me, 'You are My Word.' I told Daddy about my dreams and that they were telling me I was called to preach. Still, he didn't want me to preach, and I never got my first chance till he was so sick one Sunday he couldn't get out of bed. Momma sent me to do the Sunday service in his place. I think I was seventeen at the time. That wasn't too long before you came up to our church revival."

"Why didn't your father want you to preach?" she asked.

My face went bloodred. I could feel it. My cheeks went hot with embarrassment. I darted a glance out the window at a big truck that was turning through the parking lot. I glanced over to the people sitting on the other side of the café. Suddenly, all the sounds in the café, people talking, dishes clanging, became deafening to me. I felt my breath quicken. What was I going to tell her? My mind was racing when she broke the evil spell of my anxiety.

"Seems to be a bit of emotion there." Wanda smiled gently. She reached her hand across the table to touch my arm. "You don't have to tell me now if you don't want to. You don't have to tell me at all, if you don't want to."

The touch of her hand felt warm and reassuring. I found myself wondering if I should go ahead and confess, or if I should forever keep my final sin with Lynetta a secret. I felt myself draw a breath deep down to the bottom of my lungs and expel it in one brief gush. I set my fork to the side of my plate and looked down at the half-eaten food. I decided to confess. "I committed a horrible sin," I said without looking up.

"A horrible sin?" she questioned softly. "You didn't murder anyone, did you?"

"No," I replied quietly and humbly. "But what I did could be considered blasphemy against the Holy Spirit. There is no forgiveness for blasphemy."

"If you believe you have committed the unforgivable sin, why do you continue to preach?" she asked.

"Well, the Book of Matthew says it is speaking against the Holy Spirit," I said quietly, still not looking up. "But the Book of Mark says it is blasphemy against the Holy Spirit. I didn't speak against the Holy Spirit, but what I did was sacrilege. I have tried to repent. I hate myself for my sin, and I want forgiveness, but there is a nagging thought that I cannot be forgiven. Still, I feel compelled to preach. I feel compelled to try to bring as many as possible to the Lord. Maybe, if I have to go to hell, I can save as many as possible along the way."

"What did you do that was so bad?" she questioned softly.

I hesitated and sat there for some time saying nothing, only staring at my plate. A single tear fell from my eye. At last I brought myself to confess. "Well, you know that girl I told you about, the girl I liked but didn't love?"

"Yes," she affirmed quietly.

"I had sex with her in the church one afternoon, right on the front pew." I pulled my hands up, and buried my face in them. "Daddy caught us, and her Daddy was with him. I don't know what I would have done if we hadn't been caught. I might have just pretended like it wasn't happening, like I pretended all the other times we had sex. I knew it was wrong, but I felt like I couldn't stop myself. Daddy was horrified. He said I desecrated the Temple of the Lord."

"Pastor Dennison."

Wanda pronounced my name like she was trying to convince herself that it really was my name.

"So you are telling me you're a human being."

I said nothing but continued to sit there with my face buried in my hands.

"Look at me," she commanded.

She was older than me by at least ten or twelve years, and maybe she had gained some wisdom in those years that I didn't have. She had been married before. Maybe there were things she understood that I didn't understand.

I obeyed as I was told and slowly raised my face above my hands to see her sitting across from me, looking at me compassionately and smiling.

"I forgive you," she said. "What you did was explore your body the way normal young people want to. Where you did that is irrelevant, I think." She shifted into business mode then. "This may not be something that we would ever want leaked to the media, but it shouldn't keep you from your ministry. We will just have to be careful that your private life is kept private. People in positions of notoriety have to do that sort of thing. What the rest of the world doesn't know won't hurt it. In the meantime, you may have an opportunity to preach to untold numbers of people. However, we will have to be careful about any future proclivities you may have."

I sat there, silent. I had no idea what to say. I was trying to make sense of what she was saying to me. On one hand, it was as though she had compassion for the terrible thing I had done wrong and the horrible feelings I had about it, but on the other hand, it seemed as though she was giving me permission as long as it was kept a secret.

"I'm confused," I said, finally.

"Well, maybe by the end of the week you will have a better understanding of how all this works and a better determination of where you want to go from here," she quipped.

I just sat looking at her.

"Oh, look at the time," she bantered. "We better get on the road. It could be past dinnertime before we get into Nashville. Are you through with your meal?" She reached for her purse and motioned to the waitress.

"I guess I've had enough," I quietly responded. Truthfully, I had lost my appetite.

"Check, please!" she called to the waitress as she twisted her glance back over her shoulder. "Would you like something to go?" she said, turning back to me, "chips or something?"

"I don't know," I replied.

The waitress came to the table and laid a slip in front of us. "Well, I'll get something in case we want a snack," Wanda said as she scooted out of the booth and went to the register to pay.

I felt embarrassed that I was not paying for the meal, as though those truck drivers were going to think I was a mooch letting my female companion pay while I just sat there. I tried not to look at anyone. Wanda came back to the table with a couple of bags of chips and two bottles of cola. She plopped a dollar tip on the Formica and said, "Ready?"

"Sure," I replied and then followed her to the car.

In short order, we were back on 70 headed toward Nashville. For the rest of the trip, we talked about everything from my farm upbringing to Grandma Miller to Teddy. It seemed like she wanted to find out everything that she possibly could about my childhood. I told her more details about the dreams and the simple life where I had grown up. I could barely squeeze in any question about her. When the topic of Teddy serving in the Army came up again, she said, "You are registered for the draft, aren't you?"

"Yes, ever since I was eighteen," I replied. "I guess I've been lucky so far."

"Well, I don't think you'll have to worry about it," she commented. "You are the only surviving son in a family where your brother served in the military. I think there is a law that will give you deferment in that case. It's something we can research further if necessary."

I began to relax more as time went on, and no sooner had I done so than my little soldier began to prod my thinking. In the days before seat belts, I could turn toward her and lean back against the passenger side door, where I got a full view of the contour of her body perfectly outlined in that print dress. Her breasts sat over her chest like majestic hills in the distance, not too big and not too small. They were smooth like the knolls in a grass pasture. I watched her soft movement as she steered. I fought with myself between fantasies of making love to her and chastising myself for entertaining such thoughts. Around all this, I answered her questions. By the time we got to Nashville, I don't think there was much about me she didn't know. We pulled into the parking lot of the new Vacation Inn at about 6:00 p.m. It was one of the grandest and most beautiful things I had ever seen until that point in my life. Wanda had previously made arrangements for us to have adjacent rooms, and as soon as we got our luggage to the room, she said, "I think I would like to freshen up a bit before dinner and get into something a little more casual."

"Didn't we already have dinner back at the truck stop?" I questioned.

"Oh, that's a Southern thing, isn't it?" She giggled. "As long as I have lived in Memphis, I still haven't gotten used to referring to lunch as dinner and dinner as supper. Why don't you go get freshened up a bit yourself? I'll come knock on your door when I'm ready to go—to supper."

"Okay then," I said and turned to walk down the hall to my room. I had no idea what she was talking about—freshen up before supper? I had never heard of any such thing as freshen up, but I went obediently to my room. When I got there, I plopped my bag up on the bed and pulled out a few toiletries and set them on the counter in the adjacent bathroom. This alone was pure luxury to me. I had rarely ever even seen an indoor toilet except on trips to Jonesboro at public facilities, and I had never seen one quite as fancy as that one. I certainly had, never in my life, had a toilet of any kind all to myself, right next to my room. We always had to go to the outhouse or keep a coffee can under the bed for those physical necessities when winter nights got too cold.

After I unpacked a bit, I sat on the edge of the bed to wait. Then I decided to lie down, and about the time I felt myself drifting off to sleep, Wanda knocked on the door. I got up and opened the door to find her standing there in skin-tight blue jeans with the cuffs folded about halfway up her calves. She had on a tight little pale-blue blouse with a little black cardigan sweater over it that was so fluffy it looked like it could have been made of cat hair. She was wearing black flats for shoes.

"Ready?" she questioned with a smile, and I found myself thinking maybe "freshen up" meant that I was supposed to change clothes. However, back on the farm, we didn't have that many changes of clothes, and it was not unusual to wear the same ones for a couple of days if they didn't get too dirty.

"I guess so," I replied. "Where are we going?"

"There's a little burger joint up the street," she replied, "walking distance. It will be quick and easy."

The next thing I knew, we were walking down the street a few blocks to a little place that had blinking neon lights over the top. The windows jutted out at an angle toward the street and were outlined in chrome. Inside, gray industrial tile covered the floors, and there were little round tables that were extra high surrounded by red-cushioned chrome stools that swiveled and had a round footrest. We walked up to the counter where the menu was posted on the wall behind the fry cooks. We stood there among numerous other people examining the offerings.

"You know, I had a burger for lunch," she said. "I think I'm going to have a hot dog for dinner."

"That sounds good," I said. Things like burgers and hotdogs were an exceptionally rare treat back in the Arkansas woods and only to be enjoyed once in a while if the family happened to be in a larger town for some type of business. Momma fried ground beef patties at home sometimes, but if that got put in a sandwich, it didn't resemble a burger. I ordered a chili dog, and she ordered just a plain hotdog with mustard and nothing else. We carried our meals in little paper boxes and our sodas to a nearby table. My chili dog was a little harder to eat than I expected, and when I ended up smearing chili across my cheek, Wanda reached across the table with her napkin and gently dabbed my face. It almost felt like Momma wiping my face when I was a little boy. "Thank you," I said.

"Never knew a man who couldn't use a feminine touch," she commented. "There...good as new."

After we finished eating, we walked back under streetlights toward the hotel.

"This is really an interesting place," I commented as we walked.

"Nashville is a wonderful city," she replied. "There's a lot happening here."

"Well, I know there has been a lot of music coming out of Nashville for a while," I went on. "We listen to the radio at home, and they are always talking about somebody who recorded their song in Nashville. I kind of like Flatt and Scruggs."

"Yes, there's a lot of talent here," she said and then shivered a little, pulling her hands up to her shoulders and hugging herself.

"Are you all right?" I asked.

"You know, it might help if you put your arm around me to warm me up a little," she voiced the hint I had not taken. I placed my arm hesitantly around her shoulder as we walked. She put her arm around my waist and leaned into me. I felt her breast against my chest, and the soft smooth contour of her shoulder beneath my palm. My groin surged with desire.

"That's much better," she remarked.

"Good," I said quietly as I felt my mind and body reacting to the closeness. I had not felt anything like it since I had been with Lynetta, and although I thought Lynetta was beautiful, I had not desired her with near the intensity that I felt for Wanda Moore. I thought back to the first day I had seen her walking up in that pink dress. I wanted her, was attracted to her, like no other woman I had ever met, and now with my arms around her, I was fighting myself over it. Now that she had her arm around me, and her breast against me, I heard my mind saying, *Push her away. This is wrong.*

"This feels nice," Wanda commented.

"Yes" was my only reply. I felt myself trembling with both anxiety and lust. I ignored my mind telling me to stop. I didn't want to stop. Just as it had often happened before, my groin was overriding my intellect. I could only imagine that it must be similar to a junkie putting a needle in his arm, wanting it, longing for the high, and all the time telling himself, "Don't do it!"

When we got back inside the hotel lobby, I let go of Wanda's shoulder. Then she moved her hand from around my waist and reached down to clasp my hand in hers. I felt completely confused. As much as I wanted her, I had thought that she was all business. I may have been a naive kid from the Arkansas sticks, but I was smart enough to know when someone wanted me. I didn't know what to do. I was there for the ministry. I was there to have a greater chance to serve the Lord, and my little soldier could only think of serving itself. Wanda obviously was willing. I couldn't believe what was happening. I couldn't believe that Wanda was behaving as she was. Perhaps I had told her too much that afternoon. Perhaps I had led her on. Perhaps she was a lonely widow, but I couldn't imagine she would have any difficulty getting any man she wanted. I didn't know what to think or what to do. Part of me felt like a lamb being led to slaughter, and part of me begged for it, *"Go ahead, slit my throat, and burn me for sacrifice to this brazen god of lust."* At that moment I didn't care.

When we got to her room, Wanda turned and looked up at me with an alluring smile. "Would you like to come in for a little while?" Then she squeezed my hand. My heart was pounding so hard I could feel the pulse in my ears.

I looked up the hall in either direction to see if anyone was looking. Could there be some stranger who might spot my guilt and point an accusing finger? Would I be shamed and humiliated for these thoughts? No one was there.

"Aren't you tired?" I asked.

"Oh, I have a little vigor left in me." She grinned.

My conscience begged me to turn loose of her hand, tell her no, and go back to my room.

My little soldier demanded relief, and I wanted to spend as much time in her presence as I possibly could. "Okay, for a little while," I acquiesced, but in truth, I was begging.

She turned and placed her key in the lock, turned it, and opened the door. I followed her into the room and shut the door behind me. She pulled her sweater from her shoulders and tossed it on a chair. "Would you like something to drink?" she asked.

I figured all there would be till morning was water. I had seen glasses in the bathroom.

"Yes, I guess a glass of water would be fine," I acknowledged.

"I have something a little better than water if you want. I thought we might celebrate your first trip to Nashville," she said. "Have you ever had champagne?"

Honestly, at that point in my life, I did not have a clue what she was talking about. I had never even heard of champagne. Momma and Daddy certainly never drank, and liquor wasn't even legal in most Arkansas counties in those days. Anybody who wanted it had to drive to Missouri, and if they drank any alcohol, it was more likely to be beer or whiskey than champagne. If she had said wine, I knew what that was. I probably would have told her no. I would have known it was alcohol, and having never experienced anything to do with liquor, except for my observations of Teddy, I would have had no problems resisting, since I certainly did not want to follow the path that he had taken. Instead, I lied. "Oh sure," I gleefully quipped. "I love champagne."

"Good."

She turned and walked toward a bucket that was setting on the counter just inside the bathroom door. "I took the liberty of getting some ice earlier so it would be chilled."

She brought the bottle back to me and handed it in my direction, apparently having no problem with the idea of serving alcohol to someone under legal drinking age.

I stood there staring at it for a moment and then looked back up at her. "Am I supposed to open it?" I asked.

"Well, yes, silly." She smiled.

"I don't know how," I responded sheepishly.

She giggled. "Well, it takes a strong thumb, and I'm afraid I don't have a thumb that strong. Besides, I don't want to break a nail, but here, I'll show you."

She instructed me to remove the wire over the cork, to point it away from myself but not at a window or a mirror, and to press below the cork with my thumb.

When the cork popped off and foam spewed from the bottle, she shouted "Whoop!" and laughed.

I quickly began trying to put my palm over the mouth of the bottle to prevent the liquid from escaping.

She laughed even louder. "No, no, no," she instructed, "you don't have to do that." Then she trotted off to the bathroom for glasses.

She poured the bubbling champagne into the hotel's water glasses and handed a glass to me.

I took a sip and tasted the sweet effervescence for the first time.

"Mmmmm," I heard myself moan. "That is good."

"You've never really had it before, have you?" She grinned, eyes sparkling like the champagne. I suppose it didn't occur to her that giving me alcohol could get her arrested for contributing to the delinquency of a minor. I had not turned twenty-one yet.

"You caught me," I confessed. "It is very good though, kind of like a soda pop that is not so sweet." I still didn't know it contained alcohol.

"Yes," she said. "Let's sit down."

We sat side by side on the edge of the bed, sipping our champagne, but I swigged more than sipped. I realized that she must have planned to seduce me. I wondered if she had gone out to make arrangements for this while I thought she was freshening up. I wondered if she planned it all along, or if something I had told her about my sin with Lynetta had put the thought in her mind that day.

"Welcome to Nashville," she announced, holding her glass into the air. "A toast to Pastor Ronald Dennison, may he be phenomenally successful, and may he bring millions of lost souls to the Lord!" She tapped her glass against mine and then drank. Never having seen a toast before, I imitated what she did except I chugged the remainder in my glass all at once.

"Would you like some more?" she asked and was pouring it into my glass before I could answer.

"It's very good," I said as I began to feel lightheaded. I turned and looked at her, scanned her body up and down, allowed my eyes to float over her breasts. "Miss Moore—Wanda." I complimented nervously, perhaps having some inhibitions loosened by the alcohol. "I think that you are the most beautiful woman I have ever met."

"Thank you, Ronald," she replied, calling me by my first name for the first time without the word pastor or reverend attached. "You are a very handsome man as well."

"May I kiss you?" I begged.

She grinned shyly, unlike her. "You have to ask?" she responded.

I gulped the remainder of the champagne in my glass and moved my face over hers, first looking into her eyes and then at those incredible lips. I touched my tongue to her lipstick and slid it gently between her lips as my lips covered hers. Before I even touched her soft lips, my little soldier was pressing against my pants like a prisoner pushing against the bars of a prison cell. My hand slid down her neck to her breast, and I cupped it gently. I began unbuttoning her blouse and slipped my hand under the fabric to touch the beautiful mounds of flesh beneath. I rolled my mouth to the nape of her neck and licked her soft, tender skin. She leaned her head back in a gasp as my mouth traveled down to her breasts. She sighed. "I get the feeling you have done this before."

I was nervously doing things to her that I had wanted to do, fantasized about doing since the first day I set eyes on her. She pushed her shoes off into the floor, lay back on the bed, and pushed herself to a pillow where she finished unbuttoning her blouse. I pulled my shirt off over my head without unbuttoning it. Then I moved on my knees between her legs, unbuttoned her jeans, reached beneath her hips to the waistband of her jeans, and pulled them down and over her feet. I could not have turned back at that point even if I had wanted to. I buried my face into the crotch of her panties and licked my tongue over her skin at the edge of the seams. I rolled my fingers inside the lining and pulled them back to one side. Then my tongue went to a place where it had never been before. I lapped at her bowl like a ravenous dog. The surge of power I felt in my genitals was overwhelming, pulling with tight, tingling urgency. I couldn't help myself.

I was a slave in that moment. I surrendered to the will of my body, to the command of my little soldier. I quickly undid my pants and pulled them down to my knees. I shoved my hips over her pelvis, pulled the seams of her panties to one side, and pushed myself inside her while she was still wearing them. My little soldier buried himself in the moist warmth and begged me to move. I put my arm behind her neck and pressed my little soldier as deeply into her as I could. I licked the side of her neck and pulled back just enough to look into her eyes.

Then I began to thrust. My body begged for release. Every inch of me wanted it, wanted to let go with her, but I also wanted to wait. I had learned with Lynetta to wait, and I wanted it to last as long as it could. Several times I felt my little soldier nearing explosion, demanding to spill into her, and I stopped. *Wait…wait!* I commanded myself silently. I squeezed my groin tight, stopped moving, and leaned back. I touched her, gazed into her eyes, ran my fingers around her sensuous lips, and reveled in her beauty.

She reached up and ran her hands through the hair on my chest. When her hands glided over my nipples, I felt myself almost burst again. I could scarcely believe the depth and exhilaration of pleasure. As soon as I felt a lull, felt myself regaining command of my body, I began to thrust again. Over and over I did this until I thought I could not possibly take it any longer. At last I gave myself permission to finish. I was thrusting myself hard and deep into her when I heard her breath quicken. She moaned like a banshee, grabbed at me, and pulled at my skin, and then she convulsed into panting screams. I felt the muscles inside her tighten around my little soldier and pull on it like a hand gripping. I was at once scared and at the same time tantalized. I had never seen a woman climax like that before, much less experience it while I was inside her. I knew what it was. Lynetta had taught me enough to know that girls could climax, but Lynetta never had an orgasm like that.

Wanda was just beginning to calm down when I felt my little soldier tighten like a vise grip, then I felt the pulse from between my legs surging from deep inside me and pounding out of me like a machine gun. I didn't have time to pull out. Each pulsating release into her hit me like bullets of ecstasy. A groan came out of me that could have been confused for a man being stabbed. My whole body surged repeatedly, and then I fell into a lump on top of her. Aftershocks cascaded through me like electricity, and I had repeated surges of the most incredible eruption. If I had not been hooked before, from that moment on, I was addicted to sex.

I lay there exhausted on top of her, motionless. I am sure I felt heavy like a sack of potatoes across her chest. Then she put her hand to my shoulder to give me a nudge, a little hint without saying, "Get off me." I rolled over onto my back and said, "I've never quite experienced anything like that."

Miss Wanda Moore said, "I think you need to go to your room now."

Her tone was clear, cool, matter-of-fact. Suddenly, I felt as though the teacher were telling the student to go back to his desk. My heart fell, like a man shoved off a tower, thudding into my chest, not dead, but horribly wounded in that moment. The truth is I wanted to stay there, lie beside her all night, make love to her again and again, but it was over. My fantasy had become reality's toy. I gave no protest and simply obeyed.

"Okay," I replied and began pulling my pants back up. My disappointment must surely have been obvious, but it didn't matter.

"I think we will both sleep better," she said. Then she scooted to the edge of the bed, pulled the soiled panties over her feet, walked naked to the bathroom, and dropped them in the sink. Her change in behavior felt very cold to me. We had just consummated the most intimate thing I had ever experienced even with Lynetta, and yet it seemed no more intimate to her, at that point, than a trip to the outhouse. A flash ran through my mind of Daddy scolding me in the corn bin of the barn, but I don't think I had ever felt so dejected as in that moment. When I had dressed, I went to the door and said, "I guess I'll see you in the morning."

"I'll knock on your door about 8:00 a.m." she said. She smiled, simply smiled. That was it. We were done. We had taken care of one another's physical needs, and now we were done. What I had thought to be a glamorous sin had been no more than taking out the hedonistic trash.

"Good night," I said as I stepped into the relieving but ominous silence of the hall. I walked quietly back to my room, all the while feeling like I was going to burst into tears. There I was, trapped in Nashville with no way home, doing things I knew in my heart were wrong. As much as I wanted to say no to my body, I could only do so for the briefest of times. From the time of my first orgasm, my little soldier had always won the battles.

When I was back in my room, I fell to my knees before the bed, heaving in tears and proclaiming, "I am a miserable, worthless sinner! I deserve to burn in hell! Dear Lord, how can I teach anyone? How can I be Your Word when I betray everything You ask of me?"

In about thirty minutes, I could cry no more. My eyes were numb, and my body felt empty. After I got into bed, I lay there staring at the ceiling, thinking what a fool I must have been to have left the sanctuary of home for this. Even with the drapes drawn, I could still see bits and flashes of city lights. It seemed so surreal to me when all my life I had been used to the complete darkness of a country night where the most light that could ever be seen was the gray shimmer of the moon, and the brightest light that ever occurred at night was only when the moon was full. I lay there for quite some time, watching the flicker of dim light around the edge of the drapes.

When at last I fell asleep, there were no dreams.

CHAPTER 12

By the time Wanda knocked on the door the next morning, my bags were packed, and I was sitting on the bed staring at the door. A deep remorse had fallen over me, a grief almost as severe as losing Teddy. I kept asking myself, "What have I done?" All I could think was that I made a terrible mistake to even come to Nashville in the first place. I told myself that I was nobody, a country hick preacher who didn't know anything. I berated myself for having sex with Wanda. I berated myself for getting too big for my britches, for thinking that I could be something that I'm not. I cried myself to sleep the night before, wondering if I had ruined it all, if my behavior had destroyed my chances of becoming a well-known minister, and then telling myself I was stupid ever to think I could be such a thing in the first place. Still, I could not understand Wanda's behavior. Our indiscretions left me feeling blank, wondering if the people I was to meet that day might be even bigger hypocrites than myself. Every time I found myself lusting for a woman, I felt like I had betrayed the Lord, and then what I did with Wanda was much worse. I questioned if I deserved to even be a Christian, much less a minister.

That morning I sat motionless, numb and empty, waiting for the knock. When it came, I simply stood and took two or three steps to the door to open it. There she stood in the hall, Miss Wanda Moore, dressed in an elegant and very businesslike chocolate-brown dress. She smiled a congenial smile and said, "Good morning, Pastor Dennison," like nothing had ever happened.

At that point, I was even more confused. "Good morning, Miss Moore," I replied quietly.

"Ready to go?" she questioned still smiling, and I found myself wondering if I dreamed the whole thing or that I drank enough champagne that my fantasy seemed real.

"I think I need to go home," I said.

"Home? What do you mean 'go home'?"

"I don't think I'm cut out for this," I went on. "I don't think I belong here."

"Oh, of course you belong here," she encouraged. "You have wanted to be a minister ever since you were a little boy, right?"

"Yes, ma'am," I replied. "I wanted to be a minister, a preacher, but I did not want this. Maybe I am better off pastoring a little country church. Maybe I am better off not trying to push my raising."

"Well, you are here," she chided. "You have come all this way to explore the opportunity to become a broadcast minister. You might as well see it through. You do want to find out what your options are, don't you?"

I hesitated. I was less sure than at any time before. However, after a moment, I said, "Yes, ma'am."

"Come on then," she bubbled, seemingly ignorant of my feelings. "Let's go meet Mr. Clayburn."

She then turned and swayed cheerfully down the hall. I picked up my bags and followed like an obedient little boy. Despite my grief over my sins, my confusion, and my newborn anger at her behavior, I still watched her heart-shaped ass ticking back and forth down that hall like the pendulum of a clock. We loaded the bags in the trunk of her car, and when we got into the seat, she blabbed the question, "Sleep well?"

"Fine, I guess," was my stilted reply. I lied. I had barely slept at all. She drove for about twenty minutes, making the same little bits of inane small talk that I barely responded to, and then we pulled up in front of a two-story Victorian house with a graveled parking area in front.

"Is this it?" I asked, having expected something with more grandeur, perhaps like one of those big churches or office buildings that I had sometimes seen in magazine pictures.

"This is it," she replied. "We will leave your bags in the trunk for now. Come on."

She got out of the car, walked around to the front, and motioned for me to come on. When I met her in front of the car, she reached over, took my hand, and led me up the steps and across the porch to a door with a half-moon window at the top. There were narrow beveled windows to either side and a small brass plaque on the door that said, "Christ Beacon Broadcasting."

The porch had ornate white columns and gray-painted porch boards that ran perpendicular from the front of the house. She didn't bother to knock but simply opened the door and strolled in with me in tow. Immediately inside, there was a foyer with a chandelier and a staircase directly across from the door. To the right side of the foyer was a set of French doors that stood open to reveal what had obviously been the home's original living room. There was a fireplace directly across from the French doors and in front of the fireplace was a large sleek mahogany desk. Sitting behind the desk was a slender bald man in his middle to late fifties with a cigar sticking out of one side of his mouth. He was clean- shaven and dressed in a charcoal-gray business suit with a white shirt and a solid maroon tie. As soon as we came in, he looked straight up from the paperwork on his desk, plucked the lit cigar from his mouth, and plopped it onto a nearby brass ash tray.

"Miss Moore!" he exclaimed congenially. "It is good to see you."

When he stood up, I could see that he was a very tall man with an almost athletic build. He stepped around the desk and crossed the room where we had just entered through the French doors.

"And you must be Pastor Dennison," he said, reaching out his long-fingered thick hand to shake mine.

"Yes, sir," I replied softly and timidly. What had seemed not so grand from the outside suddenly seemed to be quite grand on the inside, and I felt intimidated.

"Come in. Sit down," he commanded.

We both followed him toward his desk. I sat in a large brown leather chair across from his desk as I had been motioned to do, and he crossed around to his seat behind the desk.

Wanda said, "I think I will get us some coffee." She then walked to a side door of his office. I had not mentioned that I had been hungry. I didn't think it would be polite, but I was not used to going without breakfast or coffee in the morning.

"Hold on a minute, Wanda!" Mr. Clayburn exclaimed, raising a forefinger into the air. Then he turned to me and said, "Son, have you had breakfast?"

"No, sir," I quietly responded.

"Country boys like their breakfast, don't they?" he proclaimed. "Wanda, see if there is some toast or something else in there for Pastor Dennison. I'm sure we have something we could feed him."

"Sure," she said and turned toward the green-tile kitchen, which I could then see through the side door that she held open.

Mr. Clayburn turned back to me immediately. "Well, young man." He smiled. "Miss Moore tells me that you have quite a gift for the Gospel."

"I don't know, sir," I replied. "People seem to like to hear me preach."

"Well, do you have any idea what Christian broadcasting is about?" he questioned. "Have you ever heard ministers on the radio? Ever heard of Jerry Patterson?"

"Yes, sir," I replied. "I have heard Reverend Patterson on the radio before."

"Well, he is one of our folks," Mr. Clayburn continued. "Unfortunately, he does not translate well to television. Beautiful speaking voice and very charismatic on the radio and in person, but the camera doesn't like him, too many little distracting mannerisms."

"Mannerisms, sir?"

"Yes. You know," he answered. "Little hand gestures, twitches and tics. The camera just exaggerates that stuff. The visual medium is different, and we can't seem to train him out of those habits."

"Okay," I replied, not having a clue what he was talking about.

"Miss Moore tells me that you present very well, and she thinks you will do well on camera," he went on.

"I hope so, sir," I said quietly, fiddling with a button on my shirt. My heart was not in the moment. On one hand, I felt that I had to go through with what I had come there to do. On the other hand, I just wanted to go home. I felt so ashamed of my behavior from the night before and so confused as to why Miss Moore was behaving as she was.

"I don't know if you will do so well if you are this timid when you get on screen," he commented. "I have to say I am a bit confused. I have been told that you are quite a dynamo, very charismatic."

"I guess I'm a little out of my comfort zone," I replied. Truthfully my remorse over my behavior had me subdued.

"Well, relax!" He grinned, picking up and relighting his cigar with a match he grabbed from a nearby tray and struck on the underside of his desk. "You're among friends here. Isn't that right, Wanda?" he called toward the kitchen.

"Yes, good friends," I heard her call back.

"How's that coffee coming?" he whooped.

"Almost there," she called back.

I sat there looking around the room, feeling like a county fair rabbit in a display cage. I noticed and began gazing at a huge painting of the crucifixion scene hanging over the fireplace mantel behind Mr. Clayburn's desk. I had seen it when I came in, but in my anxiety, I had not really allowed myself to pay that much attention to it. It showed Jesus on the cross with four little haloed angels flying on each side of him. There were people in robes at the base of the cross, and some of those also had haloes.

"You like that?" Mr. Clayburn said, catching me staring at it. "It's a copy of a Giotto Di Bondone. Special piece I think."

"Coffee's on," Wanda said as she entered from the kitchen carrying a large tray. She set it down on Mr. Clayburn's desk and poured coffee from a silver pitcher into little porcelain cups.

"Cream or sugar?" she asked, looking up at me.

"Both," I said.

She then added the requested condiments and handed the cup and saucer to me along with a small plate containing two bubbly-looking pieces of round bread with a pat of butter and a couple of pieces of bacon.

"I thought I smelled bacon!" Mr. Clayburn exclaimed.

"I hope you like English muffins," Wanda said to me as she handed Mr. Clayburn an identical plate. Apparently, she knew how he liked his coffee and prepped it for him without asking how he wanted it.

"Yes, ma'am," I lied. I had nothing of a clue what an English muffin was before that moment or what to expect of it. Had it been one of Momma's biscuits, I would have known exactly what to expect.

"You know, I think I will just have the coffee," Mr. Clayburn commented. "I've already had a little breakfast. Let's give Pastor Dennison my share. I'm sure he is used to something a little more substantial than a muffin and bacon."

Wanda pushed his plate across the desk toward me without saying a word and sat down in the adjacent chair with only a cup of coffee for herself.

"Go ahead and eat," Mr. Clayburn said when he saw me sitting there just gazing at my plate.

I put the bread in my mouth and was delighted with the buttery flavor and chewy texture even though it was initially a little disconcerting. It was nothing like Momma's biscuits.

"As I was saying," Mr. Clayburn continued, "television is quite a different medium than radio. When you are in radio, there are things you can hide. Nobody has to know what you look like, but when it comes to television, appearance becomes imperative. It is not only important that you look good—and you are a handsome man, Pastor Dennison—but you have to present well in general. You can't be picking your nose or fiddling with your pocket or blinking a lot. You have to sell yourself to the camera."

The more he talked, the more intimidated and nervous I felt. I kept questioning the whole thing, and I went back to thinking that maybe I just wanted to go back home, forget all this stuff about becoming a famous minister and live the simple country life I had been born into. However, I said politely and quietly, "Yes, sir."

Mr. Clayburn shot a look at Wanda as if to say, "What the heck is this?"

She picked up on his unspoken question and said, "You should see Pastor Dennison in front of a congregation. He is a totally different man, full of fire and charisma." She then shot a slightly stern look at me, as if to tell me to straighten up.

I looked over at her, still chewing my muffin. I didn't know what to say. I felt like a deer in the sights of a hunting rifle. My experience with Miss Moore the night before, or rather my guilt about it, had taken a lot of fire out of me. I felt undeserving, overwhelmed, intimidated, and ashamed.

I finished chewing that bite, set the muffin back on my plate, and set the plate on the edge of Mr. Clayburn's desk. Then I looked up at the two of them and tried to compose myself. "The truth is," I began, "I'm scared to death. All this terrifies me. I feel undeserving, and I feel" I glanced timidly toward Miss Moore, "ashamed."

"Ashamed?" Mr. Clayburn asked in surprise as he rose from his desk and walked around to the side on the opposite corner from me.

"I'm not a saint, sir," I confessed to him. "I am not who I need to be. I do not have what it takes to be a proper Christian, much less a minister of the Lord. I think…I think…I need to go home."

A grin crossed his face, and he glanced over at Miss Moore. She glanced knowingly back at him, and I had a brief suspicion that he had some idea what must have happened between us.

"Well, you are not perfect," he responded. "Imagine that. What Christian is perfect?"

He turned and walked behind his desk, looking up at the painting over the mantel. "Have you ever noticed, Pastor Dennison," he said, laying his forefinger across his chin, "that many of the most beloved of the Lord have been quite sinful men? King David, for example, exploited women and still unified Israel." He turned around to look at me. "I don't know that you have to be a saint, Pastor Dennison, but if this were to be something that would work out, we will need to take some steps to keep your private life… private. I also don't think that you are required to be a sinless man to be a Christian or a minister of the Lord. It is about saving souls, isn't it? Not about being perfect. It is about working toward perfection, not expecting automatically to achieve it."

He stood there, gazing at me. I said nothing.

"I assume," he went on, "that God is a forgiving God, and so long as He knows that we are making an effort to serve Him and make a better man of ourselves, that will be sufficient."

There was an excruciating silence. I felt numb, shutting down. I didn't know what to say or how to say it. I found myself longing for the days when I sat beneath a shade tree with Teddy and giggled about frivolous childhood things.

Finally, Mr. Clayburn said, "We have a screen test scheduled at ten o'clock. Wanda, would you mind transporting Pastor Dennison to the studio? I will be taking my own car." He made no mention of my statement that I wanted to go home. She ignored it as well. It was as though my plea had gone unheard.

"I would be happy to." Wanda smiled. "Wilburn Studios?"

"Yes, Wilburn," he replied.

Mr. Clayburn turned without further statement and exited out the back of the building through the kitchen.

Miss Moore motioned for me to follow her as I sat silent and unmoving in that chair with my hands resting palms down on each chair arm. I paused a moment then followed as she went back out the front door to her car. I walked quietly down the steps, opened the passenger side door, and slid into the seat just as sullen as I had been in the house.

After she pulled out of the drive, she said, "Okay. What is going on here?"

"I'm confused," I said, staring at her. "I don't understand this."

"Well, it's very simple," she responded. "I brought you here because you are talented. You need to exhibit that talent and show a little motivation toward it so you can reach the dreams you report to have."

"No, that's not what I'm talking about," I tried again. "I'm confused about you. I don't get it, how we can make love, make incredible love, and the moment it is over, you can drop it as though it was no more than a wad of paper tossed into a trash can."

"Did you think last night was a date?" she questioned. "It wasn't a date. It was a good time. I wanted you. I knew you wanted me. We're both adults. Why not?"

"See, that's what I'm talking about," I went on. "It's like it's nothing. How can it be nothing? Two human beings cannot get any closer than we were last night. Sex is so important that the Bible admonishes that it be kept within the sanctity of marriage. It can't be nothing."

"Ah," she said, glancing quickly up at the ceiling and back at the steering wheel. "Okay…I made a mistake—two mistakes. First, I think I judged you to be like most men who would consider a roll in the hay just a roll in the hay. Second, I think I forgot that you are young and that you have been isolated from the real world."

"What do you mean by that?" I snapped, suddenly feeling irritated.

"It's okay," she soothed, sensing my irritation. "I was the same way really, although the town I came from was not so small and isolated. We were close enough to Wichita that I *maybe* got a little more exposure to the way things are in the real world."

"Oh…yeah," I said sarcastically. "Kansas is such a glamorous and chic state, and you are from the *big city*."

"Newton is a town of twelve thousand people," she said in defense, "and Wichita may not be a metropolitan complex, but it is a pretty big city. How big is Ravenden?"

"I've been to Memphis before!" I defended.

"How many times?" she asked. "And for what reason? How long did you stay, an hour or two?"

I sat in sullen silence, feeling childish indignation at that point.

"Look," she said finally. "What we did may be considered a sin, but being naive is not a sin. It just means there are things about the world you still have to learn. I'm older. I've been around a little more. I think the fact that you command the pulpit the way that you do and that you showed such confidence when I met you beguiled me into believing that you are more prepared than you actually are."

"And what do you mean by that?" I questioned, still feeling miffed.

She took a deep breath. "I mean that there are things you are going to know ten years from now that you don't even realize you don't know now, and when you look back, you will not believe how you could have thought it was all going to be so simple."

She turned to look at me, then pulled the car over, and parked it at the edge of a sidewalk. She turned the key off in the ignition, turned around in the seat, and stared at me for a moment. "I'm not in love, Ronald," she informed. "I'm not romantically interested at all. You are a sexy man, and I enjoyed being with you, but if you thought we were dating, I'm sorry. I don't want to date. I don't know that I ever want to be with any man that way ever again. After what I went through, I changed. I became a widow at twenty-five. Do you know how hard it is to be a widow that young? What you don't know is that I was pregnant when David died. Barely over a month after his funeral, I miscarried our child. I was so in love. I had so many dreams of having a family, and my heart was shattered like a crystal vase thrown against a brick wall. Now I'm the brick wall. I'll never let my heart be that fragile vase again. I will never put my heart on the line again for any man, but I still have needs, and once in a while I indulge myself. I should have thought twice before I did that with you. I'm sorry."

I was speechless.

My anger turned to compassion as my mind tried to empathize with what she had just told me. I had no idea what it was like to be in love much less lose a child. Maybe I had thought there could have been more with Wanda. Blended with my guilt had been a need for closeness and companionship. I wanted to convince her to try again. I wanted her to give me a chance to be what David was to her, but I could see that brick wall in her eyes. When I could tolerate that wall no longer, I dropped my eyes to the leather seat between us and said, "I don't know what to say."

"There's nothing to say," she scolded. "Just accept that we both got our needs met. It was really great sex, and now let's move on."

"But I did wrong! I did wrong!" I shook my head, still staring at the leather seats. "I broke a commandment and committed fornication. I shouldn't have given in to temptation."

I glanced up when I heard the back of her head hit the car window on her side. She had popped her head back and was staring up at the ceiling of the car. "You know," she said, drawing her gaze back to me, "I tried all my life to be a good Christian girl. I was raised in the church marching up the steps every Sunday wearing cute little dresses on Easter, listening to every word the preacher said, taking it to heart and trying my best to be the Christian I thought the Lord wanted me to be, but after what I went through when David died, and especially after I lost the baby, I started asking myself, why. Really, why? I don't even know if there is a God anymore. I know what I was taught my whole life, but how do I know? How do you know? How does anyone know if it's true? You live your life trying to do the right thing only to have the whole promise ripped apart. I try to do right by people. I try to have compassion and care about people, but why should I deprive myself for the promise of a heaven that no one really even knows exists? I'm supposed to deprive myself now in hopes of some obscure reward when I die? I finally realized it doesn't make any sense. It doesn't make any sense, Ronald, and that's when I gave up being a Christian. If I'm a sinner, I'm a sinner. So be it. If I'm not hurting anybody, then it's nobody's business but mine."

"But you work for a Christian ministry," I pleaded.

"Exactly," she replied. "You got it. I *work* for a Christian ministry. That doesn't mean I'm a Christian. It means that I get my livelihood, a very good livelihood, from working for a Christian ministry. It puts food on the table and is a lot less complicated than prostitution, which if David had been a common man, if he had not had this connection, would have been about the only profession left for me as an uneducated woman. I could have sold myself to many men on the street, or to one man I didn't love just because he would support me. There are women who go through what I went through, and because their husbands didn't leave them anything but a name, they have got no choice but to scrub floors or fuck for money. What kind of benevolent God puts people through shit like that?"

"Satan has hardened your heart," I softly affirmed.

"Has Satan hardened my heart, or has reality hardened my heart?" she asked. "The world is a rough place, Ronald, and whether you are a Christian or not, you have got to be tough to get through it. What I want to know is, are you tough enough to get through it?"

"What do you mean?" I asked.

"I mean, do you think this is going to be easy?" she flashed back. "Because, if you think this is going to be easy, you are already defeated."

"I don't understand," I said.

"Being a minister," she replied, "being a nationally famous or maybe even a world-famous minister. Do you think that is going to be easy? Television could make you into that, but what exactly do you think that means?"

"It means I can be a fisher of men," I replied. "It means I can cast a wide net to bring souls to the Lord."

A devilish smirk crossed her face. "It means," she said, "that you are going to be under a microscope. You are going to be examined, scrutinized, picked apart, and put back together by every critic, asshole, and lunatic out there. It won't be the moms and pops of Ravenden who watched little Ronnie Dennison grow up, and *Praise the Lord he's become a preacher man!* There will be souls to save, yes. There will be people who are hungry for the Gospel just like the good folks back in Randolph County, Arkansas, but for every one of those, there will be people calling you a liar, a hypocrite, a con man, a thief, and a charlatan. For every one who praises the work that you do, there will be another one who is trying to take you down. Are you strong enough to deal with *that*, Pastor Ronald Dennison? Are you strong enough to take on the evil that will come with the good? For just like Jesus, they will persecute you for your light as much as they would your darkness."

"I-I-I guess I never really thought it through like that," I sheepishly replied.

"Well, here's the deal, Pastor Ronald," she firmly commanded as she leaned forward toward me, "as far as talent goes, you have got what it takes. You have every bit of what it takes. You have charm, good looks, a fantastic speaking voice, a command of the pulpit, and a charisma that draws people to you like flies to shit. You don't even realize that you reek of it. You haven't even noticed, have you, that everywhere we have gone people notice you as soon as you walk into the room? They are intrigued by you, can't stop looking at and wondering about you. You carry an aura about you that both allures and frightens people at the same time, and you don't even know it."

"People look at you, not at me," I said. "You are an extremely beautiful woman, and so of course they are going to notice and look at you. I heard the man whistle at you at the truck stop yesterday. I saw those men looking at you. The only reason they noticed me was because I was with you."

"That's different," she countered. "That's sex appeal. You have that too, but you have something I don't have. I can tell the difference, and I saw it when you did that revival. I had to wait a good thirty to forty minutes after you finished that service for a chance to talk to you. Those weren't just the people from your church coming up to congratulate you on a revival well done. Those were people from as far away as Missouri and Tennessee who had heard about you, word of mouth, and who wanted to experience you for themselves. Then, when they did experience you, they had to place themselves with you. They had to talk to you, be in your presence, and touch you. If I hadn't known better, I would have sworn I was watching Jesus in the multitudes with people hoping only to be able to touch the hem of your garment."

She went on. "I've worked with Mr. Clayburn for seven years, and I've been around a lot of ministers and some who were very good speakers, but I've never seen anything like that before—ever. But here is the deal… if you don't have the strength to stand up to those who are going to try to tear you down, much less the strength to cope with your own shortcomings, then you are already defeated. It is going to take more than your

God-given gift, Pastor Ronald. It is going to take a titanium backbone and diamond balls. It is going to take the ability to build a fortress around your tender Christ-loving heart that even a nuclear blast cannot shatter. If you don't have at least the willingness to build that strength, then you might as well go home. I know that's what you say you want today. You can go home. Then you can explain to God in the afterlife how you squandered your talent and hid your light under a bushel."

Her reference to the parable of the talents did not go unnoticed. I sat staring at her, almost in shock. I felt like a blast wave had just passed through me, leaving behind each cell of my body in numb but tingling awareness. I knew she was right. I had noticed everything she described, how people would linger and want more of what they felt with me, and would not move on when obviously someone else was waiting for my attention. I had not known how to deal with it. I felt rude to brush one person off because someone else wanted to talk to me, but I felt rude to continue talking to someone who had already had an ample amount of my attention knowing that someone else wanted to come to me as well. I had felt both delighted by and burdened by the attention. A part of me wanted to bury my talent and give it back to the Lord unchanged. A part of me wanted to hide the light that I had been given and go back to the simple, uncomplicated life of the country, but in that moment, I knew I couldn't do that. I knew I had to move on. I had to stand up to the challenge. My mind went back to the dreams of Jesus shouting at me, *"You are my Word!"* I still didn't know exactly what that meant. I only knew that I had to go forward. I could not go back.

"Well?" she said, at last breaking my daze.

I sighed deeply. "Well…let's go meet Mr. Clayburn and do this screen test, or whatever it is he wants me to do."

Wanda merely turned back around in the car seat, started the car, and we drove on, eyes straight ahead, saying nothing.

"I've never met anyone like you," I commented after a pause.

"There are lots of people you are going to meet who don't quite match up to what you are used to from the folks at home," she replied. "There are lots of people very much like me." She glanced over at me briefly and then returned her attention to driving. "Ronald, you are so talented, and you have so much to give," she went on, "but you are so naive. You have no idea how much you have been sheltered from the world. I understand. I was that way once. It's a hard lesson to learn that life doesn't really match what you learned in your childhood."

I was intrigued by her. I didn't know whether to run from her or embrace her. Her confession that she was not really a Christian confused me even more. Still, I decided right then, if she was the devil, I might learn as much from the devil as from Jesus. "Will you teach me?" I asked quietly.

She glanced over at me and smiled. "Life will teach you," she said. "I am only a part of it."

In short order, we were pulling up in front of a one-story unassuming brick building. I realized we must be close to downtown because I could see tall buildings a short distance away.

"Follow me," Wanda commanded as she got out of the car, swayed up a short walk to a glass push door. I followed her inside to find a secretary sitting at a desk near the door. "We are here to see Mr. Malvern," Wanda specified once inside. "Is Mr. Clayburn here yet?"

"Yes, ma'am," the secretary replied. "They have been waiting for you."

Wanda motioned with her hand for me to follow. We walked down a short hall and into a room that was almost completely dark except for some lights shining on a squared-off area that contained a desk with a painting of Jesus kneeling and praying in the background. Mr. Clayburn and another man were sitting in fold-up chairs a few feet in front of the desk. There were a couple of large cameras off to the side and figures in the darkness which I assumed to be camera men. My nerves twisted just at the sight of it. I had never seen actual television cameras, and the sight of them seemed ominous and intimidating to me. When the two men heard the door open, both rose and turned around. Wanda walked straight up, shook the hand of the man standing next to Mr. Clayburn, and said, "I'm sorry to be delayed, Mr. Malvern. I hope you weren't waiting long."

Mr. Malvern was a somewhat chubby man who appeared to be in his late thirties or early forties. He was a fair amount shorter than Mr. Clayburn and, obviously, had eaten one too many pieces of pie. His straight brown hair was combed over to one side with a small part just above his left ear.

His face was clean-shaven, and his lower lip appeared to be slightly larger than the upper one.

"Think nothing of it." He smiled and then turned to me. "Ah," he went on. "You must be the boy wonder, the miracle preacher. I've heard a lot about you."

"Yes," I replied sheepishly. "My name is Ronald Dennison."

"Well, young man," he scoffed lightly, "let me take this opportunity to teach your first lesson in the media business. When someone greets you and pays you a compliment, or even if they offer you a verbal jab, don't be half-whispering '*Yes, my name is*' while you are staring at the floor. Hold your head up and look at me. Reach out your hand to shake mine like I'm your long-lost buddy and say, 'YES, SIR! My name is Ronald Dennison. So happy to meet you, Mr. Malvern!' Now, let's try it."

I couldn't believe what was happening. Never in my life had anyone spoken to me that way or asked me to rehearse a handshake. "Come on then!" Mr. Malvern insisted. "Let's try it. Greet me like an equal. Greet me like I'm the person you most wanted to meet in all the world. Greet me like I'm your disunited brother coming home from the war!"

My heart sank. He could not have known about Teddy. Surely Wanda had not had an opportunity to tell anyone that my brother had been in the war before he died. A stab of grief pierced my heart, and then I thought back to that day in Jonesboro when I met Teddy at the bus station, how I wanted to hug him and never let go. He had been, on that day, the most beautiful sight I had ever seen. I looked up for some comfort or support, but Wanda and Mr. Clayburn were just standing there, staring at me, saying nothing, and waiting for me to comply.

"Come on!" Mr. Malvern commanded again.

I looked him straight in the eye, reached out my hand again, and said, "How do you do, sir. My name is Ronald Dennison. I am very pleased to meet you."

"Needs work," Mr. Malvern chided again. "Here let me show you."

Mr. Malvern turned to Mr. Clayburn, thrust out his hand, and proclaimed boldly, "Mr. Clayburn, it is so good to meet you. My name is Trent Malvern, and I am happy to make your acquaintance!"

After firmly shaking Mr. Clayburn's hand, he turned back to me and said, "Now you try—and put some oomph into it!"

"Ronald," I heard Wanda say from over my shoulder, "do you remember how you greeted me last year when I came to your revival? You were in your own element. You were confident and comfortable because you had your own clan all about you, so when you shook my hand, I felt affirmed and welcomed. That's what Mr. Malvern is talking about."

I had never thought about it. My mind went back to that moment when I first met Wanda. "Well, one of the things that made that easy," I half-joked, "was that you were the most beautiful woman I had ever met in my life."

"Ha! Ha!" Mr. Malvern bellowed. "She is beautiful, isn't she, son? Now, what if you thought of every person you were ever to meet as being as beautiful and alluring as Miss Wanda Moore? Would that put a smile on your face and a gleam in your eye?"

"Yes, sir." I smiled. "I think it would."

"Well, let's try it," he returned. Then he jutted his hand out to me and said, "So you are the wonder preacher I have heard so much about. My name is Trent Malvern. Good to meet you."

"Mr. Malvern!" I gleamed as I looked him straight in the eye and firmly shook his hand. "Yes, I may well be the preacher you have heard about. My name is Ronald Dennison. Very good to meet you, sir!"

"Much better! Much better!" Mr. Malvern announced. "Now let me show you something."

He reached his hand around and placed it between my shoulders. Then he nudged me toward the area that had been staged with the desk and the picture of Jesus in prayer. He led me to the desk and then leaned back on it, inviting me to do the same. He waited for me to lean back on the desk next to him. Then he pointed toward the darkness where I could barely see anything beyond the edge of the lighted area. "Young man," he coached. "Out there are your Wanda Moores. Out there are those beautiful alluring women you want to meet simply because they are beautiful and charming. You have to think of every one of them like Wanda Moore, as the person you most want to meet in all the world. They may not all look like Miss Moore. Some of them look like little old grandmothers and grandfathers, some like hardworking farmers or factory workers, businessmen or janitors. Some look like housewives who are just worn-out with taking care of the kids and cleaning house all day. Some might be teenagers or college students who are taking a break from their studies to watch a little television, and every one of them wants to meet *you!* They want to meet you because you bring something to them. You give them the Good Word, the Gospel, the cleansing water that soothes and refreshes their tired and challenged souls, and you want to meet them because they are all children of God. You want to meet them because you know the worth and value of every beloved child of God. You want to meet them because you want them to know that they can lay their burdens down at the foot of the cross and be lifted up into the eternal joy of redemption."

"Wow!" I exclaimed. "You would make a good preacher."

"Son, I'm a good director and producer," he responded. "That just might be something similar. Now what you have to understand here is that television, unlike preaching to the folks who come to church, takes a little production, a little finesse. Instead of those folks out there coming to your revival, you are going into their homes, and if you do this right, they are going to feel like you are a visitor in their home just like the pastor from the church down the road."

"Now here is a little trick. You have to speak to those cameras as though you are sitting on the sofa next to Mrs. Smith or Mr. Jones, letting them know all the good reasons why they ought to go to church with you on Sunday. If we were doing a Hollywood film, I wouldn't want you to look at or speak to the camera. You would have to pretend the camera isn't there, but in this case, I want you to talk directly to that camera just like Mr. and Mrs. Smith or Mr. Jones are sitting right inside of it. You are talking to them personally and privately. You are bringing the love of Jesus straight into their home."

"But there is more than one camera," I noted.

"Right you are," Mr. Malvern continued. "That is part of how we get the finesse—Tim!" he shouted into the darkness, half startling me. "Turn on camera one."

A red light came on atop the camera off to my left. "You see that red light there?" he said, pointing. "That light means that the camera is on. The film is rolling. You can speak directly to that camera—Jason, camera two." A red light came on atop the camera to my right. "Now, you can't speak to both cameras at once, can you?" Mr. Malvern waved his finger between the two. "But we may be running both at the same time. We may be getting secondary shots of you that we may or may not use. You just pick which camera you want to talk to, and if you want to switch from one to the other, you can do that, but you don't need to be going back and forth too much. Also, I can direct you by pointing to the camera you need to be giving your attention." He pointed in the general direction where he and Mr. Clayburn had been sitting earlier. "I'm going to be off over there, giving directions to those camera men that you aren't even going to hear."

It felt confusing, but I tried to keep my confidence up. I just kept telling myself, "You will learn how to do this."

"But first," Mr. Malvern went on, unaware of my thoughts, "we just need to see how you look on camera. So you can sit here at the desk, lean on it like we are doing now, or you can walk around within this area, but stay centered as much as possible. You don't have to do anything special to start with. All we want to know is how you are going to look as it translates to the television screen. So I'm going to go back out there to sit with Mr. Clayburn and Wanda, and all I want you to do is pick a camera to look into, and just tell us a little bit about yourself. If the camera moves, you need to follow it, at least with your eyes. I don't want you chasing it about the room, but just keep your attention on it the way you might if you were having a conversation with someone at a party who turned to pick up hors d'oeuvres off the snack table."

"Sir," I interrupted. "I've never been to a party, and I never heard of anything called a hors d'oeuvres."

"Okay, bad example." He laughed. "Just try to keep your focus on the camera. Now just tell us a little bit about you." Mr. Malvern walked into the darkness beyond the lights that were shining on me, and I could no longer see him. I could see the red lights still on both cameras.

"I…ah…I don't know what you want to know," I pleaded.

"Who are you? Where did you come from? What makes you tick? How did you get interested in the ministry?" his voice responded from the darkness.

"Well, I…ah…my name is Ronald Dennison."

"Don't stutter," the darkness commanded. "Keep the 'ahs' and 'uhms' to a minimum. Say it like you mean it. Tell Mr. and Mrs. Smith who you are and why you need to come to their church."

I collected myself, thought for a second, and thought what I might say if strangers had moved close to church back home, if I wanted to visit and let them know our church was available and that they were welcome to come.

"Hello," I began confidently. "My name is Ronald Dennison, and I am very pleased to meet you. I'm the pastor at the church down the road, and I would like to tell you a little bit about me and about our ministry. I first got interested in the ministry when I was a little boy because my father was a minster, and I very much looked up to and respected my daddy. When I was about ten years old, I began having dreams about Jesus, and Jesus was telling me, *You are My Word.* I didn't know what it meant, but I kept having the dreams until one day, when I was about seventeen, my daddy fell ill and couldn't preach one Sunday, so my momma sent me to preach instead. Oh, I was so nervous. I wasn't sure what I was going to say or how I was going to say it, but when I got up in front of that congregation, it was like the clouds parted, and the light of heaven opened."

I looked upward to my left, smiling and somewhat squinting into the light. Then I looked back to the camera. "I felt the power of the Lord move in me that day. I felt the Holy Ghost fill my being and speak the words of our Lord, and I think I was moved as much or more than the good folks I was preaching to. After that, people began telling me that I had the calling, that I was meant to be a preacher, and that I could be successful at bringing souls to the Lord. The next thing I knew, people were asking me to preach almost every Sunday, and every time I spoke, I felt the Spirit move in me. I want to share that with you. I want you to know what it feels like to have Jesus in your heart. I want you to know the joy of a closer walk with Jesus. Praise God! I want your soul to be saved, just like his and hers, and his and hers." I pointed in different imaginary places about the room.

"Cut!" Mr. Malvern shouted.

"Cut what, sir?" I questioned.

"Ha!" he bellowed. "'Cut' means stop the filming. You'll learn all this stuff in time. Jacob," he continued from the darkness, "that looked pretty good to me."

"Yeah, yeah," I heard Mr. Clayburn respond. "That came across a lot cleaner than I thought it was going to. How soon can we take a look at the film?"

"I think we can probably get it by Wednesday," Mr. Malvern responded. They bantered on, and all the while I sat there under the lights, listening to the course of my life being plotted for me. While they were chatting, Wanda came out of the darkness and joined me at the desk. She stood there, arms folded, smiling at me. "You did good, preacher man," she declared. "Very nice."

"What now?" I asked.

"Well, they are probably going to negotiate a few things, consider this and consider that. They will probably look at the film first, just the two of them, and then we will all take a look at it together later this week."

"I say we have got our title!" Mr. Malvern trumpeted from the darkness. "He said right there in that dialogue—'*The Church Down the Road*'—I say that's what we call the program. He's a little green, but he's a smart kid. We can teach him what he needs to know."

"Do you want to go ahead and set up some training and orientation?" Mr. Clayburn asked.

"Well, let's wait to see the film just to be sure," Mr. Malvern responded, "but I think we may have a winner here."

Wanda and I were both listening to this. I was still leaning against the desk, and she stood to one side. "Here we go," I said, looking to her for reassurance. She leaned back against the desk beside me, reached over, and placed her hand over mine.

"Here we go," she said, smiling.

CHAPTER 13

For the next couple of days before the screen test came back, we didn't do much. I stayed in Mr. Clayburn's guest room. He had the biggest, most beautiful house I had ever seen. There was an arch over the front entry leading to a foyer that I now realize was actually not as big and grand as it appeared to me back then. A boy who has never seen much more than a four-room shack would be impressed by anything that seemed much beyond that. There was a large formal living room to the left and a hall that led past the stairs straight by a kitchen into the den in back. From the den adjacent to the kitchen in the back of the house, large windows revealed a fenced and somewhat lush backyard with a swimming pool and a gazebo nearby. There was a dining room to the left just past the living room down that hallway as well. My room was up the stairs to the right. It was carpeted and had the biggest, plushest bed I had ever before seen. The room was a pale robin's egg blue with indigo and turquoise drapes flanking a window that was lightly shaded with white sheers. The window overlooked the rooftop of the neighbor's house. There was a door to one side of the headboard of the bed that led to a small bathroom but something grander than I had ever before experienced. When I walked back from the bathroom, I could see through that window past the neighbor's roof to a clean, well-manicured street lined with houses quite similar to Mr. Clayburn's. I walked around as though I had eggs beneath my feet, and I dared not crush one. I was afraid I might damage something, stain something. Coming from a four-room house with an outdoor toilet, Mr. Clayburn's home felt like the Taj Mahal to me. If ever we got anything fancy back home, we always took the most delicate of care with it, because anything fancy was something seldom seen and not likely to last. So I felt as though I had to treat all that luxury with kid gloves. I had not yet learned that most people who have luxury take it for granted. Things that are easily replaced are seldom treasured.

Mr. Clayburn's black maid, Sadie, oriented me to my room and showed me where to find linens. I had seen black people before but never had I ever talked to one. Northern Arkansas was populated almost entirely with white people. Just a few miles west and south was what hill folk called "the bottoms." There, cotton, soybeans, and rice were plentifully raised on the eastern plains of Arkansas. Some folks from my part of the country went to the bottoms to work the fields when money was a little scarce, and that was often. When they did, they worked right alongside black folks, so people in northern Arkansas were not quite as prejudiced as people may be in other parts of the country, even other parts of Arkansas. Down in the Arkansas Delta and along the southeastern part of the state, black folks were treated just as severely as they might have been treated in Alabama or Mississippi, but hill folk were different. Hill folk were poor folk too, and we didn't see much difference between ourselves and them, except the color of the skin. Momma and Daddy always said, "There ain't no difference between niggers and white folks except what you make of it." They didn't even think of the word *nigger* as being a bad word. It was just what you called black people. It felt odd, the first time I heard the word used in a demeaning way, but then, I understood why black people came to despise the word. It felt odd that first time that I saw another human being in a servant's role. At home we had no servants. We just helped each other.

When we first arrived at the house, Mr. Clayburn had commanded Sadie to see me to my room. She walked right over and started to take my luggage.

"It's a little heavy," I said. "I can carry it."

"Nonsense!" Mr. Clayburn snapped. "It's her job. We pay her to do these things." He didn't mention that he never paid her much. I learned later that her salary was measly even by rural Arkansas standards.

I turned to look at him, astonished. Even if she was being paid, it seemed demeaning to let this little old lady with a bad hip drag my luggage up the stairs when I knew I was much more capable.

"Go on, let her have it," Mr. Clayburn ordered. "When you get settled, come back down. I'll meet you in the den down this hall by the kitchen." He pointed down the hall to the back of the house.

I quietly let go of the luggage and watched as Sadie half-dragged it up the first couple of steps. As soon as Mr. Clayburn disappeared down the hall, I trotted up next to her and took hold of the handle of my suitcase. She glanced up at me with an odd look on her face. I raised one eyebrow, smiled at her, and nodded. Then she released the handle and allowed me to carry my suitcase the rest of the way up. When we got to the guest room door, Sadie looked up at me as she turned the knob, and whispered, "Thank ya."

"Ain't nothin'," I said. "I got younger muscles."

"Come on over here," she went on, seeming to ignore the comment. "See dat door beside de bed? Dat's yo bathroom. You need towels 'n' linens, dere's a cabinet to de left o' de door where you can find whatcha need."

She caught me gawking at the room like it was a Rembrandt in a museum.

"Purdy, ain't it?" She smiled. "Miss Clayburn brought in some silly little man from New York. Did all dat stuff, all them fancy drapes an' all— you need to freshen up afore you come down?"

There was that phrase again, "freshen up." It would take me a little time to begin to figure out exactly what that meant. "Sure," I replied, not really knowing what I was replying to.

Sadie ambled to the door, turned, and said, "Mr. Clayburn gonna meet ya in de den off de kitchen when yo ready." She then walked out and closed the door behind her.

I really didn't know what I was supposed to do at that point. I set my suitcase on the floor by the window and went in to use the bathroom.

After that, I wandered around the room, looking at different points of finery. There were paintings with ornate frames that had dabs of flowers that matched the colors of the wall. There were trinkets and little white statues on the dresser and side tables. After a few minutes of gawking, I went downstairs.

The den was not hard to find. Turning to my right at the bottom of the stairs, I could see the kitchen at the back of the house. I went down the hall toward the kitchen, and when I entered the den, there was a dark paneled room to my left with leather chairs and a sofa. A brick fireplace flanked the back wall with a large leather chair on either side of it. Mr. Clayburn sat in the chair that was to the left of the fireplace opposite the window. Beside him on a little table was a glass about half as high as any that I had ever seen. It contained some liquid that looked like tea and a little ice. He appeared to be reading a book, and when he saw me come into the room, he placed a marker in the book and set it to one side.

"Come in," he commanded. "Have a seat."

I sat on the brown leather sofa at a slight angle across from him in front of the large window overlooking the backyard.

"Would you like something to drink? Glass of wine, scotch, or something?" he went on. I had been exposed enough to know he was talking about liquor.

"No, sir," I replied politely. "The Bible admonishes us to be of a sober mind."

"You don't start losing your sober mind till you have had four or five," he responded. "But suit yourself. Would you like some tea, water, or maybe soda?"

"Yes, sir. A glass of iced tea would be nice," I replied.

"Sadie!" he shouted over his shoulder. "Get Mr. Dennison some sweet tea."

Sadie came through an archway behind him with a rag in her hand. She had obviously dropped what she was doing, apparently dusting, to obey his command. "Yes, sir, Mr. Clayburn," she said as she waddled across the room with one hip rocking over the other as though it was difficult to walk.

"Do you need any help?" I questioned as she came through the room.

"Sit tight, Pastor Dennison," she said, waving one hand toward the floor signaling me to remain in my seat. "I'll be right back wige 'yo tea."

I was uncomfortable being waited on like that. Even though Momma had waited on me my whole life, I had still offered help, had done my part around the house, and even if she didn't ask me to wash dishes, I obliged. I questioned my feelings and wondered if I might have felt differently if Mr. Clayburn had treated Sadie a little more respectfully. I had, of course, never been around any such thing as a maid before. Where I grew up, no one I knew could afford that kind of luxury, and I wondered if they would have utilized it even if they could afford it. Hill people were resilient, self-reliant, proud people. Even though help was readily available from neighbors, and most often offered without asking, you seldom asked for help, much less demanded it. You might pay someone to do something you were not capable of doing yourself, but even then, you pitched in as best you could. It took me a while to realize that Mr. Clayburn didn't really think of Sadie as another human being but more as a farm animal good only for chores. He treated her more like a milk cow than a person.

"So, tell me about yourself, young Pastor Dennison," Mr. Clayburn exclaimed as Sadie walked past him into the kitchen.

I didn't know what to say. "Well, I…ah…I love the Lord, and I love preaching His Word."

"Good! Good for you," he encouraged a bit too robustly. "So what made you love the Lord and want to preach His Word?"

"Well, sir," I began uncomfortably, "my daddy is a preacher, and I always loved and respected him, and then when I was about ten years old, I began having dreams telling me that I was called to preach."

"Really? How interesting," he patronized, apparently having forgotten what I had said during the screen test. "What kind of dreams?"

I glared at him briefly, not sure what I was experiencing or what his motives were. "In one dream," I began. "I saw Jesus crucified on the side of our barn. Then he looked down at me and said, 'YOU ARE MY WORD' and the sound of it echoed all across the farm and all around me."

"Interesting," Mr. Clayburn replied in a glib tone as though he were examining a high school science project instead of really trying to get to know me. "So do you still have these dreams?"

About this time Sadie set a tall glass of iced tea in a little glass saucer on the sofa side table beside me. "Thank you," I said politely, looking up at her.

"Yo welcome," she replied but added, "Pastor, ya thank me every time I do somethin' fo ya, yo gonna get awful tired. I'm here to do thangs fo ya. So you just relax now and let me do it." She then crossed the room and through the arch where she had been before.

I reached for my glass of tea and took a sip as I watched Sadie waddle back across the room. Then I turned my attention back to Mr. Clayburn. "Sir, the last time I had a dream was a few months back after my brother died."

"Oh, you lost a brother," he crooned. "That's tragic. How did he die?"

"It was a drunk driving accident," I responded, not really wanting to talk about it.

"I am so sorry for your loss," he halfheartedly comforted. "I hope no one else was injured."

"No, sir," I responded, trying to think of a way to change the subject. "He lost control of his car and ran off the road."

"So your brother was a heavy drinker?" he continued to interrogate.

"Yes," I replied. "He became that. When he came home from the Korean War, he was never the same. He was always maybe a little rebellious but never anything like that. Something happened to him over there. It changed him, and I guess drinking was maybe a way he tried to forget."

"No wonder you have a distaste for alcohol. Alcohol can either be soothing or sadistic," he mentioned, and then his attention was diverted to the sound of a door opening from the garage on the other side of the kitchen. As we both turned to look, a slender woman of about his same age came through the door carrying several elegant-looking paper shopping bags. Her hair was a pale brown and pulled back behind her head in a French roll. She had a little round white hat with blue buttons which was pinned to one side of her head. Her dress was a medium blue with long sleeves, and she had a matching jacket that rounded just above her waist. The dress hugged her slender body almost as though it had been painted on. It ran down to a clean perfect seam just at her knees.

"Oh, hello, darling," she cooed as she crossed from the kitchen into the den and set her bags on the floor beside the arch between the two rooms.

At first, I wasn't sure if she was referring to Mr. Clayburn, me, or both of us, but neither of us had time to answer before I heard her call, "Sadie!"

"Yes, ma'am," I heard Sadie calling from the hall behind Mr. Clayburn.

"Please come take these bags to my room," the woman commanded at least a little more respectfully than Mr. Clayburn had. She had no sooner said it than Sadie was coming through the arch from the hall behind Mr. Clayburn. "Put these in my closet," the woman ordered, "and there are a few more in the trunk of the car. I'll need you to bring those in as well."

Sadie picked up the bags without a word and carried them through the arch behind Mr. Clayburn. The woman then immediately turned her attention to me, crossed over to the sofa, where I stood to meet her.

"How do you do?" She smiled politely, extending a thin hand with red polished nails. "I'm Evelyn Clayburn."

"I am very pleased to meet you, ma'am," I replied, noticing that her thin fingers in my hand felt rather like holding a cold boney fish. "My name is Ronald Dennison."

"This is the young preacher I told you about," Mr. Clayburn said without rising from his chair.

"Well, it is a pleasure to meet you," she returned, smiling. "Jacob has told me a lot about you."

I wondered how much Mr. Clayburn could have told her about me since he had not yet gotten to know me himself.

"Please sit down." She motioned to the couch behind me. "I'll be back as soon as I freshen up a bit." She then turned and exited through the same arch where Sadie had entered earlier. I assumed their bedroom must have been back there somewhere.

As I sat back down, I made a mental note to myself to figure out what this "freshen up" thing was all about. Then I decided to turn the tables a bit. "So, Mr. Clayburn," I questioned as I reached for another sip of my tea. "What got you interested in ministry?"

"Well, I wasn't so much interested in ministry at first as I was interested in broadcasting." He sipped from the little glass that he now was holding constantly rather than setting it back on the table. "I've been in broadcasting for a very long time. I ran across a minister several years back who wanted to know if I could put him on the radio. You make money in broadcasting through your advertising and sponsorship. Companies will pay to have their products plugged on your show. I told this fellow I didn't think there would be much chance of getting sponsorship for church sermons, and he said he couldn't do that anyway because he didn't want the Word of the Lord associated with marketing products. He said it would be too much like the money changers in the temple. I said, well, is your church going to pay for it? We have to pay for air time and the salaries of folks who work at the radio station. So he suggested we could take up a collection just like they do at Sunday services, and maybe instead of passing around a collection plate, folks could mail in their contributions. I said, you know, that just might work. I gave him a six-month trial. The money came in, enough to pay everybody and have a little left over. I got a few other ministers involved in other cities. It continued to be successful, so that's when I decided to start Christ Beacon Ministries. When television came along, I saw opportunity to reach even more people. This TV thing is going to be big, Pastor Dennison. Mark my words. Television is going to be huge."

I had gotten a lot more than I had bargained for, and I wasn't sure how to respond, but I said, "I thought radio stations just did ministerial broadcasting as a service thing, you know, for free. I know up home, sometimes they broadcast the church service itself on Sunday morning. I have been sick at home on Sunday before and have listened to church services out of Jonesboro. I don't recall any kind of advertising except for reporting the service times of the church itself, and I don't recall any requests for donations."

"There might be some little country radio stations that would broadcast a church service just to fill up air time," he said, taking another sip of his drink in the middle of the sentence. "If they didn't have a broad base of advertisers, they might do that, but that does not happen much in the cities. There are so many companies wanting to get word of their product out there, and so much more can be made by the station with advertising that they aren't going to waste their time on something that has little or no financial return. No, sir, there has got to be a money flow or the thing won't work."

"Well, how do you get money flow on preaching the Gospel?" I asked.

"The larger the audience, the bigger the prize," he said, holding his glass up in the air. "Sadie! I'd like a refill, please."

Sadie came in through the arch again and took his glass from his hand as she crossed the room. She didn't say anything but waddled over to an area on the other side of the room that I had noticed but paid little attention to. At that point in my life, I didn't have enough experience to recognize that it was a bar. Sadie dumped the remaining ice from his glass into a little sink, placed a few clumps of fresh ice into the glass with a pair of tongs, and poured up more of the brown liquid from a sleek-looking bottle. She returned the glass to Mr. Clayburn who simply held his hand up, waiting for her to place the glass into his palm.

"I'll be gettin' dinner started directly," she said, "soon as I get through helpin' Miss Evelyn back here in the bedroom."

"Good!" Mr. Clayburn exclaimed. "Scotch makes me hungry." He then turned his attention back to me. "You see, Pastor Dennison, the more people you reach, the more donate. The more who donate, the larger the coffers become, and the more you have to expand what you do as well as have a bit of comfort left over for yourself."

"Yes, sir," I replied quietly as Mrs. Clayburn came back into the room wearing a broad-skirted yellow print summer skirt with a matching blouse. She flowed across the room and turned around before us.

"Don't you just love it?" she practically giggled. "I got it at Castner's this afternoon. Twenty percent off!"

"You always look ravishing, dear," Mr. Clayburn commented, barely even looking at her. She was a beautiful woman, perhaps a little older than Wanda, and I had found myself having a fleeting lustful thought toward her earlier. Now that I saw that summer blouse exposing her, and a tiny bit of cleavage, the thought was a little less fleeting. I immediately chastised my thoughts not to be coveting another man's wife.

Mrs. Clayburn strolled over to Mr. Clayburn, bent over, and playfully squeezed thumb and fingers on either side of his mouth. "Thank you, darling," she moaned as she gave him a little peck of a kiss on the lips. "Now, when are you going to take me back to New York? I'm longing to go to Macy's."

"Soon, my dear," he replied. "Are you wearing that for dinner?"

"Oh, of course not, darling!" she scolded playfully. "I'll be right back."

Sadie had come back to the arch between the two rooms to watch the spectacle. Mrs. Clayburn brushed past her as she left the room and said, "Go ahead and start dinner, Sadie. I'll take care of dressing myself."

Sadie said not a word but ambled through the room to the kitchen, and in short order, I heard pots and pans rattling as they were being removed from the cabinet.

"You'll have to forgive my wife." Mr. Clayburn grinned. "She is a bit of a flirt."

"She seems very nice," I responded.

"She has expensive tastes," he scolded.

When dinner was served, it was unlike anything I had ever seen. There were thick cuts of steak wrapped with bacon around the side and some kind of long green vegetable I had never seen before. It was a long strand of a green round thing that looked like something from outer space to me. That green vegetable became my first taste of asparagus, and it was delightful on the palate. There were roasted potatoes, also delicious, and rolls so delicate they practically melted on my tongue. I had grown up with good food, but I had never experienced anything like that. Dessert presented my first taste of cheesecake. The trip to Nashville had provided me with pleasures I never dreamed existed, from making love to Wanda, to my first bite of cheesecake. It was almost overwhelming, overstimulating, to be in the presence of such opulence. I realized that many people in the world merely took extravagance for granted.

Over dinner, Mr. Clayburn continued to tout his prophecies about television. By that time, he was more than a bit tipsy, but I was too naive at that point in my life to realize it had been due to the Scotch. "You mark my words. In another five to ten years, this thing will be in practically every home. It will be as common as the radio and the telephone are now. I see it. It's coming. We have already got major stuff coming out of New York. NBC had a national television network established in 1951. It is just a matter of time, folks. This thing is going to be huge, and we have to find a way to get Christ Beacon into it nationally. Forget all this little local church service stuff. We have to produce just like the big boys produce. We have to present a polished product that will make people want to tune in."

He reached his fork up from his plate and pointed it at me. "And, Pastor Dennison, you may just be the ticket we need to get there."

Mrs. Clayburn looked over at me and smiled. "He goes on and on about this stuff. You practically have to slap his hand to get him to talk about something else."

"Mr. Clayburn appears to be very passionate," I said as I sliced my knife through the steak for another bite. "This is really delicious." I popped the bite into my mouth and chewed then listened for a response in the conversation.

"Yes!" Mr. Clayburn spouted.

Over his shoulder, Sadie stood ready by the doorway between the dining room and the hallway behind him. "Sadie," he exclaimed to her, "the filet mignon is excellent!"

"Thank ya, Mr. Clayburn," she responded softly. "Glad ya like it."

"Thank you, Sadie," I said, feeling very uncomfortable that she stood there the whole time, watching us eat, ready at any moment to fulfill some wish that any of us might have. Nobody's glass went empty, for whatever we were drinking seemed to refill itself magically as Sadie's hand reached around to refill the glass almost without notice.

If this was Sadie's vocation, she was excellent at it. I wasn't sure what to think of all that. In my house, or anywhere I had ever visited, everyone sat at the table together unless there was some big gathering where there wasn't room for everyone. Then the children found seats elsewhere, sometimes on the floor. I had heard of things like maids, and I had read stories about maids, but the experience of it took me aback. Despite the fact that she didn't seem to be comfortable, Sadie was required to stand there all through the meal and watch us eat. I am not sure if I would have felt different about it if Sadie had been white. From the appearances, I assumed that they would have treated her differently. I couldn't imagine that Mr. Clayburn would have asked his mother to drag the suitcase of a healthy young man up the stairs or stand there watching him eat if she was physically impaired. It wasn't that they exactly mistreated her. The behavior was subtle for the time, an implied requirement of her submissiveness, an unspoken indication that she was not quite as good as the rest of us. I found myself wondering if they fed her leftovers after the meal like one might feed the family dog. My first wondering about prejudice began that day. I realized that it is not always something direct and overt but more often not uttered aloud, at least not toward the object of prejudice. Instead, it is insidious and implied, a subtle evil rising like steam through a sewer gutter, only a faint indication of a greater filth below the surface. I squelched my imagination about it and continued the conversation. I became a passive participant.

"What will tomorrow bring?" I asked, returning my gaze to Mr. Clayburn. "What do you have in store for me?"

"Tomorrow brings another day." Mr. Clayburn smiled. "We will go over to Evangelic Temple, and you will meet the pastor, Mark Woods, there. I have a voice coach I want you to meet who will possibly work with you, and if we have the film back from your screen test, we may review that."

"I'm a little nervous about it," I commented.

"What is there to be nervous about?" he asked. "The only real difference, especially at Evangelic Temple, is the size of the audience. You will do the same thing that you do when you preach a sermon in church at home, the same thing that you do when you conduct a revival. We will simply film it. Now, when it comes to the production of your television show, that will be a little different. We will want that to be a bit more intimate, more personal. You won't so much be preaching when you do that as counseling. It would be as though someone had come to you with a problem and you are going to give them spiritual counsel regarding that problem. The difference will be that the person coming to you is the family, the individuals on the other side of that camera, and the problem will be one that we have previously determined to be the focus of the show that week."

"I'm not sure I understand," I prompted.

"Well, for instance," he went on, "let's suppose a couple came to you with the problem of adultery, and you are going to give them spiritual counseling regarding that problem in their marriage. What would you tell them about what the Bible has to say about that? Whatever you might say to that couple is what we will film for the show that day. When you do a sermon for a church service, or a revival gathering, we will simply have the cameras on you and let you do what you do, but when you are doing the show, we will have to plan that a little more carefully ahead of time. This is probably going to be a live broadcast because it is less expensive to broadcast it live than it is to film it, edit it, and broadcast the film later. So you need to get it right the first time. However, it will be filmed so we can air reruns if needed."

"So, I am not going to be preaching for the television show?" I asked. I had only the vaguest idea of what he might be talking about.

"No, not exactly," he replied. "Wouldn't want to stifle your spontaneity too much, but we might even consider scripting part of that."

"Scripting?"

"Yes, you know, like a script for a play." Mr. Clayburn pushed his plate to one side, and Sadie immediately came to the table and took the plate.

"I'm through with mine too, Sadie." Mrs. Clayburn nodded toward her. Sadie came around the table to pick up Mrs. Clayburn's plate as well and glanced over at me as she reached for Mrs. Clayburn's plate. My eyes darted between her and my plate for a second, and then I said, "Yes, you can take my plate too. It was delicious, Sadie. Thank you very much for preparing this."

"Yo very welcome, Pastor Dennison," she replied. "Can I get ya somethin' else?"

"Let's sip some coffee before dessert," Mr. Clayburn cut in. "Do you like coffee, Ronald?"

I noticed that his tone had become much less formal. For the first time, he called me by my given name instead of calling me Pastor Dennison.

"Yes, sir," I replied. "I have just never had it for anything but mostly breakfast. Aren't you afraid it will keep you awake?"

"Oh, we have a few hours before bedtime." He smiled at me. I think in some ways, he was intrigued by my ignorance. "We can get you something else if you like. Perhaps you would like a sherry?"

I found myself feeling embarrassed at how little I knew about life outside northern Arkansas. "I don't know what that is, sir," I replied.

"Oh, it is a kind of wine," he answered. "It pairs very well with dessert, and I guarantee it will not keep you awake."

"I think I better steer clear of alcohol," I replied. "I will take my chances with the coffee, I guess. This is such an adventure for me that I'm not sure I will sleep well anyway."

The idea of going back home, the embarrassment and shame of sleeping with Wanda, had been replaced with a curious fascination with how different life could be in the big city. I got a taste of what it might be like to have finer things that night, and I liked it.

"Oh, your adventures are just beginning, Pastor Ronald Dennison." He grinned a kind of semi-evil-looking grin. "We have miles to go before we sleep."

"I'm sorry, sir?" I questioned, never having heard of Robert Frost at that point in my life.

His grin grew wider. "You have a big week ahead of you," he said, "and a big life ahead of you after that."

"Yes, sir," I said. "That's why I'm feeling kind of nervous."

He made no effort to offer any word of consolation. He merely called over his shoulder again, "Sadie, coffee for everyone."

The coffee was a wonderful complement to the cheesecake that Sadie served next. When they said it was cheesecake, I wondered how in the world they were going to make a cake with cheese in it. The only reference I had to cheese was blocks of cheddar and American yellow cheese that would never have appeared to me to be any kind of complement to a dessert, and the only reference I had to cake was a sweet-flour bread with icing. However, when I tasted this cheesecake, I was shocked that it did not have the consistency of cake at all, nor did it really have the consistency of cheese, but was more like a very thick, rich pudding. If those moments of discovery that evening and the discovery that I had already encountered upon arriving in Nashville were any indication, I did indeed have a grand adventure ahead of me.

Of course, I didn't sleep much that night. I don't know if it was the coffee or my mind trying to wrap itself around what I had done, leaving home, coming to Nashville, trusting these strangers, experiencing things I hadn't even read about in magazines before. Maybe it was both, but I lay there staring at the ceiling with the soft streetlight filtering through the sheers on that grand window. The sheets on the bed were smoother than anything I had ever felt before, and the bed was both soft and firm, not like the clunky mattress I had slept on my whole life. I hadn't even experienced a bed that comfortable before. I lay there on that cushy bed, not sleeping, just watching the dim light on the ceiling. There were no streetlights in Ravenden, usually only the pin lights of stars on the black blanket of night. In Nashville, it seemed like every night was filled with light. These lights were different from the ones in the hotel room. A dusty constant glow came through the window instead of the flicker created by neon signs. These streetlights made it seem like the moon was full, even though I knew it wasn't. I must have slept at some point, but over and over in my head I kept hearing myself ask, *What have I done? What have I done?* and this was quietly countered by a small voice saying, *But I like this.*

CHAPTER 14

Everyone seemed thrilled with the screen test when it came back. It was strange seeing myself on film—just one more thing I had never before experienced. My sermon at Evangelic Temple also went well. By the end of the week, I found myself sitting with attorneys, signing contracts that I did not understand but signed anyway. When a little over a week and a half had passed, Wanda took me around town to locate an apartment that Mr. Clayburn would initially pay for out of ministry funds. Then, she took me home to get the remainder of my possessions so I could move to Nashville.

The mood around home was a mixture of joy that I was going to be getting my own TV show and sadness that I was going to leave. Momma vacillated between crying and telling me how proud she was. Daddy seemed to care less. I think, on some level, it meant to him that he could get his church back and that I would be out there somewhere out of the way, no longer his competition. More than anything, I wanted him to show some sign that he was proud of me, but that sign never came. I had no idea what I was going to do. I had no idea where life was going to lead me. I just knew that I was going to follow it wherever it would lead, and lead it did.

The first few broadcasts of *The Church Down the Road* were a little stilted and difficult, but Mr. Clayburn and Mr. Malvern brought in voice coaches and someone who was a presentation expert who helped me to "define" my audience and polish my presentation. Within a few weeks, I was beginning to get the hang of it and, within a few months, the donations started pouring in from all over America. Mr. Clayburn had me do a bit at the end of the show lamenting about how poor Christ Beacon Ministries was and how much we needed their faithful donations to be able to stay on the air. I didn't know how poor the ministry might have been when I began. However, I did as Mr. Clayburn told me and was naive enough never to question what funds the ministry might actually have. In a few years, Christ Beacon and I were anything but poor. They had been, in fact, not so poor then. Mr. Clayburn had made a nice living for himself by exploiting broadcast ministry.

By 1960, we were doing a regular Sunday broadcast from Evangelic Temple. Pastor Woods would present the Sunday service, but I was the occasional guest minister who could stir the congregation into a fervor of praising the Lord and opening their pocketbooks. As well, I admonished viewers to send their donations to further the cause of the Lord. I really didn't know how much money was actually pouring in. I only did what I had come to do, which was to preach the Gospel.

I finally learned how to drive in the city, which took a bit more finesse than the back roads of rural Arkansas. I continued to live in the little apartment that Mr. Clayburn was paying for out of the ministry and didn't see any reason to be doing anything else. I received a percentage of donations and spent very little, so within the five years from 1955 to 1960, I had a substantial savings account accumulated. In 1959, I began seeking to buy my own home. Little did I know, at the time, that I would end up buying a home for my wife and family. I discovered during those five years, as well, that there was a fountain supply of beautiful women who would eagerly have sex with me. Just as groupies might follow a rock star and seek to be with him, they sought my attention. Perhaps it was not sexual attention they sought, but they accepted the attention they were given. I did not go long without the opportunity to bed some lonely damsel and satisfy my baser urges. I found myself with women of all ages from their early twenties to nearing sixty. The age did not matter to me. If the woman was beautiful in my eyes, I eagerly bedded her whether she was my age or old enough to be my mother. Some of them were single, but many were married and feeling ignored by busy husbands who would rather play golf than make love to their lonely wives. I manipulated each one of them with the promise that our indiscretion would be our little secret. After all, they would not want their name besmirched before the congregation. I also entreated them to remain quiet so I might continue to spread the good Word of the Gospel. I followed with what I actually believed was a devout promise, that I would never stoop to such an indiscretion again. Afterward, I spent untold mental energy in remorse for what I had done, only to repeat the behavior with the same or some other woman, in the upcoming few days or weeks.

Through all this I fought with myself, chastised, and punished myself, but it did no good. When my little soldier was hungry for a conquest, the conquest was made one way or another. In the meantime, I pleaded with God to forgive me and pleaded with myself to stop the sin. There were times when I was so particularly depressed and forlorn in my misery of sin that I thought about the Bible verse, "If thine right hand offend thee, cut it off."

In those times, I sat on the toilet, kitchen knife in hand, staring down at my exposed member contemplating, sometimes very seriously, if I should cut it off. There were times I had the knife to the base of my penis and times I cut a small slit only to stop myself short of going through with the full cut. At those times, I fell to my knees, beating the butt of the knife into the floor, crying and screaming as blood trickled from my wounded soldier onto the floor. Within a day or two of healing, my little soldier was demanding its usual reward for enduring my abuse. I begged God to heal me, to take this burden of overpowering sexual urges from me. I begged to be normal, to have a wife and family like any normal man would. I begged for some teacher or guide who could show me a better way. However, all I found were women who accepted sex as a substitute for the love and affection they truly desired. None of them were for me. They were married, older, or I simply did not respect them. None of them fit. None of them were any more than a fuck. I had taken a lesson from Wanda and found myself repeating her words at times. Like her, I had come to settle simply for the sex. However, unlike her, my heart knew I needed more. Then, right after a sermon in June of my twenty- fourth year, a young woman approached me after services at Evangelic Temple. She looked strangely familiar, although I was certain I had never seen her before. I stood in the back of the church, shaking the hands of congregation members as they filed past me, offering blessings and appreciation for what they had gained from the sermon. Then, I spotted a beautiful young woman looking at me adoringly as she passed through the line. Immediately, I was taken by her hazel-green eyes that stood out and glimmered like lighthouses on the distant shore of a dark night. Her hair was brown, and her cheekbones were high. She smiled as she approached and reached out her small tender hand to shake mine.

"The sermon was lovely, Pastor Dennison," she said as she gleamed at me, eyes taunting more like a siren call than a sexual enticement.

"Thank you so much," I said, holding her hand for a moment longer than all the others. "I am so grateful that you may have received spiritual nourishment."

She smiled a half smile, one side of her lip moving up slightly above the other. It was cute and quaint and somehow comforting, pleasing. I learned later that this charming enticement had actually been the result of Bell's palsy suffered at an early age.

"You don't remember me, do you?" she said softly.

"Remember?" I questioned. I could not place where or how I might have seen her before. Immediately, the dreaded thought that she might have been one of my trysts ran through my mind and anxiety ran right along beside it.

"I'm Alissa," she greeted tenderly as though I would then recall, but I did not.

"Alissa?" I pondered. "I'm sorry. I don't recall an Alissa. I encounter so many people that it is very difficult to keep any one name firmly in mind."

"From Ravenden," she said. "You healed me."

"I healed you?"

"At the church in Ravenden. I was twelve years old. My mother brought me there because she heard that you could heal the sick. I had Crohn's disease, and you healed me."

My mind went racing back to that day when a gaunt child was brought before me. I was seventeen, preaching some of the first few sermons I had ever preached. I recalled her mother's desperation, and I recalled praying with her.

"Alissa!" I exclaimed. "Oh my goodness! I do remember! You were the first person who was ever healed of a physical sickness through me. I assume it is healed. You are still well, aren't you?"

"Yes, I am well," she replied. "I am very well. I am nineteen years old now, and I moved to Nashville almost a year ago to take a job as a secretary for a recording studio. I'm still amazed that I got the job. I have a little apartment over near Berry Hill, and I am enjoying living in the city."

"Wow!" I found myself saying. "Wow! You have developed from a gaunt and frail child to a beautiful young woman."

"I owe that to you for healing me," she said.

"No," I replied. "You owe it to our Heavenly Father for healing you, and you owe it to your faith. I was nothing more than a conduit, a copper wire on a circuit, certainly not the energy that ran through it."

"Regardless," she said, "I am deeply grateful."

I looked down and realized that I was still holding her hand and that there were members of the congregation gathering anxiously behind her. "Can you stay?" I questioned. "Could we go have lunch later? I would love to take you to lunch and catch up on old times."

"Sure, I can stay," she replied.

"Have a seat in one of the pews," I commanded. "When I am finished, I will seek you out."

She released my hand and retired to a nearby seat. I watched her as she moved to a pew and sat down. It was not so much sexual enticement I felt as I watched, but more as a father might watch over his daughter to be sure that she was safe. Then I continued to shake the hands of parishioners for several more minutes. When all was finished, I went to sit beside her. I leaned into her with my arm over the pew behind her back.

"I am astounded," I said. "I can't believe what a beautiful woman you have become. From that frail child, you have morphed into a gleaming and beautiful figure of a woman." Her cheeks flushed crimson in her embarrassment. Immediately I saw it. "I'm sorry," I interjected. "I didn't mean to be forward."

"It's okay." She smiled. "I'm just not used to compliments."

I longed to look at her. I felt a kinship I had never felt before, not with Lynetta, not with Wanda, or any of the women I had bedded at that point in my life. Those green eyes gleamed at me in a way I had never seen before. This was not a woman wanting to be fucked. This was a woman wanting to be loved, and I had the distinct feeling that she already felt a love for me. I knew in that moment that I felt something deeply different for her. "Where would you like to have lunch?" I asked, breaking the spell.

"Anywhere is fine," she said. "Do you have a favorite place?"

"The wonderful thing about living in the city," I responded, "is that I never have a lack of favorite places. There is a wonderful cafeteria around the corner here, but there are lots of congregants who like to dine there after church on Sunday. I don't know that I want them speculating about me coming in with a young woman or coming over seeking more of my attention. How about if we drive to Gallatin to a catfish place I know out there? It will be a bit of a trek but more private, and the food is very good."

"That sounds wonderful," she responded.

"We can leave your car in the church parking lot, and I will bring you back later in the afternoon if that is okay."

"Yes," she replied simply.

In those days, I had prospered enough to purchase myself a 1959 Ford Galaxy 500. My ministerial career had been very profitable by Ravenden standards, but not nearly as profitable as it was about to become. I led her from the church to my red-and-white Ford.

"Oh, wow!" she exclaimed. "You have a very nice car."

"The Lord has been good to me," I responded.

She got in the car, and I drove for about forty minutes to the fried catfish restaurant in Gallatin on the very north side of town. Congregations from churches on that side of town filed into the catfish restaurant for Sunday afternoon, dining just as Evangelic Temple parishioners filed into the cafeteria near the church in Green Hills. Nashville was very different from Ravenden. There were certainly members of the congregation who still fixed Sunday dinner in their own homes as we had done back in Ravenden, and I had even been invited a few times. However, modernization and plenty of money saw more people going to restaurants after church than cooking a meal at home.

Although I was well-known for my TV broadcast, I knew that there would be fewer questions asked in Gallatin than in Green Hills. I also knew, due to the length of the drive, that many of the church members from that side of town would have eaten and left the restaurant by the time we got there.

We pulled up to a large but rustic-looking cabin with a porch across the front and rocking chairs lining the walls on either side of the door. Inside, we were quickly seated at a little rough wood table with a floral table cloth and two chairs. The waitress took our drink orders, and we both perused the menu even though there was little else to select besides fried fish.

"I think I'll have the fish." I smiled over the menu.

"Fish?" she retorted without missing the opportunity. "Imagine serving fish here—in a catfish restaurant."

"Imagine," I said, smiling.

The menu included sides and a few options such as a pulled pork sandwich, but primarily it came down to catfish.

After a moment's brief silence, I asked, "So how did you get here? How did you get to be a secretary to a recording studio in Nashville?"

"I took a yearlong stenography course over in Jonesboro, which I learned about through a radio advertisement," she responded. "Shortly after I graduated, a friend told me about an ad for this job which they had seen in a Nashville paper. The rest is history, I guess. How did you get here?"

"Humpf," I exhaled as I looked down at the floral table cloth with yellow daisies on it. "Fate, or God's will, I guess. When I did my very first tent revival, there was a woman who came from Memphis who had heard about me. She was there to check me out for Christ Beacon Ministries, see how I might do in broadcasting. She gave me her number and told me she could link me with this ministry in Nashville, and after a lot of soul- searching, I agreed to come. So here I am."

"Isn't it funny how simple questions can have such complicated answers?" she said, stirring her sweet tea with a straw. The waitress had stealthily placed the drinks in front of us as we were talking.

"Isn't it funny," I said, "how fate brings people together and brings them together again when they never dreamed that they would ever meet in the first place?"

"Funny, fate or God's will?" she mused. "I just know that my life was never the same after you prayed with me that day when I was twelve years old and sick."

I stared for a moment at those gleaming green eyes and thought to myself, *I'm already in love.* She was attractive. She was sexy, but what I felt in that moment was anything but lust. It was totally different from what I felt when my little soldier was demanding to be inside a woman. She enticed me sexually—yes—but it was not lust. It was different. I wanted to mate with her, to have children with her, to have a family with her. It was totally different and unlike anything I had ever felt. I couldn't believe the thoughts that were running through my head in that afternoon as I stared into those gleaming green eyes. From that brief reunion with a person who had previously been only a sickly child to me, I had become enthralled. Instead of thinking about how I might get her undressed and get myself into her vagina, I was thinking about nesting, a home, children, domicile, and fantasies of coming home to a loving wife with adoring children gathering around my waist. Yes, I wanted her, but sex was on a back burner that afternoon. There were more important things to think about and talk about first.

I discovered that Alissa's mother had married a man from Memphis who had moved to Jonesboro and had taken a job as a janitor at the local hospital. This had been a step down from more lucrative work as a housekeeping supervisor in Memphis, but it was a sacrifice he was willing to make to be near her mother. He hoped in time to get a promotion back into a supervisor position. Meanwhile, her mother now cared for her frail and demented grandmother, and all of them lived in her grandmother's house just outside the city limits of Jonesboro.

Alissa had dated some but never seemed to find a good Christian boy who could aspire to her values versus someone who simply wanted to bed her a few times and move on. I discovered that she was still a virgin, saving herself for the right man, the man she would commit herself to for the rest of her life. With each bit of the conversation, I found myself admiring her more.

After that day, we dated regularly for a little over a year. In that year, never once did I try to push her into giving up her virginity. I waited patiently for the time that she would willfully submit to my desires. I admit that I continued to bed other women of various sorts here and there. I couldn't seem to help myself. No matter how much I prayed for forgiveness, for God to take the sin from my heart, I continued in my secret degradation. My fascination for lipstick both taunted and haunted me. When a woman came into my presence wearing a red or burgundy lipstick, I couldn't seem to help myself. Seeing the red around her lips was as powerful as any aphrodisiac that the devil ever invented. Often my fantasies went back to the redheaded woman in my dream rising out of the silver pond water and kissing me with those burgundy lips. There were times when Wanda was in town that we would have sex again or that she would fall to her knees in the rectory and give me a quick blowjob before I went out to preach. She said it would help to relieve my nerves, and I did not offer an argument. To her, it was only sex, fun, and she didn't seem to have the remorse over it that I did. I had to make her stop doing that before services because the guilt deeply hindered my ability to deliver a meaningful sermon. It might have relieved my anxiety, but it substantially increased my guilt.

All the while I dated Alissa and kept the secret from her. None of it meant that I didn't love her or that I didn't want to have a home and family with her. It was simply something that my body demanded of me in addition to preaching the Gospel and adoring a virgin who was destined to become my wife.

Having planned it for six months ahead of time, in April of my twenty-fifth year, we married in a grand ceremony at Evangelic Temple. Pastor Woods presided over the ceremony, and we brought in family on both sides from Arkansas to stay in hotels and attend the services. Daddy didn't come, but Momma and Hannah did. He said he had to stay home to take care of the farm and the church. I really didn't care that he wasn't there. All of it was paid for by Christ Beacon Ministries at the authorization of Mr. Clayburn. I asked no questions in those days. I simply accepted the blessings that came to me in whatever form they arrived.

After the ceremony, Alissa and I flew to a resort in the Virgin Islands, where we stayed at a hotel with frosted glass French doors that opened directly onto the beach. That night, I lay down beside her in our hotel bed for the first time, naked together. We had kissed before. We had touched, caressed, and I had become aroused before with my little soldier standing at full attention at the mere anticipation of touching her, but I had never pushed her. There were times that I had masturbated after I was with her, but I had never tried to have sex with her. Somehow, to me, that seemed to be defiling her, and I never wanted to do that. She was saving her virginity for marriage, and I honored that. When the time came that she would give her virginity to me, I wanted it to be within the sanctity of our marriage.

That night in the dim light of the hotel room, I touched her naked breasts for the first time, cupped my hands around them, and rolled my thumbs over her nipples. I moved my hand down her back and felt the supple curvature of her bottom, then reached around between her legs to feel the soft padding of her womanhood. I felt exhilarated with desire. I wanted to make love to her. I wanted to touch her and be with her as I had never wanted to touch any woman before in my life, but my little soldier simply would not cooperate. The more I tried to arouse myself, the more I touched, caressed, kissed, and undulated, the more nervous I became. For the first time in my life, my little soldier lay limp in the presence of a naked woman. She smiled, touched, kissed, reached her hand to my little soldier and gently stroked along the limp exterior, wanting to make love. I knew she wanted to, and I did too, but as much as I wanted it, nothing happened.

In the time of my greatest need, the time of my utmost, heartfelt desire, my little soldier abandoned me.

"I'm sorry," I said. "I don't know what's wrong." She smiled, looked longingly into my eyes, and continued to stroke it. It felt like a doctor who was determined to revive a patient after he had already died.

"I don't know what to do," I pleaded. "I want you. Truly I do. I want you with all my heart."

"All those times we kissed before," she explained, "it stood right up without a problem, I felt it against me."

"And now that you are my wife, there is a problem," I responded. "Now that I have an opportunity to have what I have dreamed about for over a year, I can't have it. I don't know what's wrong."

"Maybe you are a little nervous," she speculated. "Maybe it is what they call the wedding night blues."

I rolled over on my back and stared at the gray ceiling. "I want to consummate our marriage, Alissa. I do. Honestly, I do." Then, I just lay there. My silence did not reveal to her the inner anguish that I felt truly unworthy of her. I felt so ashamed of my secret life, my fornication over and over again, adultery with married women, sin upon sin. I thought nothing of those women. In my mind, they were sluts and whores who deserved to be fucked, and I was the whore-monger who fucked them. I could not do that to Alissa. I could not fuck her. She was not a slut. She was pure, virgin, untouched, and worthy of so much more than me.

"It's okay," she comforted as she ran her thin fingers through the hair on my chest, "maybe later when we have rested."

"Maybe later," I said as I put my arm around her and pulled her closer to my chest. I kissed her on top of her head. "I love you so much. You know that, don't you?"

"I do know that," she replied. "You know that I love you too, no matter what."

Those words echoed in my mind, taunted me. "No matter what." I lay there staring at the ceiling, wondering if she would say that if she knew how many women I had fucked, how many I had fucked since I had been dating her, even that I had fucked one of my old standbys in the back of the church just before our wedding. Maybe that was why I couldn't get an erection on our wedding night. Maybe God was punishing me for being a whore-monger, for fornicating frivolously when I had a good, faithful Christian woman who loved me and to whom I could have turned instead. God is the only one besides myself who knows how much I wanted her that night, how much I wanted to make love to her instead of fucking all the sluts who had put themselves at my disposal. She was a gift sent to me that I had tarnished before ever opening the package. Over and over, I questioned what made me behave the way I did. I questioned what made those women surrender themselves to me, knowing full well that I was only using them, knowing that I was a hypocrite. So many times, I had been at the pulpit of Evangelic Temple looking out into the congregation and counting, as I preached God's word, the number of women I had fucked. I wondered what made them surrender to my enticements and if they were as spiritually wounded as myself. I knew for certain that no matter how much I preached the Word of the Lord, I was not living it, and neither were they.

I had not had a dream about Jesus, or the redheaded woman, since moving to Nashville. As I lay there that night in a beach front room in the Virgin Islands holding Alissa in my arms, I mentally chastised myself for my sins. Silent tears ran down my cheeks for I knew that I had forsaken God as well as my wife. I hated myself for what I had done. I hated myself that I could randomly fuck any woman who gave me the least bit of attention, especially if she wore lipstick, but I couldn't make love to the one woman I wanted most. In that silent torment, I drifted to sleep.

Before dawn I heard a moaning from outside the door toward the beach. I got up and turned to see Alissa lying there in bed, slumbering quietly. The doors rattled from a wind that blew off the ocean.

I went to the doors and opened them. The wind blew into the room, flipping back curtains, rattling lamps beside the bed in the dark room. I turned back in fear that this would wake Alissa, but she lay there sleeping peacefully and unaware. In the surf, I heard my name being called, "Ronald…Ronald…Ronald."

I walked barefoot in the warm sand to the water's edge, with full moonlight filling the night sky and playing silver light games on the black water of the sea. The waves continued to call my name as I neared the water's edge. Suddenly, a killer whale leaped from the waves in front of me then slammed back onto the surface, splashing huge streams of water into the air, over the shore, and over me. I jumped back, startled, as I heard the whale exclaim, "SINNER!" just as it disappeared back into the depths from whence it had emerged.

I heard deep wailing, a woman crying behind me. I turned to see the redheaded woman kneeling beside Jesus as he lay prostrate on the beach, his mutilated body bleeding from the piercing of swords and nails driven into his extremities. His head lay limp in her arms as she cried, "My Lord! My Lord! Why have You forsaken me?"

An overruling grief gripped me, clenched me like a rat in the talon of an eagle, and I fell to my knees weeping, "I'm so sorry! I'm so sorry! PLEASE, DEAR FATHER, FORGIVE ME! You have died for my sins!"

The redheaded woman looked up at me with a face full of vengeful rage and shouted, "MURDERER! HE DIED FOR—YOOOOOUUUUU!"

At that point, I bolted straight up in the hotel bed with a guttural scream coming up from my chest, suddenly aware that I had awakened from a dream.

Alissa was immediately jolted awake. "Ronnie! Ronnie! What's wrong?" she pleaded.

The overwhelming grief I had felt in the dream continued to grip me. I dropped my face into my hands, sobbing. "I'm sorry, Alissa! I'm so sorry! I don't want to hurt you. I don't want to hurt anyone."

"It's okay," she comforted, apparently still thinking that it was about my failures earlier in the evening. "It's just wedding night jitters."

"No, no, you don't understand," I entreated. "I am a sinner, a terrible, terrible sinner. I'm a hypocrite, a liar. I don't deserve to be a minister. I don't deserve you. You deserve so much better than me."

She reached over and flipped on the bedside lamp. Then she gently took hold of my arm. "Ronnie, look at me," she summoned.

"I can't! I can't look at you!" I pleaded, still sobbing.

"You saved my life," she gently coerced. "I don't know where my life would have been if it had not been for you. I might even be dead by now, but you healed me."

"I didn't *heal* you!" I exclaimed. "All I did was pray with you. If anyone healed you, God healed you. Your faith healed you. I didn't do anything."

"But no one else had ever prayed with me like that," she countered. "My mother had taken me everywhere trying to find someone or something that could make the pain go away. I had been to doctors, ministers, charlatans, and country witch-doctors. No one else had ever knelt down with me, touched me gently, or prayed with me, until you did on that day. No one else loved me or even wanted to touch me. No one else made me believe that I could be happy, but you did. I felt the love in your touch that day, Ronnie. I felt it. I still do."

I continued to sit there with my face buried in my hands. I was not sobbing so much, but tears continued to drip from my eyes and wet the palms of my hands.

"I've loved you ever since that day," she said quietly. "I knew one day I would find you, and I knew that if you weren't married or committed to someone else, I would do everything I could to make you mine. The truth is, I didn't move to Nashville because I was offered a job. I actively sought a job in Nashville because I knew you were there. I saw your broadcasts. I knew where you were. I came for you, Ronnie, only for you."

She placed her hand over my back and leaned her head into me. "You have no idea how much I love you," she quietly affirmed. "I have loved you from the day you first touched me when I was twelve years old. There is nothing you could ever do that would make me stop loving you."

"Yes, there is," I countered without looking up. I could not bring myself to look at her. "I do things that can make you hate me. I am a very selfish man, Alissa, and I have deceived you. I can hurt you terribly."

"Ronnie, maybe you can hurt me, but there is nothing you can do to make me stop loving you. I don't know what is tearing at your heart," she continued to affirm, "but I do know that God can heal you just like I was healed. I know that I will always love you, no matter what, and I know that with faith you can be lifted out of this."

"What if I don't have any faith?" I replied. "What if I'm just doing this to get rich and famous? Then what?"

"Is that why you preach?" she asked. "You just want to be a rich evangelist? You told me about the dreams you have had since you were a child. Is that about becoming rich and famous, or is that about serving the Lord? Ronnie, you know that you were called to serve the Lord. You know it."

"God is not happy with me," I said, moving my hands to my forehead and beginning to calm. A deep sigh came out of me.

"God is not happy with any of us," she argued. "We all have work to do. We can all be better Christians. You know as well as I do it is not about being perfect, Ronnie. It is about serving the Lord to the best of our ability."

"I just had another dream," I confessed.

"And…?"

"I was accused of murdering Jesus," I went on.

"Jesus sacrificed himself for our sins," she defended. "In that respect, you could say He committed suicide, but He didn't really die. He did it to prove that life is eternal, that we are eternal like He is. But since He died for our sins, you could say that we all murdered Him, I guess. Still He rose again."

"You don't understand," I grunted as I turned away from her.

She sat silent for a very long pause.

"All I know," she said at last, "is that God is a forgiving God, and as long as we want to do better, as long as we are trying to do better, He is going to cut us some slack."

I turned to her and kissed her on her forehead. "Go back to sleep," I said. "Show's over."

She gave me a long, confused look.

"I don't want to talk about it anymore," I said. "Let's just let it go and try to get some sleep."

She continued with her confused look a moment longer. Then she surrendered to my resistance and turned around to switch off the lamp.

We lay back down together, and I pulled her to my chest. I lay there beside her with her head resting on my chest, knowing that she couldn't understand. I had not confessed to her. She had no idea what horrible things I had done, or that I was going to do again. I had only confessed that I was a sinner and that I despised myself for it. She didn't know the sin. She had no idea that I had tried for years to make myself stop seducing women, but I couldn't. It didn't make any difference that I wanted to serve the Lord. I knew that I would sin again. I knew that some alluring woman would appear in my circles, and I would surrender to my lust. My desire to serve the Lord had never been as strong as my lust, no matter how much I wanted it to be. I had never understood how all my prayer and my need to do the right thing had never been strong enough. Maybe God had already given up on me, had given me over to my sin and considered me lost. I knew that I loved Alissa and that I wanted a life with her, but I was terrified that I was going to destroy that. At that point in my life, I felt that I had no option but to keep the secret and go on.

As was often the case, my mind reeled for a while. Alissa fell into a quiet sleep before I did, but eventually, we had both drifted into sleep again, and in the morning, as the first sunlight filtered through the frosted glass panes of the French doors, I made love to my wife for the first time. There was no foreplay. I simply rolled over on top of her with my little soldier poised and ready, a waking erection. I reached down and positioned it between her soft folds, pushed gently, and then a little more firmly. She winced and pushed her head back in pain as I felt her virginity release under the pressure of my thrust. She gripped my back momentarily and then surrendered to me. In about thirty seconds, it was over.

CHAPTER 15

Alissa and I bought a fairly nice little house in Berry Hill, which was a little town on the southwest side that had pretty much been engulfed by Nashville. I could drive to the studios from there in about fifteen minutes. I was twenty-five when we married and making enough money from the ministries that we could get a worthy house soon after we married. It was not as grand as Mr. Clayburn's home, but it was more than sufficient for us. Our home was located in a flat little neighborhood on the east side of Franklin Road, where the Civil War Battle of Nashville had been fought. It was a newer home that they called a ranch-style patterned after Frank Lloyd Wright homes, but not quite as strange as those could be. As odd as it seemed, compared to the way I had grown up, there were no porches. The house was built almost entirely of red brick, and there were manicured little boxwood hedges on either side of the tiny front landing where there was barely enough room for more than two people to stand. The white front door had a half moon window at the top and led to the east end of our living room. Just beyond the front door was a hall leading to three bedrooms on the east end of the house. The master bedroom had a half-bath with a small adjacent shower, and there was a common bath between the other two bedrooms that had pale-green tile which ran halfway up the wall around the sink and commode, then all the way to the ceiling, behind the bathtub and shower. On the west side of the living room, an arch led to the dining room, and from there, a door led to our long galley-style kitchen. On the west side of the kitchen was a door leading to a large two-car attached garage. On the east end of the kitchen, an arch led to a paneled den that had a brick fireplace on the north end of the room and a door on the south end that led back to the living room near the hallway. On the north end of the kitchen, French-style doors led down some steps to a large brick patio area. There was also a door from the den on the north end that accessed the patio as well. There was no porch to be seen on either side of the house, no cover from the rain where one might lounge in the dry during a warm summer rain and watch gentle raindrops pelting flowers. Yet it was the nicest home I had ever lived in, and I was too busy to make use of a porch anyway.

My life had become completely different. I spent about thirty hours a week at the studio preparing for two weekly broadcasts of *The Church Down the Road.* About once a month I served as a guest minister at Evangelic Temple. By that time, five years into developing myself as a broadcast minister, I was getting frequent invitations for speaking engagements all across the country. I began to learn of the business aspects of the ministry by meeting with public relations people and marketers who would promote the engagements that Mr. Clayburn arranged for me. We soon had to move from booking engagements at churches to booking auditoriums in large cities, where crowds were beginning to gather in excess of two thousand or more. The marketers would put up billboards showing flashy pictures of me and would send press releases to broadcast media in the region. My popularity really took off around 1969. In the meantime, we were building the ministry bit by bit.

Alissa quit her job at the recording studio and came to work as a secretary for Christ Beacon Ministries. Since she was employed as my personal secretary, this meant that she often could tour with me. However, more often, she preferred to stay home. She enjoyed the house, and with the exception of occasionally hiring someone to come in to clean or help with a large meal, Alissa preferred to take care of it herself. She continued this even as we became well beyond financially able to hire a full-time housekeeper.

The ministry bought a bus for me to use when I was doing an engagement out of town. It was essentially a converted Greyhound bus. They borrowed the idea from country music stars, who practically lived in their tour busses more than they lived at home. The bus had a bedroom in the back with a full-size bed and adjacent bathroom. There was a little kitchenette and a small lounge area in the middle, and there was an overhead compartment that had a small bed where the driver would sleep. However, much of the time he drove straight through from one city to the other and slept when I was delivering services. The rest of us slept while he was driving. Generally, it was just me, the driver, and Alissa on the bus, but often Alissa would stay home because she really didn't like traveling all that much, especially as it was business and not a pleasure trip.

There were times when we would have revivals or engagements in five or six different cities over the course of several weeks before we came home. We might start in Atlanta, go from there to New Orleans, from New Orleans to Houston, then to Dallas, to Oklahoma City, Kansas City, St. Louis, and then back to Nashville. I gave basically the same sermon in every city and ended it all by having people line up to come to the front for prayer and to have hands laid on them for healing. When it became evident that so many people were coming to the front after the preaching that it would take the rest of the night to get to them all, our employees began screening those who were allowed to come for prayer and those who were not. Only about twenty people were allowed to come on stage at the end of the service for healing prayer, and that would require about another hour added onto the evening to complete the whole service. My heart sank as I began to realize that there were so many people wanting prayer and healing who would never be allowed to come to the stage. On the other hand, I had to preserve myself and my energy or I would not be able to make the next city on the following day. I began to have a prayer for all at the end of each service. I reached out my hands over the audience and said what came to my mind. "There is someone here tonight who is grieving the loss of a dear loved one who recently passed of a terrible illness. God wants you to know that your. . .husband. . .and. . . someone else has a daughter who recently passed. . .the Lord wants you to know that your loved one is safe with Him in Heaven tonight and He wants you to be comforted. There is someone here tonight who recently got a diagnosis of…cancer…I see a terrible malignant growth. We are praying for you, sister. The Almighty power of the Lord is dissolving that growth. The Lord wants you to surrender the anger and hurt you have felt that has become stagnant within you. The Lord wants you to know that you can let go, release all that hurt and anguish, and your tumor will be healed!"

There were times I heard cries and wails from the audience, and times I heard shouts of AMEN or PRAISE THE LORD! There were times I heard someone speaking in tongues, and I knew I was reaching people. I knew these prayers and services were making a difference in their lives, and they were exceedingly generous in return. In addition to the funds that came in through the mail as a result of the television broadcast, there were large amounts taken in the offering at these services. We also sold autographed Bibles and other merchandise before and after services. I paid little attention to that. I did the service, then went back to the bus or to my hotel room to rest. I didn't worry about the money. I received a very abundant compensation from the ministry, more than I had ever had in my life and more than anyone in my family had ever had. I was satisfied with that.

Christ Beacon did not charge people to get into the revivals but had offering plates at the door where people entering and leaving were encouraged to make offerings. Then, the plates were passed around during the service as well. Part of my job was to stir people into a fervor of giving. The scriptures were ripe with verses that enticed people to open their coffers and render unto the Lord. Who knows how much some people would give at the revivals or in monthly donations? I had no idea how much money was coming into the ministry, but I knew that Mr. Clayburn never seemed to want for money, nor did I. I was well cared for and so didn't concern myself with it, but it was on a morning in 1963 that Alissa brought something to my attention.

It was a Saturday morning in June. The weather lingered in the upper seventies and low eighties. Blue skies filled with sunlight, and early summer breezes gently pushed soft white clouds past the windows. I had gotten up late and had initially risen to the sounds of Alissa clinking around in the kitchen preparing breakfast. The smell of hickory smoked bacon and fresh coffee enticed me to separate from the pillow that had begged my head to stay. Alissa had bacon and eggs, toast, and coffee ready to serve at the little breakfast nook between our kitchen and the garage door. Even my breakfast had changed. Unless we made a trip home, I never got the taste of Momma's pork chops with milk gravy and biscuits. Sometimes I craved that, but I didn't mind too much. I had a good life.

We had a small table in the nook which jutted up beneath a window overlooking the backyard. A bird feeder on the other side of the patio made for a pleasant view. I staggered into the kitchen, gently kissed Alissa on the back of the neck as she stood at the stove, and said, "Good morning, sweetheart." From there, I wavered across the room to sit at the breakfast nook table. I took a wakeup breath, pushed my hands up over the top of my head, and looked out the window at the pristine day and my beautiful tree-lined backyard. A couple of cardinals munched at the feeder. "Beautiful this morning," I said as I stared across the yard.

"It is, isn't it?" she replied and then set a cup of coffee on the table in front of me.

I had barely taken my first sip of coffee when she placed a plate full of food on the table and sat across from me with her own plate. "How was your tour?" she asked as she nibbled a piece of bacon held daintily between two fingers.

I had gotten in after midnight the evening before. The bus driver dropped me off on his way home, and I had managed to snuggle into the bed with Alissa an hour or so after that. When I had spooned up next to her, she grabbed my arm, pulled it around her, and softly said, "I'm glad you're home."

I watched her nibbling the bacon and didn't really have an answer as the tours seemed often very much the same. "It was all right," I quipped and reached for my coffee. "How were things at home?"

"Well, you know…different," she said as she stared at me rather intently.

"Different?" I questioned?

"Yeah, different," she responded. "And I think we need to talk about it."

"Is something wrong?" I asked.

"Well, let's just say there is nothing out of the ordinary, but yes… something is wrong."

"What?" I questioned.

"Ronnie, I normally go over to Christ Beacon to work when you are gone." She placed the half-eaten strip of bacon back on her plate. "But this time, one of the women who deals with the correspondence and counting donations had called in sick. So I offered to help."

"Yes?"

"Well, it was an interesting experience." She held her coffee in both hands just in front of her face.

"Interesting?"

"Yes," she responded. "Let's just say I learned something."

"What did you learn?"

She took a sip of her coffee, placed it back on the table, and folded her fingers together in front of her as she leaned her elbows on the table.

"Ronnie, do you have any idea how much money you are bringing into Christ Beacon?"

"No," I replied. "I never thought about it."

"Well, yesterday, between checks and cash, I counted just over twenty thousand dollars."

I stopped eating with a dead stare at her, scarcely believing what I had just heard. Finally, I spoke. "It must have been a bountiful and unusual day."

"Yes, you might think that," she pondered softly. "But I asked one of the other women in donations, and she said they have that much—usually more—coming in most days. She said it is a slim and rare day when they take in fifteen thousand, and, Ronnie, you are generating the vast bulk of it."

"Wonderful!" I responded. "I am glad that I can bring blessings."

"Are you thinking about this?" she curtly asked.

"I have not given it much thought." I stabbed my fork into the eggs for another bite.

"That means the ministry is bringing in about eight to ten million dollars a year, Ronnie." She sighed, and leaned over the table. "How much are you getting?"

"I get around forty thousand a year," I replied. "And they are paying you another ten thousand a year. We are living very well."

"Out of eight to ten million?" she asked. "Tax-free?"

"Well, there are expenses. There are several employees, public relations people, marketing. It is not all profit."

"Yes, I have thought about the expenses," she replied. "I thought even more about the expenses at the end of the day when Mr. Clayburn came in, put all the cash in a bag, and told me to prepare the checks for deposit in the bank account."

"Oh?"

"Yes—oh."

She continued. "I asked him, 'What are you going to be doing with the cash?' and he said, 'Don't worry about it. I always take care of the cash.' Ronnie, more than half of all we received for the day was cash. Mr. Clayburn walked away with about ten or fifteen thousand dollars in cash for one day. Where did it go?"

"Well, I am sure there is good reason," I still defended even though my mind was reeling with scenarios that did not seem appropriate.

"I asked one of the other women in the office about it, and she told me he does that every day." Alissa shoved her plate to the side. "Ronnie, where is that money going?"

"I...I don't know."

"Don't you think that is something we need to ask?" she pressed.

The idea of a conflict with Mr. Clayburn did not sit well with me. After all, if it had not been for him, I would still have been a backwoods preacher in Arkansas. It would have been easier for me to continue with the forty thousand a year I was getting, which was an extremely good living in 1963, than to bring myself to face him, but Alissa didn't see it the same way.

"Honey, I'm sure there is a good reason for it," I pleaded, hoping more than anything to avoid any conflict. "He probably has other accounts and pays different expenses out of those."

"And how much does he take for himself out of what gets deposited into the accounts in addition to the cash he carries off? All of it generated by your ministry."

She interrogated me as though I were a hostile witness in a court case.

"Look at his lifestyle compared to ours and ask yourself if he is not supporting himself extremely well on your back. The Clayburns have a six-bedroom house in Belle Meade now. What's that house worth, Ronnie—a quarter million or more?"

"Well, I am not the only source of income," I continued. "There are still radio broadcasters, and he is looking into setting up other television ministers."

"Yes," she responded. "You are not the only source of income, but you are the source of 90 percent or more of the income. Ronnie, every letter but one that I opened the other day was addressed to you. Twenty thousand dollars in donations was addressed to you, and that does not include what was taken in from your tours. Think about that. There were probably about two thousand people or more at each of your engagements over the last few weeks. They were cajoled to donate when they came to the event, and then the plate was passed around for further donations, and they were hit up for donations again when they left. Then, there were Bibles and trinkets sold after the services. People bought Bibles simply because they had your name on them. They bought plain handkerchiefs at a grossly inflated price because you had prayed over them. You toured five cities in the last three weeks. You probably brought in at least twenty or thirty thousand dollars in less than a month just from touring. How many engagements do you speak at in a year?"

"Last year I did twenty engagements," I responded.

"So eighty thousand dollars in addition to the twenty thousand dollars a day in mailed donations," she demanded. "The tours alone more than pay your salary and mine with money left over—and Mr. Clayburn is walking away with almost four million dollars a year free and clear with no taxes."

My face drained of blood. I felt nauseated, blank, and unresponsive.

"We need to get a lawyer," she said.

I knew she was right, but my loyalty to Mr. Clayburn still nagged at me. If it had not been for him and for Wanda, I would not have had the wealth that I already enjoyed. My home was upper middle class, and by comparison to how I was raised, it might as well have been Buckingham Palace. My heart said, "Accept what you have, and be grateful for it," but my mind told me Alissa was right. I was being grossly cheated.

"So if we get a lawyer," I asked, "then what? Do we force Mr. Clayburn to give us more? Do we force him to account for the cash that he has walked away with for the last six years? It wasn't always this much. There was a time when the ministry paid for everything. They got me an apartment, fed me, brought me from Arkansas, and gave me an opportunity when I was making nothing for them."

"And now they are using you," she said quietly. She caught herself. "No...they are not using you. Clayburn is using you."

"What do you want me to do?" I asked and pushed my chair back away from the table.

"Well, first we need to talk to an attorney and force an audit," she replied. "Although I doubt there will be any trace to be found of the four million a year in cash that he has been embezzling for the past three or four years."

"Alissa, I signed contracts," I pleaded. "I may be bound to things the way they are."

"Did you sign a contract that said Clayburn could waltz away with ten or fifteen thousand dollars every day?" she asked.

"No—I don't know." I got up and began to pace the kitchen. "I don't know what I signed. I was young and stupid."

"Well, no matter how young and stupid you were," she continued, "I seriously doubt that you signed anything that allowed him to walk away with half of your income every day while you get a miniscule percentage of it."

"I'm sure there has to be some explanation for it," I summoned.

"What?"

"I don't know." I paced in my pajamas, racking my brain to think about things I might have taken for granted. "Charities, struggling churches, widow's funds, aid for families in poverty."

"Where is the proof of that?" she asked. "Is that really something they would keep a secret?"

"Well, I know we do good works," I assured her.

"Ronnie, have you ever read any of those letters that come in with donations?" she asked.

"No, I never thought about reading them."

"Please sit down." She motioned toward my chair. "You're making me nervous."

I sat down, leaned to the back of the chair, and looked at her.

"Ronnie, you should read those letters," she expressed. "For one thing, almost all of them are asking for prayer, and I don't know that a prayer is ever said for any of those people."

"I pray for them every week during my broadcast and bless them for their donations!" I countered with defensiveness and irritability. She did not respond to my plea.

"Their money is just taken. For another thing, there are people who are obviously sending money as donations of faith that would be better spent on food, shelter, or the care of their children. A lot of those people are exceedingly poor."

"Well, I know they are not all wealthy," I continued to defend. "But I seriously doubt that they are destitute."

"I didn't really read everything that came through the day I opened envelopes," she quietly affirmed. "But I glanced over several of them, and I think you might be surprised how often very poor people send money to you."

"Well, if someone is poor and they send money, it is an act of faith," I countered. "Their faith alone blesses them. God will prosper them for their faith."

"I'm sure you are right," she said.

She got up from her chair and walked through the kitchen into the den. She picked up an envelope from the table just inside the den door and returned with it in hand. She sat back down and held the envelope under the table. "There is just one letter I would like you to read," she continued. "It is the only letter that I opened which was not addressed to Pastor Ronald Dennison and the only one I read all the way through."

"Okay—"

She pulled the letter from beneath the table and slid it across to me. I didn't look at how it was addressed or at the return address. I simply pulled it from the envelope. The letter was written on school notebook paper and two one-dollar bills were paper clipped to the letter. It was carefully written with pencil in the old-fashioned Palmer method. I set the dollars on the table and began to read.

June 5, 1963

Dear Christ Beacon Ministries,

As always, I implore you not to show my letters to Pastor Dennison. I do not want him to know that I am sending money. I watch him every week on television, but we can't afford one of our own. I go to a neighbor's house to watch The Church Down the Road, and once in a while I am lucky enough to catch a broadcast of the Evangelic Temple services. I am so grateful that you have given Ronnie Dennison this opportunity to answer his calling and speak the true Word of the Lord.

I have often worried about him, but when I see his weekly broadcast, I know that he is all right and that he is blessed and blessing others. As I have said before, he has wanted to preach since he was a child, and I am so grateful to see him fulfilling his destiny.

If I could, I would give him the whole world, because I know in my heart that he deserves all the blessings of the world. Instead, I just want to do my own little part to sustain his ministry and help him along. I wish I could afford more, but my husband and I struggle to make ends meet now that we no longer have our children to help us on the farm. My husband is in ill health, and so we have had to cut back on many of the farm activities that once brought us a decent living.

I hope that I can continue to send my $2.00 a week to support the ministry even though it is sometimes a struggle to have the extra money. Still, I know that the money will help to keep the poor ministry going. As Pastor Dennison says each week, he blesses us that we may bless his ministry and help keep the lights on and the TV show going so that lost souls can be saved. This ministry is such a blessing to the world. I just pray that I can keep doing my part to keep it from going under.

If there is anything else that I can do to help, please do not hesitate to write me and let me know.

Yours in Christ's love,
Marylee Dennison

Tears had begun to roll down my cheeks before I ever finished the letter. By the time I had finished the first paragraph, I knew who had written it. Before I finished reading it, I could barely see through blurring tears, but I wiped my eyes on my pajama sleeves and continued. When I read the last line, I looked up to see Alissa staring at me with sadness.

"I can't…I—" Sobs came out of me, and I could say no more. I held the letter in one hand over my knee and pushed my face into the crook of my other elbow on the table. All the combined guilt I had ever felt over seducing women was nothing compared to what I felt in that moment. I had been so busy with everything that I had scarcely given thought to Momma and Daddy or how life might have changed for them since I had been gone.

I don't know how long I cried, but when I stopped, I looked up to see Alissa still sitting there quietly looking at me. She had not tried to comfort me, had not attempted to ease the pain, and somehow knew that

I needed to feel the full extent of it without a hug or justification for what I was feeling. When I finally looked up, she quietly asked, "What do you want to do?"

"How soon can you pack?" I asked in reply.

"Anytime." She half smiled and knew what I was thinking.

"Pack for a couple of days," I said. "We're going to Arkansas."

Within thirty minutes, we had both packed enough for a couple of days away. We had learned from tours and vacations to keep duplicates of things like toiletries in separate bags so all we had to do was put them in a suitcase and go rather than running around the house trying to think of what we might have overlooked. It was easy enough to just throw some clothes in the suitcases with the toiletry bags and walk out the door. By 1:00 p.m., we were on our way to Arkansas.

On the way, we talked about several things, not only how I would approach Momma with the knowledge of her letters, but how we would deal with Mr. Clayburn when we got back. We mulled over the ideas of attorneys and other legal options for the ministry, and by the time we reached the Mississippi Bridge on the other side of Dyersburg, Tennessee, we were settled on what we were going to do.

By the time we got to the Black River Motor Inn, got a room and supper, it was nearing 6:30 p.m. We got to Momma and Daddy's house by 7:00 p.m. The dim light of dusk still stretched across the summer land, and the sun was about to hide behind the trees on the other side of our barn. It was still light enough that Momma was sitting on the front porch hulling Crowder peas. When I pulled my new white Cadillac Coup Deville up in the front yard and we got out, she looked up, and her eyes gleamed like she had just seen Jesus. "Oh, gracious Lord of mercy!" she shouted. She could barely get her pea pan set aside quickly enough and almost spilled the whole thing trying to get it out of the way so she could come give me a hug. She trotted over and enfolded me in her arms with a bear hug that would have made a grizzly proud.

"Momma, you would think I was a pot of gold," I spouted back to her as she hugged me and rocked me back and forth.

She stepped back, grabbed my cheeks with both hands, and kissed me on the forehead. "You are better than a pot of gold to me, dear boy!" she gleamed. She then turned, reached out her arms to Alissa, and said, "Come here, darlin'!"

Alissa obliged, and Momma hugged her just as much.

"Oh my goodness," Momma exclaimed as she stepped back from Alissa and held her shoulders. "You get more beautiful every day, sweetheart."

"Marylee, you have always been the kindest person." Alissa smiled.

"Oh my goodness," Momma exclaimed again, looking back and forth between us. "Have you kids had supper?"

"Yes, Momma," I replied. "We ate back in Pocahontas when we stopped to check in at the Motor Inn."

"Check in at a motel?" Momma chastised. "You know you have a room here. Why would you go wasting your money on motel?"

After I left, Hannah gave up the cot in Momma and Daddy's room and slept in the bed that Teddy and I once shared till she graduated high school. She had married a local boy just a little over a year after I got married and became Mrs. Hannah Cochran. Then she and her new husband moved about an hour and a half away from Momma and Daddy to Kennett, Missouri, where her husband, Drake, got a job on a dairy farm. I knew my old room was empty but didn't want to stay there.

"Momma, we just don't want to put you out," I answered. "Besides, we have gotten very comfortable with motel rooms over the last few years."

"Oh, for goodness' sakes," she chided. "You know you are not going to put me out. There is nothing I would love more than taking care of my boy and his beautiful bride. Speaking of beautiful bride." She eyed Alissa up and down. "Am I ever gonna get any grandkids outta you two? Now grandbabies are little somebodies I'd like to take care of."

Hannah had already given her a grandson just a year into her marriage, and I had been married to Alissa for almost four years at that point, with no sign that we were ever going to conceive.

"You mean spoil, don't you, Momma?"

"That too." She grinned. "Come on in the house and sit a spell. It is getting nigh onto darkness out here." She turned without waiting for an answer to her question and motioned us to follow. She began gathering up her pans and buckets of peas from the porch.

"Aren't you going to finish hulling your peas?" I asked. "Alissa and I can help you finish."

"Oh, no, don't worry about that," she replied. "I'll finish that up in the morning."

Daddy had already twisted on the overhead light in the living room, and a dull golden light was filtering through the window and door screens. Momma went in first, and I held the door as she carried her pans straight through the living room to the kitchen. Daddy was sitting in his chair, which had been pulled over by the flue, and was reading his Bible. The potbellied heating stove had been taken down for the summer and stored in the shed.

"Hello, Daddy," I said as we came into the room and sat on the sofa.

He didn't even bother to adjust the reading glasses on his nose, much less look up from the Good Book. "Hello, son," he grunted. Then, a moment later, "Hello, Alissa."

Momma stuck her head in from the kitchen and asked, "Can I get you something to drink…a glass of sweet tea, maybe?"

"A glass of tea sounds good to me, Momma."

"I'll have one too," Alissa parroted as she got up and went into the kitchen.

In those days, it was common for any woman as a guest in the house, especially family, to go into the kitchen to help another woman who might be there.

When Alissa had left the room, I looked over at Daddy and asked, "How have you been? Everything going all right?"

"Been fine," he said, still not looking up.

"Well," I went on. "How's farming?"

"The farm's fine."

"Been doing any milking lately?" I continued.

He irritably closed his Bible and held his finger in the place where he had been reading. Then he looked up at me with a snarled look on his face. "What do you want?" he said.

"I'm just trying to have a conversation with my daddy," I replied. "It has been a long time."

"Yes, it has been a long time," he continued. "Too long to try to make small talk."

"Well, do you want to make big talk?" I laughed nervously.

He glared at me, reopened his Bible, and stared into it again as though I had said nothing to him.

Alissa returned from the kitchen, handed me a glass of tea, and sat beside me with her own glass cupped in both hands. Momma sat in a chair adjacent to the sofa with her own glass of tea.

I took a big swig of my tea and commented, "Nobody can make sweet tea as good as you, Momma."

"It's an old family recipe—sugar, water, and tea." She laughed.

"Nice and cold too," I went on. "Sure makes it better than when we had to lower a jar into the spring to get some cool tea in summer."

"You never know how blessed you are till you get something better." Momma smiled. "It's nice to have a real refrigerator instead of that old icebox."

"I'm glad you have something nicer," I said.

Daddy grunted.

"You should have nice things," I went on. "You deserve nice things, Momma."

"Well, we are blessed enough," she responded.

"I wonder, Momma," I said as I reached into my shirt pocket to pull out the letter Alissa had shown me earlier in the day. I handed the letter to her with the two dollars placed back in it and waited.

As soon as she took the letter from my hand, she knew. A flush of embarrassment ran over her face, and she kept looking up and down between me, Daddy, and the letter that she now held.

"You were never supposed to see this," she finally said timidly.

"Well, I wouldn't have seen it if Alissa had not been the one opening letters that day," I said.

"What is it?" Daddy asked, suddenly interested and looking up from his Bible.

"Oh, it's nothing," Momma said. "It's not important."

Daddy closed his Bible, set it on the table beside him, and came across the room to stand over Momma.

"It's not important, but it's enough for Ronnie to drive all the way from Nashville with it?" he growled.

Momma sat looking up at him like a scolded child.

"Give it to me," he said, reaching out his hand.

Momma handed him the letter and then whispered to me as though Daddy couldn't hear. "You're gonna get me in trouble."

When he finished, he folded the letter up, put it back in the envelope, and handed it back to her. "I knew that boy didn't drive all the way over here without a hint of nothing just to visit family. You see that fancy car he drives out there?" Daddy scolded. "You think, if he can afford that, he needs two dollars a week from you?"

Momma said nothing. The truth is, when compared, the two dollars a week she was sending back then would be the equivalent to about fifteen dollars now, and the fifty thousand dollars a year that Alissa and I brought in would be equivalent to almost half a million today.

Momma looked at Daddy for a moment and then over at me. The shame on her face was palpable, not because she had done anything wrong, but because she had disappointed Daddy and me. She dropped her head and said, "I'm sorry."

"Momma, you didn't do anything wrong," I comforted. "God bless your giving heart, but we don't need the money, and the ministry does not need money that would take food out of anybody's mouth."

"Well, we eat," Momma defended. "I still have a garden, and we still have a few chickens and a pig to butcher now and then."

"But we didn't get the electric bill paid on time last month, did we?" Daddy said, still standing over her. "We are scraping to pay bills, and you go sending off money to people who are richer than Solomon!"

"Daddy, I'll be happy to pay the electric bill or any other bill you need paid," I offered.

He glared at me and said, "You shut up! We don't need you! We don't need charity, and we, for sure, don't need your scamming ways!"

"I just wanted to support Ronnie in his ministry," Momma pleaded.

I was about to tell her that her love was all the support I needed when Daddy turned on me with an accusing finger pointing in my face. "This is your fault!" He raised his voice. "You get on that television and trick people into thinking that you are poor, and they should send you their *'faith'* money! You take food out of the mouths of the poor so you can drive around in some fancy car and live some fancy lifestyle! Do you honestly think that God is not going to judge you for this?" He turned and walked back to the other side of the room. Before he got back to his chair, he turned around, pointed his finger at me again, and quoted Matthew 24:11, "And many false prophets shall rise and shall deceive many!"

I stood. "Daddy, I am not a false prophet. My heart is with serving the Lord."

"And you think what you are doing is serving the Lord?" he scolded. "Bible says you shall know them by their works. You think the Lord wants you to steal from the poor so you can make yourself rich? You think the Lord wants you to deceive people into thinking they are doing God's will by lining your pockets?"

"I don't want anybody to be poor, Daddy. I try to teach people principles of faith and prosperity. But seek ye first the Kingdom of God and His righteousness and all these things shall be added unto you."

He reached over to his table and picked up his Bible. He pointed the Bible toward me. "HOW DARE YOU PREACH AT ME!" he shouted.

"STOP IT!" Momma screamed at him. "STOP IT, PAUL!"

She rose from her chair, wringing her apron in her hands, and walked toward Daddy. "Your son has come home," she pleaded to him. "He didn't come home for judgment or condemnation. He came home to do what he thought was the right thing. He came home to bring just two dollars back to me because he knew we needed it. Sit down, please—both of you—just sit down, now."

We both did as Momma asked, and after a long silence, I said, "Daddy, you may not believe me, but I truly do want to serve the Lord. I truly do want to do the right thing. Alissa brought all this to my attention. She worked last week processing donations, and that's when she came across Momma's letter. She also noticed that a good many of the donations coming in were from very poor people and that Mr. Clayburn was walking away, every day, with huge amounts of cash that went unaccounted for."

Daddy sat there staring at me and said nothing.

I continued. "When I go back, things are going to be different. For one thing, I am going to separate myself from Christ Beacon Ministries. After that, I don't know. I expect that I will be starting my own ministry. I don't know if I will still be doing broadcasting or asking for donations, but if I do, I will be turning a large amount of those donations back to Christian charities to assist people in need, and I will *not* be pleading that our ministry is poor and broke."

"*Well…good for you,*" Daddy said sarcastically.

"Daddy, I know you don't approve of what I'm doing," I went on. "But I really do want to help people. The first people I would like to help are you and Momma."

"We don't *need* your help!" Daddy reacted. "We don't want your sin money."

"It may be sin money now," I pleaded, "but when I go back, it is not going to be sin money. I am going to change how everything is done. Please, Daddy. I can build you and Momma a nice new house. I can make sure your bills are paid."

"And how many of God's beloved will go without so you can make sure we have a nice new house and our bills are paid?" he asked. "How long will you rob Peter to pay Paul?"

"When I go back, there will be no robbing Peter to pay Paul," I responded. "It will be different."

"No, it won't," Daddy demanded. "It will be the same turd wrapped in a different pretty package. It might be a different box and different wrapping paper, but it will be the very same turd."

Alissa had been silent through all this. At last she reached her hand over and placed it on my arm. "We should probably head back to the motel," she said softly.

"Noooooo, please stay," Momma suddenly pleaded. "Ronnie's old room is available, the bed is made. The sheets are clean. You don't have to drive all the way back to Pocahontas when you could sleep right here."

"Alissa is right, Momma." I moved over to her and took her hand. "We should go, but why don't you walk us to the car."

Momma stood and had sadness in her eyes because our brief visit had been one of turmoil.

"We will see you tomorrow before we go back to Nashville," I comforted.

"Oh, you are going back tomorrow?" Her voice practically trembled. She reached a hand up to the side of my face. "But I haven't seen you in so long, son. I thought maybe you might be able to come and stay a little while."

"Momma, we will visit tomorrow," I said as I reached up to take her hand from my face and clasp it in mine. "Come on now. Walk me to the car."

The three of us turned toward the front door. As we got to the door, I turned back and said, "Bye, Daddy."

He said nothing but simply reached for his Bible and opened it again. I had long since learned to just let it go and walk away. I had long ago accepted that I was never going to get the father's love that I wanted and needed. I only hoped one day that I might be able to give to a son of my own what had been withheld from me.

The three of us went on to the car, and when we got there, I turned and took Momma's hand.

"Momma," I said urgently. "If you need anything, anything at all, you let me know, and stop sending money to me or to Christ Beacon. From now on, I'm going to be sending money to you."

The front porch light spread a dim glow across the new darkness of evening and was just enough light to see each other as we stood by the car.

"You know your daddy is not going to let me accept that," she countered. "He gets the mail. He will know."

"Don't worry about it," I said. "I will open a bank account in your name at Imboden then make monthly deposits to it. Whenever you need anything, you just get somebody to take you over there and draw out what you need. Daddy doesn't ever have to know anything about it."

"I'm so sorry, Ronnie," she atoned. "I just wanted to support your ministry. I am so sorry about your daddy's attitude. You know he loves you. You know he does."

"I know, Momma," I lied. "Now, one more thing."

I took her hand, reached into my pocket, and took out a fold of five crisp new one-hundred-dollar bills. I placed it in her hand and folded her fingers over it. She opened her hand to look at what I had given her and obviously recognized what it was even in the dim light.

"Huhuh!" she gasped. "Ronnie, it is too much!"

"No, it isn't, Momma," I argued. "It isn't enough. There is no amount of money worth all the love, support, understanding, and encouragement you have given me all of my life. Now, you take it. Hide it somewhere that Daddy can't find it, and use what you need when you need it. In the meantime, I am going to get that bank account set up for you."

Tears rolled down her face. "You are the sweetest child any mother could hope to have." She smiled.

"Goodbye, Momma," I said as I turned toward the car door. "I'll stop by to see you tomorrow."

"But aren't you going to come to church in the morning?" she petitioned. "I know everyone would love to see you."

"No, Momma," I said, "and that's exactly why. Everyone would be treating me like a big TV star and would pay little or no attention to Daddy's sermon. I'm sure he has a wonderful message to share with them tomorrow, and I wouldn't want to do anything to detract from that."

"Well, they will be so disappointed they didn't get to see you," she begged.

"I know, Momma. It's just best this way." I opened the door to the car, and Alissa got in on the other side. "We'll come have Sunday dinner with you after church tomorrow," I said. "You making some good fried chicken?"

"Absolutely!" she said.

I got in the car, and we went back to the hotel. We talked about Daddy's reaction. We talked about how we might be able to restructure my ministry when we got back to Nashville, and we talked about the changes this was going to require in our lifestyles. Essentially, we would be almost starting over.

The next day we went back to the house and had dinner with Momma and Daddy. It was a little tense, but Daddy didn't act up anymore. The conversation was trivial and mundane, as one might expect from the musings of a country life. Alissa and I had made a pact, and kept to it, that we would not discuss anything to do with the ministry. We talked about our house, that we had been thinking about getting a dog, and we talked about perhaps one day giving Momma the grandbaby she had wanted. The truth be told, Alissa simply had not gotten pregnant. We had made no efforts at all to prevent a pregnancy. It simply had not occurred. We only stayed a couple of hours, and by 2:00 p.m., we were headed back to Nashville. We were no more than about five minutes outside Ravenden when I said to Alissa, "You know, I'm really scared about all this."

"Any big change is scary," she replied.

With my hands firmly on the steering wheel watching the green Arkansas hills roll down into the flatlands, I said, "This is a real leap of faith. What do you think is going to happen?"

She took a deep breath, turned toward me in the seat and said, "You know, I watched this show one time about parachuting. Those guys jump out of a plane, who knows how high up in the sky. When they jump, they have to trust that the parachute will open. First, they have to make sure that it is packed just right. They have to trust themselves that they didn't make a mistake when they packed it, and they have to trust that all the mechanisms will work for the chute to open. Then they just jump. That's it—they just jump. When they do, the first thing that happens is gravity grabs them, and they plummet toward the earth like a rock off a cliff. But then they time themselves, and at the right moment, they pull the cord. From there they just float the rest of the way down to their destination. Sometimes they hit the mark. Sometimes they are off a little. Sometimes they can be way off, but it is a rare event that they don't at least reach the ground safely."

"So what are you saying?" I asked.

"You can't figure out what I'm saying?" She giggled.

"Just jump," I affirmed.

"First, we carefully pack our chute," she went on, "and then, yes—we just jump."

"And pray the wind will catch our chute," I stated.

"No," she corrected, "and *KNOW* the wind will catch our chute."

"You know, it's amazing," I mused, "that after all these years as a pastor, all my study of the Bible, having my way guided clearly by the Lord over and over again, I still catch myself having doubts."

"Trust is a valuable commodity," she responded. "And faith is like trust in overdrive because faith is of things unseen. Trust is based on things we see, things we know, but faith is based on what we can't see and what we don't know for sure, but we make ourselves *know* that it will all work out as it should."

"I know you're right," I said. "So we go back to Nashville, pack our chute, and then…we jump."

"Yes," she said. "We just have to keep in mind that for every leap of faith, there is a period of blind free fall in which you have no idea if your chute will open."

"Arrrrgggggghhhhhhh!" I exclaimed while beating my flat palms against the top of the steering wheel. "All right then…here we go!"

CHAPTER 16

On the way home from Arkansas, Alissa and I considered all the possible ways that we might go about confronting Mr. Clayburn and what possible consequences each approach might have. Since Clayburn's actions could be criminal, we decided that we would hire an attorney who might negotiate a settlement for us without having to make a public exposure or take matters to court. On a hot, muggy August day in 1963, I came home from the studio broadcast to find three women sitting with Alissa in our living room sipping sweet tea over ice.

When I initially came into the kitchen through the garage door, I heard Alissa call out, "Oh good, Ronnie, you're home. We're in the living room."

I set my things on the breakfast nook table, and came into the living room to see our office director, Clara Smith, as well as two other women from the office. When I came into the room, they stood up as if a dignitary had entered.

"Sit. Sit," I commanded. "We're family here."

The women sat back down, and Alissa said, "I'll get you some tea, dear," as she headed for the kitchen. I loosened my tie and sat in a chair by the front window, while two of the women sat on the sofa, and Miss Smith sat in an adjacent side chair. Alissa returned quickly with my tea and sat in the other side chair across from Miss Smith.

Over time, Alissa had gotten to know the women in the office quite well and knew that several of them held a particular disdain for Mr. Clayburn. I knew these women as well but mostly through just a passing hello or an occasional inter-office giggle. Alissa had spent considerably more time with them and had a better understanding of their complaints. Even though she was sort of the boss's wife, several women had opened up to her and liked her, perhaps because she did not hesitate to advocate for them. I knew immediately what the meeting was about but asked anyway, "Well, ladies, how can I help you this fine afternoon?"

"Pastor." Miss Smith spoke for everyone. "We want to go with you. If you leave Christ Beacon, we want to go with you."

Clara Smith had intrigued me but never really in a sexual way. In her late forties, she managed our offices with the precision of a military commander, although her deep country drawl would make you think of her as a bumpkin. She seemed to take everything in stride and was never offended or nonplussed by anything. She had never married, for what reason, I didn't know. I had never pried to ask. Her appearance was always perfect with permed hair and classic women's business attire. Her one vice, I suppose, was her glasses. You never knew what style she might wear, and she had to spend a considerable amount of her income collecting multiple different frames. Each day, she would wear a different pair plopped over her tiny pointed nose and must have owned fifteen or twenty pairs, at least. I suppose, if her prescription changed, she just had the lenses changed on her existing frames. On that particular day, she wore a pair of lime-green cat eyes with a faux-pearl embedded in the outer tip on either side. She had an eyeglass chain made of tiny white faux pearls. That's the other thing. She probably had a larger variety of eyeglass chains than she had glasses. I never realized until that day just how loyal she had been to me.

"Thank you, Clara," I replied. "I'm honored."

Alissa spoke up, "Over the past week, Clara and I have been talking, and I think most of the staff is uncomfortable with how things have been going and would go with us if we were to venture out and start our own ministry."

Clara shifted slightly in her chair to face me. "Pastor, I have never been a fan of Mr. Clayburn, and I began noticing problems when I first went to work there four years ago. However, I have been afraid to say anything about it."

"Afraid?" I queried.

"Yes, sir," Clara continued. "You never know what might cause you to lose your job, and I have observed that Mr. Clayburn can be a vindictive man.

"I am so sorry that you would have those concerns," I reflected. "However, there would also be fear you would have to face if we were to separate from Christ Beacon."

"I know, Pastor," she continued. "We all know that it might be bumpy at first, but we are here today to let you know we are committed to you and your ministry, and we are willing to work hard to help you continue your success. The truth is, Mr. Clayburn has been reaping the vast majority of the rewards from your success instead of you, and he really does nothing to deserve it."

"Thank you for your loyalty, Clara," I responded and then acknowledged the others, "Thank you, Jill. Thank you, Martha."

"Did you know that he has three other accounts in the name, or variations of the name, of Christ Beacon Ministries with three other banks?" Clara announced.

"No," I replied.

"Well, he does," she continued. "He has accounts at Hermitage Bank, First American Bank, and Bank of Nashville. He divides the cash up every day and deposits smaller amounts in each one of those accounts. This is so he stays under the radar of the federal government, and the deposits remain small enough that it does not get reported. Since those accounts are under the name of the ministry, those deposits are tax exempt. No one has check writing privileges on those accounts except him and Mrs. Clayburn. We can't pay a bill out of any of those accounts. All our bills are paid out of the main account for the ministry at First Tennessee, and his joint personal account with Mrs. Clayburn is also at First Tennessee. His personal account takes a payment weekly from the Christ Beacon Ministry just like yours does, except instead of the $769 a week that you get, the ministry deposits fifteen thousand dollars a week into his personal account.

That is in addition to the six to ten thousand dollars a day in cash that he deposits in those other accounts. So you see, Pastor, he is personally taking almost four million dollars a year from the money that you are generating."

I felt my face flush with anger. My pulse quickened to the point that I could feel it in my neck. I saw myself screaming, tearing down the curtains, throwing furniture, but I sat saying nothing.

"What about Wanda Moore?" I asked finally.

"She receives a weekly payment a little over that of yours," Clara responded. "I really don't think she knows anything about this."

I sat silent again.

At last I took a deep breath and said quietly but quite deliberately, "Do you know a good attorney?"

"As a matter of fact, I do." She smiled.

The next day we contacted Jeffrey Lawrence, attorney at law, and made an appointment. Two days later we were in his office. Clara brought evidence of the wrongdoing, and Mr. Lawrence was quick to accept our petition to address the matter, hopefully, without any of this reaching newspaper stands or television broadcasts. Since Mr. Clayburn had long known of my illicit sexual encounters, I had a fear that he might threaten to go public with that, but I comforted myself that what I had done might be wrong but not illegal, and he could potentially be sent to prison.

Mr. Lawrence was paid a percentage of the fifteen-million-dollar settlement that he was able to negotiate in exchange for releasing my contracts and in exchange for Mr. Clayburn, at least not yet, facing a prison sentence. Broadcast rights to *The Church Down the Road* were transferred to us, and we began Ronald Dennison Ministries in the Spring of 1964. As far as the public knew, nothing had changed except the name on the broadcast credits.

Wanda Moore was informed of what we were doing and why. She then accepted a 25 percent increase in income, including bonuses based on productivity, to become director of promotions for our ministry. I had stopped sleeping with her shortly after Alissa and I married. Part of that was due to my efforts at trying to be faithful to Alissa, but part of it was because

I had become bored with it. Although Wanda was an extremely beautiful woman, my sexual attraction to her had somehow worn off, and I saw her more as a business associate than anything else. She appeared to have come to the same conclusion.

Clara Smith became my personal assistant, my "everything woman," and I made sure she was paid very well. As a matter of fact, I paid her half as much as I had made with Christ Beacon. She traveled with me on most of my engagements, kept notes, intervened when people were demanding too much of my attention, made sure that I rested, and kept me abreast of all developments.

In the meantime, President Kennedy was assassinated in November 1963. Lyndon Johnson became president. The Civil Rights Movement was disrupting the South and beginning to become a part of the national consciousness. In fact, not long after we set about dissolving our ties with Christ Beacon, Dr. Martin Luther King Jr. gave his "I Have a Dream" speech. I admired him so much for what he was doing, and I compared myself quite negatively to him. While he was trying to make lives better, I was preaching for donations and doing little other than accepting those donations while growing richer. I wanted to do something to make a real difference in the world, but simply preaching the Gospel would have to suffice. I couldn't do what Dr. King was doing, so I contributed a lot of money to charities, including the ACLU and the NAACP. At least then I could pretend that I was helping. I knew the time had long passed for people like Sadie, the Clayburns' maid, to have an equal chance in the world, but I was too wrapped up in my own life to do anything more than throw money at a cause. Besides, Sadie had retired years earlier because of her health, and the Clayburns had hired a younger maid, whom they treated just as disrespectfully.

Unlike Alissa predicted, there was only a very brief period of free fall after we separated from Christ Beacon. We bought a building just off State Route 155 that would later become Briley Parkway, and many of the employees moved with us to the new location. We had to find a different studio and had to hire a new production manager, but when we did, we also began to spruce up and modernize the set. The television broadcast was beginning to become more polished, and I was beginning to become more comfortable doing it.

Donations continued to increase, but unlike Clayburn, I left the majority of money to accumulate in Ronald Dennison Ministries. For a time, I kept the same salary I previously held and used the remainder of the money to establish and build the ministry. All the while I worked very hard. My weekly television shows started to become taped for daily broadcasts in some areas. Wanda continued to live in Memphis, and I didn't see her that often. However, she didn't need to be in Nashville to book engagements for me and seek out ways of promoting the ministry. It was not long until she was establishing venues in auditoriums and stadiums that could seat five or six thousand people at a time.

All this made it even easier for me to find and seduce women. It was a rare occasion that I went to any city and did not have sex with at least one. A case of gonorrhea and a very private trip to a doctor in Seattle at least made me start purchasing condoms. Thankfully I was far enough away on tour that I didn't risk spreading it to Alissa. After that, I had to be careful to conceal the condoms, which we never used at home, and I tried to have a bit more discretion about the women I slept with.

It wasn't long before Clara caught me with my little soldier acting up in the early spring of 1964. We had finished a service at a huge auditorium in Chicago, and it had not taken long for me to spot a sultry brunet sitting at the front near my podium, and there it was, my trademark obsession. She had thick full lips covered in a frost Valentine-red lipstick. As I preached, my eyes were on her. I could barely look away. I saw no evidence of husband or children with her, and perhaps a female who sat next to her might have accompanied her to the event.

While the collection was being taken, I pulled aside one of my crew in charge of selecting people who might come to the front at the end of the service for prayer and quietly suggested that he pick her. I deluded myself into thinking that my crew members didn't know what I was doing. As long as I thought it was a secret, I could more easily justify it to myself.

When she came through the line of prayer seekers, it only took a squeeze of her hand and a whisper of "Perhaps we can talk later" to convince her to wait for me after the service. The combination of charisma and looks usually made my seductions quite easy. I knew that I was a handsome man, and I could look at a woman with my blue eyes in such a way that she found the word *no* difficult to utter. Although I suffered intense self- recrimination after every encounter, the excitement of the allurement and the intense power of my orgasms seemed to make it all worth it.

She waited a good thirty minutes after the service, standing quietly to the side, as the audience cleared the building and my crew began to dismantle our equipment. As soon as I got the opportunity, I descended down the steps of the stage, walked straight to her, extended my hand, and announced as if she didn't already know, "How do you do? I'm Pastor Ronald Dennison."

She smiled an embarrassed smile with those beautiful red lips, and I saw myself running my tongue between them and engulfing them with my mouth as my hand wedged into the hair at the base of her neck.

"I'm Darlene Meadows," she gleamed.

I knew I had her as soon as I saw those eyes light up. "Miss Meadows? Mrs. Meadows?" I queried. It really didn't matter to me whether she was married or not except that one was a little less complicated than the other.

"Miss." She almost giggled. She must have been about nineteen or twenty years old.

"Ah…Miss Meadows," I goaded. "I would think an incredibly beautiful woman such as yourself should surely be Mrs. Meadows by now."

"No…no," she fluttered. "Still looking."

She held up her left hand to show me there was no ring. I made no effort to hide the wedding band on mine.

"Miss Meadows," I pursued. "You know it gets awfully lonely when I am out traveling around the country like this, away from my family. Often, I miss having a good conversation and the comfort of feminine company. I was wondering if you might like to join me briefly in my hotel room for a little late evening tea. The room service is very good."

"Ooooh! That sounds wonderful," she bubbled like a schoolgirl.

The women at these events could be almost like the groupies of a rock band. There was more than one occasion when, instead of pursuing as I did this one, I was having to pull them off like ticks crawling over a hound's back. Some of them I put little effort into pulling back, but there were others who either did not physically attract me or who wanted to monopolize the remainder of my evening with their own personal take on my sermon. I learned early on to dart out the back as soon as possible and allow my crew to deal with the onslaught. On this particular night with Darlene Meadows, I had hidden behind a stage curtain, watching to see if she was waiting for me and waiting to see when the last congregant left the building. I was delighted to see that she waited.

"Splendid," I gleamed. "I am staying at the Congress Plaza Hotel. Do you know where it is?"

"Yes, I grew up here." She smiled.

"I'm so happy," I returned. "I'm staying in Room 414. I will need you to meet me there in about thirty minutes. I need to take a cab back with my personal assistant, who is staying on the sixth floor. I will tell her that I am very tired and I'm retiring for the evening. When you arrive, you can call from the lobby to be sure I'm in the room. I assume you have a car."

"I have my mom's car," she replied. "My friend Sally caught a ride home with another friend."

"Your mom's car?" I questioned suddenly, feeling uncomfortable. "How old are you?"

"Oh…I'm nineteen," she replied, apparently sensing my discomfort.

"Do you still live at home?" I asked.

"Well, yes," she continued. "I attend Loyola, and we live close enough that I can walk to classes. It saves on dorm expenses, and we just haven't seen the need for me to get a car of my own yet."

"I see," I replied, recognizing the well-known university by name. Internally, I felt a quiet embarrassment that I had never attended college.

There were times I wondered what normal life I might have missed. "You can meet me at the hotel then?"

"Yes," she comforted without knowing it. "I can probably stay till about midnight or maybe a little later."

"Wonderful!" I smiled, reaching out to touch the soft padding behind her upper arm.

On the way back to the hotel, I gave Clara a song and dance about being tired, which she was used to anyway. When we got back to the hotel, we each retreated to our own rooms, and I had only been back in my room for about five minutes when the phone rang. Of course, it was Darlene. I immediately ordered a snack tray and hot tea, which arrived shortly after she did. I might have ordered wine or champagne if I had thought she was of age to drink.

There was very little to seducing her. She had to have known my intentions all along. There had been no more than two bites eaten from the snack tray, and only a few sips of tea, when I picked up on the signs of her interest and wasted no time.

"May I touch your lips?" I asked as I finished a sip of tea and set the cup back into the saucer.

"You want to touch my lips?" She seemed intrigued by the question.

"Lips are so wonderful, don't you think?" I raised my hand to my own lips and gently caressed around my mouth. "So sensitive, so soft, and so sensual."

She reached her hand to touch her own lips.

"No. No," I pleaded, raising the same finger into the air that had just touched my own lips. "Let me."

She leaned forward and closed her eyes. I moved to her, gently ran my finger over her lips, and felt the wet lipstick begin to cling to my fingertip.

"The only thing better than touching lips with your finger," I softly enticed, "is touching lips with your lips."

"Yes…yes." She sighed. "Touch my lips with your lips."

I felt my little soldier pushing to full attention as I moved my hand around her face to the back of her head and brought our lips gently together. I moved to my knees on the floor, worshiping at those lips, while she sat leaned over in her chair. I ran my tongue around the soft fold of her lips and then deep into her mouth, engulfing her, consuming her. My lust was very hungry that night.

The phone rang, but I ignored it. I assumed it was probably Alissa and that I would call her back in the morning. It continued to ring several times, but I ignored it and focused my attention on the young vixen at my hand.

I moved her gently and carefully to the bed without ever ceasing my kiss of her lips, the nape of her neck, and the folds of her ears. I gently lay her back on the bed and then undressed in front of her as she watched with fascination and anticipation. Then I undressed her piece by piece, rolling her in this direction or that, kissing as I went along the edge of her blouse, down her arms. I slipped back her blouse across her soft belly and down her legs as I pulled her skirt gently and slowly toward her feet. When I had her fully naked before me, I moved my whole body gently over hers barely, ever so lightly, touching her with my face, my chest, and my hands. I softly caressed every part of her exposure with every part of mine.

When I entered her, I was relieved to feel that she was not a virgin. I had secretly feared that she would be, that I would be deflowering a young woman, and adding even more guilt upon my sin. I moved gently at first and then began gradually moving more rapidly, thrusting deep into her. She was not quiet in her pleasure and appreciation, which goaded me into doing more to please her. I worried about the noise but comforted myself that it was a hotel, and such sounds had to abound fairly frequently in the late hours of the night, also that the walls were thick.

I was nearing climax when I heard a knock at the door. I ignored it, thinking it must be room service to pick up the tray. It didn't occur to me that they would never do that. Besides, I was so close. I desperately wanted to finish. I was building to one of those eyes-rolled-back-in-head orgasms, and I didn't need any distractions.

The knock came louder and more intensely. I wanted my mind on Darlene and nowhere else, but then there came three loud bangs on the door about two seconds apart.

"SHIT!" I exclaimed as I lifted myself up and pulled out of her. I stumbled to the door with my little soldier waving in the air like a dizzy meerkat. I stepped behind the door to prevent being seen, leaned over, and opened it just enough to peek through a two-inch space and angrily shouted, "WHAT?"

There stood Clara in the hall in her pink terrycloth bathrobe, wearing a pair of round tortoise shell glasses. Her hair was in curlers, and she had some kind of pinkish white cream all over her face.

"Pastor Dennison?" she asked as though she didn't know who I was. I quickly softened my tone.

"I'm sorry, Clara. Is something wrong?"

I might have been able to hide my activities if Darlene had not chosen that very moment to whine, "Baby, come back to bed. I need to get off."

Clara's eyes widened to the size of quarters, and she knew immediately what was going on. My mind could not wrap around anything to say. Any defense I could have made would only have made matters worse. Clara collected herself as quickly as she had been surprised.

"Pastor Dennison," she said in a very matter-of-fact and professional tone. "I tried to call earlier, but I am assuming that you were…busy. I need to let you know that, due to some unexpected changes in the Cleveland venue, we are going to have to leave in the morning about an hour earlier than previously expected. I am sorry that I didn't inform you earlier, but I only received a message requesting a call back when I returned to the hotel this evening. By the time I had made the call and completed arrangements, I assumed you had already…lain down…for the evening."

"Ah—yes, Clara," I said, darting my eyes and searching for words. "I have been…a bit indisposed."

"Six a.m. departure, instead of seven, sir." She stood there looking at me firmly, and I suddenly felt as though my mother had caught me fucking my girlfriend. My mind went back to Daddy catching me and Lynetta at the church. For a moment, I couldn't decide which was worse, having Daddy knock me down and scream at me or standing before the silent court of Clara.

"Yes, ma'am," I said shyly.

"Finish your business," she said with a smirk. "I'll see you in the morning."

I closed the door and turned around to see Darlene lying on the bed, fingering her clitoris and squirming. "Come onnnnn," she moaned when she saw me turn around. "I want to get off—again." She smiled at me and widened the spread of her legs. I stood there pondering Clara's last statement. What exactly did she mean by that? *Finish my business*? Go ahead and have sex, or wrap things up and get this young woman out of my room? I stood there for a moment, watching Darlene wiggling on the bed. I realized from her most recent behavior that she was actually quite sexually experienced. So I decided to finish fucking her.

After a very fine time in bed, I discovered that she was more difficult to get rid of than I anticipated. When I finally got her to the door, she kept coming back, wanting to kiss me again and again.

"Just one more. One more. Please, just one more kiss."

"Darlene, you have to go," I pleaded.

"Okay, call me when you're in town," she teased, then whispered. "I left my number on the napkin when you were in the bathroom." I turned to see her number written in ink across one of the white linen napkins that room service had sent with the tray. Those initial sensual and enticing kisses had become like gum on the bottom of my shoe. No matter how much I tried to wipe it on the curb, it continued to stick. It felt like I couldn't pull her off me. I finally begged her, "Please. I have got to get some sleep. I have to leave early tomorrow morning for another engagement. Please…please go."

"I'll be quiet. I'll sleep," she pleaded.

"I can't sleep with someone else in bed with me," I lied. "Please, you have to go or I won't be getting any rest at all, and I need my rest to preach again tomorrow night."

Finally, "Okay, but you will call me, right?"

"Right, right, right," I lied. "Now please go home. I'm exhausted."

"I could sleep on the floor."

"No, please—I can't sleep with another person in the room."

Having spent a good twenty minutes to maneuver her to the door, I pushed her firmly, but not forcefully, into the hallway and locked the door. Even then, to the tune of "Call Me Irresponsible," I could hear her in the hallway singing, "Call me, Pastor Dennison. Call me, Pastor Dennison. Call me and I'll entertain yooooouuuuuu." I had leaned back into the hotel room door, looked upward, and said, "Are you trying to tell me something here?"

I did not berate myself as usual but simply prepared myself for bed. My wake-up call at 4:45 a.m. caught me struggling to move. I sat on the edge of the bed for a moment with my face in my hands. Then I called Clara and quickly made arrangements to meet her in the lobby. The rest of the crew had stayed at a cheaper hotel, and the bus was parked there. Clara had made arrangements for multiple boxes of doughnuts and coffee to be waiting at the bus.

I was exhausted after having played with that young woman till around two in the morning. I had showered and packed the few things I had taken out for overnight. When I met Clara in the lobby, the taxi was already waiting for us, and her bags were already in the trunk. She acted like nothing had ever happened.

"I thought you might need this." She grinned as she handed me a cup of coffee in a to-go cup. I took the cup in hand and looked at her curiously.

"Thank you."

"How did you sleep?" she asked, smiling.

For a bewildered moment, I said nothing, not really knowing what to say in a conversation that had been, until that moment, fairly routine. "Fine," I responded. "And you?"

"Like a baby as always." She grinned a quirky little grin. "Shall we go?" I followed her to the cab, where the driver took my bag and shoved it in the trunk next to Clara's.

On the twenty-minute ride to the bus, she made normal small talk.

"I think I like Chicago," she commented as we watched the scenery sail past the car windows. "I think I want to come back some time when I can take a little longer and enjoy the *pleasures* of the city."

Now I wondered if that was a hint for me to give her a vacation or just making normal conversation. Perhaps it was a dig at my activities from the night before. I knew she had me over a barrel. She could potentially ruin my marriage, my ministry, everything. She had potent goods for blackmail minus the pictures. With her meticulous follow-through, however, I wondered if she would be able to track down Darlene Meadows and entice her into a deal to extort from me. I imagined that Clara could be formidable if she decided to engage in extortion, but I underestimated Clara. We continued this small talk until we arrived at the bus. We then had about ten minutes to have doughnuts and coffee with the crew before continuing the journey, and we had refills in paper coffee cups to take with us.

There was a crew of eight who went with us on these tours, and we usually all rode the same bus, a converted Greyhound Scenic Cruiser. About a year later, we were taking a small Gospel singing group with us and had a second smaller bus, but in those days, we all rode together. The bus was set up as any passenger bus of the day with the exception that a few cots had been installed in the back of the bus for naps, and there was a restroom in the back by the cots. We stopped along the roadways for most meals, but coolers allowed for bringing on lunchmeat and drinks. It was perhaps a step down from the luxury bus I had with Christ Beacon, but it made up for luxury with more of a sense of community. On that particular day, it felt like a little too much community. Clara and I would usually sit across from one another in the middle of the bus. Sometimes we would cut up with the crew, but often we would just read. Crew members generally clustered in one part of the bus or another and usually left us to ourselves. I had a small lap desk that I used for making sermon notes and preparing for my next presentation. Any one of us might take turns on the cots for a nap. There were four cots bolted into the side of the bus in the back, and each had a set of pillows and blankets.

We had barely gotten on the bus that morning and settled into our seats when Clara suggested, "Pastor, why don't you go on to the back and take a nap. I know you must be exhausted."

Again, I was dumbfounded. I didn't have a chance to respond before she said, "Go on. Get yourself some sleep. Then I have a confession I need to make to you when you wake up."

A confession? My mind whirled. I had no clue what she was up to or what to make of her behavior. I had expected her immediately to tell me she was quitting when I got up that morning, but I also knew she was making more money with me than she could possibly make anywhere else. The only way I could figure for her to make more money was to blackmail me. I felt like a five-year-old ordered to nap time.

"Thank you, Clara," I said as I went to the back of the bus. "I think I will do that."

My mind tried to worry, but exhaustion overtook me, and I drifted quickly to sleep. I was awakened when the bus hit a pothole on the other side of Elkhart, Indiana. A couple of the crew had also lain down for naps. One didn't even notice hitting the pothole. The other lifted his head briefly and went right back to sleep. I sat up to see Clara sitting sideways in her seat, leaning against the window and reading *Mere Christianity* by C. S. Lewis. I sat on the edge of my cot briefly, then rose, and slightly staggered down the center aisle back toward my seat. As soon as Clara saw me, she bookmarked and closed her book.

"Oh, good, you're awake," she said, smiling. "Come sit beside me." She turned to face the front and patted the empty seat to encourage me next to her. I thought I was done for. I knew she was friends with Alissa, and all I could imagine was that she would chastise me for my behavior then tell my wife that I had been unfaithful to her. I contemplated, in that moment, that my marriage was over and my career lost. I imagined myself slinking back to Ravenden a scorned man. Perhaps, instead, she would tell me how much I needed to pay her to keep her mouth shut. I found her smile to be both puzzling and disconcerting. I slid into the seat beside her feeling as though I were a condemned man. "I'm so glad we could have this talk," she said, still smiling.

I looked around the bus, front and back, to see that no one was listening and said very quietly, "Clara, I know you must be appalled at my behavior. I am so very sorry to have shocked and offended you. I know that I have diminished myself in your eyes, and I am due for repentance."

"Nonsense," she said. "I'm a grown woman. You think I don't know what men do?"

"Shhhh!" I quickly interjected, nervously looking around again. "Please keep your voice down."

She collected herself momentarily and laid her folded hands over the C. S. Lewis book in her lap. "Pastor," she said, after a long sigh, "I told you that I have a confession to make." She paused. "Do you know why I have never married?"

"No, ma'am," I replied. "I have never wanted to pry into your personal affairs."

"Nor I yours," she responded. "Your life is for you to lead, not mine to lead for you. Nor is it mine to tell you how to lead it. It is my responsibility to live a Christian life as best I know how and not to try to enforce my morals upon others, even if they be brethren."

I was beginning to feel slightly relieved with her words and tone.

She went on. "I have never married because I don't trust men not to be fornicators and adulterers. I have yet to meet a man who wasn't. I am sure they exist, and I'm sure there are at least some happy and sanctified marriages, but I have never seen one, and I have doubted that I could ever have faithfulness for myself. Men—the poor souls—are at the mercy of carnal urges. Those urges may plague some women, but I think women are more likely to remain in control of themselves than men are. I personally find that women who give in to baser urges are quite humorous at the very least. At worst, they are harlots who lead men into temptation knowing full well that men are ill prepared to resist it. They are silly to be enslaved by such things that are so easily managed, or they are evil in their intent to use the greatest weakness of men against them. Personally, I have never had such desires myself. If I have ever had them, they were of such little interest to me that they caused no disturbance. I feel sorry for men, because they seem to be enslaved by the need to breed and breed broadly."

She paused momentarily and took a very deep breath. Then she continued. "My father was never faithful to my mother. She knew about it and tolerated it even though the Bible says, 'Lest it be for adultery, there is no divorce.' My mother tolerated his behavior because she had to. She was a slave to his paycheck and considered herself to be incompetent to support six children without him. She turned a blind eye to his womanizing and taught me, the oldest and only daughter, to pity him instead of hating him."

"You must then think me a fool," I shyly commented.

"No, Pastor, I do not," she replied firmly with a nod of her head. "I think you are a fine leader, and I believe that you intend your actions in the pulpit to bring about the glory of the Lord. Your behavior away from the pulpit is none of my business."

I leaned forward and placed my head in my hands. "Please don't tell Alissa," I whispered. "I love her dearly, and I don't want any of my indiscretions ever to hurt her."

"You used the plural—in-discre-tionssss." She dragged the *sss* on the end as though it were a deflating tire. "Comfort yourself in knowing that I do not make a habit of interfering in the habits of others. As I said, your behavior is none of my business, nor is your marriage. Although I am very fond of Alissa, and I pity that she is married to someone who cannot…fully commit himself to her…it would be arrogant of me to assume that I, and not the Lord, would be responsible for making any corrections."

I fought tears. "I know that I will be punished for my sins," I said, finally after gathering enough strength to speak without crying. "I want no other person to suffer for what I've done."

"Seventy times seven," she quietly affirmed. "That's how much our Savior says we are to forgive. You have not sinned against me, Pastor, so there is no forgiveness that I need give you. I need, for my sake, to make sure that I do not judge you, or I will have my own sin to repent."

"Are you going to stay with the ministry?" I asked. "I would hate to see you choose to leave, but I understand if you decided to go, given my… behavior. You are a great help to me, Clara, and I don't know that I could find another assistant of such quality."

"I have no intentions of leaving," she replied. "Even if I wanted to leave, I could not find a job that pays as well, and you have been more than generous with my benefits."

I lifted my head to look at her, reached over, and placed my hand over hers and said, "Thank you." Then I rose and moved back to my seat.

From that point on, Clara became my confidant. She was old enough, if not almost old enough, to be my mother, and I considered her to be of wise counsel. I could count on her to tell me the truth even if I didn't abide by it. There were times I asked her advice, but rather than give me advice, she gave me scripture and asked me questions.

I behaved myself in Cleveland. When the services were over the following evening, I retreated to my hotel room and called Alissa. At first, I wondered if she was going to answer, as the phone rang for a very long time. Finally, she picked up the phone and said rather breathlessly, "Hello."

"Hello, darling," I said. "You sound out of breath."

My guilt listened to her breathlessness and turned it into imaginations that she was with her own lover and had rushed from his side to grab the phone. Why wouldn't I assume that she was doing to me what I was doing to her? After all, I deserved it. Guilt turned to jealousy in a split second, a hot potato burning my own hands to then be thrown at her. "What were you doing?" I interrogated.

"I am so frustrated," she blurted. "The Carters' dog was out there digging in my flower beds again! How many times have we asked them to keep that dog contained? Ohhhhgh! It just infuriates me! I was out there chasing the darn thing with a rake trying to keep him from digging up my tulip bulbs! As soon as I get off the phone, I am going to go over there and give them a piece of my mind!"

"Calm down," I commanded, realizing that my imagination had been way off base. "I'll have a talk with them when I get home."

"Well, what am I supposed to do about my tulips in the meantime?" she asked. "He could dig up the whole yard by the time you get home. Where are you, anyway?"

"I'm in Cleveland, Ohio," I replied. "We will be in Cincinnati tomor-row night, Louisville, Kentucky, the next night, and the next day I'll be home—two more days. If he digs up any more bulbs, just save them some-where and we'll replant them."

"How are you?" she asked.

"I'm fine." I smiled just hearing her voice. "I'm just glad there isn't as much distance between these next two cities so we don't have to get such an early start, and we can all sleep in a little longer."

"I miss you," she said.

"I miss you too. I'm really looking forward to getting home to you."

She hesitated a moment. "Ronnie, when you get home, there is some-thing we need to talk about."

My guilt kicked in again. *Okay, this is it,* I told myself. *She is going to tell me she wants a divorce. She has found out about my cheating, or she has found a lover of her own, and she is going to tell me she doesn't want me anymore.*

"What?" I asked. "Can't we talk about it now?"

"No, silly." She giggled and again I realized my guilt had misled me. "It's a surprise."

"A surprise?" I teased. "It's not my birthday. What is it?"

"I'll tell you when you get here," she resisted. "I want you to be here for it."

"You know, I'm going to call and pester you about it for the next two nights, don't you?" I teased back.

"I have willpower," she validated. "I can hold out."

"You're a vixen," I joked. "What am I going to do with you?"

"Love me," she purred. "Just love me."

"I do that—more than you will ever know, much more than I show."

My feelings rumbled inside me like storm clouds stirring wind from the mix of hot and cold. I did love her with all my heart, but I had a horrible secret that I kept from her, a secret that I knew would devastate her if she ever found out.

After my incident with Clara, I had determined never again. I was going to control myself no matter what. I would never let another woman tempt me to stray from my marriage. I was going to devote myself solely to

Alissa. But the brewing storm inside me was not just my guilt and shame swirling around with my love for Alissa; it was my intense lust, my obsession for women, my weakness for lipstick. It was a hunger that I had never been able to feed enough. It tore at me, possessed me, and demanded that I submit. As much as I wanted to be faithful to the woman I truly loved, there was a doubt in my heart. I felt weak. She broke my silent contemplation.

"Ronnie? Are you there?"

"Yes," I returned.

"You didn't say anything," she went on. "Did you not hear me?"

"I'm sorry," I lied. "I must have drifted off. What did you say?"

"I said, 'I love you more than you will ever know,' too."

"I'm sorry, honey," I pleaded. "I don't know how I could have missed that."

"You must be very tired," she comforted. "Get some rest. I will look forward to talking to you tomorrow."

"Okay, baby," I responded. "Good night then."

"Good night, sweetheart," she said. Then I heard the phone click, and the dial tone returned. I hung up the phone, lay back on the bed, and stared at the ceiling.

The next two nights were fairly typical. I spoke at an auditorium in Cincinnati and a large church in Louisville. Both nights my little soldier demanded my attention. Both nights there were women I spotted in the audience whose beauty and use of makeup, especially lipstick, tugged at my groin. Still, I resisted. However, both nights I retreated to my hotel room and masturbated to fantasies of bedding them.

On the following day, we pulled into Nashville. We left the bus in the parking lot of the office building that we had purchased off State Route 155. There was plenty of parking, so we could leave vehicles there while we were away. I had purchased a second Cadillac for Alissa so she could have a vehicle of her own and wouldn't have to be dropping me off or picking me up at the office. My Cadillac was there waiting. I had called Alissa that morning before we left Louisville so she knew I would be getting home about noon. When I came through the door of the garage she met me in the kitchen with a big hug and multiple kisses all over my face. Then she kissed me softly and sensually on the mouth. When she pulled away after a long, lingering, sexy kiss, I said, "Wow! You are more exuberant than usual. Did you miss me that much?"

"I always miss you." She smiled. "But this time is a little different."

"Different?" I questioned.

"Yes, silly," she glowed. "I told you I have a surprise."

"Ohhhhhhh!" I exclaimed. "Well, please do give me the surprise!"

"Put your things away. Then come sit down," she said.

Our breakfast nook table was set with lunch. Two plates each held a diagonally cut chicken salad sandwich with wedges of apples, some grapes, and a couple of quarters of orange. While I went into the living room to set down my briefcase and toss my jacket onto a chair, Alissa poured me a glass of milk. I went back into the kitchen and sat down at my place at the table. We held hands across the table as I offered blessing for the food, and at the end of the prayer, I lifted up my head to see those spectacular hazel-green eyes and a smile gleaming across her face.

"What?" I grinned. "You look like the Cheshire Cat."

"Maybe I'm the cat that ate the canary." She giggled. "At least I might end up craving a canary as things progress."

I reached down to grab my sandwich and took a big bite. I was actually famished after the long drive. I chewed and then reached for a sip of my milk. I swallowed and said, "Craving a canary? As things progress? What are you talking about?"

Alissa had not touched a bite on her plate. "Oh, you know," she beamed.

"Noooooooo," I replied bumfuzzled at her behavior.

She got up and dashed quickly into the den. She returned with a piece of paper, set it down on the table in front of me, then folded her hands, rested her chin on them, and gleamed at me.

"What is this?" I asked, looking at the paper, still not really sure what I was looking at. She said nothing but just waited with her chin resting on folded hands smiling like she had just seen Jesus.

"What?" I asked.

"It's a lab test." She smiled. "From Dr. Stacey's office."

"A lab test? What? Are you okay?"

"Oh, I'm okay." She giggled. "I'm very okay."

I looked at the paper again. "What does this mean?" I asked.

"It means you are going to be a daddy," she simpered delightfully.

"Oh, my goodness! What?" I put the paper down and looked at her in both shock and delight. "Alissa? Oh, my goodness!" I got up and rounded the table to hug her. She stood up to meet my embrace. Then she leaned back and touched my face.

"Oh, darling, I'm so excited." She smiled. "I can't wait to have your baby."

I hugged her again, and then it hit me. I was going to be a father. A child would be in my house. I would have to try even harder to behave myself, to be true to my wife and my family. Then, the doubt stormed through my mind. What kind of father would I be? Would I be able to present a good and honorable example for my son or daughter? As I stood there holding Alissa, feelings of shame began to overwhelm me. A voice in my head screamed, *You are a worthless, no-good sinner! You are not worthy to preach or walk among the righteous, much less father a child! You are a liar and adulterer! You are scum, and you do not deserve this loving woman, much less her child!*

I began to weep.

Perceiving this to be tears of joy instead of my tears of shame, Alissa affirmed, "I know. I know. I have cried for joy for the last three days. We didn't think we could have children, but God has blessed us with this wonderful miracle, a union of our love together, such a precious, precious gift."

As I held her and wept, I asked myself, "How can this magnificent woman possibly love me? If she ever knew the kind of scum that I am, I would surely lose her forever."

CHAPTER 17

I n the months that followed, the world continued to go through the metamorphosis that was the 1960s. Almost a hundred years since the abolishment of slavery in the United States, black people were still fighting for equal rights. Dr. Martin Luther King Jr. had been awarded the Nobel Peace Prize in October of 1964. I watched the broadcasts on the news and read about it in the papers only to feel a certain kind of shame that he was a minister who made a difference, a man who changed the world, and I was a minister who solicited the masses for money while living a secret life from my family and those who followed me. I went about my life as I had come to live it. Alissa's pregnancy didn't stop me from doing what I had done all along. One might think that the pending birth of a child would make a man behave differently, but I buried my guilt deep inside. More and more, I appeased my little soldier. It seemed easier to give in to what it wanted and move on than to fight it.

I had two tours while Alissa was pregnant, one that took me up the East Coast to New York and back through Pittsburg. Another tour took me across Arkansas to Little Rock, down through Texas to Dallas, and from there, up to Oklahoma City. The folks in Little Rock seemed to be particularly appreciative of the TV star preacher from Arkansas, and my ego had become so hooked on the praise for the role I played that I scarcely noticed anymore that I was not really doing what I had always thought God wanted me to do. Perhaps it was my guilt, or my fear, haunting me, but here and there in different cities, I could swear I saw Darlene Meadows. I would see a glimpse of a woman that looked like her just before she passed through a door or just before I was tugged away by a crew member. Once in a while, I caught a glimpse on a woman's face that seemed so like the playful tease who wouldn't leave my room back in Chicago. I shook it off and went on. Now and then, I would remember my talk with Clara and try very hard to behave myself, but it only took a night or two fighting to go to sleep while my little soldier taunted me before I gave in and sacrificed to the semen god. Meanwhile, Alissa waited patiently at home, went through much of her pregnancy without me, and continued to believe in me.

On November 7th, 1965, I delivered services at Evangelic temple as I often did when I was home. I delivered services at Evangelic Temple as I often did when I was home. Alissa attended the services, although by that time, she looked like a beach ball with legs. I knew she was miserable. She had long since passed the "Get out of me!" stage and was more than ready for the baby to come. Normally after services, she would stand beside me as I greeted congregants by the front door. I would end up shaking hundreds of hands as often she would, and it was not at all uncommon for someone to hug either of us as well. On that day, a kind parishioner had moved a comfortable chair from one of the offices and placed it beside me so Alissa could sit. She was a trooper and determined to be there at my side no matter what. Of course, the attention went to her pregnancy, as it had for the several months since she had been showing. There were kind and sometimes nosey but well- meaning little old ladies who would want to place a hand over her belly and pray for the baby. I saw one of them ambling down the aisle with her cane and thought to myself, *Oh Lord, here comes Sister Langston. She is going to want to carry on about the baby for half the afternoon, and I just want to get done so we can go home.*

Sister Langston, a widow, was usually accompanied to church by her son and daughter-in-law. Osteoporosis bent her over like a rusty hinge. Regardless, every Sunday she wore classic lined dresses that she might have worn to a formal dinner party. She used bluing in her gray hair so there was a pale-blue sheen to the permed white curls. Her dark-brown eyes barely showed through the sags of her eyelids, and wrinkles crossed her face like the veins in an autumn oak leaf. *Here she comes and here we go,* I thought to myself as I watched her wobble up with her cane. Her son, daughter-in-law, and two perfectly dressed grandsons followed stonily behind, their expressions reflecting the boredom I know they must have felt. Nonetheless, the family allowed her any Sunday discretion of her choice. She ignored me and sauntered directly to Alissa.

"Oh my, you are close, my dear," her crackled voice squeaked.

Alissa, obviously tired and uncomfortable, smiled congenially and said, "You are so right, Sister Langston. Any day now."

Resting herself, half-falling on her cane, Sister Langston reached a bony, wrinkled hand out to touch Alissa's stomach. No sooner had the hand touched than Alissa chirped, and water went rushing from under her dress, over the edge of the chair, and into the floor. "Oh dear," Sister Langston creaked. "Your water just broke. I didn't think I tapped you that hard, sweetheart."

Alissa immediately reached over, took my hand, and said, "We have to go!

I had never seen anything like that ever happen. I had heard of women's water breaking before birth, but I had no idea what it meant or what we needed to do about it.

"Oh my goodness!" I shouted. "Are you okay? What do I need to do?" I didn't wait for an answer but threw my head up and shouted, "IS THERE A DOCTOR IN THE CHURCH?"

"Oh, calm down, puppy," Sister Langston commanded as she tugged at my jacket from the elbow. "She's just having a baby."

"HERE?…NOW?" I exclaimed.

"No, not here, and not now," she responded. "But you need to get her someplace."

The excitement spread throughout the sixty or eighty church members still present. Some of them who were on opposite sides of the sanctuary had no idea what was going on. My shouts had alarmed them, and many came rushing up. Shouts of "What's wrong?" rang out.

"Oh, for goodness' sakes!" Sister Langston exclaimed, turning toward her son. "Bobby, get this under control!"

Her son turned and shouted as he waved his hands in the air. "EVERYONE! MAY I HAVE YOUR ATTENTION, PLEASE?" Voices began to quiet and he continued. "EVERYTHING IS FINE. SISTER DENNISON HAS JUST GONE INTO LABOR, AND WE JUST NEED TO BE CALM AND GET HER TO THE CAR. SO IF EVERYONE COULD JUST STAND BACK, WE ARE GOING TO HELP HER TO THE PASTOR'S VEHICLE."

"Thank you, Bobby," Sister Langston proclaimed.

She turned to me and stuck her bony old finger in my face and said, "Now you just calm down. Help this girl up and walk her to your car. She can walk. She will be fine."

"Yes, ma'am," I obediently replied. I turned to Alissa, who was already reaching for me to help her up. Bobby Langston came around to her other side and got a hand beneath her armpit. Together, we lifted her out of the chair. Other parishioners had brought towels to clean up the mess. We walked Alissa to my car, and on the way, Bobby kept reassuring me. "Been through this twice, Pastor. Always scary, especially the first time."

From there, I drove Alissa to the Vanderbilt Hospital Emergency room, which wasn't far away. I had no sooner walked her through the door when nurses came rushing around her, obviously knowing from experience what was going on. It didn't take long to get her into Labor and Delivery. Then, I paced the floor.

Before I knew it, people started coming in. Sister Langston and her family had followed me there. Clara had already left church that morning, but someone had called her and told her what happened, so she wasn't far behind. A couple of other church members showed up, but that was about it. I had deliberately chosen not to make personal friends for fear my proclivities might be found out. Alissa had insisted that we spend some couple's time with one or two of the neighbors, but I really didn't want to invite church people over into my private life.

Sister Langston came in and took a seat in the lobby then motioned for her family to sit, which they dutifully did. While I was pacing and subconsciously chewing at my fingernails, I heard her exclaim, "Oh, ye of little faith. What's the matter, Pastor? Do you think your prayers ain't working?"

Until that moment, I hadn't even noticed that she had come in and sat down. I turned quickly to see her sitting there, staring at me with both hands resting over her cane, which she had standing upright in front of her.

"Sister Langston," I collected myself. "How sweet of you to come. I really didn't expect you to come. I'm fine. Really, I am."

I looked around the lobby to see her family and a couple of other people from church whom I also had not noticed.

"Sit down, Pastor. Take a load off," Sister Langston ordered. "This could take a while."

Just like her family, I did as I was told. Embarrassed, I said, "It's in the Lord's hands."

"Always has been," Sister Langston replied. "Believe in your prayers, preacher. Don't just pray—know. Faith ain't wishing, it's knowing the Lord is working it out."

I sat there smiling, not saying much. Shortly Clara came in, and it couldn't have been much more comforting if Momma herself had walked through the door. For one thing, I assumed she could meet Sister Langston toe-to-toe if I got picked on too much.

"Clara!" I exclaimed as I stood and crossed the room to her. I took both her hands in mine. "I'm so glad you came."

"How is she?" Clara immediately asked, ignoring my angst.

"We don't know," I replied. "She was taken back to Labor and Delivery maybe thirty or forty minutes ago."

"She's fine," Sister Langston declared. "I can feel it in these old bones."

"I'm so happy to hear that you have psychic bones," Clara jabbed. "Now, what does the doctor say?"

"Still waiting," I replied.

Clara sat down beside me, and all of us made small talk for another hour or so, and then a chubby, short young nurse walked through the door and called, "Ronald Dennison."

"Yes. That's me." I stood up.

"Oh, I wondered if it would be the same Ronald Dennison." She grinned. "Big fan of yours, Pastor Dennison. Love to watch *The Church Down the Road*. By the way, I know you are not Catholic, but now it's Father Dennison." She snickered at her little joke. "'Cause it's a girl!"

I stood there trembling like a leaf in an Arkansas earthquake. My hands were shaking, and my knees felt so weak I feared they wouldn't hold me up. "Wh-when can I see her?" I asked.

"Which 'her' are we talking about?" the giggly, chubby nurse responded. "Mother or daughter?"

"Both!" I snapped, finding myself suddenly irritated at her glibness.

"Well, give us about thirty minutes to get Mrs. Dennison settled in her room and I will come get you."

The young nurse changed her tone to be a bit more professional. "We should be able to bring your baby in shortly after that."

"Thank you," I said.

The young nurse turned to leave, and several of the church people rushed up to shake my hand, pat me on the back, and announce their congratulations. After that, most of them left to go home for the evening. Clara asked if I wanted her to stay, and I told her I would see her at the studio in the morning.

"I will be home all evening," she said before walking out the door. "If you need, you can always call and talk to me."

Only a few minutes later, the nurse returned to escort me to Alissa's room. "I'm sorry," I said as we went through double doors and up a hall.

"'Bout what?" she asked, waddling a foot or two in front of me.

"I'm sorry I snapped at you," I replied.

"Ah, happens all the time," she returned. "Daddies get nervous. We expect that."

Soon she led me to Alissa's room and smiled pleasantly as she held open the door. When I entered, Alissa lay there in a hospital gown tucked neatly into pure white sheets with one of those little woven hospital blankets tossed over her. She glanced over to my eyes with a look like it came from an angel and said, "Hello, Pappa."

"Hello, Momma," I said as I walked over and stroked her hair. "How are you feeling?"

"Very tired, very sore, and very hungry," she replied.

She barely had the words out of her mouth when I heard the door open behind me. The chubby little nurse brought in a tray of food and set it on the bedside table. "First, you eat," she said. She reached for the crank at the foot of the bed to roll Alissa up into a sitting position. "Then, we'll bring the baby in a little later."

"Oh, thank goodness," Alissa responded.

The nurse rolled the bedside table over the bed in front of Alissa and adjusted the height for comfort. Then, she lifted off the stainless steel plate cover like a waiter at a five-star restaurant.

"Oh, that looks so good!" Alissa exclaimed, staring at the pork chop with mashed potatoes, carrots, and peas. "Do you have strawberries?" she asked. "I'm craving strawberries right now."

"Honey, fresh berries are out of season here in November," the nurse replied. "But I can see if they might have some frozen berries in the kitchen."

"I can run see if one of the specialty stores might have imported berries," I interjected. In those days, fruit that wasn't in season was seldom found.

"No, that's all right," Alissa responded as she reached out her hand to touch my arm. "Frozen berries will be fine if they have them and, if not, I can do without or have an apple or something." At that moment, she reached out, grabbed the pork chop with her bare hand, and began chewing into it like a ravenous little dog. "Oh, this is so good!" she exclaimed. "Mmmmmhhh, that's the best pork chop I've ever had in my life."

I looked in astonishment, not believing my eyes. Alissa had always been so proper. I had never seen her eat like that, and without even using a fork and knife to cut up the meat.

The nurse must have noticed my surprise because she said, "They almost all get like that." She grinned. "It's not really the best pork chop, just standard hospital food, but when you have just had a baby, a handful of sand would taste good."

Alissa dug a spoon into the mashed potatoes and took a big gulping bite that was almost too big for her mouth. At this point, her attention was on the food, and she didn't seem to notice anyone else.

The nurse took it all in stride. She reached for the door handle and said to Alissa, "Honey, if that's not enough for you, just let me know. I'll be happy to bring you some more, and I'll see what we can come up with in the way of berries."

"Thaoank youoe," Alissa garbled, not stopping for a moment, even to try clearing her mouth before speaking. She swallowed shortly after the nurse walked out and said, "Oh, Ronnie, you should try these potatoes. They're awesome."

I stood there watching Alissa scarfing like a hog at slop, thinking that our baby was somewhere in that building, all alone, maybe crying, maybe sleeping. I wondered what the nurses might be doing with her.

"Have you seen the baby?" I asked.

"No, not yet," she replied as she reached for the carton of milk.

I suddenly felt angry with her. How could she sit there stuffing her face and not even want to see her own baby? Did she not want the baby? Was this a sign she didn't want me?

"Why not?" I said, trying to hide the irritability I was feeling and still it came out sounding terse.

"There hasn't been time," she replied just before taking a few more swigs of milk. "They brought me straight here from Labor and Delivery. I assume they took the baby to the nursery."

"You assume?" I questioned. "Don't you even want to see the baby?"

"Well, of course I want to see the baby," she said, glancing up at me before she reached to tear off a segment of her roll. "Why would you think I wouldn't want to see the baby?"

"I don't know," I continued, about to stick my foot deep in my mouth. "It just seems that you are more interested in eating than you are in our child."

She stopped suddenly, dropped her piece of bread back onto the tray, and glared at me like a mountain lion stalking a rabbit.

"RONALD DENNISON!" she pounced, her voice wavering in tone from fierce to intense. "HOW COULD YOU SAY SUCH A THING? Do you have even the slightest clue what I have been through? Let's not even consider that I spent the last NINE MONTHS carrying *your* child, cramped and uncomfortable, with an aching back and ANKLES THE SIZE OF ELEPHANT HOOVES, not being able to find a comfortable way to sleep and having our daughter PLAYING FOOTBALL INSIDE OF ME! Let's just consider TODAY, when I went through THE EMBARASSMENT OF HAVING MY WATER BREAK RIGHT THERE IN CHURCH with the entire CONGREGATION LOOKING ON, when I went through CONTRACTIONS that made my abdomen feel like it was in a SIX-FOOT VISE GRIP, and then got rolled into a cold, stark room with STRANGERS where I passed a child roughly THE SIZE OF A WATERMELON through my vagina! Would you want to pass that through ANY ORIFICE OF YOUR BODY?"

I started to mumble an answer but didn't get the chance. I had no idea what I was going to say anyway.

"I HAVE NOT HAD A BITE TO EAT since six o'clock THIS MORNING, and in case you haven't imagined what it might be like to give birth, LET ME TELL YOU! It is like running a marathon on your back with your legs in stirrups while KING KONG IS RIPPING OUT YOUR INSIDES!" She paused only a moment. "What time is it, Ronald? Look at your watch!"

"I…ah." I glanced down at my wristwatch to see the little hand on the seven and the big hand on the ten. "Ah…ten to seven," I said sheepishly.

"Oh? Ten minutes before seven o'clock," she repeated. "My, how time flies WHEN YOU'RE HAVING FUN!"

"I-I'm sorry, dear." I bowed my head. "I was being callous and unthinking."

"Well, you can have the next baby," she said. "AND SEE HOW HUNGRY YOU GET! Have you eaten?"

"No, not really," I replied, knowing this could not be going anywhere good. "I might have had a couple of snacks in the lobby."

"Oh, you poor dear," she whined. "Here…HAVE A BITE!" She then threw the remainder of her roll at me. It bounced off my upper chest and onto the bed.

As I was staring down at the roll, she said, "Are you going to eat that?"

"I…ah…I…"

"Then give it to me!" she snarled.

I carefully picked up the roll. She snatched it from my hand and stuffed the entire thing in her mouth, chewing with great long strokes of her chin.

Oh my Lord! She has lost her mind! I thought to myself. I had never seen her behave that way. In our entire marriage, we had never really had cross words with each other. There had only been a few brief disagreements that were easily settled. Just then I heard a light tapping on the door behind me. Then the nurse stuck her head in again. "Okay to come in?" she asked with her head already through the door.

"Sure," I said over my shoulder.

The nurse then pranced around the foot of the bed to the other side, grinned at Alissa, and pulled a plastic-wrap-covered bowl out from behind her back. "Honey, look what I found," she beamed.

Still chewing almost the entire roll she had in her mouth, Alissa said, "Whoaot?"

The nurse pulled the plastic wrap off the bowl and presented it to her. "Strawberry shortcake, honey. One of the cooks put together a strawberry shortcake for you. There's even a double helping in there."

Alissa took the bowl from her then stared at me while she held the dessert with both hands like a sacrifice for an altar. "I don't know," she said, finally swallowing the bread. "Do you think we should maybe see the baby first?"

"Oh, Pishaw, honey," the nurse said, apparently not even noticing the tension between us, or totally ignoring it. "You go ahead and eat that. By the time you are done, I'll have the baby ready and I'll bring her on up." The nurse then happily waddled out of the room.

I watched her leave, and when the door was closed, I looked back at Alissa. "I'm sorry, sweetheart," I pleaded. "I was totally out of line. I just have so many feelings going on right now. I don't know what to think."

Alissa took a deep breath and relaxed. "Would you like a bite?" she said. "There's an extra spoon."

"No, you go ahead," I responded. "I know you're hungry."

She quietly picked up a spoon, held it in my direction, and nodded toward the bowl that she had just set on the tray. I timidly took the spoon and looked down into the white bowl where an ample amount of partially frozen red berries in syrup topped a vanilla cake that was surrounded on the outer edges with big fluffs of whipped cream. "Oh my, that does look good," I said.

Alissa dipped her spoon into the bowl, pulled out a big chunk of berry-covered cake, slipped it into her mouth, closed her eyes, and leaned back into the pillow. "Ohhhhh." She moaned, eyes still closed as she savored the moment. "That is heaven."

I followed with a spoonful for myself. Like Alissa, I closed my eyes and let the delicious concoction play with my taste buds. "That is really good," I said as I opened my eyes to see Alissa laying there beaming at me with a peaceful smile.

"Ronnie, let's don't fight anymore," she said.

"Let's don't," I mirrored as I leaned over to give her a peck on the lips. I then dropped my spoon in the dessert bowl, took her hand, and gave a little squeeze. She squeezed back and said, "Ronnie…we're parents. We're Mommy and Daddy. How does that feel?"

"Terrifying," I said, and a single tear rolled down my cheek.

"I know." She smiled. "But wonderful too, right?"

"Right," I said, quietly gazing at her.

"We better finish that shortcake before the nurse comes back." She half giggled.

I turned to pick up my spoon, and we proceeded to finish the bowl.

We had actually finished for a few minutes before the nurse came back and had been sitting there talking about the name we had chosen for the baby: Ariel Celeste Dennison. The name seemed like a song to us. We could have named her after someone in the family, but we both decided we would rather give her some originality than have her saddled with the confusion of having the same name as some other member of the family. Had she been born a boy; her name would have been Thaddaeus Nathan. We decided to save that name in case the next child was a boy.

In a short time, the nurse brought our baby in. She put her first in Alissa's arms, and we both looked down at that crinkled little face with squinting eyes, each of us in awe of the miracle we had created. Alissa had made the decision that she wanted to breast-feed, and the nurse reminded her that the baby was probably going to be falling asleep soon, so it might be good to go ahead and give her first feeding. The nurse assured Alissa that she would be there in case she needed any assistance or had any questions. Then the nurse turned to me and said, "Pastor Dennison, you can step outside for a little while."

In those days, men were not considered to be part of the process and were often excluded. It was not until the late 1960s and the movement toward natural birth that men really began to be allowed to participate in the birthing of their children.

"Why?" I asked.

"Because this is a private matter between mother and child," the nurse replied.

"Are you going to be here?" I persisted.

"Well, of course. I'm the nurse," she replied.

"Then it is not a private matter," I responded. "Besides, I've seen them before."

"Seen what?" the baffled nurse inquired.

"My wife's breasts," I tersely replied.

"Ronnie, please don't be difficult," Alissa pleaded.

"Why can't I stay in the room?" I demanded to the nurse. "She is my wife, and this is my baby."

Alissa finally came to my rescue. "I don't see any problem with him staying," she told the nurse.

I took a seat on the opposite side of the bed and watched Ariel and Alissa interact for the first time.

"Touch your nipple to her upper lip," the nurse instructed. "You may have to tap her mouth a few times, but she should open her mouth."

Alissa did as instructed, and Ariel's mouth popped open like a baby bird. Alissa slipped her nipple into the baby's mouth, and Ariel began to suck. This had to be repeated a few times, but Ariel soon got the hang of it.

In short order, it was over. The nurse wrapped the baby, who was already falling asleep, then turned to me. "Would you like to hold her for a minute or two before I take her back?" she asked.

I must have had a surprised look on my face because she affirmed, "You can hold her. It's okay."

I nodded. Then the nurse brought Ariel around the bed, gave a brief instruction about supporting the baby's head, and laid her in my arms. I looked down at her lying there, soft, warm, and tiny by my chest, quietly in slumber. A wave of emotions suddenly swept over me. My heart felt like it was going to break. This tiny, vulnerable, and innocent person lay there in my arms, a blank slate, unknowing where life might lead her or what might happen to her. My mind began running through all the horrible things that could happen to her from which she had no protection, including my own mistakes.

"What have we done?" I exclaimed and burst into tears. "We've brought her into a horrible, sinful world where she has no protection." My eyes blurred with tears that began streaming down my face and falling onto my child.

The nurse quickly approached and said, "Let me have her."

"Will you keep her safe? Will you protect her?" I sobbed as I gently handed the baby to her. The nurse gave me the strangest look, like she had just seen the oddest animal on God's green earth for the very first time.

"Of course, I will," she replied. "Are you all right, Pastor?"

"No," I whimpered and released my child to her arms.

I turned around to face the bed, dropped my head on the rail, and continued to sob. "Alissa, she's not safe. She's not safe. She was safe with God, and we have taken her from the safety of heaven and put her here in this horrible place!"

I heard Alissa say to the nurse, "Go on."

"Protect her," I entreated the nurse, raising my head for only a moment.

"Goodness, Ronnie," Alissa pleaded. "What's the matter with you?"

When I heard the door click and knew that the nurse was gone, a terrible wave of fear swept over me. "She's going to get hurt, Alissa. She's going to get terribly hurt. We all get hurt here. We all do."

Alissa pulled herself up in bed, leaned over, and began stroking my hair. I did not raise my head from the rail.

"Ronnie, she's God's gift to us," she continued. "She is a beautiful, healthy baby, and she is going to grow up into a beautiful, healthy woman someday. Who knows what kinds of gifts she has for the world. She might be the first woman president, or she might find a cure for cancer. She could be God's gift to all of us."

"For all have sinned and fallen short of the glory of God." I sobbed. "The world is full of sinners, some of them more horrible than others, and they're going to hurt her, and it's our fault. We did this. We brought her here to be used and preyed upon by men."

"Ronnie, stop—stop," she pleaded. "Don't do this. Can't we just be happy? Can't we just celebrate the fact that we have a beautiful, healthy baby? She couldn't ask for better parents than us. She couldn't ask for two people who would love her more or try any harder to bring her up in the sanctity of the church."

"The church won't protect her!" I cried, my tears turning to anger. "Nothing will protect her! Ever since Eden, nothing protects us."

"God protects us," she argued. "God protected me. He worked a miracle through you and brought me out of that horrible illness."

"Did He?" I moaned in a low growl. "Did He? How do you know you wouldn't have gotten well anyway?"

"I know, Ronnie—I know."

I raised my head to look at her. "Do you love me?"

She reached out to wipe the tears from my cheek with the back of her hand. "With every last fiber of my being." She smiled.

Chapter 18

I was a total nervous wreck when Ariel was born. It was not just nervous father syndrome or being afraid I might break her. I couldn't get it out of my mind how some man might do to her someday what I did to women, how some man might cheat on her someday the way I cheated on Alissa. The older she got, the more frantic I became about it. I didn't want to let her out of my sight, but I had work to do and much of it was on that stupid bus with the crew, gallivanting from one city to another. I began to grow weary of preaching on the road.

Momma adored Ariel and often begged us to come home for a visit. It was certain that Daddy wasn't going to drive to Nashville, and he had never allowed Momma to drive, so we tried to make trips home at least twice a year. Watching Momma dote over Ariel gave me a kind of joy, but my biggest fear was seeing her grow up. I wished I could lock her into age three so she could keep the innocence and never have to face the realities of life. Still, she grew.

Ariel was three years old when her little brother was born on June 12, 1968. We named him Adam. Although we had planned to name him Thaddeus, Alissa thought it would be cute to have the children's names both starting with an *A*, so he became Adam Nathan Dennison.

I wish I could say I felt better about having a boy, but it made things worse. I wanted to figure out a way to discipline him so that he wouldn't do the things I had done, but that was a very tall order for a man who couldn't discipline himself. I continued to have problems. In fact, they got worse right after Adam came along.

Alissa had some minor complications with the birth, so they kept her in the hospital an extra couple of days. Clara came to the house to help with Ariel as I had no real clue how to care for a toddler. During the few days she was there, Clara stayed till about 8:00 p.m. and then went home after putting Ariel to bed. We needed Clara's help from time to time. Alissa never would allow me to hire a maid and insisted that it is a wife's duty to take care of her own home. However, without grandparents nearby, Clara often filled in as surrogate grandmother/nanny.

It was a usual routine that I would shut the TV off just after the baby went to bed so there wouldn't be any disturbing noise in the house. I might do a little Bible study or prep work on a sermon, but most of the time I would sit in bed and read by the overhead light. If Alissa had been home, we might have talked a while before shutting out the light, but it would have been just as likely for her to sit next to me reading her own book.

Two days after Adam was born, I sat in bed reading after Clara had taken Ariel to stay with her for the night. I was missing Alissa and found it very strange to be in the bed without her. The book was not all that interesting, and I was about to close it and go to sleep when I heard a rustling noise outside the house. At first, I thought the neighbor's dog had gotten lose and had come to dig in the flowerbeds, as he was prone to do, but I couldn't imagine why the dog would be digging at that hour of night. The sound came and went, and just as I was about to go outside to check, I heard, "Ah roooooo! Ah ah ah rooooo!"

Now, it might have been possible for a coyote to have found its way through the city streets of Nashville, but it wasn't very likely. Besides, it didn't sound like any coyote I had ever heard or had ever heard a recording of. It came again, "Aaaaah ROOOOOOOOOOH!" I knew then it was no coyote and wondered if a prankster from church was pulling some kind of joke about the new baby. I assumed it was benign. Yet, after fastening my robe, I reached into the bedside drawer for the pistol we kept, just in case.

I crept through the kitchen to the back door picking up the flashlight that we kept there. I sneaked carefully onto the patio, flashlight in one hand, pistol in the other. The patio was fairly well lit by the streetlamp. I began to turn the corner around the house when it sounded again, but this time it was very different.

"Ah rooooooh! Ah ah ah roooooh! Pastor Dennniiiiiissssooooon?" My heart pounded from a different kind of fear. I knew that voice.

Around the corner, half illumined by the streetlight and half in darkness stood Darlene Meadows, the liaison from Chicago. The beauty I had perceived when I met her had turned into chaos. Her hair, much longer now, danced and spiked about her head in a jagged, matted mess. She was barefoot in jeans and wearing a tattered men's shirt unbuttoned to her sternum with no bra beneath it. I vaguely recognized the shirt as one I had thought I lost when I had spoken a year earlier in Omaha. She looked very different, but there was no mistaking who it was.

"What do you think you are doing here?" I whispered sternly and as loud as I could while still trying to remain quiet, a kind of a yell-whisper. Darlene Meadows jumped back from the bushes beside my bedroom window and let out a quick little scream of surprise followed by, "Oh…Pastor Dennison…honey, baby, you scared the crap out of me!"

"I scared you?" I exclaimed. "What in the name of the Lord's Good Word are you doing here?"

"I came to see you," she teased as she wiggled in my direction.

"Don't come near me!" I commanded. "You leave, now!" I waved the gun in her direction, but it apparently did not frighten her.

"But I want you to fuck me again," she teased as she continued to wiggle toward me.

"What? WHAT? Are you out of your mind? Go away. Go back to Chicago."

"Oh, I don't live in Chicago anymore," she said. "My parents kicked me out. So did the school. I've been following you around to different speaking engagements for a couple of years now."

"You what?" I demanded.

"Do you know how hard it is to get to talk to you if you don't want to talk to me first?" she rambled, oblivious to any kind of manners. "All those people rush up to the front after you finish. They get in the way, and I guess you got these guard guys now that are supposed to keep you safe or something. I told one of them I'd let him fuck me if he would sneak me into your room, but you know what? He fucked me and then still wouldn't let me into your room, but he wasn't as good as you, Pastor Dennison. You fuck the best." She wiggled a finger in my direction and began to slink toward me again.

"Stop!" I ordered, pointing the pistol directly at her.

"But I want you," she moped as she stood in place and tilted her eyes toward the ground. "And I know you want me too." Her eyes came back to meet mine. "Sometimes, when I hear your sermons, it's like you're talking directly to me. I can hear little undertones in your voice saying, 'Darlene, I want you. I want to fuck you again.' You know I'm right."

I sighed as though the breath were coming all the way up from my toes. "What will it take to get you to leave me alone? Do you want money? Is that what you want? If I pay you, will you go away? How much do you want? How much to get you to go away somewhere and promise you'll never bother me again?"

"I don't want your money, Pastor Dennison, I want you," she persisted. "But…a few hundred bucks might buy me some things I need. It gets a little tight out there on the road sometimes when I'm following you around. Hey, but you would be amazed what some guys will pay for just a blow job."

"No, I don't think I'd be amazed," I released. "Wait here—don't move from this spot."

I went back into the house, rummaged for my wallet, and returned with two hundred-dollar bills. When I got back, she was lying on the patio looking up at the sky. I had no sooner stepped out the door when she said, "Have you ever realized how hard it is to see the stars, when you are in the city? It's not like out in the country where it is so dark. Out there, the stars are crisp and bright. In the city, they're muddled by streetlights, if you can see them at all. You know, I didn't even realize that till I started following you around. I lived all my life in the city and never laid down on a country road at night to look up at the stars. I've done that now. It's marvelous, don't you think? Have you noticed the stars?"

"No, I haven't noticed," I said.

"Come here," she commanded and patted the spot on the patio beside her. "Lay down here and look."

"No, I don't think so," I responded. "You need to go. Here, I have two hundred dollars for you. Take it, and don't ever come back here again." I shoved the money in her direction just short of throwing it at her. I stood back and held the cash at arm's length.

"Why can't I come back?" she whined.

"Because I don't want you here!" I snapped and continued to thrust the wad of cash in her direction. "I have a wife and two children now. I love my family, and I don't want you messing it up! Now, take the money and get out!"

"But we have something special, Pastor Dennison," she persisted.

"Darlene, what we had was a fuck! That's it! Nothing more. It was a fuck. I was wrong ever to have done it in the first place. It was not fair to you, to my wife, or my ministry. It was wrong. Now you have to forget it and go on with your life. Go back to Chicago. Go back to school. Meet some nice young man, get married and have babies, but please stop coming around me." Again, I pushed the money toward her.

Darlene rolled on her side, facing the opposite direction and began to cry. "You're mean!" she whimpered.

"I'm not mean," I responded. "I'm realistic. There can't be anything else between us. You have to go."

"Will you fuck me first, one more time for old time's sake?" she asked.

"What—NO!" I insisted. "Get up, take the money, and get out, or I'll call the police and have you removed!"

"You wouldn't call the police," she calmly stated. "You wouldn't want anyone to find out about me. It might upset your little family and your ministry. It would be terrible if word got out that Pastor Dennison fucks around."

"Look at you!" I demanded. "Nobody is going to believe you. All I have to do is tell them you are a crazy fan who won't leave me alone and that you belong in a mental institution. It won't be that hard to convince anyone that you are delusional, and you are. If you think I'm going to tolerate this behavior, you're wrong. Now, you have an opportunity to take a little money and be on your way, or you can spend the night in jail, get transferred to the state hospital, and get nothing. Which will it be?"

She made no reply. She got up from the ground, walked over to me, snatched the money from my hand, and walked casually into the darkness. "You were the best fuck I ever had," she said nonchalantly as she disappeared into the darkness.

I couldn't be sure she was gone. I heard no car start, so I picked up the flashlight from the patio table where I had left it and followed into the darkness, shining the light into every dark corner of the yard. I did not find her, so I went back into the house. I went back to bed, but I could not sleep. Several times I got up to check the locks. Finally, around 4:00 a.m., sleep took over, but only for a little while. I drifted in and out of light sleep. Then a little after 7:00 a.m., the phone rang. I fumbled for the phone beside the bed and half dropped it before grunting out a sleepy, "Hello."

Alissa's voice came cheerfully through the line. "Good morning, sweetheart. You sound tired. Did I wake you?"

"I was about to get up," I half mumbled.

"You're usually awake and chipper by now," she continued. "It's not like you to be so groggy. Is everything okay?"

"Yeah…yeah," I lied. "I just had a little trouble getting to sleep last night. The neighbor's dog kept me awake."

"Was he barking again?" she asked. "We may end up having to call the city on that."

"It's okay," I replied, quickly trying to think of something to cover the story. "I-I think there must have been a stray in the neighborhood, and that was getting him stirred up. If I see it out there again, I'll call the city. So why are you calling this morning?"

"Well, they are going to release me and the baby today," she said. "Can you come get us or maybe send Clara to come pick us up?"

"I thought they said you would have to stay there all week," I responded. "Well, Dr. Stacey originally thought I would have to stay, but he said the tests came back fine this morning, so he is going to let me go home." Exuberance was evident in the tone of her voice. "Adam is wonderful and doing very well, and we would both like to come home and see Papa."

"I don't have to be at the studio till ten," I said. "Let me get dressed and I'll be down to pick you up. Should I come get you on the maternity ward?"

"No, we will be waiting in the main lobby," she replied. "I'll look forward to seeing you, sweetheart."

"Me too," I said. "Bye now. See you soon."

I hung up the phone and scrounged around for my clothes, laid them out on the bed, then shaved without a shower. I wet my hair down from the sink to flatten out the bedhead, wiped off the excess with a towel, dressed and headed for Vanderbilt. As I drove, I kept seeing the images of Darlene Meadows flashing in my mind. I prayed that I had seen the last of her. I drove through the crowded streets of Nashville and begged out loud for God to forgive me of that sin and to bless her with a wonderful life somewhere else. Nonetheless, I felt a trepidation and foreboding, a premonition that I had not seen the last of her. Multiple times I could have sworn I saw her walking along the sidewalk, but a second glance always proved me wrong.

I picked up Alissa and my new son, brought them home, and resumed life as usual except for the nagging paranoia that Darlene might show up at any time or might be lurking behind some bush. After a few weeks, I began to comfort myself that she had taken the money and had gone on with her life.

Toward the end of August, I came home from the studio in the late afternoon. As usual, after parking the car in the garage, I came through the kitchen and announced, "Honey, I'm home."

"We're in the living room," Alissa's voice responded.

"We?" I questioned and tossed my suit jacket over the back of a dining chair. "Do we have company?"

I assumed some lady from church might be visiting as that was not an unusual occurrence though rarely that late in the day. I entered the living room before she had a chance to answer and was struck with a sudden jolt of terror. "Oh dear Lord!" I exclaimed before I could catch myself. I witnessed Darlene Meadows sitting there sipping sweet tea with my wife. My heart pounded, and I felt faint.

Darlene had cleaned up. Her hair had obviously been professionally permed. She had on a knee-length pale-blue sleeveless bell dress and had taken care to get her nails done as well as attend to her makeup.

"I believe you know Miss Meadows," Alissa said, motioning to Darlene.

I caught myself, straightened my shoulders, and put on my best act. I walked directly over to Darlene, extended a professional handshake, and said, "Yes, how do you do, Miss Meadows? So nice to see you again."

"How do you do, Pastor Dennison?" She smiled and shook my hand politely.

"So," I said, sitting down in the chair opposite the sofa where Alissa sat with her knees perpendicular to Darlene, who was in the adjacent chair. "To what do we owe this visit?"

"Well," Alissa replied, turning her attention to me. "First of all, I had Clara come take the children for a little while so we might have time to talk. Second, I came home a little over an hour ago to find Miss Meadows standing on our front landing doing something rather odd."

I shuddered to think what "odd" thing Darlene might have been doing and avoided the obvious question. Instead, I nervously murmured, "Mmmmm hmmm."

"You see, as I was turning into the driveway, I noticed her on the landing repeatedly reaching up under her dress and then rubbing her hand on the doorknob," Alissa said sternly.

"Oh...really?" I quietly and nervously responded, daring a quick glance at Darlene.

"I was rubbing my pussy juice on the doorknob so you would smell it and get turned on, and you would want to come fuck me again," Darlene tweeted cheerfully.

My face must have turned the color of pickled beets. "I—I—I…Why…Why…wou-would you do something like that?" I anxiously questioned.

"I read this article in a magazine that said there are these things called pheromones, and the smell of them really turns on the male animal." She paused for a sip of tea. "So I figured I would spread some of my pheromones around. You know," she gleamed an oblivious smile and whispered, "so you would get all turned on by the scent of me and want to mate."

I sat there silent, staring at her, dumfounded and shocked. I had not the slightest clue how to respond. Finally, Alissa broke the silence.

"Miss Meadows and I have been having quite the conversation for the last hour or so," she said.

My dumbfounded stare turned to Alissa.

"Miss Meadows tells me you had a tryst with her in Chicago sometime back." Alissa's stare was stern and parental.

Again, I sat silent, feeling like my whole body had been given a shot of Novocain. Finally, I lied. "I-I don't know what she is talking about. I remember meeting Miss Meadows through our entourage in Chicago. We had dinner together, but I wouldn't consider that a tryst. We had a conversation about the…the ministry."

Darlene leaned over to Alissa and whispered loud enough for me to hear, "He is uncircumcised, and when you pull his foreskin back, there is a little brown spot on the inside of his foreskin, that you can only see when the skin is pulled back, and he has got these little scars at the base of it." In reflex, my eyes shot to my crotch and then back to Alissa. Her stare was like radiation. Darlene was accurately describing my penis in more detail than I imagined she could have noticed.

"That's very interesting information," Alissa said. "I don't know that I've ever examined my husband's penis that closely. However, I would be willing to take a closer look just for curiosity's sake."

Darlene whispered again, "He's a great lover. He is really noisy when he cums, and then after he cums, he kind of lays there and like shivers or something."

"Why are you doing this?" I turned to Darlene suddenly more angry than fearful. "What could you possibly hope to gain by saying these things to my wife?"

She ignored me and again whispered to Alissa, "I hope he is as good a lover with you as he was with me. The man shook me up! Shook me uuuuuuuppppppppp!"

"Stop it!" I yelled and stood up. "Stop saying those things!"

"Why?" Alissa questioned. "Why do you want her to stop? Is it true? Did you have sex with her?"

My gaze turned back to Alissa, and a tear rolled down my cheek. "I don't want you to be hurt," I pleaded as another tear rolled across my cheek and then another. I found myself wiping my face with the back of my sleeve.

"Too late," she responded in a cold, matter-of-fact tone. "The question is, where do we go from here?"

"Oooh, I hope we can share," Darlene quipped. "I'm sure he has got plenty to go around. I mean, I don't mind him fucking you if you don't mind him fucking me."

"SHUT UP!" I screamed at her. "SHUT UP! FOR CHRIST SAKE— SHUT UP!"

They both sat there, silent. Finally, Alissa spoke. "Is that what you want to do, Ronnie? You want an arrangement so you can have your cake and eat it too? Do you want to share?"

"No," I whimpered as I gazed at her. "I want you. I don't want anyone but you. I want…her…to go away. I've tried to get her to go away, but she won't accept no for an answer. She has been following me around the country for a couple of years now, since we first met in Chicago. I've tried to get her to go away. When you called me that morning that you came home from the hospital with Adam, it had not been the neighbor's dog that kept me awake. It was her howling at the window like a dog. I had to threaten to call the police to get her to leave me alone that night."

"Well, you gave me some money too," Darlene chimed in. "That really helped 'cause I had enough to buy some clothes and get my hair done. I mean, you might not have wanted to fuck me that night 'cause I looked like hell, but maybe, now that I'm all pretty again, you might want to fuck me again."

In unison, Alissa and I both yelled, "SHUT UP!" Then we looked back at each other, realizing what we had done.

"I don't want her," I pleaded. "But I don't know how to get rid of her."

"Did…you…have…sex with her?" Alissa questioned, already knowing the answer.

A deep and confessing sigh came out of me. "Yes…one time, years ago, in Chicago before Ariel was born."

"One time," she reaffirmed as though simply restating fact.

Alissa turned to look at Darlene, who said, "Well, it wasn't for the lack of trying. He's a hard man to get to. I mean, if you could ever get past his darn security guards, you might get a little something going, but—no! Then he has to go and turn into such an asshole, telling me to go away and leave him alone. He wouldn't even lay down and look at the stars with me. I mean, he wouldn't even lay down on the patio out there and look at the fucking stars with me. All he had to do was just keep fucking me once in a while. Everything would have been fine. I mean, I wouldn't ask for much. Just bend me over a table here or there. Hump me in a hotel room once in a while. We don't have to live together or pretend like it's any more than a fuck." Darlene stared directly at me. "I'm not in love with you, you arrogant prick! I just want your cock. Just let me have that cock again."

Alissa smiled and turned back to me. "Do you think you have learned your lesson?"

"Oh Lord, I hope so," I responded, feeling somewhat relieved.

"Well," she exhaled. "The question is, what do we do now?"

"I could move in," Darlene spouted.

"No, I don't think so," Alissa countered. Alissa looked back at me and said, "Miss Meadows mentioned her mother and father's names in discussion with me before you came in. She mentioned that they live on a West

Quincy Street in Oak Park, Illinois. The information directory should be able to locate a phone number for them. Let's give them a call and see what we can find out."

"You leave my parents out of this!" Darlene yelped. "I am a grown woman. I make my own decisions! I do what I want! If I want to fuck Elvis, I'll fuck Elvis. We get together every few weeks. He's got a little dick though, not like that nice piece of meat Pastor Dennison is swinging around, but I think I might have his baby. I'm going to name him EJ for Elvis Junior."

Alissa spoke to me as she rose from the couch, "How about you refresh the tea for Miss Meadows while I make a phone call to her parents."

"NO! YOU'RE NOT CALLING MY PARENTS!" Darlene stood and protested.

"Is there some problem with calling your parents?" Alissa calmly questioned.

"No! But you leave them out of this! There is no reason why they should have any involvement in anything," Darlene snapped. "It's not like they OWN me or something!"

"Well, if there is not a problem, then you shouldn't mind my calling them," Alissa calmly continued. "Who knows, they might enjoy a trip to Nashville. We could ask them to be our guests."

Darlene looked frantically at me then back at Alissa. "NOOOOO!" she screamed. Then she ran to the front door, threw it open, leaped off the front landing, and went running across the yard to the street, pausing only long enough to throw off her high heels and keep running. After watching her from the front door, Alissa and I looked at one another in puzzlement.

"Let's go ahead and call her parents," Alissa said. "I'd like to know what's going on." She moved to the sofa, picked up the phone from the end table, and dialed the operator. I sat down and watched as she continued. "Operator, I would like information for Oak Park, Illinois, please." She sat quietly with the phone to her ear. "Mr. and Mrs. David G. Meadows on West Quincy Street, please."

In a moment, she picked up a pen to write on the notepad that we kept near the phone. "Thank you," she said. Then she looked at the number written on the pad and began to dial. I could faintly hear the ringtone in the receiver. Then I heard a click and a very faint "Hello."

"Hello, my name is Alissa Dennison, and I am trying to reach Mr. or Mrs. David G. Meadows."

I could barely hear the background affirmation.

Then, Alissa asked, "You have a daughter by the name of Darlene Meadows?" From there the conversation went on for several minutes, then Alissa finally said, "Thank you so much, Mrs. Meadows. We don't know where she is at this moment, but we will do what we can to find her if we can. Bye-bye now."

She hung up the phone and turned to me. "It seems our Miss Meadows is a fugitive of sorts."

"She is wanted by the law?" I questioned nervously.

"No, not exactly. She hasn't really committed a crime, but she is a fugitive nonetheless—hold on a second." She then flipped quickly through the phone book. She glanced at a number and dialed again. "Yes," she spoke into the phone a moment later. "I'd like to report a missing person. Well, not exactly missing, but a missing person who I have found."

"Who did you call?" I questioned.

She held her palm over the receiver and said, "It's the police department."

"The police!" I exclaimed anxiously. "There is no need to get the police involved in anything!"

"Shusssh!" she hissed and went back to the phone. "Yes, her name is Darlene Meadows. There is a missing person's report filed in Chicago from 1966…Her parents have legal guardianship of her due to chronic mental illness, and she apparently ran away from an institutional placement in 1966…I came home today to find this woman on my front landing…No, I don't know where she is at the present time. I spoke with her long enough to realize that something is wrong with her and happened to find out who her parents are. She ran away when I told her I planned on calling her parents."

"I don't want the police involved in this!" I angrily whispered. "The story could get out. I don't need anything like this hitting the papers!"

"Excuse me a moment," Alissa said into the receiver. She then held her hand over the mouthpiece again and said, "Well, you should have thought about that before you went to bed with someone who is mentally unstable!"

"I don't want the police involved in this!" I repeated.

"At this point, Ronnie, you don't have a choice." She then turned back to speak calmly into the receiver. "No…to my knowledge, she is not a danger to anyone, but she has been judged by an Illinois court to be unstable enough to not be able handle her own affairs. It is my understanding that her parents have court-appointed guardianship."

Alissa went on to give our address and our names. She informed the police that Darlene had been stalking me and following me around the country but stopped short of telling them I had slept with her. She asked them for discretion and to please try to keep the story out of the media for both Darlene's sake and ours. When she finally finished talking to them, she hung up the phone and turned back to me.

"Now…what about us?" she asked tritely.

I dropped my head in shame. "I am so sorry. I am so ashamed, Alissa. I betrayed you, and I betrayed our vows. I committed adultery, so the Bible gives you justification to divorce me…I understand."

"Ronnie, look at me," she said. I raised my eyes to meet hers. "I'm not going to divorce you." She smiled.

"You have every reason." I cried. Tears now flowed over my face, and I began wiping them with my sleeve.

"I know you are unfaithful," she continued. "I've known it a very long time. Do you honestly think this is the first woman who has told me she slept with you? There have been several."

"Why…Why, Alissa? Why haven't you left me?"

"The simple answer is that I love you," she replied. "Yes, I have been hurt, and I've worried—more about you than anything else. The first time someone came to me, I was devastated. My heart was shattered, Ronnie, and I thought long and hard about leaving you. We didn't have any children then. It would have been easier, but despite that part of you, despite your betrayal, I still see goodness in you."

"How?" I pleaded and buried my face in my hands. "How could you see anything good in me? I'm a liar, a pig, a cheat. I use women and toss them aside. I betray them, I betray you. I betray God. I betray myself! I hate myself! You have no idea how much I hate myself."

"Ronnie," she spoke quietly and reached out to take my hand. "You cannot hate yourself enough to make me stop loving you. Of course, I want you to be faithful to me, but that is something you have to work out inside yourself before you will ever be able to work it out with me."

"I'll stop. I'll stop, Alissa." I tried to convince myself more than her. "I'll stop cheating on you. I'll stop betraying my word and my commitment to the Lord. I'll make myself stop!"

"No, you won't," she said quietly. "Not until you're finished. Not until you have found and purged this demon that eats away inside you, and the only way you are going to purge it is to make peace with it."

"HOW CAN I MAKE PEACE WITH THE DEVIL?" I cried out. I stood up, and then fell to my knees beside the coffee table, both hands to my head, pulling my hair. "HOW CAN I MAKE PEACE WITH SATAN? HE CONSTANTLY TORMENTS ME!"

Alissa moved over and knelt down beside me. She placed a comforting hand between my shoulders. "Those who are most faithful are those who are most challenged. There is a way," she said quietly. "But not the way you've been trying."

After a moment, the doorbell rang. Alissa rose and went to the door. I quickly darted into the kitchen, not wanting anyone to see me upset like that. Clara had brought the children back. It was getting late at that point, and darkness was falling. From the kitchen, I heard Clara ask,

"Is he okay?"

"He's fine," Alissa said. "Everything is fine."

In that moment, I realized my big secret was really no secret at all. I wondered how many people knew the truth. How many had talked about the less-than-hidden sins of Pastor Dennison? Obviously, it had been something that Clara and Alissa had discussed. And they loved me anyway? They loved me anyway. I couldn't fathom why they loved me, but it was obvious they did.

I never saw Darlene Meadows again after that. The next day, Alissa had gotten a call back from the police that they had found her and were having her transported to a psychiatric hospital in Chicago that her parents had designated. Perhaps they institutionalized her permanently. I never knew. In those days, they could do that. I was just grateful that it didn't turn into the scandal it could have become, but I was even more grateful to know that Alissa and Clara both forgave me for it. For the life of me, I couldn't understand why. If I had been in Alissa's place, I'm not sure I could have been so forgiving of an unfaithful spouse. It made me want to try harder, and I did. Finding out that Alissa had known all along and that she loved me anyway, forgave me anyway despite my infidelity and indiscretion, made me try so much harder to be faithful to her. For several years after that, there was no woman whom I had sex with outside my marriage. For several years, I felt somewhat normal.

CHAPTER 19

Even before Adam was born, I was tired. I had long since grown weary of going out on the road and touring. I had long since come to understand that what I was doing was a business.

I was earning money through my ministry to feed my family. Yet I was earning far more than ten or twenty families needed, and I didn't like being away from my own family. I wanted to quit touring, and in fact, I stopped scheduling tours, but requests would come, in and I could not seem to make myself turn them down. When people wanted me to preach, I felt I had an obligation to them and to the Lord to fulfill my vocation to spread the Gospel.

By 1971, the only time I went on the road was when a church requested for me to come. I did my television show regularly, but otherwise, I had even stopped preaching for Evangelic Temple except on rare occasions. They had a new minister, David Wilkes, who was a very fine man and quite a good pastor. As far as I was concerned, my television ministry was more than enough. However, the broadcast had become national many years earlier and was carried by many stations. I, therefore, had fairly frequent requests to speak at various venues all over the country.

In late 1970, a request had come in for me to speak at a very large church in St. Louis, Missouri. Clara had asked me about it, and I agreed that she could schedule the engagement for late March of 1971. Around the same time, Evangelic Temple had requested that I provide a service for them. Clara had suggested we televise the service at Evangelic as we often would do when my engagements were close enough to home. Arrangements were made for me to speak at Evangelic Temple June 20, and that would give me plenty of time to prepare a broadcast after speaking in St. Louis.

A couple of days before I was to leave for St. Louis, Clara put a call through to me from their pastor with a request that I had not expected. I picked up the phone wondering if, and almost hoping that, the call would be a cancellation of the engagement. I answered the phone in my office with my usual candor, "Yes, this is Pastor Ronald Dennison."

"Pastor Dennison," the voice on the other end of the line began, "this is Pastor Simmons at Safe Harbor Church in St. Louis, where you are to speak day after tomorrow.

"Yes, sir," I replied. "How may I help you today?"

"Pastor Dennison," he went on, "I was wondering if you ever do any private counseling."

"I...well, I suppose I could," I said and was caught a little off guard. "It is not anything that I have made any habit of."

At the time, I suspected that Pastor Simmons was requesting counseling for himself or some type of consultation over the phone.

"Would you consider speaking privately to a troubled child while you are here?" he asked.

"A troubled child?" I asked.

"Yes," he continued. "We have a family in the church that takes in foster children from the state, and they have taken in a boy who is particularly troubled. I don't seem to be able to do anything with him, and I was wondering if you might be able to get through to him."

"What's the problem?" I requested, now feeling less sure if I wanted to take on the challenge.

"Well, he came from the slums," Pastor Simmons replied. "He had an extremely difficult time. His mother was murdered last year, and he never knew who his father was. The child found his mother stabbed to death, and since there was no family considered fit to take him, he was placed in state custody. He is a very confused boy right now."

"Aren't there professional counselors to work with him?" I asked.

"Well, of course he has social workers," Pastor Simmons continued, "and he has received professional counseling, but I am of the opinion, of course, that the primary problem is a spiritual problem, and I have hope that we might bring this child to Christ."

"What is it you think I might be able to do for the boy that you have not done?" I asked.

Pastor Simmons paused for a moment. "Well," he said at last, "I am not sure that there is anything you can do for him that we have not tried. However, he seems to be fascinated with your broadcast, and we are hoping that if he meets you, he might be more open to listening to you, and perhaps you can get through to him."

"Well, I suppose I could talk to the boy," I responded. "What exactly is the problem?"

There was a hesitation on the line. For a moment, I wasn't sure if I might have been cut off. Then Pastor Simmons began hesitantly, "The boy has had an extremely troubled life. His mother was a drug addict and was probably killed in relation to a drug deal. Stephen, the boy, was ten years old when he found his mother stabbed to death. There is no telling what the child went through while he was in her care. There has been a strong suspicion that he was sexually molested, perhaps multiple times. He is eleven now and has been in foster care with our church family for about a year. Perhaps, because he was molested, he has become convinced that he is a girl, and no one has been able to convince him otherwise."

"Mercy!" I heard myself exclaim, and I felt a shivering anxiety building within myself. I couldn't explain why. I only knew that the idea of speaking with this boy was making me very nervous.

"He insists that he be called Stephanie and referred to as 'her' instead of 'him,'" Pastor Simmons went on. "He becomes extremely upset and sometimes violent if other children fail to comply with those demands. It has become increasingly difficult for the family to handle him, and with other troubled children in the home there are often conflicts. The family is considering telling the state that they can no longer care for him. If that happens, he will be institutionalized in an orphanage somewhere, and I don't see much chance for him after that. Since he has had so much abandonment in his life, we are praying that does not happen. We are praying that you may be able to have some rapport with the boy and help him get onto the right path."

I was taken aback. "I…well, I…don't know that I have ever heard of such a thing. A boy who is convinced that he is a girl? He is, of course, too young to determine if—well, I assume if he has any attractions this early in his life, it would mean he is homosexual."

"I don't know either, Pastor Dennison," Pastor Simmons replied. "It is all very confusing. Since the boy is fascinated by your broadcasts, however, we thought you might be able to sway him toward a more normal path in life."

"I certainly will put the boy in my prayers," I responded. "I don't know that I can do anything to actually help the boy, but maybe the Lord can, and I will certainly be happy to talk to the boy."

"Thank you, Pastor Dennison." The voice sounded almost pleading. "Will you be able to come early or perhaps stay over a little in order to meet with the boy?"

"Let me ask my secretary if she can tweak the agenda so I might have a little time with the boy, and I'll have her call you back." I fiddled with the phone cord, feeling a little put out with what I was agreeing to. "Her name is Clara Smith. If she doesn't get back to you today, it will probably be early tomorrow."

"Thank you, Pastor Dennison," Pastor Simmons expressed again. "We will look forward to your visit. Goodbye now."

"Goodbye," I said and hung up the phone. I immediately used the intercom to contact Clara.

"Yes, Pastor," Clara's familiar voice responded.

"Clara, Pastor Simmons says there is a boy he wants me to meet with when I am in St. Louis. Do you think you can find some time in my schedule for that?"

"How much time do you need, Pastor?" she asked.

"I don't know," I pondered, "maybe an hour, maybe two."

"I don't know about inconveniencing everyone on the crew with changing start or leave times," she calculated. "However, it is only about a five-hour drive, and we should be arriving there around 2:00 p.m. I had arranged for you to have a couple of hours to rest after we get checked into the hotel, but if you don't mind using that afternoon time, I could make arrangements for you to meet with the boy around three or four p.m. before dinner."

"Splendid!" I exclaimed, having no idea what I was getting myself into. "Why don't we make it about 3:00 p.m.?"

"I will call Pastor Simmons and make the arrangements," she replied.

"Thank you, Clara," I said as I let go of the button on the intercom. I sat back at my desk for a moment and stared at the wall.

Sudden flashes from my childhood dream ran through my mind. I saw the redheaded woman coming up out of the silver-parted waters of our pond, cupping my face in her hands, and kissing me. I heard the booming voice of Jesus crucified on the side of our barn shouting, "YOU ARE MY WORD." I sighed a deep sigh, went back to the Bible I kept open on my desk, and continued to make notes for both the taping of my television broadcast as well as my upcoming sermon in St. Louis.

I came home a little early that afternoon to find that Alissa had put the children down for a nap. She no longer worked in the office and had dedicated herself to being a full-time and exceptional mother.

"Shhhhhh!" she hushed as I came into the door with my usual "Honey, I'm home."

"The babies are sleeping," she whispered.

"Oh, I'm sorry," I whispered back. "How is my beautiful bride today?" I swept my right hand around her waist with my left across her back and kissed her passionately.

"Well, better now," she responded after I finally released her lips. "You seem a little frisky today."

"I am a little frisky today," I responded. "How about a little alone time to ourselves while the kids are napping?"

"Are you saying you want to make love to me in the middle of the afternoon?" she asked.

"That's exactly what I am saying," I said as I kissed her again and nudged her slightly in the direction of the bedroom.

"Ronnie, I would love to, but I don't want to wake the children." She sighed as she patted my chest.

"Ah, not even a little quiet quickie?" I pleaded.

"No, not even that." She stood firm. "I don't want to be distracted or especially undressed in case one of the kids wakes up and needs something."

"Shucks!" I exclaimed. "Okay then, how about if we have a glass of tea in the den and you can snuggle with me on the sofa."

"Now that I can do," she replied. "Go sit down and I'll get us some sweet tea."

I went to the den, threw my jacket across a chair, loosened my tie, and sat down. I had no sooner gotten settled on the sofa when Alissa came into the room with the tea. As she entered from the kitchen, a gleam of sunlight caught the side of her face, and I thought to myself, *She is the most beautiful woman in all the world.* I had not cheated on her since the incident when Darlene Meadows had come to our house. Our sex life had become infinitely better after that. My guilt had all but gone away, and I was happy with my beautiful wife and my wonderful family. Alissa crossed the room and handed me a glass of tea.

"Dear Lord, you are beautiful," I said before she had a chance to sit down with her own tea.

"Thank you, my handsome hubby," she responded then took a sip of her tea and set the glass on the coffee table. "How was your day?"

"It was…it was an interesting day," I replied.

"Really?" she questioned. "More interesting than usual?"

"I had an interesting request from the pastor at Safe Harbor up in St. Louis," I said and then began guzzling my tea almost down to the bottom of the glass. I set the glass on the side table and went on. "He wants me to counsel this young boy who thinks he is a girl."

"That is interesting," she commented. "I've heard of that, where children are born with both male and female parts."

"Well, no mention was made of that," I said. "I didn't think about that or even think to ask. The impression I got is that he is a regular boy who has become convinced that he is a girl."

"How old is he?" she asked.

"I think he is eleven," I replied. "He came in a year ago to find his drug addict mother stabbed to death and has been in foster care since then."

"Oh my word!" she exclaimed. "That's horrible! Poor thing, no wonder he is confused."

"Do you think that's it?" I asked. "Do you think somehow growing up like that with a drug-addicted mother made him confused about what sex he is? They think he was probably molested."

"Oh, that's horrible, and I don't know," she replied. "I'm not a psychologist, but I would think growing up in a life like that would really mess with a child's head."

"What about how we grew up?" I asked. "Neither you nor I had it exactly pristine, not like the cushy life our kids have, but we don't have that kind of confusion."

"No," she went on. "At least not that kind, but we both had parents who loved us and who were there for us. I mean, if his mother was a drug addict, how could she really care for him, and what in the world must it have done to his mind when he came in to find her stabbed to death? That's just beyond horrible!"

"Well, Pastor Simmons seems to think I might be able to help the boy." I sighed. "I don't know how other than to pray for him."

"Why does he think you can help him?" she asked.

"He says the boy is fascinated with my television ministry and maybe there might be some kind of link there. Maybe I can tap into that fascination and get him to listen. I don't know." I reached for my tea and guzzled the remainder of it. Then I tried to fit an ice cube in my mouth, but it was too big. I dropped it back into the glass.

Alissa giggled. "Would you like another glass of tea?"

"Why, yes, I would," I replied and handed her my glass.

Alissa retrieved the glass and swayed into the kitchen. I watched her the way I used to watch Wanda Moore but with a different feeling in my heart, a respect and tenderness that tempered raw desire into loving appreciation. I felt free just to love and desire my wife instead of chasing every woman I could find who would let me bed her.

Alissa soon returned from the kitchen. She set the glass of tea on the side table, leaned over and kissed me, then she said, "I'm going to start supper before the kids wake up. I will never get anything done with them tugging on me." Once again, she swayed into the kitchen. I took a few more sips from my tea, laid my head back into the sofa, and soon drifted into my own nap.

There was a thunderstorm that hit us just about thirty minutes outside St. Louis. Hard pelting rain made visibility so dense the bus driver had to pull over to the side of the road and wait for the storm to pass before we could move on. This delayed our arrival into St. Louis by almost an hour, so by the time we arrived, there was barely enough time to get checked into the hotel before my scheduled appointment with this boy. It was still raining when we arrived, and I had not brought an umbrella. The quick run into the hotel soaked my blue oxford shirt, jeans, and penny loafers.

Pastor Simmons was waiting inside the hotel to escort me to the church to meet the boy. He knew from seeing the bus parked outside the lobby that I had arrived. He approached with a raincoat thrown over one arm, using an umbrella like a cane. We had never met.

"Pastor Dennison?" he questioned even though he knew who I was. His long-fingered hand extended for me to shake.

"Yes, Pastor Simmons?" I asked in return, shaking his hand.

"It is so good to meet you, sir," he went on. "I wasn't quite sure you were going to make it there for a while. Apparently, there had been a tornado that touched down just east of town. Did you encounter any damage?"

"No," I replied. "We only had to pull off the road for a little while because the visibility was so bad."

"Well, I'm glad everyone is okay," he assured. "It looks like you still need to check into the hotel, and it looks like you might need to change."

"Yes, I'm a little wet," I replied.

"Go ahead," he said. "I can wait for you here in the lobby."

He was a kind-looking man, thin, and of average height. He appeared to be perhaps in his sixties. Blue eyes accented his gay hair, and he had a gentle smile.

"Thank you," I said and turned toward the check-in desk. I had no sooner turned in that direction when Clara approached, handing me a key.

"You are all checked in, Pastor, Room 310. They have taken your luggage up for you."

"Thank you, Clara," I said as I reached for the key. "Oh," I continued, remembering my manners. I turned back around. "Pastor Simmons, this is my secretary, Clara Smith. Clara, Pastor Michael Simmons of Safe Harbor Church."

"Yes, we have spoken many times on the phone." Clara smiled as she extended a hand to him.

"I am very pleased to meet you, Clara," he responded, "very nice to put a face to the name."

For a moment, I thought I saw a gleam in each one's eye as the handshake lingered perhaps a little longer than normal.

"Pastor, please give me about ten minutes," I said as I dashed for the elevator with the key.

I got to my room, dabbed a towel against my face and hair, and quickly changed into my normal professional attire of a black suit, white shirt, and a traditional paisley tie. When I came back to the lobby, I was surprised to see Clara sitting in a chair next to Pastor Simmons. She was turned sideways toward him and seemingly engrossed in their conversation.

"I'm ready, Pastor," I said when I approached.

"Wonderful!" Pastor Simmons glanced at me, smiled, and got to his feet. Then he turned back to Clara and said, "I hope we can continue this conversation another time. I would like to hear more of what you have to say on the topic."

"Definitely," she replied. "If I don't get a chance to spend more time with you while we are here, please give me a call in Nashville. Whether Pastor Dennison is in the office or not, I am there Monday through Friday, 8:00 a.m. to 5:00 p.m."

"I will definitely call you sometime," he responded.

I looked over at Clara, and she gave me sly little knowing smirk that told me there was something more going on than just conversation. I fought the urge to say, "I thought you swore off men for life."

"Ready?" Pastor Simmons asked as he turned to me, smiling. "Yes, I think so," I said.

We walked to his car, and he drove me about four miles from the hotel to the church.

"I hope Stephen will be happy to see you," he said as he drove. "I have encouraged him that he is going to get to meet a famous TV minister."

"Well, I hope that I am more to him than a celebrity," I commented.

"I hope so too, Pastor." He leaned in slightly to get a better look at the road as the rain had gotten heavy again. The windshield wipers sloshed the gray water quickly from side to side. I began to feel more nervous as we neared the church, and the sound of the wipers seemed irritating.

When we arrived, Pastor Simmons pulled to the back parking lot. After parking the car, he came around and shared his umbrella with me as we made a quick dash for the back door. Inside, there was a short paneled hallway with office doors on either side. Pastor Simmons called out, "Miss Johnson, we're here."

"Be right there," a woman's voice called back.

Soon, an attractive slender young woman entered the hall with a skinny boy of little more than four feet in height. His mousy brown hair was longer than usual but still in a boy's cut, early 1960s Beatle's style, and it was perfectly combed. His eyes were between brown and hazel, and his face was almost gaunt, showing an expression of deep sadness. I struggled to determine if he might have been biracial. The woman stood to his side with her hand on the boy's shoulder. He didn't move and held his hands stiffly to his side. I walked up to him, extended my hand, and said, "How do you do? You must be Stephen. I am Pastor Ronald Dennison."

"I know who you are," he said bluntly. "And my name is Stephanie." His tiny hand was swallowed inside of mine when he extended it to me.

"Well, Pastor Simmons tells me you like to watch my television broadcast," I teased.

"Yes," he said and dropped his hand from mine.

"Well, shall we go somewhere and have a talk?" I questioned and looked back to Pastor Simmons.

The young woman interjected, "You can use this room, Pastor." She extended her arm toward a door on the opposite side of the hall.

"Wonderful," I said. "Stephen, shall we go talk?"

"Stephanie!" he demanded angrily.

"Okay, shall we go inside and talk?" I replied, calmly refusing to call the boy by a girl's name.

The boy turned without saying a word and went into the room. I followed. Inside, there was a sofa under a window and a desk on an adjacent wall. The boy plopped himself on the floral-print sofa and stared at me. I gently closed the door behind us and turned to face him. I didn't want to sit at the desk as I feared that would be too formal. Instead, I pulled a nearby red velvet upholstered wingback chair a little closer to the sofa. I sat down and leaned toward him.

"So…Stephen, tell me a little bit about yourself."

"I told you my name is Stephanie!" he angrily demanded. "If you keep calling me Stephen, I'm not going to talk to you!"

"Okay." I sighed. "But I'm not comfortable calling you that because it is a girl's name, and you are obviously a boy."

"I am NOT a boy!" he snarled. "Just because I was born with a pecker doesn't mean I'm a boy!" He grabbed at his crotch. "I'm not supposed to have this. This is not the body I was supposed to have."

"Ah…okay," I went on, nervous and confused. "Tell me a little bit about yourself."

"What do you want to know?" he asked.

"Well, everything I guess." I leaned back in the chair.

The next words out of his mouth shocked me to my core. Never had I heard an adult, much less a child, utter such things.

"My mother was a drug whore," he said. "She would fuck a dog for a cigarette and hump a fire hydrant if she thought it would get her some heroin. She was a cunt!"

"Ah…well…ah," I struggled for words. "Please don't use words like that."

"Ah, well, ah what!" he snarled. "My mother was scum! She deserved what she got! I wish I had fucking killed her myself!"

I knew right then I was in over my head. I didn't know what to say. What could I say to a child who had been so deeply wounded? I felt tears welling in my heart. I clasped my hands together in front of me and simply began praying. "Blessed Jesus, lift up this child. Solace his wounded heart and give him peace—"

"STOP THE FUCKING PRAYER SHIT!" he screamed and stood to his feet. "WHY DO YOU GODDAMN PEOPLE THINK YOU HAVE TO FUCKING PRAY OVER EVERY FUCKING LITTLE THING? YOU DON'T PRAY BECAUSE YOU GIVE A SHIT ABOUT ME! YOU PRAY BECAUSE YOU DON'T FUCKING KNOW WHAT TO SAY AND BECAUSE IT MAKES *YOU* FEEL BETTER! WHERE THE FUCK WAS YOUR STUPID GOD WHEN I WAS GROWING UP IN THE GODDAMN SLUMS WITH A FUCKING DRUG WHORE MOTHER?"

Never in my life had I ever heard a child speak that way to any adult or another child for that matter. If it had been Daddy instead of me, the boy would have had a hand slapped straight across his mouth, probably hard enough to loosen teeth. I was determined, however, to establish some kind of rapport. It was clearly evident why he was having trouble in a Christian home. Never in my life had I been jarred back into myself like I was at that moment.

I paused in cold silence. I was completely taken so far aback I had no words. I sat quietly, feeling almost afraid of him. Then, finally I spoke.

"I'm sorry…Steph—Stephanie." I thought maybe, if I used the female name he wanted, he might calm down. "I do care about you. I don't know you, and I won't even pretend that I have a clue about what you have been through, but I took this time to meet with you because I do care."

"And where are you going to go when this is all over?" he demanded. "Back home, that's where. Back to your cushy, bullshit life. I bet you make lots of money doing that TV show and people sending you money and shit from all over the country. I'll bet you live a pretty damn cushy life."

I sighed long and deep, contemplating where I could go with this, what I could possibly do or what I could possibly say that would solace this child. I decided that defending myself would do no good. Besides, he was right. When all this was over, I would go back to my cushy life in Nashville. I sat there looking at him and realizing that, despite all the difficulty of my own childhood, losing Teddy, struggling with my addiction to women, I had never been through a tenth of what he had been through. My life *was* cushy, blessed beyond measure. I sat there wondering why God would bless me so abundantly while leaving this little boy to suffer the torments of hell. Finally, I spoke. "So why did you agree to talk to me?" I asked.

He stood there for a moment then walked over to me and stroked his hand up my leg from my knee, halfway to my crotch as he said in a soft, sultry voice, "Because I think you're sexy."

"Please don't do that," I asked nervously as I lifted his hand off my leg and placed it back at his side.

"Why?" he responded. "Does it make you nervous?"

"Yes," I replied. "It makes me very nervous. Please sit down."

He plopped himself down on the sofa and exclaimed, "You know, men have fucked me before."

"Dear God!" I heard myself exclaim.

"What's the matter?" he asked.

"I am so sorry anyone would do that to you," I replied.

"When I was little, it hurt," he continued. "But I got used to it. I've always liked being touched by men as long as I can remember, but there was this one asshole my mother used to leave me with. His name was Jake, and he's a fucking bastard! The more it hurt me, the more he liked it."

I became increasingly anxious and felt myself trembling. "I am so sorry," I said. "I'm so sorry that anyone would hurt you."

"You want to fuck me?" he asked bluntly.

"WHAT? Absolutely not!" I exclaimed.

"Why? Don't you think I'm pretty?"

"That has nothing to do with it," I responded quickly. "You are obviously a very handsome…boy—"

"I'M NOT A FUCKING BOY!" he screamed. "I NEVER HAVE BEEN AND NEVER WILL BE A FUCKING BOY, AND I WILL NEVER BE A MAN." He grabbed his crotch. "I WILL CUT THIS SHIT OFF MYSELF IF I HAVE TO!"

"Stephen—ah—Stephanie," I responded nervously, attempting to sound calm. "Please calm down. There is no reason to shout. Surely we can come to understand each other without shouting."

He sat there and stared at me for way too long, his eyes piercing through me, his face sullen.

"Why don't you want to fuck me?" he asked finally as he leaned back into the couch.

Again, I sighed. "Because it's wrong," I said.

"Why?" he continued. "I like you. You're sexy. Most of the time, after I watch your show, I fantasize that you're fucking me. I don't like getting fucked in the ass though. I want to get fucked in the pussy like other girls."

"Dear God, give me strength," I mumbled under my breath. Then I spoke. "Ste-Stephanie—even if the Bible didn't say that it is not right for a man to lay with another man, it would still be wrong for an adult to lay with a child."

"Why?" he questioned bluntly.

"How old were you the first time someone did that to you?" I asked.

"I don't know. Maybe I was four. Maybe I was five or six," he responded.

"It does things to a child's mind," I said and leaned toward him again, my hands clasped in front of me. "Sex is something that takes maturity to understand. Many adults struggle with it. It is not possible for most people to have sex without some emotion being involved. Those emotions can be very powerful, even overwhelming, and it is far too much for a child that young to cope with or understand."

"I understand," he said, reaching into his pocket to pull out and unfold a piece of gum. He put the gum in his mouth and began to chew. "People do it because they get the urge. After they do it, they are good to go till the urge comes again. Then they do it again."

"Did you want someone to do that to you when you were four or five years old?" I asked.

He pondered for a moment. "Well," he said, "I've always liked men. I don't remember when I didn't like men. I love to touch men and be around men, but the first time, it was that asshole bastard Jake who did it. He made me do it, and it hurt. I fucking hate him! He's not a real man."

"Well, that's the other thing that makes it wrong," I said. "It is never okay to force anything on another person that they don't want, and children don't have the maturity to make a decision like that even if they think they want it. They are not even going to think about things like that if some adult has not brought it to them."

"Well, there were a couple of other times, with other guys, that I wanted it and kind of liked it, but I could never like it as much as if I had my own pussy," he said. "I don't want it in my ass, but I was older then, and it was my choice. Mike would never do it though, my friend, Mike. I wanted him to, but he wouldn't. He came and fucked my whore mother, but he wouldn't fuck me."

"A child is not mature enough to be making those kinds of decisions," I said as I watched him intently. "I have to wonder if you would have thought you liked it if you had never been molested in the first place."

"I like it," he said, "for as long as I remember, I liked men. I don't like when most women touch me."

"I don't know," I pondered.

"Have you ever been molested?" he asked.

A shock hit me with that question. I felt like I was standing before a convicting judge. Was fooling around in the same bed with Teddy being molested? Sudden flashes of Daddy yelling at me ran through my mind. Flashes of the dream of Jesus being blown across our farm in the storm and crawling up the steps in the back door of our house and the redheaded woman screaming "SINNER" ran through my mind. I had no idea why those images came to me.

"No!" I adamantly replied.

"Then, shut up. You don't know what you are talking about," he commanded.

"I do know right from wrong," I replied. "I'm a minister. It is my vocation to know right from wrong and teach people about what is right and wrong."

"Really?" He smiled. "Well, what that bastard Jake did was wrong 'cause it hurt, and he wouldn't stop. He deserves to die, and I'm going to kill him someday, I am. If it takes me the rest of my life, I'm going to find him and kill him!"

"Did going into foster care get you away from Jake?" I asked.

"Yeah, I haven't seen him since I got out of the projects, but he didn't live in the projects. He was one of my mother's stupid friends. She used to dump me with him when she wanted to run around. I just wanted him to leave me alone. I used to try to think of ways I could kill him."

"You know that killing is wrong too," I said. "Even if people do bad things."

"The state kills people," he commented. "They call it the death penalty. I would just be saving them the trouble."

"That's different," I responded. "The state doesn't kill out of anger or vengeance but out of justice, and a court decides, not just one person who is feeling vengeful."

"Jake likes pretty boys, sissies like me," he continued, apparently ignoring what I had just said. "I never wanted to be pretty for him, but I wanted to be pretty for Mike, and I want to be pretty for you." He reached into his pocket again and pulled out a tube of lipstick. I had started to say that I was glad he didn't have to be around Jake anymore, but instead, I heard myself fervently ask, "WHERE DID YOU GET THAT?"

"I stole it," he said then uncapped it and began applying red lipstick to his lips.

"Please stop," I pleaded.

"Why? I like it," he mocked. "It makes me look sexy."

"STOP IT!" I demanded. "GIVE ME THAT!" I held my hand out with insistence that he hand me the tube of lipstick.

"No!" he replied. "It's mine!" He put the tube back in his pocket and began rolling his now-painted lips together.

My heart was pounding. I didn't know why. I only knew that I was beginning to find it difficult to breathe, and my heart began to feel like it was going to pound out of my chest. "WIPE THAT OFF YOUR LIPS NOW!" I demanded.

"NO!" he shouted back. "I thought you said we could communicate without shouting, and now you're shouting."

Sweat popped out on my forehead, and I began to feel nauseated. I grabbed a box of tissue off the desk and thrust it in his direction. "Please! Please! Wipe that off your lips!" I begged.

"You look sick," he said.

I took one of the tissues from the box and began wiping my now sweating forehead. "I don't know what's wrong with me," I said. "I-I've got to go." I staggered toward the door.

"You look like you're going to puke!" he exclaimed.

My hand reached the doorknob and shook so hard I almost could not turn it. When finally the door opened, I stuck my head into the hall and shouted, "PLEASE! PLEASE, is there a restroom nearby?"

Pastor Simmons stuck his head out of another office door and, upon seeing me, quickly moved to my side. "Pastor, are you all right?" he asked as he slipped a hand under my arm. I began to wretch, and he quickly exclaimed, "This way."

He led me a few steps to another door and opened it for me. Inside was a small wash basin and a toilet. I threw myself to my knees over the toilet and began to heave. The contents of my stomach came gushing out with a terrible force. Pastor Simmons grabbed paper towels and wet them in the sink to press against my forehead and wash my face. "My goodness," he said. "You are really sick."

"I don't know what's wrong with me," I replied. "I just suddenly became deathly ill."

"My lipstick made him puke!" I heard Stephen laughingly remark. I looked up in my haze of nausea to see him standing at the door, giggling.

"Miss Johnson," Pastor Simmons commanded. "Please take Stephen aside."

She quickly rushed to the boy, placed her hands around his shoulders, and directed him down the hall to another room.

I turned back to the toilet and gave a few more unproductive lunges at the vomit-filled basin and began to catch my breath. Pastor Simmons handed me more wet paper towels. "It doesn't look to me like you are in any shape to preach tonight," he said.

"I'll be fine," I responded. "This will pass."

"Might be catching a bug or maybe caught something from being out in the rain," he continued.

I got to my feet, still trembling, and placed a hand on his shoulder. "Pastor," I assured. "I will be fine. I feel better already. Maybe I just needed to get lunch off my stomach. It didn't set well with me."

"I know you have traveled a long way and that you have put yourself out for us," he consoled, "but I will be happy to fill in the service this evening if you are not able to do it."

"It would not do for a healer to not be healed for his own presentation," I said. "Where is the boy?"

"I'm sure he is with Miss Johnson down the hall," he replied.

"Let me speak with him before I go," I insisted. "I would like one last opportunity with him."

"Very well," Pastor Simmons responded and then called down the hall. "Miss Johnson, please bring Stephen back."

Miss Johnson emerged from a room down the hall with her arm around Stephen's shoulder. His face was wiped clean, and there was no trace of lipstick left on it.

"Get your hands off me!" he demanded as he slung his shoulder away from her arm.

"Stephen, we need you to behave in a civilized manner," Pastor Simmons commanded.

"Fuck you!" Stephen snarled.

"Please," I pleaded with both of them as I walked up the hall toward Stephen. I knelt down in front of the boy. "I know you are angry," I began. "I don't blame you for being angry. I would be angry too if I had been through even part of what you have been through. You have a right to be angry…Steph—" I stopped short of calling him either Stephen or Stephanie and then continued. "I know, because of what you have been through, it is very difficult for you to believe that anyone can be trusted or that anyone might genuinely care about you. I can't fix that for you. It is only something that you can fix yourself if you really want to. I can't make you trust me or anyone else, and there is nothing I can do to prove that I deserve your trust if you believe that no one can be trusted. Is there anyone in your life, Steph, who you have ever been able to trust? Is there anyone in your life who hasn't hurt you?"

He stood silent and stared at me. I saw the anger on his face transition into sadness. After a very long pause, the tears welled in his eyes, and he answered. "Miss Mattie," his voice creaked. "Miss Mattie was always good to me, but the state took her away from me and put me HERE!" The anger returned as he shouted the last word, and with it, tears that he tried desperately to stifle.

I reached out to take his hand. "I'm sorry," I said quietly. "Have you gotten to see Miss Mattie?"

"They won't let me see her!" he accused.

I held Stephen's hand for a moment and turned back to Pastor Simmons. "Who is this Miss Mattie he is talking about?"

Pastor Simmons sighed. "She is an old Negro woman who lived in the projects," he replied.

"Why hasn't the child been allowed to see her?" I asked.

"She is not kin," he replied. "There has been no reason for him to see her, and since she lives in the projects, we question whether it would be appropriate for him to see her. Who knows what she is really like?"

"Do you know anything about her?" I asked.

"Only that she is an old Negro woman who is poor enough to live in the projects," he replied.

I turned back to Stephen. "Tell me about Miss Mattie," I pleaded.

"She's the only person who ever loved me." He sniffled. "Now, she might as well be dead too."

"How did you know Miss Mattie?" I went on.

"She took care of me most of the time," he replied. "When I could, I would beg my so-called-mother into leaving me with her instead of Jake. When my so-called-mother was into her shit or passed out, I would go see Miss Mattie. I barely even got to say goodbye to her when they took me out of there." The tears welled in his eyes again. It was obvious to me that he loved her.

I turned again to Pastor Simmons. "Was this Miss Mattie given any option to take care of the boy when he was taken into state custody?" I asked.

"There is no way to do that," Pastor Simmons responded. "She is not a foster parent for the state. The court is, of course, going to place the boy in a home that is best suited for him. He is white, for one thing, well, more white than Negro, and placing him in the care of an old Negro woman to continue in the poverty and squalor where all this happened to him was certainly not considered a viable option."

"What does it profit a man to gain the whole world and lose his own soul?" I quoted Scripture. "If the child is living in a home where he is loved, I would think that is more important than the quality of his surroundings."

"We don't know anything about the woman," Pastor Simmons defended. "The foster family has been trying to keep him away from the influences of his previous life."

I turned back to Stephen. "Would you like to see Miss Mattie?" I asked. He nodded affirmatively.

"There is no time today," I continued. "But with the permission of Pastor Simmons and your foster family, I will stay over tomorrow, before I go back to Nashville, and I will take you to see Miss Mattie."

"Pastor Dennison, I just don't think that's a good idea," Pastor Simmons pleaded. "The projects are dangerous enough for the Negros even in the daytime. It certainly would not be safe for a coat-and-tie-wearing white man to take a child into, even in the middle of the day."

"Then I won't wear a coat and tie," I argued.

"But, Pastor, it is not safe for either of you," he continued.

"Yea, though I walk through the valley of the shadow of death, I will fear no evil," I replied. "The Lord will keep us safe. Besides, you know the way, don't you, Steph?" I had decided that calling him Steph was as close as I could come to a name that was neither male nor female.

"Yes," he replied calmly.

"You see." I turned back to Pastor Simmons. "Steph knows the way."

"All right," he acquiesced.

I turned back to the child. "Tomorrow then. We will go tomorrow."

"Thank you," the boy said quietly. He stood there for a moment, I suppose contemplating if it was okay, then he leaned over and softly hugged me. His behavior had completely changed from his previous demeanor. My arms went around the boy. I held him tightly.

"I'll see you tomorrow," I said as I rose to my feet. I patted Stephen lightly on the shoulder and told Pastor Simmons, "I am ready to go back to the hotel and get ready for services."

CHAPTER 20

That evening, the service went smoothly. After having done it for so many years and having the support of a good crew, there were only rare occasions that things did not go smoothly. There were moments of hesitation in my voice that the congregation probably took as silence for the sake of effect, but in truth, I had Stephen on my mind quite a bit. For some reason, I could not stop thinking about that child and how important it would be for him to be with someone who truly did love him, who had his best interests at heart. If this Miss Mattie genuinely cared about him, if she was what he said she was, then she would be the obvious appropriate choice of someone to parent him. The next day I would find out for sure.

There were also times, during the sermon, when flashes of my own childhood dreams assailed me briefly. I saw flashes of Jesus crucified on the side of our barn, flashes of the redheaded woman intermixed with images of my meeting with Stephen. At times I saw flashes of Daddy preaching a Sunday sermon or Momma kneeling by the pond and praying. Sometimes she would do that. I never knew why, but there were times when Momma would kneel down by the water's edge, on the shallow side of the pond opposite the terrace, and pray with her hands folded to her chest, her forehead down, while she stared into the water.

I tossed and turned that night in the hotel bed. I could not get comfortable and never felt as though I had really drifted off to sleep. At times in my state of being half awake, I thought I heard the redheaded woman call out, "Sinner!" Random words that made no sense meandered around in my mind as I drifted in and out of light sleep. Things like "You should call her, Dan" or "He doesn't know how to butcher armadillos." I had a recurrence of my original dream of the redheaded woman coming up out of the mercury-glistening waters of our pond that parted when I touched it.

I had set the alarm for 7:00 a.m. and had previously discussed with Clara that we would send the crew back to Nashville and the two of us would rent a car to go back later in the day. Pastor Simmons took me to the rental car facility as soon as we had finished breakfast about 8:30 a.m., and Clara seemed to relish the idea that she would get to spend much of the day visiting with him while I took Stephen to see his friend.

Pastor Simmons did his utmost to talk me out of what I was going to do. He admonished me that not even the neighborhood around the projects was remotely safe and that I could be putting myself and the boy in danger by taking him back there. "Though I walk through the valley of the shadow of death, I will fear no evil—Psalm 23:4." I smiled back at him.

He sighed a response. "The Lord be with you. I'll pray for you both today."

With permissions given, around 10:00 a.m., I picked Stephen up from the home of his foster parents. I didn't need to know my way around the city as Stephen was an excellent guide. As we drove to the projects known as Pruitt-Igoe, I began to notice just how feminine he was. I seemed to have missed that on the day before, as well as what a waiflike figure he cast. With his cursing, I had failed to notice the lilt of femininity in his voice and the softness of his movements. It was as though he were two different people, the angry cursing boy and the gentle feminine girl. For a moment, I wondered if God, for some reason, in His infinite wisdom, really had placed the soul of a girl in the body of this boy. I couldn't imagine why that would be, but I also couldn't imagine that whatever God ordained was, in the long run, not for the greater good of all. I also wondered why God had seen fit to bring this child across my path. Of all the things I had ever encountered, this was by far the most intriguing, and it had stimulated a deep searching of my soul. We drove to the north side of St. Louis. Stephen recommended that I park the car a good ten or fifteen blocks away from the projects and lock it.

"They'll mess with you," he said. "They see a white guy driving up in a new car, don't know what they might do."

I took his advice, and we walked the long blocks to the projects. Closer in, it was obvious that the streets were littered with bits of trash or discarded beer cans. The sidewalks were broken and, in some places, narrowed down to the dirt where the concrete didn't even exist anymore. I saw the buildings in the distance long before we arrived there, multiple old ten-or-twelve-story buildings in obvious decay and disrepair. This was a prison of segregation, a place where black people and a few white poor had been separated from mainstream society and put on the fringes, where so-called good people didn't have to look at them or live around them.

We first walked through an area where there was a dilapidated playground. People of color, adults and children, stared at us with menacing glares that seemed to demand an excuse for our presence. I had deliberately dressed down that day. There was none of the preacher garb of slacks, tie, and button-down Oxford shirt. I always brought casual clothes for the ride back home. This time, I tried to be even more casual, as casual as I could be with what I had, which was a plain white T-shirt, jeans, and tennis shoes. I had thrown on a light jacket because it was, after all, late March in St. Louis. Even though the day was unseasonably warm, there was still a slight chill in the air. From my left side, I heard the cracking voice of a pubescent boy cry out, "Stephanie! Where you been, baby?"

A black boy of maybe fifteen or sixteen came up beside us and put his arm around Stephen's neck, pulling him in close to his chest, almost in a choke hold.

"Get lost, Ronza!" Stephen exclaimed.

"But, Stephanie, honey, I've missed you, baby," the boy teased. Then he leaned in close to Stephen's ear and muttered clearly enough for me to hear. "I might like to get me some, a little lovin', sweetheart. Know what I'm sayin'?"

"I told you, get lost!" Stephen blurted, as he shoved the boy away with his elbow.

"Who's your friend?" the boy questioned as he kept pace with us. "None of your business!" Stephen declared. "Now get lost!"

The boy continued his harassment. "But, baby, you know I love ya!"

I turned to face the boy, took a menacing stance, and directly lied. "I am Officer Ron Dennison with the St. Louis police investigative unit. I am here with this young man"—I nodded toward Stephen—"on official business. Is there anything I can help you with here today, young man?"

The boy's demeanor immediately changed, and he began to back away. "No, hey, I'm just playing," he said. "Having a little fun, no harm."

Just before he turned to walk away, he put his thumb to the center of his chest and then pointed at Stephen. He made a kissing motion with his lips. Then he turned and sauntered casually in the opposite direction.

Stephen turned back to me and said, "He's an asshole. Don't pay him no mind." Then, he led me to a building in the second row from the edge of the projects, where we had approached.

The old buildings were stacked like dominoes in a row, huge dominoes made of tan bricks. He led me through the door and into a stark and dirty hallway. Then he led me up two flights of stairs to a third floor. "Elevator don't fucking work," he said as we climbed the stairs.

The entire building had an unpleasant stench about it. I followed him down a dimly lit hall on the third floor. As we passed a door on the right, he motioned to it and said, "This is where me and my so-called mother used to live." Then, he led to a door farther down the hall on the left, where the number was only vaguely recognizable, and knocked.

From inside, we heard rumblings as someone approached the door. Then the door cracked open only slightly with three chain locks obviously still attached. I could barely see one eye of the woman peering through the crack between the door and the facing.

"Who are you?" she demanded, apparently keeping eyes at my level and not noticing Stephen at first. "You ain't got no business here!"

"Miss Mattie, it's me, Stephanie," he interjected. Her eyes darted downward to see him standing beside me.

"Da Lord of Mercy!" she exclaimed as she fiddled to loosen the chain locks. She opened the door, tears filled her eyes, and she immediately knelt down to give Stephen a hug.

"Oh my Lord, child, I've missed you! I thought I was never gonna get to see you again. I'm sorry de state took you away. Oh, mercy, it's so good to see you, baby." The woman hugged Stephen for a very long time, and periodically kissed him on the cheek. Finally, she pulled away from him, and held him by the shoulders.

"Oh Lord. Let me get a good look at you! Oh, it is so good to know you are safe, baby."

"Miss Mattie," Stephen said after she released his hug. "This is Pastor Dennison. He brought me to see you."

She knelt there, looking up at me for a moment, sizing me up, then got to her feet with some obvious difficulty. This skinny black woman had barely two teeth in the front of her mouth. Her skin was wrinkled with age, and I guessed her to be at least nearing seventy years old. Suddenly a look of surprise crossed her face.

"Dennison? Dennison," she pondered. "Wait a minute. You look familiar. Oh, no! You are not dat pastor on de TV? No, can't be. Man like dat would never come here to Pruitt-Igoe."

"Yes, ma'am," I replied politely as I reached to shake her hand. "I am Pastor Ronald Dennison. I am very pleased to meet you. Stephen tells me you are a very sweet woman."

"Stephanie!" Stephen exclaimed.

"De Lord of Mercy!" she exclaimed again. "What on earth bring a man like you into a place like dis?"

"It's a long story, Miss Mattie. I'm sorry, I never got your last name," I said.

"Laroquette," she replied. "Lar-ro-quette, like Larry, oh, and a cat."

"French," I stated as a matter of recognition, not as a question.

"Creole from Louisiana." She smiled. "Come in. Come in. Ain't no use in standing out here in de hall." Miss Mattie motioned us into her apartment. It was small, and the furniture was old and tattered, but there were places she had thrown blankets over things to cover the damage. She had little figurines sitting here and there, some of them chipped and old, and colored bottles sitting on the windowsills that brought in little beams of colored light as the sun hit them. It certainly was no worse than what I had grown up with except a little more decorated and colorful. Like my own momma's house, it was very clean.

"Sit down, Pastor." She smiled at me and pointed to a chair. Then she turned to Stephen. "Have you eaten anything lately? You look bone-skinny, child."

"I had breakfast. I'm not hungry," Stephen replied.

"And what was breakfast?" Miss Mattie continued.

"I had half an apple," Stephen proclaimed proudly.

"That ain't no breakfast!" she retorted. "Don't de state feed you?"

"I'm in a *Christian* foster home," he replied with a snarl in his face as he said the word *Christian*.

"Well, don't dem Christians feed you?" she went on. "Seems to me feedin' children would be the Christian thing to be doin'."

"They had food," he replied. "I only ate the apple. I don't want to get fat. I gotta keep my figure. They tried to make me eat, but I won't."

"Girl," Miss Mattie scolded, "you are gonna waste off into nothing and blow away."

"You're skinny," Stephen teased.

"I ain't skinny 'cause I don't eat," Miss Mattie defended. "I'm skinny 'cause I'm skinny. You are skinny 'cause you don't eat. You wait right here. I'm gonna go fix you a sandwich."

She turned and went toward a short hall in the back that I assumed led to the kitchen. "Pastor, you want something?" she called back over her shoulder.

"I am just fine, ma'am," I replied. "I had a good breakfast."

She stuck her head back out from the hallway. "Now don't you make me have to get on you too," she scolded.

"Are you going to have something?" I questioned.

"I might," she popped back.

"Well, I'll have something if you have something," I responded. "But please don't go out of your way or go overboard with it. I really did have a big breakfast."

She said not another word and turned back to the kitchen.

While she was in the other room, Stephen began volunteering information. "Miss Mattie takes care of me." He smiled as he looked around the room.

He seemed different in Miss Mattie's apartment, more relaxed, more like a child. It occurred to me that he felt safe with her. It had also not escaped my attention that she made no effort to insist he was a boy. She called him Stephanie as he wished to be called and made no challenge of that, but she did challenge him on taking care of himself.

"She always made sure I was fed," Steven continued. "Even when my so-called mother was passed-out drunk or drugged up and there wasn't no food in the house. One time, Miss Mattie came down there and ran this guy off who was beating up my so-called mother. I ran up the hall to get her 'cause this guy had already hit my so-called mother so hard it sent a tooth flying across the room. Miss Mattie stuck a gun right in that guy's face and told him he could get gone by getting out of the building, or he could get gone by a bullet in the head—his choice. That man backed up out the door, but he was threatening he was going to come back and kill all of us. Miss Mattie said, 'I ain't afraid of scum like you! I'd just as soon kill you dead as to look at you, and I will kill you dead if I ever set eyes on you again!' And she meant it too."

Stephen sat silent for a moment then dropped his head and stared at the floor. "I wish I could stay with Miss Mattie," he muttered quietly.

"Pastor, you like tea?" Miss Mattie called from the kitchen.

"Yes, ma'am," I called back without taking my eyes off Stephen.

My heart broke for him. He was a completely different boy in that environment than the boy I had seen the day before. I sat there thinking to myself, *What a difference a little love makes. What a difference to be in the presence of someone who he knows loves him versus being in the presence of someone who is just taking care of him.*

In a moment, Miss Mattie emerged from the hall carrying a plate and a glass of milk. She set it down in front of Stephen and said, "Now you eat, or I'm gonna tickle you."

Stephen giggled. "No, you won't."

"Yes, I will." She grinned. "You know I will." She grinned wide, and the few teeth she had glistened in her smile where gum met enamel. She glanced in my direction. "Be right back, Pastor." Then she disappeared quickly down that little hall again.

In a moment, Miss Mattie emerged with a plate and a glass of tea for me. "It's just bread and government cheese," she said as she handed the plate and tea to me. "But it'll fill you up."

Miss Mattie darted out of the room one more time and returned with her own plate. Stephen had started munching on his cheese sandwich, but I was waiting for her to return rather than to be rude. "Go ahead and eat now," she said, and motioned to me as she came back in the room.

"Yes, ma'am," I said as I picked up the sandwich and took a bite. Miss Mattie took a bite of her own sandwich, and it was obvious that she had problems chewing due to those bad teeth. Still, she managed to accomplish the task. After she was finally able to mash the bite enough to swallow, she asked Stephen, "How have dey been treating you over dare in dat Christian home?"

"It's stupid!" Stephen replied. "I mean, I have a roof over my head and a nice bed to sleep in, but these people have got a bunch of kids that are in state custody or their parents have died or something. They have got like eight kids. It's a big house, but we still have to sleep four to a room, and they keep trying to turn me into some kind of Christian, like we have to pray over every bite of food, and we have to pray every night when we go to bed. Then, they take us to this stupid big church like three times a week. That's not the hard part though. The other kids are mean to me 'cause I'm different. Everybody in there has come out of some crappy deal, but they all think they're better than me. They pick on me 'cause I'm a girl, but I don't look like a girl. Even the other girls pick on me, and I have to sleep in a room with boys. Ain't none of it as bad as living here. They think they are tough and shit, but they ain't got a clue. Still, they pick on me and make fun of me. I want to stay with you, Miss Mattie."

"You always gonna have ta deal wid da fact dat some people, probably most people, ain't gonna like you or treat you right just 'cause you ain't like dem," Miss Mattie responded. "Dere's always gonna be people who hate you for no good reason, but if you try, you'll find de ones dat love you, and dem's da only ones dat matters."

I watched as a roach crawled up over the edge of the coffee table. Miss Mattie was quick to her feet as soon as she saw it. She grabbed a nearby newspaper and swatted the bug, flattening it to the wood. "Nasty vermin!" she exclaimed as she retreated to the kitchen. "Nasty people in dis building live like pigs, don't keep dey place clean, and den bugs come crawling up everywhere." Miss Mattie soon returned from the kitchen with a wet cloth to wipe the bug residue off the coffee table. "I'm sorry, Pastor," she said as she looked over to me. "De food is clean. I keeps it sealed up, and I wash de dishes before I ever serve any food on 'em."

"Miss Mattie, I'm not concerned about it," I replied. "I can tell that you are a very clean person."

"Miss Mattie is always getting after me to do a better job of washing up," Stephen interjected.

Miss Mattie sat down again and put her plate with the half eaten sand-wich back in her lap. She started to take a bite and then put the sandwich back on the plate.

"Pastor," she said, "what's gonna happen to dis child?"

"Well, I don't know the legalities of it all," I said. "More than likely he will live out the remainder of his childhood in state custody. Pastor Sim-mons tells me that he hasn't adjusted well with the church family that took him in, and if his behavior doesn't straighten up, they may have to seek placing him in an orphanage, or worse, a home for behaviorally disturbed children."

She looked back over at Stephen. "Baby, you gotta behave now. You don't want dem puttin' you in one of dem homes."

"I might as well be in one now. I might as well be dead," Stephen cried. "What difference does it make? Nobody loves me, and nobody really wants me. Everybody thinks I'm a freak."

Miss Mattie set her plate aside and rushed immediately to his side on the sofa. She sat beside him, placed her arm around him, and pulled him toward her. "Now don't say dat, baby," she comforted. "You know old Mattie loves you no matter what. Don't you know dat?"

"But I am a freak of nature!" Stephen exclaimed as she pulled his head to her bosom. "I probably should be killed and thrown to the pigs like some of the older kids say."

"Honey, you ain't no freak," she softly said as she began to rock him back and forth. "You are de way God made you. Don't ever be ashamed of being what de good Lord made."

"But God made me a boy!" he cried. "I'm not supposed to be a boy! I don't want to be a boy! I'm not a boy! I'm a girl! I…I don't know what I am!"

"Baby, you are eleven years old. Dat's what you are," she continued. "You don't have to know nothin' right now. You don't have to have all the answers right now. You got time." Miss Mattie turned to me as she continued to hold Stephen to her breast. "Pastor," she inquired. "Is dere anything we can do to keep dis child from going to one of dem homes?"

I sat there and stared at her for a moment. I was in a bit of a daze. Watching the two of them together, it was obvious to me where he felt most safe and most comfortable—with her. It was obvious to me that she loved him, cared for him, and wanted the best for him. Even though my mind and my Christian upbringing told me he would be better off in a Christian home, my heart told me he would be better off with her.

"Would you want to keep him?" I asked finally.

"Oh, Glory of the Lord, if dere was any way I could. I wish dat I could," she said. "Problem is, I ain't kin, and I can barely afford to keep myself."

Suddenly, an idea came into my head, a different kind of idea. It was against my logic, against my Christian thinking, but it flashed into my mind in a red-hot instant, and I found myself speaking before my logic could engage.

"What if you didn't have to worry about being able to afford it?" I asked.

"Oh Lord, yes!" she replied without hesitation. "If I knew dat I could give dis child a halfway decent life, I would be happy to raise her. I have practically raised her already. Lord knows her mother was not any kind of a mother to her. Lord knows she has been through hell. I just wish dat I had a way dat I could take her out of dat hell. I know she got ta deal with all dis idea dat she ain't really no boy. I loves her anyway. I loves her no matter what. I ain't gonna try to change her, make her into somethin' she ain't. I would do whatever it takes for her ta be happy. I would do whatever it takes for dis child."

It was not lost on me that Miss Mattie had never referred to Stephen as a boy and called him by the name he had requested. There was a part of me that wanted to rebel at the idea. Part of me wanted to demand that he should be raised in the home of a good Christian family or in a Christian orphanage where he would learn to accept his rightful place as a male in the world, instead of giving in to some fantasy of being a female, that had likely come from having been molested. Yet a part of me realized he was sitting with the only person in the world who truly loved him. I had a battle raging inside my mind, not unlike the battle I had always fought between what the Bible teaches and the discrepancies that life presents in spite of it. I sat there watching the two of them, asking myself if this was a trick of the devil to lure a poor child further into the hell of sin he had been rescued from. I realized that I had always been torn between Christian teachings and the concept of sin. God sent his Son to bring us out of sin. He died on the cross for our deliverance from sin, yet in two thousand years since His death and resurrection, we have all continued to struggle with it.

As I watched the two of them, I asked myself, *What would Jesus do?* Then another question ran through my mind that ultimately is the same as the first. *What would love do?* If Jesus was the earthly manifestation of pure and perfect love, what would pure and perfect love do? Would Jesus tell me to judge what I was seeing, to condemn this union between this old woman and this little boy who had become convinced he was a girl?

Would Jesus have me follow along with the previous plan that he should grow up in a foster home where he was loved and cared for but never loved the way Miss Mattie loved him, where he would never be accepted the way she accepted him? Then another thought ran through my mind. *Love— isn't love acceptance? Is it really possible for love to condemn, and if we think we are loving but we are condemning and judging, are we then deceiving ourselves? For how is it possible that love could condemn and save at the same time?* My life had been confusion, and that moment was no exception. The difference is that I found myself in the role of observer more than in the role of participant.

"Miss Mattie…" I found myself saying. "I will do what I can to help. I will see if I can find a way for Stephen—Stephanie to stay with you. I may have the financial ability to do that. I don't know if I have the legal ability, but I can assure you that I will do everything I can to make it possible for… Stephanie to stay with you."

"Oh Lord, Pastor," she said, never releasing her embrace of the child. "Even if I could keep her, I would not want her to grow up in a place like dis. No child should ever have to grow up in a place like Pruitt-Igoe. I pity the children who ain't got no choice, who ain't got no way out of here."

"Maybe arrangements can be made," I said. "I don't know, but I will see if there is anything I can do to help. Maybe we could make arrangements for you to live somewhere else. This is all speculation, mind you. I don't know what I can actually accomplish."

"Oh, Lord, Pastor!" Miss Mattie exclaimed. "Dat would be a miracle dat I will pray hard for, not for me. I can handle dis, but for dis child to have a better place, I will pray hard!"

The morning had passed quickly, and I realized that we needed to be getting back so Clara and I could start our trip back to Nashville. I hated to separate them, and I hesitated to say anything at all, but finally I had to.

"Ste—phanie," I said hesitantly. "We have to go. It is getting late in the morning, and I have to drive back to Nashville."

"Noooo!" he whined. "I want to stay here with Miss Mattie. You go on. I'll stay here."

"I wish you could stay here," I retorted. "But we have to go. You have to go back to the family that has legal custody."

"Miss Mattie," he pleaded. "Don't let him take me back there. I want to stay here with you."

"Now, baby, dere is what we want and what we have to do," she replied. "Pastor was kind enough ta bring you here. You need ta be kind enough to go back wid him. We will find a way to visit again, baby. We will, and maybe Pastor can do what he say, and we could live together after dat."

"Nooooo!" he whined and cried even louder. "No, Miss Mattie, don't let him take me. I don't want to go back."

I should have anticipated that this would happen, but for some reason, it never occurred to me. I only thought that I was taking the child to see an old friend and that the satisfaction of the visit might give him more incentive to behave at home. However, the visit was not at all what I expected, and yet, I'm not sure what I expected. I had deluded myself about the entire thing, the poverty and squalor, as well as the bond that was obvious between Stephen and Miss Mattie. Most of all, I had deluded myself into thinking he would just gratefully return with me without resistance. For a moment, I wasn't sure how things would turn out. I couldn't exactly leave him there because he refused to go with me. I wondered if I would have to get the police involved to have him escorted back. I dreaded such a scenario, but I had to consider it.

Miss Mattie held Stephen back away from her at arm's length, held him tight by the shoulders, and looked him straight in the eye. "Now you lookie here, Miss Hot Stuff, you need to straighten up. You had your visit. You got to see Miss Mattie, and Miss Mattie is all kinds of proud she got to see you, but now you gotta go. Now you gotta put on your big girl panties and do de right thing."

Tears filled Stephen's eyes. "But I don't want to go," he cried.

"Ain't nobody in dis world who always gets what dey want," Miss Mattie said firmly. "Don't you cause no problem for de good Pastor. He was kind enough to bring you. Now you be kind enough to go back wid him."

Stephen glanced over at me pleadingly. The look on his face begged me to change my mind, begged me to let him stay with Miss Mattie, and there was a part of me that desperately wanted to do exactly that.

"Please," he said tearfully. "Pleeeaaaaase."

"Stephen—Stephanie." I sighed as I leaned forward. "You have my promise that I will do everything I can to help you come back to Miss Mattie, but that is going to take some time and some planning. Right now, we have to go back."

I stood up and walked over to him. I held out my hand to him as he sat there on the sofa looking up at me with the saddest eyes that I think I had ever seen.

"Go on," Miss Mattie encouraged.

Stephen hesitated and stared at me. For a moment, I wondered if I might see the rage that I had seen the day before. Then he reached up and placed the tips of his fingers lightly into the palm of my hand, the way a young lady might accept a beau's invitation to dance. He stood to his feet with the grace of a young girl who was about to be led to a waltz at a formal ball. I was astounded at the femininity that I not only witnessed, but felt. That kind of feminine energy was something I had never experienced emanating from any male. It was something I had always been attracted to in women, but there was, of course, no physical attraction to this little boy, just a fleeting recognition of how comfortable I felt in the presence of femininity.

"Okay," he said, once he had gotten to his feet.

I stroked my hand across the back of his head affirming, the way I would affirm my own child. "Thank you," I said.

Miss Mattie rose to her feet and lectured him. "Now you behave yoself when you get back dere. Ain't no cause for acting up, even if people make fun of you. Just 'cause dey don't know no manners don't mean you gotta get mean wid 'em."

"But, Miss Mattie, they're all mean to me," Stephen protested.

"Well, you meet meanness with kindness," she said. "Dat's how it works. For every mean thing dey say, you say three kind things back to dem. For every put down, you lift yourself up above it. It ain't about you anyway. It's about what's going on in dere heads. De world ain't won by meanness, child, no matter how many people try to make it dat way. It's de meek dat shall inherit de earth. It's dem dat offers love for hatred and kindness for injustice dat rise above it. Just like Dr. Martin Luther King Jr. said, 'We must learn to live together as brothers or perish together as fools.' You keep dat in mind now, and you will get through it. But if you offer hatred for hatred, you are gonna die right along beside dem. Dem that lives by de sword dies by de sword. Now, no matter what happens, you keep your eyes on de prize. You keep your heart tuned to a better song."

"Well said," I commented.

Miss Mattie walked around us and straight to the door. She opened it like a doorman at a fine hotel. "Take good care of my girl," she said with eyes fixed on me.

I still could not bring myself not to feel uncomfortable that she referred to Stephen as a girl. I could not bring myself to feel comfortable that he referred to himself as a girl, that he insisted he was female, but one thing I knew for sure was that this old woman loved him. He listened to her guidance, obviously very good guidance, and she was probably the only person he knew who didn't hurt him or put him down. I placed my hand on Stephen's shoulder and directed him toward the door.

"Yes, ma'am," I said as we passed by Miss Mattie into the hall.

"Bye, baby," she said to Stephen once we had stepped into the hall. "Now you promise Miss Mattie you gonna be good."

"I promise," Stephen replied in a quiet, sad tone.

Miss Mattie placed a hand on either side of his cheeks and kissed him on the forehead. "I will always love you, baby," she said. "Don't you ever forget dat." Then she turned and shut the door behind us without saying another word. I took his hand, and we walked back in the direction from where we came. Before we neared the stairs, I was certain that I heard the faint hint of crying from behind us down the hall.

The trip back across the yard at Pruitt-Igoe was similar to the crossing when we arrived, but uneventful. I returned Stephen to the church where I left him in the care of Pastor Simmons. Clara had spent the afternoon visiting with the good Pastor, and I noticed again that there appeared to be a chemistry between them. We had left our luggage at the church, so after dropping Stephen off, we packed our suitcases into the trunk. Clara got into the passenger side of the rented Chrysler, and we headed back to Nashville.

We had barely pulled out of the church parking lot when Clara asked, "How was it?"

"Heartbreaking," I replied.

I didn't say anything else, and she didn't ask. As I drove, I tried to wrap my mind around what, if anything, I might be able to do to help the boy. Finally, I asked, "Clara, are you still in touch with the attorney who helped us with separating from the Clayburn ministry?"

"Yes," she replied. "The firm continues to manage a few things for us here and there."

"Good," I said. "When we get back, I want you to do something for me."

"Yes, sir," she replied with the formality she always maintained.

"First, find out what they know about Missouri law or if they can practice in Missouri. If not, find out if they have any ties to a good firm in Missouri. Then, I want them to do whatever is necessary to get this woman Mattie Laroquette designated as Stephen's legal guardian. If she decides she wants to adopt the boy, then do whatever it takes to make that happen for her. If it cannot be arranged for her to be his legal guardian or adopt him, then I will adopt the boy and authorize Miss Laroquette to raise him. We will set aside a trust of one million dollars to make sure that Miss Laroquette and Stephen do not have to concern themselves regarding food, shelter, or any other basic needs. They don't need to be kept in absolute luxury, but make sure they have a house in a decent and safe middle-class neighborhood. Make sure the house is paid for and the taxes and utilities are paid.

"Provide Miss Laroquette with a monthly stipend of $1,000 to care for the boy. If she is still alive when he turns eighteen, pay for whatever is required to supplement her needs beyond her social security check for as long as she lives. The trust needs to have a good brokerage firm to make sure that it is wisely invested and that it draws a good rate of interest. Then, when the boy turns eighteen, he will be allowed to draw interest off the foundation of the account to support himself, attend college, or do whatever he wishes with the money. If he can justify a legitimate need for money over and above the interest he will draw, then he can be allowed to dip into the principle. If Miss Laroquette passes away, he can have whatever funds were set aside for her." When he turns twenty-one, he may assume management of all funds left to him.

"Well." She sighed. "That sounds extremely generous. Is the house to be paid for out of the trust or purchased separately?"

"Purchase it separately," I replied. "Get them a nice home and maintain it for them. It does not need to be ostentatious, but it needs to be of good quality, in a safe neighborhood, and comfortable."

"Very well, Pastor," Clara responded. "I will need to make some notes when we get back to Nashville to make sure that I am carrying out this task exactly the way you need for it to be done."

"Thank you, Clara."

She said nothing in response. She sat silent, staring directly ahead, and occasionally glancing out the side window. For a very long time, she didn't say anything at all. Finally, she asked, "Pastor, I hesitate to ask, but…is this boy a child you have fathered during one of your…adventures?"

I turned to her in shock and felt a sudden surge of anger at the implication. I would have continued to stare at her if it was not imperative that I get my eyes back on the road. I looked down the lane in front of us for a moment and then turned toward her again. I realized that setting aside that much money for a child in another state must certainly look suspicious. I took a breath to contain my anger.

"No," I said firmly. "He is not my child."

"Regardless," she continued. "We will probably want to keep this as quiet as possible. Even if the boy is *not* yours, the rumors could be damaging, and you have certain enemies we don't want finding out about this at all. There have been times we have had to pay women to keep them from going to the media, so that could be of concern, and I suspect the Clayburns might gloat over a little revenge if they could have it."

I felt my grip on the steering wheel tighten and a surge of worrisome fear ran through me. I thought about it for a moment and realized that once again she was looking out for me and that I needed to think the decision through thoroughly.

"I understand." I sighed.

"Do you plan on telling Alissa?" she pursued.

"What do you think?" I questioned.

"I think your heart and your prayer should guide you," she responded.

I took a deep breath and loosened my grip on the steering wheel. "I think it already has," I replied.

CHAPTER 21

Clara and I got back to Nashville late in the day. We first stopped at the office, where I unloaded Clara's luggage from the trunk of the rental into her own car. She then followed me to the rental place to turn in the car and drove me back to the office to get my own vehicle. By the time I got home, it was already dark. I parked as usual and came in through the kitchen adjacent to the garage. Since it was late, and the children might have already been put to bed, I didn't call out to Alissa as I usually would. However, she heard me come in and came immediately through the kitchen door from the den. "Thank God you're home!" she exclaimed with exasperation. "I've been trying to get hold of you all day."

"What's the matter?" I questioned, noticing the obvious concern on her face.

"Your mother called this morning in tears," she replied. "I've been on the phone with her off and on all day. I left a message for you at your hotel in St. Louis, but I guess you didn't get it."

"What?" I exclaimed. "What's the matter?"

"Your father is critically ill and not expected to live more than a day or two."

"Oh my goodness!" I exclaimed. "What happened?"

"Marylee said he developed a pneumonia after catching the flu that was going around, and with the increasing frailty of his health over the years, apparently, he could not shake off the infections. She said the pneumonia progressed very quickly. The doctors wanted him to stay in the hospital, but he insisted on going home. That was day before yesterday, and at this point, he is unresponsive. Marylee called and said if we want to see him again before he passes, we need to come now."

There was actually a part of me that wanted to say, "Oh well, too bad, poor Daddy," but of course I didn't say it. There was a part of me that didn't care if he died. He had been so critical of me through the years, so wicked to Teddy, I had begun to numb myself from any affection for him. However, there was a part of me that grieved the Daddy I had always adored. Over the years I had come to realize that the man I adored was a fantasy of the father I had hoped for rather than the actual man. I was exhausted at that point, and the idea of a six or seven-hour drive to Arkansas was not something I wanted to undertake. My commitment to my family determined my decision. I sighed deeply and said, "I guess we have to go, but what about the children?"

"I know you must be exhausted," Alissa continued. "I have made arrangements for the Wilson family from church to keep the kids for a few days, and I already have bags packed for us."

"My goodness. What time is it?" I asked. I glanced over at the clock above our stove and realized it was only a few minutes till 9:00 p.m. Another exasperating sigh came out of me when I realized that we probably would not be able to get out of the city limits of Nashville until about 9:30 p.m., and that would put us at Momma and Daddy's house about 4:00 or 4:30 a.m.

Alissa reached over, took my hand, and laid her head briefly on my chest. "I know this is hard, sweetheart," she said as she squeezed my hand. "I'll be more than happy to drive the whole way. I'm rested."

"I guess we have to, don't we?" I responded. "What about my broadcast?"

"I contacted the station manager earlier today," she said. "He said it would be no problem to broadcast reruns for a few days."

"Okay...okay," I said. "Let me get my stuff out of the trunk." I turned back to the garage, and Alissa waited for me to bring my luggage in. When we got to our bedroom, I dropped the bags off by the bed and left them. Over the years of touring, we had accumulated several sets of luggage, and this was not the first time I had brought in bags full of dirty clothes to exchange for clean clothes already packed in different luggage.

"I've not had dinner," I said. "Can you please make me a sandwich while I freshen up a little?" By that time in my life and career, I not only had learned the term, but had come to appreciate the act of freshening up.

"Certainly, honey," she said. Then she rubbed her hand across my back and lightly touched her head against my shoulder, just before she left the room. She was being so loving and compassionate toward me, but it almost felt off-putting, like I didn't deserve it. I didn't want it.

I spent some time in the bathroom, toileted, washed my face, and stared at myself in the mirror for a moment, thinking how much I looked like Daddy and how different I had become from the man who raised me. I then looked around for the fresh luggage, didn't see it, and went back to the kitchen to ask Alissa about it. When I came back into the kitchen, I realized that Alissa already had our luggage sitting by the kitchen door near the garage. I had not even noticed it before. I picked up the first bag and went to the car to load it. Just as I loaded the last one and was closing the trunk, Alissa met me with a brown paper bag and a canned soda.

"You eat while I drive," she said.

When I took the items from her hand, she turned to pick up a grocery bag and a small cooler she had set by the kitchen doorway along with a blanket and pillow. She kicked the door between the garage and the kitchen closed with her foot and brought the items to the car.

"I took the liberty of packing a few snacks for the trip," she said as she turned quickly around to place all of it in our back seat. She then turned, stepped behind me, and fumbled in my right pocket for the car keys.

"Get in," she commanded while pulling the keys from my pocket. I did as I was told. Alissa checked the door to the kitchen to make sure it was locked then opened the garage door from the button next to the side door. She got in the car and backed it carefully out of the garage. Then she got back out, unlocked the side door of the garage, pressed the button to close the car access, locked the side door again, and got back in the car. I sat watching all this take place with a numb complacency. Things I normally would have done and should have done for her, I simply watched her do.

When we were on our way, I opened the bag to see, in the dim light of the streetlamps, a ham sandwich and some potato chips. I reached in and began to unwrap the sandwich from the butcher paper it was folded in, now feeling unsure if I really wanted to eat.

"This is strange," I said.

"Yes?" she questioned.

"I mean, I guess I always knew I would lose my parents at some point. In the back of my mind, I always knew this day was coming, but I never really thought about it. Now that it's here, I don't know what to think. I feel confused, mixed up."

"I have wondered what it might be like when I lose my mother," she said. "We always know that time is coming, don't we?"

"I just never really contemplated what it might be like," I replied, "or how I would get through it. It is also strange that Daddy is dying before Grandma Miller. She is at least twenty years older than him and still healthy."

"Life does strange things," she said as she took her right hand from the steering wheel to reach over and pat my leg. "It deals everyone a different experience. I think you just walk through it, one step after the other. You think whatever you think. You feel whatever you feel. More than anything, it is simply a matter of taking the next step and then the next one. Look at me. I'm a healthy, grown woman with two healthy kids when I felt like I was going to die at twelve years old."

"It was different when Teddy died," I said. "It was sudden, shocking, overwhelming. I loved him dearly, and my grief was intense, but this… this…feels like I'm walking through emotional mud, like I can barely pull one foot out of the muck to take the next step. I don't know why, because as close as I always wanted to be to Daddy, we were never really close."

"Maybe the grief is different when we lose what we hoped for rather than when we lose what we actually had. You will be fine," she comforted.

She patted my leg again and returned her hand to the steering wheel. "I'll be with you the whole time."

"You know Momma is going to complain that we didn't bring the children," I said.

"I thought she might," she said while we sat briefly at a stoplight. Then she steered us onto Highway 1 and headed for I-40. "However, I think the kids are too young to really understand what is going on anyway, and I figured we would have enough taxing of our attention without having to look after them."

"You're right," I said and finally bit into the sandwich I had been holding for several minutes.

"When you get through eating, you might want to see if you can sleep," Alissa suggested.

"What about you?" I questioned.

"I took a nap this afternoon," she replied. "I'll be fine, but I know you have driven most of the day, and you have to be exhausted. By the way, how did it go with that boy in St. Louis?"

I stared out the window into bits of darkness scattered between streetlights and home lights. "He's a very troubled child," I said, keeping my gaze out the window. "About the only person he feels comfortable with is an old black woman who lived up the hall from him in the projects. He has been deprived of contact with her since his mother was killed."

"That's a shame," she commented. "Were you able to help him?"

"Not in the way I expected to," I replied. "I thought Clara might have told you when she called yesterday that we were going to be late getting home because I took him to see the old lady in the projects this morning. I figured some source of comfort for him would be better than feeling completely alone in the world."

"I didn't get the call," she said. "Clara got hold of Mrs. Jenkins, who called yesterday evening to say you would be late getting back. She didn't say why."

"I'm sorry," I apologized.

"At least he has his church family," Alissa continued without even acknowledging the problem in communication. "I'm sure they love him, and he will grow comfortable with them in time."

"I don't think so." I turned back toward her. "This boy has essentially been alone his whole life. Even when he was with his mother, he was never really cared for. This old woman was the only friend he had. He could never count on even his mother or anyone else to love him without expectations or even be there for him on a consistent basis. His mother didn't even feed him regularly. The old lady up the hall took better care of him than his own family.

"Now he is expected to share his life with other kids he does not know, who pick on him and compete for the sparse attention of the foster parents. There are too many kids in that home. None of them gets the attention they need, and they all have to need more than the average child after what they have been through. He is expected to mold himself into what the foster parents want. I know they think what they are doing is best for him, and I know this boy is extremely confused, but the only person in his life who accepts him and loves him without expectation or condemnation is that old lady in the projects."

"Yes, but living in the projects is no life for any child," Alissa retorted.

"That's why I am making arrangements so they won't have to live in the projects," I confessed.

"What?" she investigated. "What are you talking about?"

"I've instructed Clara to get hold of our legal team to set aside a trust for the boy and for Miss Mattie, Miss Laroquette, the old woman I told you about. If they have money, they can live comfortably together, and neither of them will have to live in the projects.

"A trust?"

"Yes," I went on, "a trust fund."

"It would take a lot of money to support two people," she continued. "How much are you thinking about letting them have?"

"One million," I replied.

"What?" Alissa was obviously startled. "One…million…dollars?" she exclaimed. "Are you out of your mind, Ronnie? Nobody needs a million dollars to live comfortably! Anybody could live extremely well on less than a quarter of that. Your own parents and sister don't even get anywhere near that."

"Yet we have almost twenty million at this point," I replied. "What is giving up a a small part of that going to hurt? We don't need it. We live on much less than a quarter of it, and we accumulate more every day. Think of it as a tithe."

"Honey," she retorted, "it is commendable that you want to help this child, but that much money? If you want to give away a million dollars, it would be better spent through a charity where it could help multiple children. If you were to give it to an orphanage, you could help hundreds of children instead of just one."

"Well, maybe we'll do that too," I replied. "We'll still have more than plenty left over, and I know I need your permission to allocate this money, but I want to make sure this boy never suffers poverty again. I want to make sure that he is never without someone who truly loves him and who will care for him the way he needs."

"Why? Why this child?" she queried. "Why not any number of other children who suffer just as much?"

"I just know that I have to do this," I replied.

Then she asked the same question that Clara asked, and I suppose for the same good reason. "Ronnie, is this boy your child? Was this boy born out of one of your trysts?"

I sighed deeply. I knew that question was coming.

"Clara asked me the same question," I defended. "I know you both have legitimate reasons for suspecting that, and who knows, there may be a child out there that I don't know about, but this boy is not my flesh. I had never known nor heard of his mother, and she is not the type to come across any of the paths that I travel. She was a heroin addict. I seriously doubt she ever set foot in a church, much less an evangelical event. She was a hopeless drug addict, a soul lost to Satan who never had a chance for redemption."

"Then, why this boy?" she continued.

"I don't know for sure, Alissa. I just feel something for this child. I can't put my finger on it, but I feel a connectedness with him. I might consider adopting him myself if I didn't think Miss Mattie was the best person to finish raising him. I'm not sure I know how to handle his insistence that he is a girl. I know there would likely be conflict between us, but Miss Mattie just seems to know how to handle him, and regardless of the fact that she plays along with his fantasy that he is female, she really does guide him in the way of the Word. I watched her with him. She gives him solid, and yes, Christian guidance, and he listens to her. I think she is probably the only person in the world he actually listens to."

"So, something about this boy stole your heart." she commented.

"Yes," I continued. "I just want him to have a chance to be with the one person who truly loves him for what little time they may have."

"But, Ronnie, one million dollars?" she continued. "You don't need that much to support them in comfort. Anyone could live more than comfortably just on the interest from that for the rest of their life. Why a million dollars?"

"It's a nice round figure?" I grinned.

By this time, we were pulling onto I-40 headed toward Memphis.

"Don't be coy, Ronnie," she scolded. "This is a lot of money, and it needs a lot of consideration, not just an impulsive response to a whim."

"You're right," I replied. "When we get back, let's meet with Clara and the attorneys and see what we can figure out. Maybe we will just set aside a million and let them live on the interest. Right now, I think I am going to take you up on the offer to sleep."

By that time, I had finished my sandwich and chips. I wadded the paper bag up and put it on the floorboard in front of me.

"Okay then," she said. "As long as you are going to give yourself time to think it through and we can talk about it further, I can be content with that."

"Okay then," I responded and reached for the pillow and blanket in the back seat. I propped the pillow between the door and seat on the passenger's side, turned as far as I could on my side, and pulled the blanket up over my shoulder. I don't know how quickly I drifted off to sleep, but it wasn't long.

The pond water on our farm shimmered again like thick mercury. The pond bank seemed higher than normal, and Daddy was walking around the bank, reaching into his pocket, pulling out pebbles that looked like gold nuggets. He tossed them, one at a time, into the water. When the pebble hit the surface, the splash came up like a fountain and rained back down into ripples that flowed quickly across the shimmering silver surface.

Each time Daddy would laugh a loud cackling laugh that echoed across the pastures and woodlands. I stood at the edge of the pond, a little boy again of maybe five or six. I watched him throw pebbles into the water. Then, he reached into his pocket and pulled out something I could not see. He placed it in the palm of his hand, placed his other palm over it, and rolled it round and round. As he did this, he looked at me giggling, and his eyes glared like evil, as though there was a yellow light in them.

"I got a secret." He grinned. Then he laughed a bellowing laugh, pulled back his right hand, and threw the thing forcefully into the center of the pond. It flew from his hand like a ball of light, and when it hit the water, a huge splash came up hundreds of feet into the air and rained down over the farm. Huge globs of thick silver pond water fell from the sky and pelted the ground like molten meteors from the sky.

All the while, Daddy kept laughing. Several of the globs about the size of ping-pong balls hit my face and dribbled down my cheeks into my mouth. It tasted like blood, and I tried to spit it out.

Then I looked back to the pond, and there was no water left in it, but the redheaded woman lay at the bottom of the pond. There was nothing left of her but a skeleton, draped in her white robes, with her long red hair flowing around a bleached white skull.

She began to rise up from the bottom, and when she stood up, her entire frame was nothing but dry bones, except I could see eyes staring at me from deep inside the sockets of her skull. She walked toward me as she had done in my original dream with her hair flowing in the breeze, but her hair was stringy and thin. She put her skeleton hands on either side of my face and pressed her skeleton teeth against my lips. I tried to push her back, but I couldn't. Disgusted and frightened, I began screaming and crying.

Suddenly, she shoved me backward, and I fell to the ground. I heard moaning and turned to see Jesus crucified on the side of our barn. He was flailing violently, trying to pull loose, and there was a white cloth gag tied over his mouth. The redheaded woman screamed like a banshee, which brought my view back to her. Then she drew back a huge knife and slashed it toward me.

"AAHHHHHHGGGGGGGGGHHH!" I screamed, suddenly awake, flailing back into the seat of the car and throwing my fists out to strike. The car swerved, and Alissa was startled, but she quickly regained control.

"Good grief, honey!" she exclaimed. "You scared the daylights out of me! Are you all right?"

"Pull over! Pull over!" I frantically commanded.

Alissa immediately began scanning over the hood to see if there might be a place where she could pull to the side. By that time in the journey, we were on the flat back roads of Arkansas just west of Jonesboro, and there was little option except to just pull over as close as possible to the edge, where only a ditch separated the road from rice paddies.

"Hurry!" I pleaded, panting like a dog, trying desperately to get my breath. She pulled sideways into someone's gravel driveway. I immediately opened the door and began frantically trying to draw in the cool night air. Alissa got out on the driver's side and came around to the passenger side of the car.

"Ronnie, what's wrong?" she questioned frantically. My mouth began salivating, and a wave of nausea swelled over me.

Alissa stepped toward me, but I raised my hand to signal her to stay back. I pulled myself the rest of the way out of the car, fell to my knees in the gravel, and began to vomit.

"Goodness! Ronnie!" I heard her exclaim as she went back to the other side of the car. Just as I finished throwing up, I felt Alissa's hand on the back of my neck and a wet paper towel swipe across my mouth.

"Thank you," I panted, still trying to get my breath.

"I surely didn't think there was anything wrong with that sandwich," she said, "but you must have gotten food poisoning."

I began to feel sharp gravel cutting into my knees and started trying to get to my feet. I was still breathing like I had run a marathon. Alissa lifted under my arm to help me up.

"I've got to sit down," I mumbled. I sat back down in the seat of the car with legs facing outward through the open door. I placed my elbows on my knees and bent forward to rest my forehead into my hands. I continued to breathe heavily, and my extremities began to feel tingly and numb. I felt grief welling behind my eyes and fought to keep from crying. I felt like sobbing, but I dared not allow myself. Instead, I sucked in more air, more rapidly, and felt faint. Alissa went back to the other side of the car. I heard her open the back door and fiddle with something. In a moment, she returned with another cold, wet paper towel with some ice in it and placed it against my forehead.

"Where did you get this?" I asked.

"The ice in the cooler has mostly melted," she replied. "I had a roll of paper towels in the snack bag. I'm glad I did."

"Thank you," I said, finally beginning to get back to normal breathing. "I'm better now."

"It must have been that sandwich." She sighed. "I'm sorry, sweetheart."

I looked up at her and smiled in the dim glow of the interior overhead lights. "It was a good sandwich," I said. I did not bother to explain that I had also thrown up in St. Louis.

"Well, I'm sorry it made you sick," she consoled. "Here, I brought you a lemon-lime soda from the cooler. It might settle your stomach a little."

I reached up to take the can from her hand. "Have I told you lately how much I love you?" I asked.

"You tell me a lot," she replied.

"Well, I do love you," I went on. "I always have. I know this is going to sound contradictory and ridiculous. I know it is going to sound like I'm lying, but even when I was unfaithful, even when I was in that sickness,

I still loved you, Alissa. I never loved any of those women. I just wanted them. I don't even really know why other than pure carnal desire, temptation of the devil. I have no idea why. I have no idea why I would jeopardize something as precious as your love for me, but I did. You had every reason to leave me, legally and biblically. God himself would not hold you accountable for leaving an adulterer, and when you stayed…it just made me love you more."

Tears drifted from my eyes, and my voice trembled. Alissa came and squatted down in front of me. She reached up, took my hand, and held my palm to her cheek.

"Ronnie," she began. "It's easy to forgive a good man for making mistakes. It's hard to forgive an evil man for malicious acts. I've always known that you are a good man. No matter what you have done, and no matter what you have thought of yourself, I've always known that you have holiness at your core."

My tears flowed like rain, and I pulled her to me. "I'm sorry I hurt you," I pleaded. "I want you to know there has been no one since Darlene Meadows. I've never cheated on you since then, never."

She hugged me and kissed me on the cheek. "Hurt is part of love," she said. "Always has been, always will be. It's knowing that what we have is worth hurting for that makes it last."

I hugged her tightly. "You are so unselfish," I said. "How did you become so unselfish?"

"When you grow up thinking you are going to die," she said, "you learn to be grateful for whatever you have. You learn to cherish those you love for as long as you have them. You don't want to waste a single moment of that precious time being ungrateful, angry, or selfish, because you know it is not going to last. It's all temporary, Ronnie. Everything is temporary, even the universe itself. We get a tiny snippet of time to do what we are going to do, to become what we are going to become, and to meet who we are going to meet. After that, it's over. Why would I ever want to waste a moment of my joy being selfish, angry, or ungrateful?"

"But I'm so selfish." I sobbed. "I'm the one who is supposed to live the life above reproach, and I can't. I get in the pulpit, or on TV, and I admonish people to live a life that I'm not living myself."

She pulled away from me and wiped the tears from beneath my eyes with her thumbs. She looked at me with that look of pure love that I had only ever seen in her eyes and Momma's. "No…Ronnie, you're not selfish. A selfish man would never think of giving a million dollars to a little boy he hardly even knows."

"But I've been selfish in my marriage," I debated. "I've selfishly sought to use women for my carnal desires despite the fact that it might harm them, hurt you, or cost me my marriage."

"Ronnie," she said flatly. "Desperation and selfishness are two entirely different things. You have acted out of some kind of desperation that comes from something hidden inside you. I don't know what it is, but I know that it is there. No one can figure that out but you, and until you do figure it out, you are not going to have peace."

"I hope I can," I responded. "In the meantime, at least I have been behaving myself. Where are we?"

Alissa got to her feet. "We just passed through Jonesboro about ten miles back. We have maybe another thirty or forty minutes to go."

"What time is it?" I asked and pulled my sleeve back to look at my watch. "Three-twenty a.m.," I went on. "Very late."

"Do you want to get a hotel in Jonesboro or Pocahontas and then go to your parents' house in the morning or go on through to Ravenden?"

"Let's go on to the house," I replied. "If I know Momma, she is probably sitting up with him anyway, and I don't know what kind of emotional state she'll be in."

"Okay," she said and started back to the driver's side.

"No, I'll drive," I called after her and got up to follow to the other side of the car. "You have been driving for hours, and I have rested. Now that I know where we are, I can take it from here."

"But you have been sick, Ronnie," she said. "I don't mind."

"I'm fine now, Alissa," I replied. "Let me drive."

"Okay," she said. "The keys are still in the ignition."

Alissa went back around and got in on the passenger's side. I got in, started the car, and pulled back out onto the road. She placed her head on the pillow and seemed to drift quickly to sleep. In short order, we were pulling up in front of Momma and Daddy's house in Ravenden.

You forget just how dark it can get when you live in a city where every street is lined with streetlamps. In the county without benefit of such lights, the stars literally sparkle on a blanket of black. Darlene Meadows brought that back to me that day she lay there on our patio. I had realized it all my life, but I never really started thinking about it or noticing it until that day. For some reason, after that, I always noticed.

When I pulled into the yard of our old house, the moon was just going down on the far horizon, so the night was a cauldron of darkness at that point. Of course, Momma saw the flash of the headlights as we pulled the car up to the house. There had only been a dim light shining from their bedroom, and before I had cut off the engine of the car, the front porch light came on, and Momma stuck her head out the door to see what was going on. She had no fear out there, not in those days. No one in rural Arkansas was going to come around in the night to bother anybody.

I had no sooner opened the car door to get out when Momma came trotting across the yard in house slippers calling, "Oh, Ronnie, Ronnie, Ronnie. Baby, I'm so glad you came. From what Alissa told me this morning, I didn't think you would make it before your daddy passed."

Momma threw her arms around me, hugged me, and kissed me on the cheek. She released me just as quickly to go around to the front of the car to greet Alissa. The headlights of the car cast a light across the yard that fell adjacent to the porch light.

Momma hugged Alissa and said, "Sweetheart, I'm so glad you're here." She looked around Alissa toward the back seat of the car and wondered, "Where are the children? Are they sleeping?"

"No, Momma. We didn't bring the children," I replied. "We thought it would be just too much for them and too much for us to be looking after them."

"Oh…well," she said shyly. "I'm disappointed. I haven't seen my grandbabies for at least a year, but I guess you are right." Momma wrung her hands on her house coat. "Well, I best be getting back to your daddy. Get your things and come on in." Momma turned and walked back to the house. I took the keys to the back of the car to open the trunk. Alissa reached in to get the snack bag and cooler and met me back there.

"I told you she would be disappointed," I whispered.

"Yes, I knew she would be, and I know she is heartbroken," Alissa whispered back. "But I just couldn't see putting the children through this."

"Well, let's go on in and see what we are facing," I said.

I handed one small bag to Alissa and carried the rest of the luggage myself. Although it would have been more comfortable to stay at the Black River Motor Inn, I figured, for several reasons, it might be best to stay near Momma. We carried our things into the house, and I took the bags back to the room that Teddy and I had shared as children. Then I met Alissa in Momma and Daddy's room.

Momma had pulled a kitchen chair up next to the bed, where she could sit and hold his hand. Except for labored breathing and the occasional moment where he seemed to stop breathing for a second, Daddy lay completely still. The room was dark except for a tiny lamp that barely gave off light. Sissy's cot that she had slept on as a little girl was still shoved up against the wall in the opposite corner of the room. The same faded floral print curtains that had been there when we were kids hung from a rusty cheap curtain rod.

No one ever pulled the curtains closed at night out in the country. There wasn't anyone out there to look at you anyway, but the windows always had Momma's homemade curtains draped to either side.

The smell in the room was putrid and heavy. Momma had raised the windows up about three inches, maybe not so much as to let a little cool air in as to let some of the stink out. It was still too early in the spring to raise the windows all the way without getting cold in the room at night. Momma looked up when she saw me come through the doorway. "He's been like this since yesterday," she said in a low voice, almost a whisper. "At first, he could sit up and eat a little, just sip on some soup, but then he got to where all he does is lay there and try to breathe. He might have had a chance if I could have convinced him to stay at the hospital, but he insisted on coming home."

I walked over and placed my hand on her shoulder. "They don't make them any more stubborn than Daddy, do they, Momma?" I ran my hand up over her shoulder, leaned down, and whispered in her ear, "How much sleep have you had?"

"Oh, I doze off now and then," she replied without wavering in her gaze toward Daddy. "Hannah and Drake came down for a little while in the afternoon, and I took a short nap. They had to go back though. They are running a herd of milk cows now, and you know you are married to milking twice a day when you got a dairy barn."

Drake had started out working a dairy farm, but over the years, managed to scrape enough together to get his own herd after his daddy gave him about a hundred acres to start.

"Yes, Momma, I know," I said. "So in other words, you ain't slept much. Why don't you go lay down for a while in the other room and I'll sit with Daddy?"

"Oh, I don't think I could sleep anyway," she argued.

"Well, go lay down anyway," I ordered. "You need to rest, and Daddy will be fine. I'll sit right here beside him, and I'll call you if anything seems to be changing." I stood back to full height and nudged her. "Go on now."

Momma got slowly to her feet. "I'll just lay down on the couch in the living room," she said. "Alissa might want to go to bed and get a little sleep herself."

"No, go on into the other bedroom and lie down on a proper bed," Alissa interrupted. "I'm going to sit here with Ronnie, and if I need to lie down, I have the cot right here."

Momma looked at each of us silently and then clinched the upper collar of her robe as she exited the room. I looked over at Alissa and sighed. "I don't know why she is so devoted to him."

"Your momma believes in her vows," Alissa returned in a whisper. "She made a commitment for better or for worse. It means something to her. Besides, it is awful hard to have a child with a man and not love him."

"Despite all his preaching of the Gospel, despite the fact that the Bible is called the Good Book, he always seemed to find a way to be negative," I whispered back. "It certainly frustrated me. I can't imagine that it didn't frustrate Momma."

"Maybe it did frustrate her," Alissa continued. "Some women go about their marriages with a quiet resolve. They don't complain. They endure. They pray. They stick with it. Your relationship with him is entirely different than your Momma's relationship. There are different rules for a wife than for a son."

I sat down in the chair beside Daddy's bed. I glanced over at him and watched him struggle for every breath. Suddenly, a tear rolled down my cheek.

"All I ever wanted was his approval," I whispered with trembling voice. I brought one hand up flat across my face and wiped the wet off. "It's too late for that now."

I felt Alissa's hand on my back. "Every child wants approval," she said. "To a child, one simple nurturing affirmation is worth more than all the gold in the world."

I reached over my shoulder, laid my hand over hers, and looked up at her. "How did you get to be so wise?" I asked. "You are more Christian than I will ever be, and yet I'm the one out there spouting Gospel to the world."

"Wisdom is hard fought," she replied. "It doesn't come easy. Sometimes it comes from making mistakes. Sometimes it comes from hurt and soul-searching."

"I'm sorry I hurt you," I confessed, and the tears leaked again from my eyes. "I wish I had never hurt you."

She reached out and placed a tiny gentle hand on my cheek. "I would be lying if I said you didn't hurt me," she comforted. "But you have no idea how much I admired you first. You have no idea how much I continue to admire you."

"But I am so much a liar and a sinner," I pleaded. "Despite all the wrong I've done, it seems like God just continues to bless me when He ought to cast me down."

"Ronnie, everyone is a sinner," she continued. "What makes one sin any worse than another? It's all missing the mark."

"I miss the mark so much though," I defended.

"The one thing I know about you," she encouraged, "is that you have never stopped trying to be a good man. Despite your physical failings, there is a true and genuine soul in you, and one day maybe you will be able to see that for yourself."

I reached up to take her hand from my cheek and kissed it. "Go ahead and lie down," I instructed. "Get some sleep. I'll sit here and watch him for a while, and maybe you can spare me for a while later."

Alissa leaned over and gave me a peck on the lips and did as instructed. She cuddled up on Hannah's old cot and pulled a nearby quilt over herself. Soon I heard the distinctive puff and whish of sleep breathing and realized she had drifted off. I reached over and took Daddy's hand in mine. "You have no idea how much I loved you," I said quietly to him. "All I ever wanted was for you to love me back."

A few times through the night, I might have nodded off in the chair, but when the sun came up over the hills, I was still holding his hand. Not long after sunrise, Momma poked her head around the curtain. "How is he?" she asked.

"About the same," I said as I turned to smile at her.

"Baby, it's your turn to go get some sleep," she said.

"Maybe in a few minutes," I responded.

Momma walked around me, leaned over, and kissed Daddy on the forehead. "His breathing seems to have slowed a little," she commented.

"Really?" I questioned. "I guess I didn't notice. He is barely taking a breath anyway."

"Would you like some coffee, sweetheart?" she asked as she turned around. "When have you eaten? Maybe a little breakfast might be in order."

"Momma, you don't have to do anything," I appealed. "We can go into town and get something when Alissa gets up."

"Already awake," Alissa commented.

"I won't be doing anything but making coffee," Momma replied. "The church folks have kept me piled up with food ever since your daddy came home. There are several things in the kitchen that would make a good breakfast and won't have to be cooked. Mrs. Jenkins made some sweet rolls that are pretty amazing."

"Okay then," I agreed.

"I'll bring you something in just a few minutes," Momma said as she turned for the door.

"I'll help you, Marylee," Alissa said, now sitting on the side of the bed and rubbing her eyes.

"Sure, honey, come on," Momma invited. "We can have some girl talk."

When they left the room, I felt a fearful chill come over me. Sitting alone in the room with Daddy, I suddenly began to feel unsafe, almost as though I was in danger. I shook it off and reached for his hand. Not long after I took Daddy's hand, he gasped for a rattling breath so hard his chest rose into the air.

"What? WHAT!" I shouted. "Momma come quickly."

The few steps from the kitchen only took seconds. Momma popped into the room exclaiming, "What's the matter, baby?"

About that time, Daddy took another heaving breath and rattled in his throat as he was trying to breathe.

"Momma, what's wrong?" I exclaimed.

Momma rushed to the side of the bed and placed her hand on Daddy's chest. "It's the death rattle, honey. Your daddy is dying."

"Now? RIGHT NOW?" I exclaimed.

"Yes, now," she replied.

I threw off Daddy's hand as though it had been something nasty. I rose and began pacing across the back of the room as far away from him as I could get.

Alissa came into the room and rushed over to me. She reached a comforting hand in my direction, and I slapped it away. "Don't touch me!" I shouted. "Get the hell away from me!"

Alissa backed away and stared at me in shock. "Ronnie, are you okay?" she asked. "I've never seen you behave this way."

"Leave me the FUCK alone!" I screamed as I continued to pace. I wiped my hands against my shirt like I was trying to wipe shit off them. I felt nasty, disgusted.

"Ronnie, stop!" Momma shouted and turned back to me. "Your daddy is taking his last breaths. For goodness' sake, show some respect."

Behind her, Daddy heaved again. The anxiety overwhelmed me, and I found myself choking on rapid tiny tugs of breath. I fiddled with my clothes and pulled at them. I felt like a caged animal. One more time Daddy sucked for air and then stopped. I watched and waited for another breath, stared at him like a circus freak. Another breath did not come.

"HE'S NOT BREATHING! HE'S NOT BREATHING! HE'S NOT BREATHING!" I screamed.

Momma turned back around and looked down at Daddy. He didn't move. She reached over to his neck and felt for his pulse. Then she adjusted her fingers and felt again. "I think he's gone," she said quietly.

Those words hit me in the face like a boxing glove. "OH GOD!" I screamed. Nausea rushed through me. I felt hot and cold at the same time. I didn't know if I was going to puke or pass out. I rushed madly to the living room, passed through the front door, and out onto the porch. I fell to my knees at the edge of the porch and began to heave. There was little left in my stomach after having thrown up previously, but I couldn't stop heaving.

Flashes of images began to assault my mind. I saw the redheaded woman standing in our barn, and I lurched forward as though something evil was in my stomach. I screamed as I felt a pain go through my rectum as though someone had just shoved a knife into it.

Momma and Alissa came quickly to the porch with a cold washcloth. Alissa reached to comfort me and cool my face as she had done the night before, but I slapped it from her hands. My scream was bloodcurdling, retching, and it echoed across the farm. I saw the redheaded woman again, but she had Daddy's face. Then I saw her with my face when I was a little boy, and I was looking into a handheld mirror. In that mirror I saw lipstick smeared across my lips and a red wig on my head. Then Daddy grabbed my collar and threw me across the corn bin. Again, I screamed so hard it hurt my throat. I couldn't stop screaming. I couldn't stop heaving with nausea. I saw Daddy drop his pants. Then he grabbed the back of my head and shoved my face into his crotch.

"OH GOD NO! NO! PLEASE NO!" I screamed.

I heard Momma say, "Baby, baby, my son, be comforted. Your daddy is in a better place now."

Again, Alissa reached a cool washcloth toward my face.

I stood up and screamed, "GET THE FUCK AWAY FROM ME! GET THE FUCK AWAY FROM ME!" I backed into the yard screaming at them. I began hitting myself in the head with my fists, crying. Tears ran from my eyes like rivers, and I continued pounding myself in the face, screaming, "GODDAMN IT! I'M SO FUCKING STUPID! GODDAMN IT!"

Flashes of the redheaded woman continued to be superimposed over my sight. I could see Momma and Alissa with terrified and confused looks on their faces, but I saw them in a fog as though they weren't really there. Then I saw the redheaded woman kissing me, sticking her tongue in my mouth, but she had Daddy's face, and it was Daddy's tongue.

Again, I screamed, "GET AWAY! GET THE FUCK AWAY! GODDAMN IT! LEAVE ME ALONE! LEAVE ME ALONE!"

I fell to my knees in the yard and began sobbing uncontrollably. When I did, I felt Daddy's hand on the back of my neck. I saw myself face down in piles of dried corn shucks. We were in the corn bin at the barn. A horrible pain shot through my rectum, and I heard Daddy moaning through gritted teeth.

"IT HURTS!" I screamed. Tears continued to wet my face like a rain shower. "IT HURTS! STOP! PLEASE STOP!"

I heard Daddy's voice, grunting, "Shut up! Keep your damn mouth shut, boy!" His hand went around my face with his palm over my mouth. "You tell anybody about this, and I'll cut you up in little pieces and throw you in that pond! Shut up!"

Once more an echoing scream came out of me. I felt like it was coming up from my very soul, as though my spirit was being torn out of my body through my mouth. I felt the scream come out of me like a demon escaping hell, and then I fell silent, into darkness. —Out of the silence came the soft whispering voices of Alissa and Momma.

"Maybe we should call a doctor," Momma said.

"Maybe," Alissa replied. "He's been sick a lot lately, but I've never seen anything like this."

I felt the cool wet cloth across my mouth and over my forehead. When I opened my eyes, Momma was kneeling over me, holding an old black umbrella to shield my eyes from the sun. Alissa sat beside me on the ground with a pan of ice water nearby. She was dipping the cloth into the ice water and gently wiping my face. They had rolled me over on my back.

"There you are," Alissa said, softly smiling when I opened my eyes. "You gave us quite a scare."

Tears drifted out either side of my eyes as I lay on the cool ground. They had fetched a pillow from the house and placed it under my head. "I'm sorry," I cried. "I'm so sorry. I didn't mean to scare you. I would never want to scare you."

"It's okay, sweetheart," Alissa comforted. "We just need to get you to a doctor and find out why you have been so sick lately."

"NO! No doctor!" I demanded. "I won't go to a doctor."

"Honey, you have been so sick with all this throwing up and now screaming in pain," she continued.

My mind tried to remember what had happened previously but only bits and pieces of it would come. What did I say? What did I do? I didn't remember exactly how I had reacted, but I knew why, and I was not about to have anyone know that secret. I had buried it so deep, so very deep, that I had forgotten it myself. All these years my mind tried to tell me the truth, but I wouldn't listen. I didn't want to believe it. I didn't want to believe that it was possible that Daddy could ever have done anything like that to me. I guess when he died, my mind just couldn't take it anymore, but it was my secret, mine and Daddy's. I was not about to tell anybody else.

"I am NOT going to a doctor!" I insisted. "I'm okay now." I began, trying to get up.

"No…honey, I think you still need to rest a little while," Alissa pleaded.

"Get the fuck away from me!" I demanded. "I'm getting up."

"Ronald Dennison!" Momma scolded. "Never in my life have I ever heard you use the kind of language that has come out of you this morning. It is disrespectful to me, to Alissa, and to our Lord in heaven, and I expect you to stop it right now!"

"Momma!" I responded. "If you two hovering hens don't get away from me right now, and let me get up, I promise that you will hear a lot worse."

"Ronnie, you have never talked to me that way," Momma whimpered with tears welling in her eyes. "I don't understand what is happening to you."

"I'm sorry, Momma. I'm sorry," I pleaded.

Again, the tears began to flow from my eyes. I felt like I had no control over my emotions. One moment I was yelling and the next I was whimpering like a hurt puppy.

"I'm sorry, Alissa. I don't want to be disrespectful."

"It's all right, sweetheart," Alissa consoled. "You are probably feeling a lot of confusion right now."

"Please back away from me. Give me some room to breathe and let me get up," I entreated.

Alissa looked at me as though she wanted to scold me like one of the children. Then she looked up at Momma. They both began to move back. I rolled over on my side and sat up in the grass. I sat there, quiet for a while, before I spoke. "Shouldn't we be making some arrangements with the funeral home?" I asked as I brushed grass off my stained pants. "We've got a lot to do."

"Well, I suppose…I suppose we should call them," Momma stuttered.

"How long was I out?" I asked.

"Maybe five or ten minutes," Alissa replied. "We were considering calling an ambulance when you came to."

"Well, I'm fine now," I continued. "Momma, we need to get hold of the coroner and the funeral home and get arrangements made."

My tone was cool, calm, and clear. I was not about to let anything show again. I knew they thought my reaction was all grief over losing Daddy or that I had been sick. At least that was what I hoped. I was never going to allow either of them to know the truth about where those emotions came from. I collected myself and knew I had always kept that secret, kept it so well that I had forgotten it myself. As far as I was concerned, it would always remain a secret.

Momma and Daddy had gotten a phone only about a year before that. Despite my constant offers to pay for things like phones and improved living arrangements, Daddy had always refused. I had squirreled enough money into her account for Momma to have a bathroom built off the side of the house, but I couldn't give her too much as it would make Daddy suspicious. She told him she had saved the money from selling eggs and quilts, so that's how she could afford to put in a bathroom and get a phone. That was in fact true. I had bought the quilts and paid quite a bit more than standard price.

"Yes," she said. "I'll go call right now."

Momma sauntered off toward the house, and I think, for the first time, I realized how much her age was beginning to show.

After Momma entered the house, Alissa squatted down beside me on the grass. "Ronnie, I need to tell you something," she said. "There is a lot I will forgive and tolerate. However, I am not going to tolerate my husband being sick and refusing to get any help for it."

"I'm not sick, Alissa," I responded.

"Well, I have seen you throw up, not just throw up, but fully retch twice in less than twelve hours, and have seen you screaming 'it hurts.' That looks pretty much to me like somebody who is sick."

"I don't need a doctor, and I'm not going to one," I replied.

"Then I'll move out," she said flatly.

"What?" I questioned in amazement.

"I'll move out," she said again. "You can either go see a doctor when we get back to Nashville, or I am going to leave you."

"You're kidding," I affirmed in disbelief. "This from the woman who swore she would always love me no matter what, who stood with me despite my violations to our marriage?"

"I didn't say I wouldn't always love you," she continued. "I said I will leave you if you don't see a doctor about this problem."

"You *are* kidding," I affirmed again.

"No, honey, I *am not* kidding." She went on. "I will leave you if you don't get some help."

My mind twirled. This woman who had stood by me faithfully through the worst of my infidelities was going to leave me if I wouldn't see a doctor? In part, I didn't believe her. However, I had never known her to make any promise she didn't keep. I stared at her, trying to gather some glimmer of foolery in her eyes, but it was not there. Finally, I said, "Okay. When we get back, I'll set an appointment to see Dr. Jones."

"We'll have the appointment set before we get back," she said. "I'm going to call Clara and have her schedule the first available for you. If you get sick again before we go back, then we are going to the nearest emergency room, and I will have no arguments about it."

I sat like a scolded child, playing with blades of grass between my legs.

"Are we clear about this, Mr. Dennison?" she continued.

I sighed deeply, looked up at her, and simply said, "Yes, ma'am."

CHAPTER 22

e held Daddy's funeral in the same little chapel where Teddy's had been conducted and buried him not far from where Teddy lay. The early April weather was a far cry warmer and the drama more subdued. Momma wept through much of it and repeatedly squeezed my hand as she sat between me and Hannah. Drake sat with their kids on the other side of Hannah, and Alissa sat next to me. The funeral home had suggested a preacher at our request, and honestly, it didn't really matter to me. I was grateful that Momma did not ask me to preach as she had done when Teddy was buried. The last thing I wanted to do was preach Daddy's funeral, especially with uncovered memories now repeatedly intruding into my mind. Despite any mental effort I made, the images kept coming back to haunt me—Daddy, the corn bin, and that damned red wig. I resolved to keep my cool and put on my best Pastor Dennison face for those who attended. My smiles and handshakes abounded, and I maintained the same calm composure I had for the camera or an evangelical service. I had determined that the anguish which washed over me the day that Daddy died was never going to take me again. I took control of myself and played a role good enough for an academy award. Perhaps I had always been acting. Perhaps I had learned young how to pretend that nothing was really wrong, learned it so well I forgot who I really was and what happened to me.

There were people showing up that none of us knew. I suspected that some may have read the obituary and knew of the family from attending tent revivals conducted years before. Maybe they just crashed the funeral so they could see the TV preacher. It was certainly no secret in the region that I had become a celebrity of Christ. I didn't care why they were there. I just wanted it over, and the sooner the better.

Hannah and I both worried about Momma staying there alone, but we knew she wouldn't be going anywhere as long as Grandma Miller was still alive and able to go. Grandma still lived alone in that old house over the hill. At the funeral, she sat next to Alissa, patting her hand and whispering prayers to herself. Not long after the funeral, Grandma Miller moved in with Momma and stayed with her a few more years until she passed one night peacefully in her sleep. Momma still insisted on staying there alone. She declared to everyone that if her own mother could live all those years alone, she could too. I repeatedly offered to build her a nice new house and repeatedly offered to have her move in with us in Nashville. Still she refused, even though it would have meant that she could be there to help raise her grandchildren, whom she adored. Momma was proud. We all were, and maybe far more stubborn than any of us should have been.

There is always this numb quiet after a funeral, a feeling of confusion and not knowing what to do next. When we all got back to the homestead that afternoon, that feeling, that silence, was overwhelming to me. There I sat in my daddy's house, his presence still lingering like the smell of mothballs creeping out between the cracks around a closet door. The family sat there, making small talk and discussing everything from Drake's cows to what the weather was going to do. Alissa and I had promised Momma that we would stay another day or two, and we would stay there with her instead of a hotel, but I thought if I had to spend one more minute in that house, I was going to crumble into a million pieces. I couldn't stand it anymore. I couldn't stand being in that house. I couldn't even stand being around Momma. There were times I found myself wondering if she knew and just never said anything because she was just as afraid of Daddy as the rest of us. That's the problem with secrets, when you keep them, you never really know who else is keeping them too. Finally, I said, "I think I'm going to go take a walk."

Alissa said, "Oh, that sounds wonderful, honey. I'll come with you."

"Well, actually, if you don't mind, sweetheart," I quickly interjected, "I would really rather go alone. I need some think time, some quiet time, no conversation."

"I could be quiet," she replied.

"You know, there is always going to be that temptation to speak," I defended. "Please, honey, I just need to be alone with my thoughts. Please, just let me do this myself."

"Sure." She smiled nervously.

After recent events, I knew she was worried, but I had plans for my time alone, and I absolutely did not want anyone with me. I went to my room, changed into some jeans and boots, grabbed a light jacket, and came back through the living room. I leaned over and gave Alissa a peck on the lips. "I understand your concern, honey. I will be fine. I'll be back shortly." I smiled my best congenial smile and headed through the kitchen for the back door.

"Have a good walk, baby," Momma called after me when I was halfway through the kitchen.

"Yes, Momma," I replied.

I went out the back door and down through the barn lot. The afternoon sun was beginning to lay low in the western sky. There was just enough chill in the air that I soon donned the jacket I carried with me. I cut around the back side of the barn between the barn and the pond and headed off through the tree line into the pasture, but I had absolutely no intention of walking the pastures. I just wanted anyone who might have watched my departure from the house to think that's what I did. As soon as I was around the tree line, I cut across the back side of the pasture and came up behind the barn, where the barn would block the view of anyone who might be looking out a window from the house. I made sure to walk directly behind the barn. I then cut around to one side at the back corner and opened the door to a holding stall. I climbed up over the wall to an open place at the top and went through the milking stall. I then climbed over the feeding bins into the hayloft and cut across that to the back of the corn bin.

There I began to work loose a couple of boards at the back of the corn bin and bent them out far enough so I could crawl into the bin from the hayloft.

The hayloft and corn bin were both empty. Momma and Daddy had stopped keeping cattle years before, when Daddy got too sick to take care of them himself and it was too much for Momma to try to do by herself. The floor of the corn bin was about four feet above the ground, so we could reach into the bin and grab the ears of corn without having to bend over to get them. Around the bin were old corn husks that had likely lain on that floor a good ten years since it was last used. Any ear of corn left had been nibbled down by rats to nothing more than the dried cob.

A chill went through me as I stood in that room, not so much of cold as of terror. I had come for a reason, a reason that only I knew. I had come to see if it was true. Trembling, I caught my resolve and sucked a breath in deep. I went over to the front corner, down a few feet from the front door, where we used to reach in for ears of corn to shuck them for the chickens or throw out to the hogs. I knelt down in that corner, my hands shaking like leaves and brushed old corn husks away from the floorboards.

There, in that spot, a couple of boards lay flat and fit securely against the other boards but were not nailed down like the others. I knew they were there, and I knew they didn't just come up. Those memories had come back to me as well. I pulled out my pocketknife, flipped out the blade, and wedged it between one end of one of those boards and used it like a lever. The board came loose, and ancient dust scattered around it. I set the board back to one side and looked into the hole. There inside was an old rusty tackle box. My breath quickened and shortened as I reached in and pulled the tackle box into the dim light that filtered between the sideboards. I dropped it a couple of inches onto the floor like I had hold of a hot potato. It rattled against the old boards, and a wave of fear went through me when I pondered that somebody might hear.

I sat back on my knees and looked around for fear that someone might have been close enough to hear or might be peeking between the cracks where the gray weathered sideboards were nailed to the frame.

The silence returned, and I reached for the tackle box, hesitantly. I didn't want to touch it. I didn't want to see what might be inside. I prayed like Jesus from the cross, "Dear Lord, if it be thy will, take this cup from me." Tears began to roll down my cheeks as I reached, trembling, for the latch on the tackle box. I trembled more as I pulled the latch loose and lifted the top of the box. The drawers and compartments that once held fishing lures had been removed. So it was just a metal box with a hinged lid and a flip latch. Inside the box, lying right on top, was a woman's red wig. I sobbed as I reached in and pulled it out, stifled my sobs, and held it up close to my heart. "Daddy, how could you?" I cried. My mind reeled with images.

Some images were of Daddy putting the wig on me and standing back to check and see if it was even. Then I saw his hand coming toward me with a tube of bright red lipstick. He smeared it onto my lips, stood back, and said, "Oooooh, there, baby. Ain't you a pretty girl?"

Then Daddy held a handheld mirror up to my face to show me what he had done. In the image of that mirror, I could see that I must have been no more than six or seven years old. I saw images of Daddy wearing the wig, prancing around the corn bin half tripping over ears of corn like a drunk man. Maybe he had been drinking. Maybe that was one more thing he did in secret, that he had forbidden from the pulpit. Maybe there were many secrets and not just one. As images flashed in my mind, I sat back on the floor with the wig in my hands and cried. "Daddy, Daddy, Daddy, how could you? I loved you so much, and you betrayed me."

For a time, I felt I could not stop sobbing, but when the sobs began to cease, I looked into the tackle box again and found the tube of women's bright-red lipstick. In the back of my mind, I knew it was there. I knew it didn't belong to Momma. Daddy never allowed her to wear lipstick. He always told her that it was of Jezebel and the devil, that the dogs ate the first woman who ever painted her lips. Yet there it was in that box, and since I had memories of having him smear the lipstick across my mouth, I must, therefore, have been his Jezebel, the whore he could never allow Momma to be. I was his sacrifice. I reached into the box to pull out an old handheld mirror. There was a worn-down bar of soap and a rag. Daddy had wet the rag in pond water and smeared it with that bar of soap to wash the lipstick off my face when he was done. I reached in again for a half-used tub of petroleum jelly. I picked up the petroleum jelly and immediately dropped it with a gasp as images of Daddy doing awful things with it ran through my mind. Pain shot through me, not just emotional pain, but physical pain, and I fought back a scream. I pushed myself back against the wall and whimpered like a frightened child, "Daddy, no, please don't, please don't, please don't. Don't, Daddy, please." I buried my head in my hands and begged, "God, please help me."

Suddenly a breeze came up, a quick gust of wind, strong but gentle at the same time. The wind whipped through the open space at the top of the corn bin where we used to pull the wagon up and toss the corn in. It rattled a loose board against the side of the barn near the opening and caught my attention. I looked up to the opening with the dim late afternoon light shining through and making golden streaks across the old boards. It was enough to mesmerize me and still my tears for a moment. My mind went to Stephen, and I realized for the first time why I had felt such a connection with him. Finally, I looked back into the tackle box one last time.

In the bottom of the tackle box was an envelope, and my name was written in pencil on the side. I reached in to pick it up and felt my heart pounding like a prisoner kicking at the bars of my ribs. I had no memory of that envelope ever having been in the tackle box. I sat holding the envelope out in front of me for several minutes, wondering if I should open it, not wanting to open it, wanting to wad it up and throw it into the corner, to stomp on it in a fit of rage. My ambivalence was like the pendulum of a grandfather clock. One moment, I felt compelled to open it and see what was inside, and the next moment, I wanted to burn it. I knew either way it could not stop my confusion. Finally, I opened it and pulled out the letter inside. Daddy had scrawled in pencil onto paper that may not have been yellowed and old at the time he wrote it, but the white paper had faded by the time I opened it. I began to read.

My Dear Son Ronald,

I hope, when writing this, that you will someday come to find it in my box and read it. I know that if you are reading it, I am likely dead and gone. I know, as well, that I am burning in hell for the sins I have committed against you, against my wife, and against nature. What I did to you was more than wrong. I violated your entire childhood. I put a burden on you that no child should ever have to bear. It was a grievous sin for which I deserve to burn eternally, but I have been too weak to admit it to you or to anyone else. You have no idea how many excuses I made for my behavior. You have no idea how much I hated myself for it, but still I continued. Even now, I fight myself over writing this, and the devil calls me to justify what I have done, but I cannot. I know I cannot.

I know that it will do no good to tell you I am sorry. There is not enough repentance in the world to make up for what I did to you. I know it will do no good to tell you that I felt compelled to do what I did. I felt like I could not stop myself. I felt like I was feeding an insatiable beast that would not let me stop. Every time I used you to feed my carnal urges, they began to swell in me again. I fought myself over it long before I ever touched you for the first time, and I fought myself over it every time I touched you after that. It did not matter how much I reproached myself for it, prayed about it, or read the Bible, the beast always returned. I know that you do not understand what that is like, and I know that there is no excuse for what I've done.

All these years I have criticized you and your ministry. I was jealous. I was jealous that I could not be what you had become. I was jealous that you were a nationally respected man of God, and I was nothing more than a petty, small-town hypocrite. Count that as yet another sin on my roster. I could not bring myself to tell you that I am so proud of you for overcoming the burden of sin I placed on you as a child. I see you with your family, your loving wife, how you treat her and your children with such respect, and I wish I could have done the same. I don't know why I didn't treat my own wife and children with respect except that I always felt angry. I felt a fury that I could scarce hold back, and more than once, I took that out on you.

It may not be a consolation to know that when I was a boy, a neighbor did to me things like what I did to you. That's no excuse. I make no excuse. If anyone should have known better than to do that to a child, it should have been me, but I felt compelled to hurt you the way I had been hurt. I don't really know why. It just felt like something in me that had to come out. I don't know why I picked you except that you loved me so much and wanted to be around me so much that it was easy to take advantage of that. Teddy was so rebellious and head-strong. He didn't respond to me the way you did. He never wanted to do what he was told or go with me anywhere, and Hannah hadn't even been born when I started on you, but believe me I never touched her. I finally reached a point in my shame over what I was doing to you that I couldn't bring myself to pass that down to another child.

I want you to know, even though I have never said it, I am proud of you, my son. You have broken the evil spell I tried to cast on you. You preach the Gospel to millions, and you live the Gospel you preach. I can see it. I can see that you live your life for the Lord, while I have been the worst kind of hypocrite. I dare not ask for your forgiveness. I don't deserve it. I don't deserve a place in heaven. I have secured my eternity in hell, and I have consigned myself to accept that hell is what I deserve. I am grateful that you have done better, especially despite all the horrible things I did to you. I know that precious little of what I ever did looked anything like love, but I want you to know that I really did love you, and I hate myself for all the terrible things I did to you.

Your Daddy, Paul Dennison

My teeth were clenching as I read the letter, and as I held it in my hands having read the last words, I wanted to scream. I wanted to cry. I knew as I read it that I was a hypocrite just as he was, just on a bigger, grander scale. I may not have ever touched a child, but I seduced lonely and sometimes mentally ill women. I hid the secret from my family as well, but I got caught when Daddy didn't. If Alissa had never found out, I might never have stopped. I couldn't believe Alissa had stayed with me after what I did. I can't imagine that she would ever have stayed with me if I had done what Daddy did. I can't imagine a woman ever staying with a man knowing he was abusing her children, but then I realized some women might turn a blind eye because they are scared, maybe some women don't care enough about their children to stop it, some might even do it themselves, and some don't really think they have a choice. "I'm no better than you, Daddy," I cried. "I'm a hypocrite and a sinner too."

No sooner had I uttered the words than I heard voices outside. Frantic, I folded the paper up and stuffed it into the inside pocket of my jacket. I quickly threw everything else back into the tackle box and put it back under the boards of the corn bin. Then I rushed back through the two boards I had pulled up from between the corn bin and the hayloft. As I came through, I snagged my jeans on a rusty nail and ripped a small hole. I quickly pulled the jeans loose and rushed across the hayloft, back over into the milking stall. All the while my heart was pounding like my secret was going to be found out. I finally made it over into the back stall, ran out to the edge of the pasture at the back of the barn, and turned around. Then I pretended to be casually returning from my walk. About that time, Momma and Alissa came strolling around the other side of the barn.

"Oh, there you are, Ronnie." Alissa smiled. "We were about to get worried about you since you had been gone so long."

I had no idea how long I had been gone, but the sun sat so low in the sky that it was barely peeking over the horizon, and the shadows cast long streaks of early evening darkness across the pasture.

"Since it was starting to get dark, we thought we ought to come see if you had fallen or something," Momma said.

"No, I'm fine," I replied, faking a smile.

"How did you rip your pants?" Alissa asked, pointing to the two-inch torn place to the side of my right knee.

"Oh, that." I laughed, knowing how fake it sounded. "I caught my britches on some barbed wire trying to cross through the fence to the west pasture."

"Well, you sure got yourself dusty," Alissa continued. "How did you do that?"

"Ha…ah…well, you know that old, abandoned house over there on the upside of the creek that belonged to the Troy family? I just went in and did a little exploring is all."

"Hmmm." Momma looked at me curiously. "I thought that old house fell in a couple of years ago. I didn't think there was anything left there but the foundation and some old rotted boards. Seemed like folks salvaged most of those."

I knew Momma didn't want to accuse me of lying, but she also had to know, better than I did, what was still standing around there and what wasn't.

"Well, I just kind of picked around in the pile a little," I replied quickly, and then changed the subject. "Where's Hannah and Drake?"

"Oh, they headed on back home not long after you left," Momma replied. "You know, with those darn milk barns, you are tied to them like a prison. They had to get home to do their milking."

"Just us chickens." Alissa smiled and examined me like a class project. She had learned to read me like a first-grade book, and I knew there would be questions later.

"I'm hungry," I said. "What's for dinner?"

"Oh, we got so much food in that house that people have brought over," Momma replied, "I'm probably gonna have to throw about half of it out. We can make sandwiches or just heat something up."

"That's fine by me, Momma."

I walked up between them, put an arm around each one's shoulder, and said, "Let's go to the house."

After supper, we watched a little TV, another thing Momma got from "selling eggs and quilts." When we finally went to bed, I couldn't sleep, but I lay there quietly and waited for Alissa to fall asleep. A full moon was shining that night, and the gray-blue light spread over the world like a blue lantern in the sky. Dim gray light was slinking through the same window I used to stare out when I was a boy. I had made sure that Alissa slept on the side near the window where I used to sleep, because I knew what I was going to do.

When I could hear from her breathing that Alissa was asleep, I carefully crawled out of the bed. I had hidden some jeans, my jacket, a flashlight, and some slippers behind the old potato bin that Momma kept on the back porch by the kitchen. I carefully tiptoed through the house to the back porch and pulled the jeans over my pajama bottoms in the dark. I put on the old slippers and the jacket, took the flashlight, and carefully squeezed through the back door into the moonlight. I didn't use the flashlight until I got to the barn. I wouldn't need it till later. I quietly made my way through the back gate into the barn lot and approached the corn bin. I didn't turn on the flashlight until I climbed inside through the door. Then I went directly to the boards and immediately realized I had forgotten to bring my pocketknife. I set the flashlight to one side with the beam pointing over the boards and began trying to pry up the edge of the board with my fingers. After struggling for several minutes, and several times getting the board to come up about a half inch only to drop it again, I took the flashlight and began searching around the bin for something I could use to pry open the boards.

Then I remembered the rusty nail that had snagged my jeans. I went to the back of the bin, found the nail with the flashlight, and began working it loose with my fingers. Finally, after prying the nail loose from the near- rotting wood, I took it back to the floor boards and used it to pry them open. Even then, it was not an easy task. I reached in, pulled out the tackle box, replaced the boards where they had been, and carried it to the door of the corn bin.

Then, I turned off the flashlight and allowed my eyes to acclimate to the darkness. I then opened the door and crawled out into the moonlight. The trees cast odd shadows in the silver-blue light of the full moon. I walked immediately to the pond bank and stood there holding the tackle box in front of me.

That had been the very spot where I had stood when I had the first dream of the redheaded woman coming up from the silver waters of the pond to kiss me. It was not lost on me that the moonlight made the waters of the pond shimmer with streaks of silver light like dark mercury. As I stood there, I heard Daddy's voice come to me, and more images of my childhood flashed through my mind. We were back in the corn bin. I must have been ten or twelve years old at the time, and as I remembered it, it occurred to me that it was also around the time that Daddy stopped doing what he had been doing to me. It was around the time I became a teenager, when he just stopped. Apropos of nothing, he simply stopped.

I recalled mixed feelings about it. On one hand, it was over, and I wouldn't have to worry about him taking me aside anymore. On the other hand, it was over, and my daddy stopped touching me after that. Even though it hurt when he did it, even though I felt dirty and ashamed when he did it, it was the only affection I received from him. The only way he had ever really touched me was to hit me or force his desires on me.

Then I saw him standing there, the tackle box in his hands. "Son," he was saying, both pleading and commanding. "It would kill your momma if she ever found out about this. So we are going to put this under the boards one last time. Then if anything should ever happen to me, I want you to come get the tackle box and throw it in the pond. Over time, this stuff will rot, and nobody will ever know about it except me and you. You have to promise me, boy, nobody will ever know about it but me and you."

I wondered, as I stood there by the pond in the moonlight, why he didn't just go ahead and throw it in the pond himself right then, and it occurred to me that maybe he wasn't sure it was over. Maybe he wanted to keep it just in case he decided to pull me aside and do it to me again. Then it occurred to me that this had all happened sometime after I had the first dream. I had promised him that I would never tell anyone. Then I set about wiping it from my memory, turning it into something else. I set about refusing to believe it had ever happened. I could have thrown the box in the pond at any time myself, but I never did. Maybe that would have been like admitting it happened.

There in the moonlight, I held the tackle box in my hand and remembered the dream of the redheaded woman coming up out of the shimmering pond water and kissing me. I felt such a mix of emotions as well as sexual arousal. Was I a homosexual? There were times when Daddy was gentle. I came to desire having him touch me when he was gentle, but I desired women too. I was so confused. Tears trickled down my cheeks in little streams, and I chanted over and over to myself through gritted teeth. "I am not a homosexual! I am not a homosexual! I am not a homosexual! Thou shalt not lay with a man as with a woman!"

I thought, in that moment, that the only man I had ever really desired sexually was my own daddy, and the only reason I had desired him was desperation to have his love any way that I could get it.

Shame overwhelmed me. I felt like I must be the most awful man on earth to have carnal desires for my own father. The feelings were a mix of desire, disgust, and shame. At that moment, I felt arousal as my mind went back to times when Daddy had kissed me over my mouth, when he held me like a woman, when he had kissed me the way I kissed the women I seduced. I remembered him backing away from that kiss with the red lipstick that had been smeared over my lips, now clinging to his own.

A disgusting wave of nausea filled me, filled me to the brim, but with it came a determination—an anger. "I am not a woman!" I snarled and spit through gritted teeth. I felt like I had to spit it out, that disgust, that carnage that had been left on my lips. I wiped my mouth with the back of my hand and spit again and again. I felt the nausea building like an oil well about to gush from inside me. I dropped the tackle box to the ground, turned, and with my hands on my knees, heaved great gushes of vomit. The smell rose from the ground and nauseated me further.

Again, with a burning fury, I wiped the disgust hard from my lips and screamed, "I AM NOT A HOMOSEXUAL!" I picked up the tackle box, held the old, rusted piece of crap high above my head, and screamed again, "I AM NOT...A HOMOSEXUAL!" Then I flung it with all my might out into the center of the pond.

A huge splash came up as the heavy metal box hit the water and began to sink. Silver droplets of moonlit water splattered back into the pond. I stood there, panting, looking at the dark, murky water. The moon reflected ripples that drifted across to the outer banks. I began taking deep, full breaths, deliberately battling my anxious panting. I had no idea what I was going to do next, but I had never really known where life was going to take me. Even the determination that I was called to preach led me to places I never really dreamed of or understood. At that moment, I questioned if I had really been called to the ministry or if it had all come out of my confusion, some way to make myself look and feel important when I felt so completely small and insignificant. I stood there a moment longer. I looked across the pond to see the water had settled.

"Goodbye, Daddy," I said quietly.

Then I turned and walked back toward the house in moonlit darkness.

CHAPTER 23

The next day, Alissa and I packed for the trip back to Nashville. We begged Momma to come stay with us for a few weeks so she could see the grandchildren and get away, but she would have none of it. When we packed our luggage into the trunk of the car, we stood in the yard, and I tried one last time to convince her before we left. "Momma, please. Please come stay with us even just a couple few weeks, just a week. The kids would love to see you, and you know you need a break from all this."

"Oh Lord of mercy," she said. "This place would fall apart if there wasn't somebody here to take care of it."

"Momma, maybe it needs to fall apart," I replied. "Maybe it needs to sink back into the earth and be reclaimed by nature. Think about coming to live in Nashville. You know you can have a much better life with us. We can get you a nice house, or you could even live with us. You can be near the grandkids and see them all you want."

"Oh mercy, I don't know that I could live in a city at all, much less one that size," she replied. "Besides, Momma Miller might need me and I have got grandkids here too—well, that aren't too far away."

"Momma, you don't even know how to drive," I pleaded. "How are you gonna even take care of getting groceries much less going to see Hannah and Drake's kids or anything else?"

"I've got your Daddy's truck," she replied, "and I know a little. Some of the folks at church can teach me to drive, and I'll get my license. In the meantime, I'm sure I can catch a ride into town when I need one. Lord knows country folk are accommodating."

"Well, some things are gonna change, Momma, okay?" I insisted. "For one thing, I'm going to make sure this place gets fixed up, you have a good phone line, and whatever else you decide you need, and I want you to think about just selling this place. Give it some real thought, Momma. Consider letting us get you a nice place in Nashville, even let me build you a new house here. Wouldn't it be nice to have a new house with some modern amenities?"

"Lordy," she protested. "I have lived in this house so long I don't know what I would do with a new one. I know right where everything is, and I know I can count on my old cast iron skillets to cook up a good meal."

"Momma, please, just think about it," I pleaded. "Okay?"

"Okay, son." She smiled. "Y'all be safe on your trip home now."

She hugged me, then Alissa. We got in the car and pulled away from the house, waving back at Momma till we were out of sight. I drove, and it wasn't long till we were passing through Jonesboro on the way back home. Alissa didn't say anything at first, but just on the other side of Jonesboro, she asked, "So what was that all about last night?"

"What was what all about?" I asked, not realizing that getting out of bed and leaving the house in the middle of the night would surely have awakened her. A loving mother with small children sleeps light, and there is very little that gets past her. There was very little that ever got past Alissa.

"Getting up and going down to the barn after we all went to bed?" she questioned. "What was that about?"

I didn't say anything. She cocked her head toward me and asked, "Ronnie?"

"I just needed some fresh air," I replied quietly.

"Is that why you were yelling, 'I'm not a homosexual'?" she queried.

My heart pounded. In my illusion, I had never considered that anyone could hear me but Daddy, but I guess screaming at the top of my lungs might have been something that could have been heard from the house. Again, I said nothing and just kept driving.

"Ronnie?"

"What!" I snarled. "What do you want to know? What have you already concluded? Did you consider that maybe it was something private to myself?"

"Ronnie, have you been having attractions to men?" she asked flatly.

"No! Stop It!" I exclaimed. "Stop with the interrogation."

"Honey, it's not an interrogation," she pleaded. "I've known you have struggled with sexual demons for a long time now. I have never judged you for it. I only want you to find peace within yourself, peace with God."

"I don't want to talk about this right now," I insisted. "I don't want to talk about it now, and I really don't want to talk about it with you."

"Why not talk about it with me?" she questioned. "I'm your wife. I love you, and I only want you to be at peace with your struggles."

"Well, I can't talk about it with you," I said. "I just can't."

"Could you talk about it with someone else?" she continued. "Would you talk about it with someone else?"

"And who would I talk about it with?" I growled back. "Pastor Wilkes maybe?" I laughed sarcastically. "Oh yeah! I'm sure that would go over well! I am about to do a national broadcast of services from his church in two months. I'm sure he is going to want to know that the pastor delivering the sermon, not only to his flock, but to the nation, is screwed up sexually."

"So, you have been having attractions to men?" she asked.

"NO!" I yelled. "That is *not* what I meant by what you heard last night. NO, I...DO...NOT have attractions to MEN. Alissa, you know, if anything, I have gone too far in the opposite direction. My attractions to women have been addictive. If there is anything that haunts me, it is NOT attractions to men."

"Then why did you yell that last night?" she persisted.

"Please!" I pleaded with anger. "I don't want to talk with you about it."

"Would you maybe talk with a psychologist about it?" she continued.

"ALISSA, PLEASE! STOP!" I shouted.

"Okay," she retreated. "I just want you to know that I love you, and I want the best for you."

I reached across the seat and took her hand. "I know you love me, sweetheart," I softened. "I love you too. I know you would never want to hurt me. Please just trust me that I'm working through this—I am."

Alissa stared at me for a moment, then stared out the window at the passing landscape for a few minutes, and then changed the subject. "I'll be glad when we get out of the Delta and back into some hills," she said. "I've never cared much for flat land."

When we got back to Nashville, as planned and plotted by Alissa and Clara, I had an appointment with Dr. Jones within a couple of days of our arrival. I went to see him and told him only that I had thrown up a few times and didn't know why. He poked and prodded as any doctor would. He asked questions, drew blood, and ran tests, including an EKG. A few days after that, he called the house. Alissa answered the phone, and I happened to be home at the time of the call.

"Honey, Dr. Jones is on the phone!" she shouted from the hall next to our bedroom.

"Okay," I called back, having just stepped out of the shower. "I'll get it in here."

The children were with Clara for the day, so I made no effort to cover myself as I carried my towel toward the bed.

"All right, honey," she replied. "Just so you know, I'm planning to listen in."

I was *not* happy to hear that, but I didn't want to argue with her about it when Dr. Jones was waiting for me to pick up the phone. I did say, "I would rather you not do that."

She said, "Doing it anyway. I love you."

I sat nude on the edge of the bed, still wiping my hair with the towel and picked up the receiver. "Yes, this is Ronald Dennison." I spoke professionally.

"Hi, Ronald," Dr. Jones began. "Well, your tests are essentially all negative. Your EKG is fine and blood work looks pretty good. I don't see anything to indicate any significant problems with your health other than your blood pressure is a little elevated. Like I told you when you were in the office the other day, I am a little bit concerned about that, but I don't think it is high enough to be trying any medications at this point. You will need to watch your diet and maybe keep your salt intake down. Some exercise would be called for. What I wonder is whether you are under a bit too much stress."

"Ah…no," I replied. "I have less going on now than I had a few years ago."

"Are you sure there is not something that might be bothering you?" he questioned.

"No…no, nothing is bothering me," I lied.

"Well, I know you have had the death of your father recently, and Alissa has expressed some concerns. Given that your tests are clear and given the symptoms that Alissa described, I think you may have been having panic attacks."

"Panic attacks?" I exclaimed. "What does that mean? I'm scared or something? I'm not panicked, I'm fine."

"Well, panic attacks can be extreme," he went on. "They usually occur when people are overwhelmed by stress. They can include heart palpitations, nausea, difficulty breathing. Some people become even more panicked when they have one because they think they are having a heart attack."

"Oh," I affirmed. "Nope, never thought I was having a heart attack— just needed to puke."

"There is a medication I can prescribe," he went on. "It's called Valium. It's a new medication, and there have been some successes in using it to treat panic attacks. You can keep a few pills with you and take one if you feel like you are having onset of anxiety."

"Thank you, Dr. Jones," I replied. "I don't think I need any medications."

"Honey," Alissa said from the other line, "if it might help, why not give it a try?"

"I would prefer not to take medications," I responded.

"Well, that is up to you, Ronald," Dr. Jones said, "but it is an effective medication for anxiety."

"Anxiety?" I questioned. "Anxiety, like crazy people have? I am not crazy, and I don't need any drugs."

"Well, no one is saying you are crazy, and everyone has some anxiety," Dr. Jones defended. "When people are under a lot of stress, sometimes they need a little help."

"No!" I said flatly. "If I decide I need it, I will call you."

"But, honey—" Alissa started.

"No!" I demanded, cutting her off before she could finish the sentence.

"Okay," she said quietly. Then after a moment's pause, she said, "Dr. Jones, may I pick up that prescription for Ronnie just in case I might convince him to take them later?"

"Certainly, Alissa," Dr. Jones responded. "I'll make the arrangements for you to pick it up. In the meantime, Ronald, please call me if you have any concerns at all. Try to rest and relax a little bit. Play some golf or spend the weekend in a bed-and-breakfast or something."

"All right, sir, I will," I replied. "Goodbye now."

I hung up the phone to find that Alissa had already hung up her end and was standing in the door of the bedroom, looking at me.

"You know I'm worried about you, right?" she said.

"Yes, I know," I replied, "and you needn't be."

"Okay," she said and just stood there, leaning against the door facing.

"I have to get dressed," I said, getting to my feet. "I have to meet Pastor Wilkes at Evangelic Temple to go over some of the arrangements for the broadcast in June." I went to the closet and began pulling out my usual khaki slacks and button-down shirt that I wore when not at church. Although I had grown up with jeans, they were an infrequent part of my attire. I started to dress, and Alissa went back to her television in the den. When I got ready to leave, I stopped by the den on my way out of the house to give her a peck on the lips and a quick "See you later."

"Do you know what time you'll be home?" she asked as I was walking toward the garage.

"I'm not sure how long Pastor Wilkes and I will need to meet," I replied, "but I should surely be home by five."

"Okay, I'll know when to plan dinner then. Have a good afternoon, sweetheart."

"You too," I said as I reached for the door to the garage. The thought ran through my mind that I was both blessed and cursed to have her. On one hand, she seemed to accept everything, forgive everything, and on the other, I felt a fear of her, a pressure to be good. I knew that she knew things were different since Daddy died. I felt more fearful, more intense, and she knew it. Then, the component of having met Stephen in St. Louis was added to the mix. I struggled with the *newfound* knowledge that Daddy had molested me just like Stephen had been molested. I wondered why I had not become a homosexual like Stephen, why I didn't think I was a woman, or want to be a woman like him. None of it made sense to me. I had always thought that men became homosexuals because they didn't have the right kind of father, but I didn't have the right kind of father. I had a father who had done homosexual things to me, but I was entirely attracted to women. It all frustrated and overwhelmed me. I had fantasies of running away, going to my bank accounts, drawing out all of it except what Alissa would need to take care of the kids, and just disappearing. Maybe I might go to South America, get lost in the jungles of Panama, and live in a hut by myself just using my stores of cash as I needed it. I just wanted to run away, get away from everything and everyone, away from every prying eye and every question. What I could not get away from was my own tormenting mind. Along with this, my lust came back. I found myself looking at women in a way I had not done since Darlene Meadows. I found myself looking at every curve of breast, bottom, or waist. I found myself tantalized by full, red, kissable lips, part of me fighting it and shaming myself for it and another part of me yearning for it like a drug. The fire in my groin was building like an explosion, and there seemed to be nothing I could do to quench it. I would make love to Alissa every night if she would let me and masturbate a couple of times a day in addition to that, but it didn't matter. It didn't stop the fire, the urge to make it with practically every woman who came into my vision. The demon I once thought I had conquered was on me again.

When I got to Evangelic Temple, Pastor Wilkes escorted me to his office, and as he did, I happened to notice a photo of the office staff. In that photo was a picture of a buxom and tantalizing young woman I had never seen around there before. "It looks like you have a new girl on staff," I said to Pastor Wilkes as I strolled into his office.

"New girl?" he questioned.

"Well, I noticed in the staff photograph a face I have not seen before."

"Oh, yes, yes," he answered. "That's Lovella Titwallow, a young lady who volunteers with us a day or two a week. Her husband's family owns the Chum Snacks Company, and he was sent down here from their Pennsylvania headquarters to manage their new distribution warehouse in Nashville. I think she was a little bored with staying at home all day. She has been doing our bulletins for us each week—very good at it as well."

"Maybe we should put her to work on the bulletin for my broadcast service," I suggested. I could have cared less who actually did the bulletin. I simply found myself fascinated with the idea of seducing that young woman and hoped he might take the bait without being suspicious of my intentions. He did.

"Well, I can bring it up to her." He smiled.

"That's great." I smiled back. "I will look forward to seeing her talents." We then set about planning for the broadcast, although I had a difficult time keeping my mind off fantasies of seducing Mrs. Titwallow. It did not matter to my lust that she was married. In fact, it made the potential conquest even more exciting. Not only was it forbidden fruit, but the excitement of bedding another man's wife and potentially getting caught made it even more tantalizing.

When I got home late that afternoon, Alissa had dinner almost finished. Clara had dropped the children off, and they were playing in the front room. Ariel was now big enough to come running to meet me when I came home. She ran to hug my leg as soon as I walked through the door from the garage, and Adam toddled after her. Adam was going to turn three that summer, and Ariel was six. It seemed as though they grew so fast my mind could scarcely keep up with it.

"Hi, Daddy," Ariel said as she pressed her head into my leg just above my knee.

"Hi, sweetheart," I replied. "Now turn loose. Daddy's gotta give Mommy a kiss." She didn't turn loose, so I walked her extra weight on my leg over to the sink where Alissa was washing lettuce. Ariel clung to my leg like a monkey on a tree. Adam tried to follow but tripped and fell behind me. I was just about to kiss Alissa when I heard him break into a cry. Ariel turned loose at that point, and I turned to pick him up from the floor.

"What's the matter with my little man?" I asked as I picked him up and held him over my hip. He continued to cry. Alissa saw that I had things under control and so continued with the lettuce.

"What's that?" I asked as I wiped a thumb across his cheekbone. "Are those tears? Oh my goodness. I can't believe those are tears. Let's send those up to heaven so Jesus can turn them into diamonds." I rubbed my thumb and forefingers together as I held my hand high above our heads. "Do you see that?" I asked. "Jesus is turning those tears into diamonds!" The distraction worked, and Adam soon quit crying. I carried him back to the living room and sat on the sofa while I watched them return to play.

In a few moments, Alissa called that dinner was almost ready. That was my cue to take the kids to wash their hands. Afterward, we all returned to the dining room, where Alissa had everything prepared and the table nicely set. Adam got a highchair next to Alissa so she could monitor and manage his eating. He was old enough to feed himself but not quite old enough to be trusted to do it without a mess. Alissa was trying to teach him to use a spoon. As soon as we were all seated, I said blessing over our food, and then Alissa and I both began reaching for bowls to serve the children first. "You want potatoes, honey?" I asked Ariel as I dipped the serving spoon into the potato bowl. I knew her answer would be a nod of the head, so I had half a spoon full of mashed potatoes already headed for her plate.

"How did things go with Pastor Wilkes this afternoon?" Alissa asked. "Fine," I replied. "It's old hat. We kind of have all this down after so many times of doing it."

"What are you going to speak about this time?" she questioned.

"I thought I might address some of the things that are going on politically these days," I responded. "You know, things like the Manson murders, the My Lai massacre."

"Why the interest in world affairs all of a sudden?" she continued.

"I think I have always been interested in world affairs," I responded. "I have just never preached about it before. I wish I had. I wish I had not been so shy about standing up and saying something about things going on in the world, you know, like the Martin Luther King assignation."

"You mean assassination?" she reflected.

"Well, yes—that's what I said."

"No, you said assignation," she continued. "That means an appointment to meet a lover in secret. Martin Luther King was assassinated."

"Oh," I uttered, red-faced, certain that the flush on my face was showing. Had I just given myself away? Had I just revealed my plans to have a tryst, plans only I knew of in my own fantasy?

"So what do you plan to say about world affairs?" she questioned again.

"I haven't decided yet," I replied. "I don't want to get into the rut that some preachers get into calling it all signs of the end times. I think I would rather find some way to weave a lesson into it, a lesson for our spiritual growth, not something to terrify people that the world is coming to an end."

"Good Christians know that they will be fine when the end time comes," she commented. "Those who question their worthiness and faith might be having a little fear."

I felt my heart recoil inside my chest. In my mind I heard the redheaded woman scream, "Sinner!" The fact of my hypocrisy was not lost on me. It was quite evident to me and quite tormenting as well. I pretended to be the good preacher out to save souls, but in my heart, I sought to seduce young women and defy their wedlock.

"I…ah…I…don't think I'm very hungry," I said. "I think I'm going to go to the office for a while and maybe see if I can come up with some interesting things to say in the service."

We had built a home office over the garage only a couple of years earlier. It had become my retreat when I needed to study the Bible or prepare sermons.

I laid my napkin across my still-empty plate, rose, and left the room. When I got to the office, I closed the door behind me. It was not uncommon for me to go in there and study for hours. It was rare that Alissa would bother me or allow the kids to bother me. It was my retreat at home where I might study the Word of God and prepare sermons for my services and my television show or just retreat to pray. I sat down in the stuffed leather chair at my desk, reached over, picked up my Bible, and opened it at random. My eyes fell onto a verse from 2 Corinthians, "For we must all appear before the judgment seat of Christ that everyone may receive the things done in his body according to that he hath done, whether it be good or bad." I read the words and began to weep.

On the day Mrs. Titwallow was to arrive at my office, I was nervous from the time I got up. I was half trembling with anxiety knowing what I intended to do. I had no idea how she might respond, if she would accept my attempts to seduce her, or if she might create the scandal that Darlene Meadows could not pull off. I could barely look at Alissa that morning but made myself go through the usual gestures of husband and father. My sin lingered in my mind, generating ever more intensity in my groin as I fantasized about the buxom young woman that I had seen in the photo at Evangelic Temple. The meeting was not to take place until 2:00 p.m., and I had plenty of time to both be nervous and to fantasize. I went into the office late, about 9:00 a.m., and did research for my sermon. I had Clara bring in recent newspapers that I could use for ideas about a sermon on world affairs, the status of prejudice and discrimination in our country, and the fact that the whole world seemed to be in a state of ever-intensifying insanity. The contradiction of my own insanity was not lost on me as I studied and made notes. I could scarce pay attention to the content of an article without the distraction of a fantasy about Mrs. Titwallow.

Clara and I went to lunch at a little local café. She sat across on the other side of the booth from me sporting a large pair of round glasses with the lenses surrounded by a sort of tortoise shell pink plastic. She had recently had her hair colored and permed so she was looking quite stylish for a woman her age. As she nibbled on a French fry, she said, "Is everything all right, Pastor? You seem a little distracted."

"Oh…oh," I said, turning my attention back to her from watching the waitress's ass in her tight white uniform. "I…I guess I have just been through a lot lately, what with losing Daddy and all, and being worried about Momma."

"You have been under a lot of family stress, I know," she went on, then took her fork to carve out a small bite from her hamburger instead of picking it up and shoving it in her face, as most people might have done.

"I wonder sometimes what the world is coming to," I said. "It makes me wonder if we are not in the end times. The signs are all around us with threats of nuclear war, racism, and assassinations going on, with people losing all manner of dignity about them, doing drugs and having—" I stopped midsentence before saying, "Having frivolous sex out of wedlock," knowing that Clara knew my own sins. I quickly changed the subject. "Have you heard anything from Pastor Simmons?"

"We keep in touch." She smiled.

"He seems like a very good man," I commented. "I'm really glad the two of you hit it off."

"We are good friends," she responded. "I dare not call it more than that since we live so far away from each other."

"Well, not so far that you can't see each other occasionally."

"A woman my age who has never been married dares not hope too much," she continued as she chewed gingerly on the little piece of burger she had carved off.

"God works in mysterious ways." I smiled teasingly. "You never know what might be in store for a woman your age. Love does not necessarily go by the year you were born."

"Well, Pastor," she quipped, "if love is in the stars for me, I'm sure it will find its way."

"Surely." I smiled.

Clara nibbled on her French fry and asked, "So what are your plans for this afternoon?"

"Plans?" I asked.

"Yes, plans," she replied flatly. "What do you plan to do with this young woman from Evangelic Temple?"

"Well…ah…we are going to be prepping the bulletin for the service at Evangelic," I nervously replied, knowing full well that she could read me often even better than Alissa.

"I could have done that for you." She looked at me accusingly. "I usually do."

"I know, but Pastor Wilkes suggested that someone from his staff who is familiar with some of the changes they have been making might be a good pick to do the bulletin." I knew I was lying and suspected she knew I was lying, but she simply said, "Oh," and carved another little piece out of her burger. She knew me far too well, and even though I had gone a very long time without acting out, she also knew I was most likely to do so when I was under stress.

"Have you found an attorney to handle the trust for Stephen?" I asked.

"Pastor Simmons thinks he might know someone who can handle it," she replied. "He still doesn't think it is a good idea."

"I really don't want someone associated with the church doing it." I pushed myself back into the cushion of the booth seat.

"For goodness' sakes, why not?" she asked.

I sighed deeply. "I just think this child is a special case—different. I would prefer a secular attorney handle it rather than a Christian attorney. I know that is antithetical to my own beliefs, but I just don't want someone who might be inclined to impose his own values too much."

"In other words, you want this boy to grow up thinking he is a girl and you are going to pay for him to do that?" She set her fork down on the table and looked directly at me. "Pastor, don't you think, honestly, he would be better off remaining in Christian foster care where he can be brought up in the ways of the church?"

I stared out the metal-framed window overlooking a sidewalk to the parking lot beyond. "I'm very confused about this," I said without turning my face back to her. "I'm torn between the principles of the church and by the fact that Miss Mattie obviously and dearly loves that boy. I know she will enable him in some ways. I know she will call him Stephanie if that's what he wants, but I also know that she will give him a genuine love and affirmation that I just don't think he can receive in foster care, and I don't want, perhaps when I'm gone, some attorney imposing his own values onto the situation instead of just following the rules of the trust."

"You don't think a Christian lawyer can follow legal rules without imposing his own values onto the situation?" she asked.

"I just don't want to take a chance on that," I replied. "As much as my own Christian values say that I should just leave it alone and let the church raise him, my heart says he would be better off with Miss Mattie."

"She is already an old woman," Clara argued. "She could pass away before he ever even reaches adulthood."

"I know," I went on, turning back to her and finally looking her straight in the eye. "But she has Christian values, and she is the only one in his life that he has ever been able to turn to. She was there for him in the pits of hell and it would be, to me, a greater sin to take that from him now than it would for him to grow up thinking he is female."

"Perhaps you're right, Pastor," she said as she folded her paper napkin. "There are things in life even a Christian has to learn to accept." She sighed deeply. "I think I am ready to go back to work now, how about you?"

"Yes, ma'am." I pulled out my wallet and left an oversized tip on the table then scooted off the edge of the booth to go pay at the cash register. Clara gathered her purse and waited for me by the door.

I spent that afternoon closed off in my office and had no more communication with Clara until she buzzed me on the intercom to tell me Mrs. Titwallow had arrived.

When Clara led her to the door, I rose up with my best smile and my best demeanor and chirped, "Mrs. Titwallow, how good to see you."

Immediately I noticed the little bulge in her pale green sleeveless dress telling me that she was pregnant. This must have made her bosom even more full, and I struggled to keep my eyes off her cleavage as I came around the desk to greet her. I was delighted that she was pregnant. It would make any need for a condom irrelevant, and if she would let me, I would fuck her with abandon.

By the time I reached for her hand, I could see, feel, myself kissing those rich full lips coated in wine-colored lipstick. I felt my little soldier push inside my underwear, and I fought to prevent an embarrassing erection lest she not be the type to allow my advances. I had become very practiced at testing a woman's response to me, but this one was so enticing I almost didn't care. I took her hand and led her to the chair all the while feeling like I was going to burst at the sight of her. Having seated her, I offered her a soda or coffee, then I crossed to the refrigerator near my desk to bring her a cola after she had made her decision.

I was intrigued by her. I could tell from the accent that she must be from somewhere up north, not having the usual speak common to the area. I began to ask her questions, and she babbled a bit about her husband and his snacks company, but I could have cared less. I was only making polite conversation when I knew, from the moment that I saw her, and before that, I was going to do everything in my power to bed her.

I leaned against my desk, eying her, trying to come up with some ploy to get close to her when it occurred to me that her obvious burgeoning pregnancy was the perfect opening. Perhaps I could offer to pray for the baby and make an excuse to put my hands on her belly. At that point, I was thinking of nothing else. I didn't think about my family, my wife, or kids. I didn't think about my ministry or even that Clara was sitting down the hall at her desk within easy earshot of my office. All I wanted was to be inside her. There was no other goal but that, no other desire but that, and the more I looked at her, the more I wanted her. Finally, I could take the small talk no longer and commented that it looked as though she had a baby on the way.

"I'm sorry," she responded. She said she was embarrassed that she did not wear a maternity dress, and I pounced on the opportunity.

"Oh, don't be sorry." I slithered like a snake around its prey. "Pregnancy is when a woman is most beautiful. You should be proud you are with child."

"Well, I am proud," she replied, and then I pounced.

"May I?" I asked as I went to kneel beside her and let my hand hover just above her belly. I was about to offer to pray for the baby when she nodded her approval for me to touch her. I gazed into her eyes as I gently ran my hand over her pregnant belly. Then I carefully feigned the accident of touching her breast. There was no retreat, no embarrassment, and in that moment, I knew this was a woman I could seduce. Her very presence filled me with such erotic tension I could feel it throughout my body. I found myself saying, "Your lips are like sweet red wine. They make me want to take communion with you. I want to drink the sweet nectar of your lips."

When I asked her for a kiss, she offered no resistance but only continued to gaze back at me. Eventually, I leaned in and began to kiss her gently and sensually as I moved my hand from her belly to her breast. I could feel her desire reflected back to me. I knew she wanted me as much as I wanted her. So I carefully maneuvered her to the desk. I placed a pillow behind her and began to pull her panties and hose from beneath her dress. She kicked her spiked heeled shoes to the floor as I pulled her hose down over her feet. Then I caressed her with my mouth from her feet, up her thighs, to her waiting, engorged clitoris. I made love to her with my tongue until she climaxed. Then I stood back from her, loosened my tie, and pulled my shirt off over my head. I wanted to feel my bare chest against her. I dropped my pants and entered her. I felt the warm moist wave of pleasure engulf my little soldier and knew I could not stop.

While I fucked her, I caressed her, especially her lips. I needed to feel those lips. I ran my fingers over her lipstick and smeared it down the side of her face as I kept thrusting inside her.

At last, my groin tightened, and I felt a wave of climax rushing through me. I could not hold back the ruthless screams that came out of me as I convulsed in a powerful orgasm. I would have sworn that the devil had hold of me in that moment and was shaking me like the rag doll of a raging child.

As soon as it passed, I realized what I had done. I planned it, staged it, and insisted to myself that I could not help it. Then in one moment after that storm passed, the guilt of my sin fell upon me like a tree crashing over a house. I began to weep and plead, "I'm sorry. I'm sorry. I'm sorry."

"For what?" she quipped as though it was nothing.

I didn't understand that. She had just sinned against her husband, her children, against God, and the church. I had sinned even more because I had planned the whole thing. She may have been guilty of the sin of omission in that she did not offer to stop me. She did not set a boundary when she should have rightfully done so, but I was guilty of the sin of commission. I had sinned with intent.

"I am a no-good worthless sinner!" I cried.

Then I turned and tripped over my pants that I had forgotten were around my ankles. This flipped me facedown onto the floor, and I thought to myself, *It serves you right! God has struck you down!*

"The Lord has stuck me down!" I cried.

"Your pants struck you down," she mocked. Then she began telling me, "It's just sex. It's no big deal!"

Oh, Lord Jesus, I thought. *Is she Satan sent to taunt me?* It was not just sex. It was anything but just sex. It was a continuation of a lifetime of failure to control myself. It was a continuation of a lifetime of me hurting myself and those who loved me. It was betrayal of my wife, a betrayal of her husband, and if there was anyone in the world who should have known better, and done better, it was me.

"I am a God-forsaken sinner!" I heard myself scream into the floor.

"Well, doesn't God forgive?" she questioned.

"You have no idea how sinful I am!" I cried. "All I want to do is have sex, seduce women. The devil keeps my mind constantly on women, and I've had so many women. I have defiled so many helpless women, and I've corrupted the church."

"Well, I kind of figured you had a little practice," she mocked again. "But I'm anything but a poor helpless woman. I have some responsibility in this too."

"You are responsible!" I exclaimed. "You are a Jezebel and a whore sent by Satan to lead me into sin!"

"Although I have been a bit of a slut in my day," she taunted, "I don't think I would take it quite that far." Then she began to preach to me. She had the audacity to preach to me. "God is Holy, God is Love, God made you, so you're Holy too." The more she talked, the more disgusted I became with her.

"I have sinned and fallen short," I said into the floor, never looking up at her.

"Well, join the fucking club!" she insisted. "Who hasn't?"

"I have joined the club!" I cried. "The club of hellfire and damnation!" I lay there on the floor, not wanting to look up at her, just hoping she would go away, but she didn't.

After a while, she began telling me to get up. I didn't move. Then she yelled, "RONALD! I SAID GET UP!"

"Yes," I said quietly. "Yes, I need to get up."

She had no idea what I was thinking. At that point, I just wanted to get rid of her. I didn't want to have to look at her, talk to her, or think about what we had done. I rolled over, got up to my knees, and began to pull myself up.

"Yes...I need to get up," I said. "I have work to do." I began to retrieve my clothes, and she began to retrieve hers. She asked for the powder room, and I pointed her to the bathroom adjacent to my office. While she was in there, I dressed myself and told myself I had to pull it together. By the time she came out, I had put on my professional role again. I greeted her formally, "Mrs. Titwallow...how good of you to come to my office today. I hope this was not inconvenient for you. However, I think we may be out of time this afternoon, so if I scribble some notes and send them over, do you think you might decipher my chicken scratch to put the bulletin together?"

She looked at me like a dog that just heard a strange noise. I half expected to see her cock her head to one side and perk up her ears.

"I think I can pull that off," she said.

"Good!" I smiled congenially. "I'll have Miss Smith see you out, and she can bring you the notes, tomorrow perhaps."

"That's okay," she said. "No need to involve Miss Smith. I think I can figure things out." She then walked to the door, grabbed the door facing with one hand, kicked one heel up, threw her head back, and giggled. "See you later, honey."

After she left, I sat in the nearest chair and began to sob. I put my hands up over my face and cried like a tormented child. The next thing I knew, I felt Clara's soft hand on my shoulder and heard her quiet voice question, "Pastor, are you all right?"

She knew better. I knew she had heard everything. I had denied the obvious over lunch that she knew exactly what I was up to. Yet she had done nothing to try to stop it.

"No, I'm not all right," I sobbed. "I hate myself, Clara." Then I stood up, grabbed a vase from the table, and flung it against the wall as hard as I could. The ceramic shattered, and pieces of vase, flowers, and water flew across the room. "I FUCKING HATE MYSELF!" I screamed.

"Pastor, please sit down," she pleaded.

I turned back to her with tears streaming down my face. "Clara, why am I so evil? Why can't I control myself?"

"Pastor, sit down please." She motioned to the chair.

I sat down and buried my face in my hands again. "I don't want Alissa to know."

"I don't think that is an option," she calmly replied.

"I don't want to hurt her anymore," I pleaded.

"I know," she said as she took a seat in the chair across from me. "But after a while, some things can't be hidden anymore."

"I wish I could die!" I begged God at that moment. "I wish I could just fucking die!"

"Nobody wants you to die, honey." I heard Alissa's voice and looked up to see her standing in the doorway. I looked back over at Clara. "YOU CALLED HER?" I wailed. She nodded.

I stood and crossed the room away from Alissa, turned back to Clara, and screamed, "YOU FUCKING CALLED HER?"

"Honey, it's okay," Alissa pleaded.

"Okay?" I yelled. "How can it fucking be okay? How can you put up with this kind of shit? Aren't you mad at me? You should want to hurt me more than I want to hurt myself! You should have been over this shit a long time ago. You should have kicked my ass out, taken the kids, and gone back to Arkansas. WHAT THE FUCK IS THE MATTER WITH YOU?"

"Ronnie, I know this is not you," she pleaded. "Yes, it hurts! Of course, it hurts. I would be a liar if I said it doesn't hurt. I want a husband who is faithful to me. I want a husband who puts me and his children first, and you do that. You do…in every way, except this one." Tears began to stream down her face. I turned away from her.

"This IS me! This IS me, Alissa. I am a fucking pervert! I crave sex like a drug, and if a woman has lipstick, all the better. If she doesn't have it, I will give it to her and ask her to put it on. HERE, LOOK!"

I went to my desk, pulled a drawer completely out, and dumped the contents on top of the desk. Eight or ten tubes of lipstick rolled across the desk, some into the floor.

"YOU SEE THAT?" I yelled. "YOU SEE THAT SHIT! Sometimes I will sit here in the office drawing circles around my dick with it, and I jack off while I fantasize about some bitch that I've seen that day sucking my dick! It doesn't matter. I'd fuck any of them. In fact, I practically have. I have fucked old women. I have fucked fat and skinny women, ugly women, women who stink from filth, and whores. DO YOU THINK THAT'S NORMAL?"

She trembled as she stared at me. Clara stood quietly to the side. Finally, she said, "No, Ronnie, I don't think it is normal. I think you have a sickness, and I think you need help. We need to get you some help."

"HELP? HELP? You want to get me some help?"

I grabbed a couple of the lipstick tubes off the desk, turned, and threw them against the wall behind me and turned back to her. "Do you have any idea how much I have prayed about this SHIT? Alissa, if God can't help me—if God won't help me, NOTHING ELSE IS GOING TO HELP ME!"

"Maybe—"

She began to speak, but I wouldn't let her finish. "MAYBE? There is no maybe! I have forsaken myself and my family. I have forsaken God, so God has forsaken me!"

I turned and walked back to my desk, where I pulled open another drawer. There inside was the bottle of Valium that Alissa had picked up from Dr. Jones. She had brought it to the office in case I might feel anxious and finally decide to take one. However, until that moment, it had been untouched. "I deserve to die!"

I stood there and wept, looking down at the bottle in the drawer. "I deserve to die so I can stop hurting everyone." I looked up at her, pleadingly, and wept.

"I don't want to hurt you anymore, Alissa."

I then grabbed the bottle from the drawer, opened it, and began chugging the pills down as quickly as I could. I swallowed what I could and chewed up what I could.

"STOP!" Alissa shouted. "RONNIE, STOP! PLEASE STOP!"

Both of them ran toward me, trying to grab the bottle from my hand. I had swallowed at least half the bottle before they got to me. I chunked another bunch into my mouth and chewed them as fast as I could. They tried to grab the bottle from my hand, but I held it above my head, out of their reach, until I could grab another mouthful.

"CLARA, CALL THE POLICE!" I heard Alissa scream.

She managed to knock the almost empty bottle from my hand as I saw Clara grab for the phone. I reached over and yanked the phone cord out of the wall, and Clara ran out of the room. I then grabbed a letter opener off the desk and began stabbing myself with it anywhere I could stab, into my abdomen, my chest.

"ROOOOONNNNNNYYYY!" Alissa screamed. She grabbed the desk drawer and began swinging it with both hands toward my hand and the letter opener. "PUT IT DOWN!" she screamed. "PUT IT DOWN!"

After several swings, she knocked the letter opener out of my hand. I fell to my knees with blood dripping from all over my body and sobbed. "I WANT TO DIE! I JUST WANT TO DIE! I JUST WANT TO DIE!"

Then, suddenly, the room fell black and silent.

CHAPTER 24

There was something cold against my chest. Then the sound of a rhythmic beep combined with soft voices brought me to consciousness. I opened my eyes to see Dr. Jones leaning over me and staring down at me with a big beefy smile. He had the earpieces to a stethoscope sticking out of either side of his head. On either side of the bed where I was lying, there were metal rails, and clear tubes ran down to crisscross white tape on the inside crook of my elbow. On the opposite side from Dr. Jones, Alissa stood holding my hand.

"There he is," Dr. Jones commented as he pulled the stethoscope from his ears.

Alissa squeezed my hand and smiled.

"You're a lucky man, Ronald," Dr. Jones said. "If that stab to your chest had gone a quarter inch deeper, you would have punctured your lung. A collapsed lung, that's no fun. Painful thing. Long recovery. Your intestines were nicked a little in two places, but a fairly easy stitch-up in surgery. We had to lavage you pretty good, but I think we are doing okay there. I'm going to keep you on some IV antibiotics for a while just to make sure you don't get peritonitis. You are lucky that you didn't hit any major organs. Good thing you are right-handed, and those are on the opposite side of your abdomen."

I just stared at him, thinking how very unlucky I felt to wake up. "You should have let me die," I croaked.

"Ronnie, don't say that," Alissa said as she squeezed my hand. I looked at her scornfully.

"Well, there wasn't much chance of that," Dr. Jones interjected. "Kind of hard to overdose on Valium by itself, and you gotta try a little harder if you want to stab yourself to death with a letter opener. There are better ways of doing it, but…ah…I'm not going to show you how."

Then, I looked at him scornfully. I had tried to kill myself. I seriously wanted to die, and I was pissed off that I didn't succeed. Now it seemed like he was just mocking me.

"Where am I?" I questioned.

"Vanderbilt, of course," Dr. Jones replied. "Hospital, not university." He actually chuckled.

"Where are the kids?" I turned to Alissa, ignoring him.

"They are with Clara right now," she replied. "She is going to keep them until I can get back home."

"When can I get out?" I turned back to Dr. Jones.

"Hmmm," he groaned. "Well, that's complicated."

"What do you mean 'complicated'?"

"Well," he continued. "We could place you in Vanderbilt's psych unit or the state hospital, but Alissa has something else in mind."

"What do you mean *place me* in Vanderbilt psych or the state hospital?"

I tried to sit up, but the pain put me back to the pillow. "There is no *placing* me. I'm going home!"

"Well, uh…no, you're not," Dr. Jones said.

"What do you mean no I'm not!" I intensified. "You can't put me someplace against my will!"

"Well, actually, yes I can," Dr. Jones explained, "and I will if we have to."

"NO! I'm going home!" I insisted.

"Well, Ronald," he continued. "Let me put it to you like this. You attempted to kill yourself. Actually, that is kind of against the law, and so if I, as your doctor, have concerns that you might try to do that again, I can place you in a psychiatric facility on a minimum of a three-day hold, and that can be extended if there are continued concerns that you might be suicidal. If need be, I can even have the police escort you there."

"WHAT THE—!" I began struggling to get up. "ALISSA," I looked at her pleadingly, "tell him he can't do that. I'm going home!"

"Well…actually, Ronnie, he can do that." She smiled a nervous smile. "Actually…we are all in agreement that you need to be in treatment somewhere."

"I DON'T NEED TREATMENT!" I yelled.

"So here is the deal, Ronald," Dr. Jones continued. "I can place you in Vandy or the state hospital, or there is another option, but just being discharged to go home is not an option, and I will do whatever it takes to make sure you are safe. My priority is to be sure you are safe."

I settled hesitantly back down on the bed as Alissa placed one firm but gentle hand against my shoulder. "Please, Ronnie," she pleaded as she pressed me back toward the bed.

I lay back against the mattress and sighed. "What other option?" I asked.

"Well, Alissa has located an exclusive extended residential care facility in Colorado that she would like for you to consider."

"What? No!" I demanded. "I need to go home. I have work to do. I have to do a broadcast from Evangelic Temple in just a few weeks. I'm not suicidal. I'm fine."

"Well, not according to Alissa and Miss Smith you are not," he argued. "As a matter of fact, they are reporting erratic behavior, blackouts, and loss of control leading all the way back to your father's death and perhaps before. So, after this last incident of chewing up Valium and stabbing yourself—nope, I don't think you are all right. So you have got a choice here. I can place you in a local psychiatric unit against your will, or you can go to this nice, posh extended care program that Alissa has located out in Colorado."

"I can't be out of town for an extended time," I retorted. "I have a service to give in about eight weeks. I have got to prepare for that, and I have my weekly broadcast to do. I'll be fine."

"Nope," Dr. Jones calmly responded.

I looked over at Alissa. "Honey, I'll be fine. Please don't do this to me. I won't do anything stupid again, I promise."

"Ronnie, it is a really beautiful place out there. I think you would like it. I ordered a brochure a few weeks ago, and it looks really nice."

"Wait…what?" I argued. "You ordered a brochure weeks ago? So this is *not* something new. You have been planning to spring this on me for weeks now? Trying to kill myself had nothing to do with your intent to put me away somewhere—WHAT? Are you planning to try to get me declared incompetent so you can just take everything and dump me in an institution where I can't fight you on it? Did you even arrange for that trollop to come to my office and seduce me to throw me over the edge, to make me break? Did you pay her to come in and seduce me and mess with my head? I need to speak to an attorney, NOW!"

"Ronnie, don't be ridiculous," she responded.

"Well…so," Dr. Jones interjected, "it has been evident for some time now that you have a problem, Ronald. The deal is we are down to the wire here. You have pushed it to the limit, and you can go to Colorado, or we can probably figure out a way to keep you in a local facility, for who knows, indefinitely maybe. In the meantime, the press can probably figure out what is going on, maybe they might have a lot more interest in it if you are somewhere local. It is a lot easier for word to get out when you are local than if maybe nobody knows where you are. You can always make up a story to feed to the press."

"You are blackmailing me!" I snarled.

"Let's call it blackmail for Jesus then if you want to call it blackmail," Dr. Jones retorted. "I know Jesus is important to you, and you are going to want to get back up in that pulpit where you can preach the Word. Wouldn't you feel a whole lot better about it if you could also live the Word?"

I just glared at him. There was a righteous indignation in me at that point. *How dare he say those things to me? How dare he accuse me?* I wanted to yell that at him, but I said nothing. I turned back to Alissa and pleaded, "Honey, please…don't…please don't do this."

"Ronnie, it's a really nice place. It is up in the mountains near Colorado Springs. It is kind of an exclusive place just for people who need a place that is not in the spotlight. I even heard that Jack Lemmon was treated there."

"You see!" I exclaimed. "It might be exclusive, but how private can it be if word gets out when there has been some celebrity like Jack Lemmon there?"

"Well, nobody knows for sure," she defended. "But if he was treated there, no one knows what he was treated for, or really anything about it. Maybe it's a rumor just among people on the Hollywood inside. You know, other stars and such. I mean, there has never been anything that I know of in any of the tabloids. Ronnie, please just go. You know you need it. You need the rest if nothing else."

"Is it Christian?" I asked.

"No, it is secular," she confessed. "But I'm sure they would respect your beliefs. I have talked to them, and they seem really nice."

"You what!" I exclaimed. "You talked to them without even asking me if it was okay with me? What did you tell them, that you have an insane husband who jacks off to lipstick? What? I am so angry with you for going behind my back like this, and *they seem really nice*? How do you know? It is probably all just one big scam. You know you are gullible. They are just trying to scam you."

"Okay, that's it!" she exclaimed. "I am done with the gentle convincing approach. You listen here and you listen good, buddy! You are going to go to that facility, and you are going to shut up about it because here are your options: You can go get treated, or Dr. Jones can throw your butt in the state hospital here in Nashville. Have you seen that place out there? Do you have any idea what it is like out there? I'm told they still have drains in the floors of the patient rooms where they used to hose down the schizophrenics back in the 1920s. Sound like a fun place to be? So Dr. Jones will put you in there, and in the meantime, I will be filing for divorce."

She trembled and began to cry as she spoke, but her anger came clearly through her tears. "Yes! That's right! I will file for divorce! Not only will I file for divorce, I will plaster it and the exact reason for it on every billboard, in every tabloid, talk show, or gossip column from here to Great Britain! I will also take you for every penny you can possibly cough up, and you can forget about your little trust fund for that kid in St. Louis. Why should

I pay to raise somebody else's kid when I have two of my own to raise? And you can forget about seeing the kids. I'm sure I can convince a judge that you are not a fit father, and you don't deserve to see your children. I will also tell your mother EVERYTHING! Do you HEAR ME? I will tell Marylee everything right down to the fact that your father molested you!"

"What? Wait a minute? How did you know Daddy molested me?"

"You think you are so good with your secrets. Well, you are not. It does not take a genius to figure things out." She then stuck her perfectly polished and manicured fingernail directly in my face just a few inches short of my nose.

"You listen to me!" She gritted her teeth. "You are going to that treatment program, and you are NOT going to give me another bit of lip about it!"

I lay there in silence, just looking at her, hardly believing what I was witnessing. For a moment, I was in shock. Then I wondered if the real miracle was not that I healed her when she was a little girl, but that God sent her to heal me.

"You are the strongest person I have ever known," I said, finally. "I swear to God, you could take a bullet and keep on coming. You don't give up, do you?"

"I never give up on those I love, Ronnie—never!" She took my hand again and squeezed it gently. "I…am tired though. I am tired, and I need for you to go away for a while, not die, go someplace where you can heal and come back to me whole again."

A tear drifted across my cheek. "I've never been whole, Alissa—never. I've always been damaged. I've always been fake."

"No, that's not true," she argued. "There was a time…a time before your daddy hurt you that you were whole. There was a time when you were a sweet, innocent little boy, just like our Adam. There was a time when you were not confused, not this way. There was a time when your heart was pure. I know that is still in there, Ronnie. You just have to find it."

More tears drifted down my cheeks, and I sighed as deeply as the painful stab wounds would let me.

"How did you know Daddy molested me?" I asked.

"I found the letter in your jacket pocket, Ronnie, the one your daddy wrote and left for you," she replied. "Do you think I don't go through the pockets before I put things in the laundry? I read it. The implication was clear enough what he did to you."

"How long have you known?" I asked.

In my hurry to prevent being caught with the tackle box, I had completely forgotten that I put the letter in my pocket. Until that moment, I had not recalled it and, for all I knew, had thrown it into the pond with everything else.

"Well, I have suspected that something wasn't right for years," she replied, "but when I found that letter in your jacket pocket right after we came back from Arkansas, there was no doubt. Ronnie, please. Please, let's stop pretending. Please let someone help you."

"What is the name of this place?" I asked.

She smiled and wiped a tear from her own eye. "Manitau Chalet." She sighed.

"It sounds like a ski resort," I quipped. "How much does it cost?"

"Two thousand dollars a week," she replied.

"Holy crap!" I exclaimed. "For how many weeks?"

"It's technically indefinite," she responded, "but they said the average stay is ten to twelve weeks."

"So potentially twenty to twenty-five thousand dollars?" I challenged.

"Yes," she replied simply.

"All I can say is they better serve lobster and filet mignon." I smiled nervously.

"I'm sure they do." She sighed as she wiped tears from her face.

"So, when do we make these arrangements?" I asked.

Dr. Jones, who had retired to the back side of the room, flipping through my chart and pretending not to listen, looked up from the metal flip chart and said, "Well, you are going to have to be here for a couple of more days to make sure you are not setting up any infection in your peritoneum. From there, you and Alissa can make the arrangements."

"Okay?" Alissa asked half pleadingly and half with demanding anger.

"Okay," I replied.

"Well, I think I am done here for today," Dr. Jones interjected. "The nurse will contact me if you need anything. In the meantime, I have some other patients to attend to." He then walked out of the room.

"What about my service at Evangelic Temple?" I asked Alissa.

"Well, you were not really concerned about that when you were choking down pills and stabbing yourself," she taunted. "What were they going to do if you died? But okay, we will simply cancel it and make arrangements for you to do it sometime after you get back."

"But what are you going to tell them?" I asked. "What are you going to tell people when they ask why I am not doing my weekly show?"

"We have used reruns before," she replied. "However, if need be, I will do the broadcast in your place. Who knows, they might enjoy meeting the pastor's wife."

"I never thought about you doing the show before," I said, "but that is actually a good idea. Do you think you are up to that? Are you sure you can talk to the camera without 'ahh' and 'you know' or 'err'?"

"Well, it is a casual broadcast anyway. Besides, if they don't like me, they can have you back in a few weeks."

"What are you going to tell them about me being gone?" I asked.

"Only that Pastor Dennison has been having some health problems that require recuperation and that we would appreciate their prayers."

"You don't think people are going to pry, especially the press?" I queried. "Don't you think they are going to want to know what kind of illness I have?"

"We will just tell them you have some wounds that need extensive rehabilitation," she insisted. "That would technically not be lying."

"What wounds?" I asked.

"We will just tell them that you have some old injuries that had begun to create some complications for you, and beyond that, we wish them to respect your privacy and pray for you."

"So they would be praying for me instead of my praying for them," I commented.

"I certainly think you can use it," she replied. "I won't be lying to them. If anyone requests the details, I will simply say there are some injuries from your childhood that require some health care attention."

"That is cutting pretty close, don't you think?" I argued. "I don't want anybody finding out…you know…what is really going on."

"Actually, I don't know," she replied. "I know none of the details. That is something you will have to work out in treatment, but I don't really think folks will pry further if we are vague about it. After all, it's not exactly like you are Elvis Presley or the Beatles. You are a TV minister, and although you have a certain following, I don't think the press is going to find it all that interesting."

"I hope you are right," I said. "This really scares me all the way around. I mean, what are they going to do to me in treatment? What if it does get out? What is going to happen to the ministry while I'm gone?"

"A few minutes ago, you said I am the strongest person you ever knew," she disputed. "Do you trust me with this?"

I hesitated and looked straight at her. I had to ask myself first, and there was a moment in which I wasn't sure. "Yes," I replied. "I trust you."

About five days later, Alissa met me at the hospital on the day I was to be released. Even though I was fully capable of walking and had been walking around the room, they insisted that I had to go down in a wheelchair. I had avoided going out into the halls for fear of being seen and rumors getting started. I knew nurses were sworn to confidentiality, but I also had fears about the nurses gossiping about things that were in my chart, and other patients were not sworn to confidentiality. Nonetheless, I was there, had to be there, and had to go through this thing. I donned a fedora hat, which was uncharacteristic of me, wore an ascot, also uncharacteristic, and sunglasses in hopes of not being recognized. Then, I was wheeled down through a staff elevator to a side exit where Alissa had arranged for me to have the least exposure from onlooking eyes. On the way to and coming out of the elevator, I kept my head down as though I had fallen asleep in the chair. We went through a side door to a staff parking lot where Clara sat waiting for us in her car. I turned to Alissa as we stepped out the door. "Wait, what is going on here?" I asked.

"Honey, everything is packed for you and ready to go. Clara is going to drive you straight from here to Manitau Chalet."

"But I want to go home. I want to see the kids," I protested.

"We thought it best that you go straight there," she argued. "If you go home, you are going to want to settle in, and it will be difficult to make yourself go on from there."

"You mean it will be more difficult for YOU to make me go from there," I snarled.

"We just think this is best," she replied.

"But I want to see my kids!" I growled back at her.

"Were you thinking about your kids when you were chewing up mouthfuls of Valium and stabbing yourself?" she asked.

"You are ALWAYS going to throw that up in my face, aren't you?" I snapped back at her.

"Don't raise your voice, sweetheart," she whispered as she leaned into my ear. "People might notice. There could be publicity."

I was furious. I felt like I had been tricked. My trust in her waned. I asked myself, *What is going on here? Was this some ploy to get me out of the way, cart me off to be locked up in some institution while she took over everything and had me declared incompetent to manage my own affairs?* So many evil possibilities ran through my head at that moment. I thought about just taking off running, getting a cab home, and defying her to stop me. What would she do? Would she call the cops and tell them I was suicidal again? Finally, I just opened the passenger door and got in. I turned around to Alissa with the door still open.

"What about my stuff?" I asked.

"What stuff?" she asked back.

"You know, my clothes, toiletries, and everything."

"Honey, how many years have I been packing for you to go on road trips?" she asked. "I think I got this. You have everything you need, and if I happened to have missed anything, they will have options for you to obtain it there."

"I don't want to do this," I pleaded.

"It will be okay," she assured as she began to push the car door closed. I stuck my right leg out and placed my foot on the pavement. She motioned for me to put my leg inside the car. I sat there staring at her for a moment, resisting. Then I did as she had summoned. She closed the door and motioned for me to roll down the window. When I did, she leaned in through the window, gave me a kiss, and said, "You will be fine."

I turned to look at Clara sitting with both hands on the steering wheel. Today she had on jet-black glasses with large round frames about as wide as oranges. The lenses were rose colored. Her hair was dyed and permed as usual, and she sat looking straight ahead.

I looked back at Alissa. "You are seriously going to have me driven to Colorado by an elderly woman, an employee?" I asked.

"I'm not elderly," Clara interjected without turning her gaze from the windshield. "I'm middle-aged, and I am quite capable of handling the task."

"You see?" Alissa said. "She is quite capable of handling the task."

"I am being treated like a child or an old, demented man," I protested. "I don't like this!"

"RONNIE!" Alissa snapped so I would turn my attention back to her. "Shut up and go!"

I sighed but said nothing. Alissa reached in, put hands on either side of my head, and then leaned in to kiss me. "I love you, sweetheart. I will see you in a few weeks."

"Okay?" Clara asked.

"Okay," Alissa said.

I said nothing. Then Clara pulled from beneath the canopy and waited at the street for an opportunity to pull out. It was about 8:30 a.m., and we were on our way to Colorado.

I sat there and said nothing for probably the first thirty miles of the trip. Clara also said nothing. There was no radio on, just silence and scenery. "I'm so embarrassed," I said, turning my head to the passenger side window.

"I can see how you would be," Clara responded.

"Why did you call Alissa that day in the office?" I interrogated. "I would have been fine if she had not come in. I could have handled this, but when I saw her standing there after what I did, it was too much. I couldn't take any more."

"Pastor, the implication of that statement is that I am responsible for your attempting to kill yourself," she responded. "I am not now, nor have I ever been in charge of your decisions."

"Well, who was in charge of manipulating me into this"—I held both hands to either side of my head to make a quotations gesture—"treatment center?" I said sarcastically.

"Pastor, if you would like," she said flatly. "I am willing to drop you off anywhere, including your own doorstep. What happens after that is between you and Alissa."

"You are treating me like a misbehaved child!" I exclaimed angrily.

Clara did not say a word. She immediately steered the car over to the side of the road, pulled to a full stop, put it into park, and turned to me. "You are a grown man," she said intently. "You have a right to what you think, a right to your choices and to your behavior. I am in charge of none of that. In fact, the last I recall, you are my boss. You cut my paycheck, and while I am at work, you tell me what to do. However, this is *my car*, so if I decide to ask you to get out of it, right now, that is my prerogative, and I will do exactly that if this is the kind of behavior that I am going to have to put up with all the way to Colorado. You are responsible for your behavior, for the choices you make, and for the consequences of those choices. If you thought you were going to die in that office the other day, well, I'm sorry if your party got raided. However, since your party got raided, you now have to face up to the consequences of your behavior, and you will face those consequences whether you go to that program out there, if you go back home, or if you get out of this car right now and try to find a ride to wherever you think you need to go. You decide whatever you want to decide, and I will step out of the way. I will not try to hold you back."

"Aren't you a little afraid that I might try to kill myself again?" I asked.

"You may, Pastor," she concluded. "You may, but again, I am not in charge of the choices you make. I hope and pray to the Lord Almighty that you never again make such a choice as that, but if you do, what I know is that it *is your choice*. It is not something anybody made you do. It is not something you have to do. It is not something that is caused by anything you have ever gone through. It is not something you have to do because you are in that much pain, and you just want the pain to stop. It is something you *decide* to do. You can use whatever excuse you want for making that choice, and the bottom line is that, regardless of the excuse, no one makes that choice but you.

"I pray on bended knee with heartfelt supplication, that the Lord will give you a better choice than that, but even the Lord himself does not change your mind or interfere in the choices you make. You are the only person in the world who can do that. So if you think that is something you have to do, then I will grieve and grieve hard. I know your wife and your children will grieve much harder than I will. The rest of your family will grieve, and all the people who have known you personally or through the media will grieve. It will hurt us more than you may understand right now. We will regret deeply that you made such a choice, and then, in time, the grief will fade a little, but it will never go away, and all of us who love you will have to live with the choice you have made for the rest of our lives. We will give you the finest funeral that we can, we will sing praises to the Lord and pray for your immortal soul, but we will hurt for a lifetime over missing you and will, for a lifetime, regret that you made that choice. However, nothing will ever undo the fact that suicide was the choice you made. It is a hard grief. I don't know if you have ever had a loved one who committed suicide, but Pastor, it is a very hard grief because it means that the person you love killed the person you love. That person is both murderer and victim at the same time, and you don't know whether to be furious at the murderer or cry with compassion for the victim or both. When someone you love commits suicide, you are torn between anger and anguish, and that is a very difficult place to be. No, Pastor, I can't stop you from killing yourself if that is what you are intent on doing. Really, no one can unless they put you in a straitjacket for the rest of your life, and that doesn't really seem to be an option. We can throw obstacles in your way, we can beg and plead, but none of it will matter, if that is the decision you are intent on making."

She paused then and stared at me intently. I looked back for a moment then dropped my head in shame. She continued.

"Pastor, we are offering you a chance to face this devil inside you and hopefully to beat it. I had doubts about Alissa picking a secular program instead of a Christian program, but since those of us who are God-fearing don't seem to be able to reach you, maybe we ought to give the infidels a chance." She sighed. "It's up to you. You have to weigh out which choice you want to make, given that all choices have consequences. Now, don't tell me that I'm treating you like a misbehaving child. This is not a punishment because you were a bad boy. This is an opportunity for a grown man to decide which behavior best suits the needs of himself, his family, and his future. You can make your choice right now, and I will respect whatever choice you make, but if that choice is to kill yourself, don't expect me to hand you a gun."

Without raising my head, I said, "I'm sorry, Clara. I am a selfish man. I always have been. I have imposed on Alissa and you the most. Please forgive me."

"Pastor, the forgiveness has always been there," she returned. "You of all people should know that. 'Forgive them Father for they know not what they do.' I don't take that lightly."

"You have known about my shenanigans for so long. You have known the terrible things I have done, and you said nothing. The whole time, you said nothing." I finally looked up at her. "Why?"

"Judge not that ye be not judged," she replied. "I don't take that lightly either."

"I don't understand," I pondered. "You and Alissa seem to have your Christianity down pat. You seem to be able to take things in stride. You manage your relationship with the Lord, and it works for you, but I…I just can't seem to get it. I just can't seem to have the control over myself that you have."

"Nobody gets it all right all the time," she went on. "Absolutely nobody. Even Jesus got mad and turned over the tables in the temple. All I know is that I give as much of my all to my relationship with the Lord as I possibly can. I think Alissa does the same. Maybe it's easier for women than it is for men. We don't seem to have the urges to sin as often as men do, but I say that knowing the young woman who came to your office the other day was one of those who doesn't much care about who she fornicates with. I think you must have kind of known that too, and that's what attracted you to her in the first place."

"But why?" I pleaded. "Why do I do this? Why does my own body possess me in such a way that I can't control those urges?"

"Maybe it's not your body that's the problem," she suggested. "Maybe it has more to do with something that is going on in your mind."

"But what?" I continued.

"I think that is something for you to figure out while you are out there in Colorado," she replied. "Maybe you need some psychologist who has studied the mind to help you figure that out. Maybe there is something more to it than the devil playing games with your soul."

"Maybe you're right," I acquiesced.

She sat there for a moment before speaking. "So are you ready to go?"

I looked out the front window at the long stretch of highway ahead. Cars had been coming to and fro the whole time we sat there, and I barely noticed. I was about to turn my attention back to Clara when a semitruck whizzed past us in the lane behind her and I startled. The wind shear was enough to rock the car slightly. I didn't yell, but I almost did. I felt my heart pounding in my chest momentarily. She had not even winced from the same event and waited patiently as I came to my answer.

I took a deep and stilted breath and said, "Yes…I think I am ready to go."

Clara said not a word but turned herself back in the seat and faced the steering wheel. She put her foot on the break, put the car in drive, and watched for oncoming traffic as she maneuvered the car back out on the road. A few minutes later, she asked, "Would you like to stop in Pocahontas and see your mother?"

"Oh, heavens, no!" I exclaimed. "I don't want her to know about this. I don't want her to know her son is going to a looney bin. It would worry her to death."

"Okay," she responded with both hands firmly on the steering wheel at ten o'clock and two o'clock. She said nothing else.

Later we chatted about the weather, about different cities we would be traveling through, about food, or whatever might pass the time. Clara had an eight-track player in her car and had several selections of good Gospel music by folks like The Inspirations, The Happy Goodmans, and Bill Gaither. So we listened to music for a while as well. Since you can't listen to good old Gospel music without singing along, I found myself singing to beautiful renditions of familiar hymns.

Apparently, Alissa and Clara had planned a route through Pocahontas up through Springfield, Missouri, to Kansas City, and across Kansas to Colorado. Somehow, they had speculated that I might want to stop and see Momma, but I just couldn't bring myself to do it. I really didn't see a reason for it anyway, and I certainly didn't want to have to answer questions or bring myself to lie because I felt so ashamed of what I was having to do. I felt a twinge of guilt as we passed through Pocahontas on our way to the Missouri border, but I had become accustomed to stifling and stuffing my feelings of guilt. It was actually around lunchtime when we went through Pocahontas, but I couldn't stand the idea of stopping and having someone recognize me, so I insisted we wait until we got to West Plains, Missouri, to stop for a late lunch. Even then, I asked Clara to go in to purchase something at a fast food restaurant, then bring it back to the car.

She ate while she was in the restaurant, and I sat in the car, barely looking up at those who were going to and from the restaurant. I ate mine while she drove on to Springfield, about two hours away. At Springfield, we took Highway 13 on up to Kansas City. We got to Kansas City a little before 7:00 p.m. Then Clara pulled over at a grocery store parking lot and pulled out her map. She had checked the map multiple times through the journey, and I had not noticed a specific address had been penciled into the margin. Now she was looking at that address and trying to figure out the best route there.

"What is that?" I asked. "Why are you wanting to go there?"

"It's our hotel," she replied. "Alissa booked a hotel for us."

"This was planned out to the last detail," I commented.

"Yes," she replied. "Alissa started working on this right after you were hospitalized."

"Vacation Inn," I commented as I watched her memorize the few turns that she would make from the parking lot of the grocery store to the hotel.

"Yes, I suppose so," she replied.

Clara then folded the map, set it between us, and proceeded to get her bearings to steer back out onto the street. In a few minutes, we were pulling up in front of the hotel. I waited in the car while she went in to claim our reservations. When she came back, she set the papers and room key on top of the map.

"Only one key?" I questioned as I looked down at the seat between us.

"We are going to share a room," she replied.

"What!" I exclaimed.

"We are going to share a room," she reiterated.

"What? Why?" I questioned. "That doesn't make any sense, and I don't think it is proper."

"That's the way Alissa set it up," she said flatly.

"Why would she do that?" I interrogated. "We have more than enough money to pay for separate rooms."

"I guess she doesn't trust you," Clara responded as she started the car and proceeded to drive around to the back side of the building.

"Doesn't trust me?" I insisted. "Clara, that is utterly ridiculous!"

"Since you attempted suicide a little over a week ago, she wanted some-one to be with you at all times, and that was also recommended by the treatment center."

Clara pulled the car into a parking place almost directly in front of our room. There were balconies on the second and third floors with a stairwell in the middle and at the end of the building, but our room was first floor.

"So I am under surveillance," I snidely remarked as she was opening the door on her side. She got out of the car and walked around to the trunk to open it for our luggage. I followed from the other side.

"Clara, there is absolutely no reason for this," I insisted as I met her at the trunk.

"There is a reason, Pastor," she replied while she was digging in the trunk for a small bag. "Your state of mind has been extremely erratic and impulsive ever since your father died, and trying to kill yourself was the final straw. Those of us who love you would kind of like to keep you around for a little longer."

"Clara, I won't do anything to hurt myself," I insisted. "Let me go around and secure another room."

She picked up her bag and looked at me. "I am supposed to tell you," she summoned, "if you insist on your own room that you are not to bother coming home, and Alissa has already selected an attorney to file divorce papers if she has to."

The thought of a press-covered public divorce and the thought of experiencing national scorn for my behavior as well as losing my family quickly flashed through my mind. "Okay, okay," I acquiesced. "I just don't feel comfortable because sharing a hotel room with someone is very personal."

She smirked behind those big round black glasses.

"It's a double bedroom, and I think I will be able to control myself, Pastor. I'm pretty good at that."

I had to smile. It was ridiculous that I had gotten myself into such a place, and deep down, I knew that she and Alissa both meant well.

"Are you sure about that?" I joked. "I mean, I am quite the lover you know."

"If I have to, I will pray for the Lord to give me strength." She grinned, knowing me far too well to take that seriously. "Let's go."

We settled into our room then went to a nearby café for dinner. When we came back to the room, we watched a little television and settled in for bed by 9:00 p.m. Alissa had thought of everything, including a couple of pairs of my favorite pajamas. We each changed in the tiny in-suite bathroom. Clara had a long-sleeved floor-length granny gown that she wore to bed. Before settling down, Clara sat for a time at the vanity and netted up her permed hair so that she wouldn't mess it up too much by sleeping on it. She took the bed nearest the door, and mine was only a step or two from the bathroom. I got under the cover and watched as she put the finishing touches on her hair protection system. I said "Good night" when she went to her bed and pulled back the covers.

"Good night, Pastor," she returned in kind, and then she got under the covers, laid her head gently onto the pillow, flat on her back with her arms folded over her chest like a corpse.

A dim streetlight came in around the curtains on the opposite side of her bed. I turned painfully over, facing the opposite direction, stared at the barely lit wall for a few minutes, and fell asleep wondering what it was going to be like to be in a residential treatment center.

In the middle of the night, I heard a knock on the door. I sat up on the side of my bed to see Clara sleeping peacefully in the other bed. The knock came again, but she didn't seem to hear it.

"Clara," I called. "Do you think we should answer the door?"

She didn't stir, and the knock came again. I got up, went to the door, and opened it without thinking of taking any precautions with the lock or checking through the peephole first. There stood the redheaded woman, as beautiful as she was the first time that I had encountered her. She was wearing soft white flowing almost-seethrough garments, and her face glimmered in the moonlight, accenting her voluptuous red lips.

"I thought you might like a quickie for old time's sake," she said as she ran her finger across my lips, down my chest, and over my belly to my little soldier. "Ah," she said, stroking my phallus, "standing at attention just like a good soldier should be."

I turned around to see Clara lying on the bed sound asleep, quiet, noticing nothing that was going on.

"Sure," I replied to the question. I stepped outside.

Then the door to the hotel room closed behind me. I kissed the red-headed woman passionately and pushed her back onto the hood of Clara's car. She had nothing on underneath those silky white flows of fabric. So I quickly located my entry, snapped open the front of my pajamas, pushed myself into her, and began thrusting. The bottoms of my pajamas fell down around my bare feet. While I was fucking her, a man approached. He stood there watching as I proceeded to fuck the redheaded woman on the hood of Clara's car in an open parking lot under the streetlights. He watched intently then reached down and began rubbing the palm of his hand over his crotch. The man undid his belt and dropped his blue jeans. His jeans fell away as though they had just disappeared into thin air. He started stroking his erect soldier and then began touching me, running his finger up the crack of my ass. I tried to push him away as I continued to fuck the redheaded woman. Several times I slapped his hand or pushed him away. I kicked at him while I continued to fuck, but he kept trying to touch me. I yelled at him, "LEAVE ME THE FUCK ALONE!"

Then another man approached, a younger man, perhaps in his twenties. His thick long blond hair came down just over his ears. He pulled open his shirt to reveal a bare muscular chest. Then he leaned backward over the hood of the car, grabbed the back of my head, pulled me toward him, and tried to kiss me. I pulled my head back, pulled away from him, and tried to push him off the hood of the car. All the while, I continued to fuck the redheaded woman, and the other man continued trying to touch me. I looked down at the redheaded woman to see that she had turned into Daddy when he was about thirty-five or forty years old. He looked up at me and smiled. Then I was struck by the realization I was fucking Daddy. I looked down at him while I continued to thrust. I didn't stop, but a mix of emotions ran through me, love, grief, anger, fear. It seemed like I was feeling all those things at once. Suddenly, I felt myself on the verge of climax, about to cum, when I startled awake in my hotel bed.

I sat straight up, gasping for breath, and winced with pain from the stab wounds in my chest and abdomen. "No, no, no, no," I heard myself saying. "I'm not a homosexual. I'm not, I'm not, no, no, no."

Clara awakened and reached over to turn on the bedside lamp.

I looked at her startled then looked away in shame.

"Pastor, are you okay?" she questioned as she fumbled for her glasses case that she had left beside the bed.

She found the case, opened it, sat up on the side of the bed, and put on those big round black-framed glasses.

"Don't look at me!" I cried as I scrambled over to sit on the opposite side of the bed with my face buried in my hands.

Clara got up, came around to the opposite side of the bed, placed her small warm hand between my shoulders, and said, "Pastor, it will be okay."

"You don't understand!" I sobbed. "Nobody understands! I'm so filthy! I'm so filthy!"

"Pastor, what I do understand," she comforted, "is there are a lot of people who dearly love you, and we don't think of you as filthy."

"You don't understand, Clara," I sobbed into my hands.

"No, Pastor, I don't," she explained. "I truly don't understand, and I'm not going to pretend that I know how you feel or offer false comfort by saying that I do. I don't know how you feel, and I don't know what is going on with you. I do know that I'm not a professional, and I'm not the one to help you sort this out, but I pray for you every day. I have prayed for you from the very first time I met you. I started praying a little different prayer after I caught you with that Darlene girl up in Chicago, but I still pray every day."

"Thank you, Clara," I said as I began to quiet my sobs. "It means a lot that you care for me."

Clara just sat there quietly, rubbing her hand around between my shoulder blades. It helped. She had no idea what I was thinking. What had originally seemed like a beautiful dream when I was a little boy, as a call to preach, a call to live and speak God's Word, had become a torment. The redheaded woman had become my torturous nightmare. I condemned myself for having lustful, sinful thoughts and dreams, and now those dreams expanded into homosexuality, an even greater abomination. I thought about Stephen up in St. Louis, how he thought he was a girl, how he had touched me and solicited sex with me when he was only a little boy. I felt disgusted by what had happened to him. The world was showing me things that were in direct conflict with my Christian upbringing. Even my own father was in conflict with the words he spoke from the pulpit. I thought about when he knocked me down in the church and kicked me for making out with Lynetta, how he had screamed that I was a sinner, when at the same time, he was a sinner just as great as I was. At that time, I had blocked it all out of my mind. I had pretended so hard that Daddy was a good and righteous man that I completely forgot it, like it just didn't exist. I never wanted it to exist. I never wanted to admit such a thing to myself, and I was determined that I was not going to admit it to someone else. Even if Alissa had concluded that it happened, I was never going to admit the details to her or to anyone else.

After a few minutes of sitting there in silence, receiving the patient comfort of Clara's warm hand between my shoulders, the sobs had stopped. I said, "I'm okay now, Clara. I think I am ready to go back to bed." I took my hands away from my face and placed them on my knees. I looked up at her and smiled. She reached down to squeeze my hand and said, "All right, Pastor." She got up and prepared herself for sleep again then turned out the light. I simply rolled back over into the bed and pulled the cover up around me. I didn't sleep much after that and spent most of the rest of the night staring off into the dim night.

Daylight was just beginning to peek around the curtains when our phone rang with our wake-up call. I was already awake. I reached over, picked up the phone, listened a moment, and said, "Thank you."

Clara stirred when she heard the phone ring. "Do you want to shower first?" she asked.

"Do you need the bathroom?" I returned.

"Yes, just long enough to urinate, if you don't mind, and then you can have it."

We began our preparations for the remainder of the trip at that time. We cleaned, dressed, and checked out of the hotel. Then we had breakfast at the same little café where we had dinner the night before. We were on our way again by 7:30 a.m. When we headed back out on the road, I said, "Clara, are you sure you don't want me to drive? This is an awful long trip to have to drive all the way by yourself."

"I have strict orders not to let you drive," she said. "Besides, when I have you delivered, I'm going to have to drive all the way back home anyway."

"You are such a good friend," I complimented.

"Oh, I'm getting paid." She giggled a little. "You didn't know I was getting paid?"

"No," I replied, "but I'm glad that you are, and you are still a very good friend who we do not pay enough for your diligent service."

"I'll take a raise anytime you want to give me one, Pastor," she quipped.

"Done!" I exclaimed. "We'll talk to Alissa about it when we get back."

"Oh, now you are going to pit me against the tough one in the family," she grinned. "I may not be getting that raise."

"You will," I said.

We stopped in a town called Hays, Kansas, for lunch, and by the time we got to Manitau Chateau, it was about 5:20 p.m. We had driven through downtown Manitau Springs, which was a beautiful, rustic little town nestled in the mountains. The road to the treatment center curled up around the side of a mountain to a level place, kind of hidden in the pines, and fir trees that grew along the mountainside. The building, although it appeared to be a fairly new build, was made to look like a large Swiss Chalet built into the hillside. A rock foundation encircled the building, and there were a couple of places where stone fireplace chimneys rose up the side of the building. The A-frame roof of the initial façade was bordered by rustic wood and multipaned windows that could be seen all around the building. There was a large rustic wood balcony that hovered over an entrance area where a car could pull right up to the doors. Stone pillars supported the balcony on either side of the entrance area and around part of the parking lot. There actually appeared to be two or three stories to the building, at least.

When we pulled up to the building, a valet came out to open our doors and offered to park the car. Clara handed him the keys and instructed him that she would not be staying. Apparently realizing he would also bring in my luggage, she instructed which bags to bring and which to leave. That was an easy discernment since all her bags were pale pink. We then walked through the double front doors into a large lobby and seating area. An attractive brunet woman with hair perfectly permed around her head, who was wearing a body-hugging dark-blue knee-length dress, rose from a desk near the door and came around to meet us.

"Ahhhh," she said, smiling as she approached me directly with her manicured hand extended and absolutely no bend in her elbow.

"You must be Mr. Dennison. We have been expecting you."

"Yes." I smiled as I grasped her cool, thin, long-fingered hand.

"I am Pamela Martin, the concierge for Manitau Chateau Treatment Center." She continued to smile as though it had been painted on. "It is so good to have you here, Mr. Dennison."

About that time, the valet came in with my luggage and set it on the floor near her desk.

"Thank you, Frank," she commented as she dropped her hand from mine.

"Right this way, Mr. Dennison. We have some papers to sign in order to get started." She turned to walk away, and I couldn't help noticing the swing of her ass in that tight dress. It reminded me so much of Wanda.

She slunk around the desk, sat down, then began to pull papers from a side drawer. She placed them atop the otherwise perfectly clean desk.

"Of course, Mr. Dennison, we have contracts and agreements we need to have signed before we begin your treatment process. Please have a seat." She motioned to the chairs on the opposite side of the desk. Then she reached into a drawer and brought out a pen, which she laid atop the papers.

"Like a legal agreement?" I asked.

"Of course," she replied flatly but courteously. "We are entering into a contract to provide you mental health treatment within our rules and guidelines, and you are entering into an agreement, not only to allow us to treat you, but to follow those rules and guidelines."

"What rules and guidelines?" I questioned.

"Well, of course I will explain those in detail for you and answer any questions you may have as we go over the paperwork," she explained, "but in general, we have tiers of treatment based on the level of care required, and we have rules that vary within each tier as privileges are granted. Given that you were recently suicidal, we will start you on tier one, and that would mean no access to sharps or other means by which you may be able to harm yourself."

"Okay," I replied and glanced over as Clara took a seat in the chair beside me. "So what exactly does that mean, no sharps?"

"Well, you would have no access to things like scissors, razors, pens, or metal utensils and the like until you are moved off tier one, even then, nothing other than perhaps pens and eating utensils."

"How the heck am I supposed to groom myself or eat?" I questioned, feeling the irritability rising in my voice.

"Of course, we are not going to put you on constant observation with a staff member in your presence at all times unless you become overtly suicidal," she explained, "but you will have fairly close supervision. A staff member will be present with you when you shave, and then the razor will have to be a cartridge type that you turn back over to the staff member upon completion of shaving. Your meal utensils will be light plastic. You will initially be separated from the patients on the other tiers of care and will eat separately so you do not have access to the metal utensils we allow in the main cafeteria."

"This is humiliating!" I turned to Clara then looked back at Pamela Martin. "This is absolutely humiliating!"

"I understand your concerns," Pamela Martin went on, "but we have to make sure our patients are safe and that we do not contribute toward any attempt at self-harm."

"And how will you know that I'm not going to hurt myself?" I demanded. "When I tell you I don't want to kill myself? How else would you know? I don't want to kill myself. There you have it, now can we start me with something that is not so demeaning and humiliating?"

"Actually, we have a policy that all our patients start at tier one," she commented. "That is our standard procedure until we are certain that they are not going to make an attempt to hurt themselves, and it is more than you just saying you don't want to kill yourself. The treatment team will evaluate your behavior for signs of stability before moving you to the next tier."

"So I'm going to be like a bug under a magnifying glass," I said sarcastically.

"Well, if you want to put it that way," she responded. "We see it more as caring supervision to help you through your emotional crisis so you can move on."

I turned and stared at Clara. She smiled and said nothing. "Did my wife know about this?" I asked, turning back to the concierge.

"It is my understanding that there were several telephone conversations with Mrs. Dennison," she replied. "It is generally our policy to make things clear."

I looked back at Clara then back at Pamela Martin. "Give me the stupid papers!" I demanded. "Show me where you want me to sign!"

"Well, first of all," Pamela Martin began, "this is our consent to treat and—"

"Show me where to sign," I demanded, cutting her off in midsentence.

"Sir, I need to explain this to you," she went on.

"First of all, I don't care! Second, I am not an idiot. I'm capable of reading, and I'll read it later if I feel like it!" I exclaimed. "Show me where to sign on all your papers. I agree, whatever it is, whatever you want from me. I agree."

"Mr. Dennison, it would not be ethical of me to have you sign these without giving you a summary of what each one means," she returned.

"Fine, summarize!" I demanded. "But make it quick!"

She began to explain the form to me, and I rudely turned my fingers in the air, motioning for her to get on with it. At the end, I said, "Yeah, yeah, yeah, whatever!" I snatched the paper out of her hand, scratched my signature onto it as quickly as I could, and tossed it over to the side of her desk. "Next!" I blurted irritably and kept the pen in my hand.

I did this with every form she asked me to sign. When she had no other paper in front of her, I asked, "Is that it?"

"Yes, sir," she replied calmly and confidently.

"Fine," I continued with an irritable tone. "Have someone show me to my room." I turned to Clara. "Tell Alissa I love her. You can go now."

"Pastor, please don't be this way," she pleaded. "Everyone involved in this is here to help you and care for you. Everything that is being done is for your benefit."

I got up and walked to the middle of the lobby. "Unfortunately, no one is allowing me to decide for myself what is for my benefit."

"Well, you haven't exactly done a great job of that lately," Clara said and got up to face me.

I dropped my head.

"No," I replied. "I guess I haven't."

"You know, there is a time for holding on, for being in control," she said as she crossed over to stand in front of me, "and there is a time for letting go. Pastor, this is a time for letting go."

Pamela Martin waited patiently behind her desk. I stood there, saying nothing with my head down, staring at the floor. I looked up through the windows at the beautiful mountain scenery in the distance.

"I guess you are right, Clara," I said, moving my attention back to her. "Maybe this is a time for letting go. I've been needing a vacation for a long time. I suppose this is as good a vacation as any. At least it's beautiful here."

"Good for you, Pastor." She smiled and reached over to take my hand. She clasped it warmly between her hands.

"You can't drive back tonight," I commented. "Where will you be staying?"

"It's all been arranged," she replied. "Alissa got me an overnight stay at this cute little bed-and-breakfast near downtown. I might even rest a couple of days before I go back."

"Please do," I entreated. "You need a rest, probably more than I do."

"Pastor, I know you are in good hands," she comforted. "This young lady seems very nice and professional. I'm sure the other staff will be as well."

"Yes, you are right," I said. "I know. You probably need to go now."

Clara let go of my hand and turned her attention back to Pamela Martin and nodded. Miss Martin picked up the phone at her desk and dialed. "Mr. Dennison is ready to start now," she said into the phone. Clara turned back to me.

"You're right, Pastor." She smiled. "I should go now." Clara turned to walk toward the front door.

I saw Pamela Martin pick up the phone again and dial. Through the large glass doors, I saw the valet pick up the phone at his station by the door.

"Mr. Dennison's escort is ready to leave now," Miss Martin said.

Clara turned back to me at the door and gave a little wave.

Locked metal doors behind me opened, and two male attendants dressed all in white came into the lobby beside me.

Clara pushed on through the door. The valet had already gone to get her car. She would not stand at the curb for long.

I dropped my head again and quietly began affirming, "Okay…okay…okay…okay…"

One of the attendants went to pick up my luggage. The other said, "Mr. Dennison, please follow me."

I turned and followed him with my head still down, still affirming, "Okay…okay…okay…okay…"

At the edge of the lobby by two large metal doors, the attendant programmed a code into a keypad on the wall. The doors opened, and we all walked through while I was still quietly affirming, "Okay." Shortly after we stepped into the hall on the other side of the doors, I heard them close and the metal lock click into place. I stopped my affirmations briefly as the sound of that electronic lock wedged itself into my memory. I folded my hands together above my crotch as we proceeded down the hall, one attendant in front of me and the one carrying my luggage behind me. Once again, I began to quietly affirm, "Okay…okay…okay…okay."

CHAPTER 25

My room was comfortable enough. It was not quite the Taj Mahal I had expected from seeing the brochures and hearing Alissa's description. Nonetheless, with exception for the safety precautions that had been put in place, it was as comfortable as the average hotel room, and it had a very nice view out across the mountains. However, there was a metal screen across the window so one could not access the glass. It made the view a little dim, but I suppose it was part of their precautions with suicidal patients. I accepted that I had gotten myself into this mess by acting the way I did. Maybe, just maybe, these people could teach me how to control myself.

They had fed me dinner in my room the first night, and then I was told not to eat or drink anything after midnight. I couldn't eat anything anyway. There was nothing in the room to eat and only a paper cup to use for getting a drink of water from the sink. I didn't use it and did as instructed. I was not given breakfast and told that I would see Dr. Carter that morning for a history and physical. I complained that Dr. Jones had recently done a full physical, but it did no good. I sat in my room till almost 9:00 a.m. with only a couple of magazines the nurse dropped off. Otherwise, there was no TV, radio, or clock in the room. Electrical outlets had been covered over, I guess to prevent someone from trying to electrocute themselves. I noticed that lighting all had a locked metal guard over it so bulbs could not be accessed.

Finally, one of the nurses came to get me. She took me to a different floor of the hospital, where I was weighed, and my vital signs were taken.

A male attendant took me to a standard exam room and told me to strip down and put on a hospital gown. He never left the room the whole time. I stripped, hung my pajamas on a coat hanger behind the door, and sat on the edge of the examination table with my bare feet dangling off the edge. I felt very intimidated, unsafe, and humiliated. The room was cold, and I was practically shivering before the doctor came in several minutes later. He was a tall lanky young man, probably in his early to midthirties although he looked younger. He was one of those skinny guys with cheekbones the shape of triangles and a forehead the shape of a rectangle over that. He wore wirerimmed glasses and had short blond hair. His white lab coat came to his knees, and he had a stethoscope draped around his neck. He came in with a metal flip chart in his hand. He immediately tucked the chart into his left hand, pulled it down to his side, and offered his long bony fingers in a handshake.

"Good morning, Mr. Dennison!" he exclaimed far too jubilantly. "I'm Dr. Carter. I'll be your attending psychiatrist while you are here at our lovely facility. How are you doing this morning?"

"I'm here," I said bluntly. "Let's get on with it."

"Okay," he said in affirmation as he sat on a chair by a Formica-topped cabinet. "Let's see here. Looks like your vitals are all fine, your weight is good. Pretty healthy specimen all things considered. We are going to want you to pee in a cup for us, and we need to draw a little blood. Then I need to listen to your chest, feel around on your belly, do a rectal exam—all that standard stuff."

"Wait—what?" I exclaimed. "A rectal exam? There is no need to do a rectal exam."

"It is just standard procedure for a full physical," he said. "Something you're probably going to want to start doing annually once you get a little older. How old are you?" He began to scan the chart I guess for my age or date of birth.

"I'm thirty-seven," I answered. "I don't need a rectal exam."

"Well, like I said," Dr. Carter continued, "that's just all part of the procedure."

I felt my breath quicken and noticed that my hands had begun to tremble. As I spoke, I noticed a cracking in my voice and felt myself almost on the verge of tears. "There will be no rectal exam," I repeated. "There will be NO rectal exam."

"Well, we kind of need to find out how healthy the old prostate is," he quipped without looking up from the chart.

"No…no…no…haaaa—no!" I heard myself crying. Tears began rolling down my cheeks, and I started to shake all over. "No…no…no!" I pleaded tearfully.

At this point, Dr. Carter looked up from the chart with a look of both concern and curiosity.

The attendant stood up, came to my side, and put his hand on my arm. I pulled my arm immediately away from him and leaned toward the other side of the table.

"No…no…no…no," I continued tearfully to plead. I had flashes of the corn bin and Daddy in that damn red wig in my mind.

"That's okay," Dr. Carter said with a calm and comforting voice. "We don't have to do the rectal exam then."

"No…no…no!" continued to emit from my mouth, and I felt like a scared little boy at that moment more than I felt like a man.

"So looks like we have hit an emotional tender spot," Dr. Carter concluded. Then I heard him say, "Mr. Dennison, I need you to take some deep breaths for me, okay? Can you take some deep, slow breaths for me?" He turned to the attendant.

"Carl, will you go get Mr. Dennison a cup of water, please?" The attendant immediately left the room, and for some reason, I felt a little safer having him gone.

"I need you to understand that you are safe here," Dr. Carter continued. He stood back about two feet away from me and did not touch me. "Do you realize that you are safe?"

I did not look up at him. I had stopped, whimpered, said "No," and simply stared at the tile floor off to the right side of the exam table.

"Would you try to take some deep breaths for me, Mr. Dennison?" Dr. Carter continued.

I nodded a brief affirmation and tried to take a breath. It felt like I was trying to pull gelatin into my lungs. It would have been just as easy to inhale gelatin as drawing in that one breath. The breath came in short, rapid spurts. Then I opened my mouth and drew a trembling breath in as deeply as I could.

"Good…good," I heard his cooing voice affirm. "That's good. Now I need you to keep doing that for me, okay? I want you to focus on the sound of my voice, and I want you to focus on what you see around you. I see you are looking down at the tile. What do you see in that tile? Do you see colors or patterns? Try to pay attention to the feeling of your hand as it rests there on the exam table. Can you do that? Just feel the weight of your hand on the table and keep breathing for me, Mr. Dennison. Pull the air slowly and deeply in and pay attention to how it feels to take that breath."

Again, I tried to pull in the breath. This one was a little easier than the last had been. I continued to try to breathe as he instructed, and in a few minutes, it seemed like I could catch my breath a little. I startled when I heard the sound of the door opening and closing behind me. The attendant had come in with a paper cup filled with water.

"Thank you, Carl," Dr. Carter said as he reached out to take the cup. "Please have a seat."

He pointed for Carl to sit back down in the chair against the wall where he had previously been sitting. Dr. Carter handed me the water. "Try to take a few sips," he said, "and between sips, continue to work on taking some long deep breaths for me, okay?"

I sipped on the water. It was cold and refreshing. When I finally was able to calm down a little, Dr. Carter asked, "May I put my hand on your shoulder? Do you think you would find that comforting, or would it be intruding?"

I looked up at him with a sense of shock. "No one has ever asked me anything like that before," I said.

"Well, it is about time someone asked permission before touching you," he replied.

I was even more shocked. What did that mean? I didn't recall anyone ever asking permission before touching me.

"Is it okay?" he asked.

"Yes…fine," I replied.

"Okay," he went on as he placed that long skinny hand just to the back of my left shoulder. "I want you to know that you are in charge of your body. I'm not going to do anything that you don't authorize first, and I'm not going to do anything to hurt you."

"Okay," I replied.

He then asked me if I would be willing to let him listen to my chest and my breathing. I granted permission, and he put on his stethoscope, then proceeded to place it on various spots around my torso. "Have you had this kind of procedure done before?" he asked.

"Yes," I replied. "Dr. Jones has done this, but he has never mentioned anything about a rectal exam. He just told me he needed to listen to my heart and lungs."

"Well, we try to be slightly more thorough than the average physical exam here," he commented. "I'm sorry that upset you. The truth is, you are still a little young for a regular rectal exam, but it should be something you consider as a yearly precaution once you get past forty."

"I'm okay now, I think."

"Good," he went on. "Can I get you to lay back on the table for me now, and would it be okay if I feel around on your abdomen?"

"Yes, fine," I replied as I lay back on his exam table.

He felt around my abdomen for a little bit, avoiding the bandaged wounds, then said, "I don't want to upset you again, but I need to let you know that an examination of your testicles is pretty standard for these history and physical examinations as well. Would you be okay with having me examine your testicles?"

"Why do you need to do that?" I asked, more out of curiosity than of concern, although it did raise the anxiety in me again.

"We look for lumps just like looking for a lump on a woman's breast for breast cancer," he replied. "Oh, and I might need to poke my finger up around the edge of your testicles and check for a hernia."

"Oh," I commented. "I guess that is pretty important. Do you think I might have cancer in my testicles?"

"It is not likely," he replied. "But it is possible."

"Well, if it is not likely," I said, "I would really prefer not to have you touch me there."

"Understood," Dr. Carter replied. "Then we are pretty much through with the exam except for lab work and a few questions. I will just document that you refused those more intimate examinations. I'll also ask Carl to get you some instructions on how to examine your own testicles. Please let me know if you find anything unusual."

"I'm not refusing," I said. "I just don't want to do it. If you think you have to do it, I can submit to it."

"Why should you have to submit to something you don't want to do?" he asked.

"Well, if it is required, I can do it," I mentioned.

"Mr. Dennison, it's okay." He smiled. "You don't have to do it if you don't want to."

I gave a nervous smile in return.

Soon after, he asked the attendant to escort me to the lab where I had blood drawn and gave a urine sample. From there, the attendant took me to get a snack of orange juice and crackers. He then escorted me back to my room. Before closing the door to my room, he said, "I'll bring your lunch up shortly. Until you are taken off suicide precautions, we will have you eat in your room. After that, you can begin going to the cafeteria. Do you have any preference for lunch?"

"I have options?" I asked. "When I was in Vanderbilt, I just ate what they brought to me."

"We are not like the average hospital," he replied. "You can even order room service, just like in a hotel if you like. Folks pay quite a price for treatment here. It is understandable if they might expect a little more."

He walked over to the bedside table, opened the drawer, and pulled out a menu. It looked like a small version of a menu you might find in a five-star restaurant.

"The full menu won't work for lunch today," he said as he handed it to me, "because it is too close to serve time, and generally, we prefer residents to eat in the cafeteria rather than isolating in their rooms. However, if you will look over on the back, you can see a list of Tuesday options, and you can pick one of those for your lunch."

"Oh, is it Tuesday?" I asked while taking a seat in a chair by the window. "I guess I have completely lost track of the days." I opened the menu and glanced at a few things quickly, then flipped it over to see a list of about four different options under each day of the week in three columns, for breakfast, lunch, and dinner. Tuesday's lunch options included a Ruben sandwich, soup of the day and salad, a chicken salad sandwich, or a tuna melt.

"Can I have the tuna melt?" I asked.

"Coming right up," he said as he walked for the door.

He was not one of the attendants I had met on the previous day. He was a young man, perhaps in his twenties, average looking, but with a muscular build.

"Carl?" I called when he neared the door.

"Yes, sir," he replied as he turned around.

"How does all this work?" I asked. "How is this supposed to help me? I mean, I've never been in a place like this before. I don't know what is supposed to happen."

"Well, right after lunch, you will meet your personal therapist, who I believe is Mike Sawicki." His eyes rolled upward in thought. "Yeah, you are blue team, so that's Mike. He is the therapist for that team. You will have group sessions a couple of times through the day, maybe except for weekends. There may be some outings or different things you might be able to go do out in the community as you move up the tiers. Dr. Carter will likely consider the possibility of psychotropic medications with you. So you know—think of it like a vacation. You don't have anything else that you have to do for the next several weeks except focus on yourself and whatever you need to do to heal. I will be your attendant, and I'll be here most days. You can ask for me if you need anything. I may not be able to give you what you want, but I'll certainly try."

"This is a big place," I said, looking around the room, out the window, and back at him. "Are there that many rich crazy people in America?"

"Oh, we get residents from all over the world," he replied. "Sometimes we get dignitaries or government officials of various countries, sometimes famous people, sometimes just the run-of-the-mill millionaire."

"Oh, really?" I asked in surprise. "What government officials have you had in here?"

"I can't tell you that," he replied. "You do recall signing a statement as part of your admissions packet that you will maintain the confidentiality and privacy of other residents, right?"

"No, I was a bit of an asshole when I came in," I replied. "I just signed whatever they put in front of me and didn't read it."

"Pamela probably should have briefed you on that even if you didn't read it," he commented.

"She probably did," I responded. "I wasn't in the mood to listen much. I was angry at the time and just wanted to get it over with."

"Well, because of the fact that we get people of name and fame here," he went on, "we try to go beyond what other hospitals might when it comes to protecting the identity and privacy of our residents. The staff, of any facility, are automatically held accountable for confidentiality, but we also take the step of placing responsibility on our residents. You signed a legally binding document that essentially states you are liable and can be sued by the hospital, or any resident, whose identity you might reveal outside of here. That protects you and them."

"Thank you, Carl," I said. "It's good to know we have that protection."
"You're welcome, sir," he said. "What would you like to drink with your lunch?"

"Cola would be nice," I replied.

"I'll go get your lunch now, okay?"

"Yes, thank you, Carl," I replied.

Carl left and returned in a few minutes with a covered tray. He placed the tray on the corner of the bed and left, having given me only a smile and a nod. I brought the tray to my chair near the window and sat looking out across the range of mountains as I proceeded to eat. Northwest Arkansas and East Tennessee both had mountains, but those were nothing compared to the view out my window. The peaks were sharp and snow covered with lush evergreens climbing up the sides toward the summit.

Under the stainless-steel cover of the tray had been a tuna melt on focaccia bread with Swiss cheese melting over the sides onto the bread. There were thinly sliced French fries, a fresh fruit salad, and tiny plastic containers filled with condiments of ketchup, mayonnaise, and mustard. I ate slowly and wished I could have gotten a better view of the mountains because the view was slightly impeded by the metal screen over the window. When I finished eating, I covered the tray and set it back on the edge of the bed. Then I sat in the chair by the window again and gazed at the beautiful view. I wish I could say it comforted me, but instead, my mind was on all kinds of things except the view. I wondered if my ministry might end up destroyed by all this. I wondered if Alissa might end up leaving me anyway. I couldn't blame her if she did. She certainly had put up with more than her fair share and significantly more than most women would have tolerated. I wondered if I even wanted to continue my ministry. For so long, I had covered my hypocrisy, put on a smile, and pretended to be above reproach when I had been the very kind of person that I had spoken reproach about from the pulpit. I thought about Momma and Daddy. I thought about Teddy and Hannah and whether Daddy had abused them the way he abused me. Even though Daddy said he didn't, I had to wonder if something might have happened. Why else would Teddy have been so negative and disrespectful toward Daddy? Maybe, that was why Teddy seemed to hate Daddy. Maybe, that was why he didn't have any kind things to say about Daddy. Maybe, Teddy stood up and fought for himself when I simply submitted. The thought made me feel even less like a man. My strong big brother probably stood up to

Daddy, and I was just his pussy, not a real man. I had never been a real man. I would never know the truth about it. With Teddy in the grave, it was too late to ask him, and I suspected there was a chance he never would have told me anyway.

I was startled and let out a loud yelp when a knock came at the door a few minutes later. It had not been a big knock, just a little tap, but it scared me half out of my wits, and I leapt out of the chair to face the door. Soon after the knock, the door opened slightly, and I heard a somewhat gravelly male voice from the other side. "Pastor Dennison, may I come in?"

I got up and turned around toward the door. "You scared me," I said.

"I'm sorry, Pastor Dennison. May I come in?"

"Yes, come in!" I replied with some irritability.

The man slowly and gradually opened the door and stepped into the room. It seemed like it was going to take him forever just to step past the threshold. His looks were a shock to me. He was a slim man in his late thirties, perhaps. He had a full but scraggly, mousy brown beard that came almost down to his sternum, and the hair on his head was about as long. He had that pulled back in a ponytail behind his head. He had on loose-fitting bell-bottom jeans that were worn almost through at the knees. The jeans had ragged threads hanging from the bell-bottoms around his ankles, where his bare feet filled worn Roman-style rope sandals. He had on a T-shirt with a picture of the Beatles across the front, and his arms had several woven yarn and bead bracelets on them. As well, he had little braids here and there in his beard that were tipped by beads. "Hi there!" he said, smiling. "I'm Mike Sawicki. I'll be your guide on this journey. How are you doing, man?"

"You are my therapist?" I asked, again with irritability evident.

"Yes, sir! I am your case manager," he said with enthusiasm. "How are we doing today? How's your first day?"

"You can't be my therapist," I replied. "They need to get me a real doctor. Obviously, you are some kind of quack, or you sneaked in the back door or something. You can't be my therapist."

"Oh, but I am assigned to you," he replied, grinning.

"Look at you!" I criticized. "You look like a bum off the street. Why would a place like this hire someone who looks like you? You look like you are more likely to be sitting around under a tree smoking pot than getting a degree or becoming anything professional! I'm appalled! What are your credentials?"

"Oh, okay…hmm. I am an ACSW," he replied, "certified by the National Association of Social Workers."

"A social worker!" I snarled. "They are putting me with a social worker? I pay thousands of dollars to get into this place, and they stick me with a social worker! Let me speak to someone in authority. This won't do. I need a real therapist. I need a doctor!"

"Hmm…well," he said, "that sounds like you have yourself a problem there. I wonder what we can do about that. I could call up the executive director—no, you know the executive director is pretty busy. We could go talk to the director of psychiatric services. I wonder what Dr. Clark would have to say about that."

"Dr. Clark is the Director of Psychiatric Services?" I asked in amazement.

"Yeppers, sure is," he replied. "Well, you know, kind of medical director, but he carries a small caseload too. Oh, he's your doctor, isn't he? Yeah, of course he would be, since he is covering blue team with me. Yeah, he assigned me to blue team."

"You? He assigned you?" I snapped.

"Yeah, I think he kind of likes me," he replied. "How did you like Dr. Clark?"

"He's a very nice man," I responded.

"Mmmm hmmm…yeah." He went on stroking his chin through that scraggly beard. "Yeah, Dr. Clark said he thought he had a pretty good rapport with you, took kind of a special interest in you. See, here's the problem, and we can make this change if you want to. I mean, really, you are hiring us to do a job, right? You ought to be able to pick who your providers are. So we are here to take care of you and help you get better. We want to meet your needs and…I mean, after all it is our job, really, isn't it, to make you happy? But see, we kind of have some of our own rules around doing that. One of those rules would be if you scrap me, you scrap the whole team. Yeah, you would have to be assigned to one of the other two teams. You know, luck of the draw on psychiatrist, nurse, therapists, you know, and no take backs. You can switch one time and then you are stuck with what you get."

"Why didn't they assign me to a psychologist?" I demanded.

"Yeah, well, here's how that works. There is a social worker on each team who is the case manager and who does individual therapy and some group sessions with patients assigned to that team. The psychiatrists on each team meet with the patient about medications. There is actually only one psychologist, and she kind of floats between teams, you know. She does psych testing, some specialty groups, and stuff like that. She doesn't usually do much in the way of one-on-one, but you know, if the team maybe thinks you could have a cognitive problem or something, she would test you for that." He finished what he was saying, pointed to a chair on the opposite side of the bed from me, then asked, "Do you mind if I sit down?" He was already sitting down before I could say yes or no. He plopped down in the chair, crossed his legs, and looked at me. I remained standing.

"What kind of experience do you have?" I asked.

"Oh yeah, well, um, I moved here from Los Angeles. It was really cool to find this job. They pay pretty good here for social work, but anyway…I got my degrees from UCLA and worked in the UCLA Medical Center Psychiatric Hospital for seven years. I moved to Las Vegas and had a private practice in Vegas for a few years. Then my wife wanted to move back to LA. I went back to work for UCLA Med Center, then she found an ad for this job, and she thought, 'Yeah! we can move to Colorado, ski all we want in the winter, and hang out in the mountains in the summer.' I've been here about five years. It's cool."

"Are you a Christian?" I asked, glaring at him.

"Hmmm, that is an interesting and loaded question, isn't it?" he replied. "If I say yes, I am a Christian, then I am probably going to have to meet your qualifications for being a Christian whatever that might be, you know, because there are quite a few Christians who can't seem to agree on how things are supposed to be. You know, it might depend on whether you like Catholics or not, or maybe you might not like it if I told you I'm Mormon. Oh, wow, that would really stir things up, wouldn't it? 'Cause you know there are lots of Christians who don't really consider Mormons to be Christian. If I tell you I'm *not* a Christian, then I risk having you demand that no one but a Christian can help you. The question is whether you really want the help enough to trust that I can help you and that my religious preferences are not really relevant to that, or you want to focus on the idea that only a certain kind of Christian can help you, in which case you might be significantly limiting your options and using said Christianity as a diversion instead of trying to get better."

I was furious with him at that moment. He seemed snide and condescending to me, but I also realized he had a point. "What are your religious preferences?" I asked.

"I am a bit of an eclectic," he replied. "If your religion is important to you, I am willing to see if we can use that to help you get better. I certainly am not going to recommend that you change your beliefs. You have to decide whether those beliefs are messing you up and whether you need to make any changes in them."

"Aren't you a little old to be a hippie?" I continued to interrogate.

"Yeah, well, age is just a number, isn't it?" he grinned. "I mean, how old is Timothy Leary?"

"Have you ever dropped acid or done any of that stupid crap?" I pestered.

"Wow… hmm." He paused. "You know what I'm wondering? I am wondering how long you are going to keep up this distraction, you know, focusing on me and what I'm about rather than taking a look at your problems. I mean, aren't you here for you? Aren't you here to get to know yourself better, maybe make friends with yourself instead of being such a dick to yourself?"

"I'll thank you not to use foul language with me!" I exclaimed.

"Yeah, hmm," he said as he got up from his chair. "Maybe I might come back later. Sounds like you are not ready to get started yet. You might need a little more time to stare out the window and think." He started for the door. "I'll see you later, Pastor Dennison," he said as he reached for the handle.

He walked through the door and closed it gently behind him. I stood there for several minutes staring at the door thinking about what he had said, thinking about my behavior, wondering if I had offended him, wondering if I might somehow be in trouble, wondering if they had some means of punishing patients who don't cooperate, wondering if I could tear the screen off and jump out the window. I was furious and confused, but he had planted mental seeds.

I finally sat down where I had been, and stared out across the mountains to the blue sky beyond. I just sat there, numb, and dazed, vacillating between whether I wanted to live or die, thinking about what a mess I had made of my life. I had memories coming back to me, memories of Teddy and how much I had looked up to him, how much I loved him. I remembered Momma going to her knees that night when the state trooper told her that Teddy was dead. I remembered the first time I met Alissa, a scared and sick little girl that I laid hands on and prayed for. I thought about how strong she had become, what a rock-hard soul of a woman had come out of that scared little girl. I thought about how I had let her down over and over again and how she stood up to it all. I knew, if I had been in her shoes, there was no way I could have done it. There was no way I could have stayed with a man who constantly cheated on me. She deserved so much better than what she got with me. She deserved a man who would put her first in his life, who would cherish her as a wife should be cherished. Although I loved her with all my heart, I had never been, and doubted that I ever could be what she needed. Despite the ministry, my modicum of fame, my television show, the money, I felt like a failure. I felt like I had failed everyone. I prayed for God to help me. I bent over in the chair and sobbed. I fell to my knees on the floor, cried, and begged God to help me. Then, I realized that this was my one chance. This place, these people with their expertise, this was my one chance. I had sat there for almost two hours when I decided to press my buzzer and call a nurse. Just a few seconds after I pressed the little red button on the intercom by the bed, I heard a female voice come over the intercom and say, "May I help you?"

"Yes," I said. "Please tell Mr. Sa—I'm sorry, I don't remember his name—Mike, I think. His last name starts with an *S*. Please tell Mike, the social worker, that I'm ready to talk to him now, and please give him my apologies for being rude to him."

"Mr. Sawiki is in with another patient for the next hour," the voice said. "He is due to go home after that. I will tell him you asked for him, and he can come see you tomorrow."

My head dropped, and I sighed. "Yes, thank you," I said. "Please tell him I'd like to speak to him tomorrow."

"Yes, sir," the voice said.

Then I heard the intercom click, and I knew she had signed off. I went back to my chair and sat staring out that window. Unfortunately, it was a north-facing window, so I couldn't see the sun setting, but I watched as magenta and gold reflections played on some of the clouds over the mountains and the snow peaks.

Around 5:00 p.m., I went back to the intercom and told the staff that I did not want any dinner. I had a plastic pitcher of water in my room. An attendant had come around a little after 3:00 p.m. to give me fresh water and ice. So I had a glass of water, and I chewed on some ice for dinner. Otherwise, I sat in the chair and stared out the window. Then darkness slowly engulfed the land.

I sat in the darkness of my room, with the exception of the glow of a few lights that I assumed flanked the sidewalks or parking lot outside. In a couple of hours, I lay down on the bed with no change of clothes or preparation. I drifted in and out of sleep for the remainder of the night. Several times, a staff member stuck his or her head in the door to check on me. It was generally just a brief and quiet acknowledgement. Then they quietly closed the door, but every time it was enough to wake me from whatever light sleep that I might have been able to accomplish. I awoke the next morning before daylight with a click of the intercom.

"Mr. Dennison. Good morning. Are you awake?"

"I am now," I replied as I rolled from my side over onto my back.

"This is Rhonda at the nurse's station. Have you had a chance to look at the menu and decide what you might want for breakfast?"

"Give me a second," I groaned, half asleep. I rolled over, turned on the wall lamp, and pulled the menu from the drawer. I glanced at it quickly then said. "I'll have number two."

"All right then," she responded. "I will let the kitchen know." Not long after that, a nurse came in to take my vital signs.

They were all very friendly, but I didn't have much to say. "When do you think I might be able to see Mike, the social worker?" I asked the nurse.

"Oh, I'm sure he will be around to see you sometime this morning," she replied. "He usually makes the rounds to say hello to all his patients as soon as he comes in. That's generally around eight a.m. He should be by within twenty or thirty minutes after that, unless he checks on you first."

When breakfast came, I nibbled on scrambled eggs with cheese and toast, sipped on coffee and orange juice, but otherwise didn't pay much attention to it. Then I took a shower and got dressed in jeans and an Oxford shirt. Carl had come in with a razor to sit with me while I shaved, but I told him I was going to skip shaving for a while and see how that felt. Part of my reason was the freedom to not have to look the part of a preacher and part of it was because I would rather not shave at all than have someone sit there and watch me to make sure I didn't cut myself. It was about thirty minutes after I dressed that I heard a light tapping at the door.

"Come in," I called.

"Oh, hey." I heard Mike's gravelly voice as he stepped into the room. "Hey, how are you doing this morning? I heard you changed your mind about the switcharoo."

I got up from my chair at the window, crossed around the bed, and offered him my hand. "Mike, I am sorry about my behavior yesterday," I offered. "I was out of line and inappropriate. Please accept my apology."

He shook my hand vigorously. "Hey, no problem, man. It happens. This is a tough thing coming in here and facing all this stuff. You know? I under-stand. Lots of newbies get a little pissy."

"Where do we go from here?" I asked.

"Well, I've got some time for you this morning," he replied. "Looks like you are ready to go, so why don't we meander down the hall to my office, and we will get started on your psychosocial."

"Psychosocial?" I asked as I followed him toward the door.

"Yeah, it's an assessment, kind of a life history thing." He opened the door and allowed me to step into the hall first. "Should take about an hour and a half if you are up to it."

I followed Mike down the hall to a door that led to a hall behind the nurse's station. From there we went to the very back, where he opened a door on the left. The first thing I was struck by when I walked into the office was the view. There was no screen over his large windows, and the mountains looked even bigger from that angle of the building. He also had windows on two walls as it was a corner office. He had a large mahogany desk nestled between the two windows, and in front of that were a couple of large family-style chairs. I could see that one of them was a recliner. The walls opposite the windows had colorful abstract art. One of them appeared to be an angel with light emanating from her heart, from her forehead, and above her head. There were lines of rainbow colors flowing around her and flowing from the points of light around her heart and head. Below that was a shelf which was covered across the top with large, very interesting stones. I could see that a couple of them were crystals of some sort. The shelves below had collections of books and odd little statues. I was happy to see that one of those statues appeared to be a bronze replica of a painting I had once seen of Jesus with arms outstretched to children.

"Please have a seat," Mike said as he motioned to the recliner chair.

He then passed around the desk to retrieve a clipboard with a yellow legal pad and a pen. I sat in the chair as instructed. He came back around and sat in the chair opposite the recliner. He crossed his legs with the clipboard on his lap and said, "So how are you doing today?"

"My Lord, you ask me that a lot," I snapped half-jokingly. "Aren't you tired of that same old question?"

He was wearing almost the same thing he had worn before, except this time his T-shirt had a multicolored peace sign on it. I looked down at his feet in those sandals and could tell his toenails were at least a couple of weeks past due for cutting. It was going to be a challenge for me to let go and allow this man an opportunity, but I determined that I was going to do it.

"Yeah, mmm, hmmm, and the answer to that question would be?" He smiled.

"I'm fine," I replied.

"Okay, good," he said tapping his pen against the edge of the clipboard. "Here's how this works. I'm going to ask you about every personal question you have ever dreamed of being asked. Some of those questions are extremely personal, and you may find that this can stir you up emotionally, so you may not walk out of here today feeling as fit emotionally as when you walked in. You don't have to answer the questions, but your answers are going to give me a broad overview of your life, allow me to draw conclusions, and make recommendations. Your answers to these questions certainly are maintained as confidential to Manitau Chateau and will not be released from here except by your specific written consent. Your answers to the questions are not confidential specifically to me. We will be discussing your case among members of the treatment team, and other staff from other teams may be invited to consult or may cover your care if one of the members of our team should be out sick or something. I know this is embarrassing, and I know this is difficult, but what I need most from you is absolute honesty. This is an opportunity for you to get real and get whatever secrets you have out in the open. I am not here to judge you or condemn you for anything you have been through or anything you have done, nor is any other member of this staff here to judge you. If any member of our staff were to be judgmental or treat you with disrespect, I assure you the issue would be addressed, and if it were found to be a legitimate infraction, that staff member would not long be retained in our employment. Do you have any questions about that?"

I looked at him in disbelief. It is one thing for a stranger to see you naked in the flesh but entirely another for them to see your soul naked, stripped down to the raw core of your hidden self. On the other hand, this was a stranger I was talking to. It was not like I was going to bear my soul to Momma or Hannah or one of the parishioners of Evangelic Temple. There was a certain freedom in knowing that I could tell him my secrets, leave those secrets here, and maybe never have to see him again.

"I understand," I said quietly. "Let's do whatever we need to do."

Mike then began his questioning, about my birth, about my relationship with Momma and Daddy and Teddy, about how I grew up, and about the kinds of influences around me. Then he asked me a question I did not want to answer.

"Up until your late teens," he began, "was there ever a time that anyone who was older than you, male or female, child or adult, stranger, friend, or family member who ever teased you sexually, shamed you sexually, came onto you, touched you sexually, or exposed you to pornography?"

I sat there looking directly at him and noticed that my fingers had begun to dig into the arm of the chair. I knew this was a make-or-break moment. I knew that I had to say it, but my heart did not want to say it, and there was a fear that saying it even to this stranger would overwhelm me. There was a part of me that felt like this was a betrayal of Daddy, of the family. There was a part of me that didn't trust that I wouldn't be judged, a part of me that said admitting it would mean admitting that I'm not a real man. Men aren't supposed to have this happen to them. Men are supposed to be strong enough to stand up to that, maybe like Teddy did. There was a part of me that wanted to run from the room. I noticed that I was trembling more and that tears were drifting down my cheeks.

"What do you know?" I asked. "What do you already know about me, before this, before we have talked?"

Mike took a deep breath and sat forward in his chair. "I know that you are a very troubled man," he said softly. "I know that you tried to kill yourself, and I know that was after you screwed some young lady in your office. I know that your wife walked in on that, or walked in after the fact. I know this wasn't the first time you seduced a woman or cheated on your wife. She gave us some info about that and some other things when you were admitted."

"You have talked to Alissa?" I asked, still trembling, my voice breaking with tears.

"Yes," he replied. "We had a phone conversation right after you arrived. She told me about what I just told you."

"Did she tell you anything about this?" I asked. "This question you just asked me?"

"She told me she found a letter your father had written to you and that she thought it might mean that you had been sexually abused," he replied softly.

I looked away from him, stared out the window, held my trembling fingers to my lips.

"Is she correct?" he asked. "Have you been sexually abused?"

"Yes," I said, almost inaudibly, and tried turning farther away from him.

He sat there quietly, patiently, saying nothing. More than ever, I wanted to run. I wanted to get away, to hide, to check out, and just leave, maybe go to Mexico or something, and just disappear into the countryside. I didn't want anyone to see me anymore. I didn't want to be the famous preacher, the focus of a congregation. I just wanted to hide.

"Can you tell me about it?" he said quietly.

I found myself wanting to bite my fingers. I didn't know if I was sad, hurt, guilty, ashamed, or angry. Maybe I felt all of that.

"My daddy," I said quietly, with my wadded fist now to my mouth.

Mike said nothing. He just sat there waiting, letting me stew in the silence. Finally, I turned back to him, slammed my fist into the arm of the chair and shouted, "My daddy!" I got up and paced in front of the desk. "MY DADDY! MY DADDY! MY DADDY!" I screamed.

"Shush, shush, shush," Mike softly hushed. "It's okay, buddy. It's okay. There's a lot in there, a lot of feelings. We don't have to release them all right now. We'll get to it. Can you come back over and take a seat for me?"

I stood there trembling with rage. I felt like a caged animal. I thought about picking up one of those big rocks from his shelf and hurling it through the window.

"Ronald," Mike said softly. "I'd like for you to take a deep breath for me if you could please. Can you take a deep, slow breath?"

I remembered this from the meeting with Dr. Clark and began trying to pull air into my lungs.

"I want you to breathe like you can draw that air all the way down to your toes. Okay, buddy?"

Mike's gravelly voice had become soft and comforting, almost hypnotic. I did as he instructed, and when he could see that I was beginning to get back to myself, he asked, "Can you come back and sit down now?"

I did as I was instructed.

After I sat down, I held a couple of breaths and blew them out quickly. "I'm sorry," I said.

"You haven't done anything wrong," Mike quickly responded. "There is nothing to be sorry for. I just need to know that you are going to be able to control yourself and that we're all safe, okay? I'm not asking you to control your emotions. Those emotions need to come out, but I need you to control your actions. Do you think you can do that?"

This was all so incredibly strange to me. How was I supposed to control my actions but not control my emotions?

"I don't understand," I said.

"Well, we may not get to it all today, and I don't want you to feel overwhelmed," Mike explained. "But you have got a lot to talk about. I can tell that you do, and you have been overwhelmed by these emotions. You have put a lot of effort in, for a lot of years, to keep all this choked down, and it needs to come out. It does, but not all at once, and you need to be able to trust yourself that you are in control, that you can manage yourself even as you let these emotions come out. When we can get you to the point where you understand that emotions do not require actions, and you can let yourself feel what you need to feel and talk about what you need to talk about without losing control, then we will lance that boil on your soul, but right now, I'm just going to document that you have been sexually abused, and then we will finish up the assessment. Okay? We have got a lot of time to get to this. We don't have to do it all right now. Okay? You're going to get a chance to talk to me almost every day, and I'm going to help you fight this battle that you have been fighting all by yourself all your life. You don't have to fight it all alone anymore."

I burst into tears when he said that, like I cried when I was grieving for Teddy. I had fought the battle by myself for my whole life. I had tried to keep it all choked down, and it did feel like a boil on my soul. The mere fact that someone understood made me cry tears of gratitude.

Mike let me cry.

After a moment, he asked, "You okay, buddy?"

I looked up, and he pointed to a box of tissues setting on a table beside my chair. I grabbed several and began wiping my face. When I looked up again, he said, "Thank you." The tears started again, but not as heavily as before.

"Why are you thanking me?" I cried while I wiped my face with the tissue.

"Because you are sharing your soul with me, man," he replied. "Do you have any idea what an honor that is when another human being shares their soul with you? We don't do it very often. Sometimes, it is just a little glimmer, but now and then someone opens up and lets you see through the window of their soul right down into the core of their spirit. Thank you for that."

"I don't want to do this," I said. "It's too painful."

"Unfortunately, it has to hurt for it to heal," he comforted. "It will hurt a different kind of way than it has hurt all those years before. There is a difference between a therapeutic hurt and a pathological hurt. We'll get through this. You are going to be okay."

Mike gave me a few minutes and then finished the assessment. When he finished, he said, "So I need to know something here. Are you going to kill yourself?"

I took a minute before I said, "No."

"Not quite sure about that answer?" he asked.

"No, I'm sure," I said.

"So I can count on you to be safe? You are not going to do anything to hurt yourself. You don't want to do that anymore?" he went on.

"No, I don't want to do that anymore," I affirmed again.

"So, if you were to have thoughts about killing yourself, what would you do?" he asked.

I thought for a moment. What would I do? Then I said, "I would find somebody on staff and tell them about it."

"Good answer," he encouraged. "How would you like to come off suicide precautions?"

"I don't know exactly what that means," I commented.

"Well, it means you can have a safety razor for one thing, not one of those old-fashioned ones where you can take the blade out, but one of those newfangled plastic things, and you won't have to have Carl sitting there with you when you shave. You can move to a room where the door is not going to be locked all the time. You can come out into the lounge, visit with other residents, and go to recreation and such."

"That sounds really good," I replied. "And I don't want to kill myself anymore, at least I don't think I do. I'll tell someone if I start having crappy thoughts or thoughts I don't think I can handle."

"Good deal," he said. "I still have to run it by the team. We will still need to do a suicide safety plan for you, and then Dr. Clark gets final approval, but right now, let me show you around our lovely facility. Would you like a tour?"

"Yes, please." I smiled.

For the first time in a very long time, I felt hope.

CHAPTER 26

The next day I was moved into a slightly larger room that also had a very nice view but still had the metal screen over the window. The primary difference was that the basic amenities of a television, radio, and phone were available. I wasted no time in calling Alissa. Nashville was an hour ahead on time, so when I got settled into the room about 9:00 a.m. Mountain time, it was around 10:00 a.m. Central time. This meant that unless she had taken the kids to stay with Clara or one of our babysitters so she could go out or have some time to herself, she would be dealing with the usual morning activities. For the most part, at that time of day, that meant keeping an eye on the children while they played. Of course, it was also possible she might have taken the kids to a park or something. The phone rang almost ten times before she answered it.

"Hello?"

"Hi, sweetheart," I said. "I was about to hang up. I thought maybe you had gone out or something."

"No, just sitting here watching the kids," she replied. "How are you?"

"I'm doing okay," I answered. "They moved me off suicide precautions today and gave me a room with a TV and a phone. I met my social worker yesterday. At first, I was a little taken aback. He is a scruffy-looking hippie." I laughed.

"How do you like him?" she asked.

"After I got off my high horse and decided to get with the program, I like him just fine," I replied. "Of course, it is too soon to say I'm making much progress, but he is earning my trust."

"That's good, dear," she commented.

I paused for a moment. "When do you think you might come visit, bring the kids for a visit?" I asked.

"I'm not sure that we will be visiting while you are there," she said. "It is an awful long distance."

"You could fly into Denver and get a rental car down here," I pleaded. "I would really love to see you and the kids."

"I just don't know about putting the kids on a plane as small as they are," she continued. "We are not likely to come see you."

My heart sank. I felt as though I was going to cry, and my eyes moistened.

"Okay," I said.

Then I wondered if this meant that she was divorcing me. She had me conveniently out of the way so she could consult with attorneys about getting out of the marriage. Who could blame her?

"How are the kids?" I said, after a moment of silence.

I knew she could hear the sadness in my voice. I couldn't blame her for taking them from me either. I had so often been away, but I always longed for and anticipated seeing my children when I got home. Maybe she worried that I might be a pedophile like my daddy. Maybe she wondered if it had been done to me, would I do it to my kids as well? That could not have been further from the truth. If anything, it had made me more cautious, but she wouldn't have known that.

"The kids are fine," she replied. "Adam has made a new friend at Children's Bible Study. His friend's mother works. So I have started allowing the other boy to stay here through the day so she won't have to pay for sitters or day care."

"You have always been so thoughtful," I commented.

"Well, she is a single mother," she continued, "and it's good for Adam to have a boy his own age to play with. It all works out."

"Was she an unwed mother?" I asked, half wondering if I might have fathered the child.

The truth was I never knew how many children I might have fathered in various cities across the country. I only began using protection after getting that case of gonorrhea. Although, I generally did not do much close to home and waited until I was out on the road for my escapades, there had obviously been times I was indiscrete at home as well.

"No," she answered. "The boy's father died in a car wreck a year ago."

"Oh my goodness! The child must be devastated," I exclaimed without even thinking about how young he must have been.

"Well, he is only three, about the same age as Adam," she continued. "It is not likely he will ever remember his father much."

"A tragedy and a loss for the whole family," I commented, wondering if, in the long run, my own son would have remembered me if I had been successful in killing myself. Perhaps it would have been better for him not to remember.

"Yes, dear," she said complacently. "Get well, okay?"

"Okay," I replied.

"I have to go now," she said. "I have small children to take care of."

"Okay," I said again. "I miss you."

"Bye now," she said with no response of missing me too.

It felt very cold and distant, disconnected. I felt myself hesitating but finally I said, "Bye."

I heard the click as she hung up the phone and stood there for a moment with the receiver in my hand before hanging up.

They had given me the morning to get settled into the room, and on that day, I had lunch in the patient cafeteria. There were indeed a couple of celebrities there that I recognized. However, most of the people there did not have faces you would see on a billboard or television. Most of them looked like average people from anywhere. The staff guided me to the line where I could pick up my tray and decide what I wanted to eat. This was not a cafeteria that one might find in the average hospital. It was more like a high-end cafeteria with attendants at each station from salads and entrée through to desert. As I was going through the line, a man who appeared to be maybe in his sixties was in front of me. He was bald with gray hair encircling his head like a horseshoe, and it flowed in strings down about a third of the way over his ears. His face was round, and he had on a pair of round wire-rimmed glasses. He was maybe six inches shorter than myself. He was wearing blue plaid pajamas and what appeared to be a pair of women's house shoes. When he turned around to look at me, I realized his nose was almost as round as his head.

"Oh, hey!" he exclaimed in a friendly salesman like tone. "You are new here."

He extended a thick, somewhat tanned hand to me for a handshake. I shook his hand and smiled.

"David Mathis is the name," he continued exuberantly. "And you would be?"

Suddenly, I felt embarrassed. I felt my face go warm and flush. It had not occurred to me that even with confidentiality and extra precautions taken by the hospital, I would not want someone to know my name. What if he realized I was a televangelist? What if someone were to recognize me? I had recognized a couple of celebrities in the crowd and thought nothing of it, but I felt instantly embarrassed at the question of my name. Unlike regular celebrities, I had a powerful reputation to uphold. A minister of the Lord is to be beyond reproach or at least appear so. I wasn't so much worried that my confidentiality might be broken at that point, but whether other residents would disrespect me for having fallen from my evangelistic pedestal into what I perceived to be the mire of psychiatric treatment.

"Well?" He grinned with his tray sitting on the rail.

The patient in front of him had moved a good six feet ahead, but he stood there in place, not moving, waiting for me to answer. I realized there were people gathering in line behind me.

"Ronnie," I said finally.

"That's nice, Ronnie," he chided. "Ronnie who?"

I felt my stomach getting queasy, and for a moment I thought I might faint. I mustered my courage. I could lie to him about my name, but wouldn't he find out anyway if we ended up having group together or something?

"Dennison," my voice quivered.

"Dennison—Ronnie Dennison," he pondered as he finally began to move on down the line. "Do I know that name? Hmm…sounds somewhat familiar. You know some of the people in here are pretty famous, some a little less famous than others, some just rich enough to afford this place."

"Is that so?" I asked and then turned to the cafeteria lady to ask for Caesar salad.

"Yeah…I'm not…famous, just rich enough to afford this place," he continued. "Your name sounds kind of familiar though. Where do I know that from?"

I deliberately did not answer and requested grilled salmon for my entrée.

"So, what do you do?" he pried.

"Let's talk about you," I replied. "What do you do?"

"Ever hear of Mathis Bedding Company?" he asked.

"I haven't paid much attention to bedding," I replied.

"Well, I own that company," he continued. "We manufacture sheets, pillowcases, comforters, and such. We have product in most major retail stores, but we are not as big-time as some of those guys."

"That's very interesting," I lied and then pulled a roll from beneath the glass canopy as we neared the end of the line.

David selected a roll as well and a piece of lemon icebox pie. I passed on the pie, having learned some time back that it is far too easy to put on weight when one does not pay attention during travels.

"Come on, sit with me," he encouraged as he picked up his tray and nodded toward a table by the window.

I followed him to the table where we could see a beautifully manicured lawn and a grove of trees in the distance.

"So, Ronnie Dennison?" he pondered putting his try on the table. "Dennison, Dennison—where have I heard that name?"

"Maybe it just sounds familiar," I said and took my seat.

"No…no, I know that name," he persisted. "Ronnie…short for Ronald…Ronald Dennison—Oh, bejeebers! You're that television preacher!"

My hand trembled as I opened my cloth napkin to retrieve the silverware inside and accidentally dropped the fork on the table. It clanged against the tabletop, but I said nothing. I simply picked it up, placed it on the plate, and looked out the window into the distant tree grove. Finally, I looked back at him nervously.

"You *are* him," he continued.

Again, I said nothing and began fumbling with my silverware.

"Hey, aren't you supposed to be guiding the flock instead of going to the nut house?" He grinned like the Cheshire Cat.

At that moment, I wanted to punch the man, but I was feeling too nervous to accomplish that, even if I had been inclined to follow through with the impulse. He must have noticed my hand trembling because he looked down at me fumbling with my napkin and said, "Hey, it's okay. We're all nuts here. Nobody has anything on you that you don't have on them—relax."

I still did not say anything and began trying to sink my trembling fork into the salad.

"I'm in here because I tried to kill myself," he blurted.

I looked up at him a moment, held a piece of romaine lettuce on the tip of my fork, and asked, "Why did you do that?"

"Because I wanted to die," he said flatly. "My wife died about two months ago, and I had no idea how much she meant to me until then. I spent my whole life working on that damn business most of the time, ignoring her, ignoring my kids."

He picked up his knife and began slicing the pork chop he had selected. "I'm sixty-eight damn years old. Oh! Pardon me for saying *damn* in front of a preacher. I mean, please excuse my French. Anyway, I'm sixty-eight, and the woman I loved the most, and ignored the most, was suddenly gone. The kids have all moved on, and I didn't pay enough attention to them when I had the chance. So they have their own lives to live, you know? The funeral is over, they go home. I'm in that huge house all by myself. I never felt more alone in my life. I just felt like there was nothing else."

"I'm sorry for your loss," I commented quietly.

"You know that doesn't help, right?" He looked up at me. "I'm sorry for your loss—everybody says it. Some of them really mean it, but it doesn't help. Sympathy? Sympathy doesn't fix anything. Something terrible happens to you and a little pity is supposed to fix it. Nothing fixes it."

"I'm sorry, I didn't mean to be trite," I said.

"I got up one morning to go to work," he continued. "Yeah, I was still working at sixty-eight. If she hadn't died, I would probably have worked till I fell over and died and still would never have realized how much I had ignored her, my kids, any possible life I could have had besides work. I guess my business was more important to me than my family. At least I acted like it was. Anyway, I got up to go to work. She would always stay in bed at first, you know. I would get up, get a shower, come back, and give her a kiss to wake her up. Then she would get up and fix my breakfast. In forty-six years of marriage, I can scarcely remember a day she didn't get up and fix my breakfast. She had to be really bad sick if she didn't get up and see me off to work." His eyes watered with tears.

"That morning she wouldn't wake up. She wouldn't move. I shook her and nothing. When the ambulance got there, they said she had had a heart attack in her sleep. She died lying right there beside me. She died sometime in the night, and I never even knew it till I came back to give her a kiss to wake up. At least I'm grateful she died in her sleep—peacefully, I hope."

"That must have been really painful and scary," I commented.

"We were married for forty-six years." He sighed. He took a bite of his pork chop, stared out the window at the perfectly manicured lawn, and chewed. Then he turned back to look at me. "We take things for granted you know? We have something wonderful and beautiful that we ought to be grateful for every day, and we just piss away our lives and our time, really not even noticing that the most beautiful rose of all is right there under our nose, and all we have to do is breathe in the fragrance, but we don't. We're men. We are too busy doing what we think men are supposed to do to notice that we have everything we need and more already."

My mind went immediately to Alissa and the kids. I had ignored them. I had pissed away the time. I had focused most of my time on my ministry but almost as much on how I was going to achieve my next fuck when I had a beautiful, loving wife and two beautiful children who needed my attention. I could have, and should have been paying attention to them, instead of chasing tits and ass. I had ignored my family, not only for what I had perceived to be my calling, but for carnal pleasure.

"I think I know the feeling," I said. "I've ignored my wife and my kids too."

"You know, I would sometimes work for eighty hours a week," he said. "I didn't really know, until she died, how much I had been trying to avoid having any feelings at all. Then they all came crashing down on me."

He picked up his roll without putting down his fork and took a bite out of the back side of it. I realized the sprig of romaine was still on the end of my fork, and I hadn't yet taken a bite. I finally shoved it in my mouth and chewed.

"I was gone on tours for weeks at a time," I said. "I would call every night, but it's not the same. I told myself I was doing God's work that the Lord needed me to speak His word, but my family suffered because of it."

"So why are you here?" he asked, staring me straight in the eye. "It is not just because you ignored your family to go out on the road and preach."

The question stopped me dead in my tracks. I found myself still wanting to keep the secret even though I knew it had to come out. I looked back at him as though silently pleading, *Please don't make me tell.* After a moment of bearing his unwavering glare, I said, "I tried to kill myself, too."

"Why?" he asked flatly.

My hand was trembling again. I dropped my fork onto the plate. He glanced down at my hand then brought his attention back to my eyes. I avoided his glare, looked around to a nearby table, and commented, "Look, that dessert looks good. I wish I had picked that."

He never stopped staring at me, never moved his gaze as he watched me squirm like a bug under a magnifying glass with the sun focused on it.

"You've got a secret," he said.

The breath went out of me in a sigh so big one might have thought a straight-line wind had come through. I trembled even more. I tried to smile. I worked on laughing, but what came out was anything but real laughter. If God had chosen to take me in that moment, I would have been grateful. A heart attack would have been easier.

"Yes," I said at last.

He smiled. "It's okay, preacher. Nobody's perfect."

My mind went immediately to Matthew 5:48, "Be perfect, therefore, even as your Heavenly Father is perfect." I found myself muttering the words under my breath.

"What's that?" he asked.

"It's a Bible verse," I replied. "Be perfect as your Heavenly Father is perfect."

"Yeah, I've heard that before," he commented. "That's a pretty tall order, isn't it?"

"I certainly have never been able to accomplish it," I replied, "and the harder I tried, the more imperfect my behavior seemed to get."

"Is that your secret?" he asked.

I reached over to pick up my tea and take a sip. "Yes," I said. "That's my secret."

"No, I think there is a little more to it than that," he pried.

I set the tea back down inside the cafeteria tray. "Okay!" I snapped. I was totally fed up with feeling pressed and pestered. I decided to let him have it, let him have all of it, and see if he could handle it. I leaned in and growled at him, "You want to know my secret? Here is my secret. I live a double life. I present myself as a man of God, above reproach. I preach to people about keeping the Word of God, about being perfect when I am anything but. I cheat on my wife over and over again. Even when I am not out there fucking somebody else, I'm looking for the opportunity. I watch women like a cat stalking a bird. No woman can walk by me without me checking out her ass, her tits, her lips. I have a sickness for lips, for lipstick. If a woman has full red lips smeared with lipstick, I get off ten times harder when I fuck her than if she doesn't. I even keep tubes of lipstick in my desk at the office, and sometimes I lock the door, smear lipstick on my dick, and jack off while I fantasize about fucking some woman wearing dark red lipstick, or I fantasize that the red lipstick around my dick is her mouth going down on it. I tried to kill myself when my wife walked in right after I seduced and fucked a pregnant woman from church in my office. There you have it. That's my secret! Are you happy now?"

"Ah, Evangel lipstick," he quipped and giggled. "That would be a great title for a book!"

I glared at him with the intensity of a spotlight, stood up, threw my napkin on the table, walked straight out of the cafeteria, and back to my room. I walked directly past the nurse's station and slammed the door like a temperamental teenager. Then I paced my room like a caged animal for about twenty minutes before I heard a knock at the door. "WHAT!" I yelled.

Mike stuck his head in the door. "Hey, man, can I come in?" he said gently.

"You're already halfway in, and I can't stop you!" I snarled back. He pulled himself carefully through the door.

"Hey, heard you had a little upset down in the cafeteria there."

"I want out of here!" I insisted. "I've got enough money. I'll clean out one of my accounts and go down to Mexico, find some little village where I don't have to pretend to be something I'm not, and just live in fucking peace for once. Maybe, I'll sell mangos off the back of a cart or something. Maybe, I'll fuck all the Mexican women who will have me!"

"Hmmm…yeah," he commented. "Problem is, no matter where you go, there you are, man. No matter where you go, you take your brain and all the shit that's in it. You take your guilt, your shame; it all goes with you. Ah…so what shook you off your peace down there in the cafeteria?"

"That asshole made fun of me, the preacher who fucks around, called me evangel lipstick."

"Yeah, some people don't think about what they're saying, you know," he defended. "Problem is, maybe they don't know the difference between your wounds and your funny bone, whether you are going to take it as a joke or get your heart twisted over it. David said he was just cutting up, didn't know it would upset you so much. Are you sure you weren't upset, really, before he even said it?"

I sat down, leaned over with my elbows on my knees, and buried my face in my hands. "Mike, how do I stop this? How do I stop this obsession?" I asked.

He pulled another chair across from mine and sat facing me only a couple of feet away. "Did it ever occur to you that you are fighting the wrong demons?" he asked.

"What are you talking about?" I lifted my face up to look at him.

"Well, here you are trying to control these urges, you know, trying to make yourself be a good boy. Maybe you even think you can try to be a better man than your father was."

"I've NEVER touched a child in lust!" I demanded.

"Yeah…mmm hmmm. That's right. Then, you already are a better man than your father was. You never touched a child in lust, not like your father did to you. Hey, that's good, man. That's really good. You have made sure you didn't put another child through what you have been through."

He leaned over toward me. "But lust is still your problem, isn't it? It's an evil bastard. It makes you do things you think you can't control. Then it tells you what an awful piece of shit you are for doing it. Yeah, that sucks, man."

"If I could have controlled it, I would have," I defended.

"Yeah, poor guy. You get super horny, and that shit has got to come out, right? You gotta cum, right? That can be pretty powerful. Hey, I'm a man. I know what it's like to get super horny." He sat back in his chair. "Yeah, but see, here's the deal, man. You were in control the whole time. You planned that shit. You selected those women. You looked for them in the crowd and watched for the opportunity to nail one. You made arrangements to meet them. You took precautions, sometimes not very good precautions, but you took precautions not to get caught and not to get a disease or maybe get a lady pregnant. Man, that would be embarrassing, wouldn't it? Get some woman pregnant, maybe be having to contend with paternity suits, that sort of thing. Man, there could be a huge public scandal over that one. So…but you get caught, and you want to say the devil made you do it? The court system wouldn't give a shit about why you fucked that woman. All they would be interested in is what kind of child support you are going to pay her. It sure is convenient to have the devil to blame, isn't it?"

"Who else is to blame?" I asked.

He looked at me flatly. "You tell me."

I sat there knowing the answer he wanted but not wanting to say it. I got up, walked to the window with my back to him, and stared out the window.

After a long pause, he said, "So tell me. Have you fucked enough women to prove you're a man yet, or do you still need to fuck a few more just to make sure?"

I turned immediately back around and glared at him. "WHAT?"

"So," he went on. "Have you fucked enough women to prove you're a man yet?"

"I wasn't trying to prove I'm a man," I replied. "I know I'm a man."

"Are you sure about that?" he asked.

"What are you saying?" I demanded.

"Your father molested you, right?" he asked. "What exactly did he do to you? Made you wear a woman's wig, put on lipstick. He made you look like a pussy so he could pretend you were a pussy. Did you get tired of being a pussy, man?"

"I DON'T want to talk about that!" I insisted and began to pace again.

"Okay…well, when you get ready to talk about it, let me know." He got up from his chair and walked toward the door.

"Where are you going?" I asked.

"You seem to be calm enough," he returned. "You're okay for now, and you don't want to talk about it. So I'm going to go back to my office. I have an appointment with another patient in about five minutes. You have another appointment with me tomorrow. In the meantime, I'd like for you to ponder the answer to my question."

"Okay," I groaned. "Fine."

Mike continued out the door, and I continued to pace, though at a slightly slower rate. Before he walked out the door, he said, "We have a group in room C every day at 3:00 p.m. Maybe you might want to start coming to group. I think it might be good for you."

"It's hard enough just talking to you," I replied.

"Yeah," he commented. "It takes some guts to come here. Some people can't handle it. Some leave. Some have to take a couple of shots at it before they get real, but you know what? It's not me or the other patients here you need to get real with. It's yourself, man."

"I'll think about it," I said and turned back to the window.

I was angry and dismissive to him. I had no intention of thinking about anything, but questions have a tendency to get stuck in your head. He opened the door and stood there for a moment half in and half out of the room.

"A wise man once said, 'We are as sick as our secrets,'" he said before he stepped through the door and closed it behind him.

Most of what I did after he left was pace the floor. I sat down, flipped on the television, and tried to get some comfort from afternoon game shows, but there was no comfort. I didn't really think about what he asked me to think about. I just numbed my mind with whatever I could find to numb it. I didn't go to group that afternoon. In fact, I didn't show up for my appointment with Mike the next day. I hid out in my room, brought food back from the cafeteria or called room service, and talked to as few people as I possibly could. I went through the rest of the week and over the weekend eating in isolation. I piled my tray as full as I could and immediately returned to my room sometimes brining back four or five desserts. I would fill myself with so much sugar it became sedating, and it seemed like the only other thing I wanted to do besides eat was sleep. If I couldn't hide any other way, I could be unconscious.

They left me alone and let me isolate. Mike didn't even comment or come by when I missed my appointment with him. The nurses would occasionally check in on me. Otherwise, it was just me, food, the television, and sleep. After about a week of this, I heard a knock on the door.

"GO AWAY!" I demanded.

I was lying on the bed with a half-eaten sandwich coming apart on top of the cover just a foot or two away. What was left of the ham, spread with mayonnaise, had fallen out of the bread and was smearing itself into the fibers of the coverlet. I didn't care. I had not shaved nor taken a bath in at least three days. I didn't want to see anybody. I didn't want to do anything. I only wanted to lay there and stare at the wall if nothing else.

"Hey, man." I heard Mike's voice from the other side of the door. "Can I come in?"

"LEAVE ME ALONE!" I shouted back.

The door cracked open slightly and he said, "Well…ah…see, there is a problem with that. You know. We got a problem when we have a patient who comes in and thinks of this as the gluttony Hilton where they can hold up in a box and eat all day."

"THE ROOM IS PAID FOR!" I shouted. "IT IS THE HIGHEST PRICED FUCKING HOTEL I'VE EVER STAYED IN! SO…LEAVE… ME…ALONE!"

"Well…hmmmm," he mumbled. "Yeah, that would be great, except we are not a hotel. We are a treatment center and laying up in your room eating half the grocery list is not getting treatment. We need for you to get treatment, buddy." He stepped the rest of the way into the room.

"GET OUT!" I shouted. I grabbed what was left of the half-eaten sandwich on my coverlet and threw it at him. It fell miserably short of the target. Mike briefly glanced down at the decaying food on the floor then back at me.

"Well, I could do that," he said. "Go away and let you rot in your self-imposed prison, or you could get up, get dressed, and come on down to group. We will be starting in about five minutes."

"I'm not going anywhere!" I commanded and buried my head deeper into the pillow.

"Okay…yeah…I kind of thought you might say that. So…I brought group to you."

"YOU WHAT?" I shouted.

He turned back to the outside, stuck his head through the door, and asked, "You guys ready?"

"GET OUT!" I screamed.

"Okay, come on in, guys," he said to the hallway, and people started walking into my room, some carrying fold-up chairs.

"WHAT THE FUCK!" I shrieked. "GET THE FUCK OUT!"

"Everyone, this is Ronald," Mike said, gesturing his hand in my direction. "Please introduce yourselves."

The first person through the door was a young woman, perhaps in her mid-twenties. She had soft brown hair and was a beautiful girl. She was followed by a man in his forties, a woman who was perhaps in her fifties or sixties, a young overweight man in his mid-twenties or early thirties, and last by David.

"GET...OUT!" I screamed and pulled the cover over my head. An empty plastic drink cup flipped onto the floor.

"Oh, wow," I heard Mike's gravelly voice pronounce. "Those linens look pretty rank. I think I need to call laundry and have them strip that bed."

"GET THE HELL AWAY FROM ME!" I screamed as I pulled myself from beneath the cover and threw myself into a sitting position at the headboard. I grabbed hold of the covers with both hands, made a fist around them, and pulled them with me like they were my most valuable possession.

The young woman then circled the bed, stood between me and the window, extended her hand to me and said, "Hi, my name is Gretchen."

I stared at her and did not offer my hand.

They each circled the bed introducing themselves one at a time. In the meantime, Mike had the attendant bring in more folding chairs. The last person to introduce himself was David.

"You know me," he said. "But to refresh your memory, I'm David Mathis, and I'm very sorry that I upset you."

I said nothing to any of them and did not offer to come out from under the cover, which I held up around my neck as though warding off frigid cold.

David said, "You know, Ronald, I need to apologize for my comment down in the cafeteria last week. I was totally out of line. I shouldn't have done that. I was trying to make a poor excuse for a joke. I meant nothing by it."

Still, I said nothing.

"Okay, guys, grab a chair," Mike commanded. "We can circle around the bed. That would be fine, I think."

"Nobody asked ME if it was fine!" I growled.

"Oh, sorry," Mike said cheerfully. "Is it fine, Ronald?"

"NO!" I growled again.

"Oh…jeez, I hate that," he said. Then he pulled a chair up to the foot of my bed, where he could look directly at me. "So," Mike continued, "who would like to get group started today? Any thoughts you have been thinking, any ponderings you want to share for discussion?"

"No!" I huffed.

"That's all right, Ronald." He smiled. "You don't have to talk if you don't want to. This is your first group, so it's fine if you observe and see how things work."

The woman in her fifties cleared her throat. "I would like to say something."

She turned to me. "Remember, I'm Doreen?"

I glared at her and said nothing.

"Well, I would just like to say," she continued, after a brief pause, "that this all looks very familiar to me. When I first came in, I did essentially the same thing. I hid out, wouldn't talk to anybody. It's hard…you know? You come in here, you are around total strangers, you don't know what the rules are, really. I mean, they give you the sheet of paper that has the do's and don'ts on it, but those are the hospital's rules. The rules you don't know are how you are supposed to conduct yourself socially around the staff and the patients here. I just avoided it. I held up in my room at least three days without coming out. I just avoided everything and everyone. I think that's how I have dealt with most of my problems for most of my life. I found some way to distract myself and avoid what was really going on."

"Anyone else ever feel that way?" Mike asked as he scanned his view around the circle that now enclosed my bed.

"I have," Dave commented. "I think I used work as a way of avoiding. It wasn't that I didn't love my wife or that I didn't want to spend time with her or my kids, but I was afraid of repeating the patterns I grew up with. I think I was partly afraid of doing to my kids what my dad did to me."

"Do you feel comfortable telling the group more about that?" Mike asked.

Dave took a deep breath. "I could never do anything right for my father," he went on. "No matter what I did, it was never good enough. I don't think I can remember a single time, during my upbringing, that the man ever complimented me. I got the hell slapped out of me more than anything else. I remember one time, when I was ten or twelve years old, he asked me to mow the lawn.

There was a piece of a tree limb that had fallen down next to the fence, and instead of moving it, I just mowed around it. I felt like I had finished the lawn so, I put the mower back in the garage and went inside to have some tea.

"He went out to inspect, and the next thing I knew, he was pulling me out of the chair by the scruff of my neck and dragging me by the collar to the yard. He took me to the little spot where I failed to mow. It wasn't more than about two feet maybe, and over next to the fence where it really wasn't that noticeable. 'WHAT THE HELL IS THIS?' he screamed at me. He didn't give me time to answer. The next thing I knew, I felt his hand slapped so hard against the side of my head it knocked me to the ground. Then he screamed, 'YOU WORTH-LESS LITTLE SHIT! I ASK YOU TO DO ONE DAMN THING, AS SIMPLE AS MOWING THE LAWN, AND YOU CAN'T EVEN GET THAT RIGHT!' Then he told me to get up, shoved a pair of scissors at me, and screamed, 'CUT IT!' He grabbed my collar again, shoved me to the ground, and screamed it again. 'AND GET THAT DAMN PIECE OF WOOD OUT OF THERE. PUT IT WHERE IT BELONGS!'

"I lay the scissors down and carried that little piece of tree limb over and dropped it in the garbage can. It wasn't more than about fifteen inches long and maybe the size of your wrist. It was just a little piece of rotten wood that fell into the yard somehow. He followed me the whole way, slapping me on the back of my head, cursing me, and telling me how I can't do anything right. Then as soon as I dropped it in the garbage can, he grabbed me and shoved me back toward the spot of grass. The whole time he was screaming about how he had to take time out of his day, stop what he was doing to mess with me and my fuckups. When I got back, he insisted that I take the scissors and cut the grass as evenly as the mower had cut it and to the same height. Three or four times, I thought I had finished, but he would kick me and tell me I missed a spot or that I had cut one spot lower than the other grass. Finally, he said, 'It isn't good enough, but you can go.' You can bet I never missed a spot again, but it didn't matter. He always found something, and when he did, I got it just as bad or worse."

The whole time he was talking, I thought about Daddy and his rages. The worst one was the time when he caught me and Lynetta making out in church. Sometimes, when he molested me, he told me it was punishment for something I had done wrong. I grew up feeling like everything I did was wrong. I craved attention and praise so much that I was just as addicted to attention and affirmation as I was to lusting after women. I needed the praise from the crowds, the letters, the gratitude. That pushed me as much as the lust in my groin.

"How do you think that affected you?" Mike asked David.

"I became a perfectionist," he replied. "Whatever I did, it was going to be the best of the best, and even if it was top of the line, I was never satisfied. I had to work harder all the time, try harder all the time. It might be part of what made me a millionaire. I learned to sell. Whatever I did, it was going to be better than the next ten guys, but I had to keep working, and keep working because it was never good enough. I was almost as hard on my employees as my father was on me. I made lots of money, but it cost me my family, my wife."

He didn't cry, but you could hear the nearness to it in his voice and see that his eyes were ready to flow over.

"Are you saying you feel like you killed your wife?" the overweight young man said.

"I might as well have killed her," Dave replied. "Our life was constant stress. People outside the family might look at us and think we had it made, but we didn't have what we really needed. We didn't have each other. My wife went to ball games and school events with the kids. I didn't. I didn't have time for that. She might as well have been a single mother, and after the kids were grown and out of the house, I still didn't come home. I made the job more important than her. It took her dying for me to realize what I had really given up. I missed watching my kids grow up. Oh, I was there, in and out of the house, but when I was there, more often than not, I was telling the kids to go away and stop bothering me because I was still working, even at home. I missed having beautiful times with my wife who I loved and adored. I missed it all because I was still trying to please my goddamn abusive father when I was sixty-eight years old and he was long dead!"

"Who can relate to that?" Mike asked the group.

He looked around the group one time, then directly at me. "Ronald, can you relate to that?"

I said nothing while he stared at me. Finally, I said, "David, you know you have a lot of years left ahead of you. Sixty-eight isn't really so old. You still have time to retire, relax, and enjoy your life."

"You are full of shit," David said back to me.

"No, really." I tried to smile. "You've got plenty of money. You could take trips to Europe, vacation. You could still meet a nice woman."

"Like I said," David repeated. "You are full of shit. You think you can sit there and pretend like everything is all honkey-dory and give advice to us poor suffering fools when you are obviously up to your eyeballs in your own shit. Why don't you come clean? Tell us *your* story...come on."

I looked around the group with all the eyes staring back at me.

"We are all here for a reason," Doreen said. "Nobody is here because we had a pristine life. We have all got things we have to sort through and make sense of."

I sat there staring at them all, feeling like a trapped animal.

"My neighbor molested me when I was five years old," Gretchen said, looking directly at me. "Well, it started when I was five years old. It went on until I was fourteen, and I guess I got too old for him, or maybe I was getting too old for him to have an excuse to babysit. Anyway, he stopped, finally. It didn't matter. I was damaged goods. I already felt like I had been ruined for marriage or for any decent boy. I never told anyone about it before coming here. I just turned into the town slut. Why bother saving myself for marriage when I lost my virginity at five years old, right?"

Tears began to flow softly down her cheeks, and she wiped her eyes with her forefingers.

She went on. "I would let anybody have me. I didn't care. Boys fucked me and then talked about it to their friends. Girls called me names when I walked by them at school. It just made me worse. I got into drugs and booze. I would just numb out and let guys do what they wanted. When I was sixteen, I was gang raped at a campsite. I shouldn't have been out there in the first place. Any decent girl would never have gone to a campsite alone with a bunch of boys. They all knew what was up. It didn't take much, the offer of pot and booze and I was in. I got so drunk that I was barely aware. I drifted in and out of consciousness while they were doing it. I remember one piling on top of me, then another. I have memories of them standing over me, swigging beer and calling me cunt, whore, slut… cum bucket—you name it. Later in the morning, one of them took me back to my house, walked me staggering up the sidewalk, and knocked on my parents' door. He was sweeter than syrup when he told my mom and dad how he found me passed out by the dumpster at the Dairy Freeze. So…I was grounded for two weeks for drinking, but they never knew the truth. I was too embarrassed to tell anybody what happened. Those same boys taunted me and bullied me at school. By the time I was twenty-one,

I had tried to kill myself three times. My parents put me in this treatment center and that one. They had me talking to psychiatrists. It didn't help. None of it helped till I started talking about what had really happened to me, what was really going on in my head." She looked at me like she was looking straight through me, this young woman who was probably at least fifteen years younger than me. She looked at me like she knew I could have been one of those boys. Maybe she looked at me like she knew I could have been her.

"I'm sorry," I said and felt tears rising up from my heart. "I'm so sorry."

"Do you have anything else to say?" she asked.

My face flushed hot like a hot wind blowing through my pores. I heard my heart pounding, felt it pounding in my chest. I sat there for a very long time trembling with the whole group staring at me, with Mike giving me a gentle nod as he stared at me. I felt like my heart was going to pound out of my chest. I saw an image of the redheaded woman's skeleton face right before my face, screaming, "DON'T YOU DARE TELL!"

I squeezed the coverlet so hard that my fingers began to ache. Finally, I risked a sentence. "I don't know if I can," I whimpered.

"Try," Gretchen said softly.

All eyes were on me. I looked around the room, feeling like I was on trial, feeling like I was the witness who had just been cornered in a Perry Mason episode. I looked over at Gretchen, this brave young woman, and tried to smile, but I couldn't smile. I felt sweat beading on my forehead.

"My daddy molested me," I finally managed to choke out.

There was silence in the room. No one said anything. Their eyes were on me. At last, Mike said, "I'm very proud of you, Ronnie. Would you be able to tell us a little more about that?"

Tears began to drift slowly down my cheeks. "I don't know if I can," I muttered through burgeoning sniffles.

Gretchen leaned over toward me and once again gently said, "Try."

A quick and jagged breath went into me. Tears dripped off me like rain, and the first thing I said was, "I loved my daddy! I loved him *so* much!" My fists gripped the cover like I was holding on for dear life to the only lifeline I had. My hands ached. My teeth clenched. Then with another jagged breath, I continued.

"I loved my daddy more than anything in the world. They could have told me he hung the moon in the sky, and when I was a little boy, I would have believed it." I found it difficult to talk through sobs, difficult to say what I was saying. "But he was a very sick man, and he hurt me." I buried my head into my blanket-covered fists and sobbed. "I hate telling you this!"

"All of us in this room know what it is like to be hurt," Doreen said softly. "We understand probably more than you realize."

"You said you hate telling us this," Mike spoke. "Would you be willing to talk about that, hating to tell?"

I looked up. "I feel like I'm betraying my daddy, like I'm betraying my family."

"He betrayed you first," David responded.

"Why does it feel like I'm doing something awful and wrong to tell this?" I asked.

"Because you weren't supposed to tell, were you?" Gretchen questioned. "None of us were supposed to tell. We were supposed to keep the secret for the very ones who were hurting us. I don't know about you, but I was afraid what might happen if I told. I was afraid he might hurt me more, that he might kill me if I told. I was afraid my parents would punish me for doing something wrong, and then I couldn't get out of it because I had to keep the secret. He would tell me things like, 'You want it as much as I do.' Bullshit! He implied it was my fault, that I was somehow seducing him! Bullshit! No child wants to be placed in that kind of predicament! No child wants to be manipulated and confused! No child wants to have some adult doing those things to them and then blaming them for it! No child wants to feel like they have no one on their side!"

"My momma was on my side," I said.

"Did she know what was happening to you?" Gretchen asked. "A lot of times, they know and just keep their mouth shut because it is easier to let some bastard hurt your child than to deal with your own fears and your own insecurities."

I began to tremble again. "Oh my God! Do you think she knew?" I cried. "She was always comforting to me. She was always loving, but she always stood by Daddy. She always did what she thought he wanted, 'for better or for worse,' she said. She couldn't have gotten out of that marriage even if she wanted to, even if she hadn't been determined to keep a commitment that her Christian living required her to keep. There were so many things she couldn't do, or didn't think she could do, to take care of herself—but dear Jesus! Do you think she stood passively by and let that happen to me, knowing what he was doing to me?"

"That would be a question you would have to ask her," Mike commented.

"I couldn't do that!" I cried. "What if she didn't know? It would break her heart to find out now."

"And the secret continues," Doreen commented. "The secret is like always being nauseated but never being able to throw up. Even though you know you'll feel better if you can just puke, you choke it back and try to avoid just letting it come up."

Mike leaned back in his chair.

"It might be too soon," he said. "You may not be ready to do this yet, but I think it would be important sometime for you to tell the group your story—tell them what happened to you and how you reacted to that."

"Mike...I...ah." I watched him for a moment. His face was calm, serene. I could see no judgment in it. I looked around the room and asked, "We have all been abused? Every one of us?"

"Yes," Doreen said flatly, and the two who hadn't spoken nodded their heads in affirmation.

"What was your abuse?" I asked Jack, the overweight young man. "Same as yours." He smiled nervously. "But I had some of the beatings like David talked about as well."

"Me too," I heard myself say. "Daddy used to wail the hell out of me." I felt myself feeling somewhat comforted, a little more open. I had found a community. The loneliness I had felt my entire life began to dissipate. I felt courage quicken in my chest. After all, they had already told me so much about themselves. I thought about what courage that took to tell someone, not knowing if they were going to be judged or shunned. Of course, it was safer in the hospital than out of it, and we might not ever tell anyone else, but at least we could tell each other. At least we could lean on each other.

I began to speak. "My daddy would put a redheaded woman's wig on me and put lipstick on my lips. Then he would"—I felt myself sigh deeply—"make me put my mouth on his—" Still, I was having difficulty saying it—"penis or he would penetrate me from behind. Sometimes, he would wear the wig and the lipstick, and he would want me to do things to him. I didn't want to…I didn't want to do it. I felt so ashamed about doing it, but I wanted so much to please my daddy. I wanted so much for him just to love me, and I guess I thought this game he played with me in the corn bin was love—maybe that was love."

I took another long deep breath. "I'm ashamed to say any of this, but I'm especially ashamed to tell you that…" I paused for a very long time. They waited quietly and patiently until I could find the strength to say, "I felt sexually attracted to my own daddy. Sometimes he wore the red wig and pretended to be a woman. Sometimes he made me wear it. I was confused, and sometimes I didn't know if Daddy wanted me to be a boy or a girl. I couldn't understand how I could be so attracted to girls and still become aroused with my daddy. The older I got, the more I felt like I had to prove I was really a man, and the only way I knew I could do that was to breed like a bull breeds. The only way I knew how to do that was to act like a farm bull and mount as many cows as I could. I started to be aroused early and started playing with myself, but when I had an orgasm from masturbating, and the semen came out of me, I thought I was bleeding in the dark. Then when I saw it, I thought it was puss or something, that I had a horrible disease and that I was being punished by God. Despite all the things Daddy was doing to me, I didn't know anything about sex. I was so ignorant! My brother told me it was like the cattle mating on the farm, that it was normal for me to ejaculate. What he never knew is that, in my mind, I thought that if the bull mates with many heifers and that's what makes him a bull, then that is what I had to do to prove that I'm a real man. I thought being attracted to Daddy meant that I was a homosexual." I quoted Leviticus 18:22, "Thou shalt not lie with mankind, as with womankind: it *is* abomination." Tears came, and I began to rock in place. I buried my head into the blanket again and screamed, "I WAS FUCKING SEXUALLY ATTRACTED TO MY OWN FATHER!"

There was silence throughout the room. They sat there and let me sob, all of them.

After a while, Mike softly spoke. "Ronald, do you remember the question I asked you a few days ago, after you got upset with David?"

"What question?" I groaned without raising my head.

"I asked you if you thought you had slept with enough women to prove you are a man," he said.

"Fucked!" I snarled. "You asked me if I had fucked enough women to prove I'm a man."

"Okay...fucked," he continued. "You remember the question. Have you thought about the answer?"

"No," I replied.

"No, you haven't thought about the answer?" he asked.

I looked up at him. "No, I haven't fucked enough women to prove I'm a man," I replied. "I don't know that I'll ever feel like I'm a real man. I don't know that I can. I would like to pretend that I'm not queer, but the bottom line is I started to enjoy having sex with my own father. After a while, it started to feel good. I got aroused by my own daddy! What does that make me?"

"A human being," Jack quickly responded. "So what? You got aroused by eroticized abuse. So what?"

"So it means I'm queer...a homosexual...a faggot!" I snapped back. "It means I've sinned against God and against nature, and no matter how I try, no matter what I do, no matter how many women I seduce or how powerful the orgasm, I cannot get beyond the fact that I repeatedly...enjoyed... having sex...with my own father! I can't get beyond the fact that I'm not... normal."

"It means you are a human being," Jack insisted firmly. "Nobody's normal!"

David snapped back at me. "I've never had a sexual encounter with a man in my life, but I damn sure am not normal, and I damn sure am not going to judge you. A little boy who wants his father's love above all else is trained by his father into sexual acts? A child doesn't know the difference! A child doesn't know what to think. It is not the sexual contact that does the real damage, it's the mind fuck! It fucks with a kid's head. A kid doesn't have the maturity to sort that shit out."

"So…hmm," Mike interjected. "Because you were aroused by your father, that means you are gay?"

"Doesn't it?" I asked. "I enjoyed having sex with another man. 'If a man also lie with mankind, as he lieth with a woman, both of them have committed an abomination: they shall surely be put to death; their blood *shall be* upon them.' Leviticus 20:13!"

"Mmmmm…hm…yeah," Mike went on, "Leviticus says a lot of things about a lot of things, doesn't it? Says something about sacrificing goats and lambs too, but I don't know anybody who still does that. Even the Jews don't do that. We could cherry-pick the Bible for this justification or that all day long, but…so…ah, how many other men would you say you have had sexual relations with other than your father?"

"None!" I demanded.

"Are you sure about that?" he pressed.

"Okay!" I acquiesced. "I fooled around with one kid one time after school when I was about thirteen, and once after I first moved to Nashville, a man came to my office and confessed that he was attracted to men. He wanted me to pray for him to heal him of his homosexuality. After I knelt down to hold his hands and pray with him, he started touching me. I ended up letting him give me oral sex. I never saw him again after that. Maybe I was also attracted to my brother. Maybe, but not really. We slept in the same bed. He taught me some things about sex. I knew when he jacked off, and he knew when I did, but we never touched each other that way. I loved him, and loving him, I found myself sometimes having desires for him. I'm such a confused fucking mess!"

"It gets confusing for abused kids. Sometimes it's hard to tell the difference between love and attraction. So…how often would you say you find yourself sexually attracted to other men?" Mike pressed. "You know, checking out another man. How often would you say you find yourself doing that?"

"I don't know," I quickly replied.

"Okay, some attractions to men. Hmmm, so…let's put this into percentages." Mike continued to press. "So what percentage of the time would you say you are sexually attracted to women and what percentage of time would you say you are sexually attracted to men?"

I just glared at him.

"Hey, it's an honest question." He smiled.

I found myself becoming angry again. "I don't want to say."

"Okay, so…is it…50/50, 75/25? What would you say? What percentage of your attraction time is spent in sexual fantasy about men versus sexual fantasy about women?"

Again, I glared at him, but I was thinking. Finally, I answered. "I am attracted to men about five or ten percent of the time—maybe, and to women the rest of the time."

"So…five to ten percent?" he asked. "You are sure that it is not more than that?"

"YES! I'm sure!" I snapped.

He leaned forward in his chair again. "Don't you think that is a pretty clear indication that you are heterosexual?" he asked.

"But I have attractions to men!" I argued.

"So do I." Mike smiled. "Once in a while, I wouldn't say it would ever be enough to make me want to leave my wife, but now and then I have a brief little sexual arousal toward a dude."

"So do I," Jack responded.

"I have some attractions to women sometimes," Gretchen responded.

"So do I," Doreen added.

"I don't," David entered, "have…attractions to men. I mean, I can't say I don't think some guys are attractive or that I might think, yeah, that guy is built or really good-looking, but I wouldn't say it ever turns into a desire to touch him or go to bed with him. I just don't have it, but I can understand it, and I don't care if you have attractions to men. There is no reason for me to care if you do."

"It's more normal than you think, man," Mike interjected, "and it is a very common confusion among those who have been molested, even by the opposite sex. People who have been sexually abused sometimes don't know what their real attractions are for a while. 'Cause, you know, it is not the physical contact with a child that causes the actual damage. Like David said, it's the mind fuck that takes place, all the guilt, shame, and confusion. People who have been through it are often confused. Sometimes, they don't realize that they can be loyal to their own natural orientation, but you did, man. You stayed loyal to your heterosexuality. You might have gone a little overboard trying to prove it, but you stayed loyal to your own inner urgings."

James, the man in his forties who had sat silent throughout the entire process, finally spoke. "I'm gay," he said quietly. "I'm the queer, the faggot, the abomination you talked about. All of my attractions are to men. I'm sorry if that offends you."

I felt stopped in my tracks, embarrassed, and ashamed. There was a part of me, in that moment, that wanted to shame him, tell him what a sinner he was, and how he needed to accept Jesus so he could stop doing such vile things, but there was a part of me that knew I had no right. There was a part of me that realized his sin was no worse than my own. I heard a gentle voice in my head say, "For all have sinned and have fallen short of the grace and glory of God." After a moment, I said, "I'm sorry."

"I'm sorry too," he replied. "I'm sorry nature made me this way. I'm sorry that I have felt like an outcast and a pariah for my entire life. I'm sorry I got bullied in school—ridiculed and made fun of one day, then asked by the same dude for a quick blow job on another day. I'm sorry that dude beat the hell out of me after I gave him a blow job because he couldn't stand the shame that he felt about it.

"I'm sorry I couldn't make myself be straight. I've tried my whole life to be straight. I even got married once. I did everything I knew to try to make myself attracted to her. But see, even though you might be able to have an orgasm with another man, you may still not really be attracted to men. I could have the occasional orgasm with my wife, but it wasn't the same as making love to her, and most of the time I had to fantasize about some guy to get there. It wasn't the same as my attractions to men, the way I felt when a man touched me or when I touched a man. I loved her, and we are still friends, even after the divorce, but I could never really make myself be attracted to her. Just because I was capable of having sex with her did not mean I was straight.

"I couldn't make myself be what my parents wanted me to be. I couldn't make myself be what the church wanted me to be. I'm sorry—sorry that Christians think I deserve to die, to be put to death, or shunned for being who I am. The minister who baptized me said the sin of homosexuality is worse than the sin of murder. So I deserve to die for who I am? For the longest time, that scared the shit out of me. See…I've got no excuse. I can't say I got aroused by some eroticized abuse and that made me gay. I wasn't sexually abused as a child except for being sexually bullied by other kids and called all kinds of horrible names, but that was because I was gay. I am just attracted to men, like, exclusively men. You know, like David is attracted to women but on the total flip side of the coin.

"I know when a woman is beautiful, but that doesn't make me want to sleep with her. I've never known a time when I wasn't attracted to men. When I was a little boy, I was drawn to the touch of a man like a bee to honey. I didn't really even know I was having attractions to men then. I just knew I melted when I was hugged by a man or some teacher rested his hand on my shoulder. About the time I hit puberty, maybe before, I began to find myself getting aroused by seeing men, being near men, or boys in school. I found myself fantasizing about the coach at school. Then I made a huge mistake. I told the guy who I thought was my best friend that I was having these thoughts, and it was all over from there. It must have scared him or something because the next thing I knew, it was all over school, and he wouldn't have anything to do with me anymore, except to taunt me and bully me the way the others did. It didn't matter that I wasn't feminine like people expect you to be when you are gay. He told, and my life was never the same. There was never another time I could walk into school without being taunted and bullied. They did all kinds of shit to me, from used condoms hung on my locker to spray painting 'Faggot' on the front door of our house.

"It was a small school, and I didn't know anybody who felt the way I felt. I thought I was the only one, and when all the abuse started, I felt lonelier than I had ever felt in my life. My mom and dad kind of defended me, kind of, but then there were the talks. 'Why don't you ask a girl out? Go out and have some fun. Maybe you could try out for sports.' Shit—I wasn't about to do that. The jocks were the worst about picking on me. Although, I would have loved to be in a locker room, watching all those guys walking around naked, taking showers, I knew I would get it worse than ever if I ever tried out for sports, when everyone knew. I wasn't even allowed to look at a guy in the hallway. I had to divert my eyes or some guy was yelling, 'What are you looking at, faggot?' Then the next moment I was getting shoved into a wall."

After that, James sat for a while in silence, as did we all. I was totally silenced. I didn't know what to say. I was contemplating what I might be able to say when he spoke again.

"I was fourteen the first time I tried to kill myself. This time—the time that got me hospitalized here—was the fifth time I've tried…One of these days…I'll get it right. There is no use in me being here. Nobody has any use for me except as a trick for sex and then dump me. I'm the worst kind of sinner, right? I need to be put to death, right? Even the stupid psychology books say I'm sick, that there is something wrong with me for feeling what I feel, for being who I am. So I might as well die." Tears began streaming down his face.

I sat there in shock hearing the last thing he said. I felt like I needed to say something, but I didn't know what to say. I realized that, although I had suffered, there were others in the world, perhaps more than I knew, who suffered at least as much or more than I had.

Dave was sitting right next to James. At that moment, he reached over, placed his fat hand over James's hand, and said, "James…I hope you never get it right. I hope you are finding out here that there are people in the world who will love you no matter what. There are people in the world who will accept you for who you are, no matter what. I'm a straight guy, and in high school, I might have been one of those guys who would have picked on you, but I'm here to tell you, I don't feel that way anymore. I love you just the way you are, and I want to be your friend. I want you always to remember that you have a friend in me." Dave leaned over and hugged James, pulled him close, and actually kissed him on the cheek. James, tears streaming down his face, smiled shyly, as David continued to hold him.

Mike leaned toward James. "How are you feeling, man? You doing okay? Having any thoughts about killing yourself now?"

James looked up, directly at me. I sat there for a moment, feeling like an ant under a magnifying glass. Then I said, "I don't know what to say. My world has just been turned upside down. I…I never realized, never thought…I was taught my whole life it's a sin. It's wrong."

"So was I," James quietly responded. "When I was sixteen, I heard a preacher say, 'The sin of homosexuality is worse than the sin of murder.' I went home after church that day and tried to kill myself. I couldn't change it. I couldn't make myself right, so if I'm worse than a murderer, I deserved to die, right? But I didn't choose this. Who would choose this? Any heterosexual Christian who thinks even a crazy person would choose this never stops to ask themselves exactly when it was that they chose to be straight. Who would choose to be something so rejected and despised? Who would choose abuse and bullying, discrimination and shunning? Do you know the US Constitution protects your right to choose any religion you want, even if it is Satanism, and you can file a lawsuit for discrimination if an employer fires you for your religion? You can choose your religion. I can't choose what I am. Yet I can be fired for being gay, and I have no protection at all, but you have legal protection for whatever religion you choose. So, do you think it's a sin to be who I am? Is it a sin to be the way nature created me? Is it okay to cherry-pick a four-thousand-year-old book that was written during ancient and primitive times and was compiled and rewritten multiple times over the ages to berate and put people down for being homosexuals? I am not going to call myself a sinner for having the feelings I have, no matter who thinks I should!"

Mike interjected. "And we are not going to assume being gay means you are abnormal or sick just because the diagnostic manual and the APA hasn't gotten their shit together yet."

Stephen came into my mind. I thought about this boy who was convinced he was a girl. I thought about how he insisted on that, being so young. Then I questioned, is it some abnormality, some genetic freak of nature that caused him to be that way, that caused James to be homosexual, or is it the way God made them, maybe all part of God's plan, in some way? My mind wanted to hold true to my Christian beliefs, but I was so confused. I had no excuse for my own behavior, although my heart wanted to blame Daddy for it. Mike's question about percentages made me realize that, although I might have been confused about my sexuality, what Daddy did to me did not make me gay, and James was gay even though he had never experienced that kind of sexual abuse. My mind was going in a thousand different directions. On one hand, I knew that I was called to love and have compassion. On the other hand, the Bible said what it said. I had lived by that, been taught by that, held it as my own for my entire life, even though I had violated the admonishments of the Bible myself.

Then another Bible verse came into my mind, "*Ye* blind guides, which strain at a gnat, and swallow a camel." Matthew 23:24. I asked myself, *Why this verse? Why this moment?*

Then the answer came, and I heard a voice in my mind saying, *You strain at the letter of the law and miss the whole point of the law. You strain to be perfect, never to sin, which makes you miss the one thing that is most important. "Thou shalt love the Lord thy God with all thy heart and with all thy soul and with all thy mind. This is the first and great commandment. And the second is like unto it, thou shalt love thy neighbor as thyself. On these two commandments hang all the law and the prophets."*

An awareness filled my mind like the sun emerging from long, dark, and stormy clouds, giving off great light, filling the sky with beauty so that even those once dark clouds are lined with golden light. Love is the bottom line! On this rests everything, and what is love but the wish that one should have the greatest and highest good that is possible for them to have? What is love but wanting someone to be happy? If God truly loves us, would He not, then, most desire that we be happy? An energy filled me. I felt myself fill with an instant joy, a transformation as I understood that I had spent my entire life straining at a gnat and choking on a camel. I had spent my entire life so focused on the little nitpicky should and shouldn't of the Bible that I had missed the whole point of the Bible. If I didn't have love, I was as a clanging cymbal, no more than a loud gong with no substance. So many verses ran through my mind in those brief moments, "Judge not that ye be not judged." The awareness that love cannot judge flooded me. It is impossible to simultaneously condemn and save. Love and judgment cannot share the same space at the same time, and if I judge while telling myself that I am loving, I am lying to myself and pretending for God, instead of truly living by His Word.

"OH MY GOD—JAMES!" I shouted. "I LOVE YOU!" I leapt out of bed like a madman, rushed to his chair, and commanded, "STAND UP! I WANT TO HUG YOU!"

"What?" He looked around the room, confused, almost as though hoping someone would rescue him from the idiot who suddenly stood before him.

"Stand up!" I commanded again with my arms wide open to him. "Please, let me give you a hug. You may not realize it, but you have given me answers that a lifetime of studying the Bible has not given me. You have given me my true calling, and I love you for it!"

James got carefully to his feet. I then threw my arms around him and squeezed very tightly. With my head next to his, I began to speak. "God created you in His image, in His likeness. He created you perfect like Himself. You can, therefore, be nothing less than perfect because it is impossible for Perfection to create anything less than Itself. If Perfection could create imperfection, then Perfection could not exist. You exist! I exist! We all exist! We must, therefore, be God's perfect creation. Either we believe that God is Love and Perfection, or we believe that God is insane and imperfect. It is not possible to be both. It is not possible to serve two masters. Either we serve Love, or we serve malice! Either we serve God or we perish in the hell that malice creates for us! Either we are in love or we are in fear! Either we have faith in God, or we fear that God is inadequate! OH MY GOD! JAMES!"

I held him back away from me, gripping him by the shoulders and shouted, "YOU HAVE GIVEN ME THE ANSWER! MY GOD, MAN! YOU HAVE GIVEN ME THE ANSWER!"

CHAPTER 27

James and I became good buddies over the next few weeks. We laughed and chatted and accepted one another as is, without expectation. Once I let go and let in God, everything got better.

I felt lighter, happier, and renewed. I stopped criticizing myself and other people. I stopped worrying about sin and started working on expressing genuine love and acceptance. Once I stopped judging and putting myself and other people into categories and compartments, my whole life changed for the better. There were other groups, other discussions, and there were a couple of times in which I got to be the one to bring someone a new awareness, to give them the option of healing. I can't say that I was completely healed or over it, but I was well on my way. I became willing to let God teach me to heal instead of trying to figure out what God meant and then impose that on myself and others. For the first time, I began truly to understand love, and I began to understand the commandment of "Judge not that ye be not judged." In my past, I had judged under the guise of love. On one hand, I was saying to someone that God loved them, and on the other hand, telling them that they were not acceptable to God if they did not change to suit my beliefs and expectations. I realized that love is acceptance. It allows people to be themselves without the imposition of judgment.

The greatest gifts God gave us are love, life, and choice. I realized that our lives belong to us and to us alone. Since a true gift has no expectations, and life is one of God's greatest gifts, we get to do whatever we want with the life we are given. Holy love would never try to force anyone to be anything other than what they are, for God would never force anyone to His will. Control is the result of fear, not love, and there is no fear in God. I realized that I did not really have faith if I thought I had to intervene for God. God is certainly powerful enough that He does not need me or anyone else to try to force what we personally happen to believe is His will on anyone. The truth is that the only one who knows God's will is God. My need to intervene for God had more to do with my pride and arrogance than any true desire to serve the Lord. When Jesus shouted in my dream, "You are My Word," he meant that I was to live His Word by aligning myself with God's Love, living God's Love as much as possible instead of trying to convince anyone what they should or should not do. We each have a right to choose how we will live the life God gave us, for life, choice, and love are God's gifts to us.

I stopped thinking in terms of bad people and began thinking in terms of behavior that has consequences. I began to define the difference between behavior and being. I realized that people can't help what they are, who they are, or how they are made. I began to love everyone the same, including myself. *Love thy neighbor as thyself* came to mean to me that I am also to love myself. I realized there was nothing to prove. Daddy did what he did, and I forgave him for it. There were tears in that forgiveness, but I came to realize that he was wounded too and that I would never be able to understand why he did what he did. I recognized the fact that Daddy didn't have access to many of the opportunities for healing that I had. He never could have paid for some big treatment center and never would have been pushed by Momma into going to one like Alissa did me. I understood that he had grown up in a world that was more restricted than the one I had grown up with. He had grown up without the opportunities that I had. I forgave him for not getting it, for not understanding.

More than once I heard my mind saying, "Forgive them, Father, for they know not what they do." I began to think about that. I came to understand that it is much easier to forgive someone for ignorance than it is to forgive them for malice. If I had thought Daddy was evil, I never would have been able to forgive him, but when I realized he was ignorant, I had sympathy for him. I thought about why Jesus said, "Forgive them for they know not what they do" and what he might have meant by that, and I realized the statement has three basic implications. The first implication is that Jesus had so much love He could forgive His own murderers even as He was being murdered. The second implication is that they were not murdering Him because they were evil or bad people; they were murdering him because they were ignorant. Even if they had malice in their hearts, it was there because of ignorance. They didn't get it. They didn't understand love. If they had understood love, they could not have been behaving that way. If they understood love, there would have been no place for malice in their hearts. The third implication, when I really stopped to think about it, is that even if someone is attempting to murder Christ himself, they are still forgiven. First of all, Jesus proved that it is impossible to murder Him. He rose from the dead to prove that Christ cannot be murdered, and God cannot be mocked. In that is the true recognition that He really did die for our sins because "Forgive them, Father, for they know not what they do" means there is no sin, and we need never look at anyone and see a sinner but a child of God. There is only love, and the closer we come to understanding and emulating that love, the closer we come to living a truly Christian life. In those last few weeks at Manitau Chateau, I accepted so much. I was practically giggly with joy for the first time in my life. I accepted that Daddy had molested me and that he didn't do it because he was evil. Even though he consciously and technically knew better, he did it because he didn't really know any better, because he was ignorant of real love, for himself or for me. He had deluded himself. He was fighting his urges instead of accepting his urges and accepting himself. I realized that anytime we fight an urge, we give it power, and it can seem to have power over us, but if we don't fight it, and we accept that we have the urge, it then becomes a choice we can make or choose not to make. We no longer feel like the urge is bigger than we are. We no longer feel like something has power over our choice. I realized that all those times I had felt like I was not in control of myself, I was very much in control of myself. I was trying to prove something, but there was nothing to prove. I was battling a demon of self-deprecation and shame, thinking that I had to seduce those women in order to feel better or distract myself from the real problem. Just like Daddy, it was my deluded attempt to fix something inside me that I really didn't think could be fixed. At Manitau Chateau, I came to understand there was nothing to fix. There was nothing to be undone.

I began again. I began to look at my past differently. It did not define me; it gave me opportunities to learn. Okay, my father molested me. I had sexual attractions to my own father. I had confusion, shame, and anguish over all that. Until I met Lynetta, I knew no other sexual expression other than what I had experienced with Daddy. Of course, I became aroused when stimulated during the abuse. The body responds, and regardless of the fact that my sexual orientation was toward women, my body responded to the touch of a man who I loved and wanted to please. So what? It is understandable that a child would eventually respond to sexual touch with his own arousal. It was not fair that Daddy did that to me, but it was not wrong that I felt what I felt. I was beginning to not even think of right and wrong the same way anymore. It is terrible for anyone to hurt another person—absolutely, especially a child. It is terrible to put a child in such a predicament that they might not be able to emotionally and mentally navigate their way through it. Like Daddy, some never do, not even in a lifetime. Some people end up killing themselves, trapped in the shame and self-loathing so intense that they can't seem to find their way out of it. Daddy's actions had messed up most of my life, but I was beginning to get through it. I was beginning to understand love, and that when we understand love, we never place another human being, especially a child, in such a predicament. Genuine love never seeks to do harm. When we understand love, we want the greatest and highest good for everyone, no matter who they are, and we especially want the greatest and highest good for children, even if they are not our own.

The world can be a place of such great cruelty, and the greatest tragedies are not those that come from some natural disaster or calamity of nature. The greatest tragedies are the inhumanity that we impose on one another. How cruel we are to each other, even to our own family, our own loved ones, our own community. How terrible that we impose hurt and harm on one another, that we get caught in the trap of hatred, resentment, and shame. I realized, finally, that I had been trapped in resentment and shame. I resented what Daddy had done to me, and I took it out on every woman I met, including my own wife. I used sexual release as a distraction from my pain and confused pleasure with happiness. I crucified women in sacrifice to the god of my lust and my vengeance. I say vengeance because I had to realize that there was a part of me that resented and disrespected women or I could not have behaved that way. Perhaps I picked that up from Daddy. As much as I loved my mother, I had grown up with the idea that women were objects to be used and discarded if necessary. Daddy thought of Momma more as a possession than a loved one. I had treated women as expendable, something to be used for my own selfish need. I even blamed them for my own indiscretions which further hurt them and hurt me as well. All along, I had hopes that some of those women might have been able to rise above our tryst, maybe to realize something out of it.

After I began to realize what I had done and took responsibility for it, I prayed a lot for my actions to have been seed to a harvest of love and understanding. I prayed that even though I had acted without concern for them or what effect my actions might have on them, that they would somehow grow from the experience. I thought about women like Darlene Meadows and how I had ended up using a woman who was mentally ill for my own carnal pleasure, how that backfired on me and should have been a lesson of love and understanding instead of a lesson in fear. The only lesson I had gotten from it, at the time, was that I needed to work harder at controlling my behavior so I wouldn't get in trouble. I thought about the fact that I had treated women like inflatable sex dolls made of flesh, having no more meaning to me than a doll that could be deflated and cast aside. I had not thought about them, about their person, their soul, or who they were as human beings. I had not thought about what gave them joy or what made them cry. To me, they were just another conquest, another distraction. I realized that one of the reasons I could not reach those crescendos of lust with Alissa was that she was more than an object to me. The lust came from the power of the unhealed anguish within me, and I didn't want to feel that anguish with Alissa. I didn't want to feel the need to get off with a sexual explosion that would temporarily release the emotional pressure that was constantly rebuilding inside me. I didn't want to use her for that. She was the person I loved, my wife, my mate, the mother of my children. I could not have sex with her without guilt about the women I had used. I could not have sex with her and let go, because she was more than just a liaison to me.

I determined that I was going to learn how to make love to her. I determined that I was going to learn how to set everything else aside and simply commune sexually with the woman I loved. I would no longer take my fear, guilt, rage, or shame to bed with me. I would no longer allow Daddy, the redheaded woman, or anything else to join us in my mind. When I got home, I was going to learn how to free myself so I could truly, for the first time, make love to my wife.

It is amazing how much awareness can come in such a short period of time. I walked through the same world, but it was a different world. There were the same people, with the same faces, the same clothes, the same backgrounds, the same things to say, but I didn't see any of them the same way. It was like I started seeing more than bodies. I started seeing souls. I started seeing more than men or women, I started seeing people, each one with their own struggles, their own stories, their own perceptions, their own battles to fight, their own hurts to overcome. I thought back to the last young woman I had sex with before my suicide attempt, how I had blamed her for my behavior, and what she had said to me. "God is Love, God is Holy, God created all of us in His image—that makes all of us created in the image and likeness of pure and perfect Holy Love itself." I had used her for sex, and even if she was just as into it as I was, she still became an angel sent by God to wake me up and make me realize what I was doing to myself, my family, loved ones, and others. Finally, it sank in. None of us can ever be less than what pure and perfect Holy Love created. There is no less than or greater than. There is no measure of worth because perfection created everyone's worth as equal. The only time there are problems is when we forget that. When we believe that we are better than others or that others could be better than us, is when problems are created. When we separate ourselves in any way from others in God's creation, there are problems created. Yet even in those problems, there is truth. Even when we lapse into the kind of insanity I lapsed into after my abuse as a child, there is truth, and the truth is that God is perfect, and no matter what we believe, think, say or do, in the end, God's will *is* the only will, and God's will has essentially already been done. Holy Love is like the sun. It only shines. We can retreat from it, put ourselves into emotional caves, even forget that it is there, but all the while it remains, shining on for eternity until the time comes that we choose to step back into the light.

In early June, I called Alissa to let her know I was being discharged. I could tell there was a hesitancy in her voice. After having been put through so much, it was only natural that she would have some trepidation and hesitation lest I come home and resume the same behavior I had always resumed. But things truly would be different this time. Honestly, if I could have spent the rest of my life at Manitau Chateau, with exception of not being able to see my wife and kids, I would have been happy with that. My entire perspective had changed.

The treatment center made arrangements for a shuttle to the Denver airport, and then I would fly back to Nashville. There would be no more need of the watchful eye to make sure I didn't try to kill myself. I knew that was never going to happen again. I couldn't kill what God created anyway, so I might as well learn to live my life as God intended and be joyful in every moment of it. An attempt to kill myself would be throwing the gifts God gave me right back in His face. I finally realized that regardless of what I had been through, regardless of all the pain I had experienced or caused, regardless of what the future might hold, my life was worth living, and I determined I was finally going to live it for me and my family, as well as for God.

Before I left, I said goodbye to the remaining patients in my group. James had been discharged a week earlier. He hugged me before he left and said *thank you* for accepting him and caring about him instead of judging him. He promised me that he would never try to kill himself again and that he was going to work on loving himself for who he was instead of believing the taunts of others. For many years after that, we had occasional phone calls to one another, and we always sent each other gifts at Christmas. As far as I know, he never made another attempt to kill himself, and as far as I could tell from our interactions, he was happy. He didn't always care for the way some people treated him, but regardless of the prejudice and hatred, he always knew there were many others who loved him. He came to understand that judgment says nothing about the one being judged and everything about the one who is judging. Around 1985, he contracted AIDS. Still, he maintained a positive attitude and coped with the illness gracefully despite the prevailing attitude of fear that plagued the country at that time. On an afternoon in 1990, his mother called to tell me he had passed away. I offered my condolences to her and to the family. Then, after I hung up the phone, I quietly wept.

On the day I left Manitau Chateau, I gave hugs to everyone. Dave was discharged with me and was going to ride the same shuttle to the airport. Before we left, Mike stood out front with us while the shuttle driver loaded our bags.

"Is it okay if I hug you?" I asked.

Mike held his arms open, and I hugged him tightly. "Thank you," I whispered as he held me.

"Thank you," he replied. "Thank you for sharing your soul with me. Thank you for honoring me with your pain and for giving me a chance to show you there is a better way."

I stepped back from the hug and looked past his scraggly exterior into his eyes. "You gave me God," I said. "You gave me what I thought I had my whole life but never realized that I didn't really have it. You helped me find real love."

He smiled. "All I did was give you a safe place to heal and nudge you a little. You did all the rest."

Then, Dave stepped up to give him a hug as well. I stepped back while Dave had his time with Mike. Then we loaded the shuttle for the airport along with a couple of patients from the other treatment teams.

When the shuttle pulled away from the building, I turned to look back. Manitau Chateau soon popped out of view when we rounded a curve, and I couldn't help feeling a moment of grief and sadness. I knew that I would never again experience anything like that and that I would never be coming back. It had changed me forever and the indelible mark on my soul would last for the remainder of my life. I drew a deep breath, turned around, and gazed out the side window at the incredible beauty that is Colorado.

At the Denver airport, Dave and I said our goodbyes. We hugged each other before heading off to our own respective terminals. Dave had decided he would finally retire. He was going to visit his kids and try to be more of a father and grandfather than he had been in the past. He determined that he was never again going to ignore or take a loved one for granted, but he also determined he was going to travel the world for a while and just explore.

"We've changed," he said as he pulled back from our hug.

"Haven't we though?" I smiled. "For the better—all for the better."

We promised to call, but we never did. I got a card from him every Christmas and sent one back. I learned to wait till I got his card before sending my own because the address could be different every year. He finally settled in a small village in France with a woman he had met on one of his excursions, and far as I know, he was happy.

I tried to keep up with several members of my group, but after a while, most of them faded into my memories. Gretchen would call me now and then to check on me and see how I was doing. She had been the one to see beyond the veil of my self-deception. She had been the one to see the truth and to call me on it. This young lady who could have been almost young enough to be my daughter had called me on my shit. Sometimes, I would call to check on her. When she was in her late twenties, she married a very nice man and began to raise a family. She found a man who was empathetic about her abuse and who seemed to respect her. Still, they were divorced a few years later, and she became a divorced mother with two young children. We all still had scars, but where there are scars, there is also healing. Where there is healing, there is life.

When I got to the Nashville airport, Alissa met me with a smile and a hug as well as the obvious bit of trepidation and concern that I might return to old behavior. I had heard it in her voice over the phone, and I could see it in her posture when she met me from the plane. I hugged her and kissed her then stepped back to look at her square in the eye.

"I know you're worried," I said. "I would be worried too if I were in your shoes, but I don't think you have to worry anymore. Honestly, I think I have got this. I don't expect you to just believe that. I have deceived you too much and too often for you to just believe that I'm never going to do it again. I will have to show you I've changed. I get that. I know it will take time; trust broken is harder to mend than it was to find in the first place, but if you are willing to give me the time, you'll see. I'm not the same man you sent away several weeks ago." I gazed at her and realized there was a beautiful soul behind those eyes. There was a person gazing back at me, although with a slight tinge of fear, who recognized the soul in me. She always had. Since the beginning, she had seen in me what I could not see in myself.

"I love you," I said. "I never want to hurt you again. I never wanted to hurt you in the first place. This is not going to be another empty promise that I won't cheat on you again. I don't have any need or desire to cheat on you again, and despite everything, I have always loved you."

"I know," she replied simply. "I love you too." She took my hand and walked beside me to the car. We loaded my luggage in the trunk. Then she drove us home. When we got there, I sat her down and told her everything. I told her the detail of how Daddy had molested me and how I had thrown the old tackle box into the pond on the night of his funeral. I told her about my confusion and how I had spent all those years acting out, trying to prove that I was a man after Daddy made me feel like I was anything but a real man. I told her anonymously about James, how listening to his story led me to realize that it all comes down to love and forgiveness and that forgiveness is a key that is essential in love.

She did exactly as I expected the woman who had stood by me through it all to do. She accepted. She hugged me, told me that she loved me, and that she was so glad I had come to understand. After all, she had understood love and forgiveness long before I ever actually came to that awareness. I realized that it was possible that my behavior could have pushed her to the point that she could no longer tolerate it, but I also realized that even then, she would never have stopped loving me. Even if she had been forced by my behavior to leave me, she still would have loved me. I had no more need for that behavior and that was a good thing.

I didn't want to go back to work, but I had made a commitment to Evangelic Temple before I ever went to treatment that I was going to do a televised sermon for them. We had originally intended to put it off while I was in the hospital, and make excuses for my absence, but I actually got back just in time to give the service on the twentieth of June, as had originally been planned. I determined that this was going to be my last sermon. I sat Alissa down and explained to her that I wanted to give up the ministry, at least what I thought had been my ministry. After all, I had done even that to prove something, to gain the attention that I had so ravenously craved and didn't get from Daddy. I had done that to prove that I was bigger and better at preaching than Daddy was.

Ultimately, Daddy and I were both hypocrites. We had both presented a persona for the church. We had both laid down a law from the pulpit that we broke in our own lives. I was no better than Daddy, and he was no better than me, but after my awareness, I realized I didn't have to be on television or in a pulpit or on the radio to teach God's Word. I understood that the best way to teach God's Word is simply to live it, and by example, show a way to truth.

All my caterwauling and prancing didn't really teach God's Word. It was all a show. I didn't want to be an actor anymore. I wanted my life to be an example. I understood that I would always be a student of life, always learning more, always working on practicing love. I realized that God's love was something that I could slip away from, but that I would never lose it. Like the Prodigal Son, I could always go home. I could always step back into the light of love. I had wallowed with the pigs. I had squandered my inheritance of Grace, and yet it had never been taken from me. I took myself away from it. I determined that instead of trying to be good, instead of focusing on what I should or should not be doing, I was going to focus on love. Every day, I would commit myself to God's love. Every day, I would commit myself to listening to love and to practicing love. I realized that I could, at any moment, be either existing in love or in fear, in compassion or in malice. I could be in the practice of love or in the grips of fear, but I could not serve two masters. I determined, rather than trying to make myself behave, I was going to try to live my life in the love of God.

Alissa and I both agreed that we had more than enough to live on in grand comfort for the rest of our lives. We set up a one-million-dollar trust for Stephen in St. Louis, and our attorneys were finally able to secure Miss Mattie's legal guardianship of him. I had every hope that this would allow Miss Mattie to raise him in comfort and in love and get him away from people who abused him and mistreated him, even those who unknowingly did it in the name of Jesus. I had come to understand why I felt a kinship with him. I saw myself in him. In a way, he had been the first catalyst that began my healing. Without knowing it, he had begun to bring the memories of my abuse to the surface. I had seen myself in him, and he had been a mirror reflecting back what I had repressed and avoided all my life. Like the young lady I seduced in my office, he was another angel of God, someone sent to lead me home. I had no idea what kind of life he might choose. Whatever life he came to live was really none of my business. I only wanted to make sure he had the opportunity to live a life of comfort and a life where the trust he had in Miss Mattie might give him a chance for happiness. I had already set up a trust for Momma, and I made a quick trip back to Arkansas to sit down with her and explain what I had been through and what I was going to do with the rest of my life. As expected, it hurt her. It took answering a lot of questions and explaining a lot of feelings, but in the end, she seemed to understand.

"Oh God bless! God bless, Ronnie!" she wept and hugged me. "If I had ever known, oh my Lord, child, I might have been tempted to kill that man. I know for sure I would have taken all you kids away from here. I would have called the law on him. Baby, if I had only known, I never would have let you go through that."

I really don't think Momma knew anything about what Daddy was doing, at least not consciously, and in many ways, I think she had felt as trapped as I did. There was a part of me that didn't want to tarnish Daddy's image in her eyes, but I realized that I really couldn't keep the secret any longer, especially from her. I wanted no more secrets.

Alissa and I ended up buying a simple little house on fifty acres near Momma, just outside Pocahontas. As soon as I finished my last sermon at Evangelic Temple, we began the process of going home. I found buyers for the bits and pieces that were left of my ministry. I closed down my broadcast with my last televised sermon, and a few months after I completed that sermon at Evangel, we moved back to live where we could be close to Momma and watch after her in her old age.

I never preached again, and for a time I had to expend a lot of energy explaining why. I was so well-known locally that I could scarcely go to a grocery store without someone coming up to me and asking me when I was going to preach again. My response became, "I would rather that you see the light of truth in my daily living and know that you can have that, too, than to stand on the mountainside and shout the Word."

We kept two million of the total in our own accounts. It was more than enough to live in as much opulence as we desired, but we chose to live simply, and this allowed us to use extra funds for good purposes. The land I bought with our house became more of a hobby farm than anything else, but I would occasionally make a little off the land as well. Sometimes, I would put produce on the back of a truck, park in town, and sell it, or give it away if I thought someone could not really afford it. It gave me an opportunity to meet people and to share the Word and the truth in a way that, in the end, was much more meaningful than what I had spouted from an opulently designed pulpit in a wealthy church. People talked to me and told me their troubles, sometimes confided deeply in me, and gave me a chance to teach them another way of looking at the world. I had come to realize that wealth was no more an answer than anything else although I had more than my share of it. Still, We had wealth but it didn't matter. Besides, you never see a trailer hitch on a tombstone. We can't take it with us, and whatever we accumulate here is going to go to someone else eventually, or it's going to end up in a landfill. It is all borrowed and must be returned when the contract is over. What does it profit a man to gain the whole world and lose his own soul? My soul had become my treasure. I learned to enjoy what I had while I had it, to use it for as much good as I could, and let it go when the time came to let it go.

It would be more than enough to give our kids anything they wanted for the rest of their lives. We had trusts for them to be educated. There was nothing they needed that they did not already have anyway, and we got to watch them grow up with a simple, uncomplicated life instead of the mess they might have encountered if they had gotten much older while I was still preaching.

We placed our two million in retirement investments, and the rest, which came to about seventeen million, we distributed to a collection of different charities, including programs for abused and orphaned children. Sometimes we would anonymously fix a problem for someone who was struggling, secretly pay for someone's roof to be fixed when we knew they could not afford it, or arrange for a promising child to become educated. Life became more about giving than getting. After all, the Bible does say, "Feed my sheep." Despite all we gave away, there seemed to be an unending supply. Our well of prosperity never ran dry.

We got as much arranged as we could ahead of time. We began making our plans to go home. Then on the last Sunday of June 1971, it came my time to speak at Evangelic Temple. As was usual fare, I had people in the back, adjusting my suit, and patting makeup onto my face before I was to go out before the cameras one last time. No one knew that it would be my last time except me, Alissa, Momma and Clara. I had also let Clara in on the deal. I had a long talk with her and gave her enough severance pay that she would be fine. Besides, not long after that, she moved to St. Louis and married Pastor Simmons, and as far as I could tell, they were happy together for the rest of their lives.

When the time came, I stood off to the side as usual, having been prepped as the star for Christ. I was prepped for the show and the hype of televised Christianity. Alissa stood there in the wings and watched me from a hall beside the pulpit. Then, upon introduction, I entered onto the platform at the front of the church, as I had done on many occasions. I walked back and forth and greeted the packed congregation. I looked up at the lights of the cameras and the lenses that were focused on me. I had long ago become very comfortable with all of it. This was a national broadcast shared before millions. As I walked across the stage with my microphone, I said into it, "God bless you! Thank you! Praise the Lord!" This, I had done on so many occasions. They stood and applauded as they would have any star of a show. Finally, I said, "Please be seated."

As commanded, the congregation of eight hundred to a thousand sat down. I looked over to the side and realized there were people who were standing in the wings, unable to find a seat. Any ruling of a fire marshal about overcrowding was overlooked on that day, as it had been on many other days that I had preached. They had all come to hear me preach the Gospel, but they were going to hear the Gospel as they had never heard it before.

After the bulk of the congregation was seated, I walked back and forth for a moment in my light tan suit. Then I said, "My name is Ronald Dennison, and I am a sinner!"

This was not an unusual thing for me to say in my sermons. I had used the statement since my very first sermon all those years ago in Daddy's church.

I continued to pace and then spoke again. "'For all have sinned, and have fallen short of the glory of God.' What do you think that means? Honestly—what do you think that means?"

I walked to the front of the platform, leaned into the congregation, and said again, "FOR ALL HAVE SINNED AND HAVE FALLEN SHORT OF THE GRACE…AND…GLORY OF GOD!"

I stood up straight. "My brothers and sisters in this congregation, my brothers and sisters who are tuning in to this broadcast. Listen to me when I say this, FOR ALL HAVE SINNED AND HAVE FALLEN SHORT OF THE GRACE AND GLORY OF GOD!" I continued to pace in front of them.

"Are you aware that I could be among the worst of sinners? But then, how do you measure sin? When you think about sin, do you measure it? Do you assume that one sin is worse than another sin? Do you say to yourself things like, 'Well, I gossip, but at least I am not sleeping with my neighbor's wife'? Is there one sin that is worse than another sin, or is a sin…a sin?" I paused for a moment and stood there, silent.

"Do you know what the word, the term 'to sin' really means? It means we have missed the mark. It means we did not get it right—this time! It was never intended to be a condemnation of ourselves or others, for we are all commanded by the Bible, 'JUDGE NOT THAT YE BE NOT JUDGED!' To judge…is to condemn…to criticize…to ostracize…shun…to separate ourselves from others by assuming we are somehow better than they are, that our SIN is somehow less than theirs! IF…I JUDGE…then I am judged! If I judge…I have sinned. It is not possible to condemn without guilt, even if we deny that we feel guilty about it. It is, THEREFORE, not possible to judge without placing that same judgment upon ourselves. I have judged, brothers and sisters. I have judged myself. I have judged others. I have condemned people for engaging in the SAME BEHAVIOR THAT…I…WAS ENGAGING IN MYSELF!" Again, I stood silent for a moment.

"You know…I have a confession I need to make. I need to bare my soul before you and before everyone at this moment. For the Bible does say, 'CONFESS YOUR SINS—one unto another.' Doesn't it say that? Yet often we don't. Often, we live secret lives of sin. We hide in the darkness where sin gets a foothold on our lives, while we pretend to be good

Christians. We hide in the darkness of our transgressions while we present a smiling MASK of graciousness and superiority to others. Yet the Bible says, 'Confess *your* faults one to another and pray one for another that ye may be healed.' James 5:16. My brothers and sisters in Christ…I…need to confess my faults to you…this morning. For I…have truly sinned."

I waited for dramatic effect. Then I said, "I am an adulterer. I am a womanizer. I have engaged in lust. I have manipulated and used women for pure carnal pleasure. I have had homosexual thoughts, and I have had, on at least a couple of occasions, sexual climax with other men. I might have been having fantasies about women when I did it, but I still reached sexual climax on at least a couple of occasions with other men. The first man…I experienced sexual arousal with…happened to be…my father." The collective gasp was so audible it could have been heard from space. There were mumblings among them. I waited for the ramble to quiet down, then I went on.

"You see, my daddy molested me from the time I was about five years old till the time I was maybe ten or twelve years old, and you know what? Despite the fact that he was a very sick man, he was also a good man. My daddy was a backwoods preacher. He was a country evangelist. He preached the Gospel of Christ, and as far as I know, he truly…wanted…to live it…but he didn't. He didn't live it. He was trapped in a secret life where he felt like he could not control himself even if that meant molesting his own son. I know now…that my daddy hated himself for what he was doing. My daddy was convinced that he was going to hell, and he felt like he could not stop what he was doing. Yet he CHOSE to do what he was doing. He allowed the belief that he was a condemned man to give him permission to continue to hurt me. For if we believe that we are already condemned, that we are already going to hell anyway, doesn't that then create the excuse to do whatever we want? We may not admit that to ourselves, but think about it. If I believe that I am damaged goods, that no one would want me for who I am, and that I am condemned by society and by God, does that not then create the belief that I might as well go ahead and do what I have contemplated?"

I let the congregation and television audience stew on those words for a moment, and then I continued.

"At least once or twice a week during the time I was growing up, my daddy would make excuses to have me in the corn bin by myself. He hid an old tackle box under the boards of the corn bin with a red wig and lipstick in it. Sometimes, he would put the wig on me, smear lipstick on my face, and treat me like I was a woman, right down to carnal knowledge with the woman that he pretended me to be. My daddy…sodomized me…the first time…when I was five years old. Can you imagine the pain that causes, not just the physical pain for a child that small, but the emotional confusion of a child who doesn't understand why he is being hurt…who doesn't understand that he is not being punished for some wrong he doesn't even recall? Can you imagine?"

Some people were visibly aghast. Some pulled handkerchiefs from purses to wipe tears from their eyes. Some could not take it. I saw a few people getting up and leaving and some who had been standing took their seats. About a quarter of the congregation eventually walked out, but the majority sat there and listened to me speak, and I most assuredly continued to speak.

"My daddy sodomized me till I was about ten, maybe even thirteen years old. I don't really remember how old I was when he stopped. He would put the red wig on me, but after I was reaching puberty, he would wear the wig and the lipstick and insist that I sodomize him. My first orgasm through sexual contact with another human being occurred when I was sodomizing my own father! I grew up with that shame. I grew up being shamed by my father…for…one day he would be abusing me in the barn, and on another day, he was beating me for making out with a girl. MY DADDY…PREACHED…THE GOSPEL, BUT HE DID NOT LIVE THE GOSPEL! He was living one life and presenting one face to the church and the community while he was sodomizing me at home! The rules that were preached from the pulpit were broken in our barn!"

At that moment, I went over and leaned one arm on the pulpit. "I'm here to tell you. That is a very confusing experience for a little boy. I grew up very confused about sex, love, life, men, women, the Bible—the church. You name it! Because…although it hurts, it is NOT the physical contact that does damage to a child who is being ABUSED, it is the MIND FUCK that destroys that child!" There was another gasp and rumble when I said that. Still others walked out. Those were words that I sincerely doubt anyone in that congregation or in the television audience had ever heard uttered from the pulpit. I don't know if the words got bleeped on the television broadcast, but probably not, as there was no worry about "dirty words" being uttered from church. I didn't care. It was my intent to give a sermon like no other that any of them had ever heard. So I continued.

When the rumble quieted, I said, "Oh, you think that is a BAD word that I just said? I am here to tell you that it is not! The only BAD words, the only DIRTY words ARE THE WORDS THAT ARE USED TO DEGRADE AND DEMEAN ANOTHER HUMAN BEING, ESPECIALLY A CHILD! I WOULD RATHER MY CHILD HEAR THE WORD 'FUCK' ANY DAY OF THE WEEK THAN HEAR ME SAY I THINK HE OR SHE IS WORTHLESS, USELESS, NO GOOD, STUPID, A WHORE, A FORNICATOR, A SODOMIZER, OR ANY OF THE OTHER WORDS THAT ARE PERFECTLY ALLOWABLE FOR ME TO USE FROM THIS PULPIT! If you do not use the WORD to CONDEMN…then it is NOT a BAD WORD!" I stood there for a moment then returned to my pace.

"I didn't want to believe it. My daddy, who I loved and adored, who spoke in the church, preached the Gospel, and admonished people to live by the word of Christ, WAS SODOMIZING ME IN THE BARN!" I paused for a moment and watched the reactions within the congregation. Then I continued. "When I was about ten years old…I had a dream about a beautiful redheaded woman coming up out of our pond. She was wearing long flowing white garments, and she walked up to me, brought my face to her lips, and kissed me sensually. I told myself that I didn't know what it meant, but my subconscious mind knew exactly what it meant. I just couldn't tell anyone what was happening to me any other way than to tell my momma the dream. The dream was my subconscious attempt to let someone know what was happening. I told the dream to my momma, and she told me it meant that I was called to preach. She didn't get it, and neither did I."

I had suspected Momma would be watching the broadcast, as always. I hoped that I had prepared her. Later, I discovered that she had chosen not to watch. The whole thing was a lot for her to accept. I understood that, but she put her heart into our relationship and, in the end, loved me as she always had. I thought about her in silence for that moment, then I went on. "In the next dream, the redheaded woman was at the foot of Jesus, who was being crucified on the side of our barn. Jesus turned to me and shouted, 'YOU ARE MY WORD!' and the sound echoed across the farm. After that dream, I became even more convinced that I had been called to preach, but my daddy still would not let me preach. At the time, I had blocked so much out of my mind that I didn't even realize the dreams were about Daddy and what he was doing to me. Daddy had to have known what the dreams were about, and maybe that was why he didn't want me to preach. Maybe he was afraid I might get up in front of the congregation and tell it all, as I am doing now, but I could not have told what I would not admit. I didn't realize that I had the need to prove I was better than Daddy at his own vocation. I didn't realize that I had the need to beat him at his own game. There was no other way I could beat him. I didn't realize I had the need to prove I was more of a man than he was. In fact, I had the need to PROVE that I was really…a man, because the abuse kept me from feeling anything like a real man. I blocked the memory of my daddy's abuse so thoroughly from my mind that I did not consciously recall it again till after he died!

Then it HIT ME…LIKE A BOLT OF LIGHTNING!

"I guess my mind decided once Daddy died, that I was ready to remember. Maybe, after Daddy died, the pressure to keep the secret was no longer there. Still, I tried to suppress it. I tried my best to keep it from coming out. I don't know exactly why I remembered, but remember I did. I remembered the SHAME…THE ANGUISH…THE GUILT…THE EMBARASSMENT…THE FEAR…that had been there my whole life and had been repressed through the abuse of, and sexual conquering of randomly selected women! I slept with as many women as I could because I wanted to forget! I seduced one woman after another because I wanted to prove I was a man and not the homosexual my daddy made me out to be. Of course, I grew up with the idea that homosexuality is among the worst of sins. It was the last thing I wanted to admit and the last thing I wanted to have in my mind. So I seduced as many women as I could in my effort to make up for the fact that the nagging terror that I might be queer was planted in my mind by my father's abuse. Just like my daddy, I hid my sin. It just happened to be a slightly different sin. I pretended to be something that I am not. I used sex as a distraction, but I also used it as a tool to inflate my ego, to make me feel more like a man, to make me feel like I could control others. I ABUSED MY FAME AS A TELEVANGELIST TO TAKE ADVANTAGE OF OTHERS! I ABUSED MY POSITION TO MANIP-ULATE AND TAKE ADVANTAGE OF WOMEN! There was more than one occasion that some woman had to be paid off to keep her from going to the press. There was more than one occasion that some woman tried to blackmail me because of my wealth and position! I continued to use and manipulate them for my own carnal desires so I could TRY to overcome my own insecurities as a man! However, right here, right now, today, I am here to tell you that you cannot blackmail a man who has no secrets, AND I HAVE NO MORE SECRETS!"

I held the microphone to my side and took a deep breath then pulled it back toward my lips and spoke.

"Where all that took me, my need to try to overcome the insecurities created by my abuse as a child, was right here. Right where I am…right now. That took me to the pulpit, where I tried to be a better preacher than my daddy had ever been. It took me to Nashville, to radio and television broadcasts, and to Christian stardom. It also took me to the realization that when you are famous, even as a famous preacher, some lonely, perhaps damaged women will allow you to do things to them that they would not allow from another man. It took me to the realization that even women who are not lonely or damaged can be intimidated by the power that wealth and position provide. It took me to the temptation of lust and lasciviousness. It took me to adultery against my beautiful, faithful, and loving wife. It took me to seduce one woman after another, after another…AND…WHY?"

I dropped the microphone to my side again and continued to pace in front of the congregation, then I began again.

"You know…at the time…I didn't know why. Now I know that I was trying to prove my manhood. I was trying to prove that I was not a homosexual, that I was attracted to women. After all…my first orgasm from sexual contact…was in the act of sodomy with my own father. Maybe…just maybe…if I seduced enough women, I could prove that achieving climax with my father did not mean I was homosexual or that I was condemned to hell for that. I thought I chose a better sin. The problem was that I could never believe it, because I only chose…a different sin. The problem was that every time I felt stressed or upset, I sought out lust as the antidote. THERE WAS NO ANTIDOTE!"

A thought crossed my mind as I was speaking. I couldn't believe what I was saying to an entire nation. I knew that no preacher had ever done anything like this ever before. I knew there would be repercussions; there would be press, gossip, etc. I didn't care because before that sermon was over, I was going to quit. I had started arrangements ahead of time, the trusts for myself, for Stephen in St. Louis, for Clara, for Momma, and for charity. Evangelic Temple itself was about to get a huge check from my ministry, and then I was going to be done with preaching, done with the lust for power that being a televangelist had afforded me. Like giving up my seductions of women, I knew that I had to give that up as well. I went on.

"I HAD AS MUCH LUST FOR POWER AS I DID FOR WOMEN! I used my wealth, fame, and notoriety to manipulate and control others SO I COULD FINALLY FEEL LIKE I WAS MORE THAN THE WORTHLESS…DISCARD OF A HUMAN BEING…THAT MY FATHER MADE ME OUT TO BE! You see, if we are treated as expendable when we are children, treated as worth less than others, used like some farm animal or tool, when we are beaten down—then, we can begin to believe we…are…worthless. When we are treated as worthless, we feel worthless as children. We don't know to challenge those things. We are a blank slate upon which is written the teachings of our parents or other adults, not only through what they say, but through what they do. We don't know any better than to believe that what we are being taught about ourselves and our place in life…is true. I would never have admitted it, but I believed I was worthless, and I learned that I could use sex, money, and power to compensate for that. I could use sex, money, and power to give me a TEMPORARY reprieve from those feelings of insecurity. SEX…MONEY…AND POWER…BECAME MY DRUG! I needed more and more of that drug because the effects were only temporary. EVERY TIME I GOT THE RUSH OF SEX AND POWER, I…WAS…THRILLED—for a moment. Then, the insecurities returned, then the belief that I was unlovable and unworthy returned, and when it did…I NEEDED MORE OF MY DRUG! And you paid for that! You paid through donations that you thought were going to expand the ministry of the Lord. I would like to think, and I deeply pray that some of what you gave went to the betterment of people who were touched by something I might have had to say…but the bottom line is that no matter what I was saying from the pulpit…no matter what I was teaching or preaching…I…WAS LIVING A LIE…AND NO DRUG OF ANY KIND…WAS…EVER…GOING TO MAKE ME FEEL BETTER!"

I fell silent. Tears welled in my eyes, I felt dregs of shame, but I also realized these were tears of release. In a moment, I cried as I continued. "It took…attempting…suicide for me to come to my senses! It took…seducing one last woman, FEELING LIKE I WAS CONDEMNED TO HELL and NOT WANTING TO GO THROUH ANOTHER MOMENT OF TORMENT OR ANOTHER DAY ON THIS EARTH for me to come to my senses—and you know who helped me come to my senses?"

I walked a couple of steps back, put out my hand toward Alissa, motioning for her to join me on the platform. She walked quietly from the back and took my hand. I put my arm around her, then we turned back to the congregation.

"My loving wife, who knew the hell I was going through, who KNEW I had been unfaithful to her, who KNEW…I would rather have died than to hurt her again. It TOOK…MY LOVING WIFE…to intervene, to INSIST that I get some help. It took this before I could come to my senses. IT TOOK HER REFUSAL TO ACCEPT ANOTHER MOMENT OF WHAT I WAS DOING TO MYSELF for me *FINALLY* to get some help. Oh, I resisted! I tried everything I could to talk my way out of going, but after I HAD ATTEMPTED TO KILL MYSELF AND FAILED—THANK GOD ALMIGHTY—I was in a bit of a trap. I am here to tell you that I am SO THANKFUL for my loving wife, Alissa, for without her, I might have been caught in my addiction until it destroyed me completely. Without her, I might have eventually found a way to kill myself. THANK GOD FOR HER! THANK GOD FOR THIS ANGEL WHO STOOD BY ME—PUSHED ME—AND REFUSED TO ACCEPT ANYTHING LESS THAN GETTING HELP!"

I leaned over, kissed Alissa on the forehead, took my arm from around her, held her hand, and went on.

"She was my guardian angel, but she was not my only angel. There were other angels. Those angels were a transsexual boy who is convinced he is really a girl. I was supposed to counsel him and help him understand that he IS NOT…a girl. I was supposed to help him realize that he needed to live his life as a boy and give up the nonsense that he is a girl. Instead, he—she—was the first one to force my memories out of me, the first one to reflect to me what was really going on inside my tortured mind. Others included a hippie therapist and a homosexual patient at the same treatment facility! You see…I had to be hospitalized after I chewed up Valium and stabbed myself with a letter opener. I had to go somewhere to get psychiatric help. I know that you were all told I had health problems and that's why I had to be out for a while. That's true—what you were not told is that those were mental health problems. I fought the demon of shame for my entire life. I tried to appease it with sacrifices of lust and fornication. None of it worked! Finally, I didn't see any reason in trying anymore, especially when my wife walked in to find me—after I had just seduced a young woman in my office! THAT WAS IT! The final straw…the final shame. At the time, I was thinking I might go to hell for committing suicide, but it surely couldn't be any worse than the hell I was living. I assumed I was going to hell anyway, so what did it matter? If I was going to go to hell anyway for the way I had been behaving, then it made no difference if I got there by killing myself. I decided, at that moment, that I wanted to die! But I was lucky—I am a very lucky man and a very blessed man, you know. I was lucky that I have a wife who is a saint, an angel. I am lucky to have had a woman so strong, who stood by me at my worst and never gave up on me. I have loving friends in people like my assistant, Clara Smith. I had angels around me who could see in me…what I could not see in myself."

I looked over to see that Alissa was standing there, smiling at me. "I treated the people who loved me the most…most despicably. I lost myself in shame, lust, and confusion and it took a homosexual man who was describing the hell that he went through as a child, being bullied and ridiculed, to help me realize—WE ARE ALL SINNERS! My sin was no worse than his, so WHO AM I TO JUDGE? NO SIN IS WORSE THAN ANY OTHER! This young homosexual man told me about going home and trying to kill himself when he was sixteen after his preacher told him that the sin of homosexuality is worse than the sin of murder! WHY WOULD YOU NOT TRY TO KILL YOURSELF WHEN YOU HAVE BEEN TOLD THAT YOU ARE ALREADY CONDEMNED? IS IT ANY WONDER that homosexual teenagers try to kill themselves? IS THAT WHAT WE WANT OUR CHILDREN TO DO? I know what the Bible says about homosexual acts, but at this point in my life, I don't know that I believe BEING a homosexual is wrong. I am living proof that it is just as easy for heterosexuals to engage in self-denigrating behavior as it is for homosexuals, and I know that young homosexual man was one of the angels who helped me see the truth!"

Mumbles and rumblings ran through a large portion of the congregation and still more got up and walked out. One person shouted, "Preach the Gospel, not your opinion!"

I watched as several people left. I knew that what I was saying was not what they wanted to hear. I knew that it was antithetical to the beliefs they had held, most of them, for most of their lives. For most of my life, I had held those same beliefs. I had no intent to disrespect or attempt to challenge the teachings of the Bible. I only wanted people to understand that there are other interpretations that can be made, and that if they were to take the blinders off, even for a moment, they might come closer to seeing the whole picture. At that point, about 20 percent of the seats in the congregation were empty. I stood there silent for another moment, watching as people were walking out, knowing that I was challenging the very core of their beliefs. Then I raised the microphone to my lips again. "When the Bible says, 'Be you therefore perfect, even as your Father who is in Heaven is perfect,' does it mean we are not allowed to make mistakes? Does it mean that we are supposed to deny ourselves, deny who we are, assume that we are not perfect? Are we supposed to quest for some impossible goal that no human being outside of Jesus Christ could achieve? Or does it mean to realize that Perfection cannot create less than Itself? Does it mean that we need to realize that, despite all our flaws and misgivings, all our judgments, our condemnation, and criticism of ourselves and others, we are still PERFECT even as our Father in heaven has created us, even as our Father in heaven is PERFECT? GOD is LOVE…GOD is HOLY… GOD is PERFECT…GOD created me—US—each and every one of us…IN…HIS…OWN…IMAGE! Therefore, WE ARE ALL EQUAL IN GOD'S PERFECTION—ALL EQUAL IN THE WORTH THAT GOD CREATED AND ALL DESERVING OF GOD'S LOVE!"

I took a deep breath and went on.

"For those of you out there who have children, I have a question for you. Which one of your children would you be willing to condemn to hell for all eternity? Can you choose? I don't know about you, but I could NEVER make that choice. I love my children with every ounce of my being. No matter what they become, no matter who they grow up to be, no matter what they will ever do, there is NO WAY in my heart or soul that I could EVER condemn either of them to hell! And yet…we believe that our Father in heaven…WHO LOVES MORE INFINATELY AND DIVINELY THAN ANY ONE OF US IS CAPABLE OF LOVING… could CONDEMN ANY OF US TO HELL? I NO LONGER BELIEVE IN HELL! Hell is a state of mind that is created by our feelings of separation from God. Everything we do, every thought we think, takes us in one direction or the other. It takes us toward the HOLY, INFALLIBLE LOVE OF GOD…or it takes us to feeling worthless, useless, fearful, and, therefore, places us in the state of mind. THAT…IS…HELL! YOU CANNOT SERVE TWO MASTERS! We serve one or the other at every moment of our lives! Everything, every thought, feeling, and action falls into one of two categories: We serve LOVE or FEAR. We serve COMPASSION or HATE. We serve FORGIVENESS or MALICE. We cannot serve either at the same time. Each one is mutually exclusive of the other. YOU CANNOT SERVE TWO MASTERS!"

Again, I stood in silence for a time, scanning the congregation and the variations of expressions around the church. Finally, I spoke again.

"You know, as I was struggling with all this in that mental health treatment center out in Colorado, I had Bible verses running through my mind. As I was struggling to make sense of why my daddy beat me and sodomized me, I thought about Luke 23:34, 'Forgive them Father for they know not what they do.' I thought about forgiveness and how much the Bible admonishes us to forgive—SEVENTY TIMES SEVEN—over and over again we are admonished to forgive—WHY? That is a tall order! Isn't that a tall order? It is a tall order for a child who is growing up being abused and mistreated by the very people who are called by all ethical standards to love that child most! It is a tall order for that child to forgive those who were supposed to love him, when instead, they hurt him."

Alissa stood quietly beside me, hands now folded in front of her. I glanced at her periodically, as I continued.

"How was I going to forgive my father for what he did to me? How was I going to forgive myself for what I had done to multiple women, my wife, my family, and my church? 'Forgive them, Father, for they know not what they do'? 'Be perfect even as your father in Heaven is perfect'? Then…then another Bible verse came into my mind—'YE BLIND GUIDES WHICH STRAIN AT A GNAT AND SWALLOW A CAMEL!' Then I realized it IS NOT about being perfect! We are already perfect! We get so focused on the law, the letter of the law, the nitpicky little, cherry-picking 'do and don't' of the law that we miss the point of the law! What…is…the…point…of…the…law? 'LOVE THE LORD THY GOD WITH ALL THY HEART, AND THY NEIGHBOR AS THYSELF!'

Perhaps that should be interpreted, love thy neighbor as well as thyself! 'LOVE THE LORD THY GOD WITH ALL THY HEART, AND THY NEIGHBOR AS THYSELF! ON THIS…ON THIS…RESTS…ALL…THE LAWS AND THE PROPHETS!' LOVE! LOVE! LOVE is the bottom line! AND WHAT IS LOVE? Love is wanting the best, the greatest and highest good for someone. Love is wanting those people to have peace, comfort, joy and happiness—PERIOD! THERE IS NO 'I'LL LOVE YOU IF…' LOVE IS NOT EARNED! IT IS A GIFT FROM GOD! When Jesus said, 'FORGIVE THEM FATHER FOR THEY KNOW NOT WHAT THEY DO!' HE…DID…NOT…SAY…'Well, you know, under certain conditions! You know, they have to meet certain conditions before you can forgive them.' NO! He said, 'FORGIVE THEM!' THAT'S IT! If they truly understood love, they could not be acting as they were acting. They were not EVIL! They were IGNORANT! MY DADDY WAS IGNORANT! HE DIDN'T GET IT! HE DIDN'T UNDERSTAND! He did not do to me what he did because he was evil. He did what he did because he didn't get it, and despite how much he hurt me, I CANNOT—WILL NOT—BELIEVE THAT HE IS LIVING ETERNITY IN HELL! LOVE…DOES NOT… CONDEMN! LOVE IS THE OPPOSITE OF SELFISHNESS! SELFISHNESS CONDEMNS! SELFISHNESS SEEKS ITS OWN WAY! IT SEEKS CONTROL! IT DEMANDS! LOVE DOES NOT DEMAND…ANYTHING! And if I truly seek to live the Word of God, I seek it for myself. I don't tell others how they should live, what they should or should not be doing! I do not shun others because they don't live as I believe they should. If I truly seek to live the Word of God, I JUST LOVE THEM! THAT'S IT! I seek LOVE! I return myself to it as soon as I realize I have slipped away! I seek to live LOVE AND ONLY LOVE! By doing that, I become His Word."

I stared out into the congregation, looking for various eyes that might be looking back at me, and there were many. Some had tears in their eyes. Some were stone-faced. Some looked sullen. I continued. "LOVE—'on this rests all the laws and the prophets.' I forgave my daddy for hurting me. I had to—for my sake, not for his. My anger and my denied hatred for him were only hurting me. It was destroying me, and it was preventing me from living by God's Word. I forgave myself for hurting myself, for taking advantage of women, for treating them like sex toys instead of human beings, and I forgave myself for hurting my wife—and my family. I am…a very…very lucky man. For not only was I able to forgive myself and my daddy, my saint of a loving wife…was able to forgive me. For that…I am most eternally grateful." Alissa was still standing there, still smiling. For a moment, there was a fear in my heart that she might have walked away, but there she was. I took a breath and smiled back at her then turned my gaze to the crowd one last time.

"There have been a lot of people I have hurt in my life. Some of them may be in this congregation this morning. Some of them may be tuning in to this broadcast. Many of them will not believe me and will not forgive me for what I've done. I accept that. What I want you all to know is that I regret that you were hurt. I apologize with all my heart. I wish my behavior had been better, but I am not sorry. Sorry…is what I was when I was doing those things to you. Sorry…is what I was when I was using women to exploit sexual urges and appease my own inner conflict. Sorry is what I was when I was profiting from a ministry that afforded me the opportunity to exploit. I am not sorry anymore. I am repentant—which means to feel sorrow for what I have done, but it means more than that. It means that I let go of what was there before. I am not a sorry person, but I engaged in sorry behavior. I am not a bad person. There is a core of love within me, but because of my conflict and confusion, I engaged in hurtful behavior. I repent of that behavior. I no longer need it. Those who are confident have nothing to prove. I no longer have anything to prove to you, to my daddy, to myself, or to God. I am not confident that I have come to understand love fully, and love…will be my commitment from this moment forward—to myself, to my family and others close to me, and as often as possible, to everyone I meet. I commit myself to love. I commit to make further amends wherever I can, whenever I can. I am dedicating the vast majority of the wealth I accumulated from my ministry to this and other churches, to charities, and to helping others. That's where it should have gone in the first place."

I drew a deep breath. "And Jesus said, 'Go and sin no more.' I can't promise that. I cannot promise that I will not make mistakes. I can't promise that I won't mess up. I can promise, however, that I will do my best to keep myself focused on God's HOLY LOVE, to return it to my heart every chance that I get, and to understand that love is much more than a promise. Promises can be broken, but true love cannot. That is why I know that my Heavenly Father, who is perfect in every way, who created me in His perfection, and who loves me more infinitely that I am even capable of loving, will never break His love for me, nor for you. True love cannot be broken. So…when you go from here today, do not go with the admonishment to sin no more. Go with the encouragement to love, to seek love first within yourself and then offer it to everyone you meet. Go with the encouragement to return yourself to love as often as you realize that you have slipped away. Go with the assurance that God's love is always and forever unfailing and that you are HIS BELOVED CHILD—IN WHOM HE IS WELL PLEASED!"

Some in the congregation stood to their feet at that moment and applauded. I felt tears drifting down my cheeks. I stood there for several minutes while they applauded and affirmed, "God bless you. God loves you. You ARE HIS beloved child."

When at last the roar died down, I said, "I need to let you know something else…I am relinquishing my ministry."

There was a rumbling of voices, groans, and a few shouts of "No, Pastor!" and "We need you."

Again, I waited.

When the crowd had calmed down, I said, "I am a flawed and sinful man, and although I know that there are times when God speaks through me, I would rather go and live his commandments rather than teach them. I got into the ministry because I had something to prove. I got into the ministry to show up my father and to best him at what he thought he was good at. I have nothing to prove. You have been kind and generous, and even now as I let you know, openly, just how flawed I have been, you send your love to me. What I want to say to you is don't rely on the word of some preacher who may or may not be in it for the genuine love of God. Rely on your own study, your own inner voice. Trust that God will lead you, that you are on the right path, and that you will find your way if you truly wish to find it. I…am retiring. I have done this for many years, and my prayer is that something I have said or done over all these years, despite my sins, may have touched someone, may have lifted up someone, and given them a glimmer of realization that the love of God is forever and always present— forever and always—with us, forever and always ours to claim.

"Look around. Look at each other. When was the last time that you truly extended your love to a stranger? Look at all the good things you have before you in this moment and be grateful for them. There is nothing which is not of God or from God. Ultimately, there is nothing which is not God. You don't really need me to tell you this. You already have it in your heart. Search within your heart…and there you will find God. For Jesus said, 'Lo, I am with you always.' Know this. Know this one thing, and know that love is the bottom line, and you have all you need. You have all that you will ever need. Instead of throwing your money at some TV preacher, throw your heart into understanding the love of God within yourself. You don't need me, and you certainly don't need to give me any more money. If you are going to give money, give it to the poor, to the needy. For our Lord said unto us, 'Feed My sheep.' Give it to the down and the downtrodden—'for insomuch as you have done unto the least of these, you have done unto Me,' sayeth the Lord. Make your love a living commandment and extend it wherever you can. If you want to tithe to the church, then tithe to the church, but don't sacrifice to the church. If you don't have the money to pay a tithe, then give whatever you can and don't worry about it. If you would rather give to the poor than give to the church, then give to the poor. Lord knows, these days, most churches don't need your charity. Most of all, remember that the church is there for you. You are not there for the church. For you see, religion is not what you need to be focused on. Religion is merely a tool to be used to help you construct your spirituality. To be focused on religion would be like focusing on the hammer and nails instead of on the house you want to build with it. Religion is a tool. It is only a tool. Like any other tool, it can be used for good purpose or bad. A hammer can be used to construct a home, or it can be used as a murder weapon. Those who wield the hammer decide how it will be used. Remember that religion is a tool, not a nation. The hammer does not need your faith and loyalty, the home does. Religion does not need your faith and loyalty, God does. Be careful where you place your faith, for wherein you place your faith, there is your reward. Place your faith in eternal love, and eternal Love will be your reward, but be careful that you do not make the church itself an idol before God."

I stood there in silence one more moment. "I am so humbly grateful," I said. "You have made my life complete."

Then, I took Alissa's hand and turned to walk off the platform. From behind me, I heard rumblings, some applause. There were mostly shouts of praise, but there were also some sounds of disapproval. The one who judges reveals the truth within himself and reveals no truth about the one who is being judged. I simply held Alissa's hand and kept walking.

When I stepped behind the wings of the platform, I reached down and brought her hand to my lips and kissed it. "You are my angel," I said as I watched her soul shine through her eyes.

"And you are mine." She smiled.

I never cheated on Alissa ever again. I learned to lay with her in loving communion, gently touching her, adoring her person, and gazing into her eyes. I learned that making love, being centered in the moment with the person you love without distractions of anxiety or guilt is more fulfilling and satisfying than any lust-filled tryst could ever be. Making love to my wife filled my soul with joy and my body with pleasure. My bond with Alissa grew ever stronger, and I relaxed into the comfort that we would see each other through to the end.

A few nights after I gave my last sermon, I had one last dream of the redheaded woman. I sat up in bed to see a moonlit sky above me, and the stars were barely showing in the bright, dusty blue of moonlight. Alissa was gently sleeping on the other side of the bed while lying on her back with one arm across her stomach. The bed was floating on the water at the edge of our pond at the old farm. The foot of the bed was resting at the shoreline where I could see the barn and the barn loft from the head of the bed where I was sitting. The redheaded woman came walking toward us from a distance across the pasture behind the barn. She was dressed in white robes like I had seen in the first dream, and her hair was glimmering gold and silver in the moonlight. As she approached, Daddy joined her near the barn. He was dressed in his overalls and work boots, as he would have dressed to work the fields. He came walking toward us at the same gentle pace as the redheaded woman. He had a serenity about him that I had never seen. He was smiling a gentle smile, and his eyes reflected loving kindness. When I was a child and even as an adult, I would have had an anxious trepidation to see Daddy walking toward me like that, but I felt safe.

They came to the foot of the bed and stopped for a moment, just standing there, looking at me. Then Daddy waded into the water on my side of the bed, and sat on the edge of the bed facing me. He reached out his rough, farm-worn hand and gently touched the palm of his hand to my face as he softly said, "This is my beloved son in whom I am well pleased." I looked into his eyes as he said it and saw the love of Jesus there. He was nothing like the daddy I had grown up with. He was nothing like the man who had repeatedly hurt me and withheld his love from me, nothing like the user who took me for his own carnal pleasure. He touched me the way a loving father should touch his son.

He smiled at me then leaned over to kiss me on the forehead. "I have to go now," he said.

He rose and went back to the foot of the bed and stood on the edge of the pond bank for a moment. Then he pushed the bed away from the shore out into the water.

As the bed began floating into the pond, I turned around to see that the pond had become a vast calm ocean of silver water glistening in the moonlight. I turned back toward Daddy to see that we were floating farther away from the pond bank.

Daddy and the redheaded woman stood there waving as the barn and pastures behind them were becoming increasingly distant. I looked over to see that Alissa was still lying there peacefully sleeping. When I looked back, I saw only Daddy standing there waving goodbye. I could barely see him in the distance, but the redheaded woman was gone. He was standing there alone with a soft white light shimmering around him.

Soon the farm was only a speck on the horizon as we continued to float out into that vast, calm silver sea. When at last I could see Daddy and the pond bank no longer, I lay back down on the bed, cuddled up to Alissa with my head on her shoulder, and held her close as we drifted away.

THERE IS NO SUCH THING AS THE END.

EPILOGUE

What you have just read is a purely fictional story. However, in many ways, it is also my story. There are elements of my own experience scattered throughout the book, including hearing the minister who baptized me, when I was sixteen, preach a sermon in which he stated that the "sin" of homosexuality is worse than the sin of murder. It is a fact that authors who write fiction also write themselves into their stories, whether they intend to or not. I am a survivor of childhood abuse and, although I have no overt memory of violent or coercive sexual abuse, there was violent abuse and there are some significant indications that covert and eroticized sexual abuse occurred. I am very lucky, in that, I came across resources and loving, accepting mentors at a time when few existed, and that I determined, at the age of eighteen, that there was a better way and that I was going to find it. That better way came after years of therapy, self-help groups, reading self-help books, spiritual study and self-examination. More of that is detailed in my autobiographical poetry book, *The Gulls Are Always Laughing*.

Following, is some information regarding the truth about abuse, and its effects on individuals and society. I admit that some of what you will see below is my own opinion.

Some statistics about child sexual abuse indicate that one in three girls and one in five boys are sexually assaulted before the age of eighteen. Other stats say one in four girls and one in six boys are molested during childhood. These sets of statistics are close in approximation, but one of the important things to remember is that this is an approximation based on what actually is reported. The truth is that sexual abuse is likely to be far more rampant (unreported) than the statistics, based on surveys and public reports would indicate. The bottom line is that children often don't tell, and males are less likely to report than females. The reasons males are less likely to report sexual trauma are issues of stigma, being perceived as weak, having shame which is based on the concept of masculine persona and the belief that it isn't supposed to happen to us. Part of that is the result of male acculturation that says men are not allowed to cry, not allowed to feel, not allowed to be victims or admit defeat and must, at the very least, suck it up and pretend like nothing happened. The flip side is that women, who are abused, are patronized, ignored and accused of soliciting sexual advances that they didn't want. Survivors of sexual assault are ten times more likely to attempt suicide than the general population, and if you think about it, no wonder. Suicide is the tenth leading cause of death in the United States, and it is higher among abuse survivors and LGBTQ+. What does that say about our society and how those who are victimized and marginalized are treated, as a whole?

The effects of child sexual abuse may depend on whether the abuse was violent, coercive, covert, eroticized or all the above. Covert and eroticized sexual abuse is often more insidious and difficult to spot and may take a different course in the victim's behavior than abuse that is coercive or violent, but a key indicator that a child may have been abused is a sudden or general change in their usual behavior. Children who have been abused may begin acting out, either violently or sexually. They may introduce peers to what they have been exposed to and have a difficult time defining what is and is not appropriate play. They may withdraw, shut down, begin being cruel to animals, have a drop in grades or have a lack of interest. They may defend or even idolize their perpetrator, depending on who it was and the type of abuse they experienced.

Those adults who experienced child or adult sexual trauma may be more likely to withdraw, isolate, lack trust, engage in frivolous encounters, have difficulty defining sexual boundaries, have excessive shame, have relationship and intimacy problems, abuse drugs/alcohol and engage in other addictions such as sexually acting out, gambling or compulsive eating. Those who have been violently sexually assaulted are more likely to develop PTSD than combat veterans. Those who have experienced sexual trauma are more likely to attempt suicide, more likely to have difficulties in emotional regulation, difficulties in relationships and are more likely to be raped or sexually assaulted again. Part of that susceptibility is based on the fact that abuse is a violation of boundaries, so victims of abuse (especially in childhood) have a more difficult time defining and maintaining boundaries than those who have not been abused. They may be more likely to allow themselves to be in situations that are dangerous and potentially violating than those who have not experienced abuse. The good news is that the majority of those who have been sexually assaulted do not perpetrate sexual abuse. However, those who perpetrate sexual abuse are more likely to have been sexually assaulted, themselves, usually as children.

Sexual abuse has nothing to do with sexual or gender orientation, although those who have been sexually abused are more likely to experience sexual confusion regarding their attractions. Sexual and gender orientation are things that parents often notice in their children as young as two years old. Sexual abuse, whether perpetrated by male or female on a male or female victim has nothing to do with sexual or gender orientation which develops separately regardless of whether abuse did or did not occur. Regardless, one of the most important things to remember about LGBTQ+ is that it carries with it the experience of subtle societal abuse. LGBTQ+ are the only minority at risk of being rejected by their own families. They are rejected by many churches and often experience micro-aggressions if not overt hostility in general societal interactions. LGBTQ+, even without the experience of having been sexually traumatized, are at greater risk of bullying and marginalization. LGBTQ+ teens who face rejection by both peers and family are three times more likely to attempt suicide than their heterosexual peers. Forty-one percent of transgender people in the United States attempt suicide at least once in their lives. This is not a condition of being LGBTQ+ or specifically transgender, this is a condition of living in a society in which you are considered to be an abnormality rather than a human being. Transgender women, especially black and Latina transgender women are more likely to be murdered than the general population. What this actually speaks to is the underlying and pervasive misogyny, particularly in American Culture. Trans-men are also murdered, but not nearly as commonly as transwomen. This is evidence of the generalized and covert hatred of women in our society. In the misogynistic mind of those who murder trans-women is the idea that transwomen have abandoned being men for what misogynists loathe, being a woman. They are therefore considered, by them, to be traitors of their gender and, thus deserving of punishment.

Recovery from sexual abuse, from trauma, from bullying, discrimination and marginalization begins with openness and disclosure, such as gay pride and what happened with the #MeToo movement. The way out is through. . . through the shame, through the secrets, isolation and anger that can manifest in multiple ways. The way out is through the social repression that would rather the victim keep silent than admit what happened to them. The way out is understanding that abuse of any kind may have strongly influenced those who are survivors, but it does not have to define them. We, as trauma survivors define ourselves. We have a right to define ourselves. We have a right to be vulnerable, yet safe. We have a right to reach out, to be honest with ourselves and others, and we have a right to live lives filled with as much happiness and contentment that is due to anyone who has never experienced abuse, bullying or marginalization.

I encourage anyone who has ever experienced trauma to reach out to professionals, to support groups, 12-step groups, and online resources. Some resources for possible help are listed below. Also, you may contact the state department of mental health or professional licensing in your state to find professionals in your area who may be able to help. I realize that not everyone will be able to afford professional help, but many states provide state mental health funding for agencies that serve those who do not have access to insurance and other benefits. Never overlook the benefit of reading self-help books and of involving yourself with online or local support groups. If you are not able to access professional assistance, access whatever assistance you can find. Remember always that you are not alone and there are people who will either understand or seek to understand. Be careful in your approach to potential services, but always be willing to learn that there is a better way, that you can find it, and you will find it if you commit yourself to the goal of at least internal freedom.

Consider these resources:

National Suicide Prevention Hotline: 988

National Alliance for the Mentally Ill (NAMI): https://www.nami.org/ Home

Sexual Assault Survivors Anonymous: https://www.sasaworldwide.org

Survivors Anonymous Groups: www.survivorsanonymousgroup.com

Trauma Survivors Network: https://www.traumasurvivorsnetwork.org/ pages/home

MHA (Mental Health America) LGBTQ+ Mental Health: https:// www.mhanational.org/research-reports/lgbtq-mental-health-insights-mha-screening

The Trevor Project: https://www.thetrevorproject.org

GLADD Transgender Resources: https://www.gladd.org/transgender/ resources

Find a Social Worker: https://www.helpstartshere.org/?page_id=3677 If you search online, you will find many more resources.

These are only a few of the possible resources. There are also warmlines which, unlike hotlines that you call when you are in emotional crisis, are lines that you call when you just need to talk to someone.

National Warm Lines Directory: https://warmline.org/warmdri.html

ABOUT THE AUTHOR

Karlyle Tomms is an award-winning author who grew up in the rural Ozarks. He began writing fiction later in life and has written for different regional magazines and newspapers over the years. He has often been selected to speak at both professional and nonprofessional events, as well as radio talk shows and podcasts. His first novel, *Confessions from the Pumpkin Patch*, won the 2016 New Apple Awards Medal for General Fiction and was endorsed by Marideth Sisco, who is known for her work on *Winter's Bone*, starring Jennifer Lawrence, a film which was nominated for four Academy Awards and won the 2010 Sundance Film Festival Grand Jury Prize. His general method for fiction has been to define a protagonist and allow that character (male, female, or transgender) to tell his or her own story from first-person perspective as though the protagonist is writing an autobiography. His fictional books are about people overcoming social, psychological, emotional, political, and spiritual challenges. He also has an autobiographical prose and poetry book, *The Gulls Are Always Laughing,* which is about his own journey of overcoming childhood bullying and trauma and learning to cherish life and spiritual awareness on the Coastal Bend of Texas.

Fresh Ink Group
Independent Multi-media Publisher
Fresh Ink Group / Voice of Indie / GeezWriter / Push Pull Press

&

Hardcovers
Softcovers
All Ebook Formats
Audiobooks
Podcasts
Worldwide Distribution

&

Indie Author Services
Book Development, Editing, Proofing
Graphic/Cover Design
Video/Trailer Production
Website Creation
Social Media Marketing
Writing Contests
Writers' Blogs

&

Authors
Editors
Artists
Experts
Professionals

&

FreshInkGroup.com
info@FreshInkGroup.com
Twitter: @FreshInkGroup
Facebook.com/FreshInkGroup
LinkedIn: Fresh Ink Group

Prepare to think as you explore these wildly disparate literary short stories by author, composer, and producer Stephen Geez. Avoiding any single genre, this collection showcases Geez's storytelling from southern gothic to contemporary drama to coming-of-age, humor, sci-fi, and fantasy—all finessed to say something about who we are and what we seek. Some of these have been passed around enough to need a shot of penicillin, others so virgin they have never known the seductive gaze of a reader's eyes. So when life's currents get to pulling too hard, don't fight it, just open the book and discover nineteen new ways of going with the flow, because NOW more than ever Comes this Time to Float.

Dive in now!

Fresh Ink Group
FreshInkGroup.com